Praise for *New York Times* bestselling author
NEVADA BARR

THE ROPE

"Terrifying . . . Dark and visceral, the novel is sure to appeal to Barr's legion of fans, especially those who have been clamoring for the author to light the shadows of Anna's past . . . A crisply written and revelatory entry in the Pigeon series." —*Booklist*

"Barr's exciting 17th Anna Pigeon thriller takes readers where they've wanted to go for years—to Anna's beginnings as a park ranger. . . . Misdirection and a rising body count ratchet up the tension." —*Publishers Weekly*

"Barr's luxuriant depictions of desert landscapes with [their] colors and hues and details about Lake Powell's tourist population are interwoven into the narrative as an indispensable element of her popular series. Anna emerges from this canyon escapade as a strong, determined woman . . . Verdict: Another awesome winner for Barr."

—*Library Journal*

BURN

"This uncharacteristically urban novel may not present Anna with any endangered species to protect or environmental threats to ward off, but it does give her a chance to prove that her outdoor skills are adaptable to city streets. The harrowing plot . . . provides Barr with an opportunity to sharpen her

characters . . . [With *Burn*] Barr is writing with the kind of ferocity she usually saves for her backcountry adventures."

—Marilyn Stasio, *The New York Times Book Review*

"Nevada Barr is one of the best." —*Boston Globe*

"Engrossing . . . ingenious . . . inventive and sharply observed."

—*The Washington Post*

"Anna Pigeon remains an irresistible protagonist; but, to Barr's credit, Claire Sullivan is her finest fictional creation since Anna . . . *Burn* finds Nevada Barr turning out prose that practically sizzles." —*Denver Post*

"Outstanding. . . . Anna's complex personality continues to elevate the series, and the ranger's sojourn to New Orleans further energizes this always reliable series."

—*Publishers Weekly* (starred review)

"Suspenseful plotting." —Oregon Live.com

"Abundant suspense." —*The Oklahoman*

"*Burn* will smolder in your heart long after you're done."

—*Madison County Herald*

"Barr's strong, evocative writing explores the scenery as well as the characters." —*South Florida Sun-Sentinel*

"From the fabric of fiction Barr creates real worlds, sometimes beautiful, sometimes terrifying, but always convincing."

—*San Diego Union-Tribune*

ALSO BY NEVADA BARR

NEVADA BARR

BOAR ISLAND

St. Martin's Paperbacks

This is a work of fiction. All of the characters, organizations, and events portrayed in this novel are either products of the author's imagination or are used fictitiously.

BOAR ISLAND

Copyright © 2016 by Nevada Barr.

For information address St. Martin's Press, 175 Fifth Avenue, New York, NY 10010.

ISBN: 978-1-250-06470-7

Our books may be purchased in bulk for promotional, educational, or business use. Please contact your local bookseller or the Macmillan Corporate and Premium Sales Department at 1-800-221-7945, extension 5442, or by e-mail at MacmillanSpecialMarkets@macmillan.com.

Printed in the United States of America

St. Martin's Press hardcover edition / May 2016
St. Martin's Paperbacks edition / February 2018

St. Martin's Paperbacks are published by St. Martin's Press, 175 Fifth Avenue, New York, NY 10010.

10 9 8 7 6 5 4 3 2 1

*For Julie, a most
excellent friend*

ACKNOWLEDGMENTS

With special thanks to Linda Eddings, Stuart West, Bill "the Rock Nazi" Weidner, June Devisfruto, and all the fine folks at Acadia.

Apologies to the demolition crew that took down the derelict barracks on Schoodic. I rather liked the old heap, so I put it back.

ONE

Fists white-knuckled on the crutches, sweat running into her eyes, Heath grunted like a sumo wrestler. She was walking to the window of her front room. Walking, as in proceeding forward in an upright bipedal manner by putting one foot in front of the other. For some people, toddling around a fifteen-by-twenty-foot room would be as nothing. For Heath it was a miracle, and she was sweating buckets for it.

Eight years before, she had fallen while climbing rotten ice in Rocky Mountain National Park and broken her back: no movement, no sensation below the waist. For an eternity of hopelessness she'd wallowed in self-pity. Finding in Elizabeth a daughter, and in Anna Pigeon a friend, had convinced her to abandon her plan to drink herself to death. It was then she had begun to embrace every nerve's worth of life she could win, earn, fight for, or steal.

During all those years, eye level had been precisely forty-four inches above the floor. One of the first things she noticed when she stood up—stood up out of her wheelchair on her own two feet—was that nobody had dusted any surface more than forty-five inches above the floor in at least five years. Who knew?

She smiled and looked at her reflection standing—*standing*—in the plate-glass window. Dem Bones, Elizabeth called it. Iron Woman in Dem Bones, Heath thought.

Anchored to the outside of each thigh was a long silver-colored piece of contoured metal that linked to a round hinge at knee and hip. Below, another metal lozenge ran down the side of her calf to attach to a horizontal brace that went beneath her shoe. A wide strap, reminiscent of a weight-lifter's belt, circled her waist. A battery pack the size of a hardcover book rode on the belt at the small of her back. On the right hip of her harness was a small control panel with buttons that allowed her to use the electronic exoskeleton to sit down and stand up. The rest was done with body movement. If she leaned slightly forward, wonder of wonders, she *walked* forward. If she leaned back, the walking stopped. The entire assemblage weighed twenty-one pounds three ounces and could be folded into a case slightly smaller than a golf bag.

This was her second day with the skeleton. The first time she had stood up on her own—sort of on her own—she had suffered an attack of acrophobia so sudden and severe she'd nearly fallen. She, who had led precipitous climbs up sheer cliffs for fifteen years, looked down the five feet three inches from her eyeballs to her feet and felt as if she stood on the edge of a chasm a thousand feet deep, a vacuum sucking her into oblivion. She'd managed six steps before she hummed back into her wheelchair, exhausted from movement and terror.

Terror had quickly mellowed into excitement. Still, she felt fifty feet tall, a giantess looking down on a world of dwarves. A rush of power and awe fueled her every time she stood up.

Unfortunately, the machine wasn't hers. There was no way Heath could afford it. She was testing it for her friend Leah Hendricks, the research and development brain of Hendricks & Hendricks. Leah's device had three times the electronics of other models, was smaller and lighter, executed more minute movements, and was able to "learn." Heath had yet to tap into a fraction of what it could do. One of the drawbacks was that Leah had yet to figure out how to get the thing's battery to hold a charge for more than twenty minutes.

In a couple of months Leah would take it back to the lab to tinker with its finer points.

Heath chose not to think about how she would feel, who she would be, when this miracle was taken from her.

For now, she would only think of now, walking now, standing now. Now was good.

Twice she had walked the length of the room. Forty feet. Hooray for the para brigade, she thought. Give us forty feet and we'll take a million miles.

Harsh, repetitive racket shattered her moment of triumph. Rap music, an oxymoron to Heath's way of thinking, rudely pounded down the long hallway from the direction of Elizabeth's room.

Until recently, Heath's adopted daughter had been an aficionado of the lightweight modern version of what Aunt Gwen called bubblegum rock. That and, because children never cease to amaze their elders, anything by James Taylor. Heath had been unaware Elizabeth ever listened to rap. Boulder, Colorado, wasn't much of a Mecca for rappers; too white, too rich, too much spandex. The stuff playing now was ugly and dark, "bitch" and "whore" making up a good percentage of the lyrics.

Why Elizabeth would want to listen to this brand of aural poison was beyond Heath. Why Elizabeth would think Heath would allow it to be broadcast throughout her house, smashing all good karma in its path, was an even greater domestic mystery.

Heath waited a couple of minutes, catching her breath and hoping Elizabeth would come to her senses. The first goal was met with satisfying rapidity. The second was not.

"Wily," she said to the dog laying on the hardwood, watching her workout with narrow, sleepy eyes, "go to Elizabeth's room, boy. Unplug her whatever. Good dog!"

Wily yawned hugely, his mouth wide and crooked like his spiritual guide Wile E. Coyote.

"You're a big help," Heath said.

Pivoting with painstaking slowness, she got herself turned around and centered facing the hallway, the crutch braces biting into her forearms. There was a gizmo built in that gave Dem Bones balance, but she'd not yet come to trust her mechanized lower body, hence the crutches. Leah had tried to explain the engineering to her, but Heath's brain had stalled at the gyroscope analogy.

Fear of falling was an acquired—and necessary—paranoia for paraplegics. Given her fatigue level, it would have made more sense to use her wheelchair for the journey to the back of the house. Still and all, wheeling up, no taller than a hobbit, to lay down the law to a teenager didn't appeal to her.

From behind the crutches, extended like forelegs in front of her, the view down the carpeted hallway—to be replaced with hardwood the moment her bank account caught up with her special needs—looked impossibly long, the doors at the end appearing as distant as the pins in a bowling alley.

Heath sighed and began to hum "Who Were You Thinking Of" as she clasped her crutches through the sweat on her palms and began her robotic version of the Texas two-step. When it came to the two-step, nobody could beat the Texas Tornados.

By the time she'd made it across the living/workout/rehab room to the hall, Wily padding arthritically along behind, she was regretting her impulse to stand high and mighty over her daughter and wishing she'd dropped her rear end, exoskeleton and all, into Robo-butt—Elizabeth's name for the wheelchair.

Having reached the point of no return, equidistant from the rude noise in Elizabeth's room and the security of her wheels, Heath rested a moment before pushing on. Elizabeth had more reasons than an overcrowded psych ward to be moody and rebellious. It was the miracle of the child that she was blessed with a naturally sunny disposition. One of those enviable souls whose brain seems to effortlessly create sufficient serotonin to power a lifetime of optimism in the grimmest of circumstances.

Until a week ago, when sullenness and darkness had replaced the sun.

Or was it two weeks? As much as a month? No. Even a Johnny-come-lately mom like Heath wouldn't fail to notice over that length of time.

Heath told herself what she always told herself when she worried that an unmarried, crippled, ex-rock-climber was not the mother a girl as fine as Elizabeth deserved; what she lacked in experience she made up for with love. Also, they had E's godmother—Anna—and Dr. Gwendolyn Littleton. With Anna and Aunt Gwen for backup, Heath figured she could pull off the mother thing.

Leaning against the wall for support, Heath reviewed the past couple of weeks with her daughter. There had been red flags: Elizabeth found in tears and insisting it was "nothing." That was eight or ten days ago. Elizabeth switching screens on her computer, and snapping at Heath for sneaking up on her—as if Heath-cum-apparatus could sneak up on any hearing individual. Had that been a week back? Less. Five days.

The dark, hard rap music started day before yesterday. Elizabeth was listening to it on her iPod so loud Heath could hear the beat. She'd had no idea what the lyrics were, but Elizabeth had looked as if they were driving spikes into her brain.

Then today. The rancid, hate-filled, misogynist rant

out in the air, poisoning the hearth fairies that protected the house. Aunt Gwen had made up the fairies when Heath was a little girl and afraid of the dark. This new dark was scarier.

Lots of red flags.

Heath had noticed. She'd mentioned Elizabeth's uncharacteristic behavior to Gwen. As they did with every step in the girl's development, the two of them hashed over Elizabeth's every move.

She was in the midst of the hormonal storms of puberty.

She had a fight with a girlfriend.

She had a secret boy-crush.

She had an embarrassing disappointment.

Heath and Gwen agreed not to interfere.

That was before the rap, Heath thought. This crap was not a red flag, it was a cry for help.

With an effort, Heath pushed away from the wall. White-knuckled, muttering, "Dem bones, dem bones, dem dry bones," she began the final, interminable few yards of hallway, cursing the carpeting with every laborious shuffle of her feet.

Sweat dripping from her nose, breath coming in puffs and gasps, she bumped open her daughter's bedroom door without knocking. Elizabeth was not there.

The bathroom door was ajar, rap blasting out, steam augmenting its hellishness. Forgetting the pain in her shoulders, Heath muscled her way across the room. Using a crutch as a battering ram, she bashed the bathroom door open with so much force it struck the commode.

Tail down, Wily growled.

Steam obscured the mirror and made a wraith of the girl in the tub. Momentarily disoriented, Heath would have fallen if she hadn't been wedged between crutches and doorframe. Vision cleared. What remained was a child—a young woman really, sixteen—in a bath so hot her skin had reddened below the waterline. She was holding a razor blade to her wrist. Tears and sweat poured down her face to fall like rain into the bath. A girl and a razor and an angry voice shouting "fuck that bitch" to the beat of a machine gun in the hands of a madman.

Heath reached over and pulled the iPod out of the speaker. Silence bloomed like a blessing, broken only by the drip, drip, drip of slow tears. Pressing a button on her wrist, she activated the metal bones. With a hum like that of an electric window in an older-model Cadillac, they eased her down onto the seat of the commode. She moved her crutches so they wouldn't be between her and her daughter.

"Honey . . . ," she said gently, and held out her hand. Elizabeth laid the razor carefully in her palm. Heath set it on the sink counter.

Elizabeth had been contemplating suicide with the layered blades of a Lady Schick. At best, she could have given herself what amounted to nasty paper cuts. Though she was in a hot bath, as the media always portrayed suicides for some reason, Elizabeth, being a modest girl by nature and upbringing, was wearing the iridescent blue one-piece bathing suit she wore for swim races.

Much to laugh at.

Nothing funny.

For a minute neither spoke. Elizabeth, flushed with heat, eyes and mouth swollen from crying, long dark hair sleek as a seal's pelt on her shoulders, looked so small and young.

A lump hard and hot as a burning coal formed in Heath's throat. "What can I do?" she managed, her voice burned and choking. "What can I say? Who can I kill? For you, Elizabeth, I will do it. Whatever you need, I will do it."

TWO

Denise sipped her Coke, flat and warm from neglect. Just like me, she thought sourly, then reminded herself not to let the sourness seep into her face. Pleasant expression neutralizing her muscles, she let her eyes casually wander past Peter Barnes and his entourage.

Park picnics had become exercises in self-control. Denise loathed them, but she was damned if she was going to let Peter keep her from attending. Tables were scattered on the grass behind park headquarters. Two, shoved together, were loaded down with hamburger buns and condiments in the oversized squeeze bottles that always struck her as mildly obscene given the flatulent sounds that sputtered out with the ketchup, mustard, and, especially, the pickle relish.

Peter was sitting with his new wife, Lily. *Lily.* Could it get any worse? He couldn't have married a Sheila or a Judy?

Or someone remotely his own age?

Like me, she thought again. Hatred burned like acid in the back of her throat. Peter was forty-six, four years older than she. Pretty little Lily had just turned thirty. Their baby, Olivia, was three months. Married fourteen months and a baby girl. Lucky, lucky Peter. Lucky Lily.

Three years had passed since Denise had been the one sitting next to Peter Barnes at the picnics. More. Thirty-eight months. Yet the wound had not healed. She still felt as if her skin had been peeled from her body, and her flesh, newly flayed, screamed silent and bloody for everyone to see.

For a time—months, maybe as long as a year—Denise had thought things were getting better. Then they started getting worse. Hate would roar like a lion, then tears would sting, but not fall. Thoughts of *them* flooded her mind in muddy rivers, bursting their banks. When the baby came, the flooding grew worse. Some days Denise could not escape endless tape-loops of images of that baby girl.

She hated Peter, hated Lily, though Lily hadn't been the Other Woman, just the next woman. How could she not hate Lily? Lily was young and pretty. Lily had Denise's life, Denise's man, and just to make sure the knife was twisted, the baby Denise could never have.

Could never have because of Peter.

She realized her eyes had been stuck on the happy little family too long, on the baby. Lily was holding the baby, feeding it from a bottle. Lily never nursed. The little cow had no milk.

Lily caught her, smiling, happy, welcoming.

Denise forced a smile that probably didn't work.

Peter had undoubtedly told Lily about poor, old, pathetic Denise, the reject who had taken on the role of the ghost at the manor window, always present, never invited in.

Deciding she'd stayed long enough to prove she wasn't broken-hearted, Denise stood and carried her Coke to the nearest trash bin. In an impotent act of defiance, she didn't put the can in the recycle bin. Given that Peter had chosen to trash her life and recycle his own with the lovely, fertile Lily, she was damned if she would support his pet program.

Artie, the gung-ho new district ranger, sat at a table with one of the secretaries. Young and eager, he was trying to make being a park ranger more like being an Army Ranger, itching for black ops. Denise forced herself to smile at him.

After making it a point to saunter slowly from table to table saying her good-byes so it wouldn't look like she was slinking away with her tail between her legs, Denise made it to her Miata. The last few steps she staggered like a drunk. What the hell was that about?

Holding on to the low door to keep from falling, she took deep breaths. Tremors rattled her bones. Almost as if Peter—his eyes, all the eyes—the baby, Lily, everybody knowing, had brought on some kind of seizure, as if around Peter and his postcard-perfect life she could no longer fill her lungs. Bony fingers of a monster hand wrapped around her rib cage, squeezing and squeezing.

Paranoia rampaged through her veins.

No. No monster. No seizures. Hyperventilation is all. Lily doesn't know. They are fooled. I have them all fooled, Denise told herself. For the most part she knew she was right. Certain people had a knack for seeing the ghost behind the eyes. Those people Denise avoided. The rest, when they bothered to think about her at all, believed she had moved on, that she was just as thrilled as they were with the assistant superintendent's spiffy new family.

When she could do so without stumbling, Denise opened the car door and slid into the low bucket seat. A Mazda ragtop in northern Maine was a rich man's summer toy, but a foolish purchase for a woman who could afford only one car. Denise had bought it a week after Peter announced he "needed space," then promptly gave himself that space by throwing her out of the house they'd shared for eleven years.

Two months later he threw her out of his life.

At the time she bought the convertible she hoped it would make her feel free, sexy. For a brief moment it seemed to, then it didn't, and she'd come to hate it. The list of things she was coming to hate lengthened daily, each new loathing attaching to the anchor that was Peter Barnes. The chain of hate had grown so heavy that some days Denise felt she couldn't carry it another foot, that she would collapse under it and lie helpless until all vestiges of life were crushed from her body.

Before—as in before she was ruined and dumped—Denise used to enjoy the short drive on Route 233 to Bar Harbor. August, high summer, hot days and cool nights greened the park. The coast, with its islands like jeweled rock gardens scattering in a sea of whitecaps and blue water, took on a fairy-tale beauty.

Beauty was not yet on the list of things she hated, but she supposed it would come under the pall eventually.

Bar Harbor, draped in schmaltzy cuteness, was a place she'd used to avoid during tourist season. Alcohol, in its myriad forms, was another thing she'd once scorned. This evening, after suffering through another picnic with the royal family, she craved a place as fake as the promise of Happily Ever After, and a beer. Beers. One had ceased being enough long ago.

On the outskirts of town she pulled into the wide circular drive of the Acadian Lodge. In the 1940s and '50s—the heyday of lodges and camps—the almost-wealthy summered at the Acadian, basking in the shadow of the truly moneyed.

There were cottages then. Denise had seen pictures of them—trim, freshly painted, lawns and gardens in careful rustic disarray, and "campers," looking happy and coddled by armies of servants, mostly girls who'd come up from the cities by train to earn a little money and enjoy a summer by the sea.

No more.

The cabins had long since been torn down and the property sold off in half-acre lots. The lodge had grown as sad and tacky as a drunken old woman. Touches of new paint, sporadically and inexpertly applied, soaked like cheap drugstore makeup into the wrinkles and cracks of wood that had weathered too many winters.

In its glory days, the bar had been a fashionable watering hole. Now it was the haunt of locals, lobstermen mostly. It was dark and smelled faintly of the sea and dead fish. Stale cigarette smoke had permeated the walls and carpets so deeply that all these years after indoor smoking had been legislated into a crime, the smell persisted.

Usually Denise drank at home and alone. For reasons she didn't understand—and didn't want to—she was drawn to the Acadian when things in her mind got too ugly. Slipping into a dark wooden booth in a dark corner, she took off her sunglasses. The room was dominated by a once-elegant long bar backed by a mirror easily six feet high and fifteen feet long. Black age spots pocked the silvering around the edges, contributing to the sense that the place was diseased or moldering back into the stone and lichen upon which it was built.

The bartender raised an eyebrow. "Draft, dark," Denise said, and then worked herself into the corner of the booth until the shadows closed around her. Other patrons had no business seeing memories ripping at her flesh, sharp-taloned and as vicious as harpies.

A couple of lobstermen on barstools were talking about the old guy who'd shot another old guy by the name of Will Whitman for robbing his traps and moving in on his territory. Yet another skirmish in the lobster wars that had been waged along these waters for generations and showed no sign of letting up. Law enforcement was worthless for the most part. Whose traps were where, and who ran which lines, was a mystery to everybody but the men who harvested lobsters for a living. They knew the bottom of the ocean around Maine as well as landlubbers knew the streets of their own neighborhoods.

Denise had heard that the dead man's son, Walter, had been excommunicated from the fishing community because everybody figured his dad was guilty of robbing traps—sins of the father, acorns falling near trees, chips off the old block. She smiled to herself. The bozos knew nothing.

Lobsters disappeared, lobsters were never there in the first place, lobsters were poached. These jokers in their little boats on top of the water could only guess who or what happened right underneath them.

A young couple—tourists, lost or slumming—slid into a booth on the end wall. Both on the same side. The old Denise would have thought it romantic. This new Denise wanted to bite their heads off and spit them into their imported beers.

At the near end of the bar, where the wood curved gracefully toward the mirrored wall, a lone woman sat hunched over a glass. Bleached-blond hair formed a curtain between her and the lobstermen. Denise's booth was on the opposite side of the ersatz veil, so she could see the blonde's face. She was sporting a black eye and a split lip.

Revulsion swept through Denise in a sick-making wave. She couldn't stand that the woman's outside was a public image of her own insides: battered, abused, ashamed, and drinking alone.

Despite that, every few minutes, Denise's gaze found its way back to the blonde on the barstool. Denise had been in law enforcement all of her adult life. A national park ranger, she'd seldom dealt with city-cop stuff. Parks were peaceful places for the most part, even in Acadia, where park and town and resort and sea came together in a patchwork of populations, each with its own agenda. Not once had she pulled her gun, used her baton or her pepper spray. What minimal compliance and self-defense training she'd gotten at the Federal Law Enforcement Training Center in Georgia had long since been forgotten.

Black eyes and split lips, though, were a form of violence she was familiar with. Family troubles don't go away on vacation; they get worse. The damaged face wasn't enough of a novelty to hold Denise's interest, but something was. As she sneaked peeks over the rim of her first beer glass, her second, and then her third, she tried to figure out what was so fascinating.

It became evident that the battered blonde was known to the bartender. Maybe a regular. Denise hadn't seen her here before, but then she never came to the Acadian this early in the evening. The lobstermen came here a lot. Usually, by the time Denise slunk in, they were three sheets to the wind. They might know the woman. Either the acquaintance was slight or they didn't like her. Both pointedly refused to look in her direction. This suited Denise. If they didn't look at the blond barfly, they couldn't look at her.

There was something bizarrely familiar about the woman. Had she arrested her? No, that process was long and, in many ways, intimate. Denise would have remembered.

Acadia, for all it had a large and fluid population in the summer months, was a small town for year-round inhabitants. Had she seen the blonde in a grocery store or, given the face, a hospital emergency room? In her capacity as an EMT she had been to the ER at Mount Desert Island Hospital enough times with injured people.

The woman looked to be in her late thirties or early forties. The barstool made guessing her height tricky, but Denise figured she was about the same height as she was—five foot six—and probably weighed about the same, one hundred thirty pounds. Her face— without the obvious damage—was the kind that can be dressed up or down. Makeup and a good haircut and she'd be pretty. Without it, she was fairly ordinary. Still, there was something . . .

After a while the blonde began looking back. Their eyes met, and Denise stopped her furtive surveillance. The last thing she wanted was to get into a "what're you lookin' at?" bitchfest with a stranger.

Another beer, a trip to the ladies' room.

The lobstermen got up and left. As they passed the blonde, working on her third drink since Denise arrived, one ducked his head and said, "Miz Duffy." The other nodded politely.

Miz Duffy. No lobsterman Denise had run across would call a woman "Miss" unless she was their kid's schoolteacher. Miz Duffy must be Mrs. Duffy. As Denise made her way unsteadily back to her booth, she wondered if they'd made a point of ignoring Mrs. Duffy because they didn't think a married woman should be

alone in a bar, or because they were acquainted with
Mr. Duffy, and the fact that he'd beaten on his wife
made social intercourse awkward.

Mrs. Duffy watched them go, a tired look on her
face, and something more energetic in the curl of her
upper lip, disgust possibly.

The blonde shifted on the stool. Again their eyes
met, this time in the long mirror backing the bar. Realization hit Denise with the force of near-sobriety. Not
disgust. Hatred was what burned in the blonde's eyes.
She knew. Denise had seen it. It greeted her in the bathroom mirror every morning. For a long time they
sat, eyes locked, watching a slurry of emotions, memories and shocks flickering across the faces in the glass
at dizzying speed. Never breaking eye contact, the
blonde stood, picked up her drink, and carried it over
to Denise's booth. She slid into the shadows on the
opposite side.

"I was beginning to think I'd made you up out of
whole cloth," she said, and laughed.

The laugh made the hairs on the back of Denise's
neck prickle.

THREE

Elizabeth wouldn't tell Heath why she'd been contemplating slitting her wrists. When pressed, she cried and looked so desperate it scared Heath into silence.

Dem Bones hung like a Space Age suit of armor on its stand in the corner; Heath, collapsed in the familiar embrace of Robo-butt, was putting water on for tea. While the water heated, she rolled onto the back porch to call Gwen in her persona of doctor and great-aunt. She also called Anna Pigeon in her persona of law enforcement ranger at Rocky Mountain National Park and Elizabeth's godmother. Surely, between medicine, the law, and Heath's blind determination, they could find out what had driven Elizabeth to despair and put the child back together again.

Curled up on the oversized leather sofa, and in her pajamas though it was not yet sundown, Elizabeth accepted the tea without comment. Elizabeth couldn't care less about tea, but it was all Heath could think to offer, and she was grateful her daughter took it.

Heath had not seen E this hopelessly totaled since, at nine years old, she had wandered out of the night woods weeping and nearly naked.

A year earlier, during a nightmare canoe trip on Minnesota's Fox River, Elizabeth had been as strong and canny as any battle veteran. Heath had almost forgotten she wasn't Rambo; she was a sixteen-year-old girl. Evidently, whatever this evil was, it was of a variety that struck at the heart of where that wonderful, vulnerable girl lived.

Anna arrived first. Soundless in moccasins without socks, she appeared in the doorway between the kitchen and living room. She must have dropped everything and left work as soon as Heath called. Heath probably sounded as panicked on the phone as she was. She refused to feel guilty. They were talking about Elizabeth's life.

Anna had changed out of her uniform. She was wearing Levi's so worn the knees were white and stringy with age, not artifice, and an oversized, man's white shirt, probably her husband Paul's, rolled up to the elbows.

A while back Anna had turned fifty. More gray twined through her braid now than when Heath had first met her. Decades in the sun had freckled and creased her skin in a way that suited her skull and her soul. Anna had grown to look like a person you would want to tell your darkest secrets, all the while harboring an uneasy sense she already knew what they were.

"Hey," Heath greeted her. She didn't expect a hug. Anna was not a touchy-feely kind of woman. Both in greeting and departing, Anna nodded. A modified bow of respect, Heath guessed. Or dismissal.

Perhaps because Elizabeth was so young and damaged when she'd met Anna, she had crept through those boundaries. Leaping off the sofa, the girl threw herself into the ranger's arms. As tall as Anna, and a few pounds heavier, Heath expected Elizabeth's onslaught to knock Anna back into the kitchen, but Ranger Pigeon stood staunch as an oak and wrapped her arms around the clinging girl.

Relief only slightly tainted with jealousy washed over Heath. Chest muscles loosened. She drew her first deep breath since she'd found Elizabeth in the bath. It saddened her that, physically, she could not be Elizabeth's rock. Without bitterness, Heath knew she'd gotten the harder job, to anchor and support her emotionally.

Anna folded down onto the floor, her back against the sofa, legs crossed Indian fashion. Elizabeth curled up on the seat behind her and played with Anna's pigtail the way she'd done when she was a little wreck of a girl, still in shock from the multiple ordeals that brought her into Heath's life. Holding on to the braid, Elizabeth whisked the tail over her eyes and cheekbones as if sweeping away cobwebs.

"I wish you hadn't changed out of uniform," Heath said to Anna. "I was kind of looking forward to having a gun close to hand."

Before Anna could respond, Gwen blew in through the outside door. Gwen was in her late seventies, small-boned, fragile-looking, with wildly curly hair that she ignored with the exception of taking time every three weeks to keep it as resolutely red as it had always been. Dr. Gwen Littleton was the antithesis of a little old lady. Heath thought of her aunt as a whirlwind, a dust devil, a genie in a tiny bottle, a force that, though small in size, was most definitely to be reckoned with.

She gusted into the living room, dropping the black leather doctor's bag she'd been given when she graduated from medical school—and still carried every day—on the floor. The air that came in with her was the kind that can only be found during dry high-mountain summers, a draft so light and crisp, so warm and full of optimism, you feel that if only you could spread your wings wide enough you could fly.

"I left the door open," Gwen announced. "Fresh air. My unbottled, unpatented, priceless, free cure-all." Dumping her purse, Heath's mail, and a long turquoise-and-gold scarf she'd been carrying for some reason, she put her hands on her hips, surveyed the three of them, and said, "Okay, now, what's this all about?"

Elizabeth started to cry again, mopping at the tears with the tail of Anna's braid. Though it had to be absorbing a bit of snot on the side, Anna didn't look like she had any intention of rescuing it.

Gwen swooped down onto the sofa and folded her great-niece in her thin arms. Anna took one of Elizabeth's narrrow feet between her roughened hands and began to massage it gently. Heath rolled nearer, closing

Elizabeth into a circle of love. An impenetrable circle? Probably not. Love did not conquer all, but
sometimes it made it bearable.

"Baby, what is it? You have to tell us," Gwen
crooned.

"Or we'll never go away," Anna added.

"Not even to go to the bathroom," Heath said. "How
disgusting would that be?"

"I am so ashamed," Elizabeth mumbled through her
tears and the soggy end of Anna's braid. "I swear I'm
going to die of embarrassment. Just die! I want to die,"
she said with bone-chilling sincerity. "I'm so ashamed."
Tears clogged her throat then, and she sobbed into
Gwen's boney bird-shoulder.

"I accidentally fell on a friend of mine and killed
her," Anna said. "That was pretty embarrassing."

Heath almost blurted out, "What the fuck?" Leading technical climbs for much of her adult life, Heath
was fluent in the modern vernacular, and "fuck" was
such a jolly good bad word. But when Elizabeth came
into her world, Heath had determined to clean up her
language. Saying the F-word was one thing; hearing it
on the lips of a fairylike little girl was obscene. Worse,
it was tacky, low rent.

Anyway, it had been ruined. On the Fox River one
of the thugs had, quite simply, used it up. He had used
all possible, probable, and improbable applications of
the word, finally rendering it absurd. Now, when E and
Anna and Heath heard someone say "fuck," they'd lift
an eyebrow, exchange a smile.

Left without it, Heath fell back on the classics. Twelve apostles and forty thousand cowboys couldn't be wrong. God damn it to hell, bastard, SOB. All were workable.

"The hell you say," she amended. From the corner of her eye she noted Elizabeth was listening. The sobbing had quieted.

"No kidding," Anna said somberly. "Squashed her throat. Now that's something to be ashamed of."

"I once told a woman her fetus was going to be stillborn," Gwen admitted. "She mourned and wailed through seventeen hours of labor. The baby never moved, its heart never beat, I swear it! The moment she was born, that baby girl was wiggling and giggling. The wretched little thing had been lying doggo, or hiding behind Mom's liver or some darn thing. I thought I was going to die of humiliation before the mother killed me for scaring her to death. Thank God that was back before mothers sued for every little birthmark. I was so ashamed I didn't show my face at the hospital for nearly a week. When I did, doctors, and even some nurses, started calling me Dr. Lazarus."

"I never killed anybody or scared anybody half to death," Heath said. "But in college I got drunk and made a bet with this guy that I could free-climb the front of the administration building, no lines, no belays, no shoes, no gloves, no nothing. Bet him a hundred bucks. He upped it to a hundred and fifty if I did it totally naked. I was halfway up and doing great when the cops showed up with the spotlights. I was charged with drunk and disorderly, disturbing the peace, and—this hurt worst—defacing university property, apparently by plastering my bare-naked ass on it."

"You did not!" Gwen exclaimed.

"Spent the night and half the next day in jail. I was too ashamed to call you. The only reason I wasn't expelled was that the boy who made the bet with me was the president of the university's son. Cross my heart and hope to die."

Elizabeth stared at her wide-eyed, completely engaged now. "Oh gosh, Mom, how did you stand it?" she cried.

Absurdly pleased that her tale had trumped accidental death by falling on, and nearly terrifying to death by misdiagnosis, Heath said, "This was before everybody had iPhones. I was only totally humiliated in front of twenty or thirty people, not millions on the Web."

Elizabeth's face went deathly pale. Heath had read the phrase "deathly pale" many times, but this was the first time she'd ever witnessed the phenomenon. It was as if she watched the blood drain from beneath her daughter's skin, leaving a gray pallor in its wake. For a moment she thought E was going to faint or scream or vomit. What she did was far more frightening. She began striking herself in the face with her balled fists.

Heath ached to hold her. She knew that the best she could manage was to lurch upon the pile like Frankenstein's monster. Cursing the ice that had bested her, she turned her wheelchair sharply and sped from the room, left the hardwood and hit the carpet without slowing down. Robo-butt had never moved so fast. In an instant she was down the hall and in Elizabeth's room. The pink iPhone, a gift from Gwen, was on the bedside table. Elizabeth's laptop was on her desk, holding pride of place in the midst of a landfill's worth of cosmetics, tissues, magazines, earrings, and whatever else had been dropped there over the past two years.

Heath took both electronic gadgets and dropped them into the saddlebags on her chair. Another twenty seconds and she was back in the living room parked beside the couch. "Elizabeth," she said in a tone that cut through the soft fuzzy outpourings of Gwen and the somber attentions of Anna. Elizabeth looked up, eyes and cheeks wet, lips red and swollen.

Heath held up the pink cell phone.

"Noooooo," Elizabeth begged. She covered her ears and squeezed her eyes shut as if waiting for the fuse to burn down to the dynamite.

"Yes," Heath said. "Rotten ice." Rotten ice was their code for *This will try to kill you. Face it or run away fast.*

Gwen glared at Heath. Anna nodded slightly. In the minute or less Heath had been gone, Anna must have figured it out. Heath pushed the message button. Seventeen new messages in the in-box. "I've never had seventeen messages in my entire life," Heath said. A small whimper from Elizabeth. Not funny. Heath opened the first message and read it. Then she read it aloud in a flat voice. " 'Have you been on The Page? Dweeb said you did the basketball team. TNT?' "

"Kimmy?" Heath asked as she noted who it was from.

"She's in my geometry class," E said miserably.

"TNT? Explosive?" Anna asked.

"Totally Not True," Elizabeth said. "How could she have to ask?" Tears started. She knocked them from her eyes with the backs of her hands.

E was going to be brave. Heath hoped she was. She opened the second. " 'Check The Page.' Tiffany sent this one," Heath noted. "The Page?" She raised an interrogative eyebrow.

"It's a blog the kids all read." E hid her eyes with the tail of Anna's braid. "Somebody posted that I did things I didn't do."

"Like the basketball team?" Anna said dryly.

"Like that," E said.

Heath opened the third message: " 'Who hasn't screwed you yet?' My God, this stuff is insane. Somebody is going to get their skull bashed in if I have any say in the matter."

The fifth had a picture attached, an image of a woman being mounted by a Great Dane. Heath didn't read it aloud. She passed the phone to Gwen.

" 'I guess you like being done to by dogs.' "

"Holy Mary Mother of God," Gwen whispered.

Anna had taken the laptop from the saddlebag and had it open on her thighs. "What's the address of the blog?"

E told her. Anna typed it in.

Heath rolled her chair over to read it. " 'EJ pulled a train—you hear that? After the game.' "

" 'True. I was the caboose.' That one's signed Spike," Anna said.

"It's this creep everybody calls Dweeb. He signs himself Spike," Elizabeth said. "God, the *Dweeb*!" E cried. "Nobody could think I'd have anything to do with the Dweeb!"

" 'No sloppy seconds for me.' This one is signed IceBlow."

"A slime bag Dweeb hangs with. You should have let me kill myself," E whispered.

" 'Sloppy twenty-seconds more like,' " Anna read on relentlessly. Heath considered stopping her, saving Elizabeth the pain, but she believed Anna was right in what she was doing. Elizabeth already knew what they said. Aloud, in Anna's flat, almost bored tone, they lost some of their snickers-in-the-dark malice and sounded as stupid as they were. Almost.

" 'Not in all orifices.' " Anna looked around. "Orifices?" she asked no one in particular. "Big word for this moron." She returned her attention to the computer and read the last two quickly, as if the whole thing were too foolish for words.

" 'No shit?' asks bozo," Anna said.

" 'Meat sandwich with a blow job topper.' This from thug number two. Who started this ball rolling?" she asked Elizabeth in cold even tones.

"I don't know," E sobbed. "The only names I recognize are Dweeby Spike and his creep pal, IceBrain. If cooties weren't extinct, they'd have them big-time."

Of course, Heath thought. Once the story was out, the dweebs and the creeps wanted to be part of the action. If a girl was having sex with the other boys, why not them? "This is good," Heath said. "Nobody cares what they say. They're creeps." That sounded good and might even be true.

"Your Facebook password?" Anna asked.

"WilyCoyote2015," Elizabeth said softly. "Capital W, capital C." At the sound of his name, Wily thumped his tail on the floor. Pushing to his feet, the old dog ambled over and stuck his head under Heath's hand. It was as comforting as it always had been.

Anna looked up from the laptop. "More of the same," she said. "Where else?"

"Everywhere," Elizabeth said hollowly. "There's a website the kids go to, like a Mean Girls thing. That blog. I've found three others. Things are forwarded to my whole class sometimes."

Cyberbullying: vicious, anonymous, all-pervasive. Heath forced her voice to calmness, then asked, "Who started sending these first?"

"I don't know," Elizabeth whispered. "Honest, I don't know. Don't tell anyone," she begged. "Anna, promise me, no cops. No cops, Heath, nobody. Gwen, no doctors, and please, please, please don't talk to any of my friends' parents. Pleeeeease!"

For a second, Heath suspected Elizabeth knew, not only why she was being targeted, but by whom, and her sixteen-year-old mind was telling her that if she ratted out the culprit, it would dump her into a hell worse than the one she was already in. The one that could only be escaped by razors to the wrist.

Heath changed the subject. "When did"—and she waved the cell phone rather than speak the evil words—"this stuff begin?"

"I don't know," Elizabeth said automatically. Then, "About a week after school let out for the summer." Elizabeth was a rising senior at Boulder High. Not in with the in crowd or the jocks, but at the moderately comfortable level of acceptable anonymity that allows a majority of kids to survive high school without permanent scarring.

"Who?" Anna demanded.

Shocked into honesty by Anna's tone, Elizabeth said uncertainly, "Tiffany?"

"Tiffany? Tiffany's your best friend," Heath said. Not a friend of Heath's choosing. The girl's parents were Christian fundamentalists, or at least her mother was. Heath figured Elizabeth had suffered enough at the hands of religious fanatics for several lifetimes, but Tiffany seemed like a nice girl.

In Heath's opinion the friendship was more one of opportunity than genuine attraction. Tiffany, her folks, and her two-year-old brother, Brady, moved into the house next door; she and Elizabeth were the same age and starting their freshman year together; both settled at the same level in the high school pecking order. Admittedly, Elizabeth seemed to enjoy Tiffany's company. Most days either she was at Tiffany's or Tiff was over here. It suddenly occurred to Heath she'd not seen the girls together for a while, a week or more.

Rotten mother, she scolded herself. Blind as a bat.

"I don't think we're friends anymore," Elizabeth said.

"Did you guys get in a fight?" Heath asked. She

should have asked this a week ago. She should have been paying better attention.

"Not exactly. Momma, could I have some more tea? It really helps." When Elizabeth called Heath "Momma," either they were having a moment or Heath was being conned. Obviously Elizabeth really, really did not want to talk about this. All three adults homed in on the vibe like hounds on a scent.

The only thing missing was the baying.

FOUR

Bad idea to be doing this drunk, Denise thought, but continued dragging the straps of her scuba tank up over her wetsuit. Cold water would sober her up quick enough, she rationalized. If it didn't, and she drowned, that was all right, too. Since all of her children had been murdered, and Peter had thrown her away like so much damaged goods, death didn't seem like such a bad option.

Except that Peter would be glad she was dead.

Except that the son of a bitch would go right on living his spiffy little life. With his precious Lily and the baby. They would watch the baby that should have been hers grow up without caring that Denise was fish food.

Mouthpiece adjusted, gear hooked to her harness, she made a final check of the gauges with her flashlight. How drunk could she be if she remembered to check gauges? It wasn't as if she was planning on going deep or staying down long, half an hour max. Hell, I dive drunk better than I do sober, she thought. *Drunk diver.*

The phrase amused her, and as she went over backwards into the ocean, she forgot to hold on to her mask. Cursing and sputtering, she managed to catch it before it sank and get it back on. So much for the "better drunk" theory of diving.

Mask adjusted, she got her bearings. The night was perfect. Warm, overcast, and as dark as the inside of Jonah's whale. Her navy blue runabout on a midnight sea in a great big ocean was as close to invisible as a corporeal body was likely to get.

She upended.

Following the anchor line toward the bottom, she thought about Will Whitman, the lobsterman who got shot for robbing that old guy's traps. Whitman might have been rustling lobsters, but the traps he got shot over were in her territory. The murder had renewed hostilities in the long-running feud.

Not that she cared. People shot people. People did a lot of awful things to other people. Nobody gave a damn. Her own mother had dumped her. She'd been adopted by borderline assholes. Cry me a river; nobody cares about anybody other than themselves.

Enough! she told herself and quieted her mind. Stopping thoughts from spinning was hard. It was like her mind had developed a mind of its own, and maybe neither one was her friend.

No! she shouted silently. The dueling minds couldn't have this place. Clenching her jaw, she forced herself to look outward.

She loved that only the circle of her lamp and the anchor line existed. Under the Atlantic at night was the only time she felt anywhere near free or whole any-more. Contained in apparatus and silence, held in weightlessness and peace, she savored the balm to her soul. Above, in the light, in the world of men, she de-voured herself, ripped the flesh from her bones with her teeth, like a coyote chewing off its own leg to free it-self from the jaws of the trap.

Watching the line play through her gloved hand as she descended, she let herself think about the woman she'd just met in the bar of the old Acadian Lodge.

Neither one of them had said anything for the lon-gest time after the blonde slid into the booth and made her cryptic announcement. "I'd begun to think I'd made you up."

They sat and stared at each other in the dim light of the bar. Denise was struck dumb. She'd never quite known what was meant when people said that. She did now. There were no more words in her head at that mo-ment. Had there been, she wouldn't have been able to move her tongue or push out the breath to say them. Words had become futile pathetic little things, not fit to bring into the immensity of the idea that had slipped in with the blonde.

"Takes some getting used to, doesn't it? I've been thinking on it for months now, so I'll talk while you get your mind around it, how's that?" the woman said. Her voice sounded creepy, the way Denise's always did when she heard herself on a tape recorder, familiar but alien. Not right.

"My name is Paulette Duffy. I'm forty-one." She smiled. Denise drank down the last of her beer, then waved at the bartender for another. Paulette's teeth weren't the same. Denise had gotten her front incisors busted in a schoolyard fight and had neat straight caps. Paulette's leaned in as if they needed each other for support.

"I think I'm forty-two," Denise managed. "But that could be off a year either way."

"Forty-two on March sixth of next year," Paulette Duffy said. Her hand shot out for no reason Denise could see and banged the metal napkin holder. "Sorry," she laughed. "I guess I'm turning into a klutz in my old age."

"Nerves," Denise said to be saying something. "Happens to me more and more." Her head was swimming. Too much beer. Too much everything. Sitting back, she let her head fall against the cracked leather of the booth. "Forty-one," she whispered. "Forty-two on the sixth of March. That kind of makes a person real, doesn't it? Knowing when you were born, knowing somebody cared enough to write it down."

"You never knew?" Paulette asked softly. Denise hated being pitied for her rotten childhood, hated talking about it, wouldn't talk about it. Peter was the only one to whom she'd told all the grit and grime, and now, every time he looked at her through the scrim of his new clean wife and spotless baby, she could see every bit of shit she'd ever been through clinging to her in his eyes.

Now she wanted to spew it all out like vomited beer here in this booth for Paulette Duffy. "Never knew," she said. "I'm not ready for any of this." She pulled the man's wallet she favored out of the hip pocket of her pants, then dumped the contents on the table. It was probably enough to pay for her drinks three times over. She didn't care. "I'll never be ready for any of this." Standing unsteadily, she waited a second for the room to stop spinning.

"Here," Paulette said. She scribbled on a bar napkin. When Denise didn't hold out her hand to take it, Paulette shoved it in Denise's pants pocket. "This is my address and the number of my cell phone. I got one of those prepaid ones at Walmart. I have lots of minutes left. Call me. Promise. Promise you'll call me."

Denise didn't promise. She made it to the Miata. Then to the runabout. Then to the sanctity of lobster rustling under the sea.

The ocean floor coalesced out of the gray-green circle of gloom at the farthest reach of Denise's light. Turning herself so her feet pointed earthward, she came to a gentle landing on the sand. Froglike, iridescent green in the glow of the lamp, her swim fins squeezed small swirls of liquid dust puffed from beneath her.

The depth gauge read twenty-six feet. Habit was all that made her check it. This stretch of Davy Jones's locker was, metaphorically speaking, the back of her hand.

Moving with the slow grace of a hippopotamus on the bed of the Nile she turned, letting her light drift in a circle until she saw the yellow line snaking down from the buoy she'd anchored near, the marker of a line of lobster traps. With a lazy kick she rotated to the horizontal and swam toward it.

Traps were on the end of lines connected to Styrofoam buoys on the surface. Lobstermen checked their traps every day, putting fresh bait in if they needed it. The buoys were marked with the license number of whichever fisherman owned the trap.

The traps on the ocean floor out from Somes were the old variety, wooden crates covered in rope mesh, with a circular opening just big enough for a lobster to crawl in. Occasionally, Denise mused, surely a lobster, smarter than her fellows, after having consumed the bait, would crawl back out to live and reproduce. Maybe man had created the ultimate evolution facility, and one day the giant spiders would take over Silicon Valley.

The first trap had two lobsters in it, but they were small. She passed them by. The next had one enormous old fellow. Lobsters could live a hundred years, though most didn't make it more than ten or fifteen. This guy looked to weigh close to two pounds. He had been around a while.

Careful to avoid the claws, Denise reached in and dragged him out. Her hand twitched as if she'd been hit by an electric shock, much the way Paulette Duffy's had. Her knuckles rapped on the side of the trap, and her fingers opened. With a flick of his tail, the lobster shot into the darkness.

Nerves.

Over forty and falling apart, Denise thought. The big spider would have been a good addition to the canvas sack trailing from a tether attached to her dive harness, but, in a way, she was glad it had escaped. Sad to end one's life in a tourist's stomach.

When she had ten good-sized lobsters, she switched off her light. Her bag could easily hold as many as fifteen, but she made it a rule never to take every one she found. If a trap had a couple of lobsters in it, she'd take only one. Those she emptied, if there was any bait left inside, might lure in another crustacean before the licensee came to check his catch. This way she figured the lobsterman would be pretty sure his traps had been poached, but not a hundred percent sure.

Denise rotated her lobster rustling through four different patches. All they had in common was that they were shallow and easily accessible from Somes Sound, where she moored her little boat. Other than running into somebody night diving—and probably up to no good either—while she was in the act of robbing the traps, there was no way she could get caught.

Denise liked that the lobstermen knew they'd been had, liked that she was thumbing her nose at the holier-than-thous in the park service, the Peter Barneses. Liked the feeling that, at least in this, she was the one in control. It was she, Denise Castle, who was making fools of them all. That was as important as the money she got for her catch with the less than honest owner of the Big Fat Lobster Trap, a seafood restaurant on the outskirts of Bar Harbor.

Lobster rustling was petty payback for what had been done to her since she was old enough to remember. Pathetic, if she thought about it, but it was the best she could do.

Until now.

Paulette Duffy.

There were possibilities opening to her that hadn't existed before.

Kicking off the bottom, she let herself rise gently to the surface. She had not been deep enough, nor down long enough, to make any decompression stops necessary. At the surface, she bobbed, a black sea creature in a black sea. Finding her boat was the most challenging aspect of her midnight forays into the seafood aisle of the Atlantic.

Under the gunwale, on either side of the bow, she had mounted three small LED lights. They were green. She'd been careful not to put them in a line or evenly spaced—the telltale marks of a work of man, not nature. Glimpsed by anyone, they'd be taken for a reflection, a bit of phosphorescent sea vegetation, or a trick of the light. For her they were homing beacons.

After a minute or two she saw them winking as the boat rose and fell on a gentle swell. She swam toward it. Having tied her sack of squirming arachnids to the starboard cleat, Denise heaved herself over the gunwale. As always, her first action was to remove and stow her dive gear, then pull on Levi's, a sweatshirt, and a ball cap to cover her wet hair. She'd established her reputation as a woman who enjoyed night diving. Still, diving at night, alone, was considered dangerous enough to raise questions she'd rather not answer on the off chance she ran into anyone. The lobsters she could always cut loose back into the ocean if need be.

An innocent, if nocturnal, ranger once again, enjoying the resource and preserving it for blah, blah, blah, she started her motor and headed back toward Somes

Sound. Bear Island loomed to her port side, dark and forbidding, its mysterious, reclusive owners seldom in evidence, then Boar Island, smaller and virtually tree-less. Boar had a jagged silhouette that reminded De-nise of a ruined castle, the turrets half crumbling. The lady who owned it had a bad heart and was currently in a convalescent home in Bangor.

That's what happens to women who have no chil-dren to care for them, Denise thought. In old age they become orphans and are thrown on the state for their keep. Denise did not want to end her life the way it had begun, an unwanted orphan beholden to the state of Maine for a meal and a roof over her head.

That brought her back to the battered blonde, Pau-lette Duffy.

And all the new possibilities.

FIVE

Elizabeth knew she'd stepped in it, Heath could tell. As three adult stares bored into her, she groaned and rolled her eyes toward the ceiling. This show of sass did more to cheer up Heath than a thousand clowns in a barrel full of monkeys. "You said you 'didn't exactly' have a fight. What is 'not exactly' having a fight?" Heath asked.

Regardless of the incidents that should have aged Elizabeth before her time, she retained that magnificent innocence of face one seldom sees in anyone over the age of ten. When she was with people she trusted, or too tired to keep her guard up, her emotions could be as easily read as those of a two-year-old. Heath watched in loving fascination as Elizabeth decided to lie, thought better of it, decided to cry, changed her mind, and, finally, began.

"You know Mr. and Mrs. Edleson, Tiff's mom and dad?" Elizabeth asked. The question was meant for Gwen and Anna. Of course Heath knew them. Sam was around forty, thick sandy hair, nice build. If he hadn't been cursed with a seriously weak chin he would have been a handsome man. A chin implant probably would have changed his life. As it was, Heath noticed, Sam vacillated between arrogance and obsequiousness. Terry, his wife, said he worked as an apartment and condo manager for a company that rented real estate to vacationers by the week or month. Ostensibly this job was what brought the family from Coeur d'Alene, Idaho, to Boulder, Colorado. Terry was a part-time bookkeeper for an auto-body company. In her mid-to-late thirties, she ran to fat, twenty pounds or so over-weight, no longer particularly obese by American standards. Her hair was the same color as Sam's, but hers was from a bottle. Overall she seemed pleasant: pleasant face, pleasant voice. Heath couldn't think of any serious drawbacks to her as a neighbor—or even as the mother of Elizabeth's best friend—except that Terry talked too much in general, and too much about her God and her husband in particular.

The moment she'd spot Heath outside, words would begin to flow, a river with no end in sight. Heath wasn't as quick at escaping as she'd been in her salad days. There was a long trek from the mailbox to the ramp beside the kitchen steps with nothing but a low hedge between her property and the Edlesons'. During these rolling social events, Heath had been informed in far more detail than she cared for that Sam was cut out for bigger things, Sam was unhappy in his job, Sam had always thought . . . God had a plan for Sam, but . . .

"I vaguely remember the Edlesons," Anna said,

cutting into Heath's thoughts. "You had Paul and me over as backup when you invited them for dinner last summer."

Last summer. Heath was surprised. She'd thought she'd made it a point to socialize with her neighbors, and especially the parents of her daughter's best friend, at least two or three times in the past year. Evidently not. There'd always been an excuse not to set herself up for an evening of Sam's seesaw personality and Terry's mouth.

"I say hi whenever I see them," Gwen said. "Though if it's Mrs. Edleson, 'hi' can take a chunk out of one's day."

Elizabeth laughed. If the sound had been a dead fish, both Heath and Wily would have rolled in it. A child's laughter, particularly after tears, wasn't something Heath had ever fancied getting dewy-eyed over, but she was, and not for the first time, either.

"Well, me and Tiff—"

"Tiff and I," Gwen corrected, then looked abashed that she'd interrupted at such a time.

"You and Tiff," Heath said to get Elizabeth going again. She didn't want to give her time to reconsider that lie she'd seen sneaking across her face earlier.

"We were supposed to be looking after Brady, Tiff's little brother," she explained to Anna and Gwen, in case they'd forgotten about him. "He's a monster. A real monster—he bites and spits; he just never lets his mom see him doing it, so she thinks he's like this little angel and Tiff and I are the evil stepsisters or something. Anyway, we were supposed to be watching him because it was Wednesday night—remember, Mom? I wanted to go over even though we'd be babysitting so Tiff and I could decide what to wear on the last day of school? Not like it matters, but there's always stuff on the last day and, well, you know."

Heath nodded, though she didn't know, and didn't remember that particular Wednesday.

"Wednesday nights are big church nights. Usually Tiff and her brother both go, and sometimes her dad, but Brady had been pretending to have the flu all day, so Mrs. Edleson let him stay home if Tiff would watch him. Mr. Edleson stayed home, too, though I got the feeling Mrs. Edleson wasn't happy about that. Then, around eight or so, Brady disappeared to pull the wings off of flies or whatever—"

"Does the kid torture animals?" Anna asked darkly.

Elizabeth was untouched by the ice in her voice. "No," she said. "He's not like a little Hannibal Lecter in the making or anything. At least not that I've seen. He's mostly into torturing high school girls, as in Tiff and me.

"So Tiff went out to the backyard—you know what a big yard they have, part of it borders on the creek— because that's where the little monster likes to hide out in the dark and leap out and scare the bejesus out of us. I didn't want to deal, so I stayed in the living room, where we'd been watching boring kid movies to keep Brady happy.

"Turns out Tiff wasn't in the yard looking for Brady." Elizabeth faltered to a stop.

Heath, Anna, and Gwen waited in respectful silence.

Heath wondered if they worked as hard as she did not to demand answers.

Elizabeth sighed deeply and resumed. "Her dad had intercepted her coming in and sent her and Brady out for something at the drugstore. So, anyway, I was sitting on this big couch they have in the living room playing solitaire on my phone, and Mr. Edleson comes down from upstairs and sits on the couch and starts asking me the usual lame questions. How do I like school and what do I want to be when I grow up. Then he asks if I have a boyfriend, and I say don't I wish, and he starts in this long thing about some tribe in darkest wherever, and how fabulous it is that the old guys, uncles even—gross—introduce the virgins into womanhood. Way gross."

She looked up from where her hands were picking at the edge of a fray on the hem of her pajama top, swept an inclusive glance over Heath and the others, then returned to her hands. "It reminded me of something Father Sheppard would say."

Father Sheppard—Dwayne Sheppard—was the leader of the pseudo-Mormon cult Heath and Anna had rescued Elizabeth from when she was nine years old. Sheppard believed in multiple wives, the younger the better. Heath could feel her blood pressure rising. Anna and Gwen were as stone.

"Then what happened?" Gwen asked softly.

"He like put his hand on my thigh and leaned in and kissed me. A wet sloppy kiss that Wily would be disgusted by. I was, you know, so totally freaked, for a second I didn't do anything. I mean, I didn't kiss him back, but I just froze. I guess he thought I was saying what he was doing was okay." Elizabeth's eyes filled again, and her hands came up to hide her face.

Gwen took hold of Elizabeth's wrists, prying her hands from her cheeks. "You didn't do anything wrong. Nothing. Nada. Zip," she said firmly.

"And he didn't think what he was doing was okay," Anna said. "He's nearly forty, he is your best friend's father, and he's married. He knew it was not okay. You did not bring this on yourself. Mr. Edleson is a scumbag."

Anna rose to her feet. Heath, tuned in to the finer details of human locomotion, noticed she didn't move with the effortless grace she once had; still, she rose fluidly. Only the faintest of grunts and the crack of a knee or ankle attested to the effort.

"What are you doing, Anna?" Heath asked warily.

"I'm going to pay a call on the neighbors," she replied.

"Noooo," Elizabeth wailed.

"I'll take care of that end of things," Heath said, a hint of territorial challenge in her tone.

For a moment Anna swayed like grass in a gentle breeze. Heath waited to see if she would respect the role of mother or if she would go tear Sam Edleson's house down. Heath wasn't sure which outcome she was hoping for. Anna settled, folded down, and took up her position on the floor beside the sofa.

"Was that the whole of it?" Heath asked, sensing it wasn't and dreading the rest of the story.

"No," Elizabeth admitted. "While he was slobbering

on me, and grabbing, Tiff came in. She hadn't gotten all the way to the drugstore. He'd given her the keys and told her to take Brady with her in the car! Tiff has a learner's permit, but it's not a good idea for her to be driving at night, even if it's only to the Walgreens. And not with Brady screaming and bouncing around."

Maybe because of what she'd been through in Sheppard's house of wives, Elizabeth seemed to censure Sam Edleson more for endangering his children than for making a sexual assault on her. At that moment, Heath loved her daughter so fiercely she thought she might explode.

"How long was she gone?" Anna asked. Heath moved rapidly from angry and proud of Elizabeth to shaking inside and terribly cold. Had the cretin stopped at a slimy kiss and a grope?

"If she'd've gone to the store, it would have been maybe half an hour. I don't know exactly. We've kind of quit speaking to each other. I guess she came back for something, and she came into the room while her dad was grabbing at me. I'd got over myself and was shoving and hitting to get him off me, and he was sort of flopping around. I don't know if he was trying to stay on me or get off me without getting kneed in the balls, because that was what I was trying to do.

"Tiff started screaming, and Mr. Edleson fell onto the floor. Right then Mrs. Edleson walked in, back way early from her church thing. It usually goes till nine."

"My guess is both Tiff and Terry felt there was something fishy going on," Anna said. "It probably wasn't the first time good old Sam had tried to get time alone with the girl next door. He may have been run out of Idaho for all we know. I'll check it out."

Elizabeth went on, "I managed to get up. Mr. Edleson had torn my blouse—not torn it, really, three of the buttons just popped off—and I was holding it shut, not knowing what else to do. Mrs. Edleson starts yelling, and Tiff stops screaming and starts yelling. Mr. Edleson is a creep, but I didn't want to hang around to watch him get chewed out. TMI big-time." Elizabeth stopped again and fell into what looked almost like a trance.

Staring at her hands, she turned them back and forth as if she'd never seen them before. After a few seconds Heath saw a tear fall like a raindrop on her left palm.

"Momma, they weren't yelling at *him*," she whispered. "They were yelling at *me*."

SIX

It was late when Denise parked her Miata a few houses down from the address Paulette had given her when they were at the Acadian. Several days had passed, full days for Denise. Acadia was at the peak of its busy season. That wasn't the reason she'd put off visiting, however. Twice Paulette Duffy had called her cell. Denise hadn't picked up.

There was a lot to think about before she could distill even part of it into words. Paulette Duffy—Paulette—had had years to grow used to the idea. Until they'd met in the old lodge, Paulette had no proof, but she'd long had suspicions. Not Denise, not the trained law enforcement officer, taught to seek out disparities and make sense of them. Denise hadn't had a clue.

She had always been at pains to give as little thought as possible to her so-called family. Home wasn't "the place where, when you have to go there, they have to take you in," as Frost had written. Home was where, if you had to go there, you might as well put a gun in your mouth and blow your brains out. You'd be doing yourself a favor. The Denise who had suspicions was a deep-secret Denise, a Denise that Ranger Denise Castle had thought long dead.

Three days and two phone calls passed, and finally, at quarter past ten in the evening, Denise was parked on the outskirts of the small village of Otter Creek on a two-lane road that cut through a dollop of public land still extant in the midst of Acadia National Park.

When she'd first bought the Miata, the only concession to good sense she'd made was disabling the interior light, a practice customary in police vehicles. No sense in lighting oneself up for whatever miscreant might be waiting in the dark to take a potshot at the local constabulary.

Denise was grateful for that moment of sanity. Tonight she didn't want to be seen entering or leaving Paulette's place, wasn't sure she wanted the two of them to be associated with one another. Not sure she wanted any of it to be real. Not that she loved the devil she knew, but she was used to him. Paulette would change everything.

Moving quietly and casually, she sauntered the hundred yards between her car and Paulette's cottage. Should one of the scattered residents happen to look out a window, she would appear to be an innocent out on a stroll enjoying the sweet-smelling night.

Paulette's home was what Denise's high school art teacher used to call a two-bit picture in a thousand-dollar frame. Because of its location, the smallish plot

of land had to be worth a fortune. The tiny but picturesque shack squatting on it was hardly worth the match
it would take to burn it down. It had to be family land.
Paulette's husband's, Denise guessed. Had it belonged
to Paulette, surely she would have sold it and run away
on the proceeds.

Paulette's husband, Kurt Duffy, wasn't home. Paulette had said that in the text that finally brought Denise
to Otter Creek.

She stepped into the deeper shadow of the dilapidated porch. Through the four frosted panes in the
front door shone the bluish wavering light from a television. Either the volume was off or the old house had
better soundproofing than its gaping weathered siding
suggested.

Denise rapped lightly on the frame of the screen
door.

The door opened so suddenly it startled her. Paulette
must have been waiting and watching for her. "Come
in," she whispered, as if she shared Denise's desire for
secrecy.

The house's interior was as sorry as its exterior. A
battered, stained sofa, cigarette burns on the arms and
one of the cushions, slumped against the left-hand wall,
facing off with a huge television. The TV was the old-
fashioned kind with a rounded glass front and three feet
of tubes forming an ugly black hump on its back.

A scarred coffee table filled the space between, cup
rings overlapping on the ruined finish, the surface littered with orange crumbs from a single-serving bag of

Doritos. Blinds with broken slats, dents in the plaster walls, dirty finger marks on the woodwork, and the cracking linoleum floor attested to the misery Denise had sensed in the battered blonde on the barstool.

Nausea tinged with panic rose quivering and cold in Denise's midsection. Like Paulette's bruised face, the room was an outward manifestation of the ruin Denise carried inside herself. Scrupulous attention to her outsides kept it hidden. She hoped. Her apartment was spotless, neither cluttered nor Spartan; the art was tasteful, the dishes carefully selected. The same could be said for Denise—sharply pressed clothes, well-cut hair, clean unbitten nails, painstakingly maintained so no one would suspect that her life was no better than if she were living it out in this sad room.

Anger at the tawdriness of Paulette's house flared up, hot and bitter. This place was a slap in the face, insulting.

Paulette read her expression, or maybe her mind.

"It's not me," Paulette said hurriedly. "This room, it's not mine. What I mean is . . . ." Shoving the ruin of bleached hair back from an eye now haloed in the faint yellows and greens of a fading bruise, she let her eyes wander over the desolate interior landscape. A sigh of such exhaustion Denise's anger was blown away on it emptied Paulette Duffy's lungs. "I made it nice, not rich, but orderly and clean, and, believe it or not, it had charm. I'm good with my hands."

Denise was good with her hands. For Peter's house she'd sewn curtains and created flower beds, stenciled bathrooms, and carved tiny animals on each kitchen drawer pull. For Peter's house. For Lily's house. For the baby's house.

"Kurt liked it once. Then, I guess, he knew how much it meant to me . . . I don't know. Things changed. Things got broken," Paulette finished with a resigned smile.

For Denise, too, things had changed. Things had gotten broken.

"Please, please, come," Paulette begged, and to Denise's surprise, Paulette took her hand and tugged her farther into the house. More to Denise's surprise, she didn't jerk her hand free. It was okay. It was good. It was right that her hand was in Paulette's hand. Nothing had ever been so right before. It was like she and Paulette were alone, alone together.

Paulette led her to the pathetic couch, where they sat side by side, knees almost touching. Paulette began to talk of the little girl she'd been. The joy she'd found in the tide pools, each a tiny universe of beings so incredible it was hard to believe they were real and alive.

Denise had felt the same.

Paulette spoke of a puppy she'd had in fourth grade. Rex, she'd called him. Rex was a mixed breed with dark mottled fur and a depth of intelligence in his canny brown eyes.

Denise, who hadn't been allowed pets—or much else in the way of comfort—had found solace in a stuffed dog, his fur mottled beige and brown. She'd named him Rex.

Paulette remembered winning the fifty- and hundred-yard dash in track meets all through grade school.

Speed was one of Denise's strengths. Every morning until the snow got too deep, she ran five miles before breakfast. In a strange intoxicating way, Paulette was telling the story of Denise's life, not factually, of course, but perhaps the life another Denise Castle had lived in a parallel universe. Which, in a way, was the case.

At some point they moved to the kitchen, and Paulette made tea—not coffee, tea; not fancy, Lipton. Both women drank it unsweetened with a dash of lemon juice.

Seamlessly the conversation shifted to Denise, and she found herself telling not of the wretchedness of her bouncing around the foster system but of a pair of sunglasses, the lenses shaped like hearts, the plastic frames canary yellow, that she'd had in the second grade, her prize possession, then basking in the warmth of Paulette's throaty laugh of understanding.

Paulette's had been shaped like the eyes of a cat, the frames fire-engine red.

Paulette had grown up on Isle au Haut, the only child of a lobsterman and his wife. Her mother "did" for the summer people who kept houses there. Much of Isle au Haut was part of Acadia National Park, the southernmost patch in the patchwork quilt of federal lands.

In her work as a ranger, Denise had been by the tiny one-room school where the island kids went dozens of times. She'd been by Paulette's house. There had to have been times she had missed Paulette by hours, or even minutes.

At sixteen Paulette married Kurt Duffy, the son of a lobsterman who ran lines out of Frenchman Bay, and moved to the mainland, then to a tiny house on Otter Creek Road—a thin slice of public land cutting through the main bulk of the park on Mount Desert.

At sixteen Denise had planned to elope with a boy named Chuck Miles. He had been killed when a logging truck hit his Honda as he was coming to pick her up.

Paulette worked at Mount Desert Hospital.

Emergency medical work was Denise's favorite thing about being a ranger.

Paulette worked mostly nights. She loved the night.

Denise loved the night; she volunteered for the latest shifts.

Twice Paulette had gotten pregnant, and twice Kurt Duffy had beaten her so bad she lost the baby. After the second time she could never get pregnant again; there were complications.

Denise had gotten pregnant with Peter's child. He'd slaughtered it. Slaughtered all her children.

Kurt told Paulette that if she ever left him he would track her down and kill her.

Peter had made a family that Denise was not part of. A family with a baby.

Sometime after midnight they found themselves in the cramped bedroom Paulette shared with her husband when he chose to come home. Shoulder to shoulder, hip to hip, they sat on the edge of the queen-sized bed and stared at their reflections in the wide mirror over what had once been a fine dressing table. Denise's dark hair was pulled back from her face into a low-maintenance ponytail at the nape of her neck.

Paulette pulled her desiccated blond mop back and secured it with a scrunchie. Then they stared. Smoking had roughened the skin around Paulette's mouth, and the blow to her face had discolored the flesh around her left eye. Other than this, they were the same. The ears were identical; their noses were the same, a little long with a squared tip and thin nostrils. Their eyes were the same shade of blue. Each had a brown fleck in the iris of her left eye, dead center below the pupil. Paulette's eyebrows had been plucked, but the arch and the long winged taper matched Denise's.

"I always felt you out there," Paulette said, her voice soft with wonder. "When I was little, you were my playmate. Mom said you were my imaginary playmate. I knew better."

Denise said nothing. She was afraid if she spoke she would cry or, worse, the woman beside her would vanish.

"Did you sense that I was here?" Paulette asked timidly.

Denise shook her head, fascinated at watching her sister's—her identical twin sister's—lips move on precisely the same mouth as her own. "I felt you as not here." Denise tapped her chest over her heart. "Like I wasn't all here. I felt part of me had gone missing. I thought maybe the doctors had accidentally cut off some part of me when I was born. It confused me because I couldn't see any part the other kids had that I didn't. No extra toes or arms or anything. When I got a little older, maybe eight or nine, I lived with a fairly decent family that attended a Presbyterian church. For the eight months I was with them, I went to Sunday school every week along with their kids. The teacher taught us that people had souls. After that, I assumed that I had accidentally been born without a soul. That that was the part that was missing.

"After that I put it out of my mind."

For another few minutes they sat in silence marveling at the faces in the mirror. Denise realized she must have known from the beginning that the battered blonde on the barstool was the part of her that had gone missing.

She had recovered her lost soul.

SEVEN

The specter of Sam Edleson filled the room with the stench of sulfur. Heath caught herself grinding her teeth and made herself stop.

"I'm going to make a few calls," Anna said, and slipped from the room as soft-footed as the apocryphal Indian.

Elizabeth excused herself to go to the bathroom.

Heath and Gwen waited in terror, neither saying anything, both afraid Elizabeth had gone to harm herself, both afraid they would never again feel safe when the girl was out of their sight.

"Should I go check on her?" Heath asked.

"No," Gwen said. Then, after a minute, "Do you think I should?"

"No."

Gwen began feverishly tidying the room. Heath pored over her daughter's cell phone, rereading the sordid texts, wanting to delete them but knowing she shouldn't. They were evidence. Elizabeth was adamant;

she didn't want the police involved. Elizabeth was also sixteen. Heath wasn't sure police could do anything about the cyberattacks anyway. To ease the pressure, she finally allowed herself to delete one message. It was from herself to Elizabeth reminding her to put the wash in the dryer.

After what seemed a cruelly long time, Elizabeth returned. Relief flooded Heath when she saw she'd washed her face and combed her hair, signs of hope.

Then the three of them waited, Heath spinning her mental wheels. Gwen, having straightened every cushion, and aligned every book and magazine, sat on the sofa watching her great-niece with such intensity Elizabeth finally pelted her with a pillow.

Irritation, another sign the girl was beginning to engage in the world outside her misery.

Anna returned. "Edleson left his job in Idaho for making improper advances to a seventeen-year-old high school intern. In Idaho it's only a felony if the girl is sixteen or under. Nobody wanted to press charges, for all the usual reasons. The company didn't want to fire Edleson because of the adverse publicity and/or unemployment compensation. He was told to quit, and did. Shortly thereafter the family moved to Boulder." Having delivered the message in as few words as possible, Anna waited, her weight on the balls of her feet. Heath guessed she was hoping to be shot toward Sam Edleson as an arrow is shot from a bow.

"You called the cops!" Elizabeth cried.

"I did," Anna said. "The Coeur d'Alene, Idaho, police. They have no jurisdiction over you."

Reassured, Elizabeth's attention jumped to the next awful conclusion. "He's done it before?" she demanded, sounding shocked.

"Probably more than once," Anna said. "That's how these guys are."

"Then why were they yelling at *me*?" The indignation in her voice went far to soothe Heath. Because she was female, it was inevitable Elizabeth would be thinking she had done something wrong, brought this upon herself.

"Elizabeth, would you get my boots, please?" Heath asked.

"Which boots?" Elizabeth asked warily. "Your old climbing boots?" This last was asked with a small note of hope.

"Nope," replied Heath, dashing it. "The turquoise and silver." Elizabeth groaned. Almost said something, thought better of it, and levered herself up off the sofa cushions to vanish down the hall.

"What's with that?" Anna asked.

"Now we're going to pay that nice neighborly call," Heath said. Her voice came out flat and dark. Even if his wife and daughter lied to themselves and the world about Sam, Heath wanted him to know in no uncertain terms that she knew what he had done.

"No time like the present," Anna said.

"Good cop, bad cop?" Heath asked. She felt silly saying it, but it worked on television, and was the only plan that came to mind.

"Only if I can be the bad cop," Anna said without a trace of humor. "Are you going to wear your carapace?"

Heath thought she detected a note of excitement in Anna's voice. The electronic exoskeleton fascinated the ranger. Leah, whom Anna had gotten to know on their ill-fated trip down the Fox River, had strapped Anna into the prototype. Though she'd fought the machine as if it were trying to take over her body, she'd come to respect and admire it. Whenever Heath used it, Anna would whistle through her teeth or shake her head and mutter, "I'll be damned."

"Not tonight," Heath said. "I've used up my quota of energy on that scale. Robo-butt will have to do the heavy lifting."

"Let me get my—" Gwen began.

Heath cut her off. It was best not to let the juggernaut pick up any speed. Gwen lacked self-control around people who harmed children. Though Heath wanted to rend the Edlesons limb from limb, burn their house down, and sow the land with salt so nothing would grow there for a thousand years, she suspected she would gather a lot more workable leverage and information by using subtle threats and blackmail.

"I don't think this is a good time to leave Elizabeth home alone," Heath said.

"Of course not," Gwen agreed immediately. "I'll make a fresh pot of tea." She smiled wearily. "It's good to have something to hate that can easily be dumped down the drain."

As if he understood every word that passed, Wily heaved himself to his paws with a sigh and made ready to follow them. "Protect the children and old people," Heath said fondly as she rubbed his head. There was a time she would have taken him. He was courageous and as wily as his namesake, but the years were creeping up on him.

Elizabeth returned carrying a pair of worn but beautiful turquoise cowboy boots with silver threading. "What's wrong with your sneakers?" Elizabeth asked forlornly. "Or even your hiking boots?"

"Tonight I intend to kick some ass," Heath replied. Elizabeth flopped down, her body awkward, her resentment obviously at war with what Heath suspected was the joy of having a champion, regardless of whether she rides out on a white horse or in a gray wheelchair.

Gentle, as she always was when touching her adoptive mother, Elizabeth waved away Heath's hands and put the boots on her feet for her.

"Aren't those a bit dressy for an unannounced call?" Gwen remarked, coming in from the kitchen with the threatened pot of tea.

"Power suit," Elizabeth said.

Anna said nothing, following as Heath rolled toward the front door.

The sun was behind the mountains, and though it wasn't dark, shadows pooled and the sky had grown soft and infinite. The day's warmth was drifting away from the skin of the mountains on a gentle down-canyon breeze carrying the scent of pine.

Lights were beginning to come on in the neighborhood, people home from work and cooking supper. Sam's truck was in the drive, an outsized Dodge Ram that one should not keep if one doesn't own a ranch where it can run and play. Expertly, Heath wheeled around it. Fortunately, the Edlesons' house had a wide brick walk and a front door without a step, a rarity Heath hadn't noticed before her disability. Given this was to be a confrontation, she was glad she didn't have to be dragged up a front stoop, then wait while Robo was hauled clanking up behind like an albatross.

When they arrived at the door, Anna reached over Heath's head and banged the frame of the screen door. There was a doorbell, but Heath was happier with the "Open up. Police!" sound of Anna's knuckles and left it alone. Disquiet murmured from inside, muttering, then silence, as if a television set had been switched off.

More silence.

"Curtains twitched at two o'clock," Anna murmured. Heath had caught the tiny movement from the corner of her eye—Sam or Terry or Tiffany peeking out the front-room windows to see who was at the door. The phrase "at two o'clock" threatened to make her giggle hysterically, and she wondered when her anger had turned to fear. Heath had no fear that Sam would do them physical damage. Bizarrely enough, given she would probably come out on the wrong end of a physical encounter with a well-muscled man, she would have welcomed that. A compulsion to feel his flesh under her fists—or between her teeth—coursed through her so fiercely that, for a second, she felt she could rise from her chair and kick the door down. Her fear was that something she or Anna might say or do would make it worse for Elizabeth.

Anna banged again, louder and longer this time. Heath didn't allow herself to wince.

She was beginning to think the Edlesons weren't going to answer the door when she heard the bolt thunk back. The door opened halfway. No lights were on in the front room. The one in the kitchen, a light Heath had noticed when they crossed the drive, had been turned off. Dim behind the screen door, Terry stared out at them, her eyes like black holes in a dead-gray face.

"Hi, Terry," Heath said pleasantly. "This is Anna Pigeon, a friend of the family and, for the moment, chief chair wrangler." She smiled crookedly. Poor little paraplegic couldn't hurt a fly. It wasn't one of Heath's favorite strategies, but she wasn't above using it now and then if she thought it would give her the upper hand. Maybe she heard a faint snort from Anna; she wasn't sure. "Could we come in for a minute?"

Terry didn't want to let them in. She was breathing hard through pinched nostrils. Heath could hear each sniff. Terry's lips, usually full and soft-looking, were pressed into a tight little frown.

"I'm afraid I don't handle the chill of evening as well as I did before . . ." Smiling again, Heath waved a hand over her lap to indicate just how very sad and debilitated she was. Terry still didn't want to let them in, but, like a lot of people, she was intimidated by the wheelchair. How could she say no? Heath was a *cripple*, for Christ's sake. The door opened a bit more, and Heath got a wheel in, then, with a push from Anna, she was over the sill and into the house. All Terry could do was get out of the way so Heath wouldn't run over her feet.

Before the fall from Keystone, Heath had been brash and ballsy. After, she had been angry and self-destructive. When she finally realized that, though she couldn't walk, she was still a whole person, she found she'd changed. From the bastion of Robo-butt, the world was different, more layered and complex. Heath learned patience. She learned to watch people, to really listen, to genuinely *see* them. Something she'd not done much of when she was superwoman climbing tall mountains. Another skill she'd picked up was canniness, an ability to manipulate situations to her advantage, to manipulate people when she had to. Cunning wasn't a strength much lauded in literature or the media, but it was a strength all the same, and Heath respected it.

Once they had breached the walls, as it were, Terry's mood didn't warm. She did, however, assume the role of hostess, offering them coffee. Anna didn't accept. Heath did. Hard to toss somebody out before they've finished their drink. She parked herself advantageously, blocking the big, leather, man-of-the-house chair so the only remaining seating was on a couch that was too soft or a straight-backed chair that was too hard. She didn't want Goldilocks getting too comfortable.

Anna leaned against a dark wood highboy, her ankles crossed, her arms crossed, looking deceptively relaxed.

In the minute it took for this arrangement, Terry was back with two cups of coffee on a tray along with a bowl of powdered creamer and half a dozen packets of

Sweet'N Low. "Sure you won't have anything?" she asked Anna politely. Being the hostess, probably along with the fact that neither Heath nor Anna had lit into her, seemed to have dialed her hostility down a notch. Coffee served, Terry perched on the edge of the couch, her mug hands as plump and white as the Pillsbury Doughboy's. Where there should have been knuckles there were babyish dimples. The rest of her was as amorphous; her bland oval face just missed being pretty due to a lack of definition in her features.

"The girls haven't been seeing much of one another lately," Heath opened conversationally.

"That's so," Terry said, then took a careful sip of her coffee. "I think it will be good for them to have a little time just with family." She was recovering her equilibrium. Heath wanted none of that.

"So do I," she said flatly.

Terry looked up, annoyed or startled. Sam appeared behind her, backlit in the kitchen doorway, shoulder against one side of the frame. His hair was tousled, that nice gold-shot Robert Redford hair, and he wore a plaid shirt half unbuttoned. Heath suspected he'd been in the bathroom primping until this entrance.

"I know you sexually assaulted Elizabeth," Heath said to Sam. "Elizabeth's sixteen. In Colorado that makes your behavior child molestation. A felony."

Sam stopped leaning. He, at least, was scared. Not so Mrs. Edleson. Clacking her mug down on the tray, she tried to nail Heath to the wall with a malevolent glare. "Now see here, Heath, Sam didn't do anything! Do you hear me? You daughter, your *adopted* daughter, is no better than she should be, and you don't know the half of it."

Heath looked over Terry's head. "Sam, I know you arranged to be alone with Elizabeth, then assaulted her. I'm thinking the only reason it wasn't rape was that your wife and daughter got wind of it and came home before they were supposed to."

Terry was on her feet. "Your daughter made advances to my husband!" she shrieked, looking like she might fly at Heath and claw her eyes out.

Anna's voice cut cold from where she still leaned against the sideboard, ankles crossed. "Elizabeth's sixteen. Sam's forty—"

"Thirty-eight," he interrupted, his first words since entering the fray.

"She's a minor. He touched her. Either way it's a felony. Either way Sam goes to jail," Anna finished.

Terry quivered, fumed, sat, took up her coffee cup, breathed, sipped. "There's no need for that kind of talk," she said softly. "There's no need to embarrass yourself—or your daughter—by calling the police. I don't blame Elizabeth. Girls like Sam. He's a very handsome man."

A snort from the sideboard, and a murmured "Chinless wonder."

Heath suppressed a smile. Terry pretended not to hear. Sam's hand flew to hide the lower half of his face.

"Elizabeth made a pass at Sam," Terry said. The threat of jail hadn't silenced her, but it had toned her down.

"Just like the girl in Idaho made a pass at Sam?" Anna asked. She pushed out from the table she'd been tucked against and stepped into the light from the kitchen. Menace radiated from her. Heath could never figure out how she did it. It was just there, palpable, a sense of imminent threat that could be felt against the skin of the mind.

"That girl . . . that girl was . . . she . . ." Terry, her righteous anger temporarily damped, was flailing for words to fan it back to life. Heath took this moment of vulnerability to unlock Elizabeth's cell phone and open a text. Wheeling close enough that she bumped Terry's knees, she thrust the cell phone into the other woman's hands, where she couldn't miss the photo of a woman and a dog fornicating.

"Is that why you sent this to my daughter?" Heath demanded. Terry dropped the pink cell phone as if it were a used tissue.

"This is sick," Terry hissed at Heath. "Your daughter is disgusting and sick. This proves it."

Sam pushed his wife aside, then reached down to retrieve the phone. Heath watched him narrowly as he turned the phone right side up on his palm and pushed the button to unlock it. "Shit!" he said in what sounded like genuine shock. Terry tried to slap it from her husband's hand, but he dodged her blow. Anna moved from the shadows to stand behind Heath's chair. Making plans for a quick retreat, no doubt.

Before the Edlesons could stop their squabble to launch a counterattack, Heath broke into their concentration.

"Sorry to introduce that into your world so suddenly," she said acidly. "Someone has been using the Internet and cell phones—Twitter, texting, you name it—to cyberstalk Elizabeth. I need to find out who is behind it. Since the girls were at odds, I thought Tiff might be able to help me."

"Tiff had nothing to do with that!" Terry snarled. "Nothing. I kept her away from your . . . *daughter*." She made the word sound like an epithet. "Because Tiff is a good girl." Terry's doughy round face hardened and took on a sly look. "Since there is no problem, but you are troublemakers, what about I help you, and you promise not to try and get my Sam in trouble with the police?" she asked shrewdly.

"I promise," Heath said solemnly.

"What about you?" Terry glared at Anna.

"Elizabeth doesn't want the police involved," Anna said.

"We don't know anything about these . . . these filthy things," Terry said. "We don't know people who even know where to get filth like that. Nobody we know would ever *get* anything like that on your daughter's phone. There. Now we're out of it. That's all the help I can give you."

The bitch was throwing it back on Elizabeth. Heath said nothing, and that nothing burned in her throat like fire on gasoline.

Sam, still staring at the phone, as if loath to take his eyes from the image of the woman and the dog for fear it would vanish, sat down on the sofa with a thump. "I've never seen anything like this stuff." He was thumbing forward on the touch screen, no doubt hoping for more.

Terry snatched the phone from her husband's hands. Heath was willing to bet she knew what Sam was, knew the lies she told herself so she could stay in the marriage.

"Is Tiff home?"

"You are not going to show this to Tiffany!" Terry exclaimed in horror. Marching over, she dropped the phone in Heath's lap with an exaggerated moue of distaste.

"The girls are estranged," Heath said. "Maybe Tiffany is doing this because she's angry, because you told her Elizabeth tried to seduce her dad."

"Tiff wouldn't do this," Sam said. "Tiff wouldn't even know what this is."

Heath could feel Anna hovering behind her like a brewing storm cloud. She shot her a warning glance; they needed to talk to Tiff. "I don't need to show her the photograph," Heath said with as much patience as she could muster. "But I would like to talk to her. The girls are close; Tiffany might know who wants to hurt Elizabeth."

Terry's eyes narrowed. "We're done here," she said. "Take your daughter's filth and get out."

"We need to talk to Tiffany," Heath insisted. "If you want to be around when we do, go and get her."

Sam stood, trying to pull his manhood up around him despite the missing chin. "You heard my wife," he said, and took a threatening step toward Heath.

Anna moved from the shadows behind Robo-butt.

Her right arm shot out, stiff and sudden, the heel of her hand catching him in the solar plexus. With an *oof* he sat again, his moment of macho a thing of the past.

"The girls are not close," Terry hissed. She stomped past Anna and jerked open the front door. "Elizabeth brought this on herself. She probably gets stuff like that all the time. She probably likes it."

Anna had turned the wheelchair so Heath was facing the harridan at the door. Throughout this adventure in futility Heath had remained relatively calm. Terry's smugness and accusations blasted her self-control. The old Heath rose from the ashes of the one born of the ice fall. Heath never moved, but she saw, actually saw, an image of herself rise from her chair like a zombie from the grave, arms outstretched, fingers curled into claws the better to tear out and devour the flesh of Terry Edleson's throat. Maybe Terry saw the projection. Heath didn't know. All she knew was that a look of abject, pants-wetting terror deformed the other woman's face.

Heath bared her teeth and braced her hands on the arms of her chair. Murder could be done in a state such as this. Had her legs been viable, she would have probably left the Edlesons in a squad car, never to see the outside of a prison cell again. As it was, blind rage could not be sustained more than a moment. Anna swept up behind her. Heath leaned back into the loving embrace of Robo-butt to be rolled unceremoniously over the sill and onto the brick walk. "You assaulted Sam," Terry shouted. "I helped you! So you can't call the police. They won't believe you. You promised!" She glared at Heath.

"I did," Heath said.

"You are a witness," she yelled at Anna.

"I am," Anna said.

The door slammed. The dead bolt thudded into place.

For a moment Heath and Anna stared at the door.

"Now we call the police?" Anna asked.

"Now we call the police," Heath agreed.

Empty and exhausted, she slumped back in the seat and said nothing more, letting Anna push her down the walk. The long summer dusk had settled into true night. A streetlight made shadows stark and colorless on the concrete sidewalk beside the asphalt. Black and white, Heath thought, and missed a time when she saw right and wrong that clearly delineated.

"Ms. Jarrod?" came a whisper.

Anna stopped pushing. Heath came out of her slump into full alert.

"Ms. Jarrod, it's me, Tiffany." The girl, her blond hair gray in the cold light, separated herself from the side of her dad's truck and crouched down by Robobutt. At first, Heath thought it a sign of unusual sensitivity in a teenager, but realized it wasn't. Tiffany didn't want her parents to see her consorting with the enemy.

"I gotta get back," Tiff said. "Tell Elizabeth it's not me; my folks won't let me call. They took my phone and my laptop and I'm like in a black hole. I can't call anybody or get on Facebook or anything! I hope she's okay. Tell her I'll write her and put the note under the hedge where we used to crawl through when we were little kids. Nobody'd ever think of that."

"Elizabeth's being cyberstalked," Anna said curtly. "Do you know who's behind it?"

"I know about the stalking—everybody at school does. I don't know—"

"Tiffany!"

"Gotta go. I know what Dad . . . I . . . gotta go." She stood and ran, probably hoping to get back inside the house before Mom and Dad figured out she'd defected.

Anna pushed. Robo-butt rolled. Heath rode. Only the crunch of the chair's rubber tires on bits of escaped gravel accompanied them back to the kitchen door. Gwen, Elizabeth, and Wily were waiting for them on the couch, tense and wide-eyed.

Anna parked the chair, then sank down in her former place. Heath set the brakes.

"Well, open the envelope, for heaven's sake!" Gwen exclaimed.

"No winner," Heath said wearily. "It probably isn't Tiff, which is good news. She couldn't, her folks confiscated her cell phone and her laptop."

"Gosh," Elizabeth breathed, evidently shocked at the draconian nature of the punishment. "What did she do?"

"She saw," Anna said.

"Tiff said she would write you about it and leave the note under the hedge where you kids used to crawl back and forth to each other's yards," Heath said.

"On paper?" Elizabeth asked.

"No. She's going to scratch it on a piece of slate with a stylus," Heath retorted.

"That Tiffany wasn't doing it, that's good, isn't it?" Gwen asked.

"Not really," Heath said.

"We haven't a clue as to who is behind it," Anna said. "So we have no way to make it stop. Nobody to come down on. We don't have a motive. We don't, do we, Elizabeth?" The adults again stared at the teenager in her pj's like hawks at a baby duckling.

"No," Elizabeth said sadly. "At school everybody likes me, or I don't even know them. You know how it is. There's a bunch of boys who make a game of getting girls to have sex with them, and they keep score. They're creeps, and they've done some creepy things—you know, posting about the girls who put out, and even meaner posts about the ones that didn't. Both Tiff and I got asked sort of out by one of their bottom feeders—not like a date or anything, just stupid stuff by a guy who wants to be in on the game but is a total loser. Maybe the creep boys could be doing it. I don't think so, though. I mean, at school, I'm not all that *important*. Why take the trouble to stalk me? I'd probably be worth, like, half a point."

"Half a point?" Anna asked.

"You know, a cheerleader's worth five points, a girl on the student council two points. Like that."

"Time to cull the gene pool," Anna murmured.

"God, I'm glad you're here, Anna," Heath burst out as a boil of anxiety burst inside her. "For all we know this could turn to physical stalking."

Anna said after a moment: "Starting next week, I've got a twenty-one-day detail in Acadia National Park. Acting chief ranger. Their chief is fighting that big fire in Southern California."

This last was said without affect, but Heath knew it rankled with her friend. Like many rangers, Anna neighed and fretted like an old war horse when fire season came around. Heath couldn't understand this love of fighting wildfire. For some it was about overtime and hazard pay.

For others it was an addiction. Anna belonged to the latter group. She'd taken a bullet during the Fox River adventure, and her left arm never fully recovered. Though Anna'd never admit it, she probably hadn't the strength to swing a Pulaski for long.

To be acting chief in a park as important as Acadia would be welcomed by most rangers, a nice step up the ladder to being permanent chief somewhere else. Anna had dithered about the promotion to district ranger. Money meant little to her. Being out of doors and away from human beings meant a lot.

"You're leaving?" Elizabeth wailed.

Heath flinched, not because her daughter cried out like an abandoned five-year-old but because, for an instant, she thought she'd done it herself and was mortified.

"They don't need you!" Heath said, then stooped to threats. "They're liable to give you a promotion."

"I'll be sure and offend the higher-ups," Anna said with a dry smile.

"Send someone else," Heath said, hating the whine in her words.

"Wildfires in California. Everybody is short-handed," Anna said.

Heath said no more. She'd already said too much.

Gwen, whose usual upbeat enthusiasm seemed to have been squelched by the points game and creeps and stalkers, perked up. "Acadia National Park? In Maine? Of course in Maine! For heaven's sake, I'm getting dotty. My first job out of med school was near there. I have to make some calls. Heath, Elizabeth, pack. We are going to Maine with Anna!"

Gwen kissed the air around everybody's cheeks, snatched up her black medical bag, and blew out on the wind the way she had blown in.

"Mary Poppins," Heath laughed.

"Who does Aunt Gwen know in Maine?" Elizabeth asked.

"Dez Hammond and Chris Zuckerberg. A couple of old hippies from the day," Heath said. Heath had met them on two occasions when they'd visited Boulder. She remembered liking them. "Chris comes from money. She inherited an island off Acadia. They spend most of their time rehabbing an old mansion and hosting artists."

"Where's Arcadia?" E asked.

"Acadia," Anna corrected. "Northern Maine, lobsters and nor'easters."

"I'm going to be marooned on an island with four old ladies," Elizabeth cried.

"In a crumbling old mansion," Heath said.

"You'll be there, won't you?" Elizabeth begged Anna.

Heath was annoyed that, though she had more years under her belt than Heath, Anna was not among the designated Old Ladies.

"Not me," Anna said. "A desert isle in the vast Atlantic? Too boring for this child."

Elizabeth groaned.

EIGHT

D o you want to see where I really live?" Paulette
asked. The question should have seemed sudden
or peculiar, but it wasn't. In her core—her soul if the
metaphor held—Denise knew her twin, her other self,
could not truly live in this tragic wreck of a place with
paper peeling from the walls and ancient linoleum curling at the corners and buckling along the seams.

They stood at the same instant, laughing at themselves and one another simultaneously. Denise felt as
if scales, dirt, fragments of rotting lumber, cracking
mortar, and broken roof slates were sliding off her. In
the dim light of the bedroom's single shaded lamp,
Denise imagined she could see dust rising from the
cascade of debris as her old, worn-out, worthless,
piece-of-shit life crumbled. When the dust settled, a
new, clean, sun-filled life would be built around her and
her sister. Denise communicated none of this. Paulette,
she was positive, was feeling the same sense of slough-
ing off a diseased and decrepit skin.

Wordlessly, Paulette led the way through a dilapidated kitchen—appliances right out of Sears circa 1970—and through the back door of the cottage. As they crossed the small weedy yard, a children's swing set, one chain broken, a rotted seat dangling like a broken limb, formed the yard's epitaph.

Paulette reached out. Hesitantly, Denise took her hand and was led into the black night forest.

"I don't go home much, and I always go a different way," Paulette whispered as they made their way through the darkness beneath the trees. "If Kurt found out, he'd spoil it just to be mean; just because he likes to hurt me by ruining my things. He thinks it's funny. Hitting isn't enough. He can't hurt me bad enough with his fists short of putting me in the hospital, which costs a lot, or killing me."

Holding tightly to Paulette's hand, Denise followed blindly, her story—her sister's story, their story—surging through her veins and arteries, down the capillaries until each and every cell in her body was caught up. Waves of fury crashed over deep valleys of sorrow; seas of compassion rose and receded. It had been a while since Denise had felt anything for anyone but herself. The hatred she harbored for Peter had hardened into bitterness. Wormwood and gall had been all she could taste, smell, see, touch.

Dead; she'd been dead to herself in every way that counted. Coming alive in this womb of pine-scented darkness, her hand warm and safe in her twin's, was so overwhelming she staggered like a drunk and fell to her knees, dragging Paulette with her.

Denise felt her sister patting her hand. "Shh, shh," Paulette murmured softly. "It's okay. We're together." Those words were the first and only lullaby Denise had ever heard. She began to cry.

Usually sick helplessness came on the heels of Denise's crying jags. This time, when the tears finally stopped, she felt renewed, as if the tears were poisons her body had expelled.

"We're almost there." Paulette's voice came from the darkness. Denise allowed the gentle tugging to bring her to her feet. "This land belonged to Kurt's mom," Paulette whispered as they crept along. "His grandma lived here. When she died we moved in. It's not like a city lot. It's only about forty feet wide where the house is, but it runs way way back, getting skinnier and skinnier like the tail of a comet. Kurt doesn't care anything about it except that it's his. I wanted him to sell at least part of it because he could get a lot of money for it and we wouldn't have to live in a shack. 'Shack's good enough for the likes of you' was his big-deal answer. If he ever found this, he'd kill me.

"We're here." Paulette let go of Denise's hand. The connection broken, for a second Denise felt as though she were falling, falling and freezing. It was only a dream: the twin, her soul, the Acadian blond barfly. All of it. A dream. A wail rose in her throat, as lonely as the howl of the last wolf on earth. The sound of fumbling, the scratch of a match being lit, then a flame that, born into such a lightless universe, hit Denise's eyes with the force of a supernova, aborted the cry.

Her sister was there. No dream. Tears began to flow

again. No paroxysms of grief or wrenching sobs, only warmth and joy in liquid form. Fleetingly, Denise remembered a self that was not given to emotion, a self made stoic by life. No more. In the past months emotions came in sudden overwhelming waves. These were the first that didn't threaten to tear her apart.

Paulette lit an old kerosene lamp she took from beneath a rusted overturned bucket, adjusted the wick, then handed the lamp to Denise to hold. They were standing at the door of a small shed. The eaves cleared Paulette's head by less than six inches. They would have to stoop to pass through the door without banging their skulls.

By the light of the lamp, Paulette found a short piece of dirty frayed string caught in a crack between two pieces of weathered siding. She pulled it out to reveal the key tied to the end.

"There are so many park visitors, folks would be wandering in all the time," she explained as she turned the key in the padlock that secured the door. "Visitors don't seem to know what's public land and what's private."

"Or care," Denise said.

Paulette pushed open the door, stepped inside, took the lamp, and held it up so Denise could see the room. Bitterness vanished. Delight took its place. The room— the entire house—wasn't more than a hundred and fifty square feet, roughly twelve by twelve, and the ceiling closer to seven feet than eight. On each of the four walls was a large many-paned window, the mullions, frames, and sills clean and painted white, the glass old, from back when glass had ripples and imperfections in it. The walls were painted soft gray, the color of a dove's breast, and hung with pieced fabric stretched over wooden frames, the bright bits of cloth making flowers and mountains, trees and ponds.

On the worn planks of the floor was a simple rag rug. A white crib with a small stuffed bear looking through the bars, a three-drawer chest painted China red, a round table with a lamp of the same color, and a rocking chair completed the nursery. Nothing fussy, nothing out of place, everything clean and necessary and beautiful.

As Paulette closed the door behind them, Denise walked around the room. The windows weren't windows at all. Frames with glass, sills, and half-pulled shades had been mounted on the wall. Behind them were paintings of a forest, much as it might look were the windows real and she was looking through them in the early morning. Shafts of sunlight slanted through dark trunks. The shadows of leaves dappled a small green clearing. Wildflowers surrounded a granite boulder. A bunny grazed fearlessly on new grass.

"I didn't dare make any changes to the outside," Paulette said. "Kurt doesn't come back here, but when people can look in, they can break in, and will. And if Kurt did come this way for some reason, I didn't want to call attention to this old shed."

"He'd ruin it," Denise said. It wasn't a question. She knew he would as if she'd been with Paulette each time he'd made a wreck of what little beauty she'd managed.

Denise reached over the bars of the crib and laid a

finger between the stuffed bear's ears. Though she'd never had much in the way of toys—at least not new ones—this one felt familiar to her.

"Kurt's a monster. A big fucking monster," Paulette blurted out.

At the outburst of obscenity, Denise turned to her sister.

Paulette laughed and covered her mouth the way Denise had done until Peter told her it made her look childish. Child*like,* she thought as she watched her twin. Childlike and charming. Another thing Peter had taken from her.

"I've never said that out loud before. Awful as it is, it felt good to say it. Isn't that weird?"

Denise didn't know what to say. It wasn't weird. Not at all. None of this was weird. All of it was exactly how it should be. That was what was weird.

Paulette sat in the rocking chair and let Denise explore the small ornamental boxes, the few books, the fabric art. "When I got pregnant the first time, I bought all these wonderful things for the baby's room. Then, you know, I lost the baby. Kurt said I had to take them back if I'd bought them, or sell them on eBay or whatever if they'd been gifts from my mom and dad—they were still alive then. But I couldn't. I just couldn't. I dragged them all back to this shed and told Kurt I'd given them to Goodwill. He half beat me to death for not getting any money for them. The second time I got pregnant, we got a few more things. Not as many. Mom and Daddy had passed. They were pretty old when they adopted me and died within three months of each other.

"I did the same thing with the new stuff; told Kurt I'd given it away. After that, I used to come out here and kind of fix things up, thinking it would be a nice place for the new baby. I got my nursing degree and started working at Mount Desert Hospital with newborns and infants."

"A nurse!" Denise was pleased. Another thing they had in common: nurse/ranger. Both were jobs helping people.

"When I found out there weren't going to be any more babies," Paulette said with a shrug, "I just sort of kept on coming out here to get out of Kurt's sty for a while and remember who I am."

It was easy to forget who you were, Denise thought. She'd forgotten. No, she and Paulette had not forgotten who they were; who they were had been taken from them and thrown into the garbage. Forever, Denise had thought. Now here it was, her true *self,* with her sister's *self,* in an empty nursery in the woods.

"Peter's baby's name is Olivia," she said without thinking. "Olivia Barnes. The name I got was Castle. Now you're Duffy. What was your name before that?"

"Mallory, Paulette Mallory. The Mallorys adopted me. They were good people."

"Then when we're together, I won't be Denise Castle. I will be Denise Mallory," Denise said, and they both smiled.

Paulette stood, the chair still rocking as if her ghost remained behind, and walked over to a small painted table between windows half open on an imaginary forest. "I had time to get used to the idea of us, remember me saying that?" She didn't wait for Denise to answer, as if knowing that, of course, Denise remembered. Miracles tend to stick in memory, and everything about finding a twin sister was miraculous. "I felt you, but then these started appearing in the newspapers in the personal ads. I've only found three. They could be in papers in Bangor and Portland and other places. We only get the local stuff. I've never bothered to try and do a search. I wouldn't know where to begin. Here." She handed Denise a clipping from a newspaper. It wasn't much bigger than the slip of paper found in a fortune cookie. "That one I came across four years ago and for some reason just cut it out and kept it."

Denise turned the bit of newsprint toward the lamp and made out the blurred message. *Seeking identical twins, female, born on the sixth of March and separated at birth. They would now be thirty-seven years of age. Urgent they contact me. Family legacy. If you believe you may be such a person send a postcard to P.O. Box 1597, Post Office, Bar Harbor, ME.*

"March sixth, our birthday," Paulette said.

"No name or zip code," Denise said.

"This one was from year before last." Paulette handed her another scrap. The message was the same but, this time, included a zip code. Still no name. "And this is from January this year."

"The legacy," Denise said. Her brain, unable to absorb so much so quickly, had slowed to a crawl for the moment. "It would be money, wouldn't it?"

"Or maybe a house or land, like that," Paulette said.

"Our birth parents, do you think?" Denise asked, not

sure whether she would be overjoyed or furious if she were ever to lay her eyes on her birth mother or biological father.

"Maybe," Paulette said. "Or another relative."

"A lawyer," Denise said, unwilling to have any more relatives at the moment, wanting to be just sisters alone in a magical cabin in the woods. "We're the right age, aren't we?"

"And female and twins and separated at birth. How many can there be?"

"You'd be surprised," Denise said, remembering all the studies done on identical twins separated at birth.

"Born on the sixth of March? Girls who would be forty-one years old now, thirty-seven when I found the ad," Paulette said. "The babies must have been from around here, or who would run the ad in a tiny town like Bar Harbor?"

Before Denise could think of another reason the ad wasn't for them, the sound of sleigh bells or wind chimes leaked into the room, tinny and cheap.

Paulette pulled a cell phone out of her pocket and looked at the face of it, then up at Denise.

"It's him!" she whispered with all the terror of a trapped bird. Denise could hear her sister's frantically beating wings inside her own skull.

"I have to answer," Paulette said pleadingly.

Denise nodded. Of course she had to answer. If she didn't, Kurt would kill her.

Denise sat on a tiny chair with a rattan seat and a cavalry trumpet carved into the top slat on the back, a perfect, plain, lovely chair for a child, and listened as her sister made excuses for not being in the house when her husband called the home phone; listened to her lie about where she was and who she was with; watched tears roll over Paulette's cheeks, and the way her lips curved down as she rocked herself, begging him not to be mad, promising to be at the house next time.

When she was finally able to hang up, she let the hand with the phone in it fall as if lifeless beside the rocking chair.

"Kurt really is going to kill you," Denise realized suddenly.

Paulette nodded. "I've felt it for a while. He hasn't said anything, and hasn't hit me much, and not real hard. But I know he's planning on killing me and burying my body under the house. When he looks at me I can see it in his eyes as clear as anything. I can see him thinking about how he's going to get the shovel and hide it under the house so it will be ready."

Denise had spent her life in law enforcement. There was no evidence Kurt was plotting murder. He hadn't said he was. He'd laid no concrete plan. Yet Paulette felt it, saw it in his eyes, and believed her husband was planning to murder her.

Denise did, too. She, too, could see it.

This seeing of things hidden wasn't new. It had been growing for months. Change had crept into Denise around the time the park was informed Lily was pregnant with Peter's child. Though subtle, creeping, the change was in both mind and body. Her body responded with small betrayals of the kind that had let the lobster escape. Her mind responded by focusing ever more sharply, by knowing—sometimes—what was in the minds of those around her, just as she now knew her sister believed Kurt would kill her, and knew that Kurt, her *brother-in-law,* did, in fact, plan to murder his wife.

Paulette was her identical twin. Denise knew without asking that she, too, had come to see things that others had hidden in their hearts.

"Kill him first," Denise said, and was mildly surprised that the idea was not shocking. Killing Kurt Duffy was no more than a simple act of self-defense.

"They'd know it was me. Everybody knows he beats me. Not that they care. They'd know it was me. I'd go to jail forever."

"Not if you had a solid alibi," Denise said.

NINE

"Everything is so green and blue," Aunt Gwen said for perhaps the third time. Her red curls as wild as Medusa's snakes in the wind, she was yelling over her shoulder to Heath. Robo-butt, with Heath in it, and Wily grinning on her lap, was firmly lashed in the aft of a small outboard motorboat piloted by a gruff cliché of a New Englander. At least seventy, maybe older, he smelled strongly of tobacco and bay rum, had a couple of days' worth of beard, squinted from a leathery face, and clenched an unlit pipe in his teeth. Central Casting couldn't have done it better, Heath thought.

Aunt Gwen sat in the seat next to him, no doubt charming the pants off Matthew. Luke? Something biblical and manly. Elizabeth, her back toward the rest of them, perched on a gunwale to Heath's right, her mouth set in a rigid line that added years to her face. The rest of the boat's limited deck space was piled with the women's luggage.

Anna had been sent to Acadia several days earlier.

Left in Boulder, Heath felt childishly helpless and exposed without her friend. It was embarrassing. A big chunk of the eleven days since Heath found E in the bath with the Lady Schick had been spent getting ready for this trip. The other chunks had been spent watching Elizabeth turn from the compassionate, resilient girl she'd watched grow up to an angry, whining teenager, whom she felt like she didn't know.

Who she sometimes felt hated her.

The change depressed and confounded Heath. E wanted to escape the bullying, yet seemed angry and afraid to leave it behind, as if, unattended, it would metastasize until the cancer destroyed her life. The promised solitude had gone from a reprieve to a prison sentence in the girl's mind. In Heath's as well, on bad days. Like this one. Only Gwen had maintained her optimism. It had been temporarily damped by the news of her old friend Chris's heart attacks, and finally a stroke. The sadness was touched, Heath guessed, by a fear of her own mortality; Chris was sixteen years Gwen's junior.

No one was equipped to fight invisible monsters, Heath realized. Monsters of the Id or the Internet. The kind that worked in the dark, unknowable, motives as twisted and murky as eddies in a polluted river. Creeping poisonous fog that insinuated itself through the cracks of the mind.

The kind Anna couldn't shoot and E couldn't run from.

"That be Boar," the pilot said. He lifted an arm and pointed with a hand that looked to be carved from an old oak tree. Arthritis bent his little finger at the second joint, poking it out to the side at an odd angle.

"You've got to be kidding," Elizabeth said.

"It'll be fun," Heath insisted with more determination than faith. The island was right out of *The Count of Monte Cristo,* or some other nineteenth-century romance. It looked like a broken molar thrust a hundred feet up from the ocean's surface. In the cavity of the jagged tooth, protected by a rugged cliff to the northeast, was the house they would be staying in for the foreseeable future. As luck—bad for Gwen's friend, the island's owner—would have it, it was unoccupied for the present. Chris was recuperating—or dying—in a medical facility in Bangor.

Heath hoped the house would prove less forbidding than the land it rested atop, and their sojourn there more salubrious than that of the former occupant.

The boat pulled neatly up to a stone jetty. The pilot turned off the engine, then, line in hand, jumped nimbly onto the jetty to tie the boat off. Wind keened around the granite base of the island. None of them spoke; Heath, Gwen, and E were staring up a fifty-foot cliff, steps carved into the stone.

"John, are you sure this is the right island?" Gwen asked the pilot. John Whitman, Heath remembered.

"Yup."

"This is not happening," E said.

"Why didn't you tell us?" Heath asked.

"Didn't ask," John said.

"Anybody mind if I shoot your pal Chris?" Heath asked.

"Ms. Zuckerberg is ailing." John said with mild rebuke. He tied a second line to secure the stern of the boat. Wily hopped from the boat to the jetty. Not hopped—his hopping days were behind him; scrambled was more like it.

John scratched Wily behind the ears.

"I think I might be able to do the stairs on my butt," Heath said. "Might" was the operative word. Leah had grudgingly given her permission to bring Dem Bones, but she was not to use it anywhere there was salt or damp. Not all that useful under the circumstances.

"Slippery as eel snot if there's any wind. And there's always wind," John said around the stem of his pipe, which he was lighting.

"That's insane," Elizabeth said. "This whole thing is insane."

"You could lose your balance and be killed," Gwen said.

"That would take the fun out of it," Heath admitted. She didn't have the kind of money it would take to stay in a hotel. The airfare had just about cleaned her out.

"Does this mean we get to go back to Boulder?" Elizabeth asked.

"Can you spell 'stalker'?" Heath wasn't going to let E anywhere near anywhere until she found out who was stalking her. The police didn't much care about cyberstalking—or, more probably, hadn't a clue what to do about it. Private detectives charged a fortune, and Heath doubted they could do anything she couldn't do if she put her mind—and Gwen's and Anna's—to it.

All she needed was three things: to know E was safe, a Wi-Fi connection, and time.

"This place has everything we need. I'll just carry my butt up those stairs, and we'll be moving in," she said firmly.

John puffed on his pipe and said nothing.

Wily watched with the somber attention of a fan at a tennis match.

"It's too dangerous, Heath," Aunt Gwen said.

"Could we just not do this?" Elizabeth whined.

"Can't be as hard as it looks," Heath said with the desperate good cheer she'd taken to injecting into the platitudes she seemed incapable of avoiding.

Elizabeth snorted. She sounded like Anna, Heath realized, and was careful not to smile, not to notice at all.

A metal ramp borrowed for the occasion was laid from the boat to the jetty. Heath and Robo-butt debarked in a maneuver as complex and intricate as the landing on Omaha Beach. Gritting her teeth against what she knew was going to be an event fit for the Special Olympics, she rolled to the first of the stone steps soaring in zigzags up the face of the cliff.

That she wouldn't make it, that she would slip off and tumble into the Atlantic, or worse, the rocks, that she'd get halfway and give out, and there'd be the huge humiliation of a ranger rescue: These thoughts she shoved deep into the well of hopeless thoughts in the back of her brain.

She wasn't taking Elizabeth back to Boulder. She was taking Boar Island. The temptation to yell,

"Charge!" was tempered by the fact she'd be advancing butt first.

"I'm not climbing that," Elizabeth said. "No wonder Ms. Zuckerberg had heart failure."

"Elizabeth!" Gwen admonished, then said to Heath, "Let's wait and call Anna."

"For what?" Heath responded irritably. "Her to carry me up on her scrawny back?"

"Maybe she could drag you like a sack of laundry," E suggested.

"That I'd like to see," John said. "Still and all, if it was me, I'd take the lift."

Heath and Gwen glared at him. He squinted into the wind and puffed his pipe complacently.

Heath's hope of a Batcave-like super-elevator bored into the living rock was quickly dashed. The lift was a wooden platform with rails made of old pipes. Steel cables were attached to the four corners, then tied off ten feet up on a ring at the end of another cable that snaked to the top of the cliff, where it disappeared into a rusted iron wheel.

"Electric winch," John said as he led them to where the conveyance sat, graying wood and dull pewter-colored metal rendering it almost invisible against the granite. "When Ms. Zuckerberg had her first heart attack, and Mrs. Hammond came to look after her, she got this put in. Steps too hard for carrying groceries and what-all."

"First heart attack?" Aunt Gwen asked.

"This was the third."

"She didn't tell me that. Neither did Dez," Gwen said, her voice sharp with concern.

The boatman swung open a hinged section of the welded railing. "Who's first?"

"Don't look at me," Elizabeth said.

"I'll do it," Gwen said tentatively.

"No," Heath decided. "It has to be me."

"Right," Elizabeth said scornfully. "Who's going to hold it while you roll off? Could we please go back to the real world now?"

"The real world sucks at the moment," Heath said.

"Will it haul us all at the same time?" Gwen asked.

"Might could," John said.

"Forget it. I'm not getting on that thing," Elizabeth said, and got back into the boat.

Gwen and Heath would go first, leaving John to unload and get the luggage on the lift. Heath harbored no expectations that this new Elizabeth would help him. Wily whined and yipped and showed no inclination whatsoever to get on the thing, with or without people.

"Come here, Wily," E said. She lifted the dog back into the boat with her.

Once Heath, with chair, was rolled onto the lift, she locked her wheels. John handed her a small metal box hooked to a cable. The box had two buttons on it, one red, one green.

"After you're off, just push the button. That'll send the lift back down," John said.

"I take it green is up," Heath said with a look at John.

"We'll see," he said.

"Tally ho," Heath said idiotically, and punched the

green button. Had she not been half blind with terror, the trip up would have been stunning. Through the waves of panic that crested each time the lift lurched, or Aunt Gwen squeaked, she barely managed to register the glittering expanse of unbelievably blue sea and sky, the dense green of the hardwood forest above the cliffs, breaking waves painting white lace around their feet. These were the good things. Heath kept her eyes resolutely on them. The one time she looked down, her daughter, her dog, and John were growing ever tinier, looking more and more like specks of chewed food caught in the sharp teeth of the rocks.

She wished controlling what she heard was as simple. Fear honed her ears to batlike sensitivity. Each creak of the winch wheel or groan of the platform signaled failed machinery and a splatty death before the eyes of her only child. In the end, she gave up, stared skyward at the wheel reeling in the cable, and prayed that God would not let a nice lady in a wheelchair die on such a sunny day.

"We're here," Aunt Gwen said as the last terrifying clank announced the end of the line. Heath was pleased to hear the quaver in her aunt's voice. It was not good to be the lone coward in a group. Moving from platform to clifftop wasn't as formidable as Heath had feared. The lift rose through a square hole in a larger platform, where it could be secured in place by four sliding metal plates about the size of a magazine. Ms. Zuckerberg had clearly envisioned a day when she might be commuting by wheelchair.

When the plates were set, the lift was as stable as

the platform. Heath wheeled easily out onto solid ground. High, certainly, but solid, and worthy of a quick word of gratitude to the almighty.

The luggage followed, with John to unload it. He sent the lift back down. Heath refused to roll near the edge and holler at E to come up. Not yet.

"Used to be only a lighthouse here until city folk began piddling around in 1922," John said. "Waste of a good rock, if you ask me." He left them to get a cart for the luggage.

High on an island in the ocean, Heath could feel the elements in a way she usually didn't. The sun was a force against her skin, the wind a living thing twining in her hair; the light refractions from the sea were as sharp as the salt smell. Suddenly she felt very alive. Leaning her head back, she looked up a hundred and fifty feet to the top of the old lighthouse. The base had to be at least forty feet in diameter, and the walls fourteen feet thick, at least at the bottom.

The lighthouse was the single bit of architectural grace. The rest reminded Heath of the Winchester House in California, as if each owner had been driven to keep on building regardless of how haphazard the design. Forming an awkward V, with the lighthouse at the point, two wings—one of them two stories, the other three—blew back from the original tower, then petered out in drunken angles to finally die in piles of stone and timber. A century of winds had piled the debris along the skirt of the high granite wall on the northeast side of the island.

"If this place isn't haunted, I want my money back," Gwen said.

"I'm afraid we'll turn out to be the evil spirits," Heath said, thinking of the sudden—and to her, inexplicable—changes in her daughter. "Elizabeth has gone from Junior Jekyll to Rising Senior Hyde. It's like she's turned into a different person in a matter of days. Did I ever act like that?"

"For a year or two. You went through a bad patch when your dad remarried."

"Everything I do is wrong." Tears of self-pity and frustration flooded Heath's eyes. "Wind," she said, wiping them away. "I haven't a clue how to respond to her this way."

"Do what she asked you to do about a million times," Gwen said.

Her aunt's sharp tone offended Heath. It was as if Gwen thought she was a fool, or worse. "And what is that?" Heath snapped.

"Give her electronics back," Gwen said.

"You're joking," Heath said, aghast. The night of Lady Schick and the tub, Heath had taken everything of E's that needed a charge to run.

"That's what she wants. I think she's made that clear enough," Gwen said.

E had complained bitterly for a few days, then quit speaking of it. Why? Heath asked herself. Because she accepted that Mom was right? Decided her cyberlife sucked and she was glad to be out of it?

"Give her back her iPad, iPod, iPhone—whatever-all

teens carry these days. Life as she perceives it is in the toilet, and now you're forcing her to go through withdrawal. Electronic media is an addiction of E's generation," Gwen said with exasperating patience.

"Addiction my ass!" Heath grumbled. Cocaine was an addiction. Heroin was an addiction. A telephone was not an addiction. It was an affectation.

"You saw the crap she's getting on her phone and laptop," Heath said.

"So did she. She knows what is there; is it any worse imagining what's there? Not being able to communicate with friends because *it* is there? Because we don't understand being addicted to social media doesn't mean it doesn't exist. Addicted isn't even the right word. It is the new normal. She feels like you're punishing her for something she has no control over," Gwen said.

Heath resented the intrusion into her maternal bailiwick as much as she wanted her aunt's advice. Lose-lose situation. "The last time I checked, there was one of a threesome with her face Photoshopped over the woman's. I can't bear the thought of her looking at that stuff," Heath said.

"How do you think she feels having you see it? Or me? Though I've delivered hundreds of babies, she sees me as a little old lady who doesn't know where babies come from."

"She doesn't see you that way, you know," Heath said.

"Elizabeth is drowning in shame."

"She's been through worse, real threats, and she was so strong," Heath almost wailed, and cursed herself for being a weakling. For respectable mothers, children are Achilles' heels.

"But she can't fight this one. You can't fight this one. The enemy has no face. The enemy might be her friends. Her friends might be sniggering at the pictures and talking behind her back. It's anonymous, horribly personal, and public all at the same time."

"We should have stayed in Boulder. I should have gotten her a psychiatrist," Heath said. A second mortgage on the house and it would have been feasible. Cheap if it helped E.

"Maybe. Since you didn't, you have to let her be an adult with you. She survived the Fox fiasco because she fought back. This is her fight, and you've confiscated the field of battle. You two have to come to terms about how you're going to deal with this as a team."

"So sayeth the goddess of youth," Heath said with a wry smile.

"So sayeth the goddess," Gwen affirmed.

The winch groaned to life and began spinning up steel cable.

"Give her back her electronics," Gwen said. "I'm going to help John."

TEN

Anna sat across the kitchen table from Lily, sipping extremely good coffee and watching Peter Barnes make goofy faces at Olivia.

"Nice being your boss," he said. "We don't have much crime here, so I may order you to babysit." He grinned.

"Sure," Anna said. "I met a baby once."

"This may be Gris's last fire. He's been muttering about retiring for ten years. I wouldn't be surprised if he up and does it. Your duty station here might end up being for more than three weeks. Maybe for years."

"That's a lot of babysitting," Anna said somberly.

Anna had known Peter nearly twenty years, since law enforcement training at FLETC, the Federal Law Enforcement Training Center in Brunswick, Georgia. In the day, he'd been the epitome of "tall, dark, and handsome": black hair, brown eyes, a few inches over six feet, with thick thighs and upper arms. In a test of endurance, Anna could best him. When it came to sheer physical power, she was as a spider monkey to a bull ape.

In his forties, Pete was still tall and handsome, but the dark at his temples had been painted gray—enough to suggest he was experienced, not enough to suggest he was getting old. Fatherhood was the big change. The Pete Anna knew always referred to children as ankle-biters and rug rats, harped on overpopulation, and eschewed the institution of marriage as nothing but a piece of paper.

Yet here he was, married and dangling a wee daughter on his knee, familial bliss oozing from every pore.

"They're pretty doggone cute, aren't they?" his wife, Lily, said with a smile and a wink at Anna. "I think Peter wanted progeny because a big man with a tiny baby is a megawatt chick magnet."

Anna laughed because it was true. Even she, happily married to the finest man on earth, was finding Peter positively adorable.

"I told Anna she could be chief babysitter as well as chief ranger," Peter said, never taking his eyes off baby Olivia's face.

"I could keep her alive," Anna said seriously. She was mildly offended when they laughed. "In Texas, I kept a younger baby alive under seriously adverse circumstances."

"They don't all make it," Peter said, gooey-eyed over Olivia.

"Culling the gene pool," Anna said.

"You don't mean that!" Lily said in the warm tones of a good person.

Actually, Anna did mean it, but had learned not to flaunt her darker side. Much as she liked Peter, her personal jury was still out on his new wife. So far she'd seen nothing not to like about Lily. Still, it was good to wait a few years before rushing into these sorts of decisions.

"I'd best go make myself presentable," Lily said. Having stopped to kiss first Olivia, then Peter on the head, Lily escaped upstairs.

"Sorry about the quarters. The fancy digs are getting repainted. Are you settled in on Schoodic?" Peter asked.

"I am," Anna replied. She liked the Schoodic Peninsula. Situated across Frenchman Bay from Bar Harbor, an hour by car, less than half that by boat, it was part of the patchwork of public lands that made up Acadia. The forested peninsula was mostly owned by an absentee landlord. The NPS had only the stony tip where it thrust into the sea.

With fewer tourist amenities, the peninsula received only a fraction of the park's visitors. On Schoodic, Anna could occasionally feel a hint of how it must have been when it was wilderness.

Peter was humming "Twinkle, Twinkle, Little Star" as he fed the child from a bottle.

He looked up and saw Anna watching. "Formula's not the best, I know, but sometimes, well, the magic doesn't work. Lily has no milk," he said as if Anna had asked, as if she cared, which she hadn't and didn't.

"You're the most beautiful girl in the world, yes you

are, yes you are," Pete crooned, bobbing his big square head back and forth.

"You do know you look like an idiot," Anna said kindly.

"I *feel* like an idiot! I'm a prisoner of love," he said with an exaggerated sigh and a hand to his heart. "Who knew? Your own kid is different."

Anna would have to take his word on that. She'd never wanted kids, never had kids, and never regretted the choice. Kids were great; watching them was fun, talking to them edifying, and working with them occasionally revelatory. Anna liked kids. Then, too, she liked Irish wolfhounds. She just never much wanted one in the house.

The first few notes of Alice Cooper's "School's Out" sounded from the other room. Peter groaned. "Here, you hold her."

"I can," Anna said defensively as she took Olivia into her arms. Peter went to answer his phone.

"Hello, little citizen," Anna said. Round blue-gray eyes stared unblinkingly into hers. The infant interrogation technique. Anna always felt she was being asked, "Are you worthy? Can you keep me safe?"

"No," she said, and, "I'll give it my best shot."

Olivia stared at her in the unfathomable way of infants. Then her eyes squeezed shut. Her pretty little mouth formed an ugly square. She started to cry. Anna sighed. Babies almost always cried when she held them. It hurt her feelings. Was it that she smelled funny? Or was it that she was so paranoid about dropping the squirmy little beggars that her muscles tensed up until the creatures felt more as if they'd been nailed into a peach crate than enfolded in loving arms?

Peter appeared in the kitchen doorway, cell phone in hand. "That was Artie, the district ranger for Mount Desert. Courtesy call. They got an e-mail tip that your pal on Boar is receiving contraband." The look he gave her reminded Anna of how long it had been since they'd spent any time together, as if he was thinking that if he could turn into Father of the Year, maybe she could have turned into a person who consorted with underworld types.

"I told him we'd meet them at the jetty on Boar," Peter said. "Lily!" he roared, sounding like the old Peter. "We've got to go."

Anna's cell phone buzzed. She pulled it from its case. A text from Heath: *Weird shit getting weirder. Come when you can.*

"Ready when you are," she said to Peter. He led the way to the white Crown Vic, an older model. The NPS was a frugal organization. Anna slid into the passenger side, buckled her seat belt, and prepared to enjoy the view.

Visitors often asked her which park was her favorite. She'd never come up with a satisfactory answer. Today, a body of water encompassing a universe of light and life, a thousand blues in waves that rose and broke in sun-silver celebrations, the surf whispering secrets just out of hearing, it was Acadia.

The fancy houses infesting the multitude of islands scattered in the ocean should have made the coast feel cozier, more inviting of human habitation. Instead, on the rugged coast of the Atlantic, the grandest homes man could devise seemed mere shacks. They hugged the rocky shore as if afraid to venture from sight of land. Those on the tiny islands were like orphans lost at sea.

Anna loved it when nature made humanity seemed trivial. It was a comfort to pretend that she was of a relatively harmless race; she felt safer when she could delude herself that in the battle of Man against Nature, Nature had a chance. For the short duration of the boat ride out of Somes Sound to Boar Island, she could almost believe Internet bullies and weird shit getting weirder did not matter.

The ride up the lift, accompanied by the towering form of Peter Barnes and the hulky muscle-bound district ranger, Artie Lange, was a tad more exhilarating than Anna liked. Not for the first time, she wished more of her compadres were small-boned women, less inclined to strain machinery. Still, she appreciated the view.

The bedrooms in the lighthouse, accessed one through the other by the original circular iron stairs, and the rooms around the lighthouse's base had been renovated. The rest of the place, two wings, blew northeast and west like a tattered cape in a gale. Damp, winds, and harsh winters had had their way. The remains were more ruin than mansion.

"That was quick," Heath said as the lift creaked the last few inches to its mooring fifty feet above the rocks. "And with reinforcements," she said, not sounding particularly pleased. Heath, in Robo-butt, was sitting in the shade, an iPad on her lap. Wily lounged beside her, his chin on his paws. With a deep groan he forced himself to his feet and ambled over to greet Anna. Anna and Wily were old friends; they were pack. She was glad of the sun on his old bones, and the new interesting scents for his nose.

Scratching behind Wily's ears, Anna introduced Heath to Peter and Artie. The young district ranger was looking at Heath keenly, undoubtedly hungering for a perp worth his ambitions. Anna had never worked with Artie, never met him before coming to Acadia, but she suspected he would have been happier on a SWAT team than a bucolic island getaway. She also suspected he thought—hoped—Heath might be a major drug dealer and Anna a co-conspirator.

Suppressing a sigh, she asked, "Where are Elizabeth and Gwen?"

If Artie was going to get all Long Strong Arm of the Law, she didn't want Heath accused of drug crimes—or, gods forbid, arrested—in front of her daughter.

"John took E and Gwen into Bar Harbor for mail and groceries," Heath said.

Peter shot Anna a look. Clearly he knew his district ranger and wanted Anna to take the lead. Anna folded down with her legs crossed Indian-style, the better to commune with Wily. Peter and Artie remained standing.

"You're looming," Anna said.

Peter sat down on the waist-high stone wall separating the patio from the drop to the sea.

Artie, continuing to loom, said, "I've never been on Boar. I'm not classy enough for Ms. Hammond and Ms. Zuckerberg. Mind if I poke around a bit?"

"Poke to your heart's content," Heath said easily.

Anna wished she hadn't. It was always a bad idea to let law enforcement—especially guys like Artie—"poke around." But then, Heath thought they were here to help her with weird shit, not investigate an anonymous tip. Before Artie could go more than a step or two, Anna said, "Artie got a tip. An e-mail that said you were receiving contraband goods. Drugs. That you and Elizabeth were dealing to the kids in Boulder."

"You're kidding," Heath said, obviously—at least to Anna—stunned. Heath laughed. "You are kidding?"

"Nope," Anna said.

"You've stolen my thunder for weird shit today. This is what I got." Seeming completely unconcerned with the accusation, Heath rolled over to where Anna and Wily sat shoulder to shoulder and handed her the iPad. "Hit REFRESH," she said.

Anna did as she was told. Reading the screen was almost impossible in the direct light of the sun. Shielding it as best as she could, she squinted at the line of comments scrolling down the right-hand side.

"That's usually where the comments of people Elizabeth follows on Twitter show up," Heath said. "This guy—or girl—has been tweeting like a damned canary since last night."

The expected obscenities were in evidence, but the thrust of the argument had changed. Anna read aloud,

" 'Kill yourself. The world will be better off when you're dead. Slit your wrists. Your Mother tried to abort you. When that didn't work, she dumped you. Put a bullet in your brain. You alive will make Heath kill herself. Die, bitch, die.' "

Peter rose to his feet. Artie decided this was more interesting than poking around.

"I kind of like that last one," Heath said. "It has a certain simplicity the others lack."

"Has E seen these?" Anna asked.

"All but the last few. They came in after John took them in the boat. She may have seen them by now. She has her phone with her."

"I thought you were keeping her away from electronics," Anna said, her voice flat to keep the censure from leaking through. Anna had not rushed headlong into the twenty-first century. People scarcely noticed as life was remade by cell phones, GPS, Amazon, YouTube, Google, and Facebook. Big Brother was a mere piker compared to Amazon and its fellows. Clicking "accept, accept, accept" to unread contracts, whole countries and their children became citizens of this sudden and stunning world of bread and fabulous circuses without a thought or a backward look.

Anna knew there would be a reckoning. Even in the twenty-first century she doubted there was anything like a free lunch.

"Aunt Gwen made a good argument against it," Heath replied a bit defensively.

"Like E needs to see this stuff?" Anna growled.

"Like E needs to have a sense of control. That and

addiction," Heath said with the exaggerated patience Anna knew she'd inherited from her aunt.

"Addiction?" Artie asked. Had he been a dog, his ears would have been pricked.

"Evidently," Heath said. "Aunt Gwen said it's common, almost epidemic."

"Gwen Littleton is a pediatrician," Anna explained to Artie and Peter. To Heath, she said, "Elizabeth is not an addict," and then, "Addicted to what?"

"Electronic media," Heath said.

Anna snorted. Peter wore a neutral ranger mask, the kind put on when taking reports of flying saucers and sightings of Kokopelli.

"Be that way," Heath said to no one in particular. Shaking a cigarette from a pack kept in Robo-butt's saddlebag, she went on. "For all the reasons we had talked about, I did take E's iPhone, iPad, laptop, everything but her Kindle." Cigarette in her teeth, Heath cupped her hands to protect the lighter's flame from the onshore wind and lit it. "E grew sullen, irritable, had trouble sleeping, had little appetite, trouble focusing, exhibited obsessive behaviors, paranoia, hypersensitivity—all the things she would have if she'd been a cocaine addict and I'd cut her off cold turkey."

"Or heroin," Artie said.

Heath glanced at him, mild confusion in her eyes, then went on. "The only thing missing was hallucinations." Taking a deep drag of the smoke, she glared around at the three of them.

Wily, Anna noted, was not included in the malevolence.

"She's been under a lot of stress," Anna said.

"That, too. But after Gwen convinced me, I Googled it."

"That's asking the dealer about the junkie," Anna said.

"As Ripley said, believe it or not," Heath retorted.

"So you just handed her back everything? Fornicating threesomes, goats, pederasts, and donkeys—the whole filthy business?" Anna asked.

"We talked. I told her she had to show me everything. If it was so shaming she just couldn't bring herself to let me see it, she had to forward it to you."

"Thanks a heap," Anna said, but was honored.

"I gave her electronics back and the symptoms cleared up almost immediately," Heath said.

"Freaky," Anna said, shaking her head. To her, social media was about as entertaining as mosquitoes whining around her ears.

"Yup. Strange but true," Heath said, the wind whipping the cigarette smoke from her lips.

The bell on the pole by the lift clanged; then, with a piteous groan, the machinery began paying out steel cable.

"That will be my little addict now," Heath said.

The love in her voice made Anna smile.

Minutes later the platform appeared filled with bags, Gwen, Elizabeth, and John. When the retired lobsterman saw the field of green and gray, his eyes narrowed and his teeth clamped harder on his pipestem. Acadia was one of many parks that had frequent interface with previous residents, inholdings, shared or debated boundaries, and clashing cultures. Locals often eyed park rangers askance, figuring they were only around to make up rules about things that were traditionally none of their damn business. Conserving resources for the next generation was of little interest to those of the present generation who were just trying to get by.

Anna didn't blame them, but it was of greater importance that the native plants and animals survive and thrive. Humans had much in common with kudzu, Russian thistle, and other invasive species. They needn't be wiped out entirely, only uprooted where they threatened the natural balance.

Gwen, her hair made wild with salt wind, looked fifteen years younger than she had in Boulder. The sea air? The change of scenery? No, Anna decided; it was John. Gwen was enamored. The boat pilot had the same sort of sex appeal as Spencer Tracy, Humphrey Bogart, and Robert Mitchum. The kind that doesn't depend on youth or good looks.

Even E appeared happy enough. When she saw Anna studying Gwen, she rolled her eyes and made a face. At sixteen, geriatric romance was grossing her out. A wonderful problem, given the other things that had been grossing all of them out for the last weeks.

"John, get the cart so we can get the perishables in the fridge," Gwen bossed him happily. From the look on the man's face, he was teetering between enchanted and terrified.

"Got a present," Gwen said as she dumped envelopes and a shoe-box-sized package on Heath's lap.

"Do you want me to come help put groceries away?" E asked, batting her eyes innocently.

"That won't be necessary," Gwen said.

E flopped down beside Wily and Anna. "I just offered to annoy her. For a while there in Bar Harbor I thought she was going to ask him to carry her books or give her a ride home on his bicycle. That or get a motel room. Yuck."

"Amore," Anna said, and sighed deeply.

"Somebody to sit next to at the old age home more like," Elizabeth said. Then, "Sorry, Mom. I know she'll want to park her wheelchair next to yours."

"Not if I take my medicine," Heath said, waving her unfiltered Camel. "The cure for old age."

E was not amused.

Nor was Anna.

"What's in the box, Ms. Jarrod?" Artie, the district ranger, cut in. Anna had totally forgotten why they'd been called to Boar, the anonymous tip that Heath and E were drug dealers come to the East Coast to corrupt the youth.

Now a box appears right on cue.

"Haven't a clue," Heath said and began ripping at the paper.

"Don't open it," Anna said suddenly.

"Think it's a bomb?" Heath asked, laughing as she smashed the paper beneath the box so the wind wouldn't snatch it away. She was as gleeful as a child on her birthday. Relief from stress, Anna guessed.

"It's not ticking," Heath said as torn paper revealed a shoe box.

"Bombs don't tick anymore," Anna said as she leapt to her feet.

Heath lifted the lid off. "What in the hell . . . ," she said.

The District Danger Ranger was beside Heath's chair in an instant. "I'll need that box, ma'am." Before Anna could snatch the box or slap Heath upside the head, Artie had it in his big, long-fingered hands.

Wide-eyed, curious, Heath waited like a sitting duck.

"Looks like heroin to me," Artie said with barely suppressed glee. He bounced the box in his hand as if weighing it. "An eight-ball or thereabouts."

"Like *heroin* heroin?" Elizabeth asked.

"This could be serious," Heath said. Now that it was too late, she was finally catching on, Anna thought, but Heath wasn't paying any attention to the drugs in the ranger's hand; she was staring at the wrapping paper spread across her knees.

"This wasn't forwarded from Boulder," she said. "This was sent to the PO box we rented in Bar Harbor."

"The e-mail was sent to Acadia," Anna said.

Unconsciously, Elizabeth raised her hands to her throat. "Whoever it is knows where we are," she said softly.

ELEVEN

Denise and her sister had neither seen nor spoken to one another since they'd decided something had to be done to keep Kurt Duffy from beating—or killing—Paulette. Not that Denise wanted to be alone; she never wanted to be alone again. Space to think was what she needed. After three days of thinking, of no contact with Paulette, she went to her sister's house during the day when she knew Kurt would be at sea. She moored her runabout in Otter Cove, a tiny inlet with little to lure visitors. From there she hiked overland to Otter Creek and her sister's back door. This way no one would see her car parked anywhere near Paulette's. The car was one of the things she had thought of while she was in her lonely thinking space.

Not phoning Paulette was another thing. Cell phones were wired to record every call, every text, and, with GPS, where the phone was at any given time. Denise didn't know how many of these invasive pieces of technology dwelt in her phone—it was four years old—but if they were going to do something serious about Kurt, she didn't dare take chances.

The previous night she had taken her phone apart, cooked the SIM card in the microwave for a few minutes, then cut the nuked card into pieces with tin snips. That done, she smashed all the parts of the phone that could be smashed with a three-pound sledge hammer. Over the remaining rubble, she poured lighter fluid and burned what would burn, melted what would melt. The resulting black mess she tossed overboard where the channel was deepest.

It never made sense to her that criminals couldn't destroy evidence properly. She had to suppose they never really put their minds to it. Paulette's prepaid cell from Walmart would have to be destroyed as well.

The way her sister's face lit up when she saw who was tapping on her kitchen door made Denise's heart fill her throat. Along with her soul, she'd thought unconditional love went missing when she was born. The open trust and joy she saw in her twin's eyes she'd only ever expected to see in the eyes of her newborn child.

Paulette came out onto the porch. She was wearing a calf-length skirt in lime green and pink. The pink was in geometric patterns and the green in paisley swirls. The waistband and the bottom third of the skirt were green, the rest bold pink. On her feet were mules of tan-colored canvas with green ankle ribbons and wedge heels. Over the skirt she wore a white tunic, belted with a narrow lime green ribbon.

Denise wore trousers. Always: for work, for home, for fancy dress. The palette of her wardrobe ran the gamut from dull Park Service green and gray to totally grim. Seeing "herself" in a bright skirt, she was startled at how pretty she was, they were.

Without any need for discussion, Paulette headed toward the trees. Again she led Denise in a circuitous path to the nursery so there would be no obvious trail worn in the duff. Neither spoke until they were closed behind the wooden door, lamp lit against the artificial night inside the windowless shed. This time Denise sat in the rocking chair and Paulette on the child-sized chair with the trumpet carved on the back.

"That's a nursing rocker," Paulette said of the chair Denise had taken. "That's why the arms are so low and curved; so you can hold the baby and rest your forearm on the wood."

Unconsciously rounding her arms as if she held an infant, Denise rocked gently. "It feels right, good," she marveled. For a long moment, both she and her sister gazed out at the never-changing forest painted behind the window frames, a world no one but they could inhabit, no one but they could alter.

Paulette began as if telling a story that would be important to Denise, one that Denise had been asking for in her head. "I first brought the baby things out here fourteen years, two months, and nine days ago; you don't forget the day you lose a child. I was just storing them, you know, for the next baby. Hiding them from Kurt so he wouldn't sell them or break them. He wasn't too bad back then."

"He beat you so hard you miscarried," Denise said.

"I guess. Yes, I mean, I know he did," said Paulette

with a wan smile, her head shaking slowly from side to side. She looked as if she were fighting clear of a fog she'd been lost in for a long time. "I guess what I was thinking was that back then, when he hurt me, he didn't mean it like he does now. He'd get stirred up over money, or he'd get jealous of the way I supposedly looked at some guy, or he'd get mad because I wanted to go visit Mom and Dad or whatever. He'd get mad for some reason, lose his temper, and take it out on me.

"At the hospital we've got this old man who comes in every few months. He's got this awful abscess on the side of his calf that fills up with yuck and bursts. We clean it up, the doctors prescribe salves and antibiotics, and it seems to heal. Then, in a month or two, he's back in. Kurt used to be like that, this abscess that filled with yuck. Then he'd get drunk and beat up on me, and he'd be okay for a while. Even sorry in the beginning. Shoot, by the time I was twenty-six we'd been married nearly ten years. What else did I know? I guess I figured most men slapped their wives around. I didn't have much in the way of girlfriends to compare lives with." She smiled at Denise. "I didn't have a sister."

Denise smiled back without thinking, and realized she had been so strung out, weirded out, on guard, and paranoid for the last few months that she'd reacted in the same way Paulette had to Kurt's abuse. It had become the norm, the real, the way life was. This sudden relaxing of vigilance was a revelation. Abuse was not the way life was. It was the way men made it. Women could subject it to change without notice.

"After I lost the first baby, I never forgave Kurt. Him

beating me, I could forgive that. But not beating the baby to death inside me."

That was why Denise couldn't forgive Peter. Dumping her? Sure. Marrying a younger woman? That, too. The loss of her baby? Never. Maybe Peter was another person who needed to be dead. He hadn't beaten her, but he had certainly browbeaten her into getting an abortion. Murder twice removed was still murder. Even in a species gorging on death every day, killing babies was genuinely despised. Nobody cheered baby killers. They didn't get medals. People paid more than lip service to wanting to stamp them out.

"Then, three years, three months, three weeks, and five days later, I lost a little girl, my daughter. She was fairly well along. Tiny hands and fingers, a nub of a nose, ears, all perfect. I saw her in the the bathroom overhead light. That's where I miscarried. Kurt looked sick seeing us there on the floor. I thought he was going to pick us up, but he sort of shook all over like a goose walked on his grave and said, 'Clean up the mess.' He didn't come back for a couple of days, and when he did it was like nothing happened. Nothing. He comes through the door, turns on the TV, and says, 'What do you have for supper?' That was it. After that he didn't hit me for a long time. A year or more.

"That's when I fell into a kind of sleep, I think. I gave up on the house, except for keeping it clean enough to be sanitary, and I'd come back here and tidy up. Bit by bit, this room became what it is. While I was walking in my sleep all those years, this was the dream I was dreaming. Does that sound crazy?"

"No," Denise answered. "It's a beautiful dream. A wise dream. I must have fallen asleep, too. I dreamed of dark places and rotten people. Walking around this park we so loved when we were little, I would see nothing but my pain. Finally, my world was made of pain, and that world got smaller every day."

Denise knew she hadn't been a child in Acadia National Park. While her twin was being raised by kindly old folks on Isle au Haut, Denise was being kicked around trailer parks in Brewer and Bangor and Winterport. Still, she wasn't lying; she knew that their childhood playing in tide pools was more real than hers playing on train tracks and around warehouses. Paulette would know this, too.

For an instant she was outside herself, looking at the two of them sitting in the painted room. Panic surged up her throat; she was going crazy, had gone crazy, Paulette did sound crazy.

Then she was back in her body. The terror abated. She looked around the space her sister had created, calming herself with the fabric art pieces, the windows that showed the world as it should be rather than as it was, the crib with the stuffed bear, bright-eyed, head tilted inquisitively. The true insanity was not what she and her sister dreamed. It was the actions of those who had made their lives so miserable they needed to dream it.

"Then I woke up," Paulette said simply, cutting into Denise's thoughts. Still on the little chair, her skirt flowing to the floor in a bright blossom, she spread her hands with a shrug. "About a year ago . . . six months . . .

I don't know. Around that time I started feeling again, then I started feeling everything was odd, off somehow. At first Kurt didn't notice I'd woken up. When he did, he didn't like it. He knocked me around some— not a lot, but I could feel he meant it this time. Meant to kill me."

"The Burning Bed," Denise said.

"I loved that movie."

"Self -defense. There's no way around it."

They were quiet for a moment, the only sound the soft beat as the rocker rocked back and forth on the wooden floor.

"Do you know how to kill people?" Paulette asked. "Rangers have guns and all. Do they teach you that?"

"Not in so many words," Denise said. "They use the word 'stop.' A gun has to have 'stopping' power. We shoot at targets shaped like people, and we learn to aim for center body mass—bigger and easier to hit than the pinhead of the usual criminal. We learn to hit people with batons in places that will disable them."

Paulette thought that over for a couple of minutes. Denise rocked and thought about killing. Death was standard operating procedure: Cows died for hamburgers, grass died for cows. Little lambkins were slaughtered for Easter dinners. Turkeys died by the millions for Christmas and Thanksgiving. Animals were different, the people who ate them always insisted. People pretended that killing people wasn't the same as killing animals, that killing people was horrific. Then they voted to fight in Iran, Iraq, Afghanistan, Vietnam, Korea, Libya—always somewhere, and mostly not because anybody wanted or needed soldiers marching around their backyards shooting. Humans liked killing humans. They were good at it. They celebrated it with medals and movies and songs. Then they pretended to themselves that a woman killing a violent bastard like Kurt Duffy was so horrible she had to go to prison forever. It made no sense. Either it was okay to kill people deemed bad or it wasn't. It was pretty obvious to Denise that in America, as well as the rest of the world, the consensus was in: Killing was fine and dandy, good even. Admirable.

The only thing bad about killing was *saying* it was okay. Like the "family values" politicians: They could fornicate, whoremonger, go with same-sex hookers, commit adultery, and still get reelected by the Evangelicals as long as they *said* those things were wrong.

So nobody was going to care that Kurt Duffy was killed. Not a bit. They only paid lip service to the idea that killing a Kurt Duffy was wrong. Really, most people didn't care at all; they just wanted to curl up on the sofa and watch *Saw III* or *Dexter*. What she and Paulette needed to do was find a story that would help people explain the murder of Kurt Duffy to themselves so they could stop thinking about it, stop pretending it was bad, and get back to their own rat killing, as one of her old high school teachers was fond of saying.

"I don't want to disable Kurt," Paulette said. "I think he needs to be dead for a long, long time."

"For the rest of his life," Denise said, and they both laughed at the absurdity.

"My gosh!" Paulette gasped, covering her mouth.

"Are we awful? I mean, we're laughing about killing people. Killing *Kurt*! I don't feel awful, but I know I should."

"Don't feel awful," Denise said when they'd stopped giggling. "He does need to be dead."

"Poison?" Paulette ventured.

"Do you know anything about poison? I don't," Denise replied.

"We'd have to buy it somewhere. That would make a trail," Paulette said. "I could burn him in bed, like Farrah Fawcett did in the movie. She got off on a self-defense plea."

"It wouldn't work a second time. Too obvious," Denise decided. "Besides, you can't be anywhere around when it happens. You have to have an iron-clad alibi. We could screw with the brakes on his truck. I know how to do that."

Paulette shook her head. "He only drives from here to Bar Harbor and back. Nothing bad would happen, not bad enough anyway."

"Yeah. Bad idea. Even if it worked, we wouldn't know the exact time it would happen, so maybe no alibi. How about the lobster boat?" Denise asked.

"I don't know how to sink one even if we could get near it, and his crew would go down, too. Probably they'd all drown and Kurt would swim to shore and come kill us both. If he knew there was a both. Me for sure."

"Push him off a high place?" Denise mused.

"No. He's too big and too lazy. When he's not on the boat he doesn't exert himself at all. If you managed to get him to go up on some rock, somebody could see. You can't be seen to be with us, with me."

Denise sighed. "Okay. We shoot him."

"We shoot him three times," Paulette said firmly.

TWELVE

Heath lay in the ground-floor bedroom of the tower, exhausted from the sheer effort it took to go to bed. Before she'd been hospitalized, this had been Gwen's friend Chris Zuckerberg's bedroom. Other than a few pieces of truly stunning artwork, the decor was not what Heath had expected from a woman who owned an entire island. Though the mattress and the bedding—down comforter over fine cotton sheets—were excellent, the bed was narrow, an old-fashioned kid's bed. The armoire, obviously made for this lighthouse or another round dwelling, was an antique but in bad condition. The single wooden chair and writing desk were scuffed with use.

Gwen said Chris was land- and house-poor. The place was a money pit on a grand scale. Probably most of it went to fixing leaks in roofs and buying better mousetraps. There had to be mice. The decaying wings of the house looked like prime rodent habitat.

The room still held Ms. Zuckerberg's scent, faintly spicy; her clothes still hung in the armoire, and papers were strewn across the desk as if she'd expected to return. Something Gwen thought was unlikely. In the days since they'd arrived, and Dez Hammond had phoned to welcome them to the abandoned house, Ms. Zuckerberg had suffered several more transient ischemic attacks.

Heath found the Spartan utility of Chris's room pleasing. Simplicity had always suited her. The world presented enough treats and turns for her eyeballs that she didn't feel the need to spread too many of them around indoors.

The room above Heath had been used by Dez Hammond. Dez was a childhood friend of Ms. Zuckerberg's. Aunt Gwen said Ms. Hammond moved in pretty much full-time after her husband died and Chris's health began to fail.

This second-story room was claimed by Elizabeth of the young strong legs. It boasted two wide windows. The view, so Elizabeth said, was spectacular.

The topmost room, where the lighthouse's lantern had been housed, had a three-hundred-sixty-degree view. It had been Chris's before the first heart attack had driven her to ground level. The penthouse suite was where Gwen had chosen to bunk.

Heath's ground-floor room had only two windows, slits that medieval bowmen would have found claustrophobic. Despite the lack of a view, she liked the space. There were times when only a fortress on a crag surrounded by a cold, deep moat could make one feel safe.

Pulling the comforter up under her chin, she stared at the electronic suit Leah had so generously allowed her to bring. In this historic environment it looked at home on its hanger, more like a suit of armor than an exoskeleton. Though she had yet to try it on Boar, Heath liked having it in sight.

Hah! And they said she'd never walk again.

Through the hole cut in the thick plank flooring for the stairs, Elizabeth's music—real music, thank God—trickled, punctuated by the occasional thumping footfall. Light and lithe as a gymnast, yet the girl had a habit of walking on her heels. She made more noise coming and going than a troupe of clog dancers.

The noise, like the fortress of a house, was comforting. Elizabeth was safe. Anyone who wanted to harm her would have to cross half the continent, swim icy seas, scale cliffs, and pass through Heath's bedroom.

Lord knew, tonight, if they/he/it ran the gauntlet she wouldn't be asleep when they reached her room. Annoying, vaguely electrical twitches in her legs were driving her nuts. Horrid buggers felt nothing, were useless for anything but making laps for cats; still they leapt and kicked and jerked. Obviously they could move. They just wouldn't take orders. Most irritating.

Since sleep was off the menu, Heath sifted through the poisons someone was dripping into her daughter's world. After Tiffany Edleson fell through as the favored suspect, Heath, Anna, and Gwen had assumed the cyberstalker was one—or more—of Elizabeth's fellow students at Boulder High School.

Heath had spoken with E's high school principal and her English and geometry teachers. They'd been kind but useless. As it was when Heath was in high school, the phys ed teacher was the one to whom the kids opened up. Ms. Willis knew about the points game E had mentioned. The clique of boys who played the game boasted they wouldn't date any girl who couldn't be counted on for a friendly blow job.

"They're considered the cool boys, the BMOC, go figure," Heath told Gwen.

"They are nasty pieces of work," Gwen said succinctly. "Is oral sex de rigueur?"

They'd both looked at Elizabeth, who, by choice, was in on what they'd come to call the Cybercreep Councils. Heath and Gwen were reassured by the spontaneous "Gross, like way gross!"

"The girls they get? You know, who hang with them and do the blow jobs and whatever? You'd think they'd be the school skanks, but they're not," Elizabeth told them. "They're real hotties. I think it's that Stockholm thing, where the hostages fall in love with the terrorists."

Heath hadn't thought of it that way, but she wouldn't be surprised if Elizabeth was on to something.

Gwen said, "The boys are the skanks, Elizabeth."

A sigh and an eye roll were her reward.

Could the jerk boys, the high school rotters who made a game of degrading girls have smelled Elizabeth's virgin soul, and set on the trail like hounds on the scent of a rabbit? Heath wondered as she listened to the tattoo of her daughter's feet on the planks overhead.

Bullies tended to pick on the strays, the oddballs. Though she'd never say so to Elizabeth, the child's peculiar upbringing didn't make it easy for her to blend in, be one of the crowd—an essential survival skill for a teenager.

From age four until she was nine E had lived in a polygamist compound that called itself Mormon, though the Mormon Church would have vehemently denied the relationship. Before kids in the cult reached puberty—the age when girl children were "married" off to the chosen elders, and boy children were run out of the community lest they become sexual rivals—they lived like the children of an enormous and amiable family circa 1898.

No Internet, no TV, no video games, newspapers, or magazines; they were seldom taken into the nearby town of Loveland. Their clothes were mostly homemade. All were homeschooled. They grew up knowing of the outside world only in a shadowy way. Though such an upbringing left them woefully unprepared for the challenges of the modern world, it did allow them an innocence denied children exposed from infancy to an overcommercialized, oversexualized, violent society careening into the future on laugh tracks and Big Macs.

Miraculously, Elizabeth still retained that aura of innocence. Once, Heath had attributed it to her early cloistering. Now she believed Elizabeth would have been the same had she been raised in London during

World War II, Berkeley in the sixties, or New York City in the new millennium. Nature winning over nurture.

Innocence was an almost irresistible target for kids who have lost theirs.

When Heath was in school, bullying had a bricks-and-mortar aspect: hallway taunts, locker vandalism, heads stuck in toilets. Bullies were a hands-on bunch; they liked to see the results of their work, enjoy the public humiliation, soak up the fear.

Since the Internet, things that used to be spray-painted under bridges were published for the world to see. Besides her personal electronic pages, a lot had been posted to a blog popular with Boulder kids, *whosewhoandwhocares.net*. The site was known for unflattering pictures with "funny" captions, outing romances, derogatory remarks about fashion, belittling football players who screwed up, and naming cheerleaders who—so said the blog—didn't wear panties.

Whoever was bullying Elizabeth was too cruel for a bulletin board invented for petty cruelty. The kids who ran the blog deleted the graphic attacks on Elizabeth the moment they saw them, then blocked the source. The bully got multiple URLs and reposted after every block.

Messages, fielded by the Boulder police while Elizabeth's phone was quarantined, leaned toward the threatening. Nothing overt; crawling, spiritual cockroaches afraid of the light. The wording got darker, the pictures more sadistic. Though sympathetic, the police considered cyber malice out of their jurisdiction.

Sam Edleson was in their jurisdiction, but without

witnesses or evidence, there was little they could do. A couple of female cops went to the Edlesons' home and scared the stuffing out of Terry. Two of their male counterparts "had a talk" with Sam that left him the worse for wear. Or so said the kid who raked Heath's leaves.

The detective assigned to Elizabeth's case wasn't so user-friendly. He murmured about kids being kids, modern moms being oversensitive, letting 'em duke it out—a song that he should have known went out of fashion in the eighties.

Snug behind her castle walls on Boar Island, Heath pondered the metaphorical roaches. She was not being a hysterical overprotective mom. Heath had never been given to the vapors, not even during the dark days when she was newly disabled and Gwendolyn feared she'd off herself. Easier said than done when one can no longer access high places from which to leap.

At present Elizabeth was living on a rock made of nothing but high places and deadly falls. Heath thought of the messages urging her to kill herself. How many would it take to turn E's mind back to suicide? Ten? A hundred? After all that had happened, had the vicious words lost their ability to influence her? Heath hoped so. Hope and vigilance: Those were the only weapons she had.

Her thoughts left that miserable abyss and turned to the package of heroin and the anonymous tip, a tip given before the heroin had arrived. Obviously whoever tipped off the rangers sent the heroin. This attempt at a frame job was ludicrously amateurish. That fact would have been more reassuring had the excitement the district ranger evinced made her think he'd never smelled a three-day-old red herring before.

He'd scrutinized the contents of the box. It was filled with small rectangular packets wrapped in tinfoil. There had to be a hundred of the things. Heath had thought it was a box of toothpicks, two to a pack, the way they offer them in cheaper restaurants. With a look first at her, then at Anna, suggesting they might be in cahoots, Artie bundled the box into a paper bag, which he sealed and marked with a black Sharpie.

"Evidence," he said darkly.

Heath laughed remembering his barely concealed glee. The drug bust of the century, and he was on it! She doubted it would be as amusing if he got anyone else to take it seriously. In the justice system, things did go horribly awry now and again.

As soon as the rangers left, Heath jumped on the Internet. The tiny packages—if they even contained heroin and not baby powder or whatever—were probably one-twentieth of a gram and cost ten dollars on the street. Nicely set up for resale. An eight-ball was supposedly three grams. Eight-ball. Behind the eight ball? Was that the legal limit or something?

It was so absurd, so obviously part of the harassment of E, it had not crossed Heath's mind that the district ranger would consider her guilty. But he did. He might even have arrested her had Anna not laughed when he mentioned it. In the end he said, "Well, it shouldn't be hard to catch you."

Heath smiled to herself remembering Anna's muttered "That's what you think."

The package had no return address. The postmark
was Walla Walla, Washington. A dead end, undoubtedly. Whoever was after E had spent God knew how
much money to frame Heath for drug dealing. That was
a lot of malice, a lot of planning—even if it was bad
planning.

What they'd considered high school bullying was
taking on a whole new level of threat.

Surely nothing would come of the drug charge.
Surely Artie wasn't that stupid. Surely.

Idly, she wondered if jails were handicap accessible.
In the movies they all had miles and miles of metal
stairs.

Heath readjusted her pillow. Her shadow flashed on
the tower's curving whitewashed walls. For a few minutes she amused herself making shadow puppets on
the old plaster. A bunny, a duck, a wolf with its tongue
lolling. At that, Wily groaned. Coincidence or not,
Heath laughed. Taking that as an invitation, the dog
jumped up onto the foot of her bed—not in one try, but
he made it.

Doctor's orders were no lying down with dogs for
Heath. Without sensation in her legs, the possibility of
accidental damage was too great. Still, she didn't order Wily off. He'd worked too hard to get up, and she'd
loved him too long to insist.

Scratching him between the ears, she felt the bed
shake as he echoed the pleasure with a scratching hind
leg. A year or more before, that leg had been broken,

leaving Wily with a limp, but it still worked well enough. At least as well as Anna's left arm.

"If not Tiffany, then who?" Heath whispered the question to Wily. "Who would set me up—us, me and E—for a drug charge? Why? Ruin our reputations? Make us less believable to the powers that be? Make me look like an unfit mother?" That seemed most likely. If Heath was a drug dealer and her daughter a whore, then . . . Then what? No one would care when one or both of them disappeared? Or died?

A sudden and desperate need to see E flooded Heath. She sat up abruptly. Rather, her mind told her body to sit up abruptly. Not a great deal actually happened. She twitched like a landed fish, then pushed herself up on her elbows.

Having thrown off the covers, she shoved her legs over the edge of the bed, then laboriously worked her slippers onto her feet. Gone were the days when she could unthinkingly run around barefoot. How would she know if she injured herself? Caring for her legs often felt like caring for ungrateful children.

Wily whined from his place on the foot of the bed. "It's okay, pal. Nothing you've got to catch or kill," Heath reassured him. He thumped his tail on the coverlet.

Her electronic suit, with its gyroscope-that-wasn't-a-gyroscope thingy Leah was testing, was designed to be ultrastable. Even though there was a good sturdy handrail running up the curving wall, Heath had no desire to try the suit on the narrow stairway that corkscrewed up the tower. The wheelchair, of course, was useless. There was no way she could climb the stairs in a dignified *Homo erectus* sort of way.

In the 1860s paraplegics were SOL.

Lowering herself to the cold stone floor, Heath scootched backward using her upper-body strength—a mode of travel at which she'd become quite proficient. If she could ever figure out how to do it without dragging her pants off, she would petition the Special Olympics to add the Backward Butt Traverse to their sports roster.

Wily was accustomed to Heath's unusual modes of locomotion. He eased off the bed, stretched, sketching a deep bow, and then padded over to collapse with a gusty sigh near the foot of the spiral stairway.

"Easy for you, my four-legged friend," Heath grunted.

At the bottom step she stopped, pulled up her pajama bottoms, positioned herself with her back to the step, legs out in front of her, and caught her breath. The Backward Butt Traverse might be the best way to move without mechanical aids, but it wasn't easy. Heartbeat returned to near normal, she began the long circuitous ascent. Elbows back, palms on the step behind her, push up, swing her fanny back, settle, palms on the step behind her: twenty-three steps, twenty-three ten-inch lifts.

I shall have the triceps of a god, she promised herself.

She could have simply hollered for Elizabeth to come down, or blown the whistle that E insisted she wear around her neck, but where was the challenge in that?

When she was about three-quarters of the way up—eighteen of the twenty-three steps, and sweating like a pig—the query "Mom?" came from above.

"Coming," Heath gasped back. The tower, with its coil of stairs, didn't allow for doors. As Heath looked up at the rectangle of golden light where the steps passed through the plank floor of Elizabeth's room, her daughter's face appeared, long, straight brown hair falling down around it like the tentacles of a particularly relaxed jellyfish. Whenever she caught a different angle of Elizabeth's face, Heath was struck all over again by the girl's beauty. Part of it, she suspected, was a lack of objectivity on her part. Regardless, Elizabeth was lovely, tall for her age, willowy, with flawless skin, eyes that seemed too big for her face and were the brown of expensive chocolate.

Pride in her child went cold with the realization that images of that sweet face were being defiled in the public forum. Facebook, MySpace, Google: Elizabeth's junior varsity girls soccer team made the state championships. Even though they didn't win, a team photo could have made its way into cyberspace. Elizabeth was in an online yearbook. Any pictures taken of her by her friends and posted on public media were out there. Every pervert in the world had access to her daughter's face.

"Privacy is dead," Heath said to the face floating above her.

"Yesterday's news. Can't a girl go a whole evening without her mom bum-thumping up her stairs? Why didn't you call? I'd've come down."

The mixture of irritation and concern gave Heath the strength to make the last five steps, and even hide some of the strain as she did so.

"Did you have a reason for this, or is it just your version of jogging?" E asked as Heath levered herself onto Elizabeth's floor, her feet dangling over the dark stairs.

Heath hadn't much of a reason. *I had to see you with my own eyes, know you were real and alive* was too much emo to dump on one's child in the night. "I had a question," Heath said, hoping she'd think of one.

"Um . . . you lost one slipper and couldn't wait to ask me where it went?"

Heath looked down. During her ascent she'd lost a shoe. Damn. "I'm still better off than those with no slippers at all," she said unctuously, then admitted, "I just came up to see how you're doing."

"Okay, I guess." Elizabeth stared down between their dangling feet. "You don't have to come up, Wily." Wily laid his chin on the bottom step and made a whuffing noise.

"Any more interesting slurs on your character?" Heath asked carefully.

"I asked Tiff to keep an eye out, and I've been to all the regular places. The porn gets cleared out by the websites after a while. The 'die bitch die' stuff isn't showing up too many places. I guess it's the personal touch. My phone only."

Heath was pleased E could still make jokes, and scared that she was using humor to cover uglier truths.

"Will you get arrested?" Elizabeth asked suddenly. "You know, as a drug dealer?"

"You'd think even a blind carpenter could see this was a frame job," Heath replied.

"Ha, ha," E said, then automatically corrected Heath. "Visually challenged."

Surprised, Heath asked, "Isn't 'blind' still okay?"

"I don't know what's okay anymore," Elizabeth said miserably. Heath knew she was talking about more than politically correct language.

"If I go to jail, would you bake me a cake with a file in it?" Heath asked to cheer her daughter up.

"So not funny."

"Anna doesn't think it will amount to anything," Heath said seriously. "We don't even know for sure if it is heroin until they test it. That ranger guy, Artie, and Peter Barnes were here when it came; they could see I wasn't expecting it. There was no return address. Juries like nice middle-aged ladies in wheelchairs. They'd never get a conviction. Besides, I don't even know where you could buy heroin."

"I do," Elizabeth said.

Heath cocked an eyebrow.

"I don't know it like been-there-done-that," her daughter amended, "but I've heard there used to be a place called the Silk Road on the Internet where you could get anything except hit men. There were codes and secret e-mails and special wallets—the whole bitcoin thing—all untraceable."

"I remember," Heath said. "Then they captured the Dread Pirate Roberts and it was shut down."

"Tiff says there's another Dread Pirate Roberts," Elizabeth said. "There's always another Dread Pirate Roberts."

The Princess Bride was one of Heath's favorite books. She'd read it to E when she was ten.

"Maybe there's another one up now where you could buy something and have it mailed to anybody you wanted," E said. "Maybe somebody did that with the package you got."

"What would be the point?"

"Maybe to get you out of the way. If you went to jail, who'd get me?" Elizabeth asked.

"Anna," Heath said. "That's what godmothers do."

"That's okay then," Elizabeth said.

Heath laughed. "Thanks a million."

"You know what I mean," E said. Heath did.

For a while they sat, each lost in her own thoughts. Then E asked, "Do you think the heroin sender guy was my stalker guy?"

Heath wanted to lie, say no, she didn't think it was in any way related, so she could save Elizabeth the angst of thinking herself a danger to her family. Parents lied to children all the time to calm their fears—or to increase them.

"You'll put your eye out with that."

"If you hold the knife that way, you'll cut your fingers off."

"If you make that face again it will stick forever."

"Girls who whistle come to some bad ends."

"Boys seldom make passes at girls who wear glasses."

Heath had been careful never to lie to Elizabeth. The girl had been brought up in a multilayered matrix of lies, half-truths, myths, and monsters. Their first two years together, Heath spent a lot of time sorting carefully through Elizabeth's tangled belief system trying to ascertain which lies the child needed to hang on to in order to feel secure, and which were increasingly damaging the longer they took root. Even the dangerous lies could not be snatched away. They had to be replaced by a truth that would fill the resulting hole, or heal the wound the old belief engendered.

Rescued children didn't come with baggage; they came with unexploded ordnance from former wars.

For a while neither of them spoke. Elizabeth, her long lovely legs hanging down the trap across from Heath's, was swinging her feet idly, a trick Heath would have given ten years of her life to be able to do again.

"I expect it's part of the same deal," Heath said finally. "Stalker/heroin guy is trying to make you feel responsible for the damage he's doing. It ties in with the kill yourself, kill yourself messages. He hurts me, you blame yourself, you get depressed, etcetera and so forth."

"In a way it is my fault," E said.

"If you go there, you're basically stalking yourself. We'll have to check with Anna on the legality of that," Heath said.

For a while Elizabeth said nothing. Heath couldn't tell if she was processing or sinking into the depression that had followed her around like a black dog waiting to be fed since the bullying began.

To Heath's immense relief, the girl screwed her face up, closed one eye, and looked at the ceiling with the other.

"Well, when you put it *that* way . . ." she said. Then they were both allowed to laugh. Laughter, even when forced, is a good thing.

"Aunt Gwen thinks this place might be haunted," Elizabeth said, clearly needing a change of subject. Heath wasn't sure ghosts were the best direction the conversation could take.

"She said it *ought* to be haunted," Heath corrected.

"It is," Elizabeth said sincerely. "I saw a light sort of flickering around in one of the dead wings."

E meant one of the two crumbling arms that swept back toward the northeastern crag.

"Are you making this up to scare me?" Heath asked.

"Nope."

"Broken glass, trick of the light, squatters, enterprising tourists, could be anything," Heath said.

"Or it could be a ghost," Elizabeth said.

"I think a few ghosts would be groovy," Heath said. "Maybe we could catch one."

E gave her an annoyed look. Elizabeth believed in ghosts. Sometimes Heath believed in ghosts. She'd read somewhere that forty-five percent of Americans believed in ghosts, spirits of the dead walking the earth. Ninety percent said they believed in God, which was more or less the same thing, but on an impersonal, galactic scale. Dead saints answering prayers, angels averting car accidents, the Virgin Mother healing a child: all were just ghosts costumed in robes and feathers. The cult E had been raised in was a bizarre mixture of rogue Mormonism, Christianity, spiritualism, and carnival act. The compound was funded by the myriad wives working what used to be called welfare scams: money for unwed mothers, orphans, food stamps, single-parent households; Medicaid, Medicare, any social service that could be conned, was.

The children were taught to hate the United States government, love their spiritual leader in the person of the prophet Father Dwayne Sheppard, and believe every single thing he told them. He told them if they left the compound, ghosts of late Latter-day Saints would get them. If they didn't say their prayers, Satan would reach right up through the floorboards and snatch them into a fiery pit. He told them God wanted them to serve Him by serving him—Dwayne Sheppard. He told them that the Mormon Church had the power to bring the dead into the Mormon faith, and that all their ancestors back to Adam and Eve stood by their beds at night watching them from the beyond.

Elizabeth had shaken a lot of that spiritual olio from her proverbial sandals, but, like most Americans, she'd never quite given up the feeling that Something Was Out There.

"Should we buy it some chains to clank, or have they evolved, like vampires, into cute boys with dietary issues?" Heath asked.

"Don't, Mom. Ghosts hate to be laughed at," Elizabeth said, superstitious fear lowering her voice so phantom ears wouldn't overhear.

At that, the lights went out.

No flickering, no browning down: a sudden plunge into darkness.

"Holy shit!" Heath squawked.

Elizabeth squeaked, then laughed nervously. Power on Boar Island was capricious.

"Gosh, I hate that!" Elizabeth whispered, as if an entity in the dark might be listening.

"It takes some getting used to," Heath admitted. Ghost stories around the campfire always put the fear of God into her. She could remember when she was a Girl Scout kneeling beside her sleeping bag in a tent praying as hard as she could to keep the guy with a hook for a hand, who escaped from the insane asylum, from getting her. Forcing herself to speak in a normal tone, she said, "Time for bed anyway."

"Right," E said. "You talk about ghosts, then, bang! The lights go out for no reason, in the middle of the night, in a haunted house, on a deserted island, and you think I'm going to go to my little bed? I at least get Wily."

"I get Wily," Heath insisted.

"You can't get downstairs without a light," Elizabeth retorted. "I won't help. Don't help her, Wily," she called down into the inky darkness.

Wily whined.

Down was harder than up. Moving up, Heath used her arms and towed her legs along. Since she really couldn't push noodles, the only way to go down was on her belly like a reptile, the legs bumping along behind in more or less a controlled fall. In the dark it could be dangerous.

"Loan me a blanket and pillow," Heath said. "I'll bunk up here until the lights come back on."

"You can have my bed," Elizabeth said with a sigh. "I'll sleep on the cold hard floor with the rats."

Heath laughed. "Such a gracious invitation is hard to resist. I don't mind the floor. I'm used to hard beds. Better for my back."

A sniff in the darkness, then, "Yeah, right, and Aunt Gwen comes home from her big date and sees me all snuggled in a nice comfy bed and my poor old crippled mother in a heap of rags on the floor. Like I'd ever hear the end of that!"

Heath smiled as she listened to Elizabeth creep across the room toward her bed. Eyes recovered from the sudden onslaught of night, she could see stars through the two windows and yellow gleams from houses on shore. They had power. They always had power. Boar seemed to suffer from an intermittent short somewhere in the system between it and Mount Desert, the main island. A match was struck, the sharp smell of sulfur, then the steady warm glow of the kerosene lamp.

"I like the lamplight," Elizabeth said. Heath heard wistfulness in her daughter's voice. Had they had kerosene lamps at the compound where she'd spent her childhood? Did she ever feel homesick? Heath knew the compound had electricity. That Dwayne might have kept the electricity for the "elders" and the computer cons, and made the women and children use oil lamps, wasn't beyond the pale.

From downstairs came the sound of the door to the front room opening. Then a faint susurration, like the shush of waves against the cliffs, maybe footsteps. Elizabeth heard it as well. Before she could say anything, Heath put a finger to her lips. Boar was a private island. Still and all, Heath had been a fool not to check the doors. She didn't even know if they had locks on them.

"Blow out the lamp," she hissed.

Eyes, wide and frightened, shone above the glass chimney, and then Elizabeth and the world disappeared in a puff of breath.

Heath listened with all the intensity a dark house and surreptitious sounds can put into human ears. The lighthouse was thick-walled and nearly as solid as the granite upon which it was built. The windows, a modern addition, rattled gently in the onshore breeze. Through the open casement came the sound of the sea. Elizabeth's bare feet whispered over planks worn smooth by more than a century of use.

Kneeling beside Heath, she called down, "Aunt Gwen? Is that you?"

"The lift bell didn't ring," Heath breathed.

Nothing but darkness rose from the tower rooms below.

"Anybody there?" Heath called, since the sanctity of the silence had been broken.

A creak? A tiny scrape of leather on wood? The hushed thump of a door closing? Nothing?

"A trick of the wind," Heath said firmly. "Light the lamp before we scare ourselves silly."

Before Elizabeth could find the matches, the radio blared, lights snapped on, and both women screamed.

E had been right.

Ghosts didn't like being laughed at.

THIRTEEN

Statistically speaking, getting away with murder wasn't all that hard to do. The key was to murder someone who had no connection with your life. A stranger. The thing was, nobody but a psychopath would do that. Denise found it ironic that you could only kill with impunity people whom you had no reason to kill. Cops—even rangers—tended to be rational individuals. They liked there to be a reason for a crime. If they scented a reason, a motive, they sniffed and dug and pestered until they had enough for an arrest.

The drive-by shooters, freeway snipers, the people who put poison in Advil bottles at the drugstore—those with universal malice were almost impossible to catch. Even serial killers who kept on keeping on with their personal death marches were hard to get. Lots of evidence, lots of proof of crime, but no rhyme or reason behind it. At least not that a sane person could understand. When they did get caught it was because they wanted to. A younger, nicer, Denise had thought they wanted to get caught because they wanted to be stopped, felt a need to be punished. Now she guessed it was because they wanted credit for their work.

Because she was in law enforcement, and because America was a nation in love with serial killers, Denise had read interviews with those who had finally been captured and prosecuted. Never, not once, did one of them give a satisfactory answer to why they did what they did. Son of Sam's "The dog made me do it" was one of the clearer explanations.

That was why Patricia Highsmith's *Strangers on a Train* was such a brilliant concept. Had both men been true killers, they never would have gotten caught.

Was she a true killer? Denise had never thought about it. She'd thought about killing: thought about killing Peter, Lily, and for a brief—very brief—time, she'd even thought about killing Olivia, to hurt them as she had been hurt, to take from Peter what he had taken from her.

Thinking about killing was not the same as being a killer. Thinking was not doing. The Catholics were wrong; sinning in the heart didn't count.

As she sat in the hot airless dark of the nursery in the old shed, she went again through the plan she and her sister had come up with. Paulette would go to the old Acadian bar and stay there drinking from before Kurt's boat came in until after his body was discovered. Tuesday night was bowling night for him and his buddies, bowling and getting sloppy drunk on beer. Either Kurt would get a ride to the bowling alley with a guy named Lou, who lived a couple of houses away in the tiny town, or Kurt would pick Lou up. The pattern seldom varied.

That meant Kurt would come off the lobster boat about seven in the evening. He and his pals would hoist a few and eat burgers at a joint near the docks. Then home by nine thirty to shower, put on clean clothes, and be ready to fetch or be fetched by ten o'clock. Either way there was a half-hour window when he'd be home by himself.

Then the body would be discovered.

Lou would come to pick him up and find it, or Lou would come over to find out why Kurt hadn't picked him up and find it.

Paulette would stay in the Acadian, making sure the bartender noticed her, until eleven forty-five to be on the safe side. Then she'd come home and be surprised to find police cars all over the place. Not ranger cars—or maybe just a polite presence of green and gray in the background. The national park's law enforcement didn't have jurisdiction in Otter Creek. Who did have jurisdiction was complicated. On paper, the state of Maine and the national park (aka federal government) had concurrent jurisdiction. With Bar Harbor and other small-town police and fire departments figured in, it wasn't as straightforward as it might seem. That, too, would help. For a while state and local law enforcement might not be sure who had to do what.

It also helped that the chief ranger was out of the park. Artie was a joke. Gris was the real thing. Before he'd joined the Park Service he'd been a detective in D.C. Little Miss Bird Breath from out west would be gone in three weeks. She'd probably be only too happy to let the state do its job.

Nearly five hours in the bar at the Acadian for Paulette to establish an unbreakable alibi so she would be free and could inherit Kurt's property, thirty minutes for Denise to murder her brother-in-law.

Having greater expertise in the area of violent crime, Denise had worked out the details. After choosing the day and time, she and Paulette hadn't talked about it. Maybe identical twins didn't need to verbalize as much as other people. Certainly Denise's thoughts and her sister's seemed to run down identical channels. The killing was necessary, Denise assured herself for the umpteenth time. One, Kurt would eventually beat Paulette to death, and two, he would track her down if he wasn't dead, pursue them into their new lives for the sole purpose of ruining everything for his wife.

After the dust from the killing settled and Paulette inherited, she'd sell the property; then she and Denise would leave. Law enforcement rangers could retire after twenty years of service, just like real cops. Denise could have retired six months ago. She only stayed on because she didn't want to move her hatred from Peter's field of vision. Being a thorn in his side, a shadow on his wall, a fly in his ointment, was better than having nothing. Hurting someone was something. You were there. Alive. Noticed. If she'd retired and quietly disappeared into the woodwork, what would have been left for her?

Now that was all changed. There was Paulette. There was Kurt's land to sell and, maybe, the "family legacy," if they were the twins referred to in the ads Paulette had saved. They would finish with the park. They would have the money from the land and Denise's pension.

Money was important. Denise had never been rich, but she had been dirt poor, and intended never to be that helpless and hopeless again. Besides, they would need new things; the family would need things. They would move somewhere nobody knew them and they would be able to be out in the open, two sisters, a family.

Unused to hope, Denise felt nervous entertaining the feathered thing. The picture was so pretty she wanted to stay in it, yet was afraid that would jinx it. The gods liked to snatch away hope. Accepting the risk, she allowed the movie to continue playing in her mind. They would both cut their hair short and style it the same way. Paulette could dye hers back to their natural brown—or Denise could go blond. Hard to picture that. Better brunette and short. Paulette's hair was in bad shape from all the bleach jobs. A cut would be good for it.

They wouldn't dress alike, not in public—too corny. In private they might. Denise would order her sister a pair of pajamas identical to the ones she always wore. No. She would order new pajamas for the both of them. A new start. Together. They'd settle in a small town, maybe in the hills of North Carolina or Georgia. Someplace warm; they had already suffered enough winters in their lives. Eighty-two years of winters between them; nearly a century of cold. A house in an old neighborhood full of mature trees; a neighborhood where no one would know who they had been. What they had done. A small house, maybe three bedrooms, one for each of them and one for . . .

Hoping.

Damn.

Denise knew better.

The dream winked out with the suddenness of a match dunked in water.

Pushing the tiny button on the side of her watch, she read the time by the faint green glow. Nine fifteen. Paulette would be nursing a beer at the Acadian by now. In half an hour she'd be sipping the next and Denise would be murdering Kurt.

Would she respect herself in the morning? Yes, Denise decided, she would. Being a victim shamed her. Taking charge, killing the man who beat her sister, so that she and Paulette might have a new life together almost made her proud. It did make her proud. It made her a hero.

She rose from the rocking chair, then crossed the hand-hooked throw rug to open the shed door. With ancient trees blocking a quarter moon and stars, the dark of the woods was as complete as the darkness inside the windowless room. In black jeans, black running shoes, and a black T-shirt, Denise scarcely disturbed the void. Wearing all black was kind of theatrical but practical, and these days everybody wore black a lot. If someone were to see her, it wouldn't be remarkable. Should Kurt see her, it wouldn't ring any alarm bells in her brother-in-law's booze-raddled head.

Stretching, readying herself to be quick and calm and deadly, she listened to the sounds of the island. Mosquitoes whined; car engines hummed faintly on the road; there was a distant whispering that sounded like the ocean but probably wasn't. A faint breeze in the treetops was more likely. With the quiet and the open door, she would be able to hear Kurt's car pull onto the gravel in front of the house. She and Paulette had tried it. It wasn't loud, but it was enough.

As soon as she heard the car on the gravel, she would walk softly toward the house, using Kurt's car and entry noises to cover what sounds she might make. The back porch light was already on. As long as she walked directly toward it there would be no obstacles. When she reached the back porch, she would stand with her back to the wall between the door into the kitchen and the window where the bathroom was. Though she would be in the light, the rear porch could not be seen by neighbors or from the road. After Kurt stepped into the shower, she would let herself in through the kitchen—the door was unlocked—slip through the bedroom, open the bathroom door, and shoot him. A shower scene, like in *Psycho*. Life mirrors art.

She would leave the same way she'd come, returning to the nursery. There she would collect the flashlight. Using it, she would walk cross-country the quarter mile to Otter Cove. Her blue runabout was moored in the reeds, invisible in the dark. In the runabout, she would row out about a hundred yards, start the engine, drop the pistol over the side, and be back at the dock in Somes Sound before eleven. No one would be there at that hour, and if they were, she was known for going out alone at night in her boat. They wouldn't give it a second thought.

From there she would drive home. For good measure she would burn her gloves and clothes in her tiny fireplace. No muss, no fuss, no motive, and the prime suspect in full view at the Acadian Lounge. A job well done, Denise would pour herself a double vodka, no ice, and order two pairs of pajamas from Victoria's Secret online. Not sleazy sexy ones; flannel would be better, cute and comfy.

An engine purred in the dark, got louder; tires crunched on the gravel.

Killing time, Denise thought.

FOURTEEN

Before she got under her own covers, Elizabeth helped Heath down the stairs to her bed. They had a system. Elizabeth sat with her back to Heath and one step below. She then folded Heath's legs—which weighed less than one would think—across her lap. This way they could descend step by step on a three count. "One, two, three, push up with the arms and the butts bump down."

Goofy as it was, Heath knew Elizabeth enjoyed working out new strange ways of locomotion with her. She would, of course, die of shame if anybody but Anna or Aunt Gwen saw them doing it. As long as there were no witnesses, E had fun. So did Heath. It was like being little kids, crawling around and wriggling. Better than being a kid, because what Elizabeth did really mattered; it mattered because compassion mattered. Compassion and courage.

As far as Heath was concerned, cowards were more dangerous than evil people. An evil person did an evil thing to get his evil way. It was focused, rational. If you didn't have what the bad guy wanted, you were safe.

Cowards were like broken safety rails or frayed climbing ropes. You counted on them, and one day, they gave way and down you went.

When she was a child of nine, Elizabeth had been slated to be married off to Father Dwayne Sheppard because E's mother was a coward. What happened to the biological father was a bit vague. Heath guessed the responsibility of a family scared him. He took off when E was an infant. At any rate, Elizabeth had no memory of him. Rather than to make it on her own, E's mom became Sheppard's fifth wife.

Though she'd been nine when she'd last seen her mother, E said she didn't remember her clearly. Heath did. Hard to forget a woman who had abandoned her child twice, once to Sheppard's demands and, finally, to Heath.

Even the all-powerful Prophet Sheppard had a yellow streak down his back. Why else work so hard to dominate weak people and children?

Cowards were dangerous.

Elizabeth was one of the bravest people Heath had ever known. Until this. This onslaught of threats and secrets and lies, and something E wasn't telling her or Gwen or Anna, was disabling her.

Heath knew herself to be a coward. Being disabled scared her. Being a mom terrified her. That she couldn't keep E safe made her blood run cold. As far as she was concerned her only saving grace was that she'd learned to hide what a big fat scaredy-cat she was. According to Aunt Gwen, that was courage, to be afraid and not let it stop you from doing what was right.

After what had happened to Elizabeth and the other girls when she was nine—what they had done, what had been done to them—it didn't surprise Heath that E's courage had holes in it. Being frightened was like getting a soft-tissue injury. Once, and you recovered. If injured again in the same place, it could cripple you. This web of mystery and unknown horrors was the third strike at the core of who Elizabeth was, how she fundamentally viewed herself.

The razor and the bath had been a call for help. It had also been an indicator of how deeply E had suffered—was suffering.

Elizabeth never spoke of the bad old days, not unless she talked about it with her therapist. As far as Heath knew, she'd never spoken to the other two victims about their experience, never contacted anyone from the old compound, never reached out to her mother, never even asked what became of them when the compound was shut down and the families scattered.

Once she'd admitted that sometimes she missed the compound. There were always lots of kids around. They played simple games like tag and Mother-may-I. All the girls played with dolls, handmade of rags and buttons. A lot of the dolls were pretty. The sister-wives took pride in their sewing. As an adult Heath understood that the simplicity and safety Father Sheppard promised were false, but to a little girl, they would have felt real.

For a little kid, it would all have been real: Sheppard's brand of religion, angels, plural wives, demons, pedophilia, ghosts.

For a long time after she'd moved in with Heath, E was afraid to sleep alone in her room at night for fear demons would get inside of her. Mormons—real Mormons—weren't big on ghosts or demons. Mormons were a practical people. Heath and Aunt Gwen explained over and over that Sheppard invented the evil spirits to use as another tool of control. Mostly she believed them.

Most wasn't all.

Then there were those damn ethereal footsteps. Given the situation, even Heath's skin had gone prickly and cold. Heath guessed that E, who still slept with every part of her under the covers because exposed bits were irresistible to monsters living beneath beds, had been more freaked out than she'd let on.

Elizabeth was hiding her emotions. Heath suspected it was a result of too much unconditional love. Gwen and Heath loved E way too much. Even Anna showed glimmers of it. None of them could hide the fact that they were bleeding to death behind their eyes, could diguise the great howling need to do something. If Elizabeth had said, "Hey, if you guys chop your hands off, I'll feel better," Heath would be rolling up her sleeves while Gwen ran for the surgical saw.

That kind of love had to be a burden. Like having a Dodge Ram parked on one's shoulders. Dealing with that, and the fact that she was being called a whore—with the pictures to prove it—to everybody she knew, and about a zillion people she didn't, that her social life was deader than roadkill, that there was no way she could go back to school in the fall without wearing a paper bag over her head so nobody would recognize her, and that some creep might actually be slithering out of his hole to lay his creepy hands on her to . . .

Take her, Heath thought suddenly. For a minute she thought she would vomit. Grabbing the bar over her bed, she dragged herself into a sitting position.

Take her.

The psycho who had taken her and the other little girls so long ago was dead, Heath reassured herself. Not imprisoned, not appealing his death sentence, not getting out for good behavior: dead. Good and dead.

Copycat.

She was definitely going to vomit.

Was E's stalker planning to re-create the Rocky Mountain horror?

Heath knew lightning did strike twice in the same place.

"Don't go there," Heath said out loud, but not so loudly E might hear and come down. "Not at night when there are ghosts whisking around." "There" was a place to be avoided. "There" was supposed to be where the bad things were. Tonight, "there" was here.

"Wily," she whispered. He was already awake and watching her, his eyebrows cocked. "Come up on the bed."

FIFTEEN

Using the noise of Kurt's tires crunching on gravel for cover, Denise moved through the dark as fast as she dared, heading toward the porch light. She cursed herself for not having gotten closer earlier. There were plenty of woods, plenty of darkness. It would have been safe enough to have halved the distance. More than that; she should have lain under the back porch or squatted behind the trash cans at the side of the house.

Paulette had timed the walk during the day, over country that was as familiar to her as the floor plan of her house. Denise should have timed it for herself, in the dark, with her lack of familiarity. There had been time to pace it off half a dozen times. Instead, she'd sat in the hot darkness of the nursery and toyed with the wicked imp called Hope.

The crunching stopped before she'd traveled thirty feet. Kurt's truck door screeched open, then slammed shut. One hand on a tree, a foot not yet fallen, Denise froze. The truck engine ticked as it cooled. A night bird

called. She had no idea which one. She was law enforcement, not interpretation. An image of the Indians
in old Westerns imitating birds to signal an attack
struck her as horrifically funny. Hysterical. She held the
laughter in with an effort, her chest twitching and her
throat clenching.

No more sounds from the soon-to-be dead man. Was
Kurt lighting a cigarette or checking his cell phone?
Did he stand by the truck listening, sensing danger?
Had Paulette accidentally tipped him off, and he was
waiting for Denise with a knife or a pistol? Laughter
dried up in her lungs, tickling like ashes when she
breathed too deeply.

Denise really had to pee.

Crunch, crunch, crunch: gravel tread under heavy
boots. He was coming for her. Fear paralyzed her mind,
and Denise could not run. She could not even lower her
raised foot, or draw in breath. Clomp, clomp, clomp:
ascending the three wooden steps to the front door.

All was well.

Home, to the shower, to his death, just like it was
supposed to be. As Kurt banged the screen and front
doors, Denise sucked in a lungful of air, then ran lightly
toward the lamp on the porch, her light in the darkness,
her star of Bethlehem. The flame the moth incinerated
itself in.

Panting as if she'd sprinted a hundred yards rather
than crept thirty, she stopped short of the circle of light
leaching into the dirt-bare yard.

Kurt was inside the house.

Maybe Kurt was inside. Denise had heard the front

door slam. Was it possible he'd quietly opened it again, gone back to the truck for something? No, he wasn't the quiet type; she would have heard him. Maybe he'd only pretended to go inside. Maybe he'd heard her and slammed the doors to make her think he was inside when, all the while, he was sneaking around the side of the shack with an axe raised over his head.

Don't even think that, Denise commanded herself silently. They'd been careful. He suspected nothing.

He was in the house. That was the end of it.

The end of Kurt the baby killer.

Denise breathed in slowly to settle her nerves. Everything was as it was supposed to be. No muss, no fuss, like clockwork. That was the plan. So the trek from nursery to house had cost Denise a few minutes they hadn't counted on. There were plenty of minutes left to blow Kurt Duffy into the next world. Bullets were fast, just short of Superman-fast. Three seconds. Bang. Bang. Bang. Kurt is dead. Denise is headed for Otter Cove. Paulette is making eyes at the bartender miles away. Everyone lives happily ever after.

Stiffly, she started across the dusty yard. The scratch of her sneakered feet on the sand was as the grinding of boulders in the surf, an internal cacophony more sensation than sound. Step and step and step and no matter how many steps she took, the light didn't get any closer, the kitchen door looked tiny, wrong-end-of-a-telescope tiny, Alice in Wonderland tiny. Denise noticed her hands had balled into fists. Her vision was blurring, and sweat ran from her forehead in rivulets.

Suck it up, she ordered herself. It wasn't like Duffy

didn't need killing. It wasn't like anybody would miss him. Killing him would be no worse than dropping a rock on a black widow or stomping a brown recluse. A spider, that's all Duffy was, spinning a web that caught her sister and held her paralyzed while it fed off her soul. It needed to be removed from the world. It needed to be crushed.

The porch, a couple of rickety steps up from the bare dirt of the backyard, cracked into her shins. Shocked, she blinked twice, confused by how she had closed the distance from not possible to bruising her legs. It was as if she'd gone to sleep for a while, her brain in Zombie Land while her body traversed the ground. How long had it taken her? How much racket had she made? Was Kurt in the shower yet? Paulette hadn't timed his showers. She'd just said he'd come home around nine, take a shower, and go out around ten.

Had he showered already and left to go bowling?

Denise dropped to her knees, hiding in the shadow of the raised porch. She rubbed her palms against the dirt, drying the sweat and working feeling back into her fingers. Forcing her lungs to obey, she began breathing slowly in and out through her nose. Sweat wiped from her brow with dirt-smeared hands, she put her brain back in its skull case and sat back on her heels. Nerve returned—or at least motivation. She pushed the tiny button on her watch.

Nine eleven. A good number for terrorists. A bad number for innocents. Was she both? Neither? It didn't matter. Nothing mattered but that she focused, stay on point. Back in the days when the government dared to let its officers shoot for scores, she'd been one of the best. Now there were no scores. Too many juries would want to know why an officer with a perfect score on the range didn't just shoot the gun out of the bad guy's hand since she was such an Annie Oakley.

With an act of will, Denise got to her feet. She unzipped the black nylon pack on her belt where she carried car keys and water when she went running. With two fingers she lifted out her .22 caliber Smith and Wesson revolver. The gun was untraceable. It had belonged to a foster mother's boyfriend. Denise had stolen it when she was thirteen. Ever since she'd had a nightstand that wouldn't be searched by some interfering do-gooder or rotten foster "family" member, she'd kept it in her bedside drawer.

As she eased the .22 from the rip-stop nylon, her wrist jerked as if hit by an electrical shock. Her fingers flew open, and the gun thudded into to the weeds beside the steps. For a moment she stared at the offending hand.

Nerves.

After she'd killed Kurt, when she and her sister were free of the spider, her nerves would heal. When they were free of the park and the state of Maine and settled in their cottage far away somewhere warm, the spastic nervous movements would stop.

She picked up the revolver, then checked the barrel to make sure it hadn't become jammed with detritus. Having squeegeed muddy sweat from her forehead with the side of her palm, she dried her hand on her jeans. Mentally she began singing "Itsy Bitsy Spider."

On each syllable she took a small silent step. By the time the spider was up the waterspout, Denise was between the kitchen door and the bathroom window, her back pressed against the wood. Kurt was in the house, and was in the shower; she could see the water running through the clouded glass, and hear it through the thin walls of the shack.

Back on track. Back on point. Nerves back in alignment.

Once more she dried the palm of her gun hand on her trousers, then crept to the kitchen door and turned the knob. Bless Paulette! Not only was it unlocked, it was ajar. Not enough anyone could see, just enough the closing mechanism wouldn't catch. A gentle push and she was inside.

The kitchen was small, the linoleum old—real linoleum, not vinyl. Paulette had moved the scarred table—no bigger than most TV trays—and the two wooden ladder-backed chairs against the wall between stove and refrigerator.

Clearing the way for the exterminator coming to kill the spider.

Denise loved having a sister, a twin. Nobody, but nobody, had ever looked out for her the way Paulette did. Peter had pretended for a long time. Denise had been fooled for a long time. No more. Blood was the only thing you could count on. Family.

The door to the bedroom was open, the bedroom light off. Holding the gun at her side, Denise walked in. She didn't crouch, come in low or high, sweep the room, or step back against the wall. This wasn't like that. This was straightforward. A simple task: You walk in, you dispose of the spider, you walk out. She would touch nothing. When she'd been here before, she'd touched things. At the time she hadn't known fingerprints would matter.

Today Paulette had cleaned the house, scrubbed every surface, then touched them. No fingerprints was fishy. The wife's fingerprints were expected. Did twins have identical fingerprints? Denise would have to Google that.

The bathroom door stood half open. Light spilled onto the double bed, drawing up the one bit of color in the dim room, peach blossoms on a white background, branches cutting across in slashes of black. Denise moved to the foot of the bed, shoved the door to the bathroom open with the toe of her shoe, stepped over the sill, and, holding it with both hands, raised the .22.

The shower curtain wasn't the kind you could see through. Colorful fishes swam on a dark blue sea. The spider was big, though, and Denise could see his bulk where he elbowed and shouldered the curtain as he scrubbed himself.

Nerves were quiet. No ringing or crashing in her ears; she could hear the water striking the spider's skin. Her hands did not shake, and the sweat had dried on her face. Mind still and blank and clean, she aimed for center mass and squeezed off two neat rounds. The bullets cut so cleanly through the plastic they didn't even disturb the curtain.

The spider grunted.

Denise had expected a scream of pain, or death. She

hadn't ever been shot. Probably what you'd feel first was the bullets punching you, like fists or a ball bat. It might be a while before the pain set in.

There was a loud wet thud. The spider falling down or back against the wall. The curtain pushed out as if he grasped at it for support. Denise pulled the trigger again. A hole appeared in the middle of a bright yellow fish.

Silence, roaring after the gunshots, filled the small space.

It was done. Denise lowered the gun.

The curtain exploded out. Kurt Duffy crashed into her with the force of a freight train. Air was knocked from her lungs. Plastic covered her face. Her spine cracked against the footboard of the bed. Kurt's weight threatened to snap her in two. Plastic, and a naked wet man, trapped her legs. Her arms were forced up over her head, her face smashed against his chest.

The only thought she could muster was that she should have brought the .357, something with stopping power. In the movies a .22 was the gun of choice for executions. The long bullets could spin, maximize brain damage. This was supposed to be an execution. She'd overlooked the fact that the man she was going to shoot wouldn't be on his knees with his back to her, the muzzle of her pistol pressed up against his skull.

Air rushed back into her lungs. The Smith and Wesson was still in her hand. She couldn't fire down at such a sharp angle without danger of losing the gun. She brought the grip down hard, not knowing what part of him she hit, only that the shock felt good up her arm.

He was grunting and pushing into her like a hog in rut. Disgust lent her strength. Bringing her right knee up into his groin with all the force she could muster, she simultaneously chopped down hard on his head with both elbows.

A beefy thigh took the brunt of the knee, but the pain of the elbows distracted him. Like a snake from under a boot, she coiled from beneath him, slid the rest of the way off the bed to land on hands and knees. Water and blood slicked the floor.

Blood was good. It had to be his. The more the merrier.

He should be dead. "You should be dead," she hissed.

Rearing up from the mess of the curtain, naked, hair on his chest and back and arms, streaming water, blood seeping from his shoulder, chest, and side, he growled.

Like a bear or a mad dog.

Like a monster in a horror movie.

Like a hog bent on eating long pig for lunch.

Like a bull ready to gore, his head swaying from side to side, he pushed himself up until he was kneeling. More hair blackened his groin and legs, his penis a pale worm in the matted nest. He was huge. On his knees he reached nearly to Denise's shoulder. His arms and legs were corded and muscled from a lifetime of working against the sea.

Three holes decorated his body: shoulder, left side of his belly, and, the last, nearly invisible in the hair on the right side of his chest. All were seeping blood. Seeping, for Christ's sake! They should be gushing.

Great gouts of blood should be pouring out. Blood frothed on his lips. One had hit a lung. The big bastard could live to be ninety with those three bullets in him.

"Die, God damn you," Denise gasped. A paw the size of an oven mitt came up from the monster's side. "Die," she cried as she skittered sideways out of his reach. The corner of the bedpost banged her shoulder. The .22 flew from her hand and slid under the dressing table in front of which she and Paulette had so recently sat marveling at their twin features.

This was wrong; things weren't supposed to be this way. Spiders weren't supposed to be this hard to kill. "God damn it!" Denise threw herself flat and groped under the dresser after the pistol. Her fingers touched the barrel. A beefy paw curled around her ankle. A bellow of rage; spittle and blood spattered the floor. In the faint glow of the bathroom light the blood was startlingly beautiful, rubies cast upon the ground. Another bestial roar, and Denise was yanked backward like a rag doll in the hands of a psychotic toddler.

Hunching her shoulders and ducking her head, Denise rolled onto her side, stared into the bloodshot eyes of the spider, and kicked out with the force of thighs and butt. One foot connected with his hairy gut above the navel. She was rewarded with a woof! as the air was knocked out of him. Again she kicked, aiming higher, aiming for the bullet that had collapsed his right lung. Again she made a solid hit. He fell back on butt and heels, clutching at his chest as if he could force the lung to take in air. The next kick landed on the wound in his side. Screaming, he tried to sidle backward, escape her blows. The plastic shower curtain tangled between his feet and knees, and he fell back onto the plank flooring.

Quicker than she'd thought possible, Denise was on her feet. She caught up the bottom end of the plastic curtain and fell with it on top of the struggling man. He bucked, trying to throw her. Digging a thumb into the bullet hole in his shoulder, Denise rode him until pain and blood loss slowed his thrashing. Straddling him, knees on his upper arms, she shoved the plastic over his face, cramming what she could into his mouth as he screamed and fought for breath. Hands spread like starfish, pressing down on the plastic, Denise growled, "Die. Die, God damn you. Die. For God's sake, fucking die!"

Finally he grew still. Denise did not let up. Three minutes. She thought she remembered that from emergency medical training. Three minutes without air was enough. No. Couldn't be. She knew divers who could hold their breath three minutes.

Lights slashed across the room. Headlights from a car.

"Shit." Heart and lungs fought for ascendance, both in her throat.

A horn honked.

Denise rolled off Duffy, then stood, her legs shaking, knees wanting to fold. No time for feeling around. With one great heave she toppled the dressing table. Seven years of bad luck shattered around her feet. The Smith and Wesson was against the wall. She grabbed it up.

"Duff! Hey, Duff!" Pounding at the front door loud as a battering ram.

As the front door banged open, Denise was running through the kitchen.

She kept running into the black woods.

SIXTEEN

"This is Anna Pigeon, district ranger from Rocky. We go back a long time," Peter said, introducing Anna.

"Yes, I know. The acting chief." Denise's voice had the flat amiability of old enmity. Was it a not-so-subtle reminder that she and Peter shared old stories, old times, old friends? Anna wondered. Peter used to live with a woman named Denise. This had to be her.

"Denise Castle," the ranger introduced herself before Peter could.

Anna nodded. Gray-green circles, eerily matched to the Park Service uniform, puffed beneath Castle's eyes, and her skin had the desiccated look of someone who's just come off a three-day bender.

"There was a murder in Otter Creek last night," Peter went on. "The state has this one—not on federal land—but we should go to show the colors, see if we can lend a hand. Anna will go with you. Anna is an aficionado of bullet-riddled bodies."

Anna was not amused. The people she'd killed west of the Fox River had needed killing.

"Not exactly," she replied dryly. "Although they do seem rather fond of me."

"She's only acting chief," Denise said, ignoring the exchange. "I doubt she wants to look at a corpse."

"Beats paperwork," Anna said.

To Peter, Denise said, "I don't need help on this."

"Anna's your boss," Peter reminded her coolly. "Anna?"

Despite herself, Anna was interested. When someone else saw to the dirty work, a murder could be quite entertaining. Rather like turning over stones or poking around tide pools, digging around a murder turned up all sorts of interesting flora and fauna.

"Who knows," Anna said to Denise. "I've never been the chief ranger before. I might turn out to be helpful."

Denise's smile was on the watery side, as if she'd had to dredge it up from secret depths to meet the social norm. Then she said, "I'm retiring."

"Today?" Peter sounded confused.

The statement appeared to be as great a surprise to Denise as it was to Peter. She gasped a tiny gasp, then gusted it out on a laugh. "Soon," she said. The wavering smile firmed with what looked like smugness.

"Hop in," she said to Anna as she opened the door to her Crown Vic. "We might as well get this dog-and-pony show over with."

Anna slid into the passenger side of the patrol car, then buckled her seat belt. There was a reassuring sameness to Park Service vehicles, equipment, housing, even war stories. Six degrees of separation did not apply in the NPS. After a certain number of years, often there was scarcely one degree left. Everyone knew—or knew of—everyone, and had an opinion about them. Park people were like a hugely extended cantankerous family, complete with black sheep and heirs apparent. Some rangers felt claustrophobic in such an intrinsically small world. Anna felt at home.

Seldom did she get to ride shotgun. Rangers didn't work in pairs. She leaned back in the seat as Denise pulled out of the headquarters parking lot. It was a treat to relax and look at the scenery, enjoy the park tourist-style. A park existed for every mood, and Anna was a woman of many moods.

"What did Pete tell you about the murder?" Denise asked.

"Lobsterman shot sometime last night. Possibly a domestic. State and local police notified last night. The park, this morning. Concurrent jurisdiction. That's about it. No particulars."

"Ever heard of the lobster wars?" Denise asked.

"Sounds like a bad science fiction movie," Anna replied.

"It's serious business in these parts. Kind of like range wars in the Old West. Lobstermen are rough customers."

Anna had never known a lobsterman, but she'd worked with shrimpers out in the Dry Tortugas. Very rough customers.

"Do you think another lobsterman killed him? For lobster rustling?"

"Probably. Who cares? Otter Creek isn't on park land. The state guys, or the sheriff, whoever caught this one, probably cleared it last night. Duffy's—the lobsterman's name was Kurt Duffy—bowling pal found the body. May have been some bad blood there." Denise spoke in a bored monotone, her face a mask of indifference.

Anna watched her in the sideview mirror. Law enforcement rangers were never indifferent to murder. Parks were inconvenient places to deal drugs, host gang wars, or run prostitution rings. They were bucolic places filled with potato salad–eating people whose greatest crime was feeding the chipmunks. Most rangers never worked a single murder in an entire career. Wicked as it was—or sounded to outsiders—when a nice juicy murder did come along, the dilemma wasn't getting rangers to work the case but keeping them from trampling each other to get in on it.

"My guess is it's a lobster-war thing," Denise said as she conned the big Crown Vic along the narrow road. She was a skilled driver. She worked the mirrors with her eyes, and her hands loved the steering wheel. The only other person Anna had noticed driving with that kind of innate concentration was an ex-NASCAR racer who'd taught her defensive driving. Really good drivers tended to drive fast. Yet Denise was poking along ten miles under the speed limit. Apparently she was not only bored by the prospect of a murder investigation but didn't want to reach the scene any time in the foreseeable future.

"We had a guy shot for robbing his neighbor's

traps—Will Whitman," Denise went on with a bit more enthusiasm, warming to her subject. "Whitman's son was implicated along with his dad for poaching lobsters, but he's gone AWOL. It's probably what saved his life. These guys are the Hatfields and McCoys, Earps and Clantons—you name it, feuds go back four or five generations. There's a range war going on under the waters around here that makes Texas in the ranchers-and-farmers phase look tame."

"Did they catch the man who shot this Will Whitman?" Anna asked to be asking something.

"Sure. No problem. They threw him in jail, but he's out now. Shooting a man for robbing your traps in Maine is akin to the 'stand your ground' law in Florida."

"Whitman. Any relation to John Whitman?" John Whitman was the taxi man ferrying Heath and company around.

"John is—was—Will's father. When John retired, Will got his patch. Then there was the shooting. Since John's grandson ran off, the lobstermen have been haggling over who should get his territory."

"Any relation to Duffy?"

Denise started as if Anna had poked her with a pin, then settled. "Kurt Duffy? Probably. Everybody is somebody's cousin around here." On that she closed her mouth into a firm line that suggested the conversation was finished.

Anna let the subject drop. "Any news on the package sent to Heath Jarrod?" she asked.

"That's a strange story," Denise answered, seemingly more comfortable talking of drugs than of murder.

"We field-tested a couple of the foil packs. Black tar from Mexico, the cheapest, nastiest sort. The rest we sent to the lab. If they all contain heroin there should be about three grams total. Dime bags, cut with something. I doubt the whole amount is worth more than a few hundred dollars."

Anna didn't know a lot about heroin. In the parks, other than visitors taking a tab of acid, munching a mushroom for the visuals, or smoking a little dope, drugs were urban problems. "Doesn't the stuff come in bulk?" she asked. "Then the dealer makes it up into packages?"

"I'd think so," Denise said. "I suppose there's people for that if you're willing to pay. Here we are."

As soon as they crested the gentle rise in the road, it became obvious where in Otter Creek the murder had taken place. Four cars—two police and one sheriff's and Artie's Crown Vic—were parked around a shiny blue pickup in front of a small cottage, little more than a square of weathered wood bisected by a door with a tiny pointed roof over the porch to keep the snow off the step. Two windows flanked the front door, both blinded by pull-down shades brown and curling with age. Yellow police tape crisscrossed the door. The front was not graveled, per se. It was simply stony soil that had suffered the sudden stops of too many tires.

It didn't strike Anna as the sort of home one would build on real estate that had to be worth more money than she'd ever see. Old, then, a homesteader from way back.

"Lobster fisherman and his wife," Denise said, as if

reading Anna's mind. She parked the Crown Vic fifty yards from the house and made no move to get out. "Wouldn't you know it? Artie, on his day off. What a twerp."

Anna followed Denise's sour words to the district ranger, out of uniform but with a pistol in a holster at his belt.

"Not in the mood for a clusterfuck today," Denise said, switching off the ignition.

"Beats sitting in a hot car," Anna suggested.

"Not today it doesn't."

Anna didn't know what to say to that. Miss out on murder? Ridiculous. "Mind if I go?"

"Knock yourself out. Wait," Denise said suddenly. "I would like a look inside, at the murder scene."

That was more like the rangers Anna had known.

"Let's do it," Anna said.

A civilian around sixty, arms and hands scarred, face weather-beaten, sat smoking a cigarette on the downed tailgate of the pickup truck. A short distance away, not part of the group but near it, her back turned to the men, was a woman with too much bleached-blond hair. Oversized sunglasses hid her face. She was holding one elbow, her free hand keeping a long white cigarette close to her lips between drags.

Anna walked with Denise toward where the men were standing around the pickup's tailgate. Under concurrent, or shared, jurisdiction, if the incident was not actually on park land it was customary for the NPS to give way to the state. If it was on NPS soil, the state would usually take a secondary position. Since this wasn't exactly Acadia's jurisdiction—and Acadia wasn't even Anna's park—she didn't want to ruffle any feathers. "Just a tourist," she said as she glided up next to the district ranger.

"Anna Pigeon," Denise said.

"Right." Artie looked down at her from his considerable height. All Anna could see of his eyes was her own reflection in his mirrored sunglasses. The set of his mouth was not welcoming. Anna reminded herself to corner him about the heroin and Heath. Make sure he thought it stank to high heaven as he ought to.

"Hello, Ms. Pigeon," he said coolly. "This is Sheriff Cotter."

Anna gazed at Artie expectantly, a neutral smile on her lips, until he caved in and added, "Ranger Pigeon is acting chief while Gris is out west fighting fire."

Anna nodded to Sheriff Cotter, a red-faced man in a dun-colored uniform. His skin was the type that probably burned and peeled three months of the year. Blond stubble glittered on his jowls, and his eyebrows were nearly white.

"We got this one," he said.

"Peter told me," Anna replied. Cotter nodded. No territorial fights over this murder.

"And Deputy—"

"Dremmel, Jack Dremmel," the sheriff's exceedingly young companion answered, sticking out a bony hand for Anna to shake. Anna wondered if it was just her or if law enforcement personnel were getting younger. Jack appeared to be about fourteen. Acne still clustered on one side of his chin. She couldn't imagine him shaving.

"Bar Harbor police," Artie said.

Two middle-aged men in blue nodded at Anna. No names were exchanged. They were just being nosey.

"I'd like a look inside," Denise said. If the set of her jaw was any indication, the disinterest she'd shown in the car had transformed into a grim avidity.

"Crime techs are all done," Cotter said. "We're just waiting for the coroner to come claim the body. How about you?" he said to Anna. "You want to take a look around, too?"

"Might as well," Anna said.

Cotter removed the tape. He held the door open. Denise and Anna walked into one of the most depressing rooms she'd seen in a while, and it wasn't the one where the murder had taken place.

"The bedroom," the sheriff said, pointing to a door.

There was only one door off the cramped sitting room. The house was a shotgun: sitting room, then bedroom, then kitchen at the back, no halls. Anna crossed to the bedroom door but didn't go in. Denise pushed past her, eyes searching everything from walls to floors to under the bed and dresser.

"Guy was shot three times, then wound up in the shower curtain. Cause of death might be suffocation. The shower curtain was shoved halfway down his throat. The autopsy will let us know," Cotter told her.

"Find anything else?" Denise asked. "Murder weapon?"

"No such luck," Cotter said.

"Sounds like you got another victim in the wars," Denise said, then abruptly left the room. Anna heard the front door close seconds later.

She looked over the detritus of the bedroom: a dead man, naked, blood mixing with a thick pelt of hair on his chest, face in a rictus of death, overturned furniture, plastic curtain with bright fishes. Shards of mirror reflected shards of what had been, to all appearances, a miserable life ending in a miserable death.

Murder was so often pointless and pitiful. Anna lost her fascination with who murdered whom or why.

"I've seen enough," she said, and she had. All she wanted was to get back out into the sunlight with the living things of the park around her.

Cotter followed her out the front door. As he was replacing the crime scene tape, Artie asked, "Where did Denise go? She's the one on duty today."

Anna glanced around. Denise was already back in the Crown Vic, seated behind the wheel. Her enthusiasm had been short-lived. Obviously there were undercurrents Anna was not privy to: Peter, a surprise retirement, mood swings. She felt as if she'd walked in on the end of a family fight.

"In the car," Anna replied.

Artie's lips curled into a sneer, but he said nothing.

"I'm Lou," the guy on the tailgate volunteered. "I found the body. Me and Kurt were buddies."

Close up, Anna could tell she'd misguessed the man's age by at least fifteen years. Lou was closer to forty-five than sixty. His face reminded her of the men she'd met who worked shrimp boats all their lives, or rode with a motorcycle gang back before the gangs were comprised of lawyers and doctors on pastel Harleys. Hard lives made hard faces. Lou's was carved by exposure and, most likely, alcohol. Only his hair retained the softness of youth; brown and thick, it swept over his forehead, as jarring against his creased skin as the tresses of a bad wig.

Lou was obviously proud of having found the body. Lots of people were like that. Being part of a murder investigation was their fifteen minutes of fame. Though, given the speed the Internet churned out fame, the average dose was probably closer to sixty seconds.

Whether or not he was broken up over his pal's death, Anna couldn't tell. His face was not the kind to share warm fuzzy emotions with strangers.

"I'm sorry," Anna said. "That had to be a blow."

"Yeah," Lou said. He dropped his cigarette and shifted his butt closer to the edge of the tailgate so he could grind it out with the toe of his boot. The cigarette was only half smoked. Lou moved stiffly, his head ducked as if to hide his face. Manly grief?

"Sheriff here'll be looking for a big man, and strong," Lou said as he straightened up. "Kurt put up a hell of a fight. Tore the whole bedroom up. I'm surprised I didn't find two bodies. Kurt was tough, I'll say that for him. Tough as they come."

He lit another cigarette, sucked in a lungful of smoke, then spat between his knees, the smoke trickling out his nose. "Anyway," he said on the last wisps of smoke, "glad it was me as found him. Polly isn't much good at the hard stuff."

The woman with too much hair and the wraparound blue plastic sunglasses, standing with her back to the men, said over her shoulder, "Paulette. My name is Paulette." Peeking from beneath the dark glasses was a patch of makeup, slightly off color and applied too thickly. Bruises were a bitch to cover.

Lou's lips pursed in annoyance. Paulette turned her head away quickly as if her boldness in correcting him frightened her.

"Polly," Lou said, hitting the word hard, "was Kurt's wife."

The spouse, always the number one suspect. A battered spouse, better yet.

"Hi, Paulette," Anna said, moseying over. "I'm Anna Pigeon." She smiled. Sensing the woman would be less forthcoming at a show of force, Anna downplayed her authority. "Don't be fooled by the uniform. I'm just passing through. The park brought me to cover for the chief ranger for a few weeks." She stuck out her hand. Shaking hands wasn't her favorite thing, and the modern penchant for hugging made her blood run cold, but it was a nonthreatening way to take somebody's temperature.

Paulette's hand was cold and clammy, limp as a three-day-old fish.

Before Anna loosed her grip, the fish came alive and jerked away.

"I haven't had much sleep," Paulette apologized. She

took another drag on her cigarette. The hand holding the cigarette was shaking so badly she could hardly get the butt to her mouth. She didn't look Anna in the eye.

"I bet not," Anna said sympathetically.

"I was down at the Acadian Lodge from six until nearly midnight. I didn't know what had happened until I came home and the cops were here."

Getting her alibi out right up front; not a guilty reaction exactly. Battered spouse, she had to know the sheriff was thinking she was a suspect. Lou seemed fairly hostile toward his good buddy's wife. Regardless of his talk of searching for a big burly murderer, Anna wondered if he thought she'd killed Kurt.

The insistent *Polly* chimed in her head, and she doubted it. Lou would have more respect for a murderess.

Paulette dropped her cigarette on the dirt, then ground the filter into the gravel with the toe of her wedge sandal. Her legs were pretty. Shapely and slim. The mass of fried hair and bruised cheekbone had blinded Anna to the fact that Paulette was attractive and not much past forty. Fishing a pale blue crumpled pack of menthols from the pocket of her skirt, Paulette shook out another cigarette.

"Would you like one?" she asked politely.

"No thanks," Anna said. "I'm trying to cut down."

Paulette nodded, as if to say every smoker she knew was always trying to cut down.

"How are you holding up?" Anna asked. Just because her husband knocked her around—if it was the husband who blacked her eye—didn't mean the woman wouldn't be heartbroken at his demise. Women were funny like that.

Paulette Duffy shot her a sidelong glance from beneath the temple of the glasses. She seemed to think it was a trick question. Anna smiled back with bland concern.

"I'm okay," Paulette said. She lit the fresh cigarette and took in a deep lungful. "The house is going to be creepy for a while."

"Do you have anyone you can stay with? A brother? A sister?" Anna asked.

Paulette twitched as if Anna had poked her with a hot iron. The hand holding the cigarette flicked out. The newly lit cigarette went flying. Paulette dropped the lighter she held in her other hand. Moaning, she fell to her knees to gather her belongings up.

"I'm an only child," she said as she scrabbled in the dirt.

Anna hadn't meant to push any buttons. "I have a sister," she said as a peace offering.

"Would you mind asking Sheriff Cotter if I can have my house now?" Paulette begged without raising her eyes from the ground. Her fingers closed around the bright yellow Bic lighter, but she made no effort to rise.

With a creeping crunch, a white fender brushed Anna's thigh. Willing herself not to squeak and leap, she glanced back over the long gleaming hood. Denise. The car crept forward. If Denise hadn't braked when she did, Anna would have had to leap back to avoid being eviscerated by the sideview mirror.

The passenger-side window smoothed down with an

electric hum. "Get in," Denise said shortly. "We're done here."

Paulette crawled—actually crawled on hands and knees, the tops of her canvas sandals and the front of her skirt gathering dirt as she went—several feet before rising. Without a backward look at Anna, she scurried toward the knot of men, brushing at her skirts as she walked. The lighter and the unsmoked cigarette were still on the ground.

Anna leaned down to retrieve the lighter and return it to her.

"Leave it," Denise snapped.

Straightening, Anna gave her a level stare. She considered reminding her who was the acting chief, and who was the badly behaved subordinate.

"Sorry," Denise said with a crooked smile. "Got a call. Gets my nerves crackling."

Anna decided to let whatever Denise was playing at play out. She climbed into the Crown Vic. "What's up?" she asked, and began buckling belt and harness.

"What do you mean?" Denise asked.

"The call," Anna said. "What is it?"

Denise laughed nervously. "If these guys don't need us anymore, maybe we could get a bite of lunch."

Anna gazed at her. Denise wasn't being a smartass. From what Anna could read on her face she had forgotten—more than forgotten—she'd said she had a call. Her eyes were a total blank, as if the moments before had been taken from her brain and destroyed.

Everyone reacted to violent death differently. Most people were inured to it by years of seeing it on television, on the news, in the movies. If it didn't happen to a personal friend, most people just clucked, "Oh my, how awful," and went about their business. Except in politics and football, people cared very little about anything that didn't apply to them directly.

But for the crime scene, Denise had evinced little interest in the incident. Anna realized she had been braced for the usual discussion. How much blood? How many bullet holes? Denise didn't start the conversation.

Anna sighed. She had lost interest as well. The instinct for the hunt had vanished with the sight of the pathetic dead man in his pathetic bedroom. Maybe she was mellowing with age. Maybe she was just getting old.

"Lunch is good," she said.

SEVENTEEN

Heath wasn't sure whether she was making any headway or not. There was no end to sites, articles, and blogs about cyberstalking on the Internet. As often happened, there was not a lot of content in any of them. Most simply described the phenomenon: stalking via electronic media, the cell phone the most common method. As in the schoolyard, the incidents could be anything from a snide remark to a death threat. Sex and shame were favored tools, and, though she'd thought it unique to Elizabeth, children telling other children to kill themselves wasn't all that rare. School and government sites had tabs marked "Prevent Cyberbullying," but they were little more than advice columns on how to police your own children and teach them what to post and what not to.

Several sites were informative as to how to report the incidents and get them removed from personal media. She learned there were things called "bashboards," sites where visitors could vote on who was the fattest or ugliest or meanest kid in class. There was one for Elizabeth. Someone else had already reported it. It still existed, but Heath couldn't open it.

On the subject of how to track down a cyberbully—or stalker, as she thought of the individual tormenting E—was vague and spotty. There was no clear path through the ether if the sender was even halfway clever.

A scream snatched Heath out of cyberspace.

Shoving the laptop off her legs, she yelled, "Elizabeth, are you all right?" Then, "Aunt Gwen!" Moving as quickly as long practice allowed, she levered herself off her bed, where she'd been sitting working, and into Robo-butt parked next to it. "Gwen!" she yelled again as she rolled across the old painted concrete floor of the lighthouse and toward the archway leading to the newer part of the house.

In reality the archway was a tunnel cutting through walls thirteen feet thick. Ms. Zuckerberg had painted the sides and curved ceiling with Peach Dawn at floor level and Midnight Blue with stars overhead. Heath shot through it like a mechanized comet.

"Elizabeth!" she shouted.

Wily began barking frantically.

"I'm coming," she heard her aunt call from the top of the lighthouse.

A wide living room formed an arc around the base of the lighthouse. Curved windows gave views east and west. Large overstuffed chairs and sofas, backed by heavy dark wood tables, lent the peaceful air of an old library or a high-end lodge from the turn of the century.

Heath rolled through the charming room, seeing nothing except that her daughter was not in it.

The barking escalated.

Another scream cut across Wily's shrill cries.

"I'm coming!" Aunt Gwen again. Heath could hear her footsteps rattling down the circular stairs.

The nightmare sensation of moving in slow motion through an atmosphere as thick and unyielding as bread pudding caught Heath. She felt as if her hands could not spin the wheels of the chair, as if she couldn't see properly, her vision dusky at the edges. Had she not been able to hear rubber squeaking loudly on the tile floor as she took the corner from the living room into the kitchen, she would have thought herself trapped like a fly in invisible amber.

Ms. Zuckerberg's kitchen was spacious and modern, with antique touches tying it to the island's past. The floors were of wide planks, aged and scarred, either salvaged from old ships or made to look old by an artisan. A kitchen island stood in the middle of the space. The sides were of dull beaten tin, the top of dark marble. Beyond was the sink, and more counter space beneath cupboards built of dark wood with perforated tin where glass might have been in another home.

Elizabeth was on her hands and knees atop the utility island. Wily was on the floor, hind end up in the air, forelegs on the planks, barking like crazy at something Heath could not see between the island and the sink.

Heath jerked her wheels to a stop, and her chair slid another couple of feet. The floor was covered in water.

"What in the hell is going on?" she roared, panic making her voice big and angry.

Elizabeth snatched her eyes from whatever Wily had cornered and, to Heath's relief and fury, began to laugh. She was laughing so hard she was holding her sides and gasping, feet dangling over the edge, rear end on the cutting board, when Gwen came running into the room. Before Heath could shout a warning, Gwen hit the water-slick and careened across the floor in a comic-book slide, arms windmilling, to fetch up against the island.

This sent E into another round of hysterical giggles.

"She could have fallen and broken a hip!" Heath shouted at her daughter. "We both could have been killed."

For reasons that Heath had no interest in, this struck not only E as funny, but Gwen as well.

"Damn it, Wily, shut up!" Heath roared. To her surprise he did. He grinned at her foolishly, then trotted over to her chair. Grabbing his collar, though he was the only one who appeared to be paying any attention to her, she waited with grim patience until Elizabeth and Gwen saw fit to stop snickering.

"Are you done?" she asked acidly when they'd quieted. Careful not to look at one another lest they burst out all over again, they both nodded.

"What the hell is going on?" Heath demanded.

"Elizabeth was playing with her food," Gwen said. That set them off again. Heath sat and fumed. She'd have lit a cigarette if she'd been anywhere but inside a house. There was nothing she could do when Gwen was encouraging E. Aunt Gwen was in her seventies, but when the two of them got going Heath could easily see what her aunt had been like when she was thirteen. Finally they wound down to intermittent giggles.

Wily whined.

A skritching of hard, sharp objects clawing at the floor emanated from behind the island, where now both E and her great-aunt sat swinging their legs, heels banging lightly against the tin sides. Gwen was in lime green capri pants and aqua tennis shoes, E in sweats, T-shirt, and purple flip-flops.

Brownish green and curved, a claw protruded from behind the island, then another, smaller, then the rest of the lobster.

"There are two," Gwen managed, fighting to keep her face straight. "John dropped them by for dinner tonight."

Gwen had come home at two in the morning. Heath had checked the time when the lift bell awakened her. Then she'd heard her aunt and John giggling in the kitchen. By the time Gwen had tiptoed through her bedroom and up to her tower room, Heath had been asleep. Now Gwen's paramour had come by to drop off gifts. Things were certainly moving along in that quarter, Heath thought sourly—the sourness of the proverbial grapes, she suspected.

"I took the lid off that bucket." E pointed to an overturned metal pail by the refrigerator. "And they just came out."

Again she and Gwen went into gales of giggles. Regardless of the shock of thinking her only child was being slaughtered by barbarian hordes, Heath could see the humor and allowed herself a smile.

Gwen hopped off the island. Expertly, she grabbed the first lobster behind its claws. After a lifetime of dealing with squirming children, lobsters evidently were no challenge. While E squealed, "Eeew!" Gwen dropped it in the bucket and then caught the second one.

"I've got to go down the lift and get a bucket of seawater. Our friends here will die if they stay out much longer."

"Aren't they supposed to die?" E asked. "They're food. Shouldn't they be in the refrigerator or somewhere? Not running around the kitchen frightening the children?"

"You cook them live," Gwen said.

Elizabeth's face went stiff with shock, her mouth open. "You do not!" she exclaimed.

"You do. It doesn't hurt them," Gwen said matter-of-factly. In her soggy sneakers, her pail of lobsters at her side, Gwen marched out of the kitchen toward the lift.

"It doesn't *hurt* them?" E asked incredulously. "How can being boiled alive not *hurt* them?"

Before Heath could think of an answer, Elizabeth had run out of the kitchen. Heath rolled to the doorway, but E was not standing at the lift waiting for her aunt to return. She was nowhere in sight,

Unexploded ordnance, Heath thought miserably. Gwen should have known. She didn't know who to pity most, Elizabeth for her memories, or Gwen when she realized what she had done.

EIGHTEEN

Elizabeth couldn't run far. There was no "far" on Boar. Besides, Maine wasn't flip-flop country; it was all rocky ups and downs. She wouldn't dare be gone for long. Because of her depression and suicidal impulse, she knew if she was out of Heath's sight for too long, Heath would call in the marines.

Worse. She'd call Anna.

Heath had tried to make E know she understood thinking one wanted to die, thinking what a relief it would be to let all the pain and ugly drain away while she went to sleep. She also tried to bring home to her daughter the fact that that sleep was forever. A permanent solution to a temporary problem. What life had taught Heath, and what she clung to, was that if you didn't die, things got better.

Then, of course, you did die, Heath thought as she tried to decide whether it would be better to shout for Elizabeth to come back or let her have a little time by herself. But that wasn't the point.

Heath wanted desperately to talk to E about the lobster thing, though she knew Elizabeth was drowning in talk, advice, reassurances, and platitudes. "Love claustrophobia," E had self-diagnosed, suffering from too much love in too small a space. Occasionally, Heath wondered if E couldn't take love at the level she and Gwen were dishing it out because she had gotten too little love as a child. At other times, she assumed she and Gwen were a tad overbearing, both having been childless until Elizabeth.

Parental EMO. Elizabeth insisted it was enough to shrivel a person into a Cheeto.

Heath smiled at that, then yelled, "Elizabeth! Come back! We need to talk!" despite her better judgment.

When E was nine, a psycho had captured her and two other girls. Jena, E's therapist, had helped her work through it. Fervently, Heath wished Jena were on Boar Island. Without giving advice or passing judgment, Jena had the gift of herding a patient's thoughts the way a dog would herd sheep until they were all going in the right direction, then keep the patient company until she reached the place she needed to be.

Heath knew she and Gwen committed the sin of listening too hard. They couldn't help themselves. Sometimes Heath listened so hard she could almost hear her eardrums cracking. Aunt Gwen's face looked like Wily's when somebody had a piece of cheese he really, really wanted but was too well behaved to beg for.

Because of conferences with Jena, Heath knew what the kidnapper had tried to do to Elizabeth and the other girls. Making them kill mice was only the half of it.

What the kidnapper had tried to do—had done—was rob them of themselves, then implant a version of his horrific psycho self in their brains.

The cyberstalker was trying to do the same thing, Heath realized. Using filth and threats and shame to take away E's sense of who she was and replace it with horribleness. No wonder she wanted to kill herself.

"E! Come back! Let's talk!" Heath shouted.

Wily trotted across the natural stone patio in the direction of the landward wing of ruins behind the lighthouse.

"Thank God," Heath breathed. There was no hiding from the nose. Elizabeth would never jump off a cliff in front of Wily, and Wily wasn't fool enough to jump off a cliff just because the other kids did, Heath consoled herself.

Elizabeth might not want a fairy god-dog along. She might try to evade him. E thought she knew all Wily's tricks. She didn't. Nobody knew all Wily's tricks.

Heath rolled herself across the flat apron until she could see a sliver of what existed behind the imposing buttress of granite that backed the house. Huge blocks with deep fissured shelves tumbled down toward the ocean. Beyond was a light fog, breaking like liquid in pure white waves against the shore of Mount Desert Island, poking feathery fingers into low places and humping up over rocks.

The lift bell rang. Machinery clanked. Gwen returning with her freshly seawatered lobsters. The platform clanked into place, and silence fell.

"Elizabeth!" Heath cried again.

There was no sound but for the ocean murmuring its secrets to the rock.

Gwen, slopping water from the bucket, crossed to Heath. "Why are you shouting?" she demanded.

Heath told her.

"Maybe it won't be so bad." Gwen's optimism sounded strained. "Lobsters are just big brownish green spiders, after all."

"It was the alive part. Boiling them *alive*," Heath said dully. "I don't know if she still does, but back when she said her prayers aloud she prayed to mice—prayed to rodents—begging them to forgive her. I don't want to hear her praying to arachnids."

"And me fetching a bucket of saltwater, toting living sacrifices to toss in the pot like cannibals toss missionaries in old cartoons! How could I have been so stupid!" Gwen moaned.

On the tail of the moan rode silence, the kind that sets like concrete in the ear.

NINETEEN

Anna stood at the edge of Thunder Hole, a favorite tourist spot. A keyhole-shaped inlet in the granite cliffs forced waves into a narrow aperture, creating wondrous booming thunder and geysers of silver spray, some a hundred feet high. A walkway with metal handrails descended partway into the hole for those who wished to be misted—or drenched, as the sea saw fit.

Lunch with Denise—Subway sandwiches gobbled in the car—had been uphill work. Denise said little, showed no interest in talking of the park or the park personnel, yet the silences were not comfortable. Anna had the same feeling around Ranger Castle as she had around a kid with a balloon and a pin. Any minute there was liable to be a big bang that would scare her half to death.

As acting chief, there wasn't a whole lot to do in reality. An ambitious "acting" on a short-term assignment could louse up a lot of paperwork. Anna had stepped in for other district rangers often enough to know that unless something momentous occurred—and the state of Maine had snatched the only good murder on the books—general housekeeping was the rule.

With nothing important to do in the office, Anna opted for foot patrol, asking Denise to swing back around the Mount Desert Island loop to pick her up in a couple of hours.

Being free of the Crown Vic and Ranger Castle was more of a relief than it should have been. Castle put Anna on edge in some indefinable way. The woman wasn't right. She was out of sync. Anna was a great believer in vibes. The eye and the subconscious mind were often better at reading the small print, and making sense of it, than the conscious mind.

Leaves swirling on waters suggested deep and troubling currents. Denise had enough swirling leaves to make Anna's scalp prickle. It lent her a greater appreciation of having escaped to blue sea, golden sun, salt breezes, tourists to annoy, and cigarette butts to pick up.

She was happily ensconced with a trio of visitors, holding forth in excellent ranger style, adroitly avoiding admitting she knew zip about the flora and fauna on the coast of Maine, when her cell phone vibrated.

"Excuse me," she said as she took it from its wallet and glanced at the face. "It's a call I need to take," she apologized.

As she turned away, she heard the woman say, "Isn't that nice! She apologized!" The teenaged son said, "For what?"

"The stalker is here," Heath said without preamble.

Caller ID had done away with the need for most of the old rotary niceties, an advance Anna appreciated.

"In Maine. In the park. Or says he is," Heath said.

Phone to ear, Anna walked across the loop road and into the trees. Talking to a ranger in uniform was too great a temptation for visitors to resist, regardless of what the ranger was in the middle of. She switched the phone from her left to her right hand. Since she'd taken a bullet in her left bicep a year or so before, the arm had been opposed to remaining in static tension for any length of time. Unless she kept it moving, it stiffened and ached.

Oddly, that the stalker was in the park jolted Anna. With Heath sequestered on Boar, she'd fallen into the trap of feeling Elizabeth was safe, as if she were vacationing in a secure resort, and being stalked was no more real than a death at a Mystery Dinner.

Cybercreep was here.

"This is good news," she decided, settling cross-legged on the pine straw, careful not to lean against the tree. Sap was impossible to get out of polyester.

"You're kidding, right?" Heath asked.

"No. In cyberspace we had the chance of a snowball in hell of finding him. In a national park, it may be doable."

"Good point." Heath sounded relieved. "Except that he intends on doing more than slinging porn at E. He wants to meet with her."

Cybercreep had escalated. Anonymous bullies usually stayed anonymous. If this one was calling for a face-to-face, it was because he wanted to do something more than shame and frighten. He wanted a hands-on experience.

"Start at the beginning," Anna said.

"I got two texts—in reality, Elizabeth got the texts. Her phone buzzed. I grabbed it. I've saved them," Heath said unnecessarily. She, Anna, Gwen, and E had already had that talk. "The first says, 'I know where you are.' Not very original; we knew that from the heroin. The second says, 'Come to Cecelia's Coffee Shop today at six. Come by yourself if you want your real life back.' Cecelia's is in Bar Harbor on the town square. I Google-Mapped it."

"Better and better," Anna said. "A time and place." Silence followed that. Heath was no dummy. She would know the "better and better" could involve using E as bait at some point. Without knowing who the stalker was, or what he wanted—other than the obvious: rape, white slavery, psycho amusements of all sorts—there was danger in letting him within shooting distance of E. Then again, if they did use E as bait, at least they would be there when whatever trap he had planned began to unfold.

"This is not usual for a cyberbully, is it?" Heath asked. "More like a blackmailer, but so far nobody has asked us for anything."

"You're right," Anna said. "Poison pens and cyberstalkers thrive on being hidden, anonymous, watching the havoc they create from the safety of their webs—spider or otherwise. They wouldn't want to meet for coffee in public. Has E seen the texts?"

"Not yet. She and Wily are off somewhere licking their wounds."

"Wounds?"

"John gave Gwen two lobsters. She mentioned to E that they were boiled while alive."

"The mice," Anna said, remembering the little corpses nailed to the side of the outhouse at the cabin in Rocky. Nailed while they still lived. Not an image a young girl should have burned into her brain. Or a ranger of a certain age, for that matter.

"Get your real life back," she said, changing the subject. "What do you figure that means? If they're talking reputation, that ship has sailed."

Heath groaned. "God, don't say that."

"When I was in high school there was a girl all the boys called Rosie Rotten-crotch," Anna said, remembering. "Supposedly she was the school hump. At that age, I never thought to question it. Now I wonder if Rosie said yes, or maybe no, to the wrong boy. Or if a jealous girl started it. Rosie was an American Indian girl from the local Paiute tribe. Scapegoat. Nobody cared to dig any deeper." Anna felt a stab of guilt. She hadn't cared either. "Rosie was ruined. There's no way to rehabilitate this sort of reputation wreck."

"Yes there is," Heath insisted firmly.

Anna let that stand. If Heath said it, they'd figure out a way to make it true. Later. She glanced at her watch. "It's four thirty. Our stalker might know you're in Acadia, but I bet he doesn't know you're on Boar, or he'd have given E more lead time to make the meeting. I think I can make it."

"So can I," Heath said. "I'll call a water taxi and meet you in Bar Harbor."

"No," Anna said. " 'Come alone if you want your life back.' Elizabeth was to come alone. We should assume this person knows something about you. We don't want to scare him off."

There was a long silence, then a gust of air that Anna suspected was tainted with tobacco smoke. "Right," Heath said finally. "A woman in a wheelchair is noticed. Then ignored."

"It's the first part that would wreck the surveillance."

TWENTY

Denise picked Anna up ten minutes after she called. Denise's unsettling aura, the one that made Anna's spine tingle, evaporated as Anna told her what she wanted. The abrupt loss of Denise's erratic hypervigilance made Anna wonder what she'd been expecting. What she'd been fearing. Given Ranger Castle's behavior, Anna didn't think "fear" was too strong a word. Maybe whatever had inspired her sudden retirement was still haunting her.

"So," Anna finished, "Elizabeth's stalker is here in Maine. Wants a meet-and-greet. E's off somewhere communing with the spirits, but we don't want to let the opportunity slip past."

Denise leaned forward until her chin was almost resting on the steering wheel. "Are all men such bastards?" she demanded. "Serial killing, child molesting, rape, bestiality—you name it, men do it."

"Women, too," Anna said because she was in the mood to poke a hornets' nest.

Denise sucked an audible breath through her nose, then puffed the air out of lips loose with scorn. "Sure. One, two maybe. Not enough for a decent statistic. Get real. Women do shitty things, no doubt about it, but the twisted male victimization of women is front page every day. Got a cult leader? What's the first thing he does? Makes all the women sleep with him. Got a God? First thing the guy says—and the gods are all guys nowadays—is 'Obey your husband. Put yourself in a black bag so nobody can see you.' Root of all evil, Eve and the goddamned apple my ass! More like Adam and his snake."

Anna laughed. "I like that. I have to remember to tell my husband. He's a priest."

Denise looked at her, her eyebrows in a shocked V. "Like defrocked?"

Anna laughed again. "Episcopal."

"Sorry I shot off my mouth," Denise said. She sounded more sulky than sorry. Rather like a child who got caught doing something she wasn't supposed to.

"Don't be," Anna said easily. "In this case, you're preaching to the choir. This victim is a particular friend of mine." She didn't mention that E was her goddaughter. Being married to a priest was condemnation enough to a cynical ear.

Having cleared the change in routine with Peter, Anna and Denise would swap out cars so they weren't in a marked NPS vehicle. Denise would accompany Anna to the coffee shop. It was unlikely, but whoever was behind the bullying might recognize Anna on sight. Denise had the advantage of being an unknown.

"Do you know anything about stalking via the Internet?" Anna asked as Denise pulled the patrol vehicle into the parking garage beneath her apartment building in Bar Harbor.

Denise's head jerked back as if Anna had flopped a nasty fish in her face.

"What are you implying?" she asked, an edge to her voice.

Maybe Denise had done a bit of cyberspying after the split with Peter. Before the Internet, dumped girlfriends had to drive by "his" house to see whose car was parked there. Now, armed with personal information, they could read credit reports, check Facebook. All manner of interesting new methods of self-torture were available.

"I'm pretty ignorant when it comes to this stuff," Anna replied mildly. "I hoped you might know more."

"Oh," Denise said. "No. I'm not into that. I don't even have a cell phone."

For a law enforcement officer not to have a cell phone was tantamount to dereliction of duty. More was the pity; a cell phone saw to it that no one was ever truly off duty, or home from work. Anna tossed this lack of modern technology onto the pile of Weird Denise Castle Things growing in the back of her mind.

With the nervous reluctance of a jeweler ushering in a cat burglar, Denise let Anna into her apartment. To Anna's eyes there was nothing to be ashamed of. The place was neat to a fault—no books, no magazines, no cats or dogs or dirty underpants on the floor. White

walls were decorated with framed photographs in black
and white of the park both above and below the surface of the Atlantic. The carpet was white, no off-color
spots where beasties vomited or booted feet left dirt.
The couch was white, black-and-white zebra-print
pillows standing sentinel at either end. A glass coffee
table and a flat-screen TV finished the decor.

With the air of a wary damsel inviting a vampire
over the threshold, Denise said, "This way," and ush-
ered Anna into the apartment's single bedroom. It was
as monochromatic as the living room. Both rooms had
the impersonal feel of having been "dressed" by a Realtor looking to sell.

"These should fit well enough," Denise said, pulling a pair of gray linen slacks and a white pleated-front
blouse from the closet. A narrow black belt was hooked
over the hanger by the buckle. The clothes in the closet
were all arranged in outfits. She laid the clothes on the
bed, then took a shoe box from a neat arrangement of
shoe boxes on the closet floor. "Size seven and a half,"
she said.

"That will work," Anna replied.

Denise looked around the sparsely furnished room,
then left reluctantly as if she thought Anna might
pocket any valuables left lying around.

Having put on Denise's outfit, Anna studied herself
in the mirror on the sliding closet door. In any mall in
America she would have gone unremarked. Salespeo-
ple would trust her. PTAs would welcome her as a
member. Anna felt deep, deep undercover. Still, it was

good to be free of the Kevlar vest. Anna missed the days when they were an option, not a requirement, for law enforcement rangers.

In the mirror's reflection she noted the single personal item in this impersonal lair. A photograph stood on the black wooden nightstand. Drawn to it, Anna picked it up. A narrow rectangle, matted to fit the standard frame, showed a much younger Denise in her Park Service uniform. Three fingers wrapped around her right arm. It must have been taken when she was with Peter. He'd been cut out and the mat redone to cover the excision. Symbolic, this hiding of the past with a black mask. In the photo Denise was smiling, an expression Anna had seldom seen on her face. It had been taken before Denise had gotten her teeth capped. Her old incisors, the way they neatly overlapped, struck Anna as familiar.

"Are you done?" Denise demanded. She had entered without knocking and stood in the bedroom door radiating disapproval.

"Yes," Anna said. "Is this you?" she asked, holding up the photograph.

"It was," Denise said.

"You remind me of somebody," Anna said, turning the picture to study the image.

Denise laughed, a cartoon laugh, "Heh, heh, heh." In two steps, she'd crossed the small room and taken the picture from Anna's hands. "I have that kind of face. I always remind somebody of somebody else." Opening the drawer on the nightstand, she dropped it in facedown, then snapped the drawer closed again. "Let me get dressed."

Summarily dismissed, Anna slunk back into the living room. She'd thought the woman had been warming to her. Evidently that phase of their relationship was abruptly at an end. Why? Was Denise hiding something? Shame at having cut Peter from a picture? Embarrassment at having her crooked teeth on display? Her sudden iciness seemed overkill for such minor humiliations.

Unless Anna had stumbled on a sore spot, pushed an old button. Perhaps Denise had been teased about the teeth. One never knew which closets harbored a stranger's skeletons.

In moments Denise emerged from the bedroom in black slacks and a white sleeveless mock turtleneck. "Let's get on with it," she said as she walked to the door. Opening it, she held it, whisking Anna out with a sweep of her hand.

Door closed and locked, Denise relaxed marginally. By the time they'd traveled down the stairs to the garage, she seemed nearly her usual slightly weird self.

She opened the door of a forest green Mazda Miata. The top was down. "Cool," Anna said as she slid in.

"Not very practical," Denise said as if she quoted a stern and humorless mother.

Cecelia's Coffee Shop was on the town square in the heart of Bar Harbor's tourist district. Had the Miata not been so small, parking would have been a bitch; as it was, Denise slipped into a slot between two SUVs less than a block from the square.

She and Anna were intentionally early. They bought ice cream in small foam cups from a vendor in a pseudo-nineteenth-century cart complete with horse, then wandered to a bench in the square where they could watch the coffee shop.

"Your stalker can't have too sinister an intent on his mind," Denise said as she carved out a neat bite of ice cream with her tiny plastic spork.

"Not here," Anna agreed. This wasn't the haunted house at midnight. There would be no kidnapping, raping, or pillaging. Café tables sat beneath a striped awning, mothers and students and tourists perching on the ironwork chairs. People in shorts and T-shirts carrying plastic bags emblazoned with the names of local shops entered. A few minutes later they exited, iced coffee or mochaccino in hand. Nothing fishy, nothing shady.

On such a sunny afternoon, in the middle of a town set above the glittering blue of the Atlantic, and Disneyesque in its adorability, kidnapping, raping, and pillaging seemed an alien concept. Surely a species that invented ice cream, kites, and flip-flops would be incapable of harming a hair on a puppy's head.

The mystery of humanity wasn't that people were starkly evil or magnificently good but that they were both all the time. Sanity and insanity dwelt side by side in the human brain. Only when one grew so big it overshadowed and starved the other was it noticed.

People tended to either keep their crazy to themselves or gather with others sharing the same delusion.

Churches, synagogues, temples, covens, mosques: If enough people believed a thing, it was declared sane. One person speaking to invisible beings was a nutcase. A thousand was a cult. Ten thousand, a religion.

Fortunately, most human madness was harmless, creative even; it made life rich and memorable and annoyingly real.

"Any clue as to what we're looking for?" Denise asked, cutting into Anna's thoughts.

"Nope." Anna took a small bite of pistachio ice cream and let it melt on her tongue for a moment. "Early on I would have said teenage boys or girls, but they aren't the sort who track victims across land for a couple thousand miles. That takes money and autonomy."

"Any Dirty Uncle Ernies on the radar?" Denise asked.

"Not since she was nine."

"Goddamn sons of bitches," Denise said.

Two white high-school-aged girls and a woman who could have been their mother sat at one of the tables. Both girls were on iPhones. Mom, evidently old school, read a paperback novel. An older white male with a fat dachshund on a pink leash sat at another table and read a newspaper. Two boys came, opened their laptops on the third table, and ignored each other.

The older man finished his coffee. He and his hound ambled off. A barista cleared away his paper cup. Two middle-aged black women, both in capri pants and high-heeled sandals, took his place, sipping iced coffee. Obeying some psychic—or cyber—signal, the boys simultaneously folded up their laptops and left, still not speaking.

Time for the rendezvous came and went.

As afternoon on the square melted into evening on the square, Anna told Denise the details of the bullying. "At first we figured it must be a kid—or kids—in her school. As it turns out, if the victim doesn't know the bullies or the bullies don't ID themselves, or friends rat them out, there is virtually—and in this sense I mean virtually literally—no way to track them."

"There's got to be," Denise said, settling on a bench near an old cannon on a concrete slab. "They can hack into your computer and record every keystroke you make, redirect your browser to ad sites, turn on the volume when they want to sing you a slogan, pinpoint your position anywhere on the face of the earth, find out what color panties you're wearing, then try and sell you Viagra. How can they not track some pricks bullying a girl?"

"I guess we're talking different theys," Anna said as she spooned up a bit of the green dessert and laid it neatly on the end of her tongue, where it would melt over as many taste buds as possible on its journey to her esophagus.

"The capitalist theys are more motivated and tech-savvy than the don't-bully-children theys," Anna finished.

"And you can bet not one of them gives a flying fig about lost girls. Not one," Denise said as she savagely attacked the chocolate chunk with her spork. "What makes you think it isn't scumbag kids?" she asked around a mouthful of ice cream. "It stinks of scumbag kid fun to me."

"Asking for a face-to-face," Anna replied as she watched the people coming and going at the coffee shop. "To make a trip cross-country suggests an adult with the independence and money to travel."

"What does the girl . . . Elizabeth?"

Anna nodded.

"What does Elizabeth think of the new development?" Denise asked.

"She doesn't know yet. Her mother said she needed some time by herself. The combined concern of her mother, her great-aunt Gwen, and probably me can't be all that easy to deal with. Poor kid."

"Yeah, poor kid," Denise echoed dully.

Anna was thinking of her husband, Paul. Never had anyone loved her like he did. More than she deserved. More than she could accept sometimes. There were moments it was as if she dared not feel pain because he would feel it as well, when she could not choose to spend herself as she would like because of what it would cost him.

"Unconditional love, in large doses, can be a burden," she mused.

"I wouldn't know," Denise said.

Her tone snapped Anna out of her reverie. "There's an odd one," she said to deflect the feeling of guilt Denise's sudden exposure had awakened. Using her spork, she gestured toward a woman nearing the coffee shop. She was plump, tall in platform sandals. Screaming red hair was styled in a short curly cap and set off by oversized glasses framed in turquoise. An enormous straw bag flapped at her legs as she walked, gripped by a hand as round and dimpled as that of a child, though the woman was probably in her mid-to-late thirties.

"What's that in her bag?" Denise asked.

"Damn," Anna said, then laughed. "It looks like a welding glove."

"I think we've lost our window of opportunity," Denise said finally.

"Maybe a no-show," Anna said.

"Maybe," Denise replied.

"Got cold feet?" Anna wondered.

"Made us?" Denise suggested.

"More likely, we didn't make him." Two college boys online, one old guy with a dog, one fat guy with badly behaved offspring. Woman with a Bozo hairdo. Nothing screamed stalker.

"We're nowhere," Anna admitted. Her cell phone buzzed. "Excuse me," she said as she looked at the screen. "It's our victim's mother, probably wanting to know how we're doing." Anna poked the green phone icon and put the cell phone to her ear. "Heath," she said.

"Elizabeth has gone missing."

"You said she needed time alone," Anna said, surprised at the terror in Heath's voice.

"Hours ago, damn it! Hours ago. This island is the size of a postage stamp. She hasn't come back," Heath said.

Her fear awoke Anna's. This wasn't like E, to worry people she loved.

"Is Wily with her?" Anna demanded.

"I guess," Heath said distractedly.

Anna smothered the urge to say, "That's okay then." Absurd as it was, the fact that the old dog was with E reassured her. Anna and Wily had forged an odd connection in the North Woods of Minnesota. It wasn't something Anna chose to talk about. She doubted Wily did either.

"Anna, I'm pretty sure she's not on the island," Heath almost wailed. "I've looked everywhere I can, and called until I'm hoarse."

While Anna had been neatly occupied eating ice cream in Bar Harbor, E had disappeared. Were the two connected? Had Anna been made a patsy? "Is Gwen with you?"

"No, Gwen and John went to Bangor for the evening. Dinner and a visit with Chris Zuckerberg."

"I'm on my way. Give me half an hour," Anna said. It would take her that long to talk somebody out of a boat and get to the island. Elizabeth's body—Anna shuddered as she thought the word—would be found only by boat if she had fallen.

Or jumped.

TWENTY-ONE

Heath half crouched near the wall of boulders ringing the area that had been leveled to build the tower and house. She had on Dem Bones, her high-tech robotic walking suit, legs and belly strapped in, bright silver lozenge-shaped pieces of machinery on the outside of her thighs and calves, hinges at hip and knee. The arm-brace crutches lay fifteen feet away where she'd flung them in a rage when they got in the way of her attempts to get this so-called wonder of modern technology to complete the simple task of moving her bony ass up and over the chunks of stone calved off the granite wall.

"Goddamn useless piece of shit," she cried. Her hands clawed at the slick rock as the weight of her lower limbs, and the titanium skeleton, dragged her down. Using the motions available to her, she could only manage to kick uselessly at the rock with feet like senseless clubs, and knees not worth the effort it took technology to bend them.

As she slid back for the third time, leaving long white scratches on the glossy silver finish of the thigh and calf pieces, she screamed like a wounded panther.

Frustration consumed energy that, left alone, would turn to thoughts. There was nothing Heath could think that wasn't insupportable, that wouldn't sear the marrow in her bones. Someone was stalking her daughter; now her daughter was missing. Heath had been a fool to think cyberfilth would be the sum total of it. She was a fool not to have taken E to London, put her into witness protection, hired bodyguards. Such was her arrogant stupidity, she had thought a cripple, an old dog, and a septuagenarian pediatrician could keep her child safe.

E hasn't been missing all that long, she told herself.

"Damned she hasn't," she said aloud. Only a few hours, but Boar Island wasn't a few hours' worth of adventure. Heath automatically reached down her right hand. No wheelchair, no saddlebags, no cigarettes. "Piece of shit," she muttered.

Never would E intentionally scare her or Gwen by staying away so long. Wily would have come back if he could have, if for no other reason than his dinner was served at five every day. If E was hurt, Wily would have howled when he heard Heath calling his name. There was no girl and no dog, and the only way that could happen was if they'd been taken.

Not jumped or fallen, Heath thought. E wouldn't take Wily with her into the grave, and Wily wasn't the type to leap off a fifty-foot cliff even if E did. Besides, Elizabeth was past suicide. She was.

The lift bell rang. Frankenstein-like, Heath turned, then lurched toward where the elevator would release its passenger. "It better be you, Anna," she shouted as she monstered across the level rock. Anna didn't deserve that. Scarcely thirty-five minutes had passed since Heath called. The superwoman suit didn't deserve to be called a piece of shit either, for that matter. Heath didn't care. Choices were limited: She could rage or she could fall apart.

The lift clattered into its dock with a groan that, no matter how often Heath heard it, seemed to presage immediate disaster. Anna stepped off. "It's me," she said unnecessarily. She was in her full ranger costume, gun and all. Heath was so glad to see her, she could have burst into tears.

"About time," she said.

Anna paid no attention to the snarling dog that had possessed Heath. Undoubtedly she'd seen that fear hound more times than she'd care to remember. Heath was grateful.

"Where have you looked?" Anna asked.

"Goddamn nowhere," Heath admitted. "I got back into the ruins a ways and called. There is so much crap on the ground and the floors are so rotten, I couldn't do much inside. The rest of this godforsaken rock might as well be Mars. I can't get out of this bear pit. I went up and down the lift a few times and saw what I could from the dock. I butted myself up the whole piece-of-shit tower, one hundred and seventy feet of metal stairs, and couldn't see a damn thing from the windows. Couldn't hold myself up to look over the sills for more than a second. That's it. That's it."

"How long has she been gone, and how did she go?" Anna asked.

Heath sputtered out the tale of the lobsters and Wily. "John picked Gwen up a few minutes later. It never occurred to us that E wouldn't be right back. I am an idiot," she finished.

Anna nodded as if Heath had given her a measured professional report of the search to date. She looked around the open space at the rocks and rubble, then up at the sky.

"Light's going," Anna said. "We'd better figure out where she headed and then get moving. You want to come?"

Heath wanted to. She wanted it so much she could feel her fingers curling around Anna's from where she stood.

"No," she said through stiff lips. "You'll move faster alone."

TWENTY-TWO

Denise sat behind the wheel of her car shaking. Not shaking. Twitching like a doll with its legs stuck in a garbage disposal. Tears—a luxury she seldom enjoyed—poured down her face. Before Paulette came and gave her permission to feel, one of the few times she'd cried was the day she heard Peter was engaged. Those tears had been turned to steam by white-hot anger before they'd reached the air. She'd almost missed the days when her tear ducts had been welded shut. Now great fat drops ran down the side of her nose to drip on the black linen of her trousers.

Ranger Pigeon was finally gone. She'd been in Denise's bedroom—again—changing out of Denise's clothes, then used Denise's bathroom, no doubt rummaging through the medicine cabinet, and the towel cupboard, and under the sink, looking for anything that would trigger the memory of who Denise's photo reminded her of. Her ferreting brain ticking like a bomb.

Denise had screwed up royally at the scene. She'd

acted guilty as hell, searching the murder room for traces she might have left while the pigeon watched from the doorway, running back to the car and hiding, practically running the woman over to get her away from Paulette, going part postal over the old picture. Anna Pigeon was one of those people who saw, who looked and saw the person behind the eyes. Denise had run up about a dozen red flags.

"God damn me!" Denise cried and struck a fist against the steering wheel. "I didn't think. I didn't fucking think!" When she'd offered Anna a change of clothes, and the use of her car for the undercover stint, she hadn't thought of Paulette, of the plan. She had a family now. She had to think of them first, before the job, before cyberstalkers, before endangered citizens, before herself. Family came before everything. Family was everything.

"Don't screw this up," she muttered fiercely, then turned the key in the ignition, bringing the Miata to life. She had to see Paulette. They needed to talk this through. Denise was still in her civvies, still in the Miata, her radio on the passenger seat monitoring the traffic. It would be a risk, but the sense of urgency driving her made it imperative. She looked at her watch. Seven fifteen. Paulette was a nurse. Three days a week she worked the two-to-midnight shift in the infants ward at Mount Desert Hospital. This was one of her nights. Pulling out of the NPS headquarters' parking lot, Denise texted: *mt me H pking lot. 10 min.*

By the time she reached the hospital, the sun was going down. The long summer afternoons were golden, the light softening trees to a dark haze and turning the ocean to navy blue.

When she and her sister were ready, Denise decided, they would move somewhere there was no ocean, no winter, where the world wasn't made of rock and snow and ice water. Georgia maybe. Georgia in the pines, a little cabin. That would be perfect. Maybe a lake. Too dangerous, she decided as she parked the Miata in the darkest corner behind the building. Kids drowned in lakes all the time. In Georgia there might be alligators. Alligators liked children and little fluffy dogs. She'd read that somewhere.

Turning off the ignition, Denise lay back in her seat and waited. Paulette might not be able to get away instantly, but she'd come. Denise knew she would. They were twins. They had the exact same blood and bone and brain. They didn't have identical fingerprints. Had she ever Googled that in a hurry! What a drag it would have been if Paulette's fingerprints at the murder scene lit up Denise's own on IAFIS, the federal print identification base.

In everything that mattered, they were identical. Paulette would never let her down.

Ranger Pigeon and that damned picture. "Is this *you*? You remind me of *somebody*." The memory bit Denise in the butt again. In a fit of paranoia, she leapt from the car to put the top up. Nobody would be looking; still, it was best if she and Paulette were not seen together.

With the lowering of the sun, clouds came scudding from the southwest, and fog began to tease in from its hiding places out to sea. Good, Denise thought as she clipped the top securely down. Once she had hated the fog, hated the clammy dead touch of mist, and the confusion of veils across her eyes. Now it made her feel safer. To be hidden was calming, centering, like the world beneath the sea.

As she settled behind the wheel in the tiny car, a slash of light cut the deep shadow in the back of the building; the fire stairs, that was where the nurses left the building. There were no reserved spaces; their cars had to be parked in the back lot, the dark lot, the lot where bad things could happen.

"Screw men," Denise whispered. "Screw them all. Bastards."

She thought to flash the headlights to identify herself, but there was no need. Paulette would know where she was. She would feel her in the gray cloak of encroaching fog the way one hand felt the other in a game of cat's cradle. Such an old game. Denise couldn't remember anyone teaching it to her. No cheery childhood memories of doting grandmamas or loving aunts.

Poor little Anna Pigeon and her poor little Elizabeth suffering from a surfeit of love. "Such a burden!" Denise mocked, her voice pitched low. "God, how does one bear it!" She should have gouged Pigeon's eye out with a spork.

Nope, nobody had bothered teaching poor little Denise a nice game like cat's cradle.

Maybe it was a memory of Paulette's that had traveled into her head.

God damn Anna Pigeon. God damn Denise Castle

for letting her into her apartment, leaving her alone in the bedroom, for not hiding the photograph.

Now she and Paulette were going to have to speed things up. The luxury of time was gone. It had drained away like water down a gopher hole during the time Anna Pigeon was with her. Beady eyes licking over everything, foxy ears perked, the pigeon watched and thought while Denise did everything but spray-paint GUILTY on the clean white walls of her apartment.

Paulette had to move faster on the land sale, and Denise on tracking down the legacy advertised in the papers. If there was a legacy. She also had to give the NPS notice and get her pension papers filed. Everything had to be in place so they could tie up the loose ends and be gone before anybody knew there was any reason to think there were two of them, that they had anything to do with Duffy's demise.

"I don't have long," Paulette said as she slid in the passenger door. "I said I was going out for a cigarette. The head nurse is cool with that. She smokes a pack and a half a day."

"We'll have to quit when the family is complete," Denise said, though she'd never smoked a cigarette in her life.

"Complete?" Paulette questioned.

That Paulette didn't inherently understand annoyed Denise. She pressed the sensation down hard. Paulette was her sister, her other self; she could never be annoyed with her. Not ever. "We're going be a family," Denise explained patiently. "Like we wanted. Like we are supposed to be. It's the last thing we have to do before we go. We got rid of Kurt. Now, as soon as we are complete, we can go. Have to go, and sooner rather than later."

Paulette looked confused. Or maybe Denise just felt her confusion. The little shards of streetlights and security lights refracting in the rearview mirrors weren't sufficient to read a face.

"A family. More than just you and me?" Paulette asked.

Again the stab of irritation; again Denise shoved it down. "Families have children," Denise said too sharply.

"You said Peter had murdered your babies," Paulette said in a gentle voice. "Tell me how it was."

The irritation Denise was suffering wasn't for her sister, her twin. It was like the twitches, a case of nerves. She took hold of Paulette's hand and leaned back in the seat. The memory didn't come; it was always there, sharper and more detailed each time she revisited it.

"Four years ago I got pregnant," Denise said. "It was Peter's, of course. I loved my baby. I knew I wasn't getting any younger, and I loved my baby so much."

"Did Peter beat you?" Paulette asked. That was how her babies had been murdered.

"He said he didn't want our baby. He said he never wanted children. He said he couldn't face it. He made me get an abortion." He'd said he'd leave her if she didn't get an abortion, that's what he had said, but it was the same thing.

"Something went wrong," Denise said. "Something got ripped. I was told I couldn't have any more children. Then Peter left."

"And married Lily and had a baby," Paulette finished softly.

"My baby," Denise said.

Paulette squeezed her hand. "Is that why you came? To tell me about the baby?"

Denise opened her eyes, suddenly back from the ugly trip down Memory Lane. Peter had turned what should have been a sentimental journey into a nightmare on Elm Street. "No. I came to tell you we have to move faster. It's that ranger, Anna Pigeon. I caught her looking at a photo of us. Then she peers into me. Ice-pick eyes. I got that shivery feeling you get when something bad is about to happen."

"Who took the photo of us?" Alarmed, Paulette jerked her hand out of Denise's. Hot snaps of anger cracked up Denise's spine.

Not for Paulette. Nerves.

"It wasn't us exactly," Denise said. "It was me, before I got my teeth capped. My hair was blond then, and wild." For a moment she believed that, but it wasn't right. Her teeth hadn't been capped yet, true, but in the picture her hair wasn't like Paulette's. It was the same boring brown as it always was. For a moment, in her mind, she'd seen it blond and big like her sister's. Rubbing her face, she mumbled through her fingers, "Anna Pigeon knows. She stares at the picture, then gives me this smirky look and says, 'Is this *you*? You remind me of *somebody*.' She spent a lot of time with you at the house. She knows. Why would she say 'you remind me of somebody' unless she wanted me to know she knew I had a twin?"

There was a wrongness to her logic, Denise knew that; still and all, she felt it to be the truth. Knew it to be the truth. "Anna Pigeon will ruin everything."

Paulette sat quiet for a long time. Denise could feel twitches building in her hands, her feet. The sparks of anger flared in her esophagus until she thought she might breathe fire.

"Anna Pigeon, she's the ranger who came with you when the police were at my house?" Paulette asked, her words coming slowly, as if her mind were working hard between each utterance.

"That was her," Denise said. "Shit!" She slammed the heel of her hand against the steering wheel. "I never should have let the bitch out of the car. She's got a nose as long as a dachshund's, sticking it where it doesn't belong."

"I think maybe she knew I was me," Paulette admitted. "She looked at me like you said she looked at the picture, like she knew I was inside, there behind my eyes, and she was going to scrape me out like an oyster out of its shell."

Denise became still, no twitches, no angry motions. Staring at her sister, she let the awe that had been building since they'd found each other fill her whole being. Paulette knew everything that happened in Denise's head just as Denise knew everything that happened in Paulette's head. "Exactly like that. An oyster from its shell," Denise whispered.

"Oh God," Paulette moaned. "Maybe she looks at everybody like that. She's probably just the kind of person who really looks at things."

That wasn't it. Denise knew. Paulette knew, too; she just didn't want to admit it.

For a long time neither one of them spoke. Denise didn't feel alone in the silence. She felt *together* in the silence. Mostly.

"What do we do?" Paulette asked at last.

"I'll think of something. It's us against the world." Denise laughed because she knew it was true, the only truth.

TWENTY-THREE

The agony that stretched Heath's skin thin over the bones of her face fueled Anna's own fears. "Let's get started," she said, and turned away from her friend lest their terrors coalesce into panic. Eyes long since trained to look for spoor darted over the natural patio and the boulders surrounding it. A half-chewed bone— a project of Wily's, no doubt; flecks of brown tobacco, blowing in idle circles, eddying in the breeze where the walls formed a corner; faint tracks—the tread of Robo-butt's rubber wheels leaving bits of dried mud in the light burnishing of dust.

"It hasn't rained," Anna said.

"No. Why are we talking about the weather?" Heath was fighting tears. Anna could feel fear and shame and guilt boiling off of her like heat from pavement.

"Your wheelchair left tracks. See. Dry now, but you rolled through water. Why?" Anna asked. In the zone where spoor and prey are all that matters, Anna barely heard Heath's sputtered curses as she backtracked to where the wheels had found enough water to make mud.

"The lobsters," Heath cried suddenly. "They were in a bucket there. Gwen put them down, and we forgot all about them."

"No lobsters, no bucket," Anna said. "Do you think John Whitman took them? Maybe when he came for Gwen, he took them home to eat them himself?"

Heath thought for a moment, then said, "No. I watched Gwen and John go down the lift. Gwen had her little book-pack full of things for Ms. Zuckerberg, and her purse. John wasn't carrying anything. Both hands were empty. I'm sure of it."

"Somebody took lobsters and bucket. E? Returning to the scene of the crime to rescue the lobsters from the pot?" Anna suggested.

"Yes!" Heath almost shouted. "Yes! She would have come back and gotten them. She would want to set them free. Save their creepy crustacean lives out of the goodness of her heart. Yes. Oh, God. How long does it take to let a couple lobsters go? Ten minutes? We're in the middle of the goddamn ocean. Not even five. She's been gone three hours and twenty-three minutes," Heath wailed. She looked at her wristwatch. "Twenty-six minutes," she amended.

Anna didn't bother to ask Heath if she'd called 911, the Coast Guard, or the army. She knew the drill: No-body looked for adults—and for this, E counted as an adult—until they'd been missing for forty-eight hours.

Nobody looked for an emotional teenager out of sight for a few hours.

Heath's eyes filled with tears. Anna turned her back lest the contagion spread.

Elizabeth, worrying her mother into a state of frenzy, and risking Anna's wrath, by vanishing; that wasn't the child Anna had godparented. E cared what people thought of her, especially the people she loved. Often Anna had wondered if she cared too much, spent too much of her childhood being a parent to those around her, taking care of everybody at the expense of taking care of herself.

It would take a momentous event to lift that burden from E, to make her as thoughtless as the average person. Unless Barnum & Bailey had pitched a tent on Boar Island, or Brad Pitt made an unscheduled stop, Anna couldn't think what might distract E from her customary responsibilities.

If Brad, Barnum, and Bailey were out of the picture, the landscape became darker. Either E was not on the island or she was on the island but could not get back to the lighthouse. Anna tried to picture her curled up in the fetal position beneath the overhang of a boulder, Wily beside her. Asleep maybe.

Several hours was a long time to sleep on a rock.

A sixteen-year-old girl, possibly suicidal, definitely tormented, gone for hours on a rock not big enough to register on most charts.

That line of thought served no one.

"So, E came back and got the bucket with the lobsters," Anna said. "Describe it."

"It was a bucket. A regular bucket," Heath said. Then she threw her head back like a cat and yowled, "Elizabeth!"

Anna had seen Heath under pressure before. In life-and-death situations, physical stress and emotional pain, but she'd never seen her like this, losing control, becoming a victim herself.

"Think," she demanded. Then went on, "Bucket full of water and lobsters, the bucket would weigh close to thirty pounds. So E could lift it, but not carry it easily. Buckets are awkward. So she's got the lobsters, and she's planning on emancipating them. Elizabeth would know they'd die if she just turned them loose on a rock in the sun. Might as well go ahead and boil them, if she was going to do that. At least it would be faster." Anna followed a slopping trail where water had mixed with sand particles and dust, then been dragged through with a smooth shoe, probably Elizabeth's flip-flop. It led to the wall that protected the patio from the fifty-foot drop to the ocean. Anna leaned out and looked down the precipitous fall to the rocks below. "So she dragged the bucket to the cliff and looked over. That's a long way down. If she poured them over, the fall might kill them."

"The lift," Heath said.

"The bell ringing would bring you and Gwen running," Anna said.

"And she didn't want to see us. Didn't want to talk to us. Couldn't believe we would talk about boiling living things alive so we could watch them die." Heath's voice was climbing and diving as her mind drove it from self-hatred to despair.

"I need you to focus," Anna said. "Was the bucket metal or wood?"

"Metal," Heath managed, then pressed her lips together as if holding back a horde of wasps wanting to swarm out of her mouth.

"Five gallons or thereabout?" Anna asked. Five was a standard bucket size.

"About." Heath let the word out before resealing her lips.

"Full of lobsters and water," Anna said. "Heavy." She studied the granite above where the water had spilled, then dried. "There."

"I don't see anything," Heath said, coming so close she rolled one wheel half over Anna's toes.

Anna ignored the pain. Heath had enough on her mind. "There," she pointed. "See where the metal bucket scraped the rock. E hauled it up here. Dragging." Following the marks, Anna climbed the sloping face of the boulder on hands and feet. Her left arm ached. Since she'd been wounded it had never recovered its full strength. Physical therapy had only gotten it so far. After that, Anna treated it with denial.

Eyes to the ground, she climbed and boulder-hopped past the ruined wings of the old house and around the broken upthrust of granite.

The north side of the island, scarcely as big as two football fields, was formed of enormous chunks of granite that had cracked and worn over the eons until it created steep rounded steps descending in giant leaps to the sea. Sunlight caught shining facets, making them sparkle. Scrubby mosses and lichens grew between the rocks as if they'd been there forever. Anna smiled at the thought. Of course they'd been there forever. They were rocks.

Fissures wide enough to accommodate the passage of a slender girl and a skinny dog made a grid pattern. The lines were not straight or square enough to look man-made, but nearly so. Varying heights of rocks blocked any view of the island's shoreline.

As she stared into the distance over the swells, it struck Anna how much bigger the Atlantic seemed than the Pacific. The Atlantic and Pacific would be the only two oceans Elizabeth had ever seen. Before Heath found E, she knew nothing about the world. She was homeschooled. Her reading skills were strong, as were her math skills. She scored high on the IQ test the therapist Heath had hired gave her. Elizabeth could cook and sew better than most grown women. She knew the names of the major stars and constellations. But about the world's geography and sociology she'd been taught very little.

A lot of nine-year-olds at least knew there were seven seas. Elizabeth hadn't. She hadn't even known there were fifty states. Heath said she hadn't been aware there were people of different colors or who spoke different languages. She hadn't known people were gay or monogamous.

No television. No movies. No radio.

The world of the cult compound had little variety; everybody was considered a brother or sister or cousin whether they were blood relations or not. Polygamous, white, religious, and completely contained between the dusty gold walls of a canyon west of Loveland, Colorado, was the only life Elizabeth knew until Heath had adopted her. For the seven years since, she'd been in Boulder learning to be a twenty-first-century little girl. Then a high school girl.

Then a shamed and shunned pariah.

Now she was suddenly half a continent from Colorado, from her friends, marooned on an island. A lot for a person to deal with, Anna thought.

There was little in the way of earth or plants to mark the passage of girl and dog, but Elizabeth had not been trying to cover her tracks, so Anna followed the trail easily. The heavy bucket had slopped, leaving traces of disturbance in the fine dust. Where Elizabeth slid off of one boulder and onto to a lower one, the bucket left scrapes on the stone when she'd dragged it after her. Wily, probably not with the intention of helping Anna, but one never knew when it came to Wily, had lifted his leg several times, leaving a faint darker stain on the sparse dusty grasses that clung in the wisps of blown earth.

Following the trail, Anna wended her way downward in zigzags between boulders until she reached a point where she could finally see the edge of the little island. Twenty feet directly below where she'd stopped, water lapped the rugged shore. Anna stared at waves beating themselves to a froth on ragged rocks.

E wouldn't have dumped the lobsters here; there were too many rocks to ensure they'd have a safe landing.

As Anna picked her way through the maze of giant

granite blocks tumbled together around the base of the island, she lost sight of both sea and mainland. In a slot between two great chunks of rock no more than six feet apart, the maze ended abruptly in a three-foot drop to dark water. The slot between the boulders continued several yards farther, creating a narrow inlet protected from the wind and much of the power of the sea.

Anna squatted, studying the lip of the stone above the water. The edge was sharp, squared off at a neat ninety degrees, the face making a straight line down toward the water. Getting to her hands and knees to take advantage of the low-angled afternoon light, Anna could see where Elizabeth had smudged the dust as she sat on the edge of the rock, her feet dangling over.

A wave rushed up the narrow channel and exploded against the island, coating Anna's skin with chilling spray. Beyond the mouth of the slot was a thin feathery line: fog cat-footing in.

The wave was sucked back into the gullet of the ocean, baring the boulders walling the slot. Along the stones at the waterline were scrapes of brown and a single sketch of blue. A small boat had docked here more than once.

Any legitimate visitor would bring his boat to the jetty, ring the bell, and walk in the front door.

As Anna leaned forward to study the marks, a wavering fishy silver flashed beneath the water. Fourteen inches beneath the water, on a ledge, lying on its side, was a bucket. The bucket.

This was the end of the trail. This was where E had loosed Gwen's dinner guests.

Anna lay down on her belly and reached into the water, icy even in the heat of summer, and managed to snag the handle of the bucket and haul it out of the water. Setting it carefully aside, where it wouldn't drip on anything vital, she made a minute inspection of the place from which E had vanished.

Tiny grasses were uprooted from a crack near where Elizabeth's left hand must have rested. Sand had been swept away on one side of the rocks bordering where the boat came into the island's embrace.

Elizabeth had not jumped or swum.

She'd been dragged off of Boar.

TWENTY-FOUR

Again Heath looked at her watch. Less than two minutes had passed since last time. Finally she held it up to her ear. Ticking. Time and its petty pace were making her crazy. At minute twenty-four, Anna slid back down the same rock she'd climbed out over.

"Bucket track," she said succinctly as she dropped the lobster pail to the ground. "I found where Elizabeth dumped the lobsters. There were skid marks in the loose gravel on the rock. A handful of plants were ripped from a crack as if she'd grabbed them to keep from being pulled into the water."

Heath felt her heart stop. When it started again each beat struck a blow to her rib cage from the inside. "Slipped and fell?" she croaked. "Drowned?" This had to be what dying felt like. Everything was going black but for Anna's face. Maybe Heath was falling. She couldn't tell.

"I don't think so," Anna said as she trotted toward the lift. "Wily is gone as well, and there were scrape marks on either side of the rock crack where she set the lobsters loose. A small boat is my guess."

"She took a boat?" Heath said stupidly. Her ears were hearing words. She could see Anna's lips moving, but her brain was having a hard time making sense of things. "With Wily?"

"A boat took her, and I hope they took Wily and didn't just kill him and dump the body," Anna said as she opened the lift gate. "Coming?"

Leah said saltwater could damage Dem Bones's electronics. Leah said, "You break it, you buy it." She meant it. Leah was not a fanciful genius. To her a cliché was as good as a contract.

To hell with Leah. Heath couldn't take the time to get out of the thing and into Robo-butt.

"Of course I'm coming."

Anna turned and walked toward the lift.

Heath followed, the crutches giving her balance.

Anna was piloting the small NPS runabout, a single-engine boat with a canvas shelter over the steering wheel. Heath relinquished pride in favor of speed and let herself lean heavily on Anna's shoulder as the metal and electronics lifted her feet and legs from the dock and over the gunwale one at an excruciating time. With a push and a whirr, she was seated on the plastic bench that ran along the port side of the runabout. Anna held up an orange life jacket. Heath wanted to tell her to drop the thing, get a move on. Knowing it would take longer to argue, and she wouldn't win, she clenched her teeth and held her arms out so Anna could thread the PFD onto her shoulders.

"I'll get the straps," she insisted as Anna started to do up the front of the life preserver. Anna looked at her for a second.

"I will," Heath promised.

Evidently Anna believed her. She slipped into her own PFD, leapt out of the boat, untied the lines, leapt back in, and finally, finally, thankyoubabyjesus started the boat.

Breathe, Heath told herself. Breathe. Air came in through her nostrils. She seemed unable to force it down past the concrete closing off her throat.

"Where are we looking?" Heath asked. Her voice was nearly a whine. There was nowhere to look. Just ocean and drowned land.

"We'll start where the boat met up with Elizabeth and Wily. From there we will fan out in arcs. I will be looking for boats. You will be looking for anything, no matter how small, on the water. Every thirty seconds you will blow that whistle around your neck and shout Elizabeth's name and Wily's. When we lose the light, we assume they've made land somewhere—the boat was small, rowboat sized—and we stop. I call Peter, and the rangers start searching the park."

Heath nodded. Words were backed up behind her teeth, but not one of them meant a thing.

Evening, and the encroaching fog, rapidly cooled the air. As Anna pushed the throttle open, the rush of chill wind against Heath's overheated face felt like an acid wash until her skin became acclimated to the new element.

Darkness oozed in from all directions, the ocean,

the edge of the sky, out from the islands, their skirts of rock turning black and ominous. Heath felt the world closing down, ending. "It's been hours, she's surely dead," she moaned. "I am such an idiot. I killed her."

Anna pulled the throttle to idle. Turning she stared down at Heath. "Do you want me to slap you?" she asked. "You know, the traditional cure for female hysterics?"

Heath blinked. Anna looked no softer than the granite, no warmer than the fog. Heath swallowed.

"Not necessary," she whispered.

"Good. Talk about something else. Tell me what Gwen's been up to. Anything. Watch and call and blow the whistle." Anna turned back to the control panel and pushed the throttle forward, not far enough to bring the boat up on plane, just above idle so voices could be heard over the engine noise and the wake wouldn't swamp anything that might be floating in the darkening waters.

Heath pulled the brass whistle Elizabeth had given her from under her shirt and life jacket. Sucking in as much air as her shriveled lungs would allow, she blew a long blast, then called weakly, "E! Elizabeth!"

"Good," Anna called over her shoulder. "Now talk to me for thirty seconds and do it again. Keep your eyes on the water."

Talk. About something else. Not the girl dying somewhere because Heath was a fool, a shit-for-brains fool. There was nothing else. Aunt Gwen, she thought, gone with John to Bangor. "Aunt Gwen delivered Ms. Zuckerberg's children." Heath said the words one by one like a not-so-bright schoolchild reciting a poem she didn't understand. When she'd done, she felt herself sinking, her eyes unfocused on the endless deadly expanse of water turning the color of ink. Under all that icy black was a child of light.

"And," Anna prodded. "Talk to me."

Slowly, Heath rose out of the depths and forced herself to think of anything else. "Ms. Zuckerberg isn't doing well. Heart weak. Transient ischemic attacks. She's lost the ability to talk, Gwen said."

"Good," Anna replied, as deaf to the words as Heath was. "Blow, call."

Heath blew the whistle and called Elizabeth's name. Her voice was stronger. The talking was keeping her mind off the horror that wanted to suffocate her as surely as the water had suffocated—

"Ms. Zuckerberg can't talk," Anna said sharply. "When she gets out of the hospital, is she going to her kids?"

"No," Heath said. She knew what Anna was doing. She knew she needed it, but, at the moment, she resented Anna for it. Despair pulled at her with an almost pleasurable force, the way a steep canyon would if she stood—rolled—too close to the edge. Part of her wanted to fall into the nothing that was offered. *Coward,* she cursed herself. Sucking in a lungful of breath, she forced herself to speak. "No. Her kids don't even—"

"Hush!" Anna said and cut the throttles to idle. "Listen."

Through the muffling of the coastal fog, now reaching halfway to Boar, Heath heard what sounded like a dog's yip. Then nothing. She blew a blast on the whistle. "E!" she screamed. "Elizabeth! Answer me!"

A thin, reedy bark pierced the fog.

"There," Anna pointed to where the mother-of-pearl of the sea met the pearl of the mists. A dark shape, trapezoidal, about the size of an old shipping trunk, touched the water. Then an orange smudge showed above it. The smudge moved suddenly. As they heard the splash of a body hitting the water, a girl screamed.

Anna shoved full throttle.

TWENTY-FIVE

Denise sat at her small neat table in a space between the living room and kitchen called "the dining room" on the lease. In front of her, on the shining black wood, was a spiral notebook of college ruled paper. The cover was bright red.

She laughed. The sound startled her. Covering the notebook with her forearm, she glanced around as if the laughter had emanated from another source.

She was alone.

No. That was the old Denise Castle. *She* had been creakingly, hauntingly alone. An open wound walking through a world of salt and thorns, she'd not dared let anyone close.

Being alone was not being lonely.

People liked to say that. People were full of shit. Alone echoed down hallways of the mind, shrieking with the shrill voice of icy wind through winter-bare branches. Denise had thought that she would be alone forever, but that was just a lie the world told her.

She wasn't even alone sitting by herself in her one-bedroom apartment in her single dining chair.

That was the first huge change. Massive. Making her not a ghost, but a guest, at the party. Better than a guest, family. For so many years she'd had to watch sisters and brothers, wives and husbands and children, being families while she was just herself, one hand clapping, a loose end, a fifth wheel. Families didn't even show her the courtesy of knowing they were the lucky ones. They fought and complained, disrespected each other, went years without speaking over a trifle, yelled at their children as if children were annoying pests they were forced to deal with.

Aborting babies.

Getting divorces.

Choosing not to be together on Christmas.

As if everybody had that choice, as if, for Denise, holidays hadn't been an inescapable nightmare, where, like a bird with no place to perch, she circled cold and alone high over lighted windows and laden tables, hoping that someone would invite her in, if even only for an evening. Then, if they did, it was worse because she knew she did not belong. They knew she did not belong. Once she was surrounded, all she wanted to do was get away, be by herself where the pain and shame wouldn't show.

Family cared enough to poke and nag, call too often and hug too tightly; they fell asleep with their head in another's lap, were carried to bed. They gossiped and worried and gave unwelcome advice. Family cared if you showed up for birthdays, chided if you forgot anniversaries, because your presence, mentally and physically, mattered. Family stimulated the psyche. Without it part of a person fell asleep, like a foot held in one position too long.

A part of Denise had gone to sleep like that. It was still alive, but didn't feel alive. It felt like concrete or asphalt. As time passed, the thought of trying to wake it, to suffer the miserable tingling of life returning, had become worse than knowing a portion of her being was as deadwood on a living tree.

Paulette had woken her without a twinge. Denise was fully alive for the first time in forever.

Then she'd killed a man.

Another huge new thing: life and death, both in her hands.

About life, she felt . . . That was it; that was the whole thing, she *felt*. Resentment, jealousy, spite: The stuff she'd been sustaining herself with for so long was not *feeling*. It was what replaced feeling, fake pain directed outward so the real pain would not eat the host alive. Becoming partially dead to keep the other parts from being flayed.

Life *felt* good. What did adults say when she was a kid? "You've got your whole life ahead of you." She'd thought they were idiots. Now she knew what it meant to have her whole life ahead of her.

About killing Kurt, she should feel something. Like sex, or reading *Siddhartha,* people were supposed to be changed by the experience, somehow different afterward. Killing another human being should be like that. One day she was Denise Castle who had never

killed a person. The next she was Denise Castle who
had taken a human life in sweat and blood and a plastic shower curtain with yellow fishes on it. Those two
Denises should be different, but they weren't. Sex and
Siddhartha had been like that for her as well. Not as
big a deal as advertised.

For a moment she marveled at the things that had
changed in the past week. Denise Castle: alive, feeling,
killer, family woman.

Almost a family woman. That would come, she decided.

Alone and not alone, she returned to her notebook
and her list, items that had to be checked off before
the whole life she had ahead of her could officially
commence.

Kill Kurt (Denise)
Sell Land (Paulette)
Quit NPS (retirement pension) (D)
Find out about "Legacy" (if it exists) (P)
Car, car seat, etc.
Give landlord notice
Arrange for family—Mt. Desert Hospital
(D&P)
Leave MA for GA or SC or NC (D&P&O)
Rent (D&P&O)
Buy (D&P&O)

"Kill Kurt" was checked off.

"Sell Land" had a tentative pencil mark next to it.
Kurt's house was worthless, but the land was not. The

land was paid off; Kurt's parents were dead. He had no brothers and sisters, and no children. Paulette said it was to pass to her on his death. Ownership wasn't an issue. Denise figured Paulette could get around four or five hundred thousand for the place. They should take less if it would move the property more quickly. Timing was important.

They would skip the balancing act of selling and moving. There was no way to know if it would sell in a week or six months. Banks had gotten paranoid after the big savings-and-loan scandals, but given location, location, location, Denise guessed it would move fast. They'd have to find a way to do the paperwork from out of state. By the time it was all settled, they had to be long gone.

The land sale would mean a big infusion of cash, which was good. Denise had about a hundred thousand of her own in investments, and her pension should come to around forty thousand a year, less everything. Maybe a net of thirty. They had enough.

Again she bent over the list.

Between "Sell Land" and "Quit NPS" she penciled in in tiny letters "Remove Obstacle." Not that she'd forget to take care of that particular problem. Denise had an excellent memory—or had until her nerves started going bad. Still, the lists weren't a memory aid; she made lists so she could check things off, have the satisfaction of seeing in black and white what she had accomplished.

"Obstacle" was the second most complex item on the list.

Changing from a pencil to a pen, she underlined it in ink. Denise had hoped she could erase it as unnecessary. That hope was growing slim to nonexistent. There was no doubt in Denise's mind that Anna Pigeon would remember who the Denise in the photograph reminded her of. Those kinds of things tickled at the brain until they were solved. Anna would remember it was Paulette. Given what a nuisance the pigeon was, she would put two and two together and get Murder. If they could move the project along quickly, Anna would only have to be put off for a couple of days, three at most.

Denise overwrote the underlined word in ink. To the side, in parentheses, she wrote "triazolam." Google said triazolam was common enough. As a nurse, Paulette would be able to lay her hands on a few tabs at the hospital. Needed or not, it was important to have the drug option.

For a moment Denise stared at the wall, eyes unfocused.

"Family" was next on her list, the most difficult of all the tasks. She and her sister would be getting a family. Denise smiled. When she was a kid, people would say of a pregnant woman, "She's in a family way." There was something lovely about that. Denise and Paulette were going to be in a family way.

It was poetic justice that lovely fertile Lily was going to be their accomplice.

Lily took ergotamine for her migraines. Denise had Googled the side effects.

God, but Denise loved Google.

TWENTY-SIX

The surface of the sea had embraced the night. Foam and tendrils of mist sketched the waves with iridescence. There was no horizon; the line between water, earth, and air had been erased by the fog. As the boat leapt up onto plane, Heath, in her electronic bones, was thrown backward. Nothing looked real or solid, yet the hull of the boat slammed into the Atlantic as hard as if it traveled a surface of packed dirt. For a few heartbeats, half lying along the plastic bench, Heath thought she was falling, not just to onto the bench but out of the boat, into the sky or the sea.

Since fate or bad luck had decreed Heath had to have one part of her body that refused to work and play well with the others, she was glad it was her legs. Losing her wits—even for a few moments—scared her a whole hell of a lot more than not being able to run and jump.

Sudden silence snatched her mind back into the boat. Anna had shut the engine down. Sucking the quiet into her lungs and mind, Heath struggled to right herself, ears tuned to the sound of the yip, Wily's yip. The happiest sound in the world. Second happiest.

"Blow your whistle," Anna said. Her voice was steady, familiar; it poured into Heath's ears like a homing signal.

The whistle was clutched so tightly in Heath's hand it felt hot when she put it between her mist-chilled lips. She blew two short sharp blasts.

"Elizabeth!" Anna yelled. "E!"

A litany of prayers babbled through Heath's brain: Please God let me find her, please God, let her be okay, please God, please, please, please.

The only sound was the lapping of the waves against the hull like a beast lapping at the blood of its prey. Again Heath had the sensation of falling, but this time it had nothing to do with vertigo. The place she was tumbling into was where the mothers of dead children fell. It had no bottom and no way out.

"Wily!" Anna called. She turned on a spotlight mounted on the gunwale next to the steering wheel. The beacon lanced out, an impotent light-sword. In the fog and dusk it hid as much as it illuminated, the light catching particles of water and refracting back.

A tiny scrap of orange flared for an instant between the glazed obsidian of the water and the gray blanket of fog. "There!" Heath cried, pointing. "Move the light back. There!" A bit of orange flickered in, then out, of vision as the swells moved up and down. "Keep the light on it!" Heath shouted.

Anna didn't reply. Leaving the light where it was, she pushed the throttle gently forward and nosed the boat in the direction Heath was pointing, following the long bobbing finger from the floodlight.

The ocean heaved another great sigh, and the scrap came into sight fifty yards ahead and to the right. "One o'clock," Heath shouted.

"I see it," Anna replied.

Unfortunately, Heath did, too. Every cell in her body was straining toward that orange scrap. The apparition stayed in view a moment longer this time. Not a lovely child in a life jacket. A monster. Short truncated arms poked through holes too big for them. A misshapen skull was sunk into the body of the flotation device. It looked as if the thing were covered in rotting seaweed.

Heath opened her mouth to scream.

Anna beat her to it. "Wily!" she shouted again.

"Over here," came a faint reply.

"What the . . ." Heath's mind cleared. Wily, the dog, was in the life jacket. For an LSD moment, Heath thought Wily had called out, "Over here." Elizabeth! E was invisible in the dark water, but she must be swimming next to him. Alive.

"Coming! Hang on," Heath yelled as she pushed the button to lift herself into a standing position. At the faint whirr of the machinery Anna shot her such a repressive look she immediately whirred her butt back down onto the bench.

Anna had the spotlight on the dog in the life jacket. Heath could see the sleek head of Elizabeth beside Wily, her face a pale oval against the black water. At idle, Anna eased the boat toward them.

Heath's mental litany turned from "Please, please,

please" to "Thank you, thank you, thank you," the two fundamental prayers of mankind.

As they neared, Anna ordered Heath to throw Elizabeth a life jacket. Heath pulled off her own and threw it hard in her daughter's direction. Her arms were stronger than they'd ever been, and, thanks to wheelchair basketball, her aim was good.

Elizabeth clung to the life jacket with one hand and to Wily's scruff with the other, her head barely above water. Anna picked Wily out of the water first and deposited him at Heath's feet with a slosh of cold seawater. Never had he looked so much like Wile E. Coyote as he did at that moment, water running from his ears and muzzle, orange vest hanging on his bony shoulders.

E was next, fished out and dumped on the deck with little more ceremony than Wily had received. The light was going fast, and Heath could not tell if Elizabeth or the dog was bloody or bruised.

"What happened? Are you hurt? We've been looking for hours." Questions and comments poured out of Heath so rapidly there was no time for answers. She knew it but could not help herself. Connection to her child demanded it of her, and, denied the luxury of grabbing the girl and holding her so tightly she could never escape again, words had to suffice. "Why is Wily wearing the life preserver!" she demanded as she ran out of breath.

Into the silence that followed, E said calmly, "He can't swim, Mom."

"He can swim," Anna stated flatly.

"Oh, yeah, right, *dog-paddle*," E retorted.

Wily shook, spattering them with water and making the orange vest flap around his skinny form.

Elizabeth laughed.

How could she be so goddamned calm! Heath was shaking so badly she could hear her legs rattling in their shells. Her chest muscles contracted until drawing breath was nearly impossible, and she could feel her heart pounding so hard it shook her clothes.

"How did you get out here?" Anna demanded.

"A boat took me," E said.

Heath could almost hear the "Duh!" in her voice.

"Kidnapping is a federal offense," Anna said as she snatched the radio mike from its metal holder.

"No!" E cried. "Don't go all law enforcement on me. A friend took me on a boat ride. A nice person."

Anna stopped and stared hard at Elizabeth in the growing gloom. "And you forgot you weren't Jesus Christ and decided to walk home?" she asked.

"My friend wanted to take me back, but I insisted. When we heard you calling and I realized how long we'd been gone, I was afraid you'd arrest . . ."

Silence followed that.

"Why would I arrest a nice friend?" Anna asked.

A person. A friend. Heath could guess why this mysterious individual was genderless. The friend was a boy. Heath had been asking herself what would make a wonderful, considerate child like Elizabeth so forgetful that she would terrify her mother. A boy. A nice boy. A boy/friend. God was good. She was going to shackle E to the iron stair railing in the tower and feed her nothing but bread and water until she was forty years old.

For another moment, Anna just looked at E and said nothing. Elizabeth was hugging her arms, shivering. Anna opened the tiny door under the hull, pulled out a blanket that looked as if it was made of tinfoil, then tossed it to E. "We'll sort this out later. Wrap up. Both you and Wily." She shot Wily a hard look. "You should have known better," she said to the dog.

With that, Anna pushed the throttle to full and turned the boat back toward Boar Island.

Both Wily and E had bathed and toweled off. Anna built a small fire in the great hearth in the outer room skirting the tower. The evening was mild, but girl and dog had gotten thoroughly chilled. Anna also made tea. Elizabeth wrinkled her nose, then sighed. "Hot drinks, I know, the wilderness cure-all. Does Wily have to drink tea, too?"

Neither Heath nor Anna answered. Heath was seated in Robo-butt, her knees almost touching the overstuffed chair where her daughter was curled up. Elizabeth's feet peeked out from beneath a hand-knitted throw of purple and green. In T-shirt and sweatpants, her hair damp from the bath, and no makeup, she looked like a little girl. A delightful fact Heath knew better than to share aloud.

Sprawled in front of the hearth, Wily looked old and tired, his fur ragged and spiked with damp, his pointed ears at half-mast. Elizabeth might have deserved a ducking in icy water for being so thoughtless, but Wily didn't. The cold was hard on his old bones.

"Enough," she said to her daughter. "Tell us every single thing from the beginning of time."

"Billions and billions of years ago this was a vast inland sea," Elizabeth droned in a mockery of PBS specials.

"Don't," Heath warned. She wanted to be angry. It was spoiled by the fact that she had not heard such sauciness from Elizabeth since before the razor-in-the-tub incident. That, and the fact her daughter was alive and in one piece.

"Just tell it," Anna said quietly.

"Aunt Gwen was going to boil some lobsters alive," E said. Heath saw the wince in Anna's gaze at the same moment it clutched her own chest.

"I freaked," E apologized.

Heath had come to the conclusion it was she and Aunt Gwen who needed to apologize.

"I mean boiling alive, how rotten is that? So Wily and I took the lobsters in the bucket and went over to the far side of the island to turn them loose. We'd got ourselves down to the water and were dumping the lobsters into the ocean when, whoosh! This little rowboat rushes in between the rocks and almost smacks my feet." She laughed, and then shared the memory that brought the laughter. "I dumped the lobsters right in the boat and they started sliding all around."

She sobered. "It wasn't funny then, really, only now. What with the cyber stuff and everything, I got scared.

Anyway. We became friends and I went for a boat ride, me and Wily."

"That's it?" Heath asked carefully. "You went for a ride with a friend?"

"I promised I wouldn't tell anybody," Elizabeth said. Anna snorted.

Heath waited. E could occasionally keep secrets from her and Gwen, but never Anna.

"Wouldn't tell anybody what?" Anna asked innocently.

"You know, about him, and stuff." E had a pleading note in her voice. Anna ignored it.

"If there is something about him so dangerous that he made you promise not to divulge it to your mother, I think you'd better divulge it to your mother. And me," Anna said flatly.

"Not dangerous to me," E said. "Just him. He—oh God, I've told you he's a boy!" she almost wailed.

"Twice," Anna said. "Believe it or not, given we had a fifty-fifty chance of getting it right, we got that part right. We're betting a cute boy."

Elizabeth smiled and looked down.

"Now we know we got that part right," Anna said.

Heath said nothing. Anna was much better at this sort of thing than she was.

"So," Anna said. "You're on the back of Boar, down by the water, emancipating crustaceans, and a cute boy in a rowboat floods in. Merriment ensues, and you and Wily go for a ride."

"Yes," Elizabeth admitted.

"Being as he was adorable, and you're adorable, and everything is adorable, you become 'friends' and lose track of time," Anna said.

"I guess," E said.

"Then, when he realizes grown-ups are about to ruin this idyll, he chucks you and your poor old dog into the freezing ocean so he can save his sorry ass," Anna said.

"It wasn't like that," E protested. "I was the one who wanted to do it. To help."

"And he needed help because . . ." Anna said.

E's face took on a mulish cast. She studied her fingers. Wily licked his paw. Anna stared at E. Heath tried to fit the information E had shared into a coherent picture.

"I didn't hear a boat engine," Anna said. "And I didn't hear oars in oarlocks or paddles on the gunwale. So your new pal—who cannot be named—muffles his oars? Fishy."

Studying fingers, licking paws, staring into flames, thinking.

"You know I'll find out who fishy boy is," Anna threatened.

E said nothing.

Gradually it became clear that the boy's identity was one secret E was going to keep. At least for now. Heath quashed the urge to bargain or plead. E's new "friend" had not killed or molested her, and when she asked, he'd let her go free. That, and the fact that Elizabeth was happy, allowed Heath to keep her peace. In a bizarre way she was pleased that Elizabeth refused to divulge the boy's—and of course it had to be a boy—

name. It showed backbone, honor, a sense of being in control of her own world that the Internet creep had stolen from her.

Quiet ticked by to the comforting sound of Wily working the salt from between the toes of his right paw with his tongue.

"Hey," Anna said finally. "On a lighter note, your stalker is here in Maine and wants to meet you."

Elizabeth toppled over on her side and pulled the afghan over her head.

TWENTY-SEVEN

Denise sat cross-legged on her bed. In front of her was a silver laptop. On the screen was a full-color fish-eye view of the nursery in Peter Barnes's home. Baby Olivia slept upstairs across the hall from Peter's room. Peter and *Lily's* room, she reminded herself. Where they slept on the bed that Denise had bought secondhand and refinished with such care.

Lit by the light of a Blue Fairy lamp, Olivia slept in a pink bundle. They'd let the room get too warm, Denise noticed with irritation. The baby was kicking her tiny feet, trying to get free of the rose-colored burrito *Lily* had thought suitable for swaddling. Why didn't the woman just stick Olivia in a papoose pack and lace it up tight?

It had been a week or more since Denise had allowed herself this particular torture. Paulette had taken her mind in other, more satisfactory directions. Directions that didn't all lead to a dead end. She'd missed watching Olivia. In a way, she was more a mother to the baby than Lily was. A couple of days after the baby was born, Lily had one of her migraines and checked herself back into the hospital. When she got out, though, of course Lily didn't have to work for a living; she went back to her "activities."

Not Denise. Denise had always been there.

The day Olivia was brought home, Denise stuck a Nice Lady No Bad Feelings face on the front of her skull and trotted right over to her old home, where Peter kept his family. In a beautifully wrapped box was an expensive fragile figurine of a guardian angel.

A smile pasted so tightly to her face that her lips stuck to her teeth, Denise told Lily it was to watch over the baby.

Nice, good, little Lily had put it on a table overlooking the baby's crib, right where the tiny camera hidden in the angel's armload of brightly painted flowers would capture the entire room.

Denise had invested in several snazzy little wireless cameras. This was the only one she'd planted in Peter's house, but it wasn't the limit of her knowledge of the Barnes family.

Before Paulette, when Denise had been scarcely more than a festering sore, barely able to keep her mind from pouring out through her eyes like molten lava, she'd kept herself alive by spying on the happy couple, then, when baby made three, the happy family.

She knew Lily's routine better than Peter did. Maybe better than Lily herself did. She knew when the baby napped and how often she was changed, when she was fed and what. She knew dear Lily was dry as an

Arizona gully in August and never produced a drop of milk from her pert little tits to feed her child. Denise knew what kind of formula she used and where she kept it.

After he'd summarily thrown Denise out into the cold, thinking himself oh so clever, Peter had changed all the locks. He was too stupid to remember the dog door. Denise had been in that house dozens of times over the past three years. She knew Lily preferred Tampax tampons, the kind that looked like pink bullets; she knew when Lily's period was and how many days it lasted. She knew Lily suffered from migraines and what she took for them. She'd discovered Peter took Cialis. That had been a good day when she'd found those in his medicine cabinet. He also suffered from periodic constipation and kept *Playboy* magazines in the back of his closet.

During those awful times, all Denise thought about was revenge, years fantasizing about how she would get justice. As an employee of the American justice system, she'd thought justice was catching and punishing the bad guys. She had been wrong. What American law enforcement did was not justice, it was revenge, and revenge was for people who were helpless to obtain justice.

Paulette had taught her that.

Paulette coming into her life was the first justice Denise had ever experienced. Justice wasn't about the bad guy. It was about the victim. Justice made what was wrong right again. Justice made the victim whole. Justice put the jewelry back in the jewelry box, the car back in the rightful owner's garage. Justice was restoration. When Paulette came, Denise's lost soul was restored to her. That was justice.

Understanding this changed Denise's worldview. Revenge was not necessary—not even desirable—if justice could be had.

However, her years spying on Peter Barnes's family weren't wasted. It was serendipity—or fate, kismet—that she'd done this groundwork. At the time, she'd spied and pried because she couldn't help herself. Or so she'd thought. Some part of her brain must have realized that this information would become important to the planning of the whole life she had ahead of her now.

Not revenge; justice.

"Good night, baby girl," Denise said, and closed the laptop's cover.

She checked her watch. It was nearly three A.M. Time to leave to meet with her sister. Given how fast things were moving, and how small Acadia National Park was, meeting in the flesh, even in the dark of night in the woods, was risky, but after Denise had gotten off work she found a note Paulette had left in her mailbox; their cell phones neither texted nor took voice messages.

The note read *I have to see you. Please come tonight. We have to . . .* The last words were scribbled out.

Clutching the note, Denise feared she would have a heart attack in the foyer. Paulette had waltzed right up to the boxes in Denise's apartment building, in broad daylight, and popped a motherloving note, with her handwriting on it and, undoubtedly, slathered with fingerprints matching those at the crime scene, into Denise Castle, Law Enforcement Ranger and Identical Twin's mailbox.

Had Denise been a dog, she would have been mad enough to froth at the mouth. Thank God Paulette hadn't signed the thing. Might as well just add *P.S. We killed the prick. Love, the Bobbsey Twins.*

If anyone saw Paulette slip the note into her mailbox, Denise hoped they thought nothing of it. It had been with two bills and a flyer for used tires. Had Paulette come after the mailman, or had the mailman opened the box to put in the letters, seen the note, and read it?

"Doesn't matter," Denise said aloud. By the time the shit hit the fan, Paulette would be gone. One battered widow, no family, no friends, vanishes. A nonevent.

Denise changed out of her old pajamas. The new ones she'd ordered for her and her sister had arrived, but she didn't want to wear them until she and Paulette could wear them together.

Clad in dark clothes, she slipped quietly down the stairs and into her Miata. As on the night she'd disposed of Kurt, she would take the runabout to Otter Cove, then hike the short way overland. Covering the same ground more than once made her uneasy, but not as uneasy as taking the road. The inky shadow of the boathouse by the government dock on Somes was the only place she felt safe parking the Miata. Night diving was known to be her habit. If by chance the car was seen, no one would remark it there.

The NPS was understaffed and, at present, underfunded. Two weeks ago this would have pissed Denise off. Now park poverty was her friend. Acadia couldn't afford twenty-four-hour ranger coverage. On Friday and Saturday nights the last shift ended at midnight, on weeknights at ten P.M. Even Eager Artie would be abed by three A.M.

The Miata snugged into darkness by the boathouse, Denise rowed the runabout out a hundred yards. Probably an unnecessary precaution, but just because she was paranoid didn't mean somebody wasn't watching her. This was the downside of breaking the law—even when the law needed to be broken. Denise did not have a guilty conscience. In doing away with Duffy, she'd done the world a good turn, but it was like after she'd finished reading a mystery story. Once she knew exactly who, where, how, and when the crime was committed, it seemed it would be obvious to a two-year-old. To soothe her nerves she had to keep reminding herself that most people weren't all that bright. Better yet, most people didn't give a flying fuck unless it was a cop killed, or somebody they could use to make political hay.

Having shipped the oars, Denise fired up the engine and, at slightly better than idle, motored slowly down the sound. Air and water temperatures had reached sufficient equilibrium that the fog was shredding into thin feathers along the coast, eerie fingers given life by the light of a waning moon.

Boat firm beneath her, cool, fresh sea air in her lungs, Denise felt the iron band that Paulette's hand-delivered note had locked around her lungs loosen sufficiently to let her breathe deeply.

Please come tonight. We have to . . . Then the tangle of ink lines crossing out whatever it was Paulette decided they had to do. What could she have thought of that Denise hadn't? A few days before, Denise would have answered, "Nothing." The note and a few other things Paulette had done lately led her to believe identical twins weren't identical, as in *exactly* the same.

Denise shoved that thought aside. She and her twin were two sides of the same coin, peas in a pod, identical DNA. In everything that mattered there wasn't a particle of difference between them. She patted the front pocket of her black jeans where she had the list she'd made. Tonight they should be able to check off the meds and maybe the house. Paulette had had time to contact a Realtor, as well as two entire shifts to pinch the drugs.

Calmed by the eternal strength of the Atlantic surrounding her, Denise decided she wouldn't say anything about the hand-delivered note. Too many years in law enforcement had made her hypervigilant. That was all. Paulette, an infant-care nurse, couldn't be expected to see threats lurking behind every set of eyes. Denise loved that about her sister. Or she would, once there weren't threats lurking behind every set of eyes.

Denise expertly docked the runabout out of sight between two rocks, then followed the narrow beam of her tiny flashlight over the familiar ground between Otter and the old shed that Paulette had made into a nursery and was now their sanctuary from the world.

No light showed under the door. Clicking off her flashlight, Denise stepped beneath the roof overhang and put her ear against the wood of the door. Not a sound. Tapping softly, she whispered, "Paulette?" No answer.

Turning, Denise stared toward dead Kurt's shack. The back porch light was a blazing beacon through the trees. Paulette got off work at three A.M. She should have beat Denise to the nursery. Why was she in that rotting tomb of a house instead of in their secret place?

Paulette had been arrested for stealing drugs.

She'd collapsed of a heart attack.

Been run down by an SUV full of drunken tourists.

Panic drowning caution, Denise sprinted to where the porch hung precariously on the rear of the house. She leapt up the two steps, then stopped. The police might be inside, rangers, the sheriff, anybody. Denise stepped softly to the door. The knob turned easily. With three fingers, she pushed the door open a crack so she could see inside.

Paulette was sitting in a straight-backed chair at the small, beat-up kitchen table. Overprocessed blond hair was caught back in a purple scrunchie. She'd chewed off all of her lipstick. In pink scrubs, figured with Pooh-bears and daisies, she looked very young and helpless. A cup of coffee was between her hands. She was gazing into it as if the dregs would foretell her future.

"Hey," Denise said.

With a shriek, Paulette jumped to her feet. The mug toppled. Coffee poured over the edge of the table, dripping onto the dirty linoleum floor.

"God, but you scared me half to death," Paulette said with a shaky laugh. Before Denise had time to do more than blink, her sister had thrown herself into her arms and was hugging her with such force Denise could hardly move.

A rush of sensation overwhelmed her. Since Peter, three and more years ago, no one had touched her except strangers shaking her hand, or drunks bumping into her on their way to the men's room at the Acadian.

Babies needed to be touched. She'd read that. If they weren't touched they could fail to thrive, outright die.

Maybe adults were no different. Touch was life.

"Sorry I scared you," Denise apologized, all thought of the ill-considered note gone from her mind.

Paulette stepped away to grab a roll of paper towels off the counter. Ripping off half a dozen, she let them flutter to the floor, then used her foot to push them around, sopping up the coffee. The towels didn't get it all. What was left mingled with the yuck on the floor.

Perhaps not all the squalor had been Kurt's doing, Denise thought uneasily.

Didn't matter. They weren't going to be here much longer.

"Why didn't you wait in the nursery?" Denise asked as Paulette dropped the towels on top of a bunch of other trash in an open-topped can near the refrigerator.

"Oh, I don't know," Paulette said vaguely. "I wanted a cup of coffee. I thought this would be more comfortable."

The sordid kitchen in the murder house more comfortable? More comfortable than the nursery, with its art and painted furniture and promise of things to come?

Denise let it go, just like she'd let the leaving of the note in her box go. "Why did you need to see me?" she asked.

Paulette pinched up a packet of Nescafé, shook it, ripped off the top, and dumped the contents into a plastic mug. Taking the kettle from the stove, she offered, "Coffee?"

Instant.

"I'm good," Denise said, and waited. Her nerves weren't in shape for waiting, not in the wee hours of the morning in a trailer-trash kitchen. Her knee began bouncing, her heel never quite hitting the floor.

Paulette sat down across from her and repeated her gazing-into-the-cup routine. The spill on the scarred vinyl tabletop wasn't quite dry. Denise watched a tiny finger of it being absorbed into the cuff of the pink long-sleeved T-shirt Paulette wore under her scrubs.

"Did you have trouble getting the triazolam?" Denise asked, forcing an end to what was becoming an awkward silence.

Paulette hung her head. "I didn't get it," she murmured.

"Why the hell not?" Denise demanded, shocking herself with the outburst.

Paulette reached into the pocket of her scrubs and pulled out a handful of hypodermics with capped needles, each in its sanitary packet. "I got the needles," she offered pitifully.

Afraid to speak lest she batter her twin with abuse a second time, Denise stared at the empty hypodermic needles and nodded slowly. When she felt she could speak normally, she asked, more gently, "Did you put the house on the market?"

Paulette shook her head.

Gentleness vaporized.

Paulette hadn't done anything. Nothing. Anger geysered up Denise's throat, hot and sulfurous as the fumes of hell. Given that Denise had shot Paulette's husband up close and personal three times, pilfering a few pills didn't seem like a big deal. Denise tried to force the bile down, calm herself. Pilfering a few pills, no big deal; Paulette would see it that way after Denise explained it.

The problem was Denise shouldn't have to explain it.

How could Paulette be sitting like a lump of raw dough in this filthy kitchen and not see how important this stuff was? Crucial.

Paulette, Denise reminded herself, was the gentle aspect of them. Of course she wasn't as capable of stealing or killing as Denise was. But not to put the property on the market? How much nerve did it take to call a Realtor?

Probably Paulette was afraid it wouldn't sell, afraid of being disappointed. Denise understood that. Better to pretend you don't hope than be made to look a fool when you don't get.

Denise decided that was all there was to it. She knew Paulette's lack of faith in their *themness* would have annoyed her, had it been possible for her to be annoyed with Paulette, genuinely annoyed, not just bitchy because her nerves were bad.

"I started on our legacy thing," Paulette said with a

brightness Denise knew was false, and a smile that had been perfected to ward off the blows of her ham-handed hubby. Almost as if Paulette were afraid of Denise's displeasure.

Would that be bad? Denise wondered. Or good? Good, Denise decided. It showed Paulette cared, loved her.

"I used those old newspaper ads and sent postcards to the two PO boxes, the one listed in the original ad and the one listed four years later in that ad I showed you. Of course, even that was nearly a year old, but it could be something. It could be our mother," Paulette said, looking hopeful.

"Whoever put the ads in asking for twin girls separated at birth might have died or moved on," Denise said repressively. "More likely, good old Mom has decided nothing has changed, and she doesn't want us any more now than when she decided to chuck us out like so much garbage." Denise didn't think of the person who'd given them birth as "their" mother, just "the" mother.

Paulette twitched as if Denise had struck her. Unaccountably it made Denise angry. Guilt should have been what she felt, but she didn't. The cringing made her mad. "Please don't tell me you put this house as your return address," she growled.

"I put General Delivery like you told me," Paulette said softly, not looking up from her coffee. "Tomorrow I'll check. We could have got replies by then."

It was possible, Denise thought. Not probable, but possible. The legacy thing was just gravy, at any rate.

They had enough. Counting on anybody or anything one couldn't control oneself was never a wise thing. Denise sighed, reined in her fraying nerves. Folding hands sticky with cold coffee from the tabletop one inside the other on her lap where they wouldn't betray her emotional turmoil, she said, "That's good. That's real good, Paulette. I'm sorry I got . . . Things are hard right now. Why did you drop the note by my apartment? What did you need to see me about?"

For a long moment Paulette said nothing. Denise could hear the wind soughing through the pines and imagined she could hear the surf breaking. Peaceful sounds, sounds she'd gone to sleep to for many years. This night they rasped over her eardrums like sandpaper over a sunburn.

"We have to stop," Paulette finally said, in such a tiny voice Denise had to lean halfway across the table to hear it, then couldn't believe it. A total non sequitur. Nausea washed through her. The overhead light, in its inverted bowl of dead flies, dimmed, then grew bright again.

Too weird.

Not a sudden onset of the flu or a brownout. Nerves. Putting both palms on the table to steady herself, Denise managed to say, "Stop what?"

"Oh, honey, everything. Everything!" Tears welled up in Paulette's eyes and spilled over her lids, rolling fat and oily down her cheeks. In their wake were gray trails of mascara.

Desperately, Denise reached across the little table and took both her sister's hands. "No!" she cried, not knowing what she was saying no to precisely, but aware that she needed to stop whatever tide was washing her sister away from her. Though the tide was not of water, not of physical stuff, she held just as tightly as if Paulette were caught in an undertow. Almost, Denise could see her growing smaller and smaller as the distance swallowed her. "No!" Denise gasped.

"I love working with the babies. I can't do anything else," Paulette sobbed, her tears so copious they dripped from her jaw, plopping onto Denise's forearms. "If anybody at the hospital thought I was even thinking about stealing drugs I would lose my job."

"What difference does that make?" Denise nearly shouted. The room was spinning around them. She had to hold tight lest she and her sister be flung away from the table by the centrifugal force. "We're leaving. We're going to get another house in another town and you can get another job. We've been over it and over it, Paulette. We're going to have a life, be a family."

"If we leave Acadia—you quit your job and I quit mine—and we sell and we move, they will know!" Paulette said brokenly. "That woman, that ranger lady—I was out shopping this morning and I came home and she was here! Right here at this house. She was coming out from the back where the nursery is. First she sees that picture where you look like me, then she comes here and sees the nursery and God knows what else. Why would she be snooping around here unless she thinks I killed Kurt or she thinks we are related? This isn't even her job. She's a park ranger. She knows we are doing things. We have to stop, just stop everything, don't do anything, just be quiet and normal and do our work and not be noticed. Maybe later . . ."

"Maybe the pigeon knows something, but that doesn't mean we stop. We stop her. That's all. I have a plan. We just distract her for a couple of days. No big deal. We just give her something else to think about, then we get our ducks in a row quick as anything, and we're done. No muss, no fuss," Denise pleaded.

Denise wanted to shake Paulette until her teeth rattled. How could she not realize there wouldn't be a later? They couldn't afford a maybe. This was their one shot; this was the brass ring, the lottery, the planets in alignment. It was a once-in-a-lifetime thing. And it had to be accomplished before Anna Pigeon could put two and two together and get twins.

How could Paulette be so stupid that she didn't get that?

All at once Denise understood why Kurt Duffy slapped his wife around.

TWENTY-EIGHT

nna sat with Wily, Gwen, and Heath on the stone apron overlooking the sea. The sky was scattered with a herd of ephemeral sheep, as small and puffy and regular as if a child had drawn them. The sea was impossibly blue, navy in the shallow troughs and teal where the water thinned at the crests of the waves. This far north, the afternoons slipped into evening with exquisite slowness, the sunlight, rich as wild honey, striking diamonds from both the ocean and the granite.

Anna found it hard to believe that people bothered to torment and injure one another when there were so many better ways of spending one's time. Given the choice of a moment such as this or trolling the Internet, or shooting a hairy naked man, why would anyone choose the troll or the hairy man?

"Have you recovered from E's going AWOL?" Anna asked.

Heath sipped her bourbon. "Like it never happened," she said.

"She's lying," Gwen said mildly. Gwen was fortified with a glass of white wine, her feet resting on the rounded footrest of a classic Adirondack deck chair. "After much consultation, she has decided to pretend it is okay. I have not. In my day—and I very much think today is still my day, thank you very much—boys come to the door and meet the family."

"The boy remains a state secret?" Anna asked. "Do we even know for sure it is a boy?"

"Of course it's a boy," Gwen said. "Don't be ridiculous."

Anna smiled. Of course it was a boy.

"I wanted to forbid E ever to see the little bastard again," Heath said. "But I actually think she would have disobeyed. Yesterday E asked to 'go out' for a while. Like there was a mall nearby. Jesus. I managed to say yes without spitting."

"You get points for that," Anna said.

"Fortunately I was gone," Gwen said. "I think I should have spit."

"You were in Bangor with the owner of the island?" Anna asked to be polite.

"Yes. Christine has had several heart attacks. This last was accompanied by another stroke. She can't speak, and her left side is completely paralyzed. It's hard to see her so agitated. She fell trying to get out of bed. Dez said she had scribbled something about wanting to see her children."

"Elizabeth came back from her second 'date,' " Gwen said. "You were probably right to let her go."

"Right. Because she came back when she said she

would, I should get Mother of the Year," Heath said. "If she hadn't . . ."

Heath didn't finish that thought. She didn't need to.

Maternal fear, so palpable Anna could almost see it, curled like fog around the wheels of Heath's wheelchair. "E didn't let any interesting information slip?" Anna asked, hoping to distract her friend from the nightmare possibilities.

"Nope. If she wasn't happier than I've seen her for a long time, I might consider thumbscrews," Heath said. "E is sticking with the basic 'nice friend' description of Boat Boy."

Anna would have liked to see Boat Boy behind bars, if for no other reason than that he took her goddaughter out in a boat that had but a single personal flotation device, muffled his oars, and refused to meet the parents for fear of being arrested.

"If I was trawling for a sixteen-year-old girl, a cute boy would be my bait of choice," Anna said.

"Don't think I haven't obsessed on that. And mentioned it to E about six hundred times. She insists that's not it. The child smirks and hums to herself," Heath said sourly. "If he's a pervert I will skin him with a dull Boy Scout knife, one square inch at a time, drench him with gasoline, and set him on fire." Abruptly Heath went silent.

"You two are scaring me," Gwen said mildly. "Talk about something joyful."

"Murder, then. Murder is always entertaining," Anna suggested.

"The murdered lobsterman—the second lobsterman

killed recently, right? The first was shot with a rifle for stealing . . . poaching?" Heath asked.

"There's nothing to indicate the two killings are related—" Anna began.

"Smells fishy to me," Heath said.

"John says the two incidents have nothing to do with each other," Gwen said. Both Heath and Anna looked at her.

"And John knows this why?" Anna asked.

"It turns out—and this just breaks my heart—that the first lobsterman, the one shot because he and his son were suspected of robbing traps, was Will Whitman, John's son," Gwen said.

"God," Heath groaned. Her compassion ground deep. Anna knew she was thinking of losing Elizabeth. Anna could imagine, if only intellectually, what it must be like to lose a child, like losing a particularly magical cat or a dog one had bonded with. Maybe worse.

"John says his son is innocent, for what it's worth," Gwen added. "His grandson is still missing, trying to clear his father's name and keep himself out of the line of fire, I guess."

"John is probably right about Will Whitman's and Kurt Duffy's deaths being unrelated. Whoever killed this guy Duffy appeared to be a little more personally involved than a man gunning down a poacher. Duffy was shot three times—twice through the shower curtain—"

"And, one assumes, other parts of his anatomy," Gwen said.

"With a small-caliber weapon," Anna finished.

"Then apparently smothered with the shower curtain. Since us 'acting' chiefs haven't much to keep us occupied, I cruised by the widow's house. It's not exactly park jurisdiction, but I thought I'd interview her just for the hell of it. Nobody answered the door. I walked around to see if Ms. Duffy was hanging out clothes or sunbathing.

"Talk about depressing. The yard is packed dirt with a broken swing set. The chain on one of the swings was banging against the metal pole in the wind. It was like a scene from Edgar Allan Poe, if Poe had been born in a trailer park in 1967."

"For whom the bell tolls," Heath said amiably. "Isn't the spouse the first suspect? An abused spouse in this case, wasn't she?"

"When all else fails, it's the wife," Anna said. "But I doubt that was the case this time. From the state the bedroom and the deceased were in, there was an all-out battle. Ms. Duffy doesn't seem to be the kind who could fight a sick puppy and win. What possesses a woman to marry a Kurt Duffy?" she wondered aloud. "Move into his hovel, cook his dinners, launder his sweaty fish-smelling undershorts?"

"As my father used to say, 'Perhaps Mr. Duffy has talents we are not privy to,'" Aunt Gwen said.

Anna grunted.

Heath struck a match to light her cigarette.

Elizabeth emerged from the house, "He's back," she announced.

From the sound of her voice, Anna knew it wasn't the boy with the boat.

"Read it out loud," Heath said to her daughter.

Elizabeth held the phone in front of her at eye level. "'You didn't show up you lousy pig-faced C asterisk asterisk T,'" she articulated carefully.

"You're kidding!" Heath exclaimed. "A filthy cyberstalker who balks at the C-word?"

"He also misspelled 'lousy.' L-O-W-Z-Y. Loh-zeee," she said in the tones of a demented Hollywood Chinaman. "Sheesh! Even in text-speak we have our pride."

Then she laughed.

Anna sighed. No matter how old a woman grew, there wasn't much a cute boy couldn't cure.

At least for a while.

Anna hoped Boat Boy wouldn't break E's heart. At sixteen heartbreak was a miserable thing. Age did nothing but make it worse. Hearts that didn't grow harder as the years passed acquired an ability to love that young people could only imagine.

The text didn't prove the boy with the muffled oars, and the fear of law enforcement, wasn't a monster. It did suggest that he was not the cybercreep. Unfortunately there was more than one kind of monster in the world.

Heath lit the cigarette before the match burned her fingers, breathed in a lungful of smoke, blew it out. "Our Fox River thug ruined the F-word forever. Now this toad is going to ruin all the other bad words."

"Pig-faced asterisk asterisk is my favorite so far," Elizabeth said.

Heath shot her a sideways look, squinting through

the smoke from her cigarette. "I think you're beginning to enjoy this," she said.

Anna heard the joy beneath the pretense. No one could miss how much happier Elizabeth was since her ersatz abduction, and E's happiness was Heath's happiness. "Anything else in the text?" Anna asked.

E's eyes tracked back to the cell phone. " 'Same place, same time, day after tomorrow or else.' 'Or else' is in all caps."

"Are you being stalked by a ten-year-old?" Heath growled. "What does 'else' mean?"

"I don't think I want to find out," Elizabeth said, her good humor gone, anxiety dragging down her cheeks.

Anna thought for a moment, her fingers absently ruffling the feathers of Wily's tail; he'd flopped down between Robo-butt and Anna's chair. Threats were tricky things. Most went unfulfilled. Most. However, if the stalker wanted to meet with E, it was not to do her a kindness. "Or else" could be nothing. It could also be an ugly bit of business.

It was tempting to think the stalker would be mollified by contacting his victim in the flesh. He would say what he needed to say, be heard if he needed to be heard. Anna suspected that more than one person who climbed into a clock tower with a repeating rifle did so because they felt they could not be seen, could not be heard, could not break through the indifference of the world—or the bureaucracy—any other way.

One might be tempted to believe that a meeting would cancel out the "or else." Not Anna. To stalk and bully with the intensity this creep had shown was to prove oneself beyond the pale of society. Now that he was demanding to move from the ether into the corporeal world, he went from a psychological threat to a physical threat.

Resources were limited. Jurisdictions, considering the crime was instigated in Colorado and conducted from the cloud, were a mess. Stalking was illegal, but cyberstalking? That had yet to be dealt with in any definitive way.

Information was limited. None of them had a clue as to who this was. It could be someone connected to E's past in the compound, someone connected with the kidnapper who had taken her and the other girls, an enemy of Heath's—or even Anna's—or a random psychopath. He might recognize them or not. They might recognize him or not.

"We need to set a trap," Anna said.

"Anything to end the suspense," Heath said.

"What can I do?" E asked.

"Nothing," Anna told her. "You're the bait."

TWENTY-NINE

Until Peter, the parks had been Denise's salvation. At thirteen she'd gotten drawn out of the bleak misery that was her life to become a junior ranger and never gone back. During college she worked as a summer seasonal. After graduation she got her permanent status as a GS-3 taking fees at the entrance booth. From there she'd moved on and up. Until Peter Barnes had stopped time.

Ranger Castle, that's who she'd been, who she'd respected, who she showed the world. Ranger Castle was the only persona available to her that she'd ever been able to stomach. Now she was Denise Castle, civilian: no green and gray, no flat-brimmed hat, no badge, no cordovan-colored leather belt or boots.

Denise had quit the NPS, stepped out of her life, away from the things that had once defined her, and it had been easy. So very, very, insultingly easy. It pissed Denise off just remembering it. During the drive to headquarters to start the paperwork for her retirement, she'd wasted brain energy trying to think of plausible answers to the inevitable "Why so sudden? Why now? We'll need at least two months' notice. Who can take your place? We'll need time to hire a replacement. We have to plan a retirement party! You'll need to stay to train your replacement. If you stay another three years you'll get blah, blah, blah."

Nope.

Basically it was "Don't let the screen door slap your ass on the way out."

Her whole life, and no gold watch, nothing but a bunch of forms to sign, a couple of brochures, and a teensy wad of cash every month. She'd cleaned out her office in a matter of minutes. The only thing she'd left behind was an oversized model of an outrigger canoe Peter had bought her on a trip to Hawaii. She hated the thing. She'd only taken it because he wanted it. Well, he could have it.

Shitheads. Let them rot. The NPS, potlucks on the lawn, campfire talks, scraping tourists' automobiles off rocks was not her whole life anymore. Her whole life was ahead of her. Her real life.

Bastards. Pricks. The lot of them.

At least the fact that the NPS was no longer her good buddy lessened the guilt she felt at raiding the evidence room for a couple of rufies—Rohypnol, the date rape drug. They had been taken off, of all people, a gynecologist—Denise would have thought he'd have had his fill of women's parts—up from Boston, who'd gotten himself arrested in the park a few years back. It had yet to go to trial. Probably never would. The guy was a rich doctor.

Rohypnol, added to a dash of Valium she'd had in the bottom of her medicine cabinet, should work as well as or better than the triazolam. Paulette hadn't been able to lay her hands on any at Mount Desert Hospital. At least she said she hadn't. Denise suspected her sister lacked the gumption to steal it.

Or maybe the motivation.

No, Paulette wanted this new life as much as Denise. Maybe she didn't know it quite yet, but she would. Until then, Denise could do the heavy lifting. She was used to that. Once they had a home, were a family, Paulette would come into her own. Denise was sure of it.

For the second time in as many days, Denise crept up to the shed-become-nursery behind her sister's house. Her brain fizzed with the plan she'd come up with, loose ends popping like bubbles in a Scotch and soda. Rushing these things was never good. That was when mistakes were made.

No choice, she told herself.

Denise had insisted they meet in the nursery this time. Tapping on the door, she called Paulette's name softly.

"Come in," Paulette answered. Denise slipped through the door. Paulette had a single kerosene lamp lit. She was sitting in the low rocking chair. Her clothes were all in dark colors, and she wore lace-up sneakers. Good. Denise had been afraid she'd get here and Paulette would have disobeyed her. Paulette had asked why

Denise wanted her to dress all in black, and Denise hadn't answered. Her plan wasn't something to be dealt with over the phone.

Denise dumped the heavy sack she was carrying as she folded down onto the hand-hooked rug at her sister's feet.

The sense that time was running out for them was driving Denise too hard for her to put off what she had to say. "I have been thinking about what you said, Paulette, about Ranger Pigeon being on to the fact we're twins, and then you finding her snooping around the nursery," she said without preamble.

"Not exactly around the nursery," Paulette said. "Just behind the house, really."

"Oyster out of a shell, that's how she looked at you. That's what you said."

"I guess," Paulette admitted.

Denise stared at her.

"Yes," Paulette said in a firmer voice. "I think she's been around the nursery. I felt it."

"Right," Denise approved. "You can see how that makes the death of good old Kurt not as simple as we thought. What had been a perfect murder now has a big fat hairy flaw in the ointment."

"Fly," Paulette said.

"Whatever. Anna Pigeon is that fly, that big hairy flaw. She's an obstacle," Denise insisted. "A serious stumbling block on the road to our new life."

"Oh." Paulette looked away. She stood, crossed to the crib, and picked up the little bear, her back to Denise. "If she's been back here, I haven't seen her. She hasn't tried to talk to me or anything. Maybe she was just, you know, poking around like rangers like to do." She set the bear down carefully in precisely the same place it had been before.

Why was Paulette being obstinate? "She might not have come back; more likely she did and you didn't see. The pigeon has all the pieces to you and me and Kurt dead and you at the Acadian. She's not stupid. She's an obstacle, and the obstacle has to be removed," Denise insisted.

Paulette spun around, her hands to her cheeks like a cartoon of "noooooo." "Do you mean kill her?" Paulette exclaimed. "Miss Pigeon is a ranger, law enforcement, like you. I've seen it in every movie. If a cop is killed—probably even a tree cop—the CIA and FBI and everybody start a huge manhunt!"

Denise stifled a sigh. "It's not like that. I know you're scared. I'd be, too. But we're not going to do anything drastic," she said, forcing a smile and a soothing timbre to her voice. "What I've got planned is more like a prank. It'll be seen like a prank. Ha ha, no big deal. You'll see. Rangers play pranks on each other all the time. Nobody gets their panties in a wad. We'll snatch the pigeon—like frat boys snatch each other for a joke. We'll keep her in here for a couple of days, then, when we've finished, we'll call somebody to let her out. Nobody gets hurt. We get what we deserve."

"You're sure?" Paulette asked. Denise's twin appeared to be growing younger and younger as Denise watched. Years dropping from her voice and face. Denise was growing older. At present she felt they weren't identical twins at all, that she was the much older sister and had to take care of Paulette.

"I'm sure," she said warmly. "We need more time, just a few days more to get everything we need. If we can . . . pull our prank on Anna Pigeon, it will buy us that time. We'll finish everything on our list, then we'll buy a nice big car and we'll go south until it's spring all year around, and we'll buy a nice house."

Paulette smiled wistfully. "It would be wonderful to have a nice new house," she said. "One that was clean and pretty, where nothing was broken or patched."

"That's what we're going to have," Denise promised. "Tonight we'll remove the obstacle. Over the next few days we'll tidy up, then off we'll go. An adventure."

Paulette's smile firmed up, her age steadied at about fourteen, or so it seemed to Denise. Fourteen would have to do.

"I got water for her," Denise said, pulling three liter bottles from her canvas sack. Without a word, Paulette gathered them up and carried them to a shelf next to the crib, where she arranged them in a neat row. "I brought these." Denise dug in her bag. "MREs from the fire cache. The park will never miss them. And these." She pulled two pairs of handcuffs from her belt. "Anna Pigeon will be fine. Just for a couple of days. I hoped you had an old bucket around somewhere."

"A bucket? What for?" Paulette asked as she piled the MREs in a tidy stack beside the water bottles.

"No bathroom," Denise explained.

"Yuck!" Paulette made a face. "Wait." Dropping to her hands and knees, she felt around under the crib. "If it's only for a couple days . . ." She dragged out a pink potty-training toilet. "It's nicer than a bucket." For a moment she studied it, then turned to Denise. "It's awfully small."

Paulette was so naïve, so sweet, like a little kid untouched by the whole real, nasty, shitty world. At times Denise thought maybe Paulette wasn't all there, wasn't quite right in the head. That would mean Denise wasn't right in the head either. They were identical twins. Being crazy wasn't a new thought. Things had gotten blurry and odd in the last while, maybe a year, maybe more.

Nerves.

"Anna Pigeon has a skinny butt," Denise said. "The potty is perfect. We do it tonight."

"I didn't get the triazolam," Paulette confessed. "I can look again tomorrow. We could do it tomorrow, couldn't we?"

Denise knew Paulette wouldn't have gotten the drug. Of course she knew. There wasn't anything she didn't know about her identical twin. To Paulette this was just talk, just a game. Paulette didn't think this was going to happen; she didn't think they deserved a life together. Kurt had beat that out of her.

Denise knew better. This had to happen.

"Not a problem," Denise assured her. "I got it all worked out. You don't have to worry about a thing."

"I did get this," Paulette said, brightening. "It's about the legacy. It came to General Delivery this morning." She held an envelope out to Denise. It had been opened. That irked Denise. The legacy was something they shared—or should share. Paulette should have waited until they could open it together.

Having unfolded the single slip of paper from the envelope, Denise turned it to the lamp so she could read the letters. *The woman who put the ad in the paper regarding the twins is very ill at present. I would not want to see her hurt or disappointed. To that end, I would like to meet with you before I share your card with her. There is a legacy, two to be accurate. We can talk about that when we meet.* The number of a cell phone followed.

"Sounds like a con," Denise said. "People run all kinds of con games. This sounds like one of them. Did you call her?" she demanded. Her tone was too rough. Paulette aged a little more, and her mouth turned harder. Ugly, Denise thought.

"I didn't," Paulette said. "But I want to. I think it's real."

Paulette wanted to get back with their biological mommy, Denise thought bitterly. No matter that Mommy was obviously a heartless tramp. Paulette would probably want to hang around and nurse Mommy back to health, and to hell with her sister, her identical twin sister.

Denise rode a wave of anger until it subsided, leaving her tired and determined. "We'll do whatever you want," she said. "First let's get tonight out of the way, okay? Please?"

"Tonight?"

Denise said nothing, just kept a half smile pasted on her face. Paulette looked at her for long enough that

Denise thought she was going to come up with another argument, distraction, or reason to postpone what they had to do.

"Just for a couple days, then we let her go," Paulette said.

Denise felt a rush of relief as great as the anger had been. "I love having a sister," she said.

"Me, too," Paulette said.

THIRTY

Paulette was in the boat; she had the needle with the mixture. Denise had explained what needed to be done, and Paulette had understood and seemed confident she could do her part. The sea was flat, and there was a gentle onshore breeze. Everything was as it should be, Denise told herself for the hundredth time. Once, like the whine of a mosquito near her ear, the thought surfaced that this part of the plan, disabling Anna Pigeon, wasn't crucial. A flash of the pigeon's eyes over the picture frame, or the tilt of her head as she'd interrogated Paulette, pulled the thought back into the depths. This was not a time to take even the slightest risk. If they failed, there would be no time to recover.

Since Kurt had died and Ranger Pigeon started poking her nose in, Denise had had that awful feeling she got as a child when she tried to balance a broom on her nose. Never could she run fast enough to keep it from falling down.

This was the second-to-last major step; then they were home free, free to have a home. She concentrated on that to keep the noise of the boat engine from bouncing off her sensitized eardrums with the force of a cataclysm.

Denise had coddled and pampered the little runabout's motor until it was as quiet as a fifteen-horsepower Evinrude could get. Unfortunately, on a still night, its high-pitched growl carried across the water like the wailing of an infant.

Before she could clearly see Schoodic's rocky point in the ambient light of a moonless sea, Denise cut the engine. For a minute she breathed, letting the magnificent silence erase their trespass.

The water was flat—or as flat as the restless Atlantic ever was. This was good. High seas would have postponed this adventure. Time had become a creature of three dimensions, slippery and short and sliding fast through Denise's fingers.

Having pried off the lens covers, she lifted the binoculars to her eyes.

Schoodic Point, as advertised, was pointed. It was a peninsula on the end of a peninsula that ended in a spade-shaped stone skirt digging into the ocean at the mainland's southernmost shore. Schoodic was a bleak beauty of rock, stone, sea, and sky. Fashion shoots favored it for high-end clothes, the emaciated models teetering over the round rocks in high heels, believing that people were staring because they were pretty and not because they looked like idiots. Weddings were often booked at Schoodic Point.

A hard, uncompromising beginning to married life, Denise thought as she swept the shore with the binoculars. An ugly parking lot scraped a flat place above the beach and nearly ruined the aesthetics. This night Denise forgave its existence because it had the decency to be empty. It was after three in the morning, and RVs weren't allowed to park overnight, but they often tried to get away with it.

No RVs. No sedans with thrashing bodies in the backseat.

"We're clear," she whispered to Paulette. "We paddle from here."

Frizzled blond hair tucked under a black watch cap, small body hidden under a black long-sleeved T-shirt, black sweatpants, and black running shoes, Paulette was merely a shadow in the bow. Denise thought of herself as a strong, strapping woman. She saw Paulette as fine-boned and delicate. Odd that she and her sister were the same height and weight, same shoe, glove, and bra size. Paulette's shoulders were hunched, and her chin was down, as if she tried to disappear into her own skeleton. Black ops were not her forte. Well, Denise thought, they weren't hers either. She just did what she had to do. Paulette would see that. After the fact, when done was done, she would understand.

Both women had blackened their faces with makeup. Denise didn't know what the Delta Force guys or the Navy SEALs used, or what football players put under their eyes, but she and her sister had made do with a mix of Paulette's black, gray, and dark blue eye shadows. The effect was all she could have wished for. But for her hands, Paulette looked to be little more than a texture on the night seascape.

As did Denise. Invisible twins. Could invisible people still be identical? Sort of the visual equivalent of the tree falling in the forest: Could one no-thing be exactly the same as another no-thing? Denise wondered as she watched Paulette's white hands float up like the ghosts of long-dead starfish and close around the handle of a paddle.

In an inexpert attempt to get the paddle in position she struck the blade against the gunwale. The clunk was loud enough to wake sleepers in Nova Scotia.

Maybe Denise suffered from nervous twitches, but she was beginning to think her sister was just clumsy. She swallowed an oath.

"I'll paddle," she whispered, making her voice extra kind to stifle the traitorous thoughts about her twin.

The runabout was a bitch to paddle. Denise had done it enough that she could make it work. Work was the key word. Outboards weren't meant to run on manpower. Or, in her case, womanpower. By the time she managed to catch the crest of a good wave, and ride the surf into the rocky beach on the point below the parking lot, sweat was pouring down from her temples and between her breasts.

As the swell that beached them retreated, it dragged small stones along with it, clattering back toward the ocean floor. If she timed it right, the racket of the stony surf would cover the racket of beaching the boat.

Denise was over the side in a second. Even in midsummer the water off the coast of Maine was cold. She was used to wearing a wet suit complete with booties. Cold feet were the least of the dangers, she reminded herself as she shoved hard on the stern to move the boat out of the reach of the surf before the Atlantic could turn it into flotsam. Paulette sat like a statue in the bow, making the going that much tougher. Again Denise felt irritation rise up her spine to scratch like a metal rasp on the back of her brain.

Lot of stress, she reminded herself. Lot on our plates. "Us against the world" was not as romantic as fiction writers would have it. "Us" could get real bitchy. Things would be better—like they used to be those first few times they were together—once they got straightened away, got the legacy, the pension, the money from the sale of the house . . .

Denise slammed her mind shut against the list. It grew longer every minute she dwelt on it, longer and heavier, each chore another lead weight on her metaphorical dive belt threatening to drag her down, drown her.

Paulette jumped from the boat, grabbed the bow with both hands, and began to help drag it up on shore.

See, Denise told herself. Not irritating. Good and right.

The previous day Denise had driven to the peninsula on reconnaissance to find a secluded spot to cache the boat. It didn't need to be totally hidden, just out of casual sight should a ranger be on patrol—not likely; there weren't enough green-and-gray bodies for round-the-clock coverage on Schoodic either. More likely would be a nosy insomniac out for a ride.

She'd found a shallow dry creek to the side of the point not too long a walk from the employee housing area and the old US Navy base—now a rotting hulk of dorm rooms and hallways—but far enough so that the sounds of their arrival wouldn't wake any of the summer seasonals, or the sculptors on Schoodic for an artists' retreat.

Psychically speaking, killing Kurt had been no big deal. He was a lout and a bastard, and even his best friend was over it in a beer or two. Even without killing, this would be different. Paulette was right. There would be cops all over a federal law enforcement officer going missing. Since Pigeon was "acting" chief, Denise hoped there'd be a time lag before the NPS declared her disappearance officially suspicious. Then Denise wasn't sure who-all would descend, but she was sure it was going to be a big deal. Hence: black clothes, black face, surgical gloves for the event, and a getaway boat hidden in the scrub.

Leave No Trace.

That was a Park Service motto. Good old NPS, Denise thought with a smile. Good old Superintendent Peter, moldy green and moth-eaten gray down to his grubby little soul. This was going to look bad on Happy Daddy's résumé. A perk she'd not considered before.

Paulette was making a lot of racket puffing and grunting as they dragged the boat into the wash. After they'd settled the runabout, Denise could still hear her breathing. Paulette hadn't kept herself in shape. Denise stared over the dark shape of the hull between them. Despite the black makeup and the brim of the ball cap, she could see that Paulette's face was crumpled like a little kid's before it starts to shriek.

"Are you okay?" she asked softly.

"I have to pee," Paulette said. A nervous titter escaped her lips.

"Because you're scared?" Denise asked.

"I guess." To Denise's surprise, tears started cutting white stripes through the powder on Paulette's face. All her irritation was blown away on a gust of pity. Paulette was the softer Denise, the gentle Denise she could have been if not for the foster homes and other bullshit. Tonight was going to be hard on Paulette because of her tender heart. As soon as she could afford the luxury, Denise decided, she would have the compassion Paulette had. For now, she was grateful that her heart was hard as flint, that it had been pounded and tormented until it barely beat. Right now, tonight, that hardening was going to pay off. Paulette would understand how it had to be, if not right away, then when they were in their new house and their new lives.

Sitting on the keel of the boat, Denise patted the wet fiberglass beside her. Obediently, Paulette came around the stern to sit next to her. Denise took her sister's hand between both of her own.

"This isn't like it was with Kurt," Paulette snuffled. "It's hard to take someone when you don't want to hurt them, when they're not bad, just too smart and in the way."

"It is," Denise admitted. "I can do it without you if you like," she offered, though, in truth, she didn't think she could. "We're not doing alibis or anything."

"No alibis because we both live alone, it's the middle of the night, and no one will suspect us anyway," Paulette said, repeating exactly the words and intonations Denise had used when they discussed the venture in the boat. Denise looked at her hard, trying to figure out if she was being mocked.

No, of course she wasn't. Paulette would never do that. Twin souls would sound the same, would speak as one. Of course. Same DNA.

"Can't we just not do it? Turn around and go home?" Paulette pleaded, glancing up at Denise from under the ball cap.

Denise felt as if she towered over her sister, like a Goliath, a monster. This was as much for Paulette as it was for her. More. Compassion burned out on sudden unexpected anger. Jolted by the intensity of the fury, Denise's tongue clove to the roof of her mouth.

They had been through this. "It's just for a couple of days." Denise forced herself to go through it again. "She'll sleep through most of it. Then we tell somebody where to find her. No harm, no foul."

"Sorry, sorry," Paulette said before Denise could say any wrong words and ruin everything forever. "Of course we can't just not do it. Let's do it. Let's go. Right now."

"Don't have to pee anymore?" Denise asked as Paulette rose.

"I couldn't if I wanted to. All my sphincters are slammed shut," Paulette said, and produced a wan smile.

Denise smiled back. Paulette was trying. Paulette was a trouper.

"We'll be fine," Denise promised. "Do you have the stuff?"

Paulette unzipped her waist pack and checked the contents as Denise had seen her do half a dozen times since the boat left Somes Sound.

Paulette lifted out a syringe with a plastic safety cap over the needle. Holding it near her ear, she shook it. Paulette had crushed the rufies to powder using the bowl of a teaspoon to mash the tablets against the bowl of a soup spoon. Denise had thrown in a Valium for good measure. When the powder was as fine as they could make it, they mixed it with tap water and drew the resulting liquid into a syringe.

Denise remembered how Paulette's hands shook, setting up a tiny tempest in the spoon, how her own had shaken so much they lost some of the precious stuff.

Two street-made rufies, 1.0 mg of Valium. There wasn't anything on the Internet about the mix, but enough Rohypnol could cause unconsciousness and even coma. Coma would be good, Denise thought, startling herself. She didn't want to kill the pigeon any more than Paulette did. Still, a coma would be a whole lot easier for everybody concerned.

"Two rufies and a Valium is a lot," Paulette said. "Maybe too much."

"You should know. You're the RN," Denise said. She'd meant to sound complimentary. It came out waspish.

"LPN," Paulette said in a barely audible voice.

For a moment the letters made no sense to Denise. Paulette was a nurse. Nurses were RNs, registered nurses. Then she remembered. LPN meant licensed practical nurse. No better than an EMT.

"A Candy Striper?" Denise demanded, aghast.

"It takes a year to get accredited. RNs take four or five years." Paulette hung her head so low her forehead nearly touched her knees. "Some of us do injections, but there's always a doctor's okay, or an RN to help. I don't know whether injecting Rohypnol instead of swallowing it will make a difference. What if she ODs?"

"Shit." Denise forced herself not to roll her eyes. What if she did OD? Would it be worse than if she didn't? Worse, of course, in the sense of murder, but worse all around? For her and Paulette?

"It can't kill her," Denise said firmly. "I Googled it."

THIRTY-ONE

Anna's sleeping mind conjured up a wasp. The insect was stinging her bicep. Instantly she was awake, but, for a moment, she couldn't remember where she was. Not Rocky. Acadia. No Paul, no roommates, yet a shadow, as wide as it was tall, clotted the vague light between her eyes and the ceiling.

"Hey!" Anna barked. Squeaking like a colony of bats, the shadow changed shape and squeezed toward the door. Not a shadow—this invader was corporeal in nature. Shadows were the stuff of silence. This apparition was making a hell of a racket.

"Who are you?" Anna yelled as she threw off her covers. There was a brief scuffle as the night creature tried to shove itself through an opening half its size.

Leaping free of the bedclothes, Anna yelled: "Stop!"

The black shape wrestled with itself for a moment, then popped through the bedroom door into the living room. Anna scrambled for the light switch. In the unfamiliar room, she was slow. By the time she'd flicked the light on, she could hear the sound of feet pounding down wooden stairs. More than one person, two, maybe three. A wave of dizziness overtook her; sound was behaving oddly; the light seemed to shimmer. She brushed her wrist over her eyes.

Hers was one of four apartments in the building used for employee housing on Schoodic Peninsula. The structure was divided in half, two floors on each side, an apartment on each floor, the two halves connected by an open-air breezeway and stairs. Though it often happened in cookie-cutter dwellings, these weren't drunken neighbors wandering in the wrong door. Drunken neighbors wouldn't run; besides, at present, Anna's was the only apartment occupied.

It could be park visitors. As far as vacationers were concerned, rangers were always on duty, always there to stanch the bleeding or lend a cup of sugar. Since Anna— like a lot of the old guard—still refused to lock her doors, a couple might have wandered in and been scared into running when she awakened.

"Hey!" she shouted again. "Hold up."

In three strides she'd crossed the small living room. As she reached the head of the stairs, two humanoid shapes careened through the downstairs breezeway, running out into the parking lot with more speed than grace.

Not tourists with bad manners. Sinister miscreants. "Damn!" Anna muttered. She staggered, caught herself on the railing, then turned and ran back into her apartment. For an instant, she stood beside her bed, trying to remember why she'd come back. "Intruders," she said, and she pulled on her cordovan boots, grabbed her SIG Sauer from the drawer in the nightstand, and, stark naked but for boots and gun, hurtled out of the apartment, down the stairs, and into the night.

In the middle of the employee-housing parking lot, she stopped, eyes wide, ears open. Without warning a blackness as heavy and dark as igneous rock rolled over her brain, crushed her vision, and clogged her ears. Anna's joints turned to water. She fell hard on her knees.

Pain cleared her mind. She could hear sneakered feet scratching on pavement; the intruders were headed across the access road toward the renovated Rockefeller building used as the Schoodic Education and Research Center. Beyond the Rockefeller building were the crumbling ruins of an old navy base's housing wings.

Currently the research center was home to granite sculptors doing a summer workshop. Possibly her wee-hours visitation was from feral artists, but Anna was more worried about the artists as victims or hostages than as perpetrators. Though one or two of the huge, labor-intensive granite monoliths did look like the work of troubled minds.

As her vision cleared, she saw the two figures running hard toward the plaza where the sculptures were being carved. She heaved herself to her feet and, boots ringing on the asphalt, sprinted after them.

"Stop or I'll shoot!" she yelled. She wouldn't shoot. Rangers didn't shoot fleeing suspects even if they had slithered up to one's bedside in the dead of night.

The dreamlike sensation of running ever slower through air viscous as mud dragged at her legs. Distance—or her perception of it—underwent a sea change. The ruined barracks wavered, retreating in an undulating wreck of roof lines. The Rockefeller building, no more than two hundred yards from her apartment, refused to move closer as she ran; then, suddenly, the immense granite sculptures were looming over her.

Anna didn't so much stop with intent as simply cease to move because her body chose stagnation regardless of what her mind ordered it to do. The retreating human-shaped fragments of darkness had run past the sculptures. Immobile, she watched as they reached the barracks where the wings of the ruined building came together. Her eyes told her they vanished like smoke; her mind suggested they'd probably run down one of the stairwells that let into the basement level.

Even if her legs had not ceased to function properly, and the night had not broken all the laws of physics to become a nauseating, undulating mess, Anna would not have given chase. Nothing short of a shrieking child or a mewling kitten could induce her to pursue bad guys into that haunted hulk in the dark.

The abandoned barracks was two stories of smashed desks, shattered walls, mirror shards, falling staircases, and other sharp-edged detritus. In that place, if fleeing felons didn't kill you, tumbling down stairs or broken glass would.

Broken glass would what?

With sudden alarm, Anna wondered why she was naked, why she was standing in the shadow of lowering chunks of granite with her gun in her hand. She had no recollection of kneeling, yet she was on her knees on the stone.

Stinging in her upper arm claimed her attention.

Clumsily, she brushed at it. Something clinked to the paving stones of the sculpture yard. Stupidly, Anna stared down at it, eyes and mind disconnected. Part of her brain knew she should recognize the shape. Most of her brain was atomized, loose dust blowing in a windy night.

A syringe. The item that fell from her arm was a syringe. There was quarter of an inch of liquid in it.

Evidence of something.

She picked it up, holding it like a dagger. Forget evidence. Two weapons were better than one. Weapons against what?

People were hiding in the old barracks; she'd been chasing them. They had stuck the needle in her arm while she was sleeping.

Light. She needed light if she was going to go into the garbage- and rat-infested derelict building. Light and backup; she had to get a flashlight and a radio and a pair of underpants.

First she had to get up off of her knees. At one time she knew how human legs bent and flexed to execute this intricate maneuver. No more. She wasn't even sure where her feet were. She could neither see nor feel them.

A clunk startled her in a vague way. Rolling her head carefully to the side, she looked down. Somebody had dropped a gun—a SIG Sauer—beside her right knee. Careless bastard. What kind of idiot dropped a gun?

Me, she thought. My gun. Bending at the waist to pick it up, she fell face-first onto the granite paving. A cracking jarred the interior of her skull. Nothing hurt. Her skull felt as if it had been hurled against a wall, but nothing hurt. Or if it did, she couldn't feel it.

Straightening her arms, she forced her head and shoulders up from the ground. Sculpted works in progress, high as houses and cut into fantastic shapes, moved slowly around her, waving and leaning like grasses in a breeze. The brick and stone facade of the beautiful old building beyond rose as high as Half Dome, its many windows blank and lifeless.

"Help," she creaked. The noise she made was so thin and tiny she thought of the Woozy in *The Patchwork Girl of Oz*, the creature whose roar was supposed to bring down mountains but in reality was a teeny squeak. It didn't matter. Sculptors were artists. Artists didn't go around rescuing people. When the shit hit the proverbial, nobody ever yelled, "Is there an artist in the house!"

Anna pulled her knees under her to sit on her heels. In an attempt to scrape off the toxic fog devouring her brain, she scrubbed at her face. Pain that should have come when she fell blindsided her. She cried out feebly. One hand came away black and wet. Blood was pouring down over her left eye, blinding her.

Paul will still love me, even if the corner of my head is smashed, she thought. The image of her husband,

Paul, in all his strength and calm, centered her. She was able to find her feet and push to a standing position. Her pistol was still on the ground, an infinite distance from her eyes. Teetering sickeningly back and forth in her boots, she tried to decide if it would be worse to leave her gun and go find a radio or stay with her gun and . . . what?

Just stay with her gun.

Besides, she was naked. She'd been reminded of that when she looked way, way down at the gun. No clothes. Naked outside in the weird with no clothes. This had to be a dream. That was a relief. Peculiar dreams were not strangers to Anna. There was a foolproof test to see whether one was dreaming or not. It wasn't pinching. That was silly. It was flying. If she could fly, that was proof positive she was dreaming.

Anna tried to lift her arms. They did not reach Superman-in-flight position, only zombie-seeking-edible-brain position.

No flying.

Not a dream.

Again she looked toward the ruins. The stairwell was disgorging its recent meal, bipedal shapes bulging forth to be delineated by the faint light of the stars. The creatures who'd put a wasp in her dream, a drug in her veins.

Anna raised her gun hand. "No further," she said. "Move and I soowt." She'd meant to say "shoot." The bonk on the head, or the chemical they'd injected, turned her lips to rubber. The figures halted, murmured, then came toward her.

Anna pulled the trigger. Nothing. Her hand was empty, the gun ever so far away on the ground by her foot.

The figures separated, moving slowly in her direction. Ninjas, black clothes and hoods and faces, with four white hands, fake as plastic mannequins' hands, floating along beside them. They were wearing surgical gloves.

Coming to butcher the kill, Anna thought as she tipped into nothingness.

THIRTY-TWO

Denise couldn't take her eyes off the fallen woman. In the starlight, Anna Pigeon was faintly luminescent, as if she'd been swimming in phosphorescent plankton. The boots, incongruously dark, made it appear as if her legs had been lopped off just below the knee, leaving white stumps. Anna's hair, always in a single fat braid, was spread out around her in a dark fan shot with silver, a protective cape that reached to her waist.

Denise didn't know what she had expected to happen when they'd set out on this venture, but this wasn't it. Despite the fact that three of her bullets were in him, Kurt Duffy had roared and fought. That made it self-defense in a way. Killing should be a positive or negative choice, not made in hot blood, necessarily—cold blood was fine—but with a real sense of commitment. One *committed* murder; murder didn't just happen. The gun didn't just go off; the victim didn't just run into the knife seven times.

Since she wasn't murdering Anna Pigeon, just removing an obstacle for a while, she'd pictured it happening in a prosaic, workaday kind of way. Or peacefully, like taking out the garbage on a Sunday afternoon. The unconscious body would lie in its own snug little bed, drifting quietly into deeper and deeper sleep. Then Denise and Paulette would wrap her tidily in one of her blankets and haul her to the runabout.

Not this blood-and-snot-filled gun-toting drama.

Also, in her mental picture, Anna Pigeon would wear a pair of pajamas, for Christ's sake, or a T-shirt and panties. What kind of lunatic leaps up and gives chase wearing nothing but a pair of cordovan NPS boots, even if she is drugged?

Naked was bad in an unsettling way. Naked was vulnerable and very female. Naked gave a body a gender and an age. "She should wear fucking pajamas," Denise hissed. "Rangers get called out at night."

Paulette said nothing.

The shushing sibilance of the sea washed between Denise and her sister. Usually the sounds of the ocean soothed Denise. These rasped. The clacking of rocks as they were rolled by the receding waves clattered like a plague of demented cicadas.

Anna Pigeon's hand twitched. Passed out on major drugs, the woman seemed to still be reaching for her gun.

"Oh God," Paulette whispered. "What do we do now?"

Trained to the call of "Gun!" Denise ran forward quickly and kicked the SIG out of the reach of the weak and groping hand. At a safe distance from the moribund ranger, she retrieved the weapon and shoved it into the waistband of her pants at the small of her back. Unlike Paulette, Denise had opted for black Levi's instead of sweatpants. The denim waistband held the gun firmly.

"We get her to the boat," Denise said.

"Shouldn't we get her some clothes first?" Paulette asked plaintively.

The toe of Denise's sneaker twitched out and struck the downed woman in the shoulder.

"Don't kick her!" Paulette exclaimed.

Like that was worse than drugging and snatching her.

Denise made no reply. She hadn't meant to kick her. Her foot had jerked out of its own accord. Nerves.

"We can lend her some of our clothes," Denise said. "She won't need much. She won't be there for long. Help me pick her up."

Paulette didn't move. She was looking past the naked ranger toward the housing area. "Maybe we should go back to her room. She's going to need some things. Maybe she takes medication . . . and toothpaste . . . that kind of thing," Paulette said.

Denise thought about that for an instant—not the meds or the toiletries, a blanket to cover her up. Anna had made it fifty or sixty yards from her apartment. There was nothing but open road and parking lot between where she lay and her bed. A sculptor up late smoking dope, or doing whatever sculptors did in the dead of night, might see them. "Too risky," she decided.

"I'll take her arms, you take her legs. Put a hand under each knee; it'll be easier that way."

Paulette tiptoed gingerly around the crumpled form on the paving stones. Leaning down, she lifted one of the booted feet and pulled the leg. With the leverage, the senseless woman rolled to lie upon her back, hair veiling her breasts. Half of her face was covered in a black mask. Denise stared until she realized that it was not a mask; it was blood.

"She's bleeding!" Paulette exclaimed. "Why is she bleeding?"

To Denise, it sounded as if her sister blamed her, suggested she'd kicked Anna Pigeon in the face. Her toe had only just tapped the woman's shoulder. "She must have cut her head when she fell," Denise said curtly. "Get her legs." Moving briskly to give herself more courage and authority than she felt, Denise grabbed a limp wrist in each hand and lifted the upper body.

The used syringe fell from Anna's lax fingers. Denise dropped the hands. Flesh thudded against the ground.

"Careful," Paulette whispered. "We don't want to hurt her."

Denise grunted. Stepping on the needle, she pried the plastic up until the needle snapped off. She put the syringe in the front pocket of her jacket. Both she and Paulette had worn surgical gloves when they filled it; still, forensics would be able to tell what drugs were used, maybe match them to the rufies missing from the park's evidence locker. If anybody even thought to

check there. The syringe itself might be a special kind
Mount Desert used exclusively. One never knew what
mattered and what didn't until it was too late.

The bit of evidence secured, Denise grabbed Anna's
wrists again and whispered, "Grab her legs."

Paulette grabbed the top of the boots and pulled Anna's naked legs up and apart. A whimper escaped her
as she slowly lowered them again, boot heels carefully
together. "I can't!" she wailed softly. "It's like rape.
Please, let's get her some clothes. Or put her back in
her bed and leave. She won't remember us. You said
she won't remember anything."

Denise wanted to lash out at Paulette, but a part of
her felt as her sister did. Not about putting Ranger Pigeon back and pretending it never happened, but about
one woman prying apart another woman's legs and
stepping between them when that woman was naked.
It was icky. The worst kind of icky, the kind that stuck
to the inside of your skull for years.

"Right," she said to herself; then, to her sister, "But
we can't go back. We're way beyond that. We can't
leave her. Let's do this. Come take an arm. We'll drag
her so her feet stay together and we're not . . . you know,
looking at her that way. We don't have to drag her far.
Jumping out of bed and chasing us, she did half our
work for us. Another couple hundred yards and we're
good to go. All the hard part over."

Paulette came up beside Denise but made no move
to help. Denise shoved one of Pigeon's arms into her
hands.

"Ranger Pigeon was nice to me the morning Kurt

was found," Paulette said, looking into the bloody mask of a face.

Denise heard faint accusation in her sister's tone and bit back a harsh response. Paulette was her gentler self; she had to respect the Paulette half of her personality even when it was a huge pain in the butt. "Everything is going to be fine," she said calmly. "We've come so far. We do this and we're almost free. Think of our house in the pines somewhere warm. Think of being a family and never being cold or alone again."

Paulette took in a deep breath. "Okay," she said. "You're right."

Denise exhaled in relief. "Here we go," she whispered.

Both of them pulling moved the body at a snail's pace. Anna Pigeon couldn't have weighed more than a hundred and ten pounds, a hundred and fifteen at most, yet she apparently had made a deal with gravity; the earth seemed to hold her fast. Agonizing minutes passed as they dragged her from the granite apron in front of the Education Center onto the road to Schoodic Point, where the boat was stashed.

"Shit," Denise muttered as one of Anna's boots came off. Half a yard more and her heel was red with blood. Or, in the moonlight, black with blood. Denise was imagining the red color.

"We have to stop," Paulette said. "We're scratching her bottom and her legs all up."

"We're making a ton of noise," Denise said. Dumb and Dumber move a body, she thought. Murder wasn't glamorous; she knew that from killing Kurt. Neither was kidnapping, but it shouldn't be stupid. This was stupid, like a bad movie.

For an awful moment, Denise flew free of her body. From twenty feet up in the air she looked down at herself and her sister dragging the drugged ranger. They were ludicrous, absurd. Minuscule black ants, intent on abduction, hauling along a naked human. Insane. The picture whirled, and Denise crashed back into her own skull.

Not absurd, necessary.

Okay, absurd, but necessary, Denise admitted to herself. They had to do this to get what was owed them. She was sorry about Anna Pigeon, but Anna would have sided with the Peter Barneses and the Kurt Duffys and stripped Denise and her twin of everything. Again. Thrown them out to rot with the garbage. Again.

On second thought, she wasn't that sorry about Anna Pigeon. She should have kept her nosy little pigeon beak out of things that were none of her business, kept her beady little birdy eyes off of other people's things.

"Let's get her up," Denise said as she dragged the ranger's limp arm around her neck, hoisting her half of the inert form. "Like this, like we're walking a drunk. Then we won't be scratching her. It'll be okay. Put her arm around your neck." After more fumbling clown antics, they had the unconscious woman between them and were moving forward. Denise cursed herself. Anybody with half a brain would have worked all this bullshit out before doing the deed. The pigeon was to blame. If she hadn't nosed around they wouldn't be in such a rush, moving too fast to think things through properly.

With Anna draped around their necks, they traveled at a fairly good pace. Pigeon's toes dragged, but there was nothing Denise could do about that.

Within minutes they had trundled their catch over the rough cobble-sized stones of the point to the wash where they'd hidden the runabout. Unseen. Unheard. Like they'd never been to Schoodic. Like none of it had ever happened.

"We're good, we're good," Denise gasped, breathing in gusts as much from fear as exercise. Together they lowered the body, laying it out on the stones. "Catch your breath," Denise told her sister. "Almost done." Leaving Paulette standing over their captive, Denise went to turn the runabout right side up. The boat and outboard motor were heavy, but, unlike handling dead humans, Denise was accustomed to handling the runabout. She pried it up onto her knees, then flipped it easily over onto its keel.

Looking back over the gunwales, she expected to see Paulette getting the pigeon ready to drag over the side and into the boat. Instead, Paulette was sitting on the ground, in the rocks, her palms held to her cheeks and her feet in front of her like a little kid.

"We can't do it," Paulette said, eyes fixed on the prone naked ranger. "The shed won't be a good prison. She'll get out. Everybody will be swarming the island looking for her. Kidnapping is a serious crime. We could get the death sentence."

Like murder wasn't a serious crime—but then, Paulette hadn't murdered anybody. Denise had.

"How can we can we keep her quiet, even for a day or two?" Paulette wailed, her voice rising too high, too loud. "Hikers and tourists go in the woods, they could hear. Handcuffed, how can she get to the toilet? Feed herself? If we do it, she'll see us. Or hear us. We should have thought this through. Keeping her drugged all that time could hurt her. She could OD or dehydrate or something. I won't."

Paulette sounded mulish. More than that. She sounded firm.

What a miserable time for my sister to develop a spine, Denise thought. What a miserable time to get a conscience. Rage of the kind she thought she only held for Peter and his ilk rose up in her gorge hot as lava.

Paulette was staring up at her beseechingly, the ruined blond hair wisping out from beneath the black ball cap. Though they had been born only minutes, maybe seconds, apart, Denise realized Paulette was much younger than she was. Denise had to take care of her. You didn't rage at a child. Especially not if that child was you when you were little, back before they ruined you. Besides, Paulette was right. A nutcase who would run after you naked with a gun wasn't a person who would be easy to keep as a pet for an hour, let alone a couple of days.

Swallowing the molten anger, Denise walked around to where her sister sat beside Anna Pigeon. Crouching, she lifted one of Pigeon's arms, then laid two fingers over the pulse point at her wrist. For thirty seconds she concentrated. Having laid the hand back on the stones, she shifted, put her first and second finger on the ranger's trachea, and let them slide down into the hollow where the jugular vein was closest to the skin. Again she concentrated on feeling for a pulse.

It was there, thready and faint.

Making an executive decision, Denise removed her hand.

"Too late, Paulette," she said. "She's dead. You killed her."

"Oh God," Paulette murmured, and began to rock back and forth.

Denise sat next to her and put her arms around her. "Shh, shh," she whispered. "It's all good. This is how it was meant to be. I killed Kurt; you injected the pigeon and it killed her. That's how it had to be. We did nothing that wasn't supposed to happen. Things are just happening to help us now instead of hurt us. I'm going to take care of everything. No need to worry. Shh." She laid her cheek against her sister's. Paulette was calming at her touch. Denise savored the sensation of being of use, of value, to another human being.

"Are we done?" Paulette sniffed.

"Almost," Denise said. "I just need to find a garbage bag."

THIRTY-THREE

There was sensation of a sort. Anna didn't know if it was life, death, dreams, or something altogether different. As in a dream, occurrences that would have been staggeringly bizarre to the waking mind, felt ordinary.

Zen.

That thought wafted through the utter darkness inside Anna's skull. In dreams one was truly in the moment: no worries for the future, no regrets from the past, no expectations, therefore no surprises. The entire universe created in the mind, and the mind created in that universe.

A sliding sensation followed by a hard whack to the small of her back startled Anna free of philosophy. Pain was real and actual. Pain made a person care, and damn quick, what was going to happen next, and what had happened a second ago. Pain meant she wasn't dead and she wasn't dreaming. Life was happening.

Further than that, she couldn't fathom. "Breathe," she told herself.

ABCs: airway, blood, circulation. Breathing was first. Of course she was breathing. Alive, one did that sort of thing. But it wasn't easy. Almost, she had to tell her diaphragm to drop, her lungs to expand. Not an out-of-body experience; more a trapped-in-a-worthless-body experience.

As consciousness and breath fluttered in and out, pictures came back fleetingly: the jab, the wasp, the chase. Like old Polaroids, colors were muted and images fading like ghosts at sunrise.

Shadows had come to her room and pricked her arm. She had chased the shadows. Now she was blind and couldn't move. By the slick fabric clinging to her face, and the faint rubbery smell, she guessed she was in a big plastic sack. So, perhaps not blind, merely temporarily unable to see.

Drugged. Paralyzed. In a sack.

But not scared or unhappy. To the contrary, Anna felt fairly chipper. The drug, though powerful and paralyzing, had potential as a recreational drug. Nice of her kidnappers to think of her feelings. For a moment, Anna felt warm and fuzzy toward her shadows.

Then one of them stomped on her ankle. Roaring filled her ears. The two happenings were unrelated. The roar was an engine. Her sack and she were in a boat, or had been dumped in the backseat of a car. Boat. No car had that high whiny sound. A go-cart maybe.

Who kidnapped anybody with a go-cart?

For a while Anna faded. She knew she existed, she knew she was cold, but she had little opinion regarding these things. On some level she knew she was in deep trouble. People were not drugged and bagged and carted out to sea in a go-cart unless they were going to be disposed of.

Oddly, she didn't care overmuch.

Then the whining growl of the engine was gone. Anna's mind rose from the depths as if the harsh noise had been holding it under. Silence was a balm. Opening her mouth, she tried to breathe it in. Plastic stuck to her lips and tongue. Hands grabbed at her, latex screeching on plastic as fingers plucked and slipped on her shroud, then pinched and clutched, trying for better purchase. Heavy breathing and grunts filtered through the bag, but no voices. Not that it mattered. There would be no harm in her identifying the voices. The dead tell no tales and all that.

Dead. That sounded so melodramatic.

Anna would have liked to fight, just to say she had, that she'd gone down swinging and taken a few of the bastards with her, but she was unable to lift a hand or make her lips form a word.

As she was manhandled up to where her belly pressed hard against the gunwale, the boat rocked dangerously. Just as she was thinking how grand it would be if it capsized, and her shadows had to escort her to Davy Jones's locker, her head plunged into the cold. Plastic form-fitted itself around her mouth and nose, and she couldn't breathe.

Another heave and the rest of her followed out of the

boat. Every inch of Anna was pressed with cold plastic. The ocean was too cold. Anna didn't want to die in the cold. Maybe she'd suffocate or die of hypothermia before she drowned.

"It's not sinking," came a shrill voice.

Well, that was good news.

In the fetal position inside the garbage bag, Anna felt the sea roll her onto her back; then she spun weightless into the sucking cold.

"There she goes," a calmer voice said.

Not much of an epitaph, Anna thought.

THIRTY-FOUR

They motored back to Somes Sound, Paulette as uncommunicative and dark as a lump of coal in the bow of the boat, Denise's mind fixated on Ranger Pigeon's demise. Not her drowning or suffocating or ODing or whatever finally took her out, but how weighty deadweight was. Manhandling the body was much harder than she would have believed. In the gym, Denise could bench press her own weight, one hundred twenty-five pounds—or could when she was in her early thirties. Yet moving a soon-to-be-dead body that weighed a bit less than that had been backbreaking, even though there were two of them doing the manhandling. Dead—or deadish—people were denser than living people, physically speaking, and just as uncooperative.

Denise was glad that the killing portion of her new life was at an end—maybe at an end. One thing did tend to lead to another. Obstacles would always pop up when one least expected it. Kurt had been a given, but the Pigeon thing, that was extemporaneous. Either way, Denise had reached the conclusion that killing people was more work than it was worth in a lot of ways. Hitler probably would have won World War II if he hadn't wasted so much time and energy killing people who didn't need killing.

Kurt had needed it. That hadn't made it any easier. Anna Pigeon hadn't needed it; things just got away from them, choices lopped off, until killing her was the only good one left. That didn't make it any easier.

Paulette, too, wasn't making things any easier. Denise watched her sitting in a heap as the boat cut neatly through the gentle swells. Paulette was more delicate than Denise had thought anyone who shared her DNA could be. It must be that nature made them both the same, but nurture had toughened Denise up. Nurture for Denise had been a brutal series of beatings and betrayals. Of course Paulette had been abused by her husband. Probably she was too old by then for the abuse to have any effect other than beating her down, Denise thought, whereas she—what? Had been beaten up?

However it worked, it was obvious that the removal of Anna Pigeon, though it had given them more time—a day, maybe a day and a half—had been harder on Paulette than it had been on her. Maybe it had broken some bit of her sister that could compromise the plan. Denise sensed that waiting while feds, rangers, and whoever else swarmed around looking for the missing Pigeon would be a bad idea. Paulette would fold under the pressure. Denise didn't like to think it, but she herself might have issues. Her nerves, once as strong as steel cables, had begun to fray. Age might account for it. Or Peter Barnes. Everything. Not that she'd fold under pressure, but she might explode. Either would mean disaster.

Time, in this case, would not heal all. It was a bomb. Denise could feel it ticking. Paulette or Fate or dumb luck was going to trigger the explosion soon. That this was so was felt in her viscera, as palpable as an electric current. Even with Pigeon out of the picture, things would have to be moved up. Way up. The sale of the Duffy shack, the so-called legacy, and family.

Tomorrow night they would tick "family" off the list, then get the hell out of Dodge. Do the rest long distance. Denise had no doubt that once they were out of sight, they'd be out of mind. A has-been ranger retires and moves. A bleached-blond housewife, with an iron-clad alibi for her husband's murder, sells the house where he was killed and leaves town. Nobody would connect those nonevents to a missing acting chief ranger from Rocky Mountain National Park. No connection between Denise and Anna, Anna and Paulette, Denise and Kurt, or Paulette and Denise.

All that could screw the pooch now was Paulette babbling or Denise going postal. So: tick, tick, tick.

For Denise that meant the night, though nearly spent, was not yet over.

By the time she got the runabout moored, and Paulette headed for her bed in the shack, only fifty-six minutes remained before dawn. Sunrise would be at 5:03 A.M. At five Peter would get out of bed and go to the bathroom to pee. At 5:04 he would be pulling on his running clothes; 5:10 and he'd be out the front door swinging his hands side to side and jogging in place. He would run 4.5 miles. Depending on how he was feeling, he would be gone thirty to thirty-six minutes, getting back to the house around quarter to six.

Rather than sleeping in like a sane woman, little Lily flower got her lovely little ass out of bed at 5:15 every morning, checked on the baby—didn't pee, she did that between midnight and three—and went down to make her darling hubby coffee.

Like Peter couldn't poke the button on the coffee machine before he left.

She'd poke the button, then, while she waited for it to brew, prepare Olivia's first bottle of the day, setting it in a pan of water to heat. Microwaving wasn't good enough for Lily's baby. No nuked fake milk for Olivia.

After the burner was on low, Lily would go upstairs and brush her teeth and comb her hair so she'd be all nice and minty fresh for that big sweaty kiss Peter would plant on her when he came huffing back for his coffee.

That gave Denise a four-minute window when nobody would be in the kitchen.

Years of covert surveillance were paying off bigtime, Denise thought with satisfaction. Those long nights with binoculars, the skulking in the woods, following in rental cars, hadn't been insanity, it had been foresight. A lot of what she'd seen as problems were turning out to be plusses.

She'd been going to tell Paulette about this step in the plan. Then she learned her twin wasn't a real nurse, just a nursemaid. If she'd been a real RN it would have been good because Denise would have been more confident about the dosage. Since she wasn't, Denise hadn't said anything out of spite. Now she was glad. Given how shaken the Pigeon thing had left Paulette, the less she knew of the sordid details, the better.

Originally, Denise had planned to do this when she could take her time and make sure she got everything just right, not have to rush things to get it all done in a four-minute time slot. Most days, at two fifteen, Lily put the baby's food on to warm, then went upstairs to make the bed. Picturing it, Denise shook her head in the dark as she climbed into her Miata. What kind of a nitwit makes the bed at two in the afternoon?

Still, that left a seven-minute window. Tons of time. Denise should wait until two fifteen, but she wouldn't. Couldn't.

Tick, tick, tick.

Four minutes would have to do.

Five A.M. sharp, Denise pulled the Miata into its customary space, the place she parked for her breaking-and-entering activities. A dirt road, a quarter of a mile down from Peter and Lily's house, led to a construction boneyard no more than a hundred yards behind their property. One day a home would be built there. For the past several years it had been from whence Denise's forays into the Barnes family homestead had been staged. Car tracks could link her to the place if anybody got that far into the investigation, but she wasn't too worried. Big machinery was in and out during working hours: trucks, bulldozers, front-loaders.

By noon the tracks of the Miata would be well and thoroughly squashed.

She popped the trunk, walked around to the back of the car, and unerringly laid her hands on the crumpled McDonald's bag half wedged beneath the first aid kit. Inside, wadded in a used napkin, were three white pills, crushed to a powder. Having retrieved one of the unused Mount Desert syringes, Denise filled it half full from her water bottle, poured the powder in, shook it a few times for good measure, then stowed it carefully in her jacket pocket.

"What the hell," she whispered, and threw the bag onto the ground. Maybe she'd get lucky and the litter would blow into Peter's backyard.

THIRTY-FIVE

Heath's eyes opened to unremitting black. Where in hell was she? Clearly not in her bed in Boulder. Momentary panic from watching *Premature Burial* too many times as a kid engulfed her. The adrenaline rush brought her to full alert.

This wasn't the first time she'd woken up and not known where she was. After the accident, when she was on medications and changed hospital rooms or therapy venues, it often happened. The amnesia seldom lasted more than a second or two. A calming thought.

Ah, lucidity!

She lay in her little bed on Boar Island, and the black was not unremitting. At ground level, the tower had little in the way of natural light, but halfway up the winding stairs was a bar of living dark, dark like the midnight sky or the surface of a lake on a moonless night. There was a difference between living dark and the dark, she presumed, of a coffin six feet under.

What had wakened her?

In a second, it came to her. The lift bell had rung. Or a bell on a buoy in the ocean. Heath had seen those but never knew what they were for. To let fish know the wind was blowing? As far as she knew, both Elizabeth and Gwen were asleep in the rooms above. It was possible they could have descended the iron stairs and slipped through her room undetected. Possible but unlikely; the old stairs complained bitterly when they were used.

Heath switched on the bedside lamp, found her phone, and pinched it on. Dawn had not yet creaked. Surely John Whitman had more sense than to come calling on his lady love at this hour. She smiled, imagining the crusty old seaman serenading Gwen as she leaned over the rail around the top of the lighthouse.

Wily opened his eyes from his chosen spot at the foot of the stairs, where his charges would trip over him should they try to elude his vigilance.

"I've got ringing in my ears," Heath said to the dog.

Wily thumped his tail.

The ring must have been from a buoy, or a ship's bell. Ships did have bells, Heath remembered from old books. They told time by them. Probably they now set all the sailors' cell phones to ring at the appropriate hours. Heath turned off the light and settled down to go back to sleep.

Again the bell rang.

Definitely the lift bell.

The lift bell rang when it was called down to the jetty, and it rang when it was sent—or called—to the top of the cliff. When they'd retired for the night, it had been at the top of the cliff. Two bells; somebody had called the lift down, gotten on, then sent it up. That somebody was now on the island.

In the wee hours.

"Damn," Heath muttered. Wake E? Call Gwen? Flash an SOS to the mainland? "Why aren't you barking?" she suddenly demanded of Wily. He swept his tail over the wide boards of the floor.

Since Wily wasn't alarmed, Heath felt safe enough to see what was happening before she roused the house. The last thing she wanted was to make this ivory tower—such as it was—feel unsafe when Elizabeth was experiencing just how unsafe most of the world was.

A metal bar on legs, like a spare clothing rack, but narrower and much stronger, stood over the head of the bed. One of Leah's designs, it was lightweight, stable, and easily broken down into a civilized-sized carrying package. It was a great help when Heath overnighted away from home.

Using the bar, she hoisted herself upright, then pushed her legs free of the covers and the mattress. From there it was a fairly easy swing into Robo-butt, parked next to the bed. In one of Robo-butt's saddlebags, among other things, was a small Maglight. Heath took it out, clicked the switch a couple of times. Satisfied the batteries hadn't gone dead, she dropped it into her lap.

Rolling toward the long tunnel through the tower wall of the lighthouse, she asked, "Coming, Wily?"

The steady pad-pad of his paws on the flooring behind her was reassuring.

Though there was no moon, the arc-shaped main room of the tower, with its floor-to-ceiling windows, was surprisingly light. The sea seemed to maximize ambient light, catching the stars on the whitecaps. The granite Maine was built on had that same reflective quality, thousands of tiny facets polished by the centuries until they shone like mirrors.

Heath twisted the dead bolt, then shoved open the door with the foot of her wheelchair. Still showing no signs of alarm, Wily trotted out in front of her onto the apron of granite. Warily, she rolled after him. Halfway across the natural patio the lift platform came into view. A pile of pale stuff lay on it.

Wily trotted toward it.

"Wait," Heath called, afraid whatever had been sent up at this ungodly hour was dangerous, poisonous, or vile in some other way.

Wily ignored her, stepped delicately from the landing onto the platform, sniffed the pile, and whined. Heath clicked on the tiny flashlight, shoved the butt end into her mouth, and rolled slowly toward the dog and his catch.

It looked like a mess of fish caught in a net. Another gift from the sea provided by Gwen's beau? Wouldn't fish be nasty after even a few hours lying about? Heath rolled nearer. Saliva drooled down her chin. Since she needed both hands to roll in a straight line, she ignored it. Wily wouldn't mind. He'd been known to drool a time or two in his life.

The dog turned in a tight circle, sat down, threw his head back, and howled.

It wasn't a net of dead fish. It was a dead woman. She lay on one shoulder. Both arms were stretched above her head, the wrists tied to one of the rings used to secure cargo to the lift floor. She was naked but for one boot and the wild netting of red and silver hair.

Anna.

For a heartbeat, Heath denied it was she. Anna didn't lose, didn't die, didn't quit. Anna wasn't beaten and trussed and delivered like the morning paper. If Anna wasn't invincible, what chance did ordinary people have?

Reality snapped back.

"Gwen! Elizabeth!" Heath shouted, the Maglight falling from her jaws to her lap. She jerked the brass whistle free of the neck of her pajama top, put it to her lips, and blew for all she was worth, three piercing blasts.

"Oh my God, Anna!" She rolled until one of Robobutt's wheels was on the lift. Having put the brakes on, she levered herself out and slid down next to the body of her friend. The Maglight rolled onto the lift platform to lodge against Anna's naked breast, the light shining ghoulishly up beneath her chin.

Heath laid a hand on Anna's bare shoulder. The skin was ice cold and felt firmer than it should. "No, no, no," Heath was whispering. "Gwen!" she shouted again. Gwen was a doctor. Gwen would make it okay.

"Anna," Heath said. "Can you hear me? You're going to be just fine. Fine and dandy, damn you." As Heath murmured in a kind, reassuring voice, a voice designed to bring kittens out from under houses and rangers back from the dead, she lifted the hair from Anna's face and neck. A mass of it was pasted to her back with blood. Blood showed dark on her butt and the heel of her left foot.

"What have you been up to?" Heath asked as she felt for the carotid pulse. "You're alive," she said, more for Anna than because she was positive the weak flutter against the pads of her index and middle fingers was blood being pumped through veins.

"What is it?"

Heath turned to see Gwen, tying a robe around her, trotting toward where she sat with Anna. E, in tank top and pajama bottoms, followed close behind, her small narrow feet silent against the rock.

"Move aside," Gwen said the moment she identified the incident as medical. "Elizabeth, run for blankets."

As Gwen fell to her knees beside Anna, Heath wormed herself into a position where she could attend to the binding around Anna's wrists. The ties were cut lengths of yellow line, the kind used in boats. They weren't tied tightly. Circulation wasn't compromised, and had Anna been conscious, she could easily have escaped the bonds. Balancing as best she could on her hind end, Heath untied Anna's wrists and began massaging her cold limp hands.

"She has a pulse," Gwen said, "but it is weak and too slow." Heath said nothing. Elizabeth was sprinting from the house with an armload of blankets. Gwen was running her hands over Anna's body, palpating for injuries, breaks, and bruises.

Elizabeth dumped three down comforters onto the

ground. Heath pulled one over and began covering Anna.

Gwen sat back on her knees. "Nothing I can find. Hypothermic probably. Contusions on back, buttocks, and right heel. One lump above her left temple. That might account for the unconsciousness, but it could be any number of things. We have to get her inside and get her warmed up, then get her to a hospital as soon as possible."

"She's awake," Elizabeth whispered.

Heath leaned down so she could see Anna's eyes. They were half open.

"Hi," Anna said in a voice as creaky as a rusted gate hinge.

The eyes drifted closed again.

"That was informative," Heath growled. Seeing Anna helpless frightened her. Heath had always been a person who turned fear into anger. At the moment, she was furious and terrified. Laserlike heat burned inside her skull. Heath half believed that if she ever saw whoever did this to Anna, she could flay him using just her eyes.

For a quarter of an hour there was no talking. A comforter was ruined as the three of them dragged Anna in from the lift. Gently, they hoisted her up onto the couch, then packed down quilts around her naked body. Without being told to, Elizabeth found heating pads in one of the closets.

With a last look at Anna, she slipped into the kitchen, to microwave the pads and boil water for hot drinks,

Heath assumed. While Gwen was Velcroing a blood pressure cuff around Anna's upper arm, Heath was searching the contacts list on her phone for Peter Barnes's home number.

The silence was broken by Anna.

"Stop," she croaked.

"Hey!" Heath said with relief as she put the phone to her ear.

"No calls. Not yet," Anna managed, and, "Help me up."

Sitting up was perhaps not the best of ideas, but both Gwen and Heath had known Anna too long to think telling her to stay still would be efficacious. Gwen left the pump bulb on the cuff dangling to put an arm around Anna's shoulders, helping her into a semisitting position against the pillows piled on the arm of the sofa.

"You need to go to the hospital," Gwen said as Heath was asking, "What happened?"

Anna clutched the sides of her head as if the two soft voices were a cacophony. "What happened," she echoed. "Before you . . . Tell me what happened. I'm so cold."

With use, her voice was normalizing, but the words were slightly blurred—not the slur of a drunk so much as the drawl of a person from a very, very deep South.

"A man said he thought I was a lobster," Anna mumbled, shaking her head. "No. That can't be right. Yes. He thought I was a lobster. Said he thought I was . . . And now I'm here." She dropped her hands to her lap and looked hard first at Gwen, then at Heath.

"What are you guys doing here?" she asked with a certain petulance.

"We heard the lift bell," Heath told her. "Wily and I found you on the platform."

Heath watched, letting the information sink in through whatever was clouding Anna's perception. Anna's eyes roved the room as if to see where she'd washed up. "Boar," she said finally. Heath, Gwen, and Elizabeth, drawn in from the kitchen by Anna's voice, nodded like bobblehead dolls. Gwen took two heating pads from E. Having peeled back the blankets, she began arranging them along Anna's ribs.

Anna watched her for a long moment. "I'm naked," she observed.

"That's how we found you. Wearing only one boot. That one." Heath pointed to the sodden cordovan-colored boot standing solitary watch on the cold hearth.

"E, would you please make Anna a cup of tea, real warm but not hot, lots of sugar," Gwen said.

"No sugar," Anna said as E turned to go.

Gwen tilted her chin at her great-niece. Anna would be getting sugar.

"Do you remember anything?" Heath asked.

Anna thought. Heath waited, her fingers drumming lightly against the face of her phone, itching to call for help. "May I call Superintendent Barnes now?" Heath asked.

"Not yet. I . . ." Anna's voice faded out. Her train of

thought had evidently derailed. "Let me figure out what happed first," she said, finding her way back.

Had Anna not been showing signs of returning life—if not sanity—and Gwen not been a doctor, Heath would have made the call regardless of Anna's protestations. As it was, Anna seemed to be out of danger.

Danger of what, evidently not even Anna knew.

THIRTY-SIX

Anna was awake. A dozen times before, she'd thought she was awake, only to slip back into nightmares until she could no longer tell what was real, what had happened, and what was only a dream.

Only a dream.

There was no "only" about the dreams that pulled her down. They were a force as powerful as any she had encountered. They followed her into the waking world and threatened to drag her back.

"I am awake," she said. Her voice creaked. Her tongue was as stiff and dry as weathered wood. If taste was any indication, weathered wood from the bottom rail of an old pigsty.

"You're awake," a kind voice agreed. "And alive."

Anna rolled her eyes, eyeballs scratching against lids that felt packed with sand. "We'll see," she rasped. Heath was bent over her, a huge annoying smile on her face. "I feel like shit. My face hurts."

"You're hungover," Heath said, still grinning like a

fool. "Your head got a hard whack, but it isn't broken, according to Aunt Gwen."

Anna reached up with shaking fingers and felt above her eye. There was a lump the size of a walnut, and tender to the touch. Not broken; that was good news. At least not broken on the outside. The gray matter inside of her skull felt as if it had been scrambled like eggs. Lying down was disorienting, and she struggled to sit up. The room spun. Her stomach lurched into her throat. A hammer wielded by an invisible hand slammed into her left temple.

"Do you want to sit up?" Heath asked.

"Of course I want to sit up!" Anna grumbled. "Do you think I'm flopping around because I like looking like a landed fish?"

"Somebody got up on the wrong side of the ocean today."

Elizabeth was perched on the end of the couch where Anna lay. Anna tried to glare at her, as Heath, more trouble than help, worked to get her into a seated position without falling out of her wheelchair.

"E!" Heath said. Rising smoothly, Elizabeth trotted around the back of the sofa. Between the two of them, Anna was shoved and shored up into a sitting position.

"Damn, but I feel like shit," Anna said as bile rose up her gorge. "I'm going to be sick." Heath bobbed out of her line of sight, then bobbed back up again, a bowl in her hand.

"Gwen said you might be," she said, putting the bowl between Anna's hands.

Anna retched into the bowl, spewing up thin acid and stinking chunks.

"Done?" Heath asked gently.

"Don't be so nice," Anna said. Nice made tears threaten, and Anna was too sick to cry.

Heath smiled. "Take this, would you, E?"

"Eeeeew," Elizabeth grimaced as she removed the mess from Anna's lap.

"How long was I asleep?" Anna asked.

"Half the day," Heath said. "Gwen thought rest was the best thing for you. She gave you an antibiotic, but we didn't try and clean or dress your wounds."

"I have wounds?" Anna asked, surprised. When every inch of one's body hurt, it was hard to tell.

Elizabeth was back on her perch. "One of your heels is all scraped up, and your bottom has major road rash."

An image of her booted toes, seen down the length of her naked body, bouncing along black asphalt flashed through Anna's mind.

"I was dragged," she said, more to herself than them.

A cackle of questions battered in stereo. "By who? Where? Why? Do you remember? Dragged?"

Anna ignored them. Her skin was too tight, her hair stiff and matted; thinking was difficult. Poison pervaded her being. She was sick unto her bones.

"I need a shower," she said softly. Then, raising her head, she looked into Heath's concerned face. "A shower."

Heath and Elizabeth exchanged glances. Anna glowered. "Help her with a shower, E," Heath said finally.

"I don't need any help." Anna stood up, tottered,

then fell back on the couch. For a moment she sat blinking stupidly as resistance drained away. "That would be good, E," she said with moderate civility. "Thank you."

Leaning against the tile wall for support, hot water pouring through her salt-encrusted hair, Anna began to feel slightly more human. Most of the night and the day before were a blur. She remembered going to bed. She remembered seeing the toes of her boots. She remembered plastic sticking to her face. She remembered someone saying she was a lobster.

Four memories that didn't add up to anything. Caked in salt, contusions on her butt and heel, a knot on her forehead, a small hole that ached in her left arm, up by the shoulder, probably a needle stick: drugged, dragged, and dumped into saltwater. Without the aid of memory, logic dictated that much. Since she was not dead, one could assume she had subsequently been fished out of the saltwater. Heath and Wily had found her naked, tied to the cargo ring on the lift, shortly before sunrise.

Again, since she wasn't dead, logic suggested she was put there by the fisher-of-out, either so she would receive help or as a warning to the island's residents. E, as a stalkee, being the most obvious.

Both theories were absurd.

That didn't make them untrue.

"Are you still alive?" Elizabeth asked from the other side of the shower curtain.

"Getting there," Anna said. She could see the girl's shadow where she sat on the commode, standing by in case Anna fell or drowned.

"Let me know when you're ready to do your back," E said.

Elizabeth's comfort with her own and other people's bodies was a wonder to Anna. Nudity, injury, snot, puke, washing hair, clipping toenails—E did these things for other people as casually as she did them for herself. Maybe loving someone who occasionally required personal assistance had given her these skills. More likely she was born with them, and loving Heath had brought them to flower.

John Donne said no man was an island. He didn't say anything about women. Anna keenly felt her physical isolation from the rest of the human race, with the exception of her husband, Paul, an isolation she preferred. Every woman in her own skin, every mind in its own cranium.

Until she couldn't take care of her own skin or trust her own mind.

"I'm ready," Anna said.

"Incoming," Elizabeth replied cheerfully as she opened the shower curtain. Anna braced both hands against the opposite wall, holding herself up, while Elizabeth carefully washed the scrapes on her buttocks.

"Not as bad as we thought," E said. "Sort of like a skinned knee, but all over. Not so much bleeding as oozing. Some bleeding on your bottom, but nothing as bad as your heel. Aunt Gwen did that up while you were out cold. Now that the bandage is wet, she'll have to redress it. She said your heel is pretty much like hamburger. Nothing broken, though. She didn't want to mess with your back until you'd slept. We took a look at it. Heath and I thought we should put you out of your misery, but Aunt Gwen said it wasn't too bad, and it isn't."

Whoever had dragged her across the pavement must not have dragged her far, Anna decided. A protracted trip would have left her skinned alive.

"Where is Gwen?" Anna asked, mostly to keep Elizabeth chattering. Unlike the prattle of other people, the prattle of her goddaughter was soothing, like rain on a tin roof. Usually Anna listened for clues of what was happening in E's world, and heart, and mind. Sometimes, like now, she just rode the flow of words, enjoying the murmur of a happy life burbling past her ears, a sweet cacophony more soothing to the soul than silence.

"Aunt Gwen is in Bar Harbor meeting Dez Hammond—one of the old ladies who lived here—for coffee. Aunt Gwen felt guilty about abandoning you, but she said it was very important. An errand for Chris Zuckerberg, the other lady, the one that's sick. Some sort of meeting Ms. Zuckerberg was too sick to go to.

"Aunt Gwen took her medical bag. She said she was going to get a DNA sample or something. She had a glass tube and Q-tips and everything. Very *CSI*. Of course she wouldn't tell us what it's about since it's a doctor thing."

Anna's knees were growing weak. Her arms, bracing her against the shower wall, were tiring. "Are you about done?" she asked.

"Done," E said. Anna felt a towel being draped over her shoulders. Pulling her aching arms away from the wall, she noticed a red mark on the inside of her arm at the elbow. "Another needle stick," she said, turning to show Elizabeth the way a little girl might show her mother a splinter.

"That was Aunt Gwen. She took blood while you slept. You didn't even move an eyelid," Elizabeth said with obvious pride in her aunt's needlework.

"Took blood?" Anna echoed stupidly.

"*CSI* on every channel today. She's getting it tested for drugs," E said matter-of-factly.

"She's not in law enforcement," Anna said.

"She's a doctor. They do all that blood stuff."

Of course. "I'm not thinking straight," Anna admitted.

"Duh," E said, holding out a second towel for Anna's hair. "Sit."

Obediently, Anna sat on the lid of the commode and let Elizabeth towel-dry her hair. Gray splotches floated in the corners of her eyes, as amorphous and will-o'-the-wisp as her recollections of the previous night. The shower had washed away the salt, the blood, and the last of the anger she'd brought with her from the other side. Without the anger, her brain was a cold and sluggish thing, thoughts being forced out like the last of the toothpaste from the tube.

"Was I raped?" she asked, before her brain had time to mention that might not be an appropriate question to ask a sixteen-year-old girl, and one's goddaughter at that.

"Nope," E said as if it were the most obvious question in the world—and it was. "Aunt Gwen said there was no evidence to indicate any kind of sexual trauma. She did a rape kit anyway. Don't worry. The rest of us, even Wily, were banished from the entire house while she did her exam."

Anna was absurdly relieved. Bad enough if E and Heath had seen that sort of thing, but if Wily had, she'd have had to resign from the pack in shame.

Three taps sounded on the door. "Are you guys about done?" Heath asked. "E, your visitor has finally seen fit to come, so make sure Anna has something decent on."

Both caught the sour emphasis Heath put on the word "visitor." Anna raised an eyebrow.

Turning to take a terrycloth robe from a hook on the back of the bathroom door, Elizabeth said, "It's my friend."

"The one with the boat," Anna said.

"Yes."

"What made you decide to blow Boat Boy's cover?" Anna asked.

"Before, he needed you not to know more than you needed to know. It's the other way around now," Elizabeth said as she held out a thick yellow chenille bathrobe.

Anna snorted. Now she was on a need-to-know basis with her goddaughter. Elizabeth had grown from a skinny little kid into an entire human being, and Anna had seen every bit of it, a terrifying miracle.

"Are you going to arrest him?" Elizabeth asked.

Anna stood and let her goddaughter help her into the robe.

"I sure as hell feel like arresting somebody," she said.

THIRTY-SEVEN

The shower worked wonders. Anna was fairly steady on her feet. Her mind was clear enough for minor calculations. The mirror proved unkind. There was a nasty bruise on her forehead, her skin was pasty, and her eyes had dark circles beneath and red rims around. No beauty contests would be won today.

As she walked from the bath into the room around the tower, the lift bell rang.

"That will be Aunt Gwen," E said, hovering behind Anna's right shoulder. "She wanted to be in on this, and her meeting with Mrs. Hammond was over."

Elizabeth settled Anna on the sofa with so little fuss, Anna didn't even mind. Heath rolled in from the kitchen to hand Anna a mug of steaming cream of tomato soup. Tears stung the corners of Anna's eyes. Tomato soup was just the thing, the only thing, her stomach wanted. When she was growing up it was the food for ailing children. Dotted with chicken pox, she and Molly had sat across from each other at the scarred old kitchen table spooning soup with oyster crackers. Later it had been mumps and tomato soup and ginger ale. Then measles. Because of tomato soup, she and her sister had lived to adulthood.

She sipped, sighed, and silently blessed Heath with a smile. "Where's Boat Boy?" she asked.

"He went to meet the lift," Heath said, rolling over to one of the wide windows. "Seems Gwen decided John Whitman should be here."

Despite the healing magic of soup, Anna wasn't up for a party. "Why?"

"Boat Boy is named Walter. Walter is John's grandson," Elizabeth said.

"Curiouser and curiouser," Anna said. Then, "Walter Whitman? As in *Leaves of Grass*? A poet, no less?"

Evidently E hadn't heard of Walt Whitman. Anna would fix that another day. She took another fortifying slurp of soup.

Gwen, John, and Walter Whitman came in from the patio.

Boat Boy was so handsome Anna scowled. Light brown hair waved back off a square brow in what had been called a surfer cut when she was in college. Shoulders were broad and arms muscled—from rowing boats with muffled oars, no doubt. Lips were chiseled, eyes wide set and a deep rich hazel. The plaid shirt straining across his chest was almost a cliché in its woodsy perfection.

Unless John had more than one son, Boat Boy Walter was the son of the lobsterman shot for poaching, the boy accused of being an accomplice.

Gorgeous, an orphan, and a fugitive.

Anna had to admit, had she been sixteen and marooned on an island with annoying adults, she would have jumped ship with this boy in a heartbeat.

"This is my grandson Walter," John said.

Anna opened her mouth to introduce herself. What came out was "I'm not a lobster." Clapping her mouth shut, she frowned. Kaleidoscope fashion, parts of her lost night were spinning through her gray matter.

"A lobster trap," Walter said apologetically. "I thought you were a lobster trap. It was wicked hard gettin' you out of the drink."

"Lobster" was pronounced *lobstah;* "hard" was *hahd.* Coming from the Apollo-meets-Ralph-Lauren vision, the hard New England accent sounded out of place, yet it, too, was charming. Anna reminded herself that often as not, Prince Charming turned out to be just another clown.

"Let's all sit," Gwen said sensibly. "This may take a while."

Walter and his grandfather sat on the outer edge of the chairs, elbows on knees, hands clasped, the way Anna remembered the hired hands sitting when she was a kid. Comfortable, assured, but not wanting to be seen to be taking the boss's hospitality for granted.

"You saved my life," Anna said to Walter. "Let's start there and work our way back. That way I'll be in a more forgiving mood when we get to the kidnapping of my goddaughter."

Anna had been shooting for a spot of humor, a little levity to ease the proceedings. Through a furry brain and a swollen lip, the words came out more like a threat. John started a low grumble in his throat. Wily echoed it from the cold hearth, where he lay watching the proceedings with interest.

"Her bark is worse than her bite," she heard E whisper.

"She bites?" Walter whispered back, then caught Anna's eye and grinned sheepishly. "No disrespect meant," he apologized.

"I do bite," Anna admitted with a sigh. "But I'm not rabid, so, if it happens, you'll survive."

"Tell the woman your story," John said, jutting his chin in Anna's direction.

"You'll know by now, it was my dad was shot by Billy Gomer. Killed for poaching," Walter began uncertainly.

"I didn't know the shooter's name, but I'd heard," Anna said. It had been two, maybe three weeks since this boy's father was murdered. Walter's words—and, to give him credit, tone of voice—were matter-of-fact. The eyes and the small muscles around his mouth told Anna of the grief and strain. "You were accused of doing the same," she said before sympathy could get the better of her.

"That's right. But we were no poachers. Neither my dad nor me. It was about a patch of good fishing that was being fought over and we won. We were taking forty to fifty percent more lobsters out than Gomer ever did, so he starts saying we were taking from his line. He and my dad got into it, and Gomer shot Dad. Killed him right there." Walter clamped his lips together and stared at the floor. These were not men who wore their hearts on their sleeves. Pain was not for public consumption.

"Is this Gomer fellow in jail?" Anna asked.

Walter's grandfather barked a bitter laugh. "Billy is goin' on eighty. Twelve kids, nine of them boys, and all got a patch and a vote. There won't be any goin' to jail for Billy Gomer."

"Mr. Gomer is mean to the soles of his boots," Walter said, shaking his head. "But he's known to be honest. I think he believed me and Dad were poaching because he couldn't believe the truth, which is we're better fishermen than he ever was."

"I'd say that's about right," John added. "I'd say old Gomer believes himself. Since he's sworn he'll shoot Walter if he gets a chance, I don't much care what he believes or doesn't believe." The older man's jaw set in a concrete square. Anna would not want John Whitman as an enemy.

"I don't think he will," Walter said. "The fight was always between him and Dad. Much as I'd like to see it, I don't think there's any good to be had by lockin' Mr. Gomer up. He's sure to die in a few years anyway."

Another day Anna might have been fascinated with the ins and outs of lobster fishing in Maine. At present her head was heavy and her face hurt her, and undoubtedly hurt them to look at. "I'm sorry about your dad," she said as kindly as she could manage. The soup had helped. She almost liked herself.

Her well-meant words started to eat away at Walter's

stoicism, so she went on. "But how does this relate to saving my life and kidnapping my goddaughter?"

John Whitman stood abruptly. "There was no kidnapping." His scarred hands were balled into fists. Suddenly he wasn't quaint or colorful.

"It's okay, John," Gwen said quickly. "Ranger humor."

"I don't have much use for park rangers," John grumbled.

"They grow on you eventually," Heath said dryly.

Slowly, John lowered himself back onto the edge of the chair, his hands again folded between his knees.

Walter took his time, looking first to his grandfather, then to Elizabeth. He must have found what he was searching for, because he went on. "Mr. Gomer's talk got my fishing license suspended, pending investigation."

"An investigation that isn't going to happen," John said grimly.

"Probably not," Walter agreed. "People forget others' troubles pretty quick. The lines Mr. Gomer shot Dad over are right here off the island, between Boar and Mount Desert. Rich beds. I figured if I could find out who was stealing from the traps, I could clear Dad's name and get my license back."

"So you went into hiding, and have been watching the area?" Anna asked.

"That I have. I'd been camping out in the old wing of the house, the one seaside."

"Walter was our ghost, remember, Mom?" Elizabeth asked.

Heath nodded. A story Anna would have to hear later. Clearing his father's name, and his own, to get his fishing license back might have struck Anna as a silly piece of teenage posturing in another place. In Maine, once the Whitmans' licenses were suspended, their trap line would have been farmed out to another fisherman.

Chances were good Walter had worked with his dad and granddad since he was old enough to mend traps. He'd probably apprenticed for two years under his father to get a license. Lobster fishing might very well be all he knew and all he wanted to know.

"You've been living on Boar and watching the water at night?" Anna clarified.

"That's about it," Walter said.

"You were watching last night," Anna said.

"I was. I saw a boat I've seen before. A small dark-colored outboard. Both times before, I lost it. Weather once, and once it was just plain too dark to see where it went. It has no running lights. There are three green LED lights near the bow, but they're no bigger than that." With his thumb, Walter indicated the tip of his little finger. "And they aren't bright. Decoration maybe. Whoever owns the boat dives at night. Robbing traps is my guess. Last night, there was some light and the seas were calm. I saw that same boat coming onto the line of traps, so I rowed out as close as I could without them noticing me."

"Muffled oars," Anna said.

"That's right, and their engine noise to cover for me."

"More than one?" Anna asked.

"This time there were two in the boat. Last two times just the one. I saw them throw something over the side. I figured they were up to something, so I pulled out what they'd tossed in."

"My exceeding good luck," Anna said. "Which way did they go?"

"They came from the north up by Schoodic, and headed down toward Somes Sound when they left."

"And you were stuck with a very strange catch," Gwen said.

"Odd things get thrown in the ocean," John said.

"Anna is an odd thing," E said.

"You put me on the lift?" Anna asked.

"I knew the bell would wake up Elizabeth, and I knew her great-aunt was a doctor," Walter said. "I suppose I could have stayed, but I couldn't see what use it would be to anybody."

Anna thought about that for a moment. There was really no point in his staying. Her desire to dislike young Walter was slowly being overwhelmed by warm cozy feelings.

"Why did you tie me down to the cargo ring?" she asked in a last attempt to find fault with the boy who stole Elizabeth's heart—and kidnapped Wily.

"So you wouldn't fall off," he said simply.

The tail end of Anna's dislike vanished like a snake down a hole. All in all, she was glad to see it go. Disliking people was labor intensive at the best of times, and today wasn't the best of times.

THIRTY-EIGHT

There had been little more either John or his grandson could tell them. Anna had been wrapped in black plastic—either a bag or a sheet. Walter had torn it open. The plastic had been lost at sea. If there was anything in the bag with her, he hadn't noticed. Nor could he tell them any more about the mystery boat than he already had.

The Whitmans left for Bar Harbor, promising to look for the dark boat on their way into town. Walter promised he'd call E in the morning.

Elizabeth was positively wriggling with delight at having her beau outed and approved. Walter seemed as pleased as she to be out of the shadows. Another point for him.

Anna held out no hope the Whitmans would find the runabout that had nearly served as her hearse. Not only had it been headed in the opposite direction—Somes instead of Bar Harbor—but there were coves and jetties, private boats and commercial, in a thousand places in the waters around Acadia. Small, dark-colored, outboard—didn't narrow it down much.

The lift bell had barely rung, lowering the Whitmans to the jetty, when Gwen had a blood pressure cuff around Anna's upper arm. "A friend of a friend, a doctor at Mount Desert Hospital, was more than kind. She ran the tox screen on your blood. A heavy dose of Rohypnol and a muscle relaxant. You should be feeling better by tomorrow, almost your old self," she told Anna.

That was good news. Anna had been doped once, and once slipped LSD. By good fortune she'd never been given anything highly addictive or—so far—fatal.

"I wish rufies were harder to come by," Heath said. "If you pay attention to the news, it seems there are more date rape drugs than sex ed classes in most school districts."

"I'd hate to have a daughter in this day and age," Anna said.

"Ah, but you do," Gwen murmured.

That was another drawback when it came to children. One got fond of them, and then they went speeding away in a convertible with a bottle of Jack Daniel's and no seat belt.

"Have you yet seen fit to share with Heath why you didn't want the medical establishment or law enforcement called?" Gwen asked as she pumped the rubber bulb tightening the cuff.

"She did," Heath said. Heath was sitting in Robo-butt near the cold hearth, one hand idly playing with Wily's right ear, the other holding a glass half full of bourbon-and-water.

"Murdering me doesn't make sense," Anna said, feeling the slight claustrophobia the tightening of a blood pressure cuff always gave her. "I've been trying to work it in with the cyberstalker and/or the Duffy murder—not because either makes sense, but because they are the only items of interest I've been involved in since coming to Maine. I think I might have a better shot at getting to the bottom of it if I remain dead for a while."

"A hundred twenty over seventy. Better than most twenty-year-olds," Gwen said, deflating the blood pressure cuff. "I can see wanting to stay dead—no one pesters the dead. But won't the Acadia people wonder where you are? Aren't you acting chief ranger?"

"I called in sick, told Peter what I was up to. We argued. I won," Anna explained succinctly.

A cell phone played a few bars of "Yankee Doodle Dandy." "That's mine," Gwen said. "Would you get it, E?"

Elizabeth picked up the phone. "It's Mrs. Hammond," she said, passing the phone to Gwen, who sat on a stool at Anna's side.

"Dez," Gwen said into the phone. Her face went tight and tired. Without the burning energy within, her flesh pulled down. Pouches showed beneath her eyes. Shadows hollowed her cheeks.

Shangri-La, Anna thought as she watched her friend aging in front of her.

"Okay," Gwen said. "Okay. Let me know if I can do anything. Soon as it comes in, I promise. No, I don't doubt it either. It's a crying shame, that's what it is. Call me tomorrow?" Gwen pushed the OFF button but continued to stare down at the phone.

"What is it?" E asked.

Anna knew it was death. Death masks weren't just for the dead. Many times she'd seen them slipped onto the faces of survivors. Gwen wore one now.

"Chris died today, while Dez and I were in Bar Harbor," Gwen said.

Heath rolled over and put her arm around her aunt. E knelt on Gwen's other side and laid her head in her lap. Gathering of warmth and strength, being enfolded in the arms of loved ones, Anna knew, was beneficial for most people, so she watched in respectful silence. Wily, probably feeling sorry for her because she was not exactly of the human race, jumped up beside her on the sofa. A pain-filled whine let her know what the thoughtful gesture had cost his old injuries.

Gwen sniffed and rubbed her eyes. "It's not as if Chris and I were close. For the past twenty years it's been mostly Christmas and birthday cards, maybe a call now and then," she said after blowing her nose. "It's not a surprise. Chris—and Dez and I—knew she wasn't going to live to a ripe old age. It's just that the timing couldn't be more tragic."

"Because she was so young?" Heath asked. To Anna she said, "She wasn't even sixty."

"Fifty-seven," Gwen said. "Had her first heart attack at fifty-four."

"Is that usual?" Anna asked.

"More so now than it used to be, what with obesity, blood pressure drugs, and so on. Chris wasn't obese.

She had a weakening of the vessel walls in her heart muscles. Every doctor has a theory, but none of us agree—not that I know much about hearts over the age of ten."

"Is that what you and Dez met about? Ms. Zuckerberg's health?" E asked. As for Anna, Chris was just a name to Elizabeth.

"No. Worse in a way. Because we were out, Dez wasn't with Chris when she died. That will be hard on her. They've been together over fifteen years," Gwen said. Sighing, she moved from the stool to a comfortable armchair. "I could do with what you're having, Heath."

"Anna?" Heath asked as she rolled toward the kitchen where the bourbon bottle lived.

"No more drugs for me in this lifetime," Anna said.

"Lesbians?" E asked.

"Why does everybody have to be a lesbian!" Gwen snapped. "They became friends when they were girls. Dez was the maid here when the babies were born. After Dez's husband died, and Chris's health started to go, she came to live here with Chris. Lesbians! For heaven's sake. Can't anybody just be friends with anybody anymore?" Gwen grumbled.

Heath rolled back in with an obviously much-needed bourbon. Anna had never seen Gwen irritable. The pediatrician's mood was always so bubbly Anna occasionally wondered if she prescribed a little something for herself.

"This baby thing is new," Heath said. "Until we got to Boar, I didn't know Chris had children. I didn't know she'd ever been married."

"You said she didn't have kids," E said accusingly.

"So I did," Gwen admitted. "That was an attempt to keep you out of more misery and keep Chris's secret. I failed at both. It's been a long day. Now that Chris is gone, I guess her old secrets can't hurt her. Chris never married, but she did have children. Forty years ago— forty-two now, I guess—when Chris was fourteen, she gave birth to twin girls. Here on Boar Island. I was the doctor. It was my first paying job out of medical school. Her mother—a witch spelled with a *b*—didn't want anyone to know her daughter had gotten pregnant. Because Chris was a minor, the witch didn't need her consent to give the babies up for adoption—or so she said. There was enough family money to make her right, no doubt.

"A few years ago a couple of things happened. First, Chris's mother finally had the decency to kick the bucket—Chris had never gotten free of her, not really— and Chris had her first heart attack. That was when she decided to find her daughters if she could."

"Nearly sixty and still afraid to admit she'd had twins when she was fourteen?" Elizabeth asked. "People now would be going on talk shows and writing books about it."

"Not Chris. From age eleven to age thirteen, Chris was molested by their rabbi. When she became pregnant, she told her mother. Her father tried to beat the truth of who the real father was out of her. Her mother packed her off to Boar Island with only herself and a maid—Dez, all of twelve years old—for company," Gwen explained.

"Her own mother didn't believe about the rabbi?" Elizabeth asked. "What a rat."

"Worse," Gwen said. "Her father didn't believe her, but her mother knew she was telling the truth. The rabbi was beloved and rich and the witch didn't want to damage her own social standing by crying 'Pervert!' "

"Did she find her daughters?" Heath asked.

"Three or so years ago she put an ad in the papers, you know the sort of thing—seeking identical twins separated at birth, would now be thirty-something, legacy involved," Gwen said. She took a swig of bourbon and held it in her mouth for a moment before she swallowed. Anna took over the task of fiddling with Wily's ears.

"She didn't get an answer to that ad, or the next one, or the one after that. Assuming the girls would have been adopted out locally, and quietly, and without any paper trail, Chris only put ads in papers around this area," Gwen told them. "All of a sudden, last week, somebody answered an ad from a while ago. Chris was so excited. Not a good thing when your blood vessel walls are disintegrating. She insisted that Dez and I go meet with the woman—Dez to question her, me to get a DNA sample if the woman was willing."

"You'd have to," Anna said. "The word 'legacy' should have brought out every greedy woman for miles. I'm surprised there were no responses to the first ads."

"Mainers are a decent people," Gwen said.

"When they're not shooting each other for poaching," Anna whispered to E, who'd joined her and Wily on the sofa.

"I took the sample, a cheek swab, but Dez and I think she's legitimate—"

"Not literally," Heath said.

Gwen frowned at her, then went on. "Other than the bleached-out hair, she is the spitting image of Chris when she was in her early forties: same color eyes, same overlapping front incisors, same oval face and straight eyebrows."

The description tugged at Anna, but she let it pass. After being drugged, bagged, and dumped, a little paranoia was surely normal.

"How did she know she was a twin?" E asked. "I mean if they were separated at birth and all that, you wouldn't know, would you?"

"That was the only fishy part," Gwen said. "We asked her that same question—though believe it or not, neither one of us thought of it at first. She said she had recently found her sister, but she wouldn't tell us who it was, or if the sister knew about our meeting—nothing. Though she seemed like a good woman, if on the naïve side, I couldn't help but wonder if she planned on sharing the legacy with her twin, and of course she has to. Chris needs to give them both the news. Needed to."

The sun was low over Mount Desert, knifing into the room in a wedge of rich coppery light. Gwen squinted into the shaft of dancing motes for a moment. "Chris died. Damn. She will never get to see her daughters—not even one of them. It just makes my heart ache."

"What's the legacy?" E asked. Anna had been wondering the same thing but had become too civilized to blurt it out at the graveside, so to speak.

"Boar Island, this house," Gwen said. "There isn't much left in investments, but I imagine one could get a pretty penny for a private island off the coast of Acadia National Park. The historic value of the lighthouse would be worth something, I would think."

"Jeeze, yuh think?" Heath mocked gently. "I bet this rock would be worth millions of dollars to some rich New Yorker who wants a six-thousand-square-foot summer cottage to use for a couple of weeks each year. Not a bad legacy. Juicy enough to want to steal it from your sister."

"That's the good news part of the legacy," Gwen said, then sighed again, more deeply this time. "The bad news is that their biological father—"

"The child molester the witch was so into protecting," Heath butted in.

"Died of Huntington's disease," Gwen finished.

"Shit," Heath breathed. Gwen shot her a reproachful glance.

Elizabeth stared at her mother, then turned to Anna. "What's the big deal? He was a pervert. Who cares if he died? It's not like they'd want to look up dear old Dad for the holidays. I sure wouldn't."

"Huntington's is hereditary," Anna said. "There's a fifty-fifty chance the child will have the disease if one parent carries it."

"It is a terrible disease," Gwen said. "Pitiless. It's a neurodegenerative genetic disorder, which means the nerve cells in the brain break down. There's a whole host of symptoms ranging from loss of motor control to severe psychiatric disorders and dementia."

"Gosh," Elizabeth said. "You'd think they'd know they had it already."

"Most people start showing symptoms in their late thirties and early forties. Sometimes it manifests earlier or later, but if you didn't know your family history, you might not know what was happening to you," Gwen told E. "That's what Chris was worried about, that they wouldn't get medical care if they had it, or that, without the money from the sale of Boar, they couldn't afford it. A person with Huntington's can live twenty or more years after the first onset of symptoms, getting progressively worse and worse."

"Is there anything you can do about it?" Heath asked.

"Not much," Gwen said.

"Then who'd want to know they had it till they had it?" E asked.

Anna suspected she wasn't so much asking anybody in particular as demanding answers of the universe. Why would anyone want to get tested? A fifty percent chance of no longer worrying about it. Why would anyone who wasn't worrying about it want to know?

Gwen answered E's question. "There are some drugs that show promise. There's also the issue of safety to self and others."

"Driving," E said.

"Gas stoves, matches, babysitting, getting lost, knocking over hot coffee, the whole gamut of dangers, and we haven't even gotten to psychiatric issues," Gwen said. "At some point it becomes unsafe not to seek medical care."

"My biological father is dead and I don't know his medical history," E said. "Could I have it?"

"You could," Gwen answered slowly. "But you're more likely to get cancer or pneumonia or hydrophobia. Huntington's is rare. If you're going to dwell on it, I'll get you tested."

"You don't have the gene," Heath said. "Your father died in a motorcycle accident when he was fifty-five, remember?"

"Right," E said, sounding relieved rather than sad. Anna was unsurprised. E's father had been absent since she was eighteen months old. "Did you tell her—the daughter?"

"We didn't. Chris wanted to do that," Gwen said. "Now Chris is gone. I'm afraid the twins do have the gene. This poor woman seemed to have some cognitive dysfunction. We had to repeat ourselves. Sometimes she appeared confused, unnaturally docile."

"Maybe she just isn't very bright," Heath offered.

"She also showed chorea. Involuntary movement in her hands." Gwen flicked her wrist.

Suddenly, what had niggled in Anna's brain snapped into place: bleached blonde, overlapping front teeth, cigarettes being flipped out on the ground.

"Paulette Duffy?" she asked.

THIRTY-NINE

Once again Anna was sitting at Peter Barnes's kitchen table. As superintendent, he could keep a nine-to-five, Monday-through-Friday schedule if he wanted. Since the baby had been born, he did. Lily was watching television in the front room; Olivia, in a soft pink Onesie, was curled up on the couch beside her, making tiny grunting sounds like a piglet.

Anna set her teacup down and gazed past Peter at the charming picture on the couch. Mother and daughter, happy, safe, beautiful. Would that it would always be so.

"Elizabeth's cyberstalker has sent an ultimatum," she said more abruptly than she'd intended. "E's supposed to show up alone, in person, at a time and place to be determined. Or else."

"Preying on children! God, but it makes my stomach turn! Throw in sexual perversion and I'm ready to change my stance on the death penalty," Peter said. He didn't glance at his baby girl, but Anna noticed his head jerk as if he'd been going to and stopped himself. Attitudes changed when one had skin in the game. Taking a hit while fighting for the principle of a thing was fine, but when the good fight began to cause collateral damage to innocents, how to be a hero became more complex.

"Heath would be too conspicuous in her wheelchair, and logically, the stalker is someone who knows Elizabeth; ergo, he might know Heath or me or even Gwen. I was hoping to borrow an unknown face so it won't be only me and Gwen. Though smart and fierce, Gwen is small and somewhere north of seventy-five."

"There's always the Bar Harbor police, the Maine State Troopers, the sheriff's department," Peter said drily. "All perfectly legitimate and, from what I've experienced, competent options. Not as reassuring as an elderly pediatrician, I'm sure, but they do their best."

"I have great respect for small-town police and sheriff's departments," Anna said. "They see a little of everything and have to deal with it by themselves. They tend to be generalists, the way rangers were in the good old days, before we carried guns. It's the time-frame and subject matter that make me want to keep it personal."

"How so?" Peter asked.

"With cyberbullying, police don't yet know what to do, where they stand, what the procedure is; nobody really does. The police back home more or less blew Elizabeth off. Not out of malice, more out of this-isn't-my-jurisdiction.

"The or-else meeting is tomorrow. That's not much time to coordinate with officers who may not deal well with a girl from Boulder, Colorado, hiding out in Maine, who says she's meeting a stalker who posts dirty things about her on the Internet. I doubt we'd get things sorted out in less than the twenty-odd hours we've got."

"Put the guy off. Tell him you'll meet day after to-morrow, or next week," Peter suggested. "That might give you time to get things set up with local law enforcement."

"It might. It also might scare him back into the cyber woods. Then E will have to live not knowing when the bastard is going to pop out again."

"I wouldn't wish that on anybody, especially not a teenaged girl," Peter said.

"Marriage and fatherhood have made you downright sensitive," Anna joked.

"Estrogen seems to have a civilizing effect on me," he admitted. "I can't give you anybody. I shouldn't have let you and Denise go on NPS time. Bad judgment on my part, and let's hope it stays our little secret, at least until I'm retired. What I can do is give Artie the day off—you're on sick leave—and if you and Artie choose to spend the day hanging out with septuagenarian aunts and underage girls, that's your business."

Anna's eyes were blurring. Drug residue. She blinked rapidly to clear them.

"You look like shit," Peter told her kindly. "You should have let me come out to Boar."

"I had cabin fever," Anna said. Talking hurt—her upper lip was bruised—but nothing like the pain in her left heel or her butt. Gwen had bandaged her various scrapes. Anna felt like she was wearing diapers under her jeans. "I needed to get off the island. I'll be back in Schoodic tonight."

"Hoping for another attack?" Peter asked. He took a sip of hot tea, raising his eyebrows over the rim of the cup at her.

"No. I'm dead, don't forget," she said.

"Right. How's that supposed to work for us?" he asked.

Anna rubbed her face. "I must admit I wasn't thinking too clearly when I wanted to stay dead. I had a sort of half-baked notion that I could appear like the ghost of Hamlet's father, and the guilty parties would fall down and confess, or at least look much amazed. Trouble is, this ghost doesn't know to whom it would be profitable to appear. Now I think I'd like to stay dead until we get this business with the stalker over with. If I'm dead, nobody will be taking potshots at me."

"Artie and I made a quiet visit to Schoodic today and had a look around," Peter said. "We found a broken needle—the kind that fits in a plastic syringe—in front of the Rockefeller building. It's been bagged and will be tested."

"Gwen went through the Mount Desert lab," Anna told him. "Rohypnol and muscle relaxants were in my blood."

"Good to have friends in high places," Peter said. Being superintendent of a major national park couldn't get evidence tested in a four-hour time frame: lack of funds and facilities, the need to stand in line behind other law enforcement organization at shared labs. "We found your other boot," he went on. "Once it's been through the system, you can have it back. It was about halfway between the Rockefeller building and Schoodic Point. Schoodic was probably where the boat was beached. Nothing interesting in your apartment or on the stairs."

"No *CSI Acadia*?" Anna asked with a smile. "No tiny thread or droplet to lead us to the bad guys?"

"Sorry," Peter said. "Have you remembered anything new?"

"I don't know," Anna said honestly. "The Rohypnol has an amnesiac built in. It's not total, but everything is stretched and warped, like the memory of a dream. Walter said there were two people in the boat, and I sort of remember two people in my apartment—or the parking lot or somewhere. I haven't any idea whether I really remember two or, because I was told there were two, I think I remember. Most of the day I've been poking at my poor raddled brain. I think I might think the two were small. I think I might think they were dressed like ninjas, all in black. I think I might think they wore white gloves like Mickey Mouse. I don't trust my own memories. Before I can believe myself I need corroboration from people that weren't stoned out of their minds."

"We talked to the sculptors," Peter said. "Nobody saw anything or heard anything. We talked to your boyfriend—Walter Whitman—"

"Don't speak ill of my savior," Anna said. She sipped her tea. Earl Grey. Right up there with tomato soup for curing what ails.

"Seems like a good kid. A little monomaniacal about clearing his dad's name, but I can understand that."

"Good thing he is, or I'd be sleeping with the fishes," Anna said.

"He gave us a statement about the boat that dumped you, and precisely when and where that dumping occurred. We put out an APB to the Coast Guard and local marinas. Today I'd hoped to get a diver down where you went in. Something might have fallen from the bag you were in, or their boat. Problem is, Denise Castle, the ranger who drove you around, is our only certified diver, and she just retired."

"She went through with it?" Anna was surprised at that. Denise didn't strike her as a woman who had anyplace else to go. It wasn't anything the woman had said or done, it was the starkness of her apartment: nothing personal, no pictures with people in them, family, friends, or even co-workers. Just that one bedside photo from which Peter Barnes had been amputated.

"She did. I think she was as shocked as everybody else."

"Struck me that way, too. She'd not talked about it before?" Anna asked.

Peter looked into the other room, where his wife and child nestled in the flickering light from the television. "Why do you ask?"

"Not sure," Anna said.

Peter sighed and rubbed his jaw like a bad actor trying to indicate he's thinking. "Yes and no," he said finally. "She seemed to be happy here, but—you know Denise and I lived together for eleven years?"

"I remember, vaguely," Anna said.

"After the first shit was done hitting the fan, Denise seemed okay. Then Lily came and the baby. Denise seemed fine with that, seemed totally over the split. She brought Olivia a really beautiful coming-home gift—an angel figurine from Lenox, not cheap—and has been nice to Lily. I happen to know Denise has no family and no real friends, so on the one hand, I was surprised she just up and retired without any notice. On the other hand, there have been a few times I've caught her looking at Lily or me, or seen her face go kind of odd when somebody mentions our house, that makes me think she might not be as much over the split as she acts. So I wasn't surprised she up and re-tired. Does that make sense?"

"Why now?" Anna asked. The timing of an incident could tell one a great deal. That was the moment when something changed. "After hanging on through the split, the marriage to Lily, the birth of Olivia, why did Denise choose now to retire?"

"Who knows," Peter said wearily. "I haven't a clue as to why Denise does anything. We got Walter Whit-man squared away with the local police," he said, changing the subject. "There wasn't an arrest warrant out for him. Town police try and stay out of lobster wars. If there's any danger to Walt, it'll come from other lobstermen. John Whitman thinks blood has cooled enough the kid could come out of hiding, but that won't get him his line back. Without fishing rights, he hasn't got a future. At least not around here. I told him to talk with Gwen. If he's going to be squatting on Boar to do his spying, it should be with the owner's permission."

"The owner is dead," Anna said. "Chris Zuckerberg bought the farm this afternoon."

Peter sat back in his chair. Inwardly, Anna flinched. Wrapped up in her own troubles, she'd forgotten that Peter probably knew Ms. Zuckerberg. Not only was Acadia a small world during the winters, and people got to know one another, but any self-respecting superintendent would want to have some kind of relationship with his rich, private-land-owning neighbors.

"Sorry," Anna murmured as she hid her nose in her teacup. "Did you know Chris had kids?"

"I didn't," Peter said.

"Twins, girls, adopted out at birth. Chris was trying to find them when she died. Actually had found one—or thought she had. Paulette Duffy."

"Mrs. Kurt Duffy?" Peter asked.

"That's the one," Anna said. "Odd, isn't it, how one day you've never heard of Paulette Duffy, then she's popping up everywhere?"

"Not so odd. Every time I learn a word I've never heard before, guaranteed I'll hear it three times before the week is out."

"There was a legacy, enough to make murdering a husband worthwhile if one didn't wish to share. Though, from what I hear, most women would have murdered Kurt Duffy for free," Anna said.

"Iron-clad alibi," Peter said. "Half a dozen acquaintances and strangers can attest that she was in the Acadian at the time of the murder."

"But if Paulette is Chris Zuckerberg's long-lost child, she has an identical twin sister," Anna said.

Peter digested that for a minute. "Damn," he said finally. "So mysterious twin sits at the Acadian while Paulette kills her husband?"

"Maybe," Anna said. "Or maybe the other way around. Or maybe they're both innocent."

"Speaking of innocents."

Lily was standing in the kitchen door, Olivia in her arms. "It's Livvy's bedtime."

Peter leapt up like a terrier offered a treat. "Come on," he said to Anna. "You can be an aunt."

Because they clearly thought she would like nothing better than to watch them tucking their baby into its bed for the night, Anna obligingly rose and followed the familial parade up the stairs.

As she would have expected, the nursery was a froth of girly pink, but well done and spotlessly clean. An old-fashioned white antiqued-wood dressing table, with a large looking glass in a matching frame, mirrored the bassinette with its rows of white lace, a mobile of pink and blue and yellow ducklings hanging from the hood.

Peter and Lily cooed and prattled. Anna looked at the guardian angel. It was a lovely thing, not the usual flowing skirts and tiny feet, but a bell-shaped dress with many colors and sturdy handsome wings. On its arm was a basket of flowers.

Anna picked it up.

"Denise gave Livvy that," Lily said. "Wasn't that sweet of her?"

Anna turned it over.

"Sweet," she said, but either it wasn't a Lenox or it had been broken and repaired. The bottom was patched with plaster of paris.

FORTY

It was late when Denise finally staggered into the foyer of her apartment building. Her mailbox was empty. She'd half expected a note from Paulette reporting on her latest betrayal.

There was nothing. Good, she guessed. Maybe.

Using the handrail as if she were a woman twice her age, Denise dragged herself up the stairs to her apartment, fumbled the key into the lock, and nearly fell into the front room.

This had been one of the longest days of her life, and it had come at the end of one of the longest nights. Exhaustion swelled like a balloon in her chest. Her head throbbed. Her hands jumped with nerves. Exhausted, but not sleepy, not the least little bit. High-pitched, sharp-edged nervous energy sang through her veins, sawed through her bones, and squirted acid into her belly until her throat burned nearly to her back teeth.

The Miata, her pathetic attempt at joie de vivre after

Peter had summarily tossed her out, was gone. She wouldn't miss it. In its place, paid for in cash—it took as long to pay the idiot salesman in cash as it would have to get a loan and buy it on time—was a midsized Volvo XC90. Safe. That was what she wanted in a car now, safe and family-friendly. The car had cost a good chunk of her savings, but there was no choice. A family couldn't drive around in an accident waiting to happen.

For color, she'd chosen white. There were a zillion white sort-of SUVs with mommies and kiddies in them on every road in America. The Volvo would blend in.

Dropping keys and purse onto the coffee table, Denise let gravity suck her butt down onto the sofa. Her apartment. Sterile and neat and utterly hers. Nothing where it shouldn't be. Everything where it should. This was gone, too. Or as good as. She'd turned in her two-week notice to the landlord. In winter, she would have been stuck with six weeks' rent money. In summer, apartments were at a premium, so she'd only had to flush two weeks' worth of rent down the rat hole.

Rat.

Paulette.

"No, no, no," Denise muttered, banging her head against the soft back of the couch with each word.

Denise had quit her job, bought the most expensive car she'd probably ever own, given up her apartment, and killed two people, for Paulette. Not to mention the hundreds of dollars she'd dumped at Walmart that afternoon. All the while she was hacking off chunks of her life so that their new life together might have a chance at success, Paulette was betraying her.

It was because of the Walmart shopping spree that Denise knew this. Thinking it would look odd for a retired ranger, who had given two weeks' notice to her landlord and was supposed to be moving out, to be carting armloads of goods upstairs to her apartment, Denise had taken the risk of driving the lot of it to Paulette's house in broad daylight. In a new Volvo, she figured if any rangers saw her, they'd never think it was her. Fancy Volvos and GS-9s didn't exactly go together.

Paulette hadn't been home. At first, Denise was relieved. This wasn't the time to be arguing about what she'd bought and why and where it should be kept.

Denise had driven behind the house to unload her purchases into the nursery. Paulette wasn't in the nursery. Where was Paulette if she wasn't at work and she wasn't at home?

Denise trotted through the trees to the house. Forcing the kitchen door didn't take much brute strength. A firm shove of her shoulder overwhelmed Paulette's flimsy attempt at security. Since they were family, Denise didn't consider it breaking and entering, more like she'd forgotten her key. Paulette should have been home. Denise needed to reassure herself that nothing had happened to her sister; that she hadn't panicked or gotten sick.

Denise needed to know where Paulette was.

The old ads for twins separated at birth, along with the postcard with the cell number on it, were on the kitchen table amid the coffee rings. That was all Denise had to see. She knew what Paulette had done. She'd called the person to ask about the legacy. While Denise was buying and selling and giving notice, Paulette was meeting with their *mother,* or some lawyer or con woman. Undoubtedly Paulette was drinking up whatever bullshit this individual was pouring out. Undoubtedly Paulette was babbling out their secrets with girlish gusto, hoping for a big fat legacy or, worse, the loving arms of the bitch that had whelped them.

Denise groaned. Sitting forward, she held her head between her hands, pushing hard on her temples with her palms. Her disposable cell phone had fallen from her bag and lay on the coffee table. She could call Paulette, let her know this shit wasn't going to fly.

A hand detached itself from Denise's head, floating into her field of vision. Not like it was her hand reaching for her phone, more like it was a detached hand, like a balloon-hand in the Macy's Thanksgiving Day parade, floating on wires high above the crowd, then settling down toward the tiny phone on the table.

Denise reached out with her other hand, caught the one floating, and shoved both of them between her knees. "Poison thoughts," Denise whispered. "If you think poison thoughts you'll die."

Instead of taking up the phone, she opened her laptop. A glance at the time told her Olivia would be in her crib. If she was lucky, Peter and Lily would have finished their bullshit cooing and baby-talking, and cleared out of the room. Seeing a baby, a new life, free of the crap that was dripped into every human's veins over time until the whole person was a toxic waste dump, would settle her, calm her mind. Keep the poison thoughts from killing her. At least for a while.

She tapped on the mouse pad, opening the live feed to the camera in Olivia's nursery. Peter and lovely little Lily bent over the bassinette making faces they thought were amusing but, in truth, were scary and ugly. Then the world spun, the camera showed the wall, the ceiling, then . . .

"Shit!" Denise screamed, throwing herself back against the couch cushions, covering her eyes. When she uncovered them, all was as it had been, Peter and Lily cooing, the world right way up, Olivia in her bed.

For an instant Denise could have sworn she had seen a face. The face of a dead woman. Anna Pigeon's face. The video wasn't recorded; she couldn't go back. Had she been able to, there would have been no point. She had seen Anna Pigeon's body in a black plastic sack sinking beneath the waves of the Atlantic.

The fear and paranoia burning like acid in her gut were from fatigue, not because of anything real. She'd not slept for over forty hours. Too tired and thoughts got crazy. Way too tired and one could even hallucinate.

Anna Pigeon was dead.

Paulette was her soul, her gentle self, her family.

Obstacle removed; identical twin good and right and safe.

There was no Anna.

Paulette might have gone to meet somebody, but she wouldn't break trust with her sister, her identical twin sister. The legacy was for them, for their family. Denise herself had told Paulette to pursue it. Paulette might even be meeting with a Realtor. Could be Denise was wrong about the meeting with the legacy person.

But Denise wasn't wrong. She could hear how right she was barking down among the chunks of disappointment and misery in her brain's junkyard.

"Doesn't matter," she said aloud.

The day—and the night before—had been good, she told herself. Better than good. Denise took out the slip of paper she'd been carrying in her front pants pocket so long it was growing soft. From her bag she got a pen, one with red ink.

Kill Kurt (Denise)

"Check," Denise said, and put a neat red check mark next to it.

Sell Land (Paulette)

"Better be soon," she muttered as she passed that one over.

Remove Obstacle (D&P)

Denise paused. The dead pigeon's upside-down face blinked like a strobe light, setting parts of her mind afire. "Check," she hissed, and scribbled out the words with such force that the pen tore through the paper.

"Stop it," Denise said aloud. Her hand flicked. The pen flew from her fingers, fell to the white sofa, and rolled, leaving a thin red trail. Denise forced herself to look away from the bloody little snake-track on the perfect white of the fabric. "Calm. Slow and steady wins the race. Nerves. Fatigue. Finish and rest. That's a girl," she crooned to herself. When she felt the spate of rage diminish, she went back to the list, carefully avoiding glancing at the ink stain.

Quit NPS (retirement pension) (D)

"Check!" Denise said as she marked it.

Find out about "Legacy" (if it exists) (P)

Denise was sorely tempted to check that off, as a sign that she believed in her sister. That her sister believed in them. If she didn't know for sure, though, she couldn't do it. She never broke her own rules. Well, hardly ever.

In a spirit of compromise, she set aside the pen, fished a pencil from her purse, and put a pencil mark next to that item on the list, a faint gray check mark. For now that would have to do.

Car, shopping, etc.

"Check!" and check.

Give landlord notice

"Check!" and check.

Family—Mt. Desert Hospital (D&P)

The injection into the four-ounce, hermetically sealed waxy box, the seventh of those in Lily's cupboard, would be used by lovely little Lily late in the afternoon tomorrow. Lily used sixteen ounces each day.

That wasn't enough to check it off the list.

After nearly two days without rest, the pen that had so recently flown from her hand of its own accord became too heavy to lift. The list blurred. Denise leaned back on the couch cushion and rubbed her burning eyes, wishing she hadn't sacrificed the last of her Valium to the obstacle issue. Tomorrow *Family* would get checked off, then, one by one, the rest of the list. She would do it tomorrow. After all, tomorrow was another day.

Scarlett O'Hara had said that.

But then, Scarlett O'Hara was one crazy bitch.

FORTY-ONE

Denise's scalp stung, her eyes stung, her nose stung. In law enforcement training at FLETC, the students had been pepper-sprayed—"to know what it feels like." Sadistic bastards; they just liked tormenting the new kids. Right now, right here in Paulette's kitchen, she felt the same sensations. Besides that, her neck was going to snap.

"What's next? Waterboarding? Do you do this once a month?" she asked.

"Every six weeks. You get used to it," Paulette said as she finished rinsing the bleach from Denise's hair. "Done. You can get your head out of the sink."

Lifting her head with the care she'd use lifting a bowling ball with a soda straw, Denise straightened in the chair while Paulette wrapped a towel around her head.

"You're going to be beautiful as a blonde," she said, disappearing into the bedroom.

Denise wasn't sure about that. There were other

reasons she'd decided to bleach her hair tonight, reasons she chose not to share with Paulette—at least not yet.

Paulette reappeared brandishing a blow-dryer.

"As beautiful as you?" Denise teased.

"Just exactly as beautiful," Paulette said with a laugh.

"Identical," Denise said with an answering smile. She was teasing her twin sister, in fun. If the painful process of stripping the color from her hair had no other use, Denise still would have done it. Playing beautician, Paulette was relaxed, smiled more, even laughed. For a while she seemed to have forgotten the dark web they were weaving, some strands already destroyed forever, some yet to be spun. Denise felt the glow of awe she had experienced that first night as they sat in front of the mirror in the bedroom looking at themselves, at each other, at *theirself*.

This was what it would be like all the time. Once they had a place of their own, safe in a warm part of the world, every night they would laugh and tease, watch movies and eat popcorn. That wasn't part of Denise's childhood, yet she'd done that sort of thing with Peter. At the time it must have been nice, but that recollection had been rotted and discolored by the times between then and now. As a memory, it was a corpse, and that corpse stank like carrion.

Paulette plugged the blow-dryer into an outlet on the counter. Hot air blew over Denise's neck, breathed past her right cheek and ear. She closed her eyes. Her sister was fixing her hair. Right out of one of those books she

used to vandalize at the library when she was a kid.
The happy family bullshit that infuriated her. Maybe
it wasn't fiction after all. Maybe all those Dick-and-
Jane children's authors weren't lying through their teeth.

The new Volvo was parked behind the shack. The
back porch light was off. Still, it was a risk for Denise
and Paulette to be together. The closer they got to end-
game, the more dangerous it was to be seen in one another's proximity. People didn't remember much about
random days. They remembered where they were when
Kennedy was shot, what they were wearing when the
World Trade Center towers came down, what they had
for dinner before they'd gone to see *The Dark Knight
Rises* in a movie theater in Aurora, Colorado. Denise
didn't want anyone popping out of the woodwork and
saying, "Yeah. I saw Denise Castle and Paulette Duffy
together right before the shit hit the fan. You know, they
were real chummy. They even kind of looked alike."

Denise wanted to leave Maine unremarked and un-
remembered. She wanted Paulette to drift out of the
minds of the people who knew her the way perfume
drifts out of a bottle. The best way to get away with
murder is never to be suspected in the first place. Once
law enforcement decides on a person of interest, they
keep sticking their noses up that person's ass if for no
other reason than it makes it look like they're doing
something when they don't know what the hell to do.

Unfortunately, they had to be in the house; the bleach
job required running water. That turned out to be a
perk. Denise didn't want Paulette going out past the
Volvo and seeing all the things she had bought. Later,

Paulette would be glad, grateful even, but it might be hard for her to understand at the moment. Besides, they were having fun! Good, clean family fun. Like a couple of Mormons, Denise thought, and was taken aback at her sourness.

Having fun must be like a lot of things in life. To do it right required practice and training.

Denise's hair was dried. Paulette had set the electric rollers next to the sink and plugged them in. She insisted Denise wasn't to look in a mirror until the process—she called it a "transformation"—was complete. After the transformation would be the "reveal."

Though she'd lost the thread of why they were happy, while the curlers heated, Denise went on pretending she was. Paulette rolled her hair as the television played a reality show where people made assholes of themselves and a laugh track, like Denise, pretended it was funny.

Paulette combed out her hair and insisted on putting makeup on her. Feeling like a clown, Denise went on pretending. Maybe fun was like faith for alcoholics, fake it till you make it.

Eyes closed, promising not to peek, she let Paulette lead her through the bedroom and into the bathroom.

"The mirror's smaller than the one on the bureau, but the light's better," Paulette said, excitement bubbling in her voice. "You can look now."

Denise opened her eyes, expecting to see hair like Paulette had, broken and dried out like an overused broom. Regardless of her decaying attitude, Denise was impressed by the reveal. In the mirror was a beautiful woman. Smooth, blond, gleaming hair waved down past her chin. Soft rose colored her cheeks. A darker hue made her lips look fuller, younger. Mascara rimmed her eyes, turning the muddy hazel to dark green.

For a long, long moment Denise didn't know who she was looking at. She knew she was in the body of the person reflected in the mirror, but that face, that hair, those lips had no connection whatsoever with Denise Castle, dour and green and gray to the shattered remnants of her soul.

"Do you like it?" Paulette asked anxiously.

Denise nodded. The beautiful blonde in the mirror nodded.

If she'd had Paulette five years ago, if she'd gone blond, curled her hair, worn makeup, would Peter have needed space? Would he have chucked her out? Fallen in love with Lily?

"Doesn't matter," Denise snarled, and the plump pink lips in the mirror snarled with her.

"You hate it!" Paulette cried. Over her shoulder, reflected in the glass, Denise saw her sister's eyes fill with tears, her open happy-face curl into a pained wad.

"No. I love it. I was thinking of something else." Denise tried to undo the damage, but the moment had gone.

Though she primped and complimented her own reflection over and over, Paulette wouldn't cheer up. Denise was never so glad to see the back of anyone as she was to see the last of the pink scrubs disappear out the front door when Paulette left for work at seven forty-five.

"I'll lock up," Denise promised from where she sat on the sagging dirty couch. "I just want to finish this episode of . . ." Denise had no idea which show was on. Assholes. That was what was on. Fortunately, Paulette was more intent on leaving the dudgeon than she was on what Denise was saying.

The moment Denise could no longer hear the burr of the Duffys' pickup truck on the asphalt, she leapt to her feet.

She worked quickly, not because she was afraid Paulette might come back for some reason but because she wanted to get out of that house, out of the room where she'd killed Kurt, and away from the ammonia fumes of her new persona.

Under the bed, she found a suitcase. Rummaging through drawers with the insensitivity of a hardened burglar, she grabbed what she thought Paulette would need. One suitcase would have to be enough. What Paulette had was cheap and tired. They would both buy new wardrobes once they were settled. Cosmetics, shampoo—all the gooey stuff—they could pick up on the road.

Suitcase slammed shut and zipped, Denise snatched a set of scrubs and a pair of Crocs out of the closet. Stopping, she looked around the room. This was the last time she would see it. If things went as planned, Paulette would never see it again.

On the back porch, suitcase in hand, scrubs over her shoulder, Denise stopped again. Turning back, she stared at the weathered wood on the side of the house, the torn screen door, the peeling paint of the trim. Too bad a fire would call attention to the place. But for that, she might have thrown a match into the tinderbox.

Given her mood, if she could have, she might have burned down the world.

FORTY-TWO

Cybercreep had mandated a night meeting. Because it was the height of the season, bars, cafés, and many shops were open until eight or later. Cecelia's Coffee Shop was open until nine thirty. The cybercreep said they needed to be there at nine.

Everything about the time bothered Heath.

Poor little creep probably was hoping for darkness, she thought. Too bad the sun wouldn't set until nearly ten o'clock. That failed to comfort her. Dusk was probably worse. Often it was harder to see at dusk than it was in the middle of the night. Dusk was like a gray fog; normal shapes fooled the eye, strange shapes appeared familiar.

Of course, Bar Harbor would be lit up for the tourists.

Light was probably worse than dusk. Light meant shadows. Black shadows under docks, between boats floating in black water.

Everything about the place bothered Heath.

Why not midnight in a haunted house, or in the deep dark of the forests? Anna said the lonelier the place, the easier it was to spot the bad guy coming, to see where he parked, to hide in place until the appointed hour. In towns there were crowds; plenty of people that wouldn't be him, and only one son of a bitch who would. Hard to tell the good guys from the bad guy.

Meeting in town probably meant that he wasn't planning on kidnapping E. That, too, bothered Heath. Since it was almost a guarantee he meant Elizabeth no good, if he didn't intend to take her, then he must intend to harm her. An attack in town would be sudden, like a lightning bolt from a cloud of tourists, all but one of whom were innocent. A gunshot? A head shot? Heath shuddered at the image and gasped.

"You okay, Mom?" E asked. They were just rounding Bald Porcupine Island. E was seated beside Heath in the stern of John's boat as it turned toward the dock at Bar Harbor. They were holding each other's hands, leaning close to be heard over the noise of the engine. Gwen was at the console with John.

"Never better," Heath muttered. "Never better."

"Would it cheer you up if I told you that you look like a whale that got spray-painted at a 'Back to the Sixties' party?" Elizabeth asked.

Heath stared down at her lap. She was wearing Dem Bones beneath a riotously colored maxiskirt. Over that was a long fuchsia tunic with turquoise embroidery down the front that Anna had picked up at the thrift store where she bought the skirt. Heath's punishment for insisting on being part of the festivities. Sunglasses were out since Cybercreep had opted for night ops, but she wore a moderately battered purple sun hat with a wide brim. All in all she was, if not a perfect picture, at least a pretty good likeness of an overweight tourist with a good heart and bad taste.

If the pervert did recognize her, she would never forgive him.

He won't, she told herself, as she had insisted to Anna. For the past seven years—all of her life with Elizabeth—anyone who knew her knew her in a wheelchair. Many never saw past the wheelchair. Upright, walking, even with canes, was the ultimate disguise. Heath Jarrod was "the lady in the wheelchair," not "the fat lady hobbling down the sidewalk."

"And you look like a fourteen-year-old boy," Heath teased her daughter.

Elizabeth smoothed her palm down the flat front of her shirt, her breasts squashed beneath the Kevlar. "This thing is more uncomfortable than a bra. I'm surprised Anna wears one."

"I don't think Anna's worn a bra since she burned her last one in 1971," Heath said.

"The bulletproof vest," E said with exaggerated patience. Heath had known what she meant; she'd just wanted to make herself think things were a joking matter when they weren't.

"Regulations," Heath said. "Otherwise, I expect she wouldn't."

"Will she have somebody else's tonight?" E asked. "I hadn't thought about that. If I have hers, will she be, like, vulnerable and stuff?"

"Anna can take care of herself," Heath said. As the words came out of her mouth she remembered Anna tied to the lift, naked, unconscious, and covered in blood.

As if her mind were running along the same channels, Elizabeth said, "Anna isn't getting any younger."

"Older is tougher, like beef and redwoods," Heath said.

"Do you know where she'll be?"

"No. Not exactly. She's sort of wandering the general area. But she'll be close."

Cybercreep had insisted Elizabeth come alone. Unless he was a total idiot, he had to know that there would be watchers, that this was a trap as much for him as for E. He must be gambling that no one would dare be too close, that he would have space to do whatever it was he wanted to do, then get away before they could catch him.

"Maybe he just wants to talk," Elizabeth said.

"Let's hope so," Heath replied grimly. "We're here."

John had cut power. Under his experienced hands the boat was gliding effortlessly alongside a dock below a large parking lot that served the picturesque downtown area of Bar Harbor. Nimble as his own grandson, John Whitman leapt over the gunwale to snick two yellow lines fast, one at the bow and one near the stern.

Walt had wanted to be a member of the party. Anna had nixed that. Heath had no doubt the nixing was a waste of breath. What red-blooded young hero wouldn't want to save the damsel if he got the chance? Walt would be lurking somewhere around the town square. Since he had been unknown—even to her—until the previous day, Heath wasn't worried his appearance would scare the cybercreep into hiding or precipitous action. In fact, Heath hoped he would disobey Anna. If Heath had her way, the town would be full of young, strong, kind, brave boys in love with her daughter.

Young, strong, kind, brave, *sane* boys.

Were boys who bullied, took sexual advantage, loved pornography, and the shame and subjugation of women, technically insane? Given that society at large behaved in much the same manner, didn't that make the nasty boys the norm? Was virtue, once its own reward, now a symptom of a mental disease?

Physical demands chased away the bitter thoughts as, with the help of John and Elizabeth, Heath disembarked and got herself squared away on the pier: hat firmly on head, crutches in hand, tunic over thick waist and legs, feet pointed toward the landing ramp.

From the low dock, Heath could see that the town was lit up and the parking lot was full, but little else. It wasn't more than a couple hundred yards—and two ramps—to where she had chosen to plant herself for the duration. Over the past couple of weeks, she'd gotten good with Dem Bones. Two canes were still needed for balance, but her gait was relatively smooth and her endurance far greater than it had been at the start. Still, she didn't want to use up her strength getting up to city level and through the parking lot, so she waited while John unloaded Robo-butt and Gwen unfolded it.

Gwen stayed with the boat while John rolled Heath

up to the pavement, then halfway down the long parking area. There, he took the wheelchair and left her and Elizabeth standing in the shadow of a Chevy Suburban. He and Gwen would wait with the boat, ready to leave if leaving suddenly became necessary.

The time was eight fifteen; the sun was low in the west, veiled with clouds, the sky a deep lavender. Heath's eyes took a moment to adjust to the bright lights and big city. They had expected some foot traffic at this hour, but the square was packed with bodies. "What in hell . . ."

"People are wearing their pajamas!" Elizabeth exclaimed.

"And bathrobes and slippers," Heath said. "And I thought I looked silly."

For a minute or more they stared at what looked like a combination sleepover and shop-a-thon. "Lookie," Elizabeth said, pointing east of the parking lot where a lush lawn stretched in a smooth green apron down to the Atlantic. A vinyl sign, hung between two poles, read SEASIDE CINEMA! TONIGHT SHOWING *THE PAJAMA GAME*. Though it was not yet dark enough to start the movie, blankets were already spread, and pajama- and nightgown-clad moviegoers were lined up buying popcorn and sodas at a snack bar made to look like an old horse-drawn wagon.

Around the grassy area, the shops had doors open and lights on. Handwritten signs advertising Night Owl Specials, Midnight Snacks, and Pajama Party Sales were stuck on sandwich boards on the sidewalks and taped in windows.

"Holy shit," Heath breathed. "Talk about the unexpected."

"I bet this is why Creep-O wanted to meet 'day after tomorrow.' I wondered about that, but just thought he had a dentist appointment, or date, and wasn't free to torture people yesterday. I bet he was waiting because there'd be this big crowd today."

Heath bet her daughter was right. She bet she wanted to call this whole thing off, run—or walk mechanically—back to the boat, escape to Boar Island, disable the lift so nobody could call it down, and barricade her daughter in the tower.

Anna was here, she reminded herself, and a beefy ranger named Artie. Walter was surely here somewhere. Elizabeth was wearing a bulletproof vest. She knew not to eat or drink anything given to her by anybody, including waitstaff. She would never be out of Heath's sight or Anna's.

Damn, but Heath wished she knew where Anna was. It took an effort of will not to try to find her in the flannel-and-fleece crowd.

"Are we ready?" Elizabeth asked. "I feel overdressed."

To Heath's eyes Elizabeth looked beautiful, and as fragile as a butterfly fresh from the cocoon. She wore skinny jeans, tennis shoes—for running, Anna had insisted—and a loose boy's plaid shirt Walter lent her to disguise the thickening of the vest. Heath gazed at her daughter so long that Elizabeth started to roll her eyes. "Sorry," Heath said. "You look fine."

"Fat," E said. "Somebody should tell Anna that Kevlar makes you look fat."

"Go," Heath made herself say.

E walked farther down the parking lot. A few rows before the street, she stopped and hid in the shadow of a pickup truck, the kind that look like they're on steroids and have never hauled anything heavier than the ego of their owner. Both E and Heath would stay out of sight until twenty minutes of nine. At that time, Heath would make her way across the grassy square and pretend to window-shop in the stores to either side of Cecelia's Coffee Shop. At ten minutes of nine, Elizabeth would enter the square from the parking lot, walk straight across the center of the lawn where the most light and people were, and take a seat at one of Cecelia's outdoor tables. If no tables were free, she would stand with her back against the wall of the coffee shop, watching the square, until she was contacted. Artie, the only person other than Walt that they were sure would be a stranger to the cybercreep, would already be in place, seated at an outdoor table absorbed in the American obsession of drinking caffeinated beverages while staring at electronic devices.

If the creep did contact Elizabeth, and did not attempt anything hostile, both Heath and Artie would photograph him with their devices. Artie and Anna would tail him when he left. No attempt to capture him would be made near Elizabeth. Less dangerous that way.

If the creep made hostile motions, Artie would take him down.

Heath ran through this in her mind as her legs were propelled off of the concrete and, with scarcely a hitch, onto the lawn. Canes were a great help. People tended to make way for a wheelchair, not so much for canes, but some. When they didn't, she batted them gently with the end of the cane, and apologized. Dem Bones was miraculous, but running obstacle courses and doing ballet had yet to be programmed into it.

Crowds. Dense crowds.

This bothered Heath more than the time and the place.

Artie was armed, and licensed to carry concealed weapons when off duty, as was Anna. The density of the crowd made that problematic. A bullet could easily pass through the villain and into two or three innocents before it came to a stop. At the moment, Heath didn't care if it mowed down all of Pajama Land, as long as E was safe.

Anna would care, as, Heath presumed, might Artie. Better no guns, she told herself as she maneuvered around a big man with a bushy beard wearing blue footy pajamas and a Red Sox baseball cap. E would be too close to the action; it would be too easy for a bullet to go astray. If the cybercreep had a gun—

No, Heath told herself firmly. That was not a thought she had allowed herself to entertain for the past forty-eight hours, and she wasn't going to entertain it now. If the bastard had a gun he wouldn't need all this meeting business. He could wait outside their house, or E's school in Boulder, and just blow her away at his convenience: no waiting, no air travel, no coffee date.

Sweating so profusely her hands were slick on the rubberized handles of the canes, Heath reached the far side of the square where Cecelia's was located. Twelve o'clock—that was what had been decided so they could tell one another where to look: The green was a clock face, Cecelia's was twelve o'clock, the grassy point— now the cinema—was at nine o'clock, the parking lot where she and E entered six o'clock, and the west part of town three o'clock.

Heath was across the narrow street from the coffee shop at twelve o'clock, the outdoor movie theater at nine o'clock on her left. For a minute or two she stood still, breathing, trying not to sweat, to fit in as a general-issue tourist at a pajamarama. If such a thing existed.

After a moment she spotted Anna. Had she not seen her in costume before she left Boar, she wouldn't have recognized her. Munching popcorn, Anna was leaning against a tree at about ten o'clock, ankles crossed. Her long braid was concealed beneath a loose flowing shirt over wide-legged soft palazzo pants. A Greek fisherman's cap, the cheap kind available in most of the souvenir shops, was pulled low on her forehead. The greatest disguise was the makeup. Anna Pigeon wore red lipstick, smoky eye shadow, and mascara. Beautiful and urban on someone else, it was oddly disturbing on the ranger, rather like seeing false eyelashes on a young Clint Eastwood.

Anna had to have seen her; Heath looked like the *Mayflower,* as envisioned by Peter Max, under full sail, but her gaze wandered past and through without a flicker of recognition.

Encouraged by the sight of her friend, Heath managed the step off the curb and crossed the street to the shops. Artie looked up as she passed. He didn't recognize her. Heath felt a mild lift of her spirits.

Facing a children's bookstore as if she were shopping, she watched the reflection of the front row of cars in the big parking lot at six o'clock appear and disappear as waves of people ebbed and flowed over the green space. She didn't see Elizabeth until she was halfway across the square, seeming very small in the big shirt and dark, tight jeans. Shoulders slightly hunched, she looked around as she walked, peering into the faces of the people she passed.

That was okay. Cybercreep would expect Elizabeth to appear frightened. After all, he'd spent weeks carefully fraying every single one of the girl's nerves. One of these happy people in bunny slippers was feeding on E's fear at that very moment. Anger, so intense it dimmed her vision, flooded Heath's entire being.

Her vision didn't clear. The world was viewed through a glass dimly. Heath's head swam; her balance faltered.

Lights had gone from the windows. Gone from the square.

Her tenuous vision of her daughter's reflection had vanished.

FORTY-THREE

First the streetlights around the green went dark, then the lights on the storefronts. The sky had faded from lavender to deep blue. The pajama-clad throng melted into amorphous shuffling grays and blacks, an occasional spark of red or green as beams of flashlights startled color from a sleeve or back.

Sharp pieces of the previous night flickered through Anna's brain: shadows shifting into ninjas, gun falling from her hand, darkness sucking her down. Dizziness overtook her. Blindly, she reached out for the tree trunk. Coarse bark brought her back to her body; the ancient strength of the tree steadied her.

Slowly, Anna squatted, carefully set her box of popcorn on the ground, then rose, stepping away from the tree.

Music began, a loudspeaker playing the Broadway overture to *The Pajama Game*.

Specters that had been born on the residue of Rohypnol faded. This was not a flashback, not a vast conspiracy to throw Elizabeth into the dark. The movie was about to start. Simple, prosaic, *Pajama Game* in pajamas, quaint, colorful, charming, and a huge pain in the ass.

Irritation burned in the pit of Anna's stomach. She had not foreseen this. A blind woman should have known that when the movie started the lights would go down. Cybercreep had known it. The people in the square had known it. Anna was the fool. Had she time, she would have cursed herself. Taken by surprise, none of them might have time, especially Elizabeth.

A chill of hypervigilance shivered through Anna. Cold tingled in her feet and hands and the top of her scalp. Whatever was going to happen would happen now, while people were on the move, while the lights were down and the area still crowded.

Counting on the invisibility cloak created by her shade tree and the lowered lights, Anna leapt onto a park bench. Her skinned left heel cursed her with a stab of pain. She ignored it. From the higher vantage point, she could see over the milling crowd. Most were drifting toward the lawn in front of the movie screen. A few continued to shop, eat, and talk in the shadows beneath awnings of stores and branches of the maples in the park. Blankets were being shaken and spread. Last purchases were being made at the snack bar.

Soft, fleecy, plaid stuffed animals in the arms of children and some adults, pillows and blankets in baskets: This was not the stuff of creepiness. Who looked like a sexually perverted bully in footy pajamas? Fuzzy slippers and terry robes could disguise a lot of sinister intent.

Despite the sudden change in atmosphere, Elizabeth was staying on track, walking a little slower than before but still heading straight—or as straight as she could through the pajama swamp—for Cecelia's.

Good girl, Anna thought.

Keeping E in her peripheral vision, she began searching in ever wider concentric circles out from her goddaughter, automatically discarding the very young, the very old, and families holding hands as parents walked children toward the cinema. A young man, rising and walking in the opposite direction of the crowd, his stride that of a man on a mission, caught her attention. Walter Whitman. He had been sitting on a low stone wall between the grassy movie space and the sea. As she could have predicted, he was making a beeline for Elizabeth. Clearly he, too, had been watching her.

Heath was in front of the children's book store beside the coffee shop, her back to the windows. By the panicked way her head bobbed and craned, she had lost sight of her daughter.

On the west side of the grass, at about two o'clock on their imaginary clock face, a single man wearing khakis, a short-sleeved blue shirt, and sandals with socks stood on the sidewalk. In the dim light, age was hard to guess, but he had a full head of dark hair and stood, hands in pockets, with the slouch of a man in his twenties or thirties.

Anna punched *WM2* into the text line on her cell

phone, then hit SEND. Artie, attention torn from his laptop by the change in illumination, turned back to it. Heath took her cell phone from a pocket in her smock and looked down into the pale blue square of light. Then both looked for the white male at two o'clock.

A shake of the head let Anna know Heath didn't recognize him, but then she wouldn't necessarily.

Artie stayed with WM2. Anna continued her scan. Elizabeth was nearly across the grassy area, about fifty feet from the coffee shop. Two of the tables had been vacated by moviegoers. Once E was seated, she could take out her cell phone, put it on the table, and see the texts. Anna had wanted her to keep her hands free at all times and, when approaching the meeting place, to do nothing that might scare Cybercreep away.

Three doors down from Cecelia's, a dumpy woman emerged from an ice cream shop, her head a puff of pink lace in a many-tiered curler cap, her robe a tatty old blue-and-white-striped cotton. Plump doughy hands clutched a large satchel to her chest. By the contours of her figure, Anna guessed it must be filled with Red Hots, Jujubes, Goobers, and other treats one only ate at the movies.

A stride or two behind Elizabeth, and five yards to her right, a man paralleled E's path. Paunchy, hair thinning, stoop-shouldered: Anna put him in his early forties. He wore red-and-blue plaid flannel pajama bottoms and a pale blue, zip-front, lightweight jacket. On his feet were hiking boots. His face was unremarkable except for a simian brow that didn't match the ordinariness of his other features.

WM//E3, Anna texted. She knew they would understand the white male at three o'clock and hoped they would understand the parallel mark.

Artie glanced in WM3's general direction. Sitting, he wouldn't be able to see the man. Heath was having trouble spotting the guy as well, her head moving back and forth and looking suspicious as hell.

BCOOL, Anna typed. Shrinking in on herself, Heath settled. Then the shrinking ceased. Heath regained her stature the way a resurrection fern will after a good rain. Heath had seen Elizabeth.

E had reached the road that separated the shops from the grassy space. Walter, Anna noted, was making his way toward Cecelia's using the sidewalk. A clever boy. Anna was sorry she'd nixed his coming.

No one else stood out from the thinning crowd. No beady-eyed perverts slinking around in their pj's. Had the cybercreep seen Heath or Anna and disappeared back into whatever hole he lived in? Was he standing them up to throw them off guard the next time he called for E to meet with him, or the time after that, so he could strike when they were no longer alert?

The crowd on the green had thinned to twenty or so stragglers. Stores were still doing a desultory business. The man in sandals went into the ice cream shop. Paunchy ceased to parallel E's path and veered onto an intersecting course. The woman in the curler cap stumped stolidly down the sidewalk, evidently bent on getting a Frappuccino to wash down the candy.

Elizabeth reached the coffee shop. She slid into a

chair at one of the abandoned tables, took out her cell phone, and began fiddling with it.

The man with the paunch stopped fifteen feet shy of Cecelia's. Standing on the curb before the narrow street, he squinted as he stared across the road to where E was sitting. Artie moved his laptop so he could watch him without seeming to take his eyes off the screen.

Paunchy shoved both hands into the pockets of his windbreaker, his protruding brow shadowing his face.

Anna's brain, still tainted with the Rohypnol, reeled: the doughy hands, the oversized bag clutched to the woman's breast. This was important, this was trying to take her mind from its set track.

The man on the curb pulled a black rod from his pocket. Anna couldn't make out what it was, but it wasn't flat; it wasn't a cell phone. Pink Curler Cap was almost to Heath, her small sneakered feet marching determinedly along the dull gray concrete of the sidewalk.

Anna's brain locked between the dumpy little woman in the old housecoat and the man with the black rod. Walter bolted through the fog swaddling her mind to smash into the man on the curb. The boy didn't hit him with a football tackle or a fist; he plowed into him like a ship at ramming speed, the entirety of his strong young body smashing into the smaller man, knocking him ten feet onto the green.

"Get off me! Get off me!" the man screamed as Walter followed him down and pinned him to the turf with his weight. "Help! Help!" the man cried. No one moved to help. Anna had worked in tourist destinations most of her life. Tourists had no connection to other tourists, no knowledge of who was who, no faith in their instincts. They seldom sprang into action. There were too many unknowns in an alien environment.

The rod had flown from the downed man's hand. Rolling across the asphalt of the road, it flashed a bluish beam of light. A flashlight; the man had taken a flashlight from his pocket to fight the gloom.

Artie was on his feet and running toward where Walter held the shrieking little man down.

Doughy hands. White. Plump. Dimples for knuckles. Anna had seen her before, at the first coffee shop meeting. She'd had curly red hair then, but the same hands, the same bag. Whirling, she saw the woman in the pink curler cap drawing on a welding glove, the glove she'd seen peeking from the bag the last time.

One hand gloved, the other dipped into the capacious bag and came out with a can, the flat, squarish, metal kind that holds lighter fluid. She was passing Heath, whose attention was fixed on the tangle of men yelling and wrestling on the green.

"Run, E!" Anna shouted. "Run!" Galvanized by decision, Anna shot across the lawn, legs pumping, lungs filling to bellow again: "Run!"

Heath's head jerked in her direction. "The woman!" Anna screamed.

Ten yards separated her from her goddaughter.

The woman with the lighter fluid dropped her bag. Pinching the can in both hands, she aimed a stream of fluid at Elizabeth's face.

FORTY-FOUR

From out of a swirling mist of blind panic, Elizabeth emerged into focus. Heath felt her blood pressure drop twenty points. Without a glance at her mother, E slid into a chair at a table near Artie. She took her cell phone from her pocket and laid it on the small round tabletop. Heath's fingers closed around her own phone in the pocket of her brightly embroidered tunic. It took all of her self-control not to snatch it out and text E just to feel some small line of connection.

Tearing her eyes from her daughter, Heath forced herself to continue her search of the people straggling from shops or toward the cinema. Anna's WM3 was stopped at the curb. This man had pervert written all over him, from his baggy-butt pajama bottoms to his beetling brow.

Seemingly from nowhere a dark shape, like that of a black bird of prey stooping on an unwary rabbit, crashed into the man so hard his feet left the ground and he flew sideways several yards. Elizabeth squeaked. Heath might have squeaked herself. It was Walter. God bless him, Heath thought. God bless the boy.

Abandoning his laptop, Artie leapt from his table and went to help E's boyfriend. Elizabeth, per Anna's orders, was remaining seated until the all-clear was sounded, but her eyes were as round as a startled child's as she watched her tormentor exposed and laid out by two men.

Heath hadn't recognized the man. He didn't even look familiar. Such was the virulence of the attacks he'd mounted, so imbued with specific hatred, she'd expected Elizabeth's stalker to have a personal agenda. How could a total stranger develop such an oozing rotten loathing of a lovely young woman he'd never even met?

Then again, they might have met. Perhaps a fleeting exchange in a Best Buy or at a Walgreens. Twisting it in his mind, the man had imagined a relationship. Elizabeth failed to play her part, so he imagined betrayal. Then he plotted revenge.

Relief washed through Heath, weakening her, floating her physical fatigue to the surface. Fortunately, they would soon know why and who. Knowing would lay a lot of ghosts to rest. Knowing would keep Heath, and more importantly E, from wondering if black slime underlay the warm smiles and kind words of friends and acquaintances. Heath doubted knowing would promote understanding. Perverts had a perverted way of looking at the world. In their heart of hearts, they believed everyone would behave as badly as they did if they got the chance. Virtue was only a mask. Reality, the pervert believed, was what he lived.

Before Heath could finish drawing in her sigh of relief, she heard a scream.

"Run!"

Anna was pelting across the green, sprinting toward the coffee shop.

Elizabeth looked up from her cell phone.

"Run!" Anna screamed a second time.

Elizabeth half stood, then sat down again, evidently remembering her orders to stay put.

A short woman in a pink curler cap passed Heath, blocking her view of the men struggling on the lawn.

"The woman!" Anna cried.

Confused, Heath turned toward Elizabeth. The stumpy little figure was stopped at Elizabeth's table, standing so close, E couldn't get up without overturning her chair. A large, shiny, purple tote bag slid from the woman's arm, exposing an enormous paw.

It was a hand in a welding glove. In that hand was a can of what looked like lighter fluid.

Heath was easily ten feet from her daughter. Without thought, she dropped her canes and lunged. The legs Leah had crafted from electronics and metal responded to the sudden weight of her upper body moving forward. Dem Bones propelled her at nearly a run. Torso foremost, metal and hinges activated to their utmost, Heath was hurtling toward Elizabeth's attacker, utterly out of control.

The woman raised the can, pointed the nozzle at

Elizabeth, and started to squeeze. E shoved her chair back and tried to rise. Heath slammed past the frumpy woman and careened into Elizabeth. Both of them went down in a tangle of arms, legs, and chairs.

"Whore, Jezebel!" a woman's voice drilled into Heath's back. Sizzling and popping like a firecracker booth going up in flames seared the air. The small of Heath's back began to burn.

A loud thud and the crashing of more chairs cut off the shrieked epithets. "Stay down!" she heard Anna yell. "Stay down, God damn you."

"It's on me!" A high-pitched scream. "It's on me."

"Artie!" Anna again. And, "Keep her down."

A gasp came from nearby, and then Heath heard a small voice in her ear. "Mom, you're squishing me."

All of her weight and all of her electronics were pinning Elizabeth to the pavement. Heath tried to lever her upper body off, but her arms were shaking, muscles as weak as overcooked pasta. "I can't move," Heath panted. "Push me."

Small strong hands shoved against her shoulders. Heath was raised far enough that she could see her daughter's face. So beautiful. "Are you all right, E?" Heath's voice quavered with tears. Some good she was in a crisis. Dead wailing weight.

"I think so," Elizabeth said uncertainly.

"Help me! It's on my face!" the obscene woman screamed.

Elizabeth pushed Heath until she could roll off. There she lay on her back, helpless as a stranded beetle, the electronic legs still twisted.

Anna moved into the airspace above. "You okay?" she demanded.

"Yes," Heath managed.

"You?"

Heath heard Elizabeth repeat, "I think so."

"What's that smell? What's making that noise?" Anna asked. Elizabeth was sitting up now; Heath could see her if she craned her neck sideways.

"I don't know," E said.

Heath drew in a breath, tasting the air: singed fabric, burning plastic, a biting acridity. She listened to the sizzling crackling noise coming from beneath her. The small of her back burned like fire. Though there was no flame and no smoke, the woman must have managed to ignite the lighter fluid before Anna tackled her. Some of it must have struck Dem Bones' power pack, where it sat across Heath's hips.

Heath sighed. "I think the smell is me on fire. I'm afraid the racket is the sound of a couple hundred thousand dollars' worth of electronics being destroyed."

Anna had her rolled over and her shirt ripped up the back before Heath could say anything else.

"Artie, call an ambulance," Anna said.

"What's burning? Where is it burning?" Elizabeth was asking.

"No fire," Anna said. "Acid. Battery acid is my guess. E, go into the coffee shop and bring as much clean water as you can and scissors or a sharp knife. Do it now, and do it quickly." Heath felt her hips being jerked sideways and heard what sounded like fabric ripping. Facedown, a view of nothing but table legs and an overturned chair, Heath felt helpless.

Nothing made her angrier than feeling helpless.

"Talk to me!" she said through clenched teeth.

Instead of a reply she felt a cold wet cloth drop onto the small of her back. "Dab gently. As much water as you can without dripping. We don't want to spread the stuff," Anna said.

"Got it," E said.

"Artie, see if you can get Cybercreep to shut the hell up and get some water on her face to dilute the acid," Anna said.

"Talk to me or I'm going to bite you!" Heath said.

"Sorry, Mom." E's voice was shaking as bad as Heath's. "The can had battery acid in it. A little got on your skin above Dem Bones. Anna has cut away the shirt and the straps so we can get anything that has acid on it away from your skin. It ate right through your skirt. It's like horror movie special effects. Dem Bones is practically melting. Most of it got on the power pack."

Heath groaned. "There goes your college education."

A wet sobbing litany of "My face, my face, oh no, my face, she wouldn't be pretty without her face, little baby-faced whore, he wouldn't look at her with no face, not my face, no, no . . ." burbled in a monologue from the other side of the table.

"Are the cuffs on?" Anna asked.

"In front, so she can wash her face," Artie said.

"Help me sit up," Heath told Elizabeth. Before E could start to argue, Heath said, "Please," in a tone that was so pathetic she was almost embarrassed to use it to manipulate her only child.

As they'd done a thousand times before, Elizabeth braced her knees to either side of Heath's and, locking wrists, pulled her to a seated position. Once Heath was stable, E moved behind her and knelt, making herself into a living backrest.

Not more than a couple of yards away the woman in the pink curler cap was sitting on the ground, dribbling words and snot as she dabbed at her face with fat little white hands forced closed with silver handcuffs. Acid had splashed onto one of her cheeks and the side of her mouth. The flesh was red and beginning to blister.

This mewling miserable creature was the person who had filled E's life with threat and filth, then tried to burn her face off with battery acid.

"Who in the hell is this?" Heath asked.

Anna, who was standing slightly behind the woman talking on her cell phone, reached down without interrupting her conversation and pulled off the curler cap and, with it, a red curly wig.

Blond hair tumbled out. Blue-framed glasses fell from her nose. Heath didn't recognize her, although, through the snot, the blistering, and the smeared, mud-colored lipstick, she did seem familiar.

"Mrs. Edleson?" Elizabeth gasped.

FORTY-FIVE

The adrenaline dumped into Anna's system during the excitement of capturing Elizabeth's cybercreep had drained away. Despite the fact that she had slept a good portion of the day, Anna was so tired she could scarcely breathe. Drugged sleep did not refresh the way natural sleep did. Rather than resting, she felt as if she'd spent those hours in a morass of thick oily dreams and mind-numbing traps from which she could not escape into consciousness.

Hunched over the steering wheel of the patrol car used by erstwhile ranger Denise Castle, Anna was aware of her vision tunneling until all she could see was the red taillights in the lane ahead as she followed the second of two ambulances to Mount Desert Hospital.

In the first, with two female officers from the Bar Harbor Police Department, was Mrs. Sam Edleson, the flesh of half her jaw and lower lip eaten away by the acid she'd intended to use to disfigure Elizabeth. Often the why of a crime remained unknown long after the who, what, when, where, and how had been solved. Not so this time. Regardless of the pain talking must have caused with her ruined lip, Terry Edleson wouldn't shut up about why.

According to her, E had lured poor chinless Sam to the dark side with her wanton ways. So bewitched was Sam that he talked of Elizabeth, raved about her firm young flesh, and spied on her through the hedge between the houses.

Abused himself.

First, goodwife Terry had tried to warn E of the dangers of harlotry by destroying her reputation on the Internet, using pornographic images to shock her into good behavior, as well as to make it clear to Sam just what sort of girl he was obsessed with.

Such was the power Elizabeth held over Sam that he actually liked the pornographic images.

Go figure.

Then came the night when Elizabeth was at the Edleson house, when Tiffany had been sent out with her little brother, the night when Elizabeth had all but forced darling Sam to sexually assault her. That was when Terry realized she had to take it to the next level.

She began making threats.

Even then Elizabeth failed to loose her hold on Sam's libido. A couple of off-duty cops roughed Sam up. A rude "uniformed female" visited Terry in her home. That was the handwriting on the wall, Terry told Anna and the Bar Harbor policewomen, and in big black letters it said ELIZABETH WOULD NEVER LEAVE SAM ALONE.

Unless she was made hideous with acid burns to her face.

When her smooth soft flesh was furrowed and scarred, her gentle mouth melted, her brown fawn eyes white with blindness, then and only then would Sam be free.

At that moment, except for the fact that it was illegal to execute an insane individual, Anna could have wrung Terry's fat little neck with as little remorse as a turkey farmer on Thanksgiving eve.

Breathing deeply, Anna banished the wretched Mrs. Edleson from her mental jurisdiction. If the woman died in the ambulance, her face rotted off, if she went to hell, to prison, or back to Boulder—it was all the same to Anna.

Rohypnol hangover and fatigue ruined her powers of concentration. Fantasies of a long sauna to sweat out the toxins, a massage to unknot the muscles, and a husband's shoulder to lay her head on were about all she was willing to hold in her tattered cerebrum for more than a second or two.

That and the taillights.

The second ambulance, the one Anna followed with such dogged determination, carried Heath, E, and Gwen. The area of Heath's back affected by acid burns was small. Most of the acid had struck Dem Bones' power pack, only a small amount hitting bare skin. Cool water, quickly applied, kept the burns superficial, probably second degree at worst. Anna had no way of knowing what Heath's leaping, lunging, falling, and floundering with chairs and girls and electronic exoskeletons had done to the unfeeling half of her friend's body.

The dual red eyes of the taillights wavered as Anna's eyes watered and strained. Blinking, she pushed her face closer to the windshield. The movement set off the scrapes on her butt and heel, scabs cracking, blood oozing. Considering the possibilities, she'd gotten off lightly. Yesterday's contusions, and the shoulder she'd used to take down Terry Edleson, were the worst of it.

After a miserable eternity, the ambulances turned off the winding road out of the town of Bar Harbor and into the front lot of Mount Desert Hospital. As hospitals went, Mount Desert was small. Its age and the warm brick facade robbed it of the sterile futility the sight of most hospitals stirred in Anna's breast.

The ambulances pulled up beneath a bright sign reading EMERGENCY. In a fog, Anna nearly rear-ended the vehicle carrying Heath before she realized the flare of taillights meant it had stopped. Cursing softly, she backed out, drove around the corner into the dimly lit lot, and parked the borrowed Crown Vic.

Levering herself out of the driver's seat, Anna grunted. Gone were the days she could tackle someone and wrestle them to the ground without paying for it. Tomorrow, no doubt, she would discover a medley of bruises where Terry had managed to get in a few licks before she was subdued.

As she walked back to the emergency room entrance, she nearly bumped into Peter Barnes. Staring up at the towering form blocking out the light, she was momentarily disoriented. "Did I call you?" she asked stupidly.

"No," Peter said, taking her arm as if she needed steadying. "Are you okay?"

"Fine," Anna said. "Who called you?"

"Nobody. Anna, let's go in and sit down, maybe get somebody to look at you." He began steering her into the harsh lights of the ER waiting room. "Lily will be here in a sec. Why don't you tell me how it went tonight with your stalker, why you're here."

Peter was talking in the gentle tones used to calm crazy people, or people too sick to stand any kind of shock.

"It went fairly well," Anna said. His assumption of her frailty annoyed her, but since she couldn't think of anything she'd rather do than sit down for a minute, she let him lead her to a chair.

"Who got hurt?" Peter asked.

"Heath, but not badly, I don't think. The perp has facial burns, fairly severe I hope. The stalker was Elizabeth's best friend's mother. A woman who baked the girls cookies. Her husband had a hard-on for Elizabeth, so his wife trashed her on the Internet. A couple of weeks ago, he tried to molest Elizabeth, and the woman went psycho. Blamed E. Tried to squirt acid in Elizabeth's face."

Anna let her head drop back and closed her eyes against the fluorescent lights.

"But you're not hurt?" Peter insisted.

"You mean in addition to being dead?" Anna asked.

"Yes, in addition to that." Peter's chuckle, low and throaty, almost like the purr of a cat, washed reassuringly over her.

"Bumps and bruises," she said. "Other than that, nary a scratch."

"Oh my God! What happened to you!" came an exclamation.

She opened her eyes. Lily Barnes.

It finally occurred to her to wonder why, if she hadn't called him, Peter was here, and why Lily was here at all.

"What happened to you?" Anna countered, wincing as she dragged her butt over the plastic, pulling herself up straight in the chair

"Olivia got real sick," Lily said. "Vomiting, diarrhea, then a seizure. God, it was terrifying. The doctor thinks she may have an allergy or ingested something toxic. We've been wracking our brains. Paint on the bassinet? Dog fur? I'm going to have to go over the whole house with a Q-tip."

"Is she okay?" Anna asked, rubbing her eyes. Fine grit scraped across the sclera as if she'd spent the day at a windy beach.

"Yes. She's sleeping. The doctor thinks she'll be fine. They just want to keep her overnight for observation because of the seizure," Lily said. The young woman's brave smile looked ragged around the edges. Sinking down, she settled on the edge of the chair next to Anna. Lily laid her hand gently on Anna's arm and, with seemingly genuine concern, asked, "What happened to you?"

A nurse pushed through the glass double doors on

the far side of the waiting room. One of the doors flashed Anna's reflection at her. The mystery of why people kept asking what happened to her was solved. In the fracas, her braid had come undone; her hair was hanging witchlike around a face drawn and white with fatigue. Unused to wearing makeup, she'd rubbed her eyes until they were ringed with black mascara. What lipstick remained on her lips was only in the crevices, like red stitches.

Anna laughed abruptly. "I'm better than I look." She laughed again. A worried frown formed two lines between Peter's dark eyebrows. "No. I'm good," Anna said to put him out of his misery. "Just tired and, obviously, frighteningly disheveled. No new wounds. I'm sorry about poor little Olivia."

"Why don't you stay at our house?" Lily offered. "It's nearly an hour's drive to Schoodic. We have plenty of room."

Anna accepted gratefully. "I'll be over after I check on Heath," Anna said. "I'll try and be quiet."

"Don't worry," Peter said. "I doubt we'll be getting a whole lot of sleep until we have Olivia home safe and sound." A pained expression crossed his face. "I hate to ask . . ." he began.

"Ask," Anna said.

"Denise forgot a model in her office. She bought it when we went to Hawaii once. I was going to drop it by her apartment as a sort of good-bye peace offering. Given the situation, would you mind?"

Anna would, but she didn't have a baby in seizures, and a checkered past with the model's recipient.

"Not a problem."

"You go ahead and find your friend. I'll stick it in your car." Peter took her keys. "I'll leave these at the front desk."

Anna nodded her thanks and went to find Heath.

FORTY-SIX

Denise watched Peter and Lily leaving the hospital. Hand in hand. Enough to make a person want to puke. When Denise and Peter had been together, Peter wouldn't hold hands in public. Too much like a Hallmark card, he said. Big ranger man was self-conscious showing his softer side, he joked. What a load of crap.

Didn't matter. Tonight he was going to lose that softer side. She wasn't after revenge, Denise told herself. The fact that Peter would suffer was just a perk. Denise was all about justice.

The radio she'd conveniently forgotten to return to the NPS when she retired lay on the passenger seat. She looked from Peter Barnes to the radio. All day she'd had the thing on, waiting for the shit storm about the missing Anna Pigeon to hit the airwaves. Nothing. Either nobody noticed the pigeon's comings and goings or they weren't talking about it. Maybe they booted it upstairs and were quietly waiting for the FBI to come and save their collective ass. Denise didn't believe that. The NPS considered itself the search-and-rescue experts. They would have mounted a search. Everybody would have been on the radio all day to show how important they were.

Never mind, Denise told herself. Not her problem. Silence was golden.

After the adorable Mr. and Mrs. Barnes had driven out of the parking lot, Denise punched a number into her disposable cell phone and waited. Three rings. Four. What was Paulette doing that was so important she couldn't answer the goddam phone?

"Hello," came a whisper in Denise's ear.

"Time to take a smoke break," Denise said. "Bring a face mask, hairnet, and one of those sterile coat thingies." She punched the END CALL button without waiting for her sister's response.

From various trips to Mount Desert Hospital on EMT business, and, once, to have her tonsils out—a thing like mumps or measles, a real bitch when you were an adult—Denise had a fairly good idea of the layout. What she needed from Paulette was specific locations of patients, things that were fluid and couldn't be easily predicted. That, and where there were cameras, if there were any.

Ten minutes later by the dashboard clock in the new SUV, Paulette finally saw fit to emerge from the rear door of the hospital beside the Dumpster. In the wan light of the single security bulb, she looked around furtively, the items Denise had asked for clutched to her breast. Even in pink teddy-bear scrubs she managed to look as guilty as hell.

"Holy shit," Denise breathed. Paulette had to be kept out of any kind of heat that might be generated by this night. She probably lacked the capacity to lie about her age or weight, let alone a felony murder and all the rest.

Denise tried to tell herself that this was good, this was the honest half of herself, this was her innocence lost, but she wasn't buying it. Paulette needed to grow a backbone if they were going to have a good life together. At least for the first couple of years. After that they could let down a little, relax, and enjoy themselves.

Finally deciding the coast was clear, Paulette trotted toward the Volvo.

Denise leaned across the console and pushed the passenger door open. Paulette climbed in. "What are we doing? Oh my gosh! Look at you! In scrubs and the new hair color you could be me." She laughed.

Paulette had a lovely childlike laugh. Denise smiled, feeling better for the moment. They looked more alike. That meant they were more alike. It was the ravages of the world that had driven them apart, even in Denise's mind. This felt better. Them laughing. Or at least, Paulette laughing.

"Did you come to show me the new outfit?" Paulette asked.

Annoyance returned.

Like she'd call her out of the hospital in the middle of the night when the world was about to stop spinning to show off her new hair and matching scrubs. The ignorance wasn't Paulette's fault. Denise's decision not to share tonight's activities with her sister had been a hard but necessary one. She wouldn't change her mind now.

"No," Denise answered, and was proud at how upbeat and normal she sounded. "There's one last thing I have to do before we can—" She started to say, "Leave this shithole," but that, too, was not something Paulette needed to know at this point. "Get on with things," she finished.

This next part was key to her plan working well. Without it, the plan would still work, but it would be a good deal riskier. "Are there any women in the maternity ward who have babies, born babies, I mean, not fetuses?" she asked, trying for nonchalance and managing only monotone.

"There's Mrs. Frazier in 307," Paulette said. Then, "Oh no! You don't mean to take that poor woman's baby! She was in labor for twenty-two hours. The baby is only a day old. Not that it matters how old she is. Honey, I love you for thinking how much I wanted a baby, and I did, but you can't take her baby."

"No, no, nothing like that," Denise lied. "I just wanted to know if you had extra duties or anything that would keep you away from the infant care ward."

"No. Mother and baby are resting comfortably," Paulette said, parroting a phrase she'd heard the real nurses use, Denise assumed.

"There's a camera at the ER doors and one on the nurses' station on the second floor that I know about," Denise said. "Are there any others?"

Paulette thought about that for a moment, then ticked a list off on her fingers. "There is one at the main entrance. One in ICU. One in the infant care observation room. I don't know about the adult rooms on the first or third floor. There aren't any in the patient rooms—patients don't like that. None in the operating rooms or halls—the doctors don't like that. I think that's all. Maybe one in the pharmacy, but I don't know for sure. I've never seen it. Why? Denise, what are you going to do?"

"Where is the infant care observation room?" Denise asked.

"Second floor, between the nurses' station and the stairs. Why? Denise, tell me what you're going to do." Paulette was demanding. That was new. Though she'd wanted her sister to show a little spunk, Denise didn't like it.

"Nothing scary," Denise said. "Tying off a few loose ends."

"Do I have to do anything?" Paulette asked. "I wouldn't like to do anything that would be against doctors' orders or hospital policy."

Denise stifled a sigh of exasperation. This part would soon be over. From then on it would be smooth sailing. "Not a thing," she assured her sister. "All you have to do is stay near the nurses' station where you will be on camera for an hour or so."

"I can't just hang around. People will wonder. I have work to do," Paulette whined.

Whined.

Denise couldn't believe it. They were on the cusp of

their new life, with all the things they'd always wanted, and her twin—her twin, for Christ's sake—was whining about what people might think.

"Just stay there, or go to the ER, or find an excuse to go to the main entrance foyer. All that matters is that you stay on camera so you can prove where you were."

"What are you going to do?" Paulette asked again. Tears welled up in her eyes, green and glowing in the light of the dashboard, lending them the sinister effect of eyeballs floating in a poison soup.

"I'm going to save a life," Denise said. "Don't forget to wedge open the door." She handed Paulette an old flip-flop she'd purloined from Paulette's closet. Planning was everything. Rushing was an invitation to disaster. Too bad one seldom got a choice.

She waited until Paulette was back inside the building, then waited five more minutes to give her time to reach the nurses' station. Having squirmed into the sterile yellow paper jacket, Denise used the lighted mirror on the back of the sun visor to tuck all of her hair beneath the hairnet—a white paper cap—then put the face mask on, securing the straps firmly behind her ears and pulling the cap down until not so much as a lobe showed.

She'd overthought this portion of the plan. Cameras wouldn't matter. The fact that she was identical to Candy Striper Paulette Duffy wouldn't matter. The sterile gear hid her identity far better than the Lone Ranger's mask hid his. Surgical gloves finished her preparations. She let herself out of the Volvo, beeped it locked, and walked toward the back door of the hospital.

Denise retrieved the flip-flop Paulette had used to keep the door from closing, tossed it into the Dumpster, and slipped inside. The fire escape stairs were as expected: metal treads, pipe hand-railing, concrete floor and walls and ceiling, no windows, dim lighting, and devoid of human life. Like most people, nurses avoided physical effort in even its most modest guises. Moving quietly, she climbed to the second floor. Opening the heavy metal door an inch, Denise peeked out.

Nothing but a long hallway with doors to either side. Some were open, the light from televisions and reading lamps spilling out along with the desultory murmur of TV shows. A nurse carrying a tray with half a dozen miniature paper cups, the kind hospitals put meds in, walked past the semicircular desk where two other nurses sat, eyes on computer monitors. As far as Denise could see, Paulette had been telling the truth. There were no cameras at either end of the hallway, just a single round black eye pointing at the space in front of the desk. Halfway between the fire stairs and the nurses' station, just as Paulette had said, was a large window beside a glass door.

The observation room.

For no apparent reason, Denise's foot shot out, smacking into the door with a hollow thud. The nurse with the tray of pills stopped. She looked back over her shoulder as if she'd heard. Holding her breath, Denise waited, afraid to move the door even the half inch it would take to close it. Finally the woman shrugged and went about her business.

No worry, no worry, Denise chanted silently. Hospitals had to be full of things that went bump in the night. Bedpans falling, patients banging on their bed rails, doctors dropping wads of cash on the polished floors, interns fornicating in broom closets. Maybe that was only on television; still, hospitals had to have noises.

No worry.

Denise stood stock-still until her breathing slowed, then silently closed the door and began to ascend the steps. Between the second and the third floors was a smell of cigarette smoke. Midstride, she halted. A nurse or doctor too lazy to walk down to the parking lot might have stepped into the fire stairs for a quick puff. Denise waited for the sound of an inhalation, a butt hitting the floor, a door opening or closing. Nothing.

The smoke smelled stale. Maybe it was from earlier, even a day or more earlier. Cat piss had nothing on cigarette smoke when it came to the staying power of the odor. That was a habit Paulette was going to have to break.

Denise did a quick peek around the bend in the stair. No smoking gun. She crept up to the third floor and opened the door a crack for surveillance.

The door closest to the fire escape, from where Denise watched, had a square metal plate with the number 311 on it in black numerals. If the numbers followed the rule of even on one side and odd on the other, 307 would be four doors down and to the right.

The hallway was empty. Denise's fingers scampered over her face and head, reassuring her that the mask and hairnet were in place. They were. Forcing herself not to walk too fast or too slow, Denise went down the hall, noting the numbers on the doors. Room 307 was where it was supposed to be. No light showed from the little rectangular window in the door. Peeking in, Denise could see it was a private room. This was good. Retirement was making her stupid; she hadn't thought what she'd do if it was a double. It wasn't. This was a sign this was meant to happen.

In the single bed was a woman-sized lump limned by the pink of a nightlight. Between the woman and the door was a low crib bed. In it was an infant lying on its belly, a hand no bigger than a quarter spread like a starfish on its cheek. Denise took a deep breath, stepped briskly in, gathered up the infant, turned, and stepped briskly out.

"Point of no return," she whispered as she carried the baby toward the stairs.

The new mom hadn't woken. The child didn't scream.

All good. All signs this was meant to happen.

FORTY-SEVEN

Heath's burns had been dressed, and, as Anna had surmised, they weren't severe. There was bruising of her lower limbs, and a hairline fracture of her left shin. Both her palms were skinned and one finger broken. Given the night's events, all of them had gotten off lightly.

Anna should have taken her leave after the reassuring results of Heath's exam were delivered, but she'd stayed on, feeling a sense of comfort in the company of Heath, Elizabeth, and Gwen. When she'd been younger—like last week—she'd craved solitude and silence, the peace of wide open spaces and infinite sky. Now the small room, crowded with people she cared about, all alive, all warm, fed, and sheltered, wrapped comfortingly around her like a soft blanket.

A loud click announcing the opening of the door startled Anna's eyes open. She had dozed off in the chair beside Heath's bed. A nurse in pale green scrubs stuck her head in. Maybe a hospital shift change; Anna hadn't seen this woman before. She was in her fifties with small, brown, very bright eyes in a narrow lined face. Frowning, she glanced around the room.

"What is it?" Gwen asked.

"Nothing, not a thing," the nurse said. "Sorry to bother you." She pulled her head back and closed the door softly.

"Odd," Gwen said.

"She probably can't remember where she left her last patient," Elizabeth said. "That or visiting hours are over."

"Visiting hours have been over for a while," Heath said.

"Then why—" E began. Heath raised her eyebrows and tilted her head toward Gwen. "Right," E said. "It's who you know.

"I've been thinking, it's going to be weird seeing Tiff," E said after a moment. "After us getting her mom arrested and what not, I don't think we can really be friends anymore. I mean, how would that work?"

"It probably wouldn't," Anna said. "Too much blood under the bridge."

"Too bad," Heath said. "Tiffany is a nice girl. None of this is her fault or," she said, looking pointedly at her daughter, "yours."

"I know," E said. "Even though I know it, it feels like I could have done *something.*"

No one argued with her. Anna felt as if there must have been something she could have done or seen or sensed that would have kept things from going as far as they had. Only the fact that Elizabeth wasn't in ICU, blinded with severe acid burns to her face, kept her from dwelling on what might have been.

"What will happen to Mrs. Edleson?" Elizabeth asked Anna.

"She'll be charged with assault—not just attempted; the acid got on Heath. That's a charge she'll have to face here in Maine, I expect. It was Maine law she broke. As for the cyberbullying, I'm not sure if there are statutes in place for that in Colorado or Maine state law. It's my guess she'll get a slap on the wrist. Community service. I doubt she'll do any jail time. If she does, I expect it will only be sixty days or so. If she gets a half-way decent lawyer, he will plead her out with time served and probation. Maybe an order not to go within _X_ number of feet of you or your home."

"Not fair!" E cried.

"Life is not fair," Heath said. "Who knew?"

Gwen laughed.

Again the door to the room was opened. In hospitals no one knocks. This time it was a security guard, easily over sixty and overweight. Anna hadn't seen any security around the building or the ER when she'd arrived. Maybe he came on for the night shift.

"'Scuse me, ladies," he said, smiling an apology for the interruption. "I hate busting in on you like this. I just need to take a look in your bathroom."

"Sure," Heath said. In silence they watched him waddle to the bathroom, open the door, and look in. He did the same with the tiny closet.

"What's going on?" Gwen asked.

"Nothing for you to worry about," he said. "Good night." And he was gone.

Gwen got up and smoothed down the front of her blouse. "I'm going to find out what the fuss is about. Anybody want me to bring them back anything? Coffee? Coke?"

Nobody wanted any more caffeine.

"It is getting late," Heath said to Anna. "I think you've saved the world enough times today. Why don't you go home? You look worse than I feel."

"I'm good," Anna said automatically.

"I'm staying," Elizabeth said.

Anna managed a smile. Elizabeth had been attacked by the neighbor lady, shamed before her entire high school, and probably lost her best friend in the bargain, but she was happy. Her joy showed through the layers of concern she had for her mother and for Anna. By E's lights, Walter was the handsome prince on the white horse who had slain her personal dragon. Never mind that Walter had mowed down an innocent man, and managed to lure Artie away from his post, or that her mother had taken a splash of acid meant for Elizabeth, or that Anna had smashed her shoulder and elbow all to hell taking down Terry Edleson.

The cybercreep was out of Elizabeth's life, and a beautiful boy was in it. God was in his heaven and all was right with her world.

Anna wouldn't have had it any other way.

Gwen popped back into the room. "Nothing to be alarmed about," she said. "A baby has been misplaced.

It will turn up. They always do." Stifling a yawn, the older woman sank down on the foot of Heath's bed.

"None of you need to stay any longer," Heath said firmly. "We're all worn out. You were snoring, Anna."

"I don't snore," Anna said.

"Hah!" E snorted.

Heath rolled her eyes. "You have taught my child to snort," she accused Anna.

"I taught myself to snort! Anyway, I don't snore," E insisted.

"I'm staying," Gwen said. "Hospitals aren't much about caring for patients anymore. They are about following doctors' orders and medical protocols. Without an advocate, a patient gets about as much TLC as you might expect if we abandoned you under an overpass."

"I'm staying, too," E said.

Anna rubbed her eyes with her fists, smearing more mascara around. Nothing remained for her to do but sleep. "Okay, I'm for bed. If you need me, I'll be at Peter and Lily's."

As she tried to shove herself up from the plastic chair, the shoulder of the arm that had taken a bullet during the Fox River misadventure, the one she'd used to slam Terry Edleson to the ground, locked up. Squeaking, she held herself halfway out of the chair, unable to get up, unable to lower herself back down. "Damn," she said as Elizabeth and Gwen leapt up to help her.

Standing, she shook out her arms. "Good as new," she said, balling her hand into a fist to prove everything was working.

"Get that shoulder X-rayed," Gwen said.

"It's not broken," Anna insisted. "Just banged up."

She had no intention of spending the rest of the night being alternately pestered and ignored by a bunch of people in scrubs. Straightening her back, she walked to the door without limping, wincing, or whimpering. Success beyond her wildest expectations. Fortunately they were on the first floor and not far from the main doors. Anna picked up her keys at the registration desk, then made it to the parking lot without scaring any children with her likeness to a zombie, or attracting unwanted attention from medical personnel.

Having unlocked the Crown Vic, she crawled into the darkness of the rear seat and closed the door. In the privacy of the cramped chamber she managed to escape from the long-tailed shirt. The Velcro straps of her borrowed Kevlar vest—E had worn hers—released with a satisfying ripping sound. Sighing, she let the thing fall to the seat beside her. Beneath the vest, her tank top was soaked with sweat.

For several minutes she sat reveling in freedom from the Kevlar and the grating fluorescent lights of the hospital. Fluorescent lights made Anna feel brittle and tired. Someday scientists would undoubtedly discover the light penetrated flesh and corroded bone matter. Rubbing the ache in her shoulder, she tried to remember whether or not she'd seen a bathtub at Peter and Lily's. A long hot bath would be a passable stand-in for the sauna, the massage, and the husband.

Once she felt sufficiently recovered to drive the six miles to the Barneses' house, she gathered her courage. For decency's sake, she put on the shirt and fastened a few buttons. Traversing from the rear seat to the front to climb behind the wheel wasn't as easy as she'd pictured it. Finally in place, she closed her eyes and leaned her head back against the headrest for a moment.

"I'm getting too old for this shit," she whispered. Opening her eyes, she saw the item she was to deliver before she could go to bed. A two-foot-long model of a Hawaiian outrigger canoe was sitting on the passenger seat. "And miles to go before I sleep." She groaned and turned on the ignition.

The way to the Barneses' home led back through Bar Harbor, then to the east a quarter of a mile before the road forked, the western fork crossing the narrow land bridge connecting Mount Desert Island to the mainland. Denise's apartment complex was on the way. Anna slowed as she drove by. A light showed in the upstairs apartment where she'd changed into Denise's clothes for the first fruitless attempt at the cybercreep.

Denise's little green Miata wasn't in evidence in the parking spaces beneath the complex. A white Volvo had taken its place. Anna snugged the Crown Vic neatly, and illegally, behind the Volvo. Her errand would only take a second. Even if the car didn't belong to Denise, she should be back to move the Crown Vic before anyone needed to leave the complex.

On her first two visits the stairs had made no impression on Anna: short, one level, a romp in the park. This trip she felt all of thirteen. Good deeds were never a good idea. Leaning against the doorframe of Denise's apartment, she knocked, then rang the doorbell. A long silence followed. Relief crept in. Anna wasn't up for even the short exchange of "This is yours" and "You're welcome."

"Who is it?" Denise's voice came from behind the door.

"It's me," Anna said.

There was no peephole.

Feeling foolish, Anna opened her mouth to announce herself properly, but "me" must have been sufficient. Anna heard the slide of bolts and the rattle of a door chain. The knob turned, and the door swung open.

Paulette Duffy stood in the spill of light, her blond hair falling around her face, her pink scrubs rumpled, the front stained, a silver laptop computer held at her side. Anna stared stupidly. Paulette gaped at Anna in absolute shock, mouth open, lips pulled back showing nice, neat front teeth.

Pieces fell like bricks through Anna's mind and into place: the photo by the bed of a younger Denise before she'd gotten the overlapping front teeth fixed, Mrs. Duffy's blond hair, identical twins, Huntington's disease, the uncontrolled movements of chorea, short-term memory loss. Mood swings.

This was Denise. Denise was the other twin.

In the instant it took for this to flash through Anna's mind, she realized that Denise might have murdered Kurt Duffy while Paulette was establishing her alibi in the Acadian Lounge, and here Anna had come gimping up the stairs in the middle of the night with no weapon, no backup, no vest, and no radio.

"Hey, Denise," Anna said. "Love the hair. Peter said you'd left this in your office." She held up the canoe in both hands.

"Thank you," Denise said. She didn't reach out for the canoe.

Anna took a step back.

From within the apartment came the high gasping wail of a baby crying.

Denise swung the laptop at Anna's head. Reflexively, Anna threw up her arms, using the canoe to deflect the blow. Her shoulder locked. The laptop smashed through the thin balsa wood, shattering the model, to strike her above her eye where the knot from her last head trauma had yet to begin to heal.

"You're dead" was the last thing Anna heard.

When she regained consciousness, or what she assumed might be consciousness, she was blind. She tried to open her mouth to scream, but it was sealed shut. Struggling, she tried to figure out where one arm started and the other left off. A soft smelly pillow was hot against her chest. Her legs had been welded into a single unit, like the tail of a mermaid.

"Stay still or you'll kill her."

The whisper was close. Without eyes, Anna couldn't tell if the whisperer was in front of her or behind her. "Denise?" she said. What came to her ears was a muffled "Hunhh?" Duct tape, or something very like, had been put over her mouth. Probably her eyes as well. She could feel the pull on her eyelids when she tried to open them.

"In your arms is a baby. If you fall down, or fight, or do anything except exactly what I tell you to, you might crush her. You might asphyxiate her. You might snap her little neck." As directionless as fog, as sibilant as wind in the eaves, the whisper rasped around Anna. "You might jam your chin through the soft spot in her skull and get baby brains in your mouth."

Words hissing in her ears, Anna became aware of the life she held in her arms. The smell was a dirty diaper, the heat a tiny body, the softness the rounded contours of an infant. Lowering her head, she felt downy hair tickle the underside of her chin. This had to be the baby Gwen had so airily assured them would turn up. Denise had taken it.

Ransom? Anna wondered. Was the child the child of a rich person? Auction the little creature off to a barren couple, or sex traffickers? It seemed a bit ambitious for a retired park ranger. Kidnapping was America's least favorite sport. Hard to pull off, severe penalties, and a live product: Anna doubted law enforcement officers would risk it. At least not sane law enforcement officers.

Denise Castle might not be entirely sane. Huntington's could cause mental disorders; Gwen had said that. If Huntington's mixed with regular craziness, the results might be bizarre.

Peter Barnes had spoken of how Denise looked at Lily, how she looked at Olivia, how she reacted to the mention of her previous home. Was the baby some kind of compensation for losing her relationship?

Did it matter?

Not much, Anna thought. What mattered was the life duct-taped in her arms. If there was life.

There was no movement. If the baby breathed, she couldn't hear it. Had she crushed it already? Squeezed the little rib cage until the baby couldn't draw breath? While unconscious, had she folded over and smothered the child? Darkness greater than blindness gripped Anna. Her heart grew cold and still. Her hands, each taped tightly to the opposite elbow to provide a cradle for the infant, were useless but for the little finger on her left hand. She could bend that one. Denise had missed it in her wrapping. Gingerly, Anna poked the baby. It didn't move or cry. She poked it again harder.

Feeble squirming, then tiny baby feet kicked into her damaged joint, making it throb. "Thankyoubabyjesus," she meant to say. "Mmmghhh" was what reached the air. Anna allowed her heart to recommence beating.

Craning her neck until her shoulder knifed her in the back in self-defense, Anna managed to nuzzle the infant's face. The baby's mouth was not duct-taped shut. Anna allowed herself a meager trickle of relief. At least the child would be able to breathe as long as Anna could keep her exhausted muscles from collapsing and squashing the poor thing.

"I'm going to cut the tape on your ankles," the whisper said. "You're going to get up and walk quietly where I tell you to." The tip of a sharp object poked into Anna's cheek under her right eye. "If you are not absolutely compliant, I will poke out this eye, then the other, and so on. Nothing I do can be bad because you are a dead pigeon, and dead pigeons have no rights. If you understand, nod your head."

The prick of flesh beneath her eye receded. Anna nodded. Strands of hair were plucked from her head. Her hair had been taped down along with her eyelids and arms, effectively pinioning her head in one place. An image of Gulliver, surrounded by mallet-wielding Lilliputians, his head staked to the ground by his hair, flashed through her mind. The benefits of a reading life, she thought absurdly.

Again she nodded, more firmly this time. Maybe there was some slippage. Maybe she could trade hanks of hair for greater movement. Something to keep in mind.

A hand insinuated itself beneath her left elbow, where it was taped tightly to her ribs. "Up," the voice breathed. The hand pulled. Anna floundered to her knees, mindful of not crushing the baby, of not losing her balance and falling on it, while the voice—Denise Castle's, she assumed—continued popping, "Up, up, you. Get up. Up."

Without sight, the Rohypnol remaining in her system, combined with fatigue and shock, compromised Anna's balance, making her unsteady on her feet, unsure where this "up" was. Her inner ear insisted she was listing to starboard, but when she tried to compensate, she was jerked the other direction by the hand beneath her elbow.

"You hurt that baby and you're dead meat," Denise said, full voice this time.

Anna shuffled her feet further apart, centering her weight carefully around her spine. The sense of toppling to one side diminished. Palpable mist slid over her skin. Anna staggered back.

"It's just a shawl, you stupid bitch. Stand still," Denise ordered. The shawl was arranged around Anna's face. A few more hairs were plucked from her head as Denise tucked the fabric around her arms and the child held in them.

"You are going to be a good little pigeon. Don't even think of trying to fly the coop or make any kind of noise. If you do, you could fall down the stairs and kill the baby," Denise said.

Hands landed hard on Anna's shoulders, sending a crippling wave of agony down her side. The hands propelled her forward. The baby began a thin wail.

"Then your eyes would be gouged out and there'd be no more of your peeking and pecking," Denise said as she turned Anna to the left. They stopped. There was the sound of a door shutting. "Keep that baby quiet."

Again Denise was muttering. They must be out of the apartment, in the hall.

"Stairs," Denise said.

With Denise muttering, "Step, step, step," Anna felt her way down, relying on the hand under her elbow for balance.

Thirteen, Anna counted in her head. They were down in the parking area.

"You can't make anything easy, can you?" Denise growled.

Hands fumbled at Anna's crotch, and she wondered

if she was being sexually assaulted, but Denise was only digging the keys to the Crown Vic out of her pocket.

A beep, then Denise poked, prodded, and cursed Anna and her burden into the seat of a car. By the height of it, Anna guessed it was the white SUV parked where the Miata had been on her first visit.

"Stay," Denise ordered. "Or you're dead."

You're dead.

Denise had said that the instant before Anna lost consciousness from the blow to her head with the laptop. It hadn't been a threat; it had been a statement. When Denise first opened the door, her face had gone slack with shock at the sight of Anna.

That was when the scene with the ghost of Hamlet's father should have played out. Anna's one shot at acting in a Shakespeare play and she'd blown it.

No one but Heath's family and Peter knew Anna had been "killed." Denise had gone pale because she believed Anna was dead. Ergo Denise had been the one to dump her body into the sea. Denise and Paulette. Walter had seen two people in the boat.

Anna felt the shoulder strap slide across her arms, pushing the baby more tightly against her chest. A click let her know her seat belt was fastened. Since Denise had killed her once, thrown her into the ocean, then knocked her unconscious and taped her up like a mummy, this nod to safety had to be about the baby. Denise wanted the baby safe, her talk of Anna killing it notwithstanding. The baby was what was important.

Anna was just being moved from point A to point B. Never a good thing for a victim. Point B was always nastier than point A. Once they were there, Anna could be disposed of without interference. That was the reason point B held such an attraction for kidnappers, rapists, and murderers.

The baby continued to whine.

Anna wished she'd called Paul before she'd left the island, wished she had taken the first plane home, never stopped to do her good deed for the day, wished the child would stop crying, while at the same time taking comfort in the fact that it had sufficient air with which to cry.

"Hmm, hmm," she crooned, and brushed the infant's head with her duct-taped lips. The baby wailed louder, its fragile skin abraded by the rough tape.

The driver's door opened. "All set?" Denise asked as if she and Anna were going on a routine campground patrol.

Not knowing what else to do, Anna nodded as much as her netting of hair would allow, then a bit more, hoping to loosen the tape.

"Good," Denise said. Denise had been gone less than two minutes; she had to have put the NPS patrol car in another of the parking spaces beneath the rental units. If the apartment the slot was assigned to was occupied, it would be found as soon as the renter came home and wanted to park. If the apartment was vacant, it could be days. Still, Peter and Lily were expecting Anna. Peter knew where she'd been going. When she didn't show in an hour or two, he'd come looking. He'd find the car.

That was something.

Being on the move seemed to soothe Denise. Gone

were the hissing and the hurrying. Anna heard mirrors being adjusted, a seat belt fastened, the engine coming to life. The SUV backed out of the narrow space. Off to point B.

Had Anna decided to set a trap to catch herself, she couldn't have done it more thoroughly. She was alone, unarmed, injured, fog-brained, and had delivered herself into the hands of a deranged kidnapper. The proverbial handwriting had not merely been on the wall, it had been all but tattooed across Anna's fore-head. Denise liked to dive at night. Denise had a boat at her disposal. Denise had refused to be seen near Paulette the morning after the murder, was paranoid about Anna being in her apartment, reacted bizarrely when Anna had asked about the photograph where her teeth were identical to Paulette's, showed the same chorea as Paulette Duffy.

Shaking her head, Anna groaned.

"Okay?" Denise asked.

Anna nodded.

The distraction of the cybercreep had kept her from paying attention to what was going on in the park, the park she'd been brought in to help protect and preserve. Instead, she'd played hooky, worked on personal issues, and one of the rangers nominally under her supervision had gotten away with the attempted murder of Anna and, probably, the actual murder of Paulette's husband.

Almost, Anna felt she deserved what she was get-ting, what she was going to get when Denise reached point B.

Almost.

FORTY-EIGHT

W e're here," Denise announced.

Here, Anna knew, was between fifteen and thirty minutes by car from Denise's apartment. First, Anna guessed, they were headed to Paulette's house, but they didn't go into a house. They went into the woods. Pine needles slithered underfoot as they walked the last hundred yards or so, and the smell of sap was strong in the night air. They were in a shed or garage; Anna surmised. She'd heard the unmistakable sound of a padlock being unlocked.

"Sit," Denise ordered.

Blind, a baby bound to her chest, the best Anna could do was get to her knees and sit back on her heels. Duct tape made for secure bondage. Little of Anna remained mobile.

"God," Denise fumed. "You're such a pain in the ass."

A hand pushed hard on Anna's shoulder, toppling her onto her side. To keep the child from harm, Anna took the full weight of the fall on the point of her left shoulder. Her face was ground into rough carpet as her legs were pulled out of their bend. The baby began to cry, a few decibels higher and angrier than its ongoing pitiful mewling.

Ripping sounds filled Anna's ears; then she felt her legs being taped together again, once at the ankles and once at the knees. Clearly, Denise had a higher opinion of Anna's threat level than Anna did. She doubted she could best a fly even if she had a swatter and a head start.

"There," Denise declared, when Anna was trussed up again. "Sit up."

Struggling like a landed fish, Anna tried to bring her torso up to right angles with her legs. She failed.

An exaggerated sigh heralded the coming assistance. Hands slid under her shoulders and pushed her up.

"This will hurt," Denise said.

Since a significant portion of Anna hurt, she hardly winced as Denise carefully pulled the tape off of her eyes.

"Won't have to get those brows waxed for a couple years," Denise said.

Her face was so close it was all Anna could see, and it was out of focus.

"No reason you can't talk," Denise said. "You can even scream if you want. Nobody will hear you." Crouching in front of Anna, Denise gently worked the duct tape free of Anna's mouth.

Drool ran from her newly freed lips and dripped on the baby's head. Air, constrained by fear and pinched nostrils, rushed in through Anna's mouth. She felt her chest expand against the tight wrapping of tape and the soft bundle of life she held in her arms.

"Better?" Denise asked, her head cocked to one side like that of an alert Chihuahua.

"Yes," Anna said. "Thanks." Absurd as it was, Anna was genuinely grateful for these small kindnesses. Beggars couldn't be choosers, but they could show gratitude for the scraps given them.

As Anna's eyes cleared of tears from the stinging removal of the tape, the room that coalesced around her was not what she had expected from her garage or shed theory. Lit only by the light of a single kerosene lantern was a room built of rough wood. The curtains on the windows were open, showing a warm sunny forest outside. They weren't windows, she realized dazedly, but mullions and frames over a painting of a summer forest scene. A crib with a stuffed bear in it sat in the corner. Beside it were a child's tiny chair and a potty-training toilet

Denise had brought her—and the baby—to a nursery.

"Nice, isn't it?" Denise sat down in a rocking chair with low arms and looked around the small space with obvious pride. "It's a shame we won't get to use it. We'll have to build another just like it at our new place. It could be like a playhouse."

Despite the kindly light of the kerosene lamp, Anna's captor's face looked drawn and pale. The youthful glow the blond hair lent her had faded.

"Tired," Denise said, as if affirming Anna's thought.

Dragging her hand down over her face, fingers pressing gently on her eyelids, she mimicked a gesture that Anna equated with the living closing the eyes of the dead.

A thousand questions boiled in Anna's mind with such fury that she couldn't get any to separate themselves from the maelstrom to form words. Her palms, each fastened tightly to the opposite forearm to make a basket for the infant, were growing numb. She could no longer feel the child breathing, but, with her eyes uncovered, she could see the tiny baby she held. Snot bubbled out of a nose as small and soft as a peony petal. The crying had stopped. Now the child looked up into Anna's face with vaguely trusting gray-blue eyes.

"You took the baby from the woman in the hospital," Anna said to Denise. Her voice cracked from a throat so dry Anna could barely swallow. Without being asked, Denise got up, crossed to a shelf, and took out a bottle of water from half a dozen stored there. There were also several army surplus MREs, the kind Anna hadn't seen for years, and two pairs of handcuffs. Anna looked longingly at the cuffs. After her time in duct tape, they looked positively humane.

"Sort of took the woman's baby, but not exactly," Denise said, unscrewing the cap on the water bottle. She held it while Anna drank. Water was a fluid of many magical properties. Anna's throat opened; her mind perked up; hope flickered where the water left its trail of strength.

"What do you mean sort of?" Anna asked. "How do you sort of take a baby?"

Denise smirked as she regained her seat in the rocker. "That isn't the baby you think it is. Guess who you're holding?"

Anna stared down into the baby's face. To her, all babies looked pretty much alike. This one was pink and round with a blank little face and wide open eyes. Why would she be expected to know this baby?

Disparate facts, stored in unrelated places in her cerebrum, began to flock together like blackbirds into a pine tree: Paulette Duffy, an infant care LPN, Peter and Denise together, Peter and Denise apart, Lily and Olivia, Denise's sudden retirement, Olivia mysteriously ill and transported to the hospital where Duffy worked.

"Peter Barnes's baby," Anna said.

"My baby," Denise flared. "Olivia. What a stupid name. We'll give her a better one."

"Olivia wasn't the baby that went missing," Anna said.

"Hah!" Denise leaned forward, her elbows on her knees so her face was on a level with Anna's. "The camera over the door in the infant care observation room is pointed at the crib. I walked in, back to the camera, carrying one baby, backed out, still not facing the camera, with another baby. Peter doesn't even know his child has gone missing. That's how much he cares about her. Do you think the baby should have water?" Denise asked, her face suddenly worried.

"Probably, but done up like she is, I'm afraid she would choke. Don't you want to hold her?" That was a question new mothers and grandmothers asked Anna.

For some reason, women were supposed to want to hold infants. If Denise was among them, maybe Anna would be given an opportunity to do . . . well, some damn thing.

For a long moment, Denise sat, chin in hands, elbows on knees, studying Anna and the baby. "I don't want to hold it," she admitted at last. Anna didn't think Denise was talking to her so much as thinking out loud. "I thought I would. I really thought it would be like when my sister and I realized we were two parts of a whole. But when I carried the baby out of the hospital and didn't feel much, I figured it was because things were so, you know, tense. Then back at my apartment all she did was cry. I tried holding her, doing the rocking thing. She kept on crying. She didn't feel like a part of me, not like Paulette, more like a fish trying to flop its way out of a soggy newspaper."

"Babies aren't for everybody," Anna said sympathetically. "No big deal. I never went much for babies. Tell you what, nobody knows she's gone. We could take her back and nobody would be the wiser."

Denise straightened up. She actually appeared to be considering the suggestion, and Anna felt a tiny spark of hope.

Then Denise shook her head. "No," she said firmly. "The closeness will come. It will just take a while."

"Why don't you cut the tape so we can let her out of my arms? Then at least she can have water," Anna said.

"Soon," Denise promised. "If Paulette comes back from work and everything is hunky-dory, we won't need you for a hostage. Then we'll leave, and in a few hours, I'll send an anonymous message saying where you are and that will be that. No muss, no fuss."

Anna doubted she would be left alive. In their previous encounter, Denise had proved to be an individual who chose not to strain the quality of mercy in any meaningful way. A bullet to the back of the head or a one-way night dive was more likely.

Again Denise wiped her face, fingertips pressing on her eyelids. Anna took the opportunity to see if she could bite the duct tape closest to her chin. She couldn't, not without crushing the baby.

"I know Paulette is your sister," Anna said.

Denise laughed. "My identical twin sister." Shaking her head, she smiled to herself. "I'm still having trouble believing it's true. Too good to be true usually isn't."

"Oh, it's true," Anna said. "I know a lot about your family."

Denise had lifted the water bottle she'd used to give Anna a drink partway to her mouth. Her arm froze, suspending it midway between the chair's arm and her face. Her eyes narrowed. It didn't take a psychic to see the aura of paranoia and suspicion that darkened her visage. Paranoia: That was one of the symptoms Gwen had mentioned for Huntington's. Committing murder could make a person a tad jumpy as well. Kidnapping, Anna suspected, was hell on the nerves. Denise would have to be crazy not to be paranoid.

Since Anna had nothing to lose, she chose to feed it.

"I know she's your identical twin," Anna said, shooting for the tone of someone starting on a long list of sins. "I know the woman who delivered you as babies. I know the legacy that your biological mother wanted to share with you."

The water bottle flew from Denise's hand. Rolling, it left a dark wet trail across the rag rug where Anna sat. Denise hadn't thrown the water intentionally. Her hand had spasmed.

"Now look what you've done," Denise cried. Rising from the chair, she retrieved the bottle and set it on a small table beneath the pretend window. Hair whipping wildly, Denise looked around the room. "There's nothing to wipe it up with."

"It's only water. It will dry," Anna said calmly. "I know about your dropping things, too. You didn't used to be clumsy; now you drop things. Same with Paulette." Anna wasn't quite sure where she was going with this, just hoping that things would shake loose in a way that was more conducive to her surviving the night.

Denise growled, or grunted—a sound associated with animals, not humans. Reaching behind her back, she drew something from her waistband.

No surprise, a SIG Sauer 9 mm. Most likely the one Anna lost that night on Schoodic. The gun had never looked as big in Anna's hand as it did in Denise's. Viewed from the wrong end, the gun barrel seemed to take up half the room.

"Stop playing games with me," Denise said coldly. "If you know something, tell me. Otherwise, I'll blow your head off. I might do it anyway. You are supposed to be dead already, so what difference would it make?"

The thin yellow flame from the lantern reflected in

Denise's eyes. There wasn't much else there that Anna could see. Not the panic at the spilled water, the confusion at not wanting to hold "her" child, the warmth when she spoke of her sister: Her face reminded Anna of a patient her sister, a psychiatrist, treated. Molly had taken Anna along on a visit to the mental health facility to see a woman who suffered from severe autism. A screaming fight between three other patients had overloaded the woman's senses and she'd shut down.

Denise had that same look, as if the soul had moved a very long way from the windows, so far it almost couldn't be seen. Denise didn't look insane. In fact, she looked saner than anyone Anna had ever seen, if sanity could be measured by control. She exuded the vibe of an individual totally detached and completely dedicated to the task at hand.

A few times in her life Anna had thought she might be going to die. She thought that now. No one knew anything about death. No one came back to report on how it went down, what followed. Dead people gave no interviews, wrote no books.

Perhaps that was the reason that, though afraid, Anna wasn't nearly as afraid as she would have been if she'd been asked to speak in front of a crowd, or crawl down a skinny cave passage. Those things were real and scary. Death wasn't real. It was the last page, the fade to black. It was hard to be truly terrified of an event that wasn't quantifiable, that wasn't quite real.

"No games," Anna said evenly. The baby quieted. Glancing down, she checked to see if it had expired. Olivia's eyelashes were unbelievably long. They quivered on her round cheeks as her eyes moved beneath the closed lids. Still alive.

"No games," Anna repeated. "A woman I know, Dr. Gwen Littleton, delivered twin girls forty-some years ago. The babies were given up for adoption. Gwen and the mother became friends. The mother's health was failing, and she decided to try and find her daughters."

"Makes sense," Denise said. "She's about to kick the bucket. Don't want to die with abandoning two little girls on your conscience. Might go to hell. Tidy up with a quick 'so sorry I fucked up your lives,' and off to heaven goes Mommy."

Denise's voice, hands, and trigger finger were rock steady. If she'd gone over the edge in the past few minutes, she hadn't landed on Anna's side. "Is there anything you want to get off your chest?" Denise asked in a flat voice. "I'm the closest thing you're going to get to final absolution."

"You'll lose your hostage," Anna said. She'd wanted to sound reasonable, but her voice cracked, and she had to swallow to clear her throat.

"We can work around it," Denise said, and her finger tightened on the trigger.

"If you shoot me, you could hit your baby daughter," Anna said.

"I'm a crack shot," Denise said.

"No. You used to be a crack shot. The legacy is you have Huntington's disease; you can't control your hands," Anna said. "You put three bullets in Kurt Duffy from no more than ten feet away and none of them were anywhere near fatal."

"Bullshit." Denise pressed the muzzle of the gun hard against Anna's forehead. "Now I can't miss."

"Wait," Anna begged desperately. "You pull the trigger, this close, and the report will deafen Olivia. Rupture her eardrums. She'll be deaf as a post her whole life, and it will be all your fault."

"Put your fingers in her ears," Denise snarled.

"I can't," Anna said.

Denise glared at her. Turning suddenly, she yanked open the door and stormed out of the room. Through the open doorway all was in darkness until, about forty yards away, the overhead light in the SUV came on. Denise dove into the vehicle, only her legs sticking out.

Anna took the time to look around the room. The place was childproofed. Nothing that could be used as a weapon, even if she had use of her arms and hands, came to her attention.

A squawk made Anna's heart lurch; then a voice called her number, then Artie's. An NPS radio lay on the low table under the fake windows.

The caller was the superintendent. They'd discovered Olivia was missing. Panic vibrated in his voice. Anna had to stop herself from shouting that Olivia was okay, that she had her. Not only would Peter not hear, but Denise would be interrupted in whatever she was doing in the Volvo and hurry back to the shed.

Without fingers or even toes, pushing the TALK button on the side of the radio to reply would be an interesting exercise in ingenuity. Since that was Anna's only option, she wriggled around until her back was to the radio and, shoving with her heels, began pushing herself along the rag rug an inch at a time toward the low table. "Sorry, Olivia," Anna said as she managed to lever herself to her knees by bracing one elbow on the tiny chair by the crib. If she'd already killed Peter's child, it wouldn't matter. If she hadn't, this wouldn't be the fatal move.

Anna nosed the unit over to the wall, then pressed her chin as hard as she could into the TALK button. Maybe she depressed it a hair, maybe not; still she said, "Anna Pigeon, maybe near the Duffy house. Help!"

Denise banged back into the shed, slamming the door behind her. "Stupid bitch," she hissed. In two strides she'd crossed the room. The radio was slapped onto the floor. "Sit." Denise shoved Anna until she fell back against the wall and her rump slid down to the floor.

A pair of Bose earphones was in Denise's free hand. She squatted beside Anna, then carefully settled the phones over the baby's ears.

"There!" she said, standing. Snatching the gun out of the waistband of her pants, she pressed the muzzle to Anna's temple. "This time, promise me you'll die."

Anna closed her eyes and wondered what a person was supposed to think at a time like this.

"Denise? Honey?" The door was pushed open. Paulette stood in the faint spill of lamplight, her pink scrubs as rumpled as pajamas in the morning. "My God!" She stepped in and closed the door behind her. "Denise, what are you doing? Put that gun down." Her eyes on the baby, she stepped onto the rug in front of Anna. Dropping to her knees, she wailed, "No! You promised you wouldn't take the baby." She reached out as if she'd scoop it out of Anna's tape-and-bone bassinet, then froze. "This isn't the Frazier baby. Denise! What have you done?"

"She's kidnapped Peter Barnes's daughter, Olivia," Anna said. "The baby is sick. It was in the hospital for observation."

"Shut up!" Denise snarled.

"You're dead!" Paulette exclaimed, noticing Anna for the first time.

"Yes I am," Anna replied, wondering if it was true. "I've come back to save this child. If we don't get her back to the hospital, she'll die."

"Olivia Barnes? The three-month-old admitted for a seizure? Denise, you said you were going to save a life!" She looked up at her twin accusingly.

"I did, Paulette," Denise said, the gun lowered to her side. "I did. It was the only way. Lily, her mom, has Munchausen-by-proxy syndrome. She poisoned Olivia with ergotamine so she could go to the hospital and be the big hero. If we don't get the baby away, eventually Lily will kill her."

Paulette rocked back on her heels. "How could any mother . . . Oh, Denise! This is so awful. What can we do?"

"We have to get the baby and ourselves away from here, leave no hint to where we've gone, or that it was us who saved the baby," Denise said.

Mood swings was an understatement; she sounded so rational, so believable, that for a second Anna wondered if it could be true. "Ergotamine," Anna said suddenly. "How do you know the baby was poisoned with ergotamine?"

Paulette looked from her sister to Anna, then back to her sister. "The doctors didn't know what made the baby sick," Paulette said. Tears flooded her eyes. "Oh, Denise! You did it! You poisoned one of my babies. You . . .

"Help!" she screamed, scrambling to her feet. "Help! Somebody help me!" She reached the door and pulled it open.

The gun rose from Denise's side, leveled on Paulette's back.

"Gun!" Anna yelled because that's what she'd been trained to do.

A flash of muzzle fire and a blast, so loud in the small room that it numbed Anna's eardrums, shook the shed. Denise was turning, gun in hand. Before she could aim a second shot, Anna fell to her side, the baby affixed to her chest toppling with her, and whipped her legs out, knocking Denise's feet from under her. The gun hit the floor and skittered to the center of the round rug.

Cursing, Denise crawled for it. Whiplashing her feet, Anna managed to kick the SIG Sauer. The pistol slid over and stopped against Paulette's thigh. Paulette Duffy lay facedown, halfway in and halfway out of the nursery, a stain of blood blooming across the pink teddy bears on the back of her scrubs. There might have been life left in the woman, but Anna doubted it. The bullet had entered the left side of Paulette Duffy's back below the shoulder blade near the spine. The heart had probably been next on its trajectory.

Denise followed the gun. Trying to beat her to it, though the gun was out of her reach now and, she expected, forever, Anna flipped open and shut like a broken jackknife, getting nowhere. No crying from the baby. She hoped she hadn't smashed it.

Denise didn't grab up the SIG Sauer. Coming to her knees beside her sister's bleeding body, she covered her mouth with both hands. Moving in slow motion, she turned her head toward Anna. The hands floated down.

"What have I done?" she asked in a bewildered tone.

"You've killed your identical twin sister," Anna said. "Shot her in the back."

With a keening wail, Denise dragged Paulette up from the floor, cradling her in her lap. Denise's newly blond hair fell over Paulette's face, mingling with Paulette's bleached mess until no difference could be seen between them. Identical noses close, one face in repose, the other in a rictus of grief, Denise's tears dripped onto Paulette's cheeks.

From somewhere in the room the radio crackled. "Anna . . . Duffy house . . . Roadblocks . . ." Anna's message had gotten through.

Arms wrapped her around her sister, Denise began to rock. As if an invisible hand arrested her movement, she stopped suddenly. Misery blinked out, cheeks still awash with tears, Denise looked almost happy. Anna watched as her hand dipped into the pocket of Paulette's smock. Pulling out an empty unused syringe, she held it up to the lantern light and smiled.

Using her teeth, Denise uncapped the needle. Thumb on the plunger, she jammed the needle into her carotid artery and ripped downward. Blood sprayed out in a crimson wave, then pulsed ever smaller fountains of red. The sisters' blood mixed until both were dyed red with it and Anna couldn't tell where Denise began and Paulette left off.

Sirens sounded in the distance. "Your daddy is coming," Anna whispered to Olivia.

Expelling a sigh, Anna looked away from the tragedy clogging the door, her eyes moving to the painted sunlight through the fake windows.

There had been an instant, a moment in time, when Anna might have been able to say or do something that would have stopped Denise, saved her life.

But it would not have been a kindness.

W9-CAJ-39

KRISTAN HIGGINS

Too Good to Be True

entertain, enrich, inspire™

Recycling programs
for this product may
not exist in your area.

ISBN-13: 978-0-373-77791-4

TOO GOOD TO BE TRUE

Copyright © 2009 by Kristan Higgins

www.Harlequin.com

Printed in U.S.A.

This book is dedicated to the memory
of my grandmother, Helen Kristan,
quite the loveliest woman I've ever known.

ACKNOWLEDGMENTS

At the Maria Carvainis Agency... Thanks as always to the brilliant and generous Maria Carvainis for her wisdom and guidance, and to Donna Bagdasarian and June Renschler for their enthusiasm for this book.

At Harlequin HQN, thanks to Keyren Gerlach for her graceful and intelligent input and to Tracy Farrell for her support and encouragement.

Thanks to Julie Revell Benjamin and Rose Morris, my writing buddies; and to Beth Robinson of PointSource Media, who makes my website and trailers look so great.

On the personal side, thanks to my friends and family members who listen endlessly to my ideas—Mom, Mike, Hilly, Jackie, Nana, Maryellen, Christine, Maureen and Lisa. How lucky I am to have such a family and such friends!

Thanks to my great kids, who make life so enjoyable, and especially to my honey, Terence Keenan. Words, in this case, are just not enough.

And finally, thanks to my grandfather, Jules Kristan, a man of steadfast devotion, keen intelligence and innate and boundless goodness. The world is a better place because of your example, dearest Poppy.

Too Good to Be True

PROLOGUE

MAKING UP A BOYFRIEND is nothing new for me. I'll come right out and admit that. Some people go window shopping for things they could never afford. Some look at online photos of resorts they'll never visit. And some people imagine that they meet a really nice guy when, in fact, they don't.

The first time it happened was in sixth grade. Recess. Heather B., Heather F. and Jessica A. were standing in their little circle of popularity. They wore lip gloss and eye shadow, had cute little pocketbooks and boyfriends. Back then, going out with a boy only meant that he might acknowledge you while passing in the hall, but still, it was a status symbol, and one that I lacked, right along with the eye shadow. Heather F. was watching her man, Joey Ames, as he put a frog down his pants for reasons clear only to sixth-grade boys, and talking about how she was maybe going to break up with Joey and go out with Jason.

And suddenly, without a lot of forethought, I found myself saying that I, too, was dating someone…a boy from another town. The three popular girls turned to me with sharp and sudden interest, and I found myself talking about Tyler, who was really cute and smart and polite. An older man at fourteen. Also, his family owned a horse ranch and they wanted me to name the newest foal, and I was going to train it so that it came for my whistle and mine alone.

Surely we've all come up with a boy like that. Right? What was the harm in believing—almost—that somewhere out there, counterbalancing the frog-in-the-pants types, was a boy like Tyler of the horses? It was almost like believing in God—you had to, because what was the alternative? The other girls bought it, peppered me with questions, looked at me with new respect. Heather B. even invited me to her upcoming birthday party, and I happily accepted. Of course, by then I was forced to share the sad news that Tyler's ranch had burned down and the family moved to Oregon, taking my foal, Midnight Sun, with them. Maybe the Heathers and the rest of the kids in my class guessed the truth, but I found I didn't really mind. Imagining Tyler had really felt… great, actually.

Later, when I was fifteen and we'd moved from our humble town of Mount Vernon, New York, to the much posher burg of Avon, Connecticut, where all the girls had smooth hair and very white teeth, I made up another boy. Jack, my Boyfriend Back Home. Oh, he was so handsome (as proved by the photo in my wallet, which had been carefully cut from a J.Crew catalog). Jack's father owned a really gorgeous restaurant named Le Cirque (hey, I was fifteen). Jack and I were taking things slow…yes, we'd kissed; actually, we'd gotten to second base, but he was so respectful that that was as far as it went. We wanted to wait till we were older. Maybe we'd get preengaged, and because his family loved me so much, they wanted Jack to buy me a ring from Tiffany, not a diamond but maybe a sapphire, kind of like Princess Diana's, but a little smaller.

Sorry to tell you, I broke up with Jack about four months into my sophomore year in order to be available to local boys. My strategy backfired…the local boys were not terribly interested. In my older sister, definitely…Margaret would pick me up once in a while when she was home from college, and boys would fall silent at the mere sight of her sharp, glamorous beauty. Even my younger sister, who was only in seventh grade at the time, already showed signs of becoming a great beauty. But I stayed unattached, wishing I'd never broken up with my fictional boyfriend, missing the warm curl of pleasure it gave me to imagine such a boy liking me.

Then came Jean-Philippe. Jean-Philippe was invented to counter an irritating, incredibly persistent boy in college. A chemistry major who, looking back, probably suffered from Asperger's syndrome, making him immune to every social nuance I threw his way. Rather than just flat out tell the boy that I didn't like him (it seemed so cruel) I'd instruct my roommate to scrawl messages and tack them to the door so all could see: "Grace—J-P called *again,* wants you to spend break in Paris. Call him *toute suite.*"

I *loved* Jean-Philippe, loved imagining that some well-dressed Frenchman had a thing for me! That he was prowling the bridges of Paris, staring sullenly into the Seine, yearning for me and sighing morosely as he ate chocolate croissants and drank good wine. Oh, I had a crush on Jean-Philippe for ages, rivaling only my love for Rhett Butler, whom I'd discovered at age thirteen and never let go.

All through my twenties, even now at age thirty, faking a boyfriend was a survival skill. Florence, one of the little old ladies at Golden Meadows Senior Village, recently offered me her nephew during the ballroom dancing class, which I help teach. "Honey, you would just love Bertie!" she chirped as I tried to get her to turn right on her alamaena. "Can I give him your number? He's a doctor. A podiatrist. So he has one tiny problem. Girls today are too picky. In my day, if you were thirty and unmarried, you were as good as dead. Just because Bertie has bosoms, so what? His mother was buxom, too, oh, she was stacked…"

Out came the imaginary boyfriend. "Oh, he sounds so nice, Flo…but I just started dating someone. Drat."

It's not just around other people, I have to admit. I use the emergency boyfriend as…well, let's say as a coping mechanism, too.

For example, a few weeks ago, I was driving home on a dark and lonely section of Connecticut's Route 9, thinking about my ex-fiancé and his new lady love, when my tire blew out. As is typical with brushes with death, a thousand thoughts were clear in my mind, even as I wrestled with the steering wheel, trying to keep the car from flipping, even as I distantly realized that voice shrieking "OhGodohGod!" was mine. First, I had nothing to wear to my funeral *(easy, easy, don't want to flip the car)*. Second, if open casket was an option, I hoped my hair wouldn't be frizzing in death as it did in life *(pull harder, pull harder, you're losing it)*. My sisters would be devastated, my parents struck dumb with sorrow, their endless sniping silenced, at least for the day *(hit the gas, just a little, it will straighten out the car)*. And God's nightgown, wouldn't Andrew be riddled with guilt! For the rest of his life, he'd always regret dumping me *(slow down gradually now, on with the flashers, good, good, we're still alive)*.

When the car was safe on the shoulder, I sat, shaking uncontrollably, my heart clattering against my ribs like a loose shutter in a hurricane. "JesusJesusthankyou-Jesus," I chanted, fumbling for my cell phone.

Alas, I was out of range for cell service (of course). I waited a few moments, then, resigned, did what I had to do. Got out of the car into the cold March downpour, examined my shredded tire. Opened the trunk, pulled out the jack and the spare tire. Though I'd never done this particular task before, I figured it out as other cars flew past me occasionally, further drenching me with icy spray. I pinched my hand badly enough for a blood blister, broke a nail, ruined my shoes, became filthy from the mud and axle grease.

No one stopped to help. Not one dang person. No one even tapped their brakes, for that matter. Cursing, quite irritable with the cruelty of the world and vaguely proud that I'd changed a tire, I climbed back into the car, teeth chattering, lips blue with cold, drenched and dirty. On the drive back, all I could think of was a bath, a hot toddy, *Project Runway* and flannel pajamas. Instead, I found disaster waiting for me.

Judging from the evidence, Angus, my West Highland terrier, had chewed through the child safety latch on the newly painted cabinet door, dragged out the garbage can, tipped it over and ate the iffy chicken I'd thrown out that morning. There was no *if* about it, apparently. The chicken was bad. My poor dog had then regurgitated with such force that the walls of my kitchen were splattered with doggy vomit so high that a streak of yellow-green bile smeared the face of my Fritz the

Cat clock. A trail of wet excrement led to the living room, where I found Angus stretched out on the pastel-shaded Oriental rug I'd just had cleaned. My dog belched foully, barked once and wagged his tail with guilty love amid the steaming puddles of barf.

No bath. No Tim Gunn and *Project Runway*. No hot toddy.

So what does this have to do with another imaginary boyfriend? Well, as I scrubbed the carpet with bleach and water and tried to emotionally prepare Angus for the suppository the vet instructed me to give, I found myself imagining the following instead.

I was driving home when my tire blew out. I stopped, reached for my cell phone, yadda yadda ding dong, blah blah blah. But what was this? A car slowed and pulled in behind me. It was, let's see, an environmentally gentle hybrid, and ah, it had M.D. plates. A Good Samaritan in the form of a tall, rangy male in his mid-to-late-thirties approached my car. He bent down. Hello! There it was…that moment when you look at someone and just…kablammy. You Just Know He's The One.

In my fantasy, I accepted the kind Samaritan's offer of help. Ten minutes later, he had secured the spare on the axle, heaved the blown tire in the trunk and handed me his business card. Wyatt Something, M.D., Department of Pediatric Surgery. Ah.

"Call me when you get home, just so I know you made it, okay?" he asked, smiling. Kablammy! He scrawled his home number on the card as I drank in the sight of his appealing dimples and long lashes.

It made cleaning up the puke a lot nicer.

Obviously, I was quite aware that my tire was not changed by the kindly and handsome doctor. I didn't tell anyone he had. Just a little healthy escapism, right? No, there was no Wyatt (I always liked the name, so authoritative and noble). Unfortunately, a guy like that was just too good to be true. I didn't go around talking about the pediatric surgeon who changed my tire, of course not. No. This was kept firmly private, just a little coping mechanism, as I said. I hadn't publicly faked a boyfriend in years.

Until recently, that is.

CHAPTER ONE

"AND SO WITH THIS ONE ACT, Lincoln changed the course of American history. He was one of the most despised figures in politics in his day, yet he preserved the Union and is considered the greatest president our country ever had. And possibly ever will have."

My face flushed...we'd just begun our unit on the Civil War, and it was my favorite class to teach. Alas, my seniors were in the throes of a Friday afternoon coma. Tommy Michener, my best student on most days, stared longingly at Kerry Blake, who was stretching so as to simultaneously torment Tommy with what he couldn't have and invite Hunter Graystone IV to take it. At the same time, Emma Kirk, a pretty, kindhearted girl who had the curse of being a day student and was thus excluded from the cool kids, who all boarded, looked at her desk. She had a crush on Tommy and was all too aware of his obsession with Kerry, poor kid. "So who can sum up the opposing viewpoints? Anyone?"

From outside came the sound of laughter. We all looked. Kiki Gomez, an English teacher, was holding class outside, as the day was mild and lovely. Her kids didn't look dazed and battered. Dang. I should've brought my kids outside, too.

"I'll give you a hint," I continued, looking at their blank faces. "States' rights vs. Federal control. Union vs. secession. Freedom to govern independently vs. freedom for all people. Slaves or no slaves. Ring a bell?"

At that moment, the chimes that marked the end of the period sounded, and my lethargic students sprang into life as they bolted for the door. I tried not to take it personally. My seniors were usually more engaged, but it was Friday. The kids had been hammered with exams earlier in the week, and there was a dance tonight. I understood.

Manning Academy was the type of prep school that litters New England. Stately brick buildings with the requisite ivy, magnolia and dogwood trees, emerald soccer and lacrosse fields, and a promise that for the cost of a small house, we'd get your kids into the colleges of their choice—Princeton, Harvard, Stanford, Georgetown. The school, which was founded in the 1880s, was a little world unto itself. Many of the teachers lived on campus, but those of us who didn't, myself included, were usually as bad as the kids, eager for the last class to end each Friday afternoon so we could head for home.

Except this Friday. I'd have been more than happy to stay at school this Friday, chaperoning dances or coaching lacrosse. Or heck, cleaning the toilets for that matter. Anything other than my actual plans.

"Hi, Grace!" Kiki said, popping into my classroom.

"Hi, Kiki. Sounded like fun out there."

"We're reading *Lord of the Flies*," she informed me.

"Of course! No wonder you were laughing. Nothing like a little pig killing to brighten the day."

She grinned proudly. "So, Grace, did you find a date?"

I grimaced. "No. I didn't. It won't be pretty."

"Oh, shit," she said. "I'm so sorry."

"Well, it's not the end of the world," I murmured bravely.

"You sure about that?" Like me, Kiki was single. And no one knew better than a single woman in her thirties that hell is going to a wedding stag. In a few hours, my cousin Kitty, who once cut my bangs down to the roots when I was sleeping over at her house, was getting married. For the third time. In a Princess Diana–style dress.

"Look, it's Eric!" Kiki blurted, pointing to my eastern window. "Oh, thank you, God!"

Eric was the guy who washed Manning Academy's windows each spring and fall. Though it was only early April, the afternoon was warm and balmy, and Eric was shirtless. He grinned at us, well aware of his beauty, sprayed and squeegeed.

"Ask him!" Kiki suggested as we stared with great appreciation.

"He's married," I said, not taking my eyes off him. Ogling Eric was about as intimate as I'd been with a man in some time.

"*Happily* married?" Kiki asked, not above wrecking a home or two to get a man.

"Yup. Adores his wife."

"I hate that," she muttered.

"I know. So unfair."

The male perfection that was Eric winked at us, blew a kiss and dragged the squeegee back and forth over the window, shoulder muscles bunching beautifully, washboard abs rippling, sunlight glinting on his hair.

"I should really get going," I said, not moving a muscle. "I have to change and stuff." The thought made my stomach cramp. "Kiki, you sure you don't know anyone I can take? Anyone? I really, really don't want to go alone."

"I don't, Grace," she sighed. "Maybe you should've hired someone, like in that Debra Messing movie."

"It's a small town. A gigolo would probably stand out. Also, probably not that good for my reputation. 'Manning Teacher Hires Prostitute. Parents Concerned.' That kind of thing."

"What about Julian?" she asked, naming my oldest friend, who often came out with Kiki and me on our girls' nights.

"Well, my family knows him. He wouldn't pass."

"As a boyfriend, or as a straight guy?"

"Both, I guess," I said.

"Too bad. He's a great dancer, at least."

"That he is." I glanced at the clock, and the trickle of dread that had been spurting intermittently all week turned into a river. It wasn't just going stag to mean old Kitty's wedding. I'd be seeing Andrew for only the third time since we broke up, and having a date would've definitely helped.

Well. As much as I wished I could just stay home and read *Gone with the Wind* or watch a movie, I had to go. Besides, I'd been staying in a lot lately. My father, my gay best friend and my dog, though great company, probably shouldn't be the only men in my life. And there was always the microscopic chance that I'd meet someone at this very wedding.

"Maybe Eric will go," Kiki said, hustling over to the window and yanking it open. "No one has to know he's married."

"Kiki, no," I protested.

She didn't listen. "Eric, Grace has to go to a wedding

tonight, and her ex-fiancé is going to be there, and she doesn't have a date. Can you go with her? Pretend to adore her and stuff?"

"Thanks anyway, but, no," I called, my face prickling with heat.

"Your ex, huh?" Eric said, wiping a pane clear.

"Yeah. May as well slit my wrists now." I smiled to show I didn't mean it.

"You sure you can't go with her?" Kiki asked.

"My wife would probably have a problem with that," Eric answered. "Sorry, Grace. Good luck."

"Thanks," I said. "It sounds worse than it is."

"Isn't she brave?" Kiki asked. Eric agreed that I was and moved on to the next window, Kiki nearly falling out the window to watch him leave. She hauled herself back in and sighed. "So you're going stag," she said in the same tone as a doctor might use when saying, *I'm sorry, it's terminal.*

"Well, I did try, Kiki," I reminded her. "Johnny who delivers my pizza is dating Garlic-and-Anchovies, if you can believe it. Brandon at the nursing home said he'd hang himself before being a wedding date. And I just found out that the cute guy at the pharmacy is only seventeen years old, and though he said he'd be happy to go, Betty the pharmacist is his mom and mentioned something about the Mann Act and predators, so I'll be going to the CVS in Farmington from now on."

"Oopsy," Kiki said.

"No big deal. I came up empty. So I'll just go alone, be noble and brave, scan the room for legs to hump and leave with a waiter. If I'm lucky." I grinned. Bravely.

Kiki laughed. "Being single sucks," she announced. "And God, being single at a wedding…" She shuddered.

"Thanks for the pep talk," I answered.

Four hours later, I was in hell.

The all too familiar and slightly nauseating combination of hope and despair churned in my stomach. Honestly, I thought I was doing pretty well these days. Yes, my fiancé had dumped me fifteen months ago, but I wasn't lying on the floor in fetal position, sucking my thumb. I went to work and taught my classes... very well, in my opinion. I went out socially. Granted, most of my excursions were either dancing with senior citizens or reenacting Civil War battles, but I did get out. And, yes, I would (theoretically) love to find a man—sort of an Atticus-Finch-meets-Tim-Gunn-and-looks-like-George-Clooney type.

So here I was at another wedding—the fourth family wedding since The Dumping, the fourth family wedding where I'd been dateless—gamely trying to radiate happiness so my relatives would stop pitying me and trying to fix me up with odd-looking distant cousins. At the same time, I was trying to perfect The Look—wry amusement, inner contentment and absolute comfort. Sort of a *Hello! I am perfectly fine being single at yet another wedding and am not at all desperate for a man, but if you happen to be straight, under forty-five, attractive, financially secure and morally upright, come on down!* Once I mastered The Look, I planned on splitting an atom, since they required just about the same level of skill.

But who knew? Maybe today, my eyes would lock on someone, someone who was also single and hopeful without being pathetic—let's say a pediatric surgeon, just for the sake of argument—and kablammy! We'd just know.

Unfortunately, my hair was making me look, at best,

gypsy beautiful and reckless, but more probably like I was channeling Gilda Radner. Must remember to call an exorcist to see if I could have the evil demons cast out of my hair, which had been known to snap combs in half and eat hairbrushes.

Hmm. There was a cute guy. Geeky, skinny, glasses, definitely my type. Then he saw me looking and immediately groped behind him for a hand, which was attached to an arm, which was attached to a woman. He beamed at her, planted a kiss on her lips and shot a nervous look my way. *Okay, okay, no need to panic, mister,* I thought. *Message received.*

Indeed, all the men under forty seemed to be spoken for. There were several octogenarians present, one of whom was grinning at me. Hmm. Was eighty too old? Maybe I *should* go for an older man. Maybe I was wasting my time on men who still had functioning prostates and their original knees. Maybe there was something to be said for a sugar daddy. The old guy raised his bushy white eyebrows, but his pursuit of me being his sweet young thing ended abruptly as his wife elbowed him sharply and shot me a disapproving glare.

"Don't worry, Grace. It will be your turn soon," an aunt boomed in her foghorn of a voice.

"You never know, Aunt Mavis," I answered with a sweet smile. It was the eighth time tonight I'd heard such a sentiment, and I was considering having it tattooed on my forehead. *I'm not worried. It will be my turn soon.*

"Is it hard, seeing them together?" Mavis barked.

"No. Not at all," I lied, still smiling. "I'm very glad they're dating." Granted, *glad* may have been a stretch, but still. What else could I say? It was complicated.

"You're brave," Mavis pronounced. "You are one brave woman, Grace Emerson." Then she tromped off in search of someone else to torment.

"Okay, so spill," my sister Margaret demanded, plopping herself down at my table. "Are you looking for a good sharp instrument so you can hack away at your wrists? Thinking about sucking a little carbon monoxide?"

"Aw, listen to you, you big softy. Your sisterly concern brings tears to my eyes."

She grinned. "Well? Tell your big sis."

I took a long pull from my gin and tonic. "I'm getting a little tired of people saying how brave I am, like I'm some marine who jumped on a grenade. Being single isn't the worst thing in the world."

"I wish I was single all the time," Margs answered as her husband approached.

"Hey, Stuart!" I said fondly. "I didn't see you at school today." Stuart was the school psychologist at Manning and had in fact alerted me to the history department opening six years ago. He sort of lived the stereotype…oxford shirts covered by argyle vests, tasseled loafers, the required beard. A gentle, quiet man, Stuart had met Margaret in graduate school and been her devoted servant ever since.

"How are you holding up, Grace?" he asked, handing me a fresh version of my signature drink, a gin and tonic with lemon.

"I'm great, Stuart," I answered.

"Hello, Margaret, hello, Stuart!" called my aunt Reggie from the dance floor. Then she saw me and froze. "Oh, hello, Grace, don't you look pretty. And chin up, dear. You'll be dancing at your own wedding one day soon."

"Gosh, thanks, Aunt Reggie," I answered, giving my sister a significant look. Reggie gave me a sad smile and drifted away to gossip.

"I still think it's freakish," Margs said. "How Andrew and Natalie could ever… Gentle Jesus and His crown of thorns! I just cannot wrap my brain around that one. Where are they, anyway?"

"Grace, how are you? Are you just putting up a good front, honey, or are you really okay?" This from Mom, who now approached our table. Dad, pushing his ancient mother in her wheelchair, trailed behind.

"She's fine, Nancy!" he barked. "Look at her! Doesn't she seem fine to you? Leave her alone! Don't talk about it."

"Shut it, Jim. I know my children, and this one's hurting. A *good* parent can tell." She gave him a meaningful and frosty look.

"Good parent? I'm a great parent," Dad snipped right back.

"I'm fine, Mom. Dad is right. I'm peachy. Hey, doesn't Kitty look great?"

"Almost as pretty as at her first wedding," Margaret said.

"Have you seen Andrew?" Mom asked. "Is it hard, honey?"

"I'm fine," I repeated. "Really. I'm great."

Mémé, my ninety-three-year-old grandmother, rattled the ice in her highball glass. "If Grace can't keep a man, all's fair in love and war."

"It's alive!" Margaret said.

Mémé ignored her, gazing at me with disparaging,

rheumy eyes. "I never had trouble finding a man. Men loved me. I was quite a beauty in my day, you know."

"And you still are," I said. "Look at you! How do you do it, Mémé? You don't look a day over a hundred and ten."

"Please, Grace," my father muttered wearily. "It's gas on a fire."

"Laugh if you want, Grace. At least my fiancé never threw me over." Mémé knocked back the rest of her Manhattan and held out her glass to Dad, who took it obediently.

"You don't need a man," Mom said firmly. "No woman does." She leveled a significant look at my father.

"What is that supposed to mean?" Dad snapped.

"It means what it means," Mom said, her voice loaded.

Dad rolled his eyes. "Stuart, let's get another round, son. Grace, I stopped by your house today and you really need new windows. Margaret, nice job on the Bleeker case, honey." It was Dad's way to jam in as much into a conversation as possible, sort of get things over with so he could ignore my mother (and his). "And, Grace, don't forget about Bull Run next weekend. We're Confederates."

Dad and I belonged to Brother Against Brother, the largest group of Civil War reenactors in three states. You've seen us…we're the weirdos who dress up for parades and stage battles in fields and at parks, shooting each other with blanks and falling in delicious agony to the ground. Despite the fact that Connecticut didn't see a whole lot of Civil War action (alas), we fanatics in Brother Against Brother ignored that inconvenient fact. Our schedule started in the early spring, when we'd stage a few local battles, then move on to the actual sites throughout the South, joining up with other reenactment groups to indulge in our passion. You'd be amazed at how many of us there were.

"Your father and those idiot battles," Mom muttered, adjusting Mémé's collar. Mémé had apparently fallen deeply asleep or died…but no, her bony chest was rising and falling. "Well, I'm not going, of course. I need to focus on my art. You're coming to the show this week, aren't you?"

Margaret and I exchanged wary looks and made noncommittal sounds. Mom's art was a subject best left untouched.

"Grace!" Mémé barked, suddenly springing back to life. "Get out there! Kitty's going to throw the bouquet! Go! Go!" She turned her wheelchair and began ramming it into my shins, as ruthless as Ramses bearing down on the fleeing Hebrew slaves.

"Mémé! Please! You're hurting me!" I yanked my legs out of the way, which didn't stop her.

"Go! You need all the help you can get!"

Mom rolled her eyes. "Leave her alone, Eleanor. Can't you see she's suffering enough? Grace, honey, you don't have to go if it makes you sad. Everyone will understand."

"I'm fine," I said loudly, running a hand over my uncontrollable hair, which had burst the bonds of bobby pins. "I'll go." Because damn it, if I didn't, it would be worse. *Poor Grace, look at her, she's just sitting there like a dead possum in the road, can't even get out of her chair.* Besides, Mémé's chair was starting to leave marks on my dress.

Out onto the dance floor I went, as excited as Anne Boleyn on her way to the gallows. I tried to blend in with the other sheep, standing in the back where I wouldn't really have a chance of catching the bouquet. "Cat Scratch Fever" came booming over the stereo—so classy—and I couldn't suppress a snicker.

Then I saw Andrew. Looking right at me, guilty as sin. His date was nowhere in sight. My heart lurched.

I knew he was here, of course. Him coming was my idea. But seeing him, knowing he was with another woman today in their first appearance as a couple, made my hands sweat, my stomach turn to ice. Andrew Carson was, after all, the man I thought I'd marry. The man I came within three weeks of marrying. The man who left me because he fell in love with someone else.

A couple of years ago, at Cousin Kitty's second wedding, Andrew had come as my date. We'd been together for a while, and when it was bouquet toss time then, I'd gone up more or less happily, pretending to be embarrassed but with the smug contentment of a steady boyfriend. I didn't catch the bouquet, and when I left the dance floor, Andrew had slung his arm around my shoulder. "I thought you could've worked a little harder out there," he'd said, and I remembered the thrilling rush those words had caused.

Now he was here with his new girlfriend. Natalie of the long, straight, blond hair. Natalie of the legs that went on forever. Natalie the architect.

Natalie, my much adored younger sister, who was understandably lying low at this wedding.

Kitty tossed the bouquet. Her sister, my cousin Anne, caught it as planned and rehearsed, no doubt. Torture time over. But, no. Kitty spied me, picked up her skirts and hustled over. "It will be your turn soon, Grace," she announced loudly. "You holding up okay?"

"Sure," I said. "It's déjà vu all over again, Kitty! Another spring, another one of your weddings."

"You poor thing." She gave my arm a firm squeeze, smug sympathy dripping out of her, glanced at my bangs (yes, they'd grown out in the fifteen years that had passed since she'd cut them) and went back to her groom and the three kids from her first two marriages.

THIRTY-THREE MINUTES LATER, I decided I'd been brave long enough. Kitty's reception was in full swing, and while the music was lively and my feet were itching to get out there and show the crowd what a rumba was supposed to look like, I decided to head for home. If there was a single, good-looking, financially secure, emotionally stable man here, he was hiding under a table. One quick pit stop and I'd be on my way.

I pushed open the door, took a quick and horrifying look in the mirror—even I didn't even know it was possible for my hair to frizz that much, holy guacamole, it was nearly horizontal—and started to push open a stall door when I heard a small noise. A sad noise. I peeked under the door. Nice shoes. Strappy, high heels, blue patent leather.

"Um…is everything okay?" I asked, frowning. Those shoes looked familiar.

"Grace?" came a small voice. No wonder the shoes looked familiar. My younger sister and I had bought them together, last winter.

"Nat? Honey, are you okay?"

There was a rustle of material; then my sister pushed open the door. She tried to smile, but her clear blue eyes were wet with silvery tears. I noted her mascara didn't deign to run. She looked tragic and gorgeous, Ilsa saying goodbye to Rick at the Casablanca airport.

"What's wrong, Nat?" I asked.

"Oh, it's nothing…." Her mouth wobbled. "It's fine."

I paused. "Is it something to do with Andrew?"

Natalie's good front faltered. "Um…well…I don't think it's going to work between us," she said, her voice cracking a little, giving her away. She bit her lip and looked down.

"Why?" I asked. Relief and concern battled in my heart. Granted, it sure wouldn't kill me if Nat and Andrew didn't work out, but it wasn't like Natalie to be melodramatic. In fact, the last time I'd seen her cry was when I'd left for college twelve years ago.

"Um…it's just a bad idea," she whispered. "But it's fine."

"What happened?" I asked. The urge to strangle Andrew flared in my gut. "What did he do?"

"Nothing," she assured me hastily. "It's just…um…"

"What?" I asked again, more forcefully this time. She wouldn't look at me. Ah, dang it all. "Is it because of me, Nat?"

She didn't answer.

I sighed. "Nattie. Please answer me."

Her eyes darted at me, then dropped to the floor again. "You're not over him, are you?" she whispered. "Even though you said you were…I saw your face out there, at the bouquet toss, and oh, Grace, I'm so sorry. I should never have tried—"

"Natalie," I interrupted, "I'm over him. I am. I promise."

She gave me a look loaded with such guilt and misery and genuine anguish that the next words came out of my mouth without my being fully aware of them. "The truth is, Nat, I'm seeing someone."

Oops. Hadn't really planned on saying that, but it worked like a charm. Natalie blinked up at me, two more tears slipping down her petal-pink cheeks, hope dawning on her face, her eyes widening. "You are?" she said.

"Yes," I lied, snatching a tissue to dab her face. "For a few weeks now."

Nat's tragic expression was fading. "Why didn't you bring him tonight?" she asked.

"Oh, you know. Weddings. Everyone gets all excited if you come with someone."

"You didn't tell me," she said, a slight frown creasing her forehead.

"Well, I didn't want to say anything until I knew it would be worth mentioning." I smiled again, warming to the idea—just like old times—and this time, Nat smiled back.

"What's his name?" she asked.

I paused for the briefest second. "Wyatt," I answered, remembering my tire-changing fantasy. "He's a doctor."

CHAPTER TWO

LET ME JUST SAY THAT THE REST of the night went a lot better for everyone. Natalie towed me back to the table where the rest of our family sat, insisting that we hang out together a little, as she had been too nervous to actually speak to me yet this day.

"Grace has been seeing someone!" she announced softly, eyes shining. Margaret, who had been painfully listening to Mémé describe her nasal polyps, snapped to attention. Mom and Dad stopped midbicker to pelt me with questions, but I stuck with my "it's still a little early to talk about it" story. Margaret raised an eyebrow but didn't say anything. Out of the corner of my eye, I scanned for Andrew—he and Natalie had been keeping a bit of a distance from each other out of concern for my tender feelings. He wasn't in range.

"And just what does this person do for a living?" Mémé demanded. "He's not one of those impoverished teachers, is he? Your sisters managed to find jobs that pay a decent wage, Grace. I don't know why you can't."

"He's a doctor," I said, taking a sip of the gin and tonic the waiter brought over.

"What kind, Pudding?" Dad asked.

"A pediatric surgeon," I answered smoothly. Sip, sip. Hopefully, the flush on my face could be attributed to my cocktail and not lying.

"Ooh," Nat sighed, her face breaking into an angelic smile. "Oh, Grace."

"Wonderful," Dad said. "Hold on to this one, Grace."

"She doesn't need to hold on to anything, Jim," Mom snapped. "Honestly, you're her father! Do you really need to undermine her this way?" Then they were off and running in another argument. How nice that Poor Grace was finally off the list of things to worry about!

I TOOK A CAB HOME, CLAIMING a misplaced cell phone and a pressing need to call my wonderful doctor boyfriend. I also managed to avoid speaking directly with Andrew. Pushing Natalie and Andrew out of my head à la Scarlett O'Hara—*I'll think about that tomorrow*—I focused instead on my new imaginary boyfriend. Good thing my tire had blown out a few weeks ago, or I wouldn't have been nearly so quick on my feet.

How nice it would've been if Wyatt, pediatric surgeon, were a real guy. If he'd been a good dancer, too, even if it was just a little turning box step. If he could've charmed Mémé and asked Mom about her sculptures and not cringed when she described them. If he was a golfer like Stuart and the two guys made plans for a morning on the links. If he just happened to know a little bit about the Civil War. If he occasionally broke off midsentence when he was talking because he looked at me and simply forgot what he was saying. If he was here to lead me upstairs, unzip this uncomfortable dress and shag me silly.

The cab turned onto my street and cruised to a stop. I paid the driver, got out and just stood for a minute, looking at my house. It was a teensy little three-story Victorian, tall and narrow. A few brave daffodils stood bobbing along the walk, and soon the tulip beds would erupt in pink and yellow. In May, the lilacs along the eastern side of my house would fill the entire house with their incomparable smell. I'd spend most of the summer on my porch, reading, writing papers for various journals, watering my Boston ferns and begonias. My home. When I bought the house—correction, when Andrew and I bought it—it had been tattered and neglected. Now, it was a showplace. *My* showplace, as Andrew had left me before the new insulation was installed, before the walls were knocked down and repainted.

At the sound of my high heels on the flagstone path, Angus's head popped up in the window, making me grin…and then wobble. Apparently, I was a little buzzed, a fact underscored as I fumbled ineffectively for my keys. There. Key in door, turn. "Hello there, Angus McFangus! Mommy's home!"

My little dog raced up to me, then, too overcome by the miracle of my very being, raced around the downstairs in victory-lap style—living room, dining room, kitchen, hallway, repeat. "Did you miss Mommy?" I asked every time he whizzed past me. "Did you… miss…Mommy?" Finally, his energy expended somewhat, he brought me his victim of the night, a shredded box of tissues, which he deposited proudly at my feet.

"Thank you, Angus," I said, understanding that this was a gift. He collapsed in front of me, panting, black button eyes adoring, his back legs straight out behind him, as if he were flying, in what I thought of as his Super Dog pose. I sat down, slipped off my shoes and scratched Angus's cunning little head. "Guess what? We have a boyfriend now," I said. He licked my hand in delight, burped, then ran into the kitchen. Good idea. I'd hit the Ben & Jerry's for a little snack. Hoisting myself out of my chair, I glanced out the window and froze.

A man was creeping along the side of the house next door.

Obviously, it was dark outside, but the streetlight illuminated the man clearly as he walked slowly along the side of the house next to mine. He looked in both directions, paused, then continued on to the back of the house, climbed the back steps, slowly, tentatively, then tried the doorknob. Locked, apparently. He looked under the doormat. Nothing. Tried the doorknob again, harder.

I didn't know what to do. I'd never seen a house being broken into before. No one lived in that house, 36 Maple. I'd never even seen someone look at it in the two years I'd lived in Peterston. It was sort of a bungalow style, pretty worn down, in need of a good bit of work. I'd often wondered why no one bought it and fixed it up. Surely there was nothing inside worth stealing....

Swallowing with an audible click, I realized that, should the burglar look in my direction, he'd see me quite clearly, as my light was on and the curtains open. Reaching out slowly without taking my eyes off him, I turned off the lamp.

The suspect, as I was already calling him, then gave the door a shove with his shoulder. He repeated the action, harder this time, and I flinched as his shoulder hit the door. No go. He tried again, stepped back, then walked to a window, cupped his hands around his eyes and peered in.

This all looked very suspicious to me. Sure enough, the man tried to open the window. Again, no luck. Perhaps, yes, I'd watched too many episodes of *Law &*

Order, friend to single women everywhere, but this seemed pretty cut-and-dried. A *crime* was in progress at the vacant house next door. Surely this wasn't good. What if the burglar came over here? In his two years on earth, Angus had yet to be put to the test of home protection. Ripping up shoes and rolls of toilet paper, that he had mastered. Protect me from an average-size male? Not too sure. And was the burglar average? He looked pretty brawny to me. Pretty solid.

I let the usual stream of horrific images slide through my head and acknowledged the slim odds of their actually happening. The man, who was currently trying another window, was probably not a murderer looking for a place to stash a body. He probably didn't have a million dollars' worth of heroin in his car. And I hoped quite fervently that he had no plans to chain an average-size woman in the pit in his cellar and wait for her to lose enough weight so he could use her skin to whip up a new dress, like that guy in *Silence of the Lambs.*

The burglar tried the door a second time. *Okay, pal,* I thought. *Enough is enough. Time to call the authorities.* Even if he wasn't a murderer, he clearly was looking for a house to burgle. Was that a verb? *Burgle?* It sounded funny. Granted, yes, I'd had two gin and tonics tonight (or was it three?), and drinking wasn't really a strong suit of mine, but still. No matter how I broke it down, the activity next door looked pretty damn criminal. The man disappeared around the back of the house again, still, I assumed, searching for a point of entry. What the heck. Time to put my tax dollars to use and call the cops.

"911, please state your emergency."

"Hi, how are you?" I asked.

"Do you have an emergency, ma'am?"

"Oh, well, you know, I'm not sure," I answered, squinting one eye shut to see the burglar better. No such luck; he'd disappeared around the far corner of the house. "I think the house next door to me is being robbed. I'm at 34 Maple Street, Peterston. Grace Emerson."

"One moment, please." I heard the squawk of a radio in the background. "We have a cruiser in your area, ma'am," she said after a moment. "We'll dispatch a unit right now. What exactly can you see?"

"Um, right now, nothing. But he was…casing the joint, you know?" I said, wincing. Casing the joint? Who was I, Tony Soprano? "What I mean is, he's walking around, trying the doors and windows. No one lives there, you know."

"Thank you, ma'am. The police should be there any moment. Would you like us to stay on the line?" she asked.

"No, that's okay," I said, not wanting to seem too much of a wuss. "Thank you." I hung up, feeling vaguely heroic. A regular neighborhood watch, I was.

I couldn't see the man anymore from the kitchen, so I slipped into the dining room (oops, a little dizzy… maybe that *was* three G&Ts). Peeking out the window, I saw nothing irregular at the moment. And I didn't hear sirens, either. Where were those cops? Maybe I should've stayed on the line. What if the burglar realized there's nothing to steal over there, but then took a look over here? *I* had plenty of nice things. That sofa set me back almost two grand. My computer was state-of-the-art. And last birthday, Mom and Dad had given me that fabulous plasma screen TV.

I looked around. Sure, it was dumb, but I'd feel safer if I was…well, not armed, but something. I didn't own a handgun, God knew…not the type. I glanced at my knife block. Nah. That seemed a little over the top, even for me. Granted, I had two Springfield rifles in the attic, not to mention a bayonet, along with all my other Civil War gear, but we didn't use bullets, and I couldn't quite imagine bayoneting someone, no matter how much fun I had pretending to do just that at our battle reenactments.

Creeping into the living room, I opened the closet and surveyed my options. Hanger, ineffective. Umbrella, too lightweight. But wait. There, in the back, was my old field hockey stick from high school. I'd kept it all these years for sentimental reasons, harking back to the brief period of time when I was an athlete, and now I was glad. Not quite a weapon, but some protection nevertheless. Perfect.

Angus was now asleep on his bed, a red velvet cushion in a wicker basket, in the kitchen. He lay on his back, furry white paws in the air, his little bottom teeth locked over his uppers. He didn't look like he was going to be much help in the case of a home invasion. "Cowboy up, Angus," I whispered. "Being cute isn't everything, you know."

He sneezed, and I ducked. Did the burglar hear that? For that matter, did he hear me on the phone? I chanced a peek out the dining-room window. Still no cops. No movement from next door, either. Maybe he was gone.

Or coming over. Coming for *me*. Well, my stuff, anyway. Or me. You never knew.

Holding the field hockey stick reassured me. Maybe I'd just slip upstairs and lock myself in the attic, I thought. Sit next to those rifles, even if I didn't own bullets. Surely the police could handle the thief next door. And speaking of cops, a black-and-white cruiser glided down the street, parking right in front of the Darrens' house. Great. I was safe. I'd just tiptoe into the dining room and see if Mr. Burglar Man was in sight.

Nope. Nothing. Just the ticking of the lilac branches against the windows. Speaking of the windows, Dad was right. They did need to be replaced. I could feel a draft, and it wasn't even that windy. My heating bill had been murder this year.

Just then, a quiet knock came on the door. Ah, the cops. Who said they were never around when you needed them? Angus leaped up as if electrocuted and raced to the door, dancing happily, leaping so that all four paws left the ground, barking shrilly. *Yarp! Yarpyarpyarpyarp!* "Sh!" I told him. "Sit. Stay. Calm down, honey."

Stick still in hand, I opened the front door.

It wasn't the cops. The burglar was standing right in front of me. "Hi," he said.

I heard the stick hit him before I realized I'd moved, and then my frozen brain acknowledged all sorts of things at once—the muffled thunking of wood against human. The trembling reverberation up my arm. The stunned expression on the burglar's face as he reached up to cover his eye. My shaking legs. The slow sinking of said burglar to his knees. Angus's hysterical yapping.

"Ouch," the burglar said faintly.

"Back off," I squeaked, the hockey stick wavering. My entire body shook violently.

"Jesus, lady," he muttered, his voice more surprised than anything. Angus, snarling like an enraged lion cub, took hold of the burglar's sleeve and whipped his little head back and forth, trying to do some damage, tail wagging joyfully, body trembling at the thrill of defending his mistress.

Should I put the stick down? Wouldn't that be the prime moment for him to grab me? Wasn't that the mistake most women make just before they're tossed into the pit in the cellar and starved till their skin gets loose?

"Police! Hands in the air!"

Right! The police! Thank God! Two officers were running across my lawn.

"Hands in the air! Now!"

I obeyed, the field hockey stick slipping out of my hands, bouncing off the burglar's head and landing on the porch floor. "For Christ's sake," the burglar muttered, wincing. Angus released the sleeve and pounced instead upon the stick, snarling and yapping with glee.

The burglar squinted up at me. The skin around his eye had already turned livid red. And oh, dear, was that blood?

"Hands on your head, pal," one of the cops said, whipping out his handcuffs.

"I don't believe this," the burglar said, obeying with (I imagined) the wearied resignation of someone who's been through this before. "What did I do?"

The first cop didn't answer, just snapped on the cuffs. "Please step inside, ma'am," the other officer said.

I finally unfroze from my hands-in-the-air position and staggered inside. Angus dragged the field hockey stick in behind me before abandoning it to zip in joyous circles around my ankles. I collapsed on the sofa, gathering my dog in my arms. He licked my chin vigorously, barked twice, then bit my hair.

"Are you Ms. Emerson?" the cop asked, tripping slightly over the field hockey stick.

I nodded, still shaking violently, my heart galloping in my chest like Seabiscuit down the final stretch.

"So what happened here?"

"I saw that man breaking into the house next door," I answered, disentangling my hair from Angus's teeth. My voice was fast and high. "Where no one lives, by the way. And so I called you guys, and then he came right up on my porch. So I hit him with a field hockey stick. I played in high school."

I sat back, swallowed and glanced out the window, taking a few deep breaths, trying not to hyperventilate. The cop gave me a moment, and I stroked Angus's rough fur, making my doggy croon with joy. Now that I thought of it, perhaps whacking the burglar wasn't quite…necessary. It occurred to me that he said "Hi." I thought he did, anyway. He said hi. Do burglars usually greet their victims? *Hi. I'd like to rob your house. Does that work for you?*

"You okay?" the cop asked. I nodded. "Did he hurt you? Threaten you?" I shook my head. "Why did you open the door, miss? That wasn't a smart thing to do." He frowned disapprovingly.

"Uh, well, I thought it was you guys. I saw your car. And, no, he didn't hurt me. He just…" *said hi.* "He looked, um…suspicious? Sort of? You know, he was creeping around that house, that's all. Creeping and looking, sort of peeking? And no one lives there. No one's lived over there since I've lived over here. And I didn't actually mean to hit him."

Well, didn't I sound smart!

The cop gave me a dubious look and wrote a few

things in his little black notebook. "Have you been drinking, ma'am?" he asked.

"A little bit," I answered guiltily. "I didn't drive, of course. I was at a wedding. My cousin. She's not very nice. Anyway, I had a cocktail. A gin and tonic. Well, really more like two and a half. Possibly three?"

The cop flipped his notebook closed and sighed.

"Butch?" The second officer stuck his head in the door. "We have a problem."

"Did he run?" I blurted. "Did he escape?"

The second cop gave me a pitying look. "No, ma'am, he's sitting on your steps. We've got him cuffed, nothing for you to worry about. Butch, could you come out here a second?"

Butch left, his gun catching the light. Clutching Angus to me, I tiptoed to the living-room window and pushed back the curtain (blue raw silk, very pretty). There was the burglar, still sitting on my front steps, his back to me, as Officer Butch and his partner conferred.

Now that I wasn't in mortal fear, I took a good look at him. Bed-heady brown hair, kind of appealing, really. Broad shoulders…it was a good thing I didn't get into a scuffle with him. Well, into more of a scuffle, I supposed. Burly arms, from the look of the way the fabric strained against his biceps. Then again, it could just be the pose forced on him by having his hands cuffed behind his back.

As if sensing my presence, the burglar turned toward me. I leaped back from the window, wincing. His eye was already swollen shut. Dang it. I hadn't planned on hurting him. I hadn't planned anything, really…just acted in the moment, I guess.

Officer Butch came back inside.

"Does he need some ice?" I whispered.

"He'll be fine, ma'am. He says he's staying next door, but we're gonna take him to the station and verify his story. Can you give me your contact information?"

"Sure," I answered, reciting my phone number. Then the cop's words sank in. *Staying next door.*

Which meant I just clubbed my new neighbor.

CHAPTER THREE

THE FIRST THING I DID UPON awakening was roll out of bed and squint through my hangover at the house next door. All was quiet. No sign of life. Guilt throbbed in time with my pounding head as I recalled the stunned look on the burglar's—or the not-burglar's—face. I'd have to call the police station and see what had happened. Maybe I should alert my dad, who was a lawyer. Granted, Dad handled tax law, but still. Margaret was a criminal defense lawyer. She might be a better bet.

Dang it. I wished I hadn't hit the guy. Well. Accidents happen. He *was* skulking around a house at midnight, right? What did he expect? That I'd invite him in for a coffee? Besides, maybe he was lying. Maybe "staying next door" was just his cover story. Maybe I'd just done a community service. Still, clubbing people was new to me. I hoped the guy wasn't too hurt. Or mad.

The sight of my dress, which I hadn't hung up in my furor last night, reminded me of Kitty's wedding. Of Andrew and Natalie, together. Of Wyatt, my new imaginary boyfriend. I smiled. Another fake boyfriend. I'd done it again.

You may have gotten the impression that Natalie was…well, not spoiled, but protected. You'd be right. She was universally adored by our parents, by Margs, who didn't give her love easily and, yes, even by Mémé.

But especially by me. In fact, my very first clear memory in life was of Natalie. It was my fourth birthday, and Mémé was smoking a ciggie in our kitchen, ostensibly watching us while my cake baked in the oven, the warm smell of vanilla mingling not unpleasantly with her Kool Lights.

The kitchen of my childhood seemed to be an enormous place full of wonderful, unexpected treasures, but my favorite spot was the pantry, a long, dark closet with floor-to-ceiling shelves. Often would I go in and close the door behind me, eating chocolate chips from the bag in delicious silence. It was like a little house unto itself, complete with bottles of seltzer water and dog food. Marny, our cocker spaniel, would come in with me, wagging her little stump of a tail as I fed her kibbles, eating one myself once in a while. Sometimes Mom would open the door and yelp, startled to find me there, curled up next to the mixer with the dog. It always felt so safe in there.

At any rate, on my fourth birthday, Mémé was smoking, I was lurking in the pantry with Marny, sharing a box of Cheerios, when I heard the back door open. In came Mom and Dad. There was a flurry of activity... Mommy had been away for a few days, and then I heard her call my name.

"Gracie, where are you! Happy birthday, honey! We have someone who wants to meet you!"

"Where's the birthday girl?" boomed Dad. "Doesn't she want her presents?"

Suddenly aware of how much I missed my mother, I bolted from the cabinet, past Mémé's skinny, vein-bumpy legs, and charged toward my mother, who was sitting at the kitchen table, still in her coat. She was holding a baby wrapped in a soft pink blanket.

"My birthday present!" I cried in delight.

Eventually, the grown-ups explained to me that the baby wasn't just for me, but for Margaret and everyone else, too. My present was, in fact, a stuffed animal, a dog. (Later that day, according to family lore, I put the stuffed dog in the baby's crib, delighting my parents with my generosity.) But I never got over the feeling that Natalie Rose was mine, certainly much more than she was Margaret's, a feeling that Margaret, who was seven at the time and horribly sophisticated, nurtured in order to get out of her sisterly responsibilities. "Grace, your baby needs you," she'd call when Mom asked for help spooning yogurt into Nat's mouth or changing a poopy diaper. I didn't mind. I loved being the special sister, the big sister after four long years of being bossed around or ignored by Margaret. My birthday became more about Natalie and me, our beginning, than the day I was born. No, now my birthday was much more important. The day I got Natalie.

Natalie did not fail to delight. A stunning baby, she became more beautiful as she grew, her hair silky and blond, her eyes a startling sky-blue, cheeks as soft as tulip petals, eyelashes so long they touched her silken eyebrows. Her first word was *Gissy,* which we all knew was her attempt to say my name.

As she grew, she looked up to me. Margaret, for all her gruffness and disdain, was a good sister, but more of the type to take you aside and explain how to get out of trouble or why you should leave her stuff alone. For playing, for cuddling, for company, Nat turned to me, and I was more than willing. At age four, she spent hours putting barrettes in my kinky curls, wishing aloud that her own blond waterfall of smoothness was, in her words "a beautiful brown cloud." In kindergarten, she brought me in for show-and-tell, and on Special Person's Day, you know who was at her side. When she needed help in spelling, I took over for Mom or Dad, making up silly sentences to keep things fun. During her ballet recitals, her eyes sought me out in the audience, where I'd be beaming back at her. I called her Nattie Bumppo after the hero of *The Deerslayer,* pointing to her name in the book to show her how famous she was.

Thus went our childhood—Natalie perfect, me adoring, Margs gruff and a little above it all. Then, when Natalie was seventeen and I was in my junior year at William & Mary, I got a call from home. Natalie had been feeling crummy for a day or so. She was not one to complain, so when she finally admitted that her stomach hurt pretty badly, Mom called the doctor. Before they could get to the office, Nat's appendix ruptured. The resulting appendectomy was messy, since infected fluid had spread throughout her abdomen, and she came down with peritonitis. She spiked a fever. It didn't come down.

I was in my dorm room when Mom called me, nine hours away by car. "Get home as fast as you can, Grace," she ordered tightly. Nat had been moved to the ICU, and things weren't looking good.

My memories of that trip back home alternated between horribly vivid and completely blank. A professor drove me to Richmond International Airport. I don't remember which professor, but I can see the dusty dashboard of his car as clearly as if I were sitting in that hot vinyl front seat right now, the crack in the windshield that flowed lazily down from its source like the Mississippi bisecting the United States. I remember weeping in the plastic seat in front of my gate, my fists clenched as the airplane crept with agonizing slowness toward the terminal. I remember my friend Julian's face at the airport, his eyes wide with fear and compassion. My mother, swaying on her feet outside Natalie's cubicle in the hospital, my father, gray-faced and silent, Margaret tight and hunched in the corner near the curtain that separated Natalie from the next patient.

And I remember Natalie, lying in a bed, obscured by tubes and blankets, looking so small and alone that my heart cracked in half. I took her hand and kissed it, my tears falling on the hospital sheets. "I'm here, Nattie Bumppo," I whispered. "I'm here." She was too weak to answer, too sick even to open her eyes.

Outside, the doctor spoke in a somber murmur to my parents. "…abscess…bacteria…kidney function… white count…not good."

"Jesus God in heaven," Margaret whispered in the corner. "Oh, shit, Grace." Our eyes met in bleak horror at the possibility we couldn't imagine. Our golden Natalie, the sweetest, kindest, loveliest girl in the world, dying.

The hours ticked past. Coffee cups came and went, Natalie's IVs were changed, her wound checked. A day crawled by. She didn't wake up. A night. Another day. She got worse. We were only allowed in for a few minutes at a time, sent off to a grim waiting room full of old magazines and bland, nubby furniture, the fluorescent lights sparing no detail of the fear on our faces.

On day four, a nurse burst into the room. "Natalie Emerson's family, come now!" she ordered.

"Oh, Jesus," my mother said, her face white as chalk. She staggered, my father caught her and half dragged her down the hall. Terrified that our sister was slipping away, Margaret and I ran ahead of our parents. It seemed to take a year to get down that hall—every step, every slap of my sneakers, every breath was punctuated with my desperate prayer. *Please. Please. Not Natalie. Please.*

I got there first. My baby sister, my birthday present, was awake, looking at us for the first time in days, smiling weakly. Margaret careened in behind me.

"Natalie!" she exploded in typical fashion. "Jesus Christ hanging on the cross, we thought you were dead!" She wheeled around and charged out to smite the nurse who'd taken a decade off of each our lives.

"Nattie," I whispered. She held out her hand to me, and you can bet that I promised then and there to make sure God knew how grateful I was to have her back.

"YOU DID WHAT?" JULIAN ASKED. We were strolling through the four-block downtown of Peterston, eating apricot danish from Lala's Bakery and sipping cappuccinos. I'd already dazzled my friend with my story of clubbing the neighbor, completely outranking his tale of having successfully cooked chicken tikka masala from scratch.

"I told her I was seeing someone. Wyatt, a pediatric surgeon." I took another bite of the still-warm pastry and groaned in pleasure.

Julian paused, his eyes wide with admiration. "Wow."

"Kind of brilliant, don't you think?"

"I do," he said. "Not only have you taken a stand

against crime in your neighborhood, you've invented another boyfriend. Busy night!"

"I just wish I'd thought of it earlier," I said smugly.

Julian grinned, bent down to give Angus a piece of his pastry, then resumed walking, only to pause again in front of his place of business. Jitterbug's Dance Hall, tucked between a dry cleaner and Mario's Pizza. He peered in the windows, checking that everything was perfect within. A woman walking behind us glanced at Julian, looked away, then did a double take. I smiled fondly. My oldest friend, though he'd been a pudgy out- cast when we'd first met, now resembled a clean-shaven Johnny Depp, and the woman's reaction was fairly typi- cal. Alas, he was gay or I would have married him and borne his children long ago. Like me, Julian had been burned romantically, though even I, his oldest friend, didn't know the details of his long-ago breakup.

"So now you're Wyatt's girl," he said, resuming our stroll. "What is his last name?"

"I don't know," I said. "I haven't invented that yet."

"Well, what are we waiting for?" Julian thought a minute. "Dunn. Wyatt Dunn."

"Wyatt Dunn, M.D. I love it," I said.

Julian turned to flash a smile at the woman behind us. She turned purple in response and pretended to drop something. Happened all the time. "So what does Dr. Wyatt Dunn look like?" he asked.

"Well, he's not terribly tall…that's sort of overrated, don't you think?" Julian smiled; he was five foot ten. "Kind of lanky. Dimples. Not too good-looking but he has a really friendly face, you know? Green eyes, blond hair. Glasses, don't you think?"

Julian's smile faded. "Grace. You just described Andrew."

I choked on my cappuccino. "Did I? Crap. Okay, scratch that. Tall, dark and handsome. No glasses. Um, brown eyes." Angus barked once, affirming my taste in men.

"I'm thinking of that Croatian guy from *E.R.* Dr. Good-looking," Julian said.

"Oh, yes, I know who you mean. Perfect. Yes, that's Wyatt to a T." We laughed.

"Hey, is Kiki joining us this morning?" he asked.

"No," I said. "She met someone last night and really thinks he's The One." Julian chorused the last few words along with me. It was Kiki's habit, this falling madly in love. She excelled at finding The One, which she did often, and usually with disastrous results, becoming obsessed by the end of the first date, scaring the man away with talk of forevermore. If history repeated itself (and it usually did, as this history teacher knew quite well), she'd be crushed by this time next week, possibly with a restraining order filed against her.

So no Kiki. That was okay. Julian and I shared a love of antiques and vintage clothes. I was, after all, a history teacher, so it made sense. He was a gay man and dance instructor, so that made sense, too. Strolling along the crooked and quiet streets of Peterston, stopping in at the funky shops, the promise of leaves and flowers just around the corner, I felt happy. After a long, sloppy winter, it was good to be outside.

Peterston, Connecticut, is a small city on the Farmington River, accessible only by locals and clever tourists who excel in map-reading. Once famed for making more plow blades than any other place on God's green earth, the town had gone from desolate neglect to a scruffy charm in the past decade or so. Main Street led right down to the river, where there was a trail for walking. In fact, I could get home by walking along the Farmington, and often did. Mom and Dad lived five miles downriver in Avon, and sometimes I walked there, too.

Yes, I was content this morning. I loved Julian, I loved Angus, who trotted adorably at the end of his red-and-purple braided leash. And I loved having my family think I was in a relationship, not to mention completely over Andrew.

"Maybe I should get a new outfit or two," I mused outside of The Chic Boutique. "Now that I'm seeing a doctor and all. Something never worn by another."

"Absolutely. You'll need something nice for those hospital functions," Julian seconded immediately. We entered the store, Angus in my arms, and emerged an hour or so later, laden with bags.

"I love dating Wyatt Dunn," I said, grinning. "In fact, I may get an entire makeover. Haircut, mani, pedi…God, I haven't done that in ages. What do you think? Want to come?"

"Grace," Julian said, pausing. He took a deep breath, nodded to a passerby, then continued. "Grace, maybe we should…"

"Get lunch instead?" I suggested, petting Angus, who was licking the bag that contained my new shoes.

Julian smiled. "No, I was thinking more like maybe we should really try to meet someone. Two someones. You know. Maybe we should stop depending on each other so much and really get out there again."

I didn't answer. Julian sighed. "See, I think I might

be ready. And you having a fake boyfriend, well, that's cute and all, but…maybe it's time for the real thing. Not that your fake boyfriends aren't fun, too." Julian had known me a long time.

"Right," I said, nodding slowly. The thought of dating made a light sweat break out on my back. It wasn't that I didn't want love, marriage, the whole shmear… I just hated the thought of what one had to do to get to that point.

"I will if you will," he prodded. "And just think. Maybe there is a real Wyatt Dunn out there for you. You could fall in love and then Andrew wouldn't…" His voice trailed off, and his dark eyes were apologetic. "Well. Who knows?"

"Sure. Yeah. Well." I closed my eyes briefly. Pictured Tim Gunn/Atticus Finch/Rhett Butler/George Clooney. "All right. I'll give it a shot."

"Okay. So. I'm going home to register on a dating website, and you do the same."

"Yes, General Jackson. Whatever you say." I saluted, he returned the gesture, kissed me on the cheek and headed for his place.

Watching my old friend walk away, I imagined with an unpleasant jolt what it would be like to have Julian as half of a happy couple. Imagined him not coming over once or twice a week, not asking me to help at his Dancin' with the Oldies class at Golden Meadows, not going shopping with me on Saturday mornings. Instead of me, some gorgeous man would be sitting in my place.

Now that would really suck. "Not that we're selfish or anything," I muttered. Angus chewed on the hem of my jeans in response. We headed for home, down the narrow path that followed the river, Angus straining on the leash and getting tangled in my bags. My dog wanted to investigate the Farmington, but it was so fat and full and loud that it would sweep him away. Red buds swelled on the swamp maples, but only a few bushes had any actual green on them. The earth was damp, the birds twittered and hopped in their annual search for a mate.

The last man I'd been in love with was Andrew, and try though I might, I couldn't remember how it had felt when we first fell in love. All my memories of him were tainted, obviously, but still…to belong to someone again, someone right this time. Really meant for me.

Julian had a point. It was time to start over. Sure, I'd tried to scare up a date for Kitty's wedding. But a relationship was different. I wanted to meet someone. I *needed* to meet someone, a man I could really love. Surely, somewhere out there, there was a man who would see me as the most beautiful creature on earth, the one who made his very heart beat, made the breath in his lungs sweet and all that sappy garbage. Someone who would help me put the final nail in the Andrew coffin.

It was time.

MY ANSWERING MACHINE LIGHT was blinking when I got home. "You have five messages," the mechanical voice announced. Wow. That was unusual for me. One each from Nat and Margaret—Nat was dying to get together and hear about Wyatt; Margaret sounded a bit more sardonic. Number three was from Mom, reminding me about her upcoming art show and suggesting I bring my lovely doctor. Number four was from Dad, giving me my assignment for next week's battle and also suggesting I bring Wyatt, as Brother Against Brother was low on Yankees.

Looked like my family had swallowed my tale of Wyatt pretty well.

The final message was from Officer Butch Martinelli of the Peterston Police Department asking me to return his call. Oh, crap. I'd almost forgotten about that. The clubbing. Beads of sweat jumped out on my forehead. I dialed the number immediately and asked for the good sergeant.

"Yes, Ms. Emerson. I have some information on the man you assaulted last night."

Assaulted. I *assaulted* someone. The guy was a burglar last night; now he was the vic. "Right," I said, my voice squeaking. "I didn't exactly assault him—more of a…misplaced act of self-defense." *Because he said hi, and we can't have that, can we?*

"He's legit," the officer continued, ignoring me. "Apparently, he just bought the house, long-distance, and the key was supposed to be left for him, but it wasn't. He was looking for it—that's why he was wandering around." The officer paused. "We kept him overnight, because we couldn't verify the story until this morning. We just released him about an hour ago."

I closed my eyes. "Um…is he okay?"

"Well, nothing's broken, though he does have quite a shiner."

"Oh, good God!" What a way to make friends! Another thought occurred to me. "Um, Officer Butch?"

"Yes?"

"If he was legit, why did you arrest him? And keep him overnight? That's kind of above and beyond the call, isn't it?"

Officer Butch didn't answer.

"Well, I guess you can do a whole bunch of things without just cause now, right?" I babbled. "Patriot Act, the death of civil liberties. Well, I mean…"

"We take 911 calls very seriously, ma'am. It appeared that you were engaged in a physical dispute with the man. We felt it was worth checking out." Disapproval dripped from his tone. "Ma'am."

"Right. Of course, Officer. Sorry. Thanks for calling."

I peered out my dining-room window toward the house next door. No signs of life. That was good, because though I clearly needed to apologize, the idea of seeing my new neighbor made me nervous. I hit him. He spent the night in jail because of me. Not exactly my best foot forward.

So, okay, I'd have to apologize. I'd make the poor man some brownies. Not just any brownies, but my Disgustingly Rich Chocolate Brownies, a sure way to soothe any wounded soul.

I opted against calling any of my family members back. They could think that I was with Wyatt, as I'd been with Julian. Except instead of parting ways, Wyatt and I had gone to the movies. Yes. We'd seen a flick, come home and were now, in fact, shagging. Then perhaps we were planning to go out for an early dinner. Which would be, I admitted, a very nice way to spend a Saturday afternoon.

"Come on, Angus, me boy-o," I said. He followed me into the kitchen and flopped on the floor, rolling on his back to watch me upside down as I got to work on those brownies. Ghirardelli's chocolate, nothing but the best for the man I sent to jail, a pound of butter, six eggs. I melted, stirred, blended, then set the timer. Spent thirty minutes checking my email and responding to three parents who were protesting their kids' grades and wanting to know what their little prodigy would have to do to get an A in my class. "Work harder?" I suggested to the computer. "Think more?" I typed in a more politically correct response and hit Send.

When the brownies were done, I took them out of the oven. Looking over at the house next door, I decided that, yes, I could wait a little longer. I had papers to correct, after all. The bathroom could use a scrubbing. The brownies needed to cool, anyway. No need to race over and face the music.

Somewhere around 8:00 p.m., I woke up from where I'd dozed off over Suresh Onabi's paper on the Declaration of Independence, Angus asleep on my chest, half of a page damp and chewed in his mouth. "Down we go, boy," I said, setting him to the floor and retrieving what he'd eaten. Drat. My policy was that if *my* dog ate the homework, I'd have to assume the kid did perfectly.

Standing up, I peered out the dining-room window. There were no lights on next door. My heart seemed to be beating rather fast, my palms a little sweaty. I reminded myself that last night was simply an unfortunate misunderstanding. Surely we could all just get along. I arranged the brownies on a nice plate and took a bottle of wine from the kitchen rack, stashed Angus in the cellar so he wouldn't get out and bite the guy and headed over with my peace offerings. Brownies and wine. Breakfast of champions. What man could resist?

Walking up to 36 Maple Street was quite intimidating, really…the crumbling walkway, the broken-down house, the long grass which, who knew, could be full of snakes or something, the utter silence that hovered over the house like a malevolent, hungry animal. *Relax, Grace. Nothing to fear. Just being a good neighbor and apologizing for the head-whacking.*

The front porch of the house sagged wearily, the steps soft and rotting. Still, they supported my weight as I carefully and quietly negotiated them. I gave the front door a little knock with my elbow, as my hands were full, and waited. My heart clattered in my chest. I remembered that little…tug…I felt when I took a look at the not-burglar as he sat handcuffed on my porch…his boyish cowlick, the broad shoulders. And in that second before I hit him…he had a nice face. *Hi,* he'd said. *Hi.*

There was no answer to my feeble knock. I imagined what I most wanted to happen. That he'd open the door, and some soft music—let's make it South American guitar, shall we?—would drift out. My neighbor's face, which will sport only the slightest bruise under one eye, barely noticeable, will light in recognition. "Oh, hey, my neighbor!" he'll exclaim with a grin. I'll apologize, he'll laugh it off. The scent of roasting chicken and garlic will waft out. "Would you like to come in?" I'll agree, apologizing once more for my unfortunate mistake, which he'll simply wave off. "It could happen to anyone," he'll say. We'll chat, immediately comfortable with each other. He'll mention that he loves dogs, even hyperactive terriers with behavior issues. A glass of wine will be poured for the lovely girl next door.

See? In my mind, this guy and I were well on the way to becoming great friends, quite possibly more. Unfortunately, he didn't seem to be home right now, so he remained unaware of this pleasant fact.

I knocked again, albeit quietly, because I actually

felt a little relieved that I didn't have to see him, pleasant fantasies aside. Setting my offerings in front of the
door, I eased back down the rotting steps.

Now that I knew he wasn't home, I took a better look
around. The streetlight gave an eerie, peachy glow to
the yard. I'd never been over here before, but obviously,
I'd wondered about the house. It had been neglected for
a while…roof tiles were missing, and plastic covered
an upstairs window. The latticework under the porch
gapped like a mouthful of missing teeth.

It was a beautiful, soft night. The damp smell of distant rain filled the air, mixing with the coppery smell of
the river, and far away, the song of springtime peepers
graced the night. This house could be really charming,
I thought, if someone restored it. Maybe my neighbor
was here to do that very thing. Maybe it would become a gem.

The crumbling cement path that led from the street
continued around the side of the house. No sign of the
guy. However, a rake lay right across the walkway.
Someone could trip over that, I thought. Trip, fall, hit
head on the concrete birdbath just a few feet away, lie
bleeding in the grass… Hadn't he suffered enough?

I went over and picked it up. See? Already being a
great neighbor.

"Are these from you?"

The voice so startled me that I whirled around. Unfortunately, I was still holding the rake in my hand.
Even more unfortunately, the wooden handle caught
him right along the side of his face. He staggered back,
stunned, the bottle of wine I'd just left at his door slipping from his grasp and shattering on the path with a

crash. The scent of merlot drifted up around us, canceling out the smells of spring.

"Oops," I said in a strangled voice.

"Jesus Christ, lady," my new neighbor cursed, rubbing his cheek. "What is your problem?"

I winced as I looked him in the face. His eye was still swollen, and even in the dim light, I could see the bruise. Pretty damn impressive.

"Hi," I said.

"Hi," he bit out.

"Uh, well… Welcome to the neighborhood," I squeaked. "Um… Are you…are you okay?"

"No, as a matter of fact."

"Do you need some ice?" I asked, taking a step toward him.

"No." He took a defensive step back.

"Look," I said, "I'm so, so sorry. I just came over to… well, to say I'm sorry." The irony of further wounding him while on a mission of mercy hit me, and I gave a nervous laugh, sounding remarkably like Angus when he vomited up grass.

The man said nothing, merely glared, and I found myself thinking that the beat-up look was kind of…hot. He was wearing jeans and a light-colored T-shirt, and, yes, he had very nice arms. Big, powerful, thick muscles, not the overly defined, ripped kind that smacked of too many hours at a heavily mirrored gym. No. These were blue-collar arms. Iron-worker arms. Man-who-can-fix-car arms. An image of Russell Crowe in *L.A. Confidential* flashed to mind. Remember when he's sitting in the backseat at the very end of the movie, and his jaw is wired shut and he can't talk? I found that *very* horny.

I swallowed again. "Hi. I'm Grace," I said, trying to start over. "I wanted to apologize about…last night. I'm so sorry. And of course, I'm sorry again, for all this. Very sorry." I glanced down at his feet, which were bare. "I think you're bleeding. You might've stepped in glass."

He looked down, then turned an impassive gaze to me. Call me paranoid, but he looked quite disgusted.

That was all it took. Bruised, bleeding, smelling like a wino, and the pièce de résistance, disgust. I was undeniably attracted to this guy. Heat rose to my cheeks, making me glad for the dim light.

"Well," I said slowly. "Listen. I'm really sorry. It looked like you were breaking in…that's all."

"Maybe you should be sober the next time you call the police," he returned.

My mouth fell open. "I was! I was sober." I paused. "Mostly."

"Your hair was all wild, you smelled like gin, and you hit me in the face with a walking stick. Does that sound mostly sober to you?"

Sweat broke out on my back. "It was a field hockey stick, actually, and my hair is always like that. As you can see."

He rolled his eyes. Well, the eye that wasn't swollen shut. Apparently that movement hurt, because he winced.

"It's just…you looked suspicious, that's all. I wasn't drunk. Buzzed, maybe, okay. A tiny bit, yes." I swallowed. "But it was past midnight, and you definitely didn't have a key, did you? So…you know. It looked suspicious. That's all. I'm sorry you spent the night in jail. Very, very sorry."

"Fine," he grunted.

Okay, well, that wasn't exactly as nice as my wine-drinking, South American guitar fantasy, but it was something. "So," I said, determined that we would part on good terms. "I'm sorry. I didn't catch your name."

"I didn't give it," he said, crossing his arms and staring.

Sweet. "Okay. Nice meeting you, whatever your name is. Have a good night." He still said nothing. Very carefully, I put the rake down, forced a smile, walked past the shards of broken glass, past *him,* painfully aware of my every move. The walk home, though it was only a matter of yards, felt very long. I should've cut through the yard, but there was the question of the long, snake-concealing grass.

He didn't say another word, and from the corner of my eye, I could see that he hadn't moved, either. Fine. He wasn't friendly. I wouldn't invite him to the neighborhood picnic in June. So there.

For a second, I imagined telling Andrew about this. Andrew, whose sharp sense of humor had always made me laugh, would've howled over this apology gone wrong. But no. Andrew didn't get to hear my stories anymore. To quash the Andrew image, I instead summoned to mind Wyatt Dunn. Gentle, dark-haired Wyatt, who'd have to possess a lovely sense of humor and kind, kind heart, being a children's doctor and all.

Just as had been true in the old days of my painful adolescence, the imaginary boyfriend took away some of the sting imparted by the surly neighbor whose head I'd just bruised for the second time.

And while I knew all too well that Wyatt Dunn was a fake, I also knew that someday I was going to find someone wonderful. Hopefully. Probably. Someone better than Andrew, possibly better looking than my grouchy neighbor, and just as great as Wyatt, and just thinking about this made me feel a little more chipper.

CHAPTER FOUR

ANDREW AND I HAD MET at Gettysburg—well, the reenactment of the battle here in fair Connecticut. He
was assigned to be a nameless Confederate soldier,
instructed to shout, "May God condemn this War of
Northern Aggression!" then fall dead in the first cannon barrage. I was Colonel Buford, quiet hero of Gettysburg's first day, and my dad was General Meade. It was
the biggest reenactment in three states, and there were
hundreds of us (don't be so surprised, these things are
very popular). That year, I was the secretary of Brother
Against Brother, and before the battle, I'd been running
around with a clipboard, making sure everyone was
ready. Apparently, I was adorable…at least, that's what
I was told later by one Andrew Chase Carson.

Eight hours after we started and when a sufficient
number of bodies littered the field, Dad allowed the
dead to rise, and a Confederate soldier approached me.
When I pointed out that most Civil War soldiers didn't
wear Nikes, the man laughed, introduced himself and
asked me out for coffee. Two weeks later, I was in love.

In every way, it was the relationship I had always
imagined. Andrew was wry and quiet, appealing rather
than good-looking, with an infectious laugh and cheerful outlook. He was on the scrawny side, had a sweetly
vulnerable neck, and I loved hugging him, the feel of

his ribs creating in me the overwhelming urge to feed and protect him. Like me, he was a history buff—he was an estate attorney at a big firm in New Haven, but he'd majored in history at NYU. We liked the same food, the same movies, read the same books.

How was the sex, you ask? It was fine. Regular, hearty enough, quite enjoyable. Andrew and I found each other attractive, had mutual interests and excellent conversations. We laughed. We listened to the other's tales about work and family. We were really, really happy. I thought so, anyway.

If there was a hesitation on Andrew's part, I only noticed it in hindsight. If certain things were said with the smallest edge of uncertainty, I didn't see it. Not until later.

Natalie was at Stanford during the time of Andrew, having finished up at Georgetown the year before. Since her near-death experience, she'd become only more precious to me, and my little sister continued to delight our family with her academic achievements. My own intellect was on the vague side, not counting American history...I was good at Trivial Pursuit and able to hold my own at cocktail parties, that sort of thing. Margaret, on the other hand, was razor sharp, scary intelligent. She'd graduated second from Harvard Law and headed up the criminal defense department at the firm where my dad was a partner, making him prouder than he could say.

Nat was a blend. Softly brilliant, quietly gifted, she chose architecture, a perfect mix of art, beauty and science. I talked to her at least a couple of times a week, e-mailed her daily and visited her when she opted to stay in California for the summer. How she loved hearing about Andrew! How delighted she was that her big sister had met The One!

"What does it feel like?" she asked one night during one of our phone calls.

"How does what feel?" I said.

"Being with the love of your life, silly." I could hear the smile in her voice and grinned back.

"Oh, it's great. It's so…perfect. And easy, too, you know? We never fight, not like Mom and Dad." Being different from my parents was a clear sign that Andrew and I were on the right track.

Nat laughed. "Easy, huh? But passionate, too, right? Does your heart beat faster when he comes into the room? Do you blush when you hear his voice on the phone? Does your skin tingle when he touches you?"

I paused. "Sure." Did I feel those things? Sure, I did. Of course I did. Or I *had,* those dizzying new feelings having matured to something more…well, comfortable.

Seven months into the relationship, I moved into Andrew's apartment in West Hartford. Three weeks later, we were watching *Oz* on HBO—okay, not the most romantic show, but still, we were cuddled together on the couch, and that was nice. Andrew turned to me and said, "I think we should probably get married, don't you?"

He bought me a lovely ring. We told our families and chose Valentine's Day, six months away, as our wedding day. My parents were pleased—Andrew seemed so solid and reliable, so trustworthy. He was a corporate lawyer, very steady work, very well paid, which put to ease my father's worries that my teacher's salary would render me eventually homeless. Andrew, an only child, was doted on by his parents, and while they weren't quite as ecstatic as my parents, they were friendly enough. Margaret and he talked law, Stuart seemed to enjoy his company. Even Mémé liked him as much as she liked any human.

Only Natalie hadn't met him, stranded out there at Stanford as she was. She spoke to Andrew on the phone when I called to tell her we were engaged, but that was it.

Finally, she came home. It was Thanksgiving, and when Andrew and I arrived at the family domicile, Mom greeted us at the door in her usual flurry of complaints about how early she'd had to get up to put the "damn bird" in the oven, how she'd dry-heaved stuffing it, how useless my father was. Dad was watching a football game and ignoring Mom, Stuart was playing the piano in the living room while Margaret read.

And then Natalie came flying down the stairs, arms outstretched, and grabbed me in a huge hug. "Gissy!" she cried.

"Hey, Nattie Bumppo!" I exclaimed, squeezing her hard.

"Don't kiss me, I have a cold," she said, pulling back. Her nose was red, her skin a little dry, she was clad in sweatpants and an old cardigan belonging to our father, and yet she still managed to look more beautiful than Cinderella at the ball, her silken blond hair tied up in a high ponytail, her clear blue eyes unaccented by makeup.

Andrew took one look at her and literally dropped the pie he was holding.

Of course, the pie plate was slippery. PYREX, you know? And Nat's face flushed that way because…well, because she had a cold, and isn't flushing and blushing part of a cold? Of course it was. Later, of course, I admitted it wasn't any slippery PYREX. I knew the kablammy when I saw it.

Natalie and Andrew sat at opposite ends of the Thanksgiving table. When Stuart broke out the Scrabble board and asked them if they wanted to play after dinner, Andrew accepted and Natalie instantly declined. The next day, we all went bowling, and they didn't speak. Later, we went to the movies, and they sat as far away from each other as possible. They avoided going into a room if the other was there.

"So what do you think?" I asked Natalie, pretending that all was normal.

"He's great," she said, her face going nuclear once more. "Very nice."

That was good enough for me. I didn't need to hear more. Why talk about Andrew, after all? I asked her about school, congratulated her on winning an internship with Cesar Pelli and once again marveled at her perfection, her brains, her kind heart. After all, I'd always been my sister's biggest fan.

Andrew and Natalie saw each other again at Christmas, where they leaped away from the mistletoe like it was a glowing rod of uranium, and I pretended not to be disturbed. There couldn't be anything between them, because he was my fiancé and she was my baby sister. When Dad told Nat to take Andrew down the back hill on our old toboggan and neither of them could find a way to get out of it, I laughed when they crashed and rolled, becoming entangled in each other. No, no, nothing there.

Nothing, my ass.

I wasn't about to say anything. Each time the irritating little voice in my soul brought it up, usually at 3:00 a.m., I told her she was wrong. Andrew was right here with me. He loved me. I'd reach out and touch his knobby elbow, that sweet neck of his. We had something real. If Nat had a crush on him...well. Who could blame her?

My wedding was in ten weeks, then eight, then five. Invitations went out. Menu finalized. Dress altered.

And then, twenty days before our wedding, Andrew came home from work. I had a pile of tests beside me on the kitchen table, and he'd very thoughtfully brought home some Indian food. He even dished it out, spooning the fragrant sauce over the rice, just as I liked it. And then came the awful words.

"Grace...there's something we need to talk about," he said, staring at the onion *kulcha.* His voice was shaking. "You know I care about you very much."

I froze, not looking up from the exams, the words as ominous as *Sherman's in Georgia.* The moment I'd successfully avoided thinking about was upon me. Knowing I would never look at Andrew the same way, I couldn't take a normal breath. My heart thundered sickly.

He *cared* about me. I don't know about you, girls, but when a guy says *I care about you very much,* it seems to me that the shit is about to rain down. "Grace," he whispered, and I managed to look at him. As our untouched garlic naan cooled, he told me that he didn't quite know how to say this, but he couldn't marry me.

"I see," I said distantly. "I see."

"I'm so sorry, Grace," he whispered, and to his credit, his eyes filled with tears.

"Is it Natalie?" I asked, my voice quiet and unrecognizable.

His gaze dropped to the floor, his face burned red, and his hand shook as he ran it through his soft hair. "Of course not," he lied.

And that was that.

We'd just bought the house on Maple Street, though we weren't living there yet. As part of our divorce settlement or whatever you want to call it—blood money, guilt, emotional damages—he let me keep his portion of the down payment. Dad reworked my finances to tap into a few mutual funds that my grandfather had left me, reduced the size of my mortgage so I could swing it alone, and I moved in. Alone.

Natalie was wrecked when she found out. Obviously, I didn't tell her the reason for our breakup. She listened to me lie as I detailed the reasons for our breakup… *just wasn't right…not really ready…figured we should be sure.*

She asked only one quiet little question when I was done. "Did he say anything else?"

Because she must have known it wasn't me doing the breaking up. She knew me better than anyone. "No," I answered briskly. "It just…wasn't meant to be. Whatever."

Natalie had no part of this, I assured myself. It was just that I hadn't really found The One, no matter how deceptively perfect Andrew had looked, felt, seemed. Nope, I thought as I sat in my newly painted living room in my newly purchased house, power-eating brownies and watching Ken Burns's documentary on the Civil War till I just about had it memorized. Andrew just wasn't The One. Fine. I'd find The One, wherever he was, and, hey. Then the world would know what love was, goddamn it.

Natalie finished her degree and moved back East. She got a nice little apartment in New Haven and started work. We saw each other often, and I was glad. It wasn't like she was the other woman…she was my sister. The person I loved best in the world. My birthday present.

CHAPTER FIVE

On Sunday, I had the misfortune of attending my mother's opening at Chimera's, a painfully progressive art gallery in West Hartford.

"What do you think, Grace? Where have you been? The show started a half hour ago. Did you bring your young man?" my mother asked, bustling up as I tried not to look directly at the artwork. Dad lurked in the back of the gallery, nursing a glass of wine, looking noticeably pained.

"Very...very, uh, detailed," I answered. "Just... lovely, Mom."

"Thank you, honey!" she cried. "Oh, someone is looking at a price tag on *Essence Number Two.* Be back in a flash."

When Natalie went off to college, my mother decided it was time to indulge her artistic side. For some reason unbeknownst to us, she decided on glassblowing. Glassblowing and the female anatomy.

The family domicile, once the artistic home only for two Audubon bird prints, a few oil paintings of the sea and a collection of porcelain cats, was now littered with girl-parts. Vulvae, uteruses, ovaries, breasts and more perched on mantels and bookshelves, end tables and the back of the toilet. Varied in color, heavy and very anatomically correct, my mother's sculptures were fuel for gossip in the Garden Club and the source of a new ulcer for Dad.

However, no one could argue with success, and to the astonishment of the rest of us, Mom's sculptures brought in a small fortune. When Andrew dumped me, Mom took me on a four-day spa cruise, courtesy of *The Unfolding* and *Milk #4*. The *Seeds of Fertility* series had paid for a little greenhouse on the side of the barn last spring, as well as a new Prius in October.

"Hey," said Margaret, joining us. "How's it going?"

"Oh, just great," I answered. "How are you?" I glanced around the gallery. "Where's Stuart?"

Margaret closed one eye and gritted her teeth, looking somewhat like Anne Bonny, she-pirate. "Stuart... Stuart's not here."

"Got that," I said. "Everything okay with you guys? I noticed you barely spoke at Kitty's wedding."

"Who knows?" Margaret answered. "I mean, really. Who the hell knows? You think you know someone... whatever."

I blinked. "What's going on, Margs?"

Margaret looked around at the voyeurs who flocked to Mom's shows and sighed. "I don't know. Marriage isn't always easy, Grace. How's that for a fortune cookie? Is there any wine here? Mom's shows are always better with a little buzz, if you know what I mean."

"Over there," I said, nodding to the refreshments table in the back of the gallery.

"Okay. Be right back."

Ahahaha. Ahahaha. Ooooh. Ahahaha. My mother's society laugh, heard only at art shows or when she was trying to impress someone, rang through the gallery. She caught my eye and winked, then shook the hand of an older man, who was cradling a glass…oh, let's see now…ew. A sculpture, let's put it that way. Another sale. Good for Mom.

"Are we still on for Bull Run?" Dad asked, coming up behind me and putting his arm around my shoulder.

"Oh, definitely, Dad." The Battle of Bull Run was one of my favorites. "Did you get your assignment?" I asked.

"I did. I'm Stonewall Jackson." Dad beamed.

"Dad! That's great! Congratulations! Where is it?"

"Litchfield," he answered. "Who are you?"

"I'm a nobody," I said mournfully. "Just some poor Confederate hack. But I do get to fire the cannon."

"That's my girl," Dad said proudly. "Hey, will you be bringing your new guy? What's his name again? By the way, your mother and I are thrilled that you're finally back on the old horse."

I paused. "Uh, thanks, Dad. I'm not sure if Wyatt can make it. I— I'll ask, though."

"Hey, Dad," Margaret said, coming up to smooch our father on the cheek. "How are the labias selling?"

"Don't get me started on your mother's artwork. Porn is what I call it." He glanced over in our mother's direction. *Ahahaha. Ahahaha. Oooh. Ahahaha.* "Damn it, she sold another one. I'll have to box that one up." Dad rolled his eyes at us and stomped off to the back of the gallery.

"So, Grace," Margaret said, "about this new guy." She glanced around to make sure that we weren't being overheard. "Are you really seeing someone, or is this another fake?"

She wasn't a criminal defense attorney for nothing. "Busted," I murmured.

"Aren't you a little old for this?" she asked, taking a slug of her wine.

I made a face. "Yes. But I found Nat in the bathroom at Kitty's wedding, writhing with guilt." Margs rolled her eyes. "So I figured I'd make it easy for her."

"Yes. Life must be easy for the princess," Margaret muttered.

"And another thing," I continued in a low voice. "I'm sick of the pity. Nat and Andrew should just get on with it, you know, and stop treating me like some crippled, balding cat who has seizures and can't keep down her food."

Margaret laughed. "Gotcha."

"The truth is," I admitted, "I think I'm ready to meet someone. I'll just pretend to be seeing someone and then, you know…find someone real."

"Cool," Margaret said with a considerable lack of enthusiasm.

"So what's going on with you and Stuart?" I asked, moving out of the way as an older woman sidled up to *LifeSource,* a sculpture of an ovary that looked to my nonmedical eye like a lumpy gray balloon.

Margaret sighed, then finished off her wine. "I don't know, Grace. I don't really want to talk about it, okay?"

"Sure," I murmured, frowning. "I do see Stuart at school, of course."

"Right. Well. You can tell him to fuck off for me."

"I…I won't be doing that. Jeez, Margs, what's wrong?" While theirs was a case of opposites attract, Margaret and Stuart had always seemed happy enough. They were childless by choice, rather well-off thanks to Margaret's endless success in court, lived in a great house in Avon, took swanky vacations to Tahiti and

Liechtenstein and places like that. They'd been married for seven years, and while Margaret was not the type to coo and gloat, she'd always seemed pretty content.

"Well, crap, speaking of disastrous couples, here come Andrew and Natalie. Shit. I need a little more wine for this." She fled back to the table for another glass of cheap pinot grigio.

And there they were indeed, Andrew's fair hair a few shades lighter than Natalie's honey-gold. Considerably more relaxed than at the wedding, when they dared not get within ten feet of each other lest I burst into sobs, they now radiated happiness. Their hands brushed as they approached, fingers giving a little caress though they stopped just short of actual hand-holding. The chemistry crackled between them. No, not just chemistry. Adoration. That's what it was. My sister's eyes were glowing, her cheeks flushed with pink, while a smile played at the corner of Andrew's mouth. Gack.

"Hey, guys!" I said merrily.

"Hi, Grace!" Natalie said, flushing brighter as she hugged me. "Is he here? Did you bring him?"

"Bring whom?" I asked.

"Wyatt, of course!" she chuckled.

"Right! Um, no, no. I think we should be dating longer than a few weeks before I bring him to one of Mom's shows! Also, he's…at the hospital." I forced a chortle. "Hi, Andrew."

"How are you, Grace?" he said, grinning, his green eyes bright.

"I'm great." I looked down at my untouched wine.

"Your hair looks gorgeous!" Nat exclaimed, reaching out to touch a lock that was for once curly and not electrocuted.

"Oh, I got a haircut this morning," I murmured. "Bought some new tamer." Had to practically sell an ovary of my own to afford it, but, yes, along with the clothes, I figured some better hair control was in order. Couldn't hurt to look my best when seeking The One, right?

"Where's Margaret?" Natalie asked, craning her swanlike neck to look around. "Margs! Over here!"

My older sister sent me a dark look as she obeyed. She and Natalie had always scrapped a bit...well, it would be more fair to say that Margaret scrapped, since Natalie was too sweet to really fight with anyone. As a result, I got along better with each than they did with each other—my reward for generally being taken for granted as the poor neglected middle child.

"I just sold a uterus for three thousand dollars!" Mom exclaimed, joining our little group.

"There is no limit to the bad taste of the American people," Dad said, trailing sullenly behind her.

"Oh, shut it, Jim. Better yet, find your own damn bliss and leave mine alone."

Dad rolled his eyes.

"Congratulations, Mom, that's wonderful!" Natalie said.

"Thank you, dear. It's nice that some people in this family can be supportive of my art."

"Art," Dad snorted.

"So, Grace," Natalie said, "when can we meet Wyatt? What's his last name again?"

"Dunn," I answered easily. Margaret smiled and shook her head. "I will definitely get him up here soon."

"What does he look like?" Nat asked, reaching for my hand in girlish conspiracy.

"Well, he's pretty damn cute," I chirruped. Good thing Julian and I had gone over this. "Tall, black hair…" I tried to recall Dr. Handsome from *E.R.*, but I hadn't watched since the episode where the wild dogs got loose in the hospital, mauling patients and staffers alike. "Um, dimples, you know? Great smile." My face felt hot.

"She's blushing," Andrew commented fondly, and I felt an unexpectedly hot sliver of hatred pierce my heart. How dare he be thrilled that I'd met someone!

"He sounds wonderful," my mother declared. "Not that a man is going to make you happy, of course. Look at your father and me. Sometimes a spouse tries to suffocate your dreams, Grace. Make sure he doesn't do that. Like your father does to me."

"Who do you think pays for all your glassblowing crap, huh?" Dad retorted. "Didn't I convert the garage for your little hobby? Suffocate your dreams. I'd like to suffocate something, all right."

"God, they're adorable," Margaret said. "Who wants to mingle?"

WHEN I FINALLY GOT HOME from my mother's gynecological showcase, my surly neighbor was ripping shingles off his porch roof. He didn't look up as I pulled into the driveway, even though I paused after getting out of my car. Not a nice man. Not friendly, anyway. Definitely nice to look at though, I thought, as I tore my eyes off his heavily muscled arms, unwillingly grateful that it was warm out, warm enough that Surly Neighbor Man had taken off his shirt. The sun gleamed on his sweaty back as he worked. Those upper arms of his were as thick as my thighs.

For a second, I pictured those big, burly, capable arms wrapped around me. Imagined Surly Neighbor Man pressing me against his house, his muscles hard and hot as he lifted me against him, his big manly hands—

Wow, you need to get laid, came the thought, unbidden. Clearly, the pulsating showerhead wasn't doing the trick. Surly Neighbor Man, fortunately, had not noticed my lustful reverie. Hadn't noticed me at all, in fact.

I went into the house, let Angus into my fenced-in backyard to pee and dig and roll. The scream of a power saw ripped through the air. With a tight sigh, I clicked on the computer to finally follow Julian's advice. Match.com, eCommitment, eHarmony, yes, yes, yes. Time to find a man. A good man. A decent, hardworking, morally upright, good-looking guy who freakin' adored me. *Here I come, mister. Just you wait.*

After describing my wares online, I took a look at a few profiles. Guy #1—no. Too pretty. Guy #2—no. His hobbies were NASCAR and ultimate fight clubs. Guy #3—no. Too weird-looking, let's be honest. Acknowledging that perhaps my mood wasn't right for this, I corrected World War II quizzes until it was dark, stopping only to eat some of the Chinese food Julian had brought over on Thursday, then going right back to correcting, circling grammatical errors and asking for more detail in the answers. It was a common Manning complaint that Ms. Emerson was a tough grader, but hey. Kids who got an A in my classes earned it.

When I was done, I sat back and stretched. On the kitchen wall, my Fritz the Cat clock ticked loudly, tail swishing to keep the time. It was only eight o'clock, and the night stretched out in front of me. I could call Julian…no. Apparently, my best friend thought we were codependent, and while that happened to be completely true, it stung a little nonetheless. Nothing wrong with codependence, was there? Well. He emailed me, at least, a nice chatty note about the four men who'd been interested in his profile online, and the resultant stomach cramps he'd suffered. Poor little coward. I typed in an answer, assured him that I, too, was now available for viewing online and told him I'd see him at Golden Meadows for Dancin' with the Oldies.

With a sigh, I got up. Tomorrow was a school day. Maybe I'd wear one of my new outfits. Angus trotting at my heels, I clumped upstairs to reacquaint myself with my new clothes. In fact, I thought as I surveyed my closet, it was time to purge. Yes. One had to ask oneself when vintage became simply old. I grabbed a trash bag and started yanking. Goodbye to the sweaters with the holes in the armpits, the chiffon skirt with the burn in the back, the jeans that fit in 2002. Angus gnawed companionably on an old vinyl boot (what was I thinking?), and I let him have it.

Last week, I saw a show on this woman who was born without legs. She was a mechanic…actually, not having legs made her job easier, she said, because she could just slide under cars on the little skateboard thing she used to get around. She'd been married once, but was now dating two other guys, just enjoying herself for the time being. Her ex-husband was interviewed next, a good-looking guy, two legs, the whole nine yards. "I'd do anything to get her back, but I'm just not enough for her," he said mournfully. "I hope she finds what she's looking for."

I found myself getting a little…well, not *jealous,* exactly, but it did seem this woman had an unfair advantage in the dating world. Everyone would look at *her* and say, *Wow, what a plucky spirit. Isn't she great!* What about me? What about the two-legged among us, huh? How were we supposed to compete with *that?*

"Okay, Grace," I told myself aloud, "we're crossing the line. Let's find you a boyfriend and be done with it, shall we? Angus, move it, sweetie. Mommy has to go up to the attic with this crap, or you'll chew through it in a heartbeat, won't you? Because you're a very naughty boy, aren't you? Don't deny it. That's my toothbrush you have in your mouth. I am not blind, young man."

I dragged the trash bag full of stuff down the hall to the attic stairs. Drat. The light was out, and I didn't feel like tromping downstairs to get another. Well, I was only stashing the stuff till I could make a trip to the dump.

Up the narrow flight of stairs I went, the close, sharp smell of cedar tickling my nose. Like many Victorian homes, mine had a full-size attic, ten-foot ceilings and windows all around. Someday, I imagined, I'd put up some insulation and drywall and make this a playroom for my lovely children. I'd have a bookshelf that ran all the way around the room. An art area near the front window where the sun streamed in. A train table over there, a dress-up corner here. But for now, it held just some old pieces of furniture, a couple of boxes of Christmas ornaments and my Civil War uniforms and guns. Oh, and my wedding dress.

What does one do with a never-been-worn, tailored-just-for-you wedding dress? I couldn't just throw it out, could I? It had cost quite a bit. Granted, if I did find some flesh-and-blood version of Wyatt Dunn, maybe I'd get married, but would I want to use the dress I bought for Andrew? No, of course not. Yet there it still sat in its vacuum-packed bag, out of the sun so it wouldn't fade. I wondered if it still fit. I'd packed on a few pounds since The Dumping. Hmm. Maybe I should try it on.

Great. I was becoming Miss Havisham. Next I'd be eating rotten food and setting the clocks to twenty till nine.

Something gnawed my ankle bone. Angus. I didn't hear him come up the stairs. "Hi, little guy," I said, gathering him up and removing a sesame noodle from his little head. Apparently, he'd gotten into the Chinese food. He whined affectionately and wagged. "What's that? You love my hair? Oh, thank you, Angus McFangus. Excuse me? It's Ben & Jerry's time? Why, you little genius! You're absolutely right. What do you think? Crème Brûlée or Coffee Heath Bar?" His little tail wagged even as he bit my earlobe and tugged painfully. "Coffee Heath Bar it is, boy. Of course you can share."

I disentangled him, then turned to go, but something outside caught my eye.

A man.

Two stories below me, my grumpy, bruised neighbor was lying on his roof, in the back where it was nearly flat. He'd put on more clothes (alas), and his white T-shirt practically glowed in the dark. Jeans. Bare feet. I could see that he was just…just lying there, hands behind his head, one knee bent, looking up at the sky.

Something contracted down low in my stomach, my skin tightened with heat. Suddenly, I could feel the blood pulsing in parts too long neglected.

Slowly, so as not to attract attention, I eased the window up a crack. The sound of springtime frogs rushed in, the smell of the river and distant rain. The damp breeze cooled my hot cheeks.

The moon was rising in the west, and my neighbor, too irritable to tell me his name, was simply lying on the roof, staring at the deep, deep blue of the night sky.

What kind of man did that?

Angus sneezed in disgust, and I jumped back from the window lest Surly Neighbor Man hear.

Suddenly, everything shifted into focus. I wanted a man. There, right next door, was a man. A *manly* man. My girl-parts gave a warm squeeze.

Granted, I didn't want a fling. I wanted a husband, and not just any husband. A smart, funny, kind and moral husband. He'd love kids and animals, especially dogs. He'd work hard at some honorable, intellectual job. He'd like to cook. He'd be unceasingly cheerful. He'd adore me.

I didn't know a thing about that guy down there. Not even his name. All I knew was that I felt something—lust, let's be honest—for him. But that was a start. I hadn't felt anything for any man in a long, long time.

Tomorrow, I told myself as I closed the window, I was going to find out my neighbor's name. And I'd invite him to dinner, too.

CHAPTER SIX

"So although Sewell Point wasn't a major battle, it had the potential to greatly affect the outcome of the war. Obviously, Chesapeake Bay was a critical area for both sides. So. Ten pages on the blockade and its effects, due on Monday."

My class groaned. "Ms. Em!" Hunter Graystone protested. "That's, like, ten times what any other teacher gives."

"Oh, you poor little kittens! Want me to prop you up while you type?" I winked. "Ten pages. Twelve if you fight me."

Kerry Blake giggled. She was texting someone. "Hand it over, Kerry," I said, reaching out for her phone. It was a new model, encrusted with bling.

Kerry raised a perfectly waxed eyebrow at me. "Ms. Emerson, do you, like, *know* how much that *cost?* Like, if my father knew you *took* it, he'd be, like…totally unhappy."

"You can't use your phone in class, honey," I said for what had to be the hundredth time this month. "You'll get it back at the end of the day."

"Whatever," she muttered. Then, catching Hunter's eye, she flipped her hair back and stretched. Hunter grinned appreciatively. Tommy Michener, painfully and inexplicably in love with Kerry, froze at the display, which caused Emma Kirk to droop. Ah, young love.

Across the hall, I heard a burst of sultry laughter from Ava Machiatelli's Classical History class. Most Manning students *loved* Ms. Machiatelli. Easy grades, false sympathy for their busy schedules resulting in very little homework, and the most shallow delving into history since…well, since Brad Pitt starred in *Troy*. But like Brad Pitt, Ava Machiatelli was beautiful and charming. Add to this her low-cut sweaters and tight skirts, and you had Marilyn Monroe teaching history. The boys lusted after her, the girls took fashion notes from her, the parents loved her since their kids all got A's. Me…not such a fan.

The chimes sounded, marking the end of the period. Manning Academy didn't have bells—too harsh for the young ears of America's wealthiest. The gentle Zen chimes had the same effect as electric shock therapy, though—my seniors lunged out of their seats toward the door. On Mondays, Civil War was the last class before lunch.

"Hang on, kids," I called. They stopped, sheeplike. They may have been, for the most part, overindulged and too sophisticated for their tender ages, but they were obedient, I had to give them that. "This weekend, Brother Against Brother is reenacting the Battle of Bull Run, also known as First Manassas, which I'm sure you know all about, since it was in your reading homework from Tuesday. Extra credit to anyone who comes, okay? Email me if you're interested, and I'd be happy to pick you up here."

"As if," Kerry said. "I don't need extra credit that bad."

"Thanks, Ms. Em," Hunter called. "Sounds fun."

Hunter wouldn't come, though he was one of my more polite students. His weekends were spent doing things like having dinner with Derek Jeter before a Yankees game or flying to one of his many family homes. Tommy Michener might, since he seemed to like history—his papers were always sharp and insightful—but more than likely, peer pressure would keep him home, miserably lusting after Kerry, Emma Kirk's wholesome appeal lost on him.

"Hey, Tommy?" I called.

He turned back to me. "Yeah, Ms. Em?"

I waited a beat till everyone else was gone. "Everything okay with you these days?"

He smiled a bit sadly. "Oh, yeah. Just the usual crap."

"You can do better than Kerry," I said gently.

He snorted. "That's what my dad says."

"See? Two of your favorite grown-ups agree."

"Yeah. Well, you can't pick who you fall for, can you, Ms. Em?"

I paused. "Nope. You sure can't."

Tommy left, and I gathered up my papers. History was a tough subject to teach. After all, most teenagers barely remembered what had happened last month, let alone a century and a half ago, but still. Just once, I wanted them to *feel* how history had impacted the world we lived in. Especially the Civil War, my favorite part of American history. I wanted them to understand what had been risked, to imagine the burden, the pain, the uncertainty President Lincoln must have experienced, the loss and betrayal felt by the Southerners who had seceded—

"Hello, there, Grace." Ava stood in my doorway,

doing her trademark sleepy smile, followed by three slow, seductive blinks. There was one...and the second...and there was three.

"Ava! How are you?" I said, forcing a smile.

"I'm quite well, thank you." She tipped her head so that her silky hair fell to one side. "Have you heard the news?"

I hesitated. Ava, unlike myself, had her ear to the ground when it came to Manning's politics. I was one of those teachers who dreaded schmoozing with the trustees and wealthy alumni, preferring to spend my time planning classes and tutoring the kids who needed extra help. Ava, on the other hand, worked the system. Add that to the fact that I didn't live on campus (Ava had a small house at the edge of campus, and speculation was that she'd slept with the Dean of Housing to get it), and she definitely heard things.

"No, Ava. What news is that?" I asked, trying to keep my tone pleasant. Her blouse was so low-cut that I could see a Chinese symbol tattooed on her right boob. Which meant that every child who came through her classroom could see it, too.

"Dr. Eckhart's stepping down as chairman of the history department." She smiled, catlike. "I heard it from Theo. We've been seeing a lot of each other." Super. Theo Eisenbraun was the chairman of the Manning Academy board of trustees.

"Well. That's interesting," I said.

"He'll announce it later this week. Theo's already asked me to apply." Smile. Blink. Blink. And...wait for it...blink again.

"Great. Well, I have to run home for lunch. See you later."

the importance of the past, and, yes, sometimes they needed it jammed down their throats. Gently and lovingly, of course.

I pulled into my driveway and saw the true reason for my trip home, Angus's bowels notwithstanding. My neighbor stood in his front yard by a power saw or some such tool. Shirtless. Shoulder muscles rippling under his skin, biceps thick and bulging…hard…golden… *Okay, Grace! That's enough!*

"Howdy, neighbor," I said, wincing as the words left my mouth.

He turned off his saw and took off the safety glasses. I winced. His eye was a mess. It was open a centimeter or two—progress from being swollen completely shut yesterday—and from what I could see, the white of his eye was quite bloodshot. A purple-and-blue bruise covered him from brow to cheekbone. *Hello, bad boy!* Yes, granted, I'd given him the bruise—actually, make that plural, because I saw a faint stripe of purplish-red along his jaw, right where I'd hit him with the rake—but still. He had all the rough and sultry appeal of Marlon Brando in *On the Waterfront*. Clive Owen in *Sin City*. Russell Crowe in everything he did.

"Hi," he said, putting his hands on his hips. The motion made his arms curve most beautifully.

"How's your eye?" I asked, trying not to stare at his broad, muscular chest.

"How does it look?" he grumbled.

Okay, so he wasn't over that. "So, listen, we got off to a bad start," I said with what I hoped was a rueful smile. From inside my house, Angus heard my voice and began barking with joy. *Yarp! Yarp! Yarp! Yarpyarp-*

yarpyarpyarp! "Can we start over? I'm Grace Emerson. I live next door." I swallowed and stuck out my hand.

My neighbor looked at me for a moment, then came toward me and took my hand. Oh, God. Electricity shot up my arm like I'd grabbed a downed wire. His hand was most definitely a working-man's hand. Callused, hard, warm...

"Callahan O'Shea," he said.

Ohh. Oh, wow. What a *name*. Regions of my anatomy, long neglected, made themselves known to me with a warm, rolling squeeze.

Yarpyarpyarpyarpyarp! I realized I was staring at Callahan O'Shea (sigh!) and still holding on to his hand. And he was smiling, just a little bit, softening the bad-boy look quite nicely.

"So," I said, my voice weak, letting go of his hand reluctantly. "Where'd you move from?"

"Virginia." He was staring at me. It was hard to think.

"Virginia. Huh. Where in Virginia?" I said. *Yarpyarpyarpyarpyarp!* Angus was nearly hysterical now. *Quiet, baby,* I thought. *Mommy's lusting.*

"Petersburg," he said. Not the most vociferous guy, but that was okay. Muscles like that...those eyes...well, the unbruised, unbloodshot eye...if the other one was like that, I was in for a treat.

"Petersburg," I repeated faintly, still staring. "I've been there. Quite a few Civil War battles down there. Assault on Petersburg, Old Men and Young Boys. Yup."

He didn't respond. *Yarp! Yarp! Yarp!* "So what were you doing in Petersburg?" I asked.

He folded his arms. "Three to five."

Yarpyarpyarpyarp! "Excuse me?" I asked.

"I was serving a three- to five-year sentence at Petersburg Federal Prison," he said.

It took a few beats of my heart for that to register. *Ka-bump...ka-bump...ka...* God's nightgown!

"Prison?" I squeaked. "And um...wow! Prison! Imagine that!"

He said nothing.

"So...when...when did you get out?"

"Friday."

Friday. *Friday.* He just got out of the clink! He was a criminal! And just what crime did he commit, huh? Maybe I hadn't been so far off with the pit-digging after all! And I had clubbed him! Holy Mother of God! I clubbed an ex-con and sent him to jail! Sent him to... oh, God...sent him to jail the night after he got out. Surely this would not endear me to Callahan O'Shea, Ex-Con. What if he wanted revenge?

My breath was coming in shallow gasps. Yes, I was definitely hyperventilating a bit. *Yarpyarpyarpyarp-yarpyarp!* Finally, the *flight* part of the *fight or flight* instinct kicked in.

"Wow! Listen to my dog! I better go. Bye! Have a good day! I have to...I should call my boyfriend. He's waiting for me to call. We always call at noon to check in. I should go. Bye."

I managed not to run into my house. I did, however, lock the door behind me. And dead bolt it. And check the back door. And lock that. As well as the windows. Angus raced around the house in his traditional victory laps, but I was too stunned to pay him the attention he was accustomed to.

Three to five years! In prison! I was living next to an ex-con! I almost invited him over for dinner!

I grabbed the phone and stabbed in Margaret's cell phone number. She was a lawyer. She'd tell me what to do.

"Margs, I'm living next to an ex-con! What should I do?"

"I'm on my way into court, Grace. An ex-con? What was he in for?"

"I don't know! That's why I need you."

"Well, what do you know?" she asked.

"He was in Petersburg. Virginia. Three years? Five? Three to five? What would that be for? Nothing bad, right? Nothing scary?"

"Could be anything." Margaret's voice was blithe. "People serve less time for rape and assault."

"Oh, good God!"

"Settle down, settle down. Petersburg, huh? That's a minimum-security place, I'm pretty sure. Listen, Grace, I can't help you now. Call me later. Look him up on Google. Gotta go."

"Right. Google. Good idea," I said, but she'd already hung up. I jabbed on my computer, sweating. A glance out the dining-room windows revealed that Callahan O'Shea had gone back to work. The rotting steps of his front porch had been removed, the shingles mostly gone. I pictured him stabbing trash along a state highway, wearing an orange jumpsuit. Oh, shit.

"Come on," I muttered, waiting for my computer to come to life. When the Google screen came on, finally, I typed in *Callahan O'Shea* and waited. Bingo.

Callahan O'Shea, lead fiddler for the Irish folk group We Miss You, Bobby Sands, *sustained minor injuries when the band was pelted with trash Saturday at Sullivan's Pub in Limerick.*

Okay. Not my guy, probably. I scrolled down. Unfortunately, that band had quite a bit of press, recently... they were enraging crowds by playing "Rule Britannia" and the clientele wasn't taking it well.

It was then that my Iinternet connection, never the most reliable of creatures, decided to quit. Crap.

With another wary glance next door, I let Angus into the fenced-in backyard, then went back into my kitchen to scare up some lunch. Now that my initial shock was wearing off, I felt a little less panicky. Calling on my vast legal knowledge, obtained from many happy hours with *Law & Order,* two blood relatives who were lawyers and one ex-fiancé of the same profession, I seemed to believe that three to five in a minimum-security prison wouldn't be for scary, violent, muscular men. And if he *had* done something scary... well. I'd move.

I swallowed some lunch, called Angus back in, reminded him that he was the very finest dog in the universe and not to so much as look at the big ex-con next door, and grabbed my car keys.

Callahan O'Shea was hammering something on the front porch as I approached my car. He didn't *look* scary. He looked gorgeous. Which didn't mean he wasn't dangerous, but still. Minimum security, that was reassuring. And hey. This was my house, my neighborhood. I would not be cowed. Straightening my shoulders, I decided to take a stand. "So what were you in for, Mr. O'Shea?" I called.

He straightened up, glanced at me, then jumped off the porch, scaring me a little with the quick grace of his move. Very...predatory. Walking up to the split rail fence that divided our properties, he folded his arms again. Ooh. *Stop it, Grace.*

"What do you think I was in for?" he asked.

"Murder?" I suggested. May as well start with my worst fear.

"Please. Don't you watch *Law & Order?*"

"Assault and battery?"

"No."

"Identity theft?"

"Getting warmer."

"I have to get back to work," I snapped. He raised an eyebrow and remained silent. "You dug a pit in your basement and chained a woman there."

"Bingo. You got it, lady. Three to five for woman-chaining."

"Well, here's the thing, Callahan O'Shea. My sister's an attorney. I can ask her to dig around and uncover your sordid past—" *already did, in fact* "—or you can just come out and tell me if I need to buy a Rottweiler."

"Seemed to me like your little rat-dog did a pretty good job on his own," he said, running a hand through his sweat-dampened hair, making it stand on end.

"Angus is not a rat-dog!" I protested. "He's a pure-bred West Highland terrier. A gentle, loving breed."

"Yes. Gentle and loving is just what I thought when he sank his little fangs into my arm the other night."

"Oh, please. He only had your sleeve."

Mr. O'Shea extended his arm, revealing two puncture marks on his wrist.

"Damn," I muttered. "Well, fine. File a lawsuit, if a felon is allowed to do that. I'll call my sister. And the second I get back to school, I'm going to look you up on Google."

"All the women say that," he replied. He turned back to his saw, dismissing me. I found myself checking out his ass. *Very* nice. Then I mentally slapped myself and got into my car.

RECALCITRANT CALLAHAN O'SHEA might not be too forthcoming about his sordid past, but I felt it certainly behooved me to know just what kind of criminal lived next door. As soon as my Twentieth Century sophomores were finished, I went to my tiny office and surfed the Net. This time, I was rewarded.

The *Times-Picayune* in New Orleans had the following information from two years ago.

Callahan O'Shea pleaded guilty to charges of embezzlement and was sentenced to three to five years at a minimum-security facility. Tyrone Blackwell pleaded guilty to charges of larceny...

The only other hits referred to the ill-fated Irish band.

Embezzlement. Well. That wasn't so bad, was it? Not that it was good, of course...but nothing violent or scary. I wondered just how much Mr. O'Shea had taken. I wondered, too, if he was single.

No. The last thing I needed was some sort of fascination with a churlish ex-con. I was looking for someone who could go the distance. A father for my children. A man of morals and integrity who was also extremely good-looking and an excellent kisser who could hold his own at Manning functions. Sort of a modern-day General Maximus, if you will. I didn't want to waste time on Callahan O'Shea, no matter how beautiful a name he had or how good he looked without a shirt.

CHAPTER SEVEN

"VERY GOOD, MRS. SLOVANANSKI, one *two* three snap, five *six* seven pause. You got it, girl! Okay, now watch Grace and me." Julian and I did the basic salsa step twice more, me smiling gamely and swishing so my skirt twirled. Then he twirled me left, spun me back against him and dipped. "Ta-da!"

The crowd went wild, gingerly clapping their arthritic hands. It was Dancin' with the Oldies, the favorite weekly event at Golden Meadows Retirement Community, and Julian was in his element. Most weeks, I was his partner and co-teacher. Also, Mémé lived here, and though she was about as loving as the sharks who ate their young, a Puritanical familial duty had been long drilled into my skull. We were, after all, Mayflower descendants. Ignoring nasty relatives was for other, luckier groups. Plus, dancing opportunities were few and far between, and I loved to dance. Especially with Julian, who was good enough to compete.

"Does everyone have it?" Julian asked, checking our couples. "One *two* three snap…other way, Mr. B.—five *six* seven, don't forget the pause, people. Okay, let's see what we can do when the music's on! Grace, grab Mr. Creed and show him how it's done."

Mr. and Mrs. Bruno had already taken the dance floor. Their osteoporosis and artificial joints couldn't quite pull off the sensuality the salsa usually required, but they made up for it in the look on their faces…love, pure and simple, and happiness, and joy, and gratitude. It was so touching, so lovely, that I miscounted, resulting in a stumble for Mr. Creed.

"Sorry," I said, grabbing him a little more firmly. "My fault." From her chariot of doom, my grandmother made a disgusted noise. Like a lot of GM residents, she came each week to watch the dancers. Then Mrs. Slovananski cut in—she'd had her eye on Mr. Creed for some time, rumor had it—and I went over to one of the spectators as Julian carefully dipped Helen Pzorkan so as not to aggravate her weak bladder.

"Hey, Mr. Donnelly, feeling up to a turn on the dance floor?" I said to one of the many folks who came to watch, enjoying the music from eras gone by, but a little shy or stiff to venture out.

"I'd love to, Grace, but my knee isn't what it used to be," he said. "Besides, I'm not much of a dancer. I only looked good when my wife was with me, telling me what to do."

"I'm sure that's not true," I reassured him, patting his arm.

"Well," he said, looking at his feet.

"How did you and your wife meet?" I asked.

"Oh," he said, smiling, his eyes going distant. "She was the girl next door. I don't remember a day that I didn't love her. I was twelve when her family moved into the neighborhood. Twelve years old, but I made sure the other boys knew she'd be walking to school with me."

His voice was so wistful that it brought a lump to my

throat. "How lucky, to meet when you were so young," I murmured.

"Yes. We were lucky," he said, smiling at the memory. "Lucky indeed."

You know, it sounded so noble and selfless, teaching a dance class to the old folks, but the truth was, this was usually the best night of my week. Most nights I spent home, correcting papers and making up tests. But on Mondays, I put on a flowing, bright-colored skirt (often with sequins, mind you) and set off to be the belle of the ball. Usually I went in early to read to some of the nonverbal patients, which always made me feel rather holy and wonderful.

"Gracie," Julian called, motioning for me. I glanced at my watch. Sure enough, it was nine o'clock, bedtime for many of the residents. Julian and I ended our sessions by putting on a little show, a dance where we'd really ham it up.

"What are we doing tonight?" I asked.

"I thought a fox-trot," he said. He changed the CD, walked to the center of the floor and held out his arms with a flourish. I stepped over to him, swishing, and extended my hand, which he took with aplomb. Our heads snapped to the audience, and we waited for the music. Ah. The Drifters, "There Goes My Baby." As we slow-slow-quick-quicked around the dance floor, Julian looked into my eyes. "I signed us up for a class."

I tipped my head as we angled our steps to avoid Mr. Carlson's walker. "What kind of class?"

"Meeting Mr. Right or something. Money-back guarantee. You owe me sixty bucks. One night only, two-hour seminar, don't have kittens, okay? It's sort of like a motivational class."

"You're serious, aren't you?" I said.

"Quiet. We need to meet people. And you're the one faking a boyfriend. Might as well date someone who can actually pick up the check."

"Fine, fine. It just sounds kind of...dumb."

"And the fake boyfriend is smart?" I didn't answer. "We're both dumb, Grace, at least when it comes to men, or we wouldn't be hanging out together three times a week watching *Dancing with the Stars* and *Project Runway* with this as the highlight of our social calendar, would we?"

"Aren't we grouchy," I muttered.

"And correct." He twirled me swiftly out and spun me back in. "Watch it, honey, you almost stepped on my foot."

"Well, to tell you the truth, I'm meeting someone in half an hour. So there. I'm way ahead of you in the dating game."

"Well, good for you. That's a killer skirt you're wearing. Here we go, two three four, spin, slide, ta-da!"

Our dance ended, and our captive audience once again applauded. "Grace, you sure live up to your name!" cooed Dolores Barinski, one of my favorites.

"Oh, pshaw," I said, loving the compliment. The old folks, male and female, thought I was adorable, admired my young skin and bendable limbs. Of *course* it was the highlight of my social life! And it was so *romantic* here. Everyone here had a story, some hopelessly romantic tale of how they met their love. No one here had to go online and fill out forms that asked if you were a Sikh looking for a Catholic, if you found piercings a turnoff or a turn-on. No one here had to take a class to figure out how to make a man notice you.

That being said, I did have a date from one of my websites. eCommitment had come through. Dave, an engineer who worked in Hartford, wanted to meet me. Checking out his picture, I saw that, aside from a rather dated and conservative haircut, he was awfully cute. I emailed back, saying I'd love to meet for coffee. And just like that, Dave made a date. Who knew it was so easy, and why had I waited so long?

Yes, as I smooched withered cheeks and received gentle pats from soft, loving hands, I couldn't help the hope that prickled in my chest. Dave and Grace. Gracie and Dave. As early as tonight, I might meet The One. I'd go into Rex Java's, our eyes would meet, he'd slosh his coffee as he stood up to greet me, flustered and, dare I say, a little bit dazzled. One look and we'd just know. Six months from now, we'd be planning our wedding. He'd cook me breakfast on Saturday mornings, and we'd take long walks, and then, one day, when I told him I was pregnant, grateful tears would flood his eyes. Not that I was getting ahead of myself or anything.

Mémé left before the dance was over, so I didn't have to undergo the usual criticism of my technique, hair, clothing choices. I bid goodbye to Julian. "I'll call with the time and date of the class," he said, kissing my cheek.

"Okay. No stone left unturned."

"That's my girl." He winked and hefted his bag across his shoulder, waving as he left.

My hair felt a bit large, so I hit the loo to spritz on a little more frizz tamer/curl enhancer/holy water before my date with Dave. "Hi, Dave, I'm Grace," I said to my reflection. "No, no, it's natural. Oh, you love curly hair? Why, thank you, Dave!"

As I left the bathroom, I caught a glimpse of someone at the end of the hall, walking away from me. He turned left, heading for the medical wing. It was Callahan O'Shea. What was he doing here? And why was I blushing like some schoolkid who was just busted for smoking in the bathroom? And why was I still staring after him when I had a date, a real live date, hmm? With that thought in mind, I headed out to my car.

REX JAVA'S WAS about half-full when I got there, mostly high school kids, though none from Manning, which was in Farmington. I glanced around furtively. Dave didn't appear to be here…there was a couple in their forties in one corner, holding hands, laughing. The man took a bite of the woman's cake, and she swatted his hand, smiling. Show-offs, I thought with a smile. The whole world could see how happy they were. Over against the wall, a white-haired older man sat reading a paper. But no Dave.

I ordered a decaf cappuccino and took a seat, wondering if I should've changed out of my skirt before coming. Sipping the foam, I warned myself about getting my hopes up. Dave could be nice or he could be a jerk. Still. His picture was nice. Very promising.

"Excuse me, are you Grace?"

I looked up. It was the white-haired gentleman. He looked familiar…had he ever come to Dancin' with the Oldies? It was open to the public, after all. Possibly a Manning connection?

"Yes, I'm Grace," I said tentatively.

"I'm Dave! Nice to meet you!"

"Hi…uh…" My mouth seemed to be hanging open. "You're Dave? Dave from eCommitment?"

"Yes! Great to see you! Can I have a seat?"

"Um…I…sure," I said slowly.

Blinking rapidly, I watched as Dave sat, easing his leg out from the table. The man in front of me was sixty-five if he was a day. Possibly seventy. Thinning white hair. Lined face. Veiny hands. And was it me, or was his left eye made of glass?

"This is a cute place, isn't it?" he said, scootching his chair in and looking around. Yep. The left eye didn't move a bit. Definitely man-made.

"Yes. Um, listen, Dave," I said, trying for a friendly but puzzled smile. "Forgive me for saying this, but your photo…well, you looked so…youthful."

"Oh, that," he laughed. "Thank you. So you said you're a dog lover? Me, too. I have a golden retriever, Maddy." He leaned forward and I caught a whiff of Bengay. "You mentioned that you also have a dog?"

"Um, yes. Yes, I do. Angus. A Westie. So. When was that taken? The picture?"

Dave thought a minute. "Hmm, let's see now. I think I used the one taken just before I went to Vietnam. Do you like to eat out? I love it myself. Italian, Chinese, everything." He smiled. He had all his own teeth, I had to give him that, though most of them were yellow with nicotine stains. I tried not to wince.

"Yeah, about the photo, Dave. Listen. Maybe you should update that, don't you think?"

"I suppose," he said. "But you wouldn't have gone out with me if you knew my real age, would you?"

I paused. "That's…that's exactly my point, Dave," I said. "I really am looking for someone my own age. You said you were near forty."

"I *was* near forty!" Dave chuckled. "Once. But listen, sweetheart, there are advantages to being with an older man, and I figured you gals would be more open to them if you met me in person." He smiled broadly.

"I'm sure there are, Dave, but the thing is—"

"Oh, excuse me," he interrupted. "I really should empty this leg bag. You don't mind, do you? I was injured at Khe Sanh."

Khe Sanh. Being a history teacher, I knew quite well that Khe Sanh was one of the bloodiest battles of the Vietnam War. My shoulders slumped. "No, of course I don't mind. You go ahead."

He winked his real eye and rose, walking to the restroom with a slight limp. Great. Now I'd have to stay, because I couldn't walk out on a Purple Heart, could I? It would be unpatriotic. I couldn't just say, *Sorry, Dave, I don't date elderly wounded veterans who can't pee on their own*. That wouldn't be nice, not a bit.

So, in honor of my country, I spent another hour hearing about Dave's quest for a trophy wife, his five children by three women, the amazing AARP discount he got on his La-Z-Boy recliner and which type of catheter worked best for him.

"Well, I should get going," I said the moment I felt my duty to America had been served. "Uh, Dave, you have some very nice qualities, but I really am looking for someone closer to my own age."

"You sure you wouldn't like to go out again?" he asked, his good eye glued to my boobs as his fake eye pointed in a more northerly direction. "I find you very attractive. And you said you liked ballroom dancing, so I bet you're quite…flexible."

I suppressed a shudder. "Goodbye, Dave."

Julian's class was sounding better and better.

"No DADDY YET," I SAID TO ANGUS upon my arrival back home. He didn't seem to care. "Because I'm all that you need, right?" I asked him. He barked once in affirmation, then began leaping at the back door to go out. "Yes, my darling. Sit… Sit. Stop jumping. Come on, boy, you're wrecking my skirt. Sit." He didn't. "Okay, you can go out anyway. But next time, you're sitting. Got it?" Out he raced toward the back fence.

I had one message. "Grace, Jim Emerson here," said my father's voice.

"Better known as 'Daddy,'" I said to the machine, rolling my eyes with a smile.

The message continued. "I dropped by this evening but you were out. Your windows need replacing. I'm taking care of it. Think of it as a birthday present. Your birthday was last month, wasn't it? Anyway, it's done. See you at Bull Run." The machine beeped.

I had to smile at my father's generosity. Truthfully, I made enough to pay my bills, but as a teacher, I didn't make nearly as much as the other folks in my family. Natalie probably made three times what I made, and it was only her first year in the working world. Margaret earned enough to buy a small country. Dad's family "came from money," as Mémé liked to remind us, and he made a very comfortable salary on top of that. It made him feel paternal, paying for home repairs to be done. Ideally, he'd have liked to do it himself, but he tended to injure himself around power tools, a fact he learned only after getting nineteen stitches from what he still called a "rogue" radial saw.

Returning to the living room, I sat on my couch and looked around. Maybe it was time to repaint a room, something I tended to do when down in the dumps. But no. After almost a year and a half of nonstop renovations, the house was pretty perfect. The living-room walls were a pale lavender with gleaming white trim and a Tiffany lamp in one corner. I'd bought the curved-back Victorian sofa at an auction and had it reupholstered in shades of green, blue and lavender. The dining room was pale green, centered around a walnut Mission-style table. The house wanted for nothing, except new windows. I probably needed another project. I almost envied Callahan O'Shea next door, starting from scratch.

Yarp! Yarp! Yarpyarpyarp! "Okay, what now, Angus?" I muttered, hauling myself off the couch. Opening the slider in the kitchen, I saw no sign of my furry white baby, who was usually easy to spot. *Yarp! Yarp!* I moved to the dining-room windows for a different view.

There he was. Crap. In a move he was bred for, Angus had tunneled under the fence and stood now in the yard next door, barking at someone. Three guesses as to whom. Callahan O'Shea was sitting on his stair-less front porch, staring at my dog, who yapped from the yard, leaping and snapping, trying to bite the man's legs. With a sigh, I headed out the front door.

"Angus! Angus! Come, sweetie!" Not surprisingly, my dog failed to obey. Grumbling at my dog, I walked across my front yard to 36 Maple. The last thing I needed was another confrontation with the ex-con next door, but with Angus snapping and snarling at him, I didn't have much choice. "Sorry," I called. "He's afraid of men."

Callahan hopped off the porch, cut me a cynical glance. "Yes. Terrified." At those words, Angus launched himself onto Callahan's work boot, sinking his teeth into the leather and growling adorably. *Hrrrrr. Hrrrrr.* Callahan shook his foot, which detached Angus momentarily, only to have my little dog spring upon the shoe with renewed vigor.

"Angus, no! You're being very naughty. Sorry, Mr. O'Shea."

Callahan O'Shea said nothing. I bent over, grabbed my wriggling little pet by the collar and tugged, but he didn't let go of the boot. *Please, Angus, listen.* "Come on, Angus," I ground out. "Time to go inside. Bedtime. Cookie time." I tugged again, but Angus's bottom teeth were crooked and adorable, and I didn't want to dislodge any.

However, I was hunched over, my head about level with Mr. O'Shea's groin, and you know, I was starting to feel a bit warm. "Angus, release. Release, boy."

Angus wagged his tail and shook his head, the laces of the work boot clenched in his crooked little teeth. *Hrrrrr. Hrrrrr.* "I'm sorry," I said. "He's not usually so—" I straightened up and bang! The top of my head cracked into something hard. Callahan O'Shea's chin. His teeth snapped together with an audible clack, his head jerked back. "Jesus, woman!" he exclaimed, rubbing his chin.

"Oh, God! I'm so sorry!" I exclaimed. The top of my head stung from the impact.

With a glare, he reached down and grabbed Angus by the scruff of his neck, lifted him—there was a small snap as the laces were tugged out of Angus's mouth—and handed him to me.

"You're not supposed to lift him like that," I said, petting Angus's poor neck as my dog nibbled my chin.

"He's not supposed to bite me, either," Callahan said, not smiling.

"Right." I glanced down at my dog, kissed his head. "Sorry about your, um…chin."

"Of all the injuries you've given me so far, this one hurt the least."

"Oh. That's good, then." My face actually hurt from blushing. "So. Are you going to live here, or is this an investment or what?"

He paused, obviously wondering whether I was worth the effort of an answer. "I'm flipping it."

"Oh," I answered, relieved. Angus spotted a leaf blowing across my lawn and convulsed to be put down. After a second's hesitation, I complied, relieved when he ran off to give chase. "Well. Good luck with the house. It's very cute."

"Thank you."

"Good night."

"'Night."

I took a few steps toward my house, then stopped. "By the way," I added, turning back to my neighbor, "I did search you on Google and saw that you're an embezzler."

Callahan O'Shea said nothing.

"I have to say, I'm a little disappointed. Hannibal Lecter, at least he's interesting."

Callahan smiled at that, an abrupt, wicked smile that crinkled his eyes and lightened his face, and something twisted hard and hot in my stomach and seemed to surge toward my burly neighbor. That smile promised all kinds of wickedness, all sorts of heat, and I found that I was breathing rather heavily through my mouth.

And then I heard the noise, and so did Callahan

O'Shea. A little pattering noise. We both looked down. Angus was back, leg lifted, peeing on the boot he'd tried to eat a few moments before.

Callahan O'Shea's smile was gone. He raised his eyes to me. "I don't know which one of you is worse," he said, then turned and headed for his house.

CHAPTER EIGHT

THIRTEEN MONTHS, TWO WEEKS and four days after Andrew called off our wedding, I thought I was doing fairly well. The summer after had been pretty rough without the daily presence of my students, but I threw myself into the house and became a gardener. When I was antsy, I tramped through the state forest behind my house, following the Farmington River miles upriver and down, getting chewed on by mosquitoes and scratched by branches, Angus leaping along beside me on his festive leash, pink tongue lapping the river, white fur spattered with mud.

I spent Fourth of July weekend at Gettysburg—the real Gettysburg, in Pennsylvania—with several thousand other reenactors, forgetting the ache in my chest for a few days in the thrill of battle. When I got back, Julian put me to work at Jitterbug's, teaching basic ballroom. Mom and Dad invited me over often, but, fearful of upsetting me, they were painfully polite to each other, and it was so tense and freakish that I found myself wishing they'd just be normal and fight. Margaret and I drove up the coast of Maine so far north that the sun didn't set till almost 10:00 p.m. We spent a few quiet days walking the shore, watching the lobster boats bob on their moorings and not talking about Andrew.

Thank God I had the house. Floors to sand, trim to

paint, tag sales to attend so I could fill my little wedding cake of a home with sweet, thoughtful things that weren't associated with Andrew. A collection of St. Nicholas statues that I'd line up on the fireplace mantel come Christmas. Two brass doorknobs carved with *Public School, City of New York.* I made curtains. I painted walls. I installed light fixtures. I even went on a date or two. Well, I went on one date. That was enough to show me that I didn't want to get involved with anyone just yet.

School started, and I'd never loved my kids more. They may have had their little foibles, the overindulgences and the horrible speech patterns laden with *like* and *totally* and *whatever,* but they were so fascinating, so full of potential and the future. I lost myself in school, as I always did, watching among the resigned for the spark in one or two, the glow that told me someone connected with the past the way I had when I was a kid, that someone could *feel* how much history mattered to the present.

Christmas came and went, New Year's, too. On Valentine's Day, Julian came over armed with violent movies, Thai food and ice cream, and we laughed till our stomachs ached, both of us pretending to ignore the fact that this should've been my first anniversary and that Julian hadn't been on a date in eight years.

And my heart mended. It did. Time did its work, and Andrew faded to a dull ache that I mostly only thought about when I was lying alone in bed. Was I over him? I told myself I was.

Then, a few weeks before Kitty the Hair Cutting Cousin's wedding, Natalie and I went out for dinner. I had never told her the real reason Andrew and I had broken up. In fact, Andrew had never even said those words aloud. He didn't have to.

Natalie picked the place. She was working at Pelli Clarke Pelli in New Haven, one of the top architectural firms in the country. She'd had to work late and suggested the Omni Hotel, which boasted a restaurant with a nice view and good drinks.

When I met her there, I was a little shocked at her transformation. Somewhere along the line, my little sister had gone from beautiful to stunning. Each time I'd seen her in grad school or at home, she'd been dressed in jeans or sweats, typical student clothing, and her long, straight, blond hair was all one length. Then, she looked like a classic American girl next door, wholesome and lovely. But when she started working for real, she invested in some clothes and a stylish haircut, started wearing a little makeup, and wow. She looked like a modern day Grace Kelly.

"Hi, Bumppo!" I said, hugging her proudly. "You look gorgeous!"

"So do you," she returned generously. "Every time I see you, I think I'd sell my soul for that hair."

"This hair is the devil's hair. Don't be silly," I said, but I was pleased. Only Natalie could be sincere about that, the sweet angel.

I ordered my standard, generic G&T, not being a really sophisticated drinker. Nat ordered a dirty martini. "What kind of vodka would you like?" the waiter asked.

"Belvedere if you've got it," she answered with a smile.

"We do. Excellent choice," he said, obviously smitten. I smiled, wondering when my little sister had learned to drink good vodka.

And so we chatted, Natalie telling me about the team she was on at Pelli, the house they were designing that would overlook the Chesapeake Bay, how much she loved her work. By comparison, I felt a little…well, a little pedestrian, I guess. Not that teaching wasn't incredibly fulfilling, because it was. I loved my kids, my subject, and I felt like Manning, with its faded brick buildings and stately trees, was part of my soul. But despite Natalie's genuine interest in hearing about how Dr. Eckhart fell asleep at the department meeting when I suggested revamping the curriculum and why it bugged me that Ava had never given so much as a B-, my news sounded pale.

It was at that moment that we heard a burst of laughter. We turned and saw a group of six or eight men just coming off the elevator into the bar, and right in front was Andrew.

I hadn't seen him since the day he dumped me, and the sight of him was like a kick in the stomach. The blood drained out of my face, then flooded back in a sickening rush. A high-pitched whine shrilled in my ear, and I was hot, then cold, then hot again. Andrew. Not very tall, not all that good-looking, still on the scrawny side, his glasses sliding down his sharp nose, his sweet, vulnerable neck…. My entire body roared at his presence, but my mind was completely blank. Andrew smiled at one of his buddies and said something, and once again, his compadres burst into laughter.

"Grace?" Natalie whispered. I didn't answer.

Then Andrew turned, saw us, and the same thing that had just happened to me happened to him. He went white, then red, his eyes grew wide. Then he forced a smile and headed our way.

"Do you want to go?" Nat asked. I turned to look at her and saw, without much surprise, that she looked, well, utterly beautiful. A rosy flush stained her cheeks, not like mine, which could grill a steak. One of her eyebrows was arched delicately in concern. Her slender hands with their neat, unpolished nails reached out to touch my hand.

"No! No, of course not. I'm fine. Hi, there, stranger!" I said, standing up.

"Grace," Andrew said, and his voice was so familiar it was like a part of me, almost.

"What a nice surprise," I said. "You remember Nat, of course."

"Of course," he said. "Hello, Natalie."

"Hi," she said in a half whisper, cutting her eyes away.

I wasn't sure why I asked Andrew to join us for a few minutes. He pretty much had to say yes. We all sat together, so civilized and pleasant it could've been high tea at Windsor Castle. Andrew gulped upon learning that Nat lived in the same city where he worked, but covered well. *Ninth Square, nice renovations over there. Oh, really, you're at Pelli, how exciting... Funny. Small world. And you, Grace? How's Manning? Kids good this year? Great. Um...are your parents well? Good, good. Margaret and Stu? Great.*

And so we sat there, Nat, Andrew, me and the fourton elephant that was tap-dancing on the table. Andrew chattered like a nervous monkey, and though I couldn't hear over the roaring in my ears, I could see everything as clearly as if I were on some sense-enhancing drug. Natalie's hands were shaking just slightly, and to hide this fact, she'd folded them primly on the table. When she glanced at Andrew, her pupils dilated, though she was trying not to look at him at all. Above the neckline of her silky blouse, her skin was flushed, nearly blotchy. Even her lips looked redder. It was like watching the Discovery Channel's show on the science of attraction.

If Natalie was…affected, well, Andrew was terrified. His forehead was dotted with sweat, and the tips of his ears were so red they looked ready to burst into flame. His voice was faster than usual, and he made a point to smile at me often, though he couldn't seem to look me straight in the eye.

"Well," he said the minute he could escape, "I should get back to my workmates there. Um, Grace…you…you look great. Wonderful to see you." He gave me a fast hug, and I could feel the damp heat from his neck, smell the childlike sweetness of his skin, like a baby at naptime. Then he stepped back abruptly. "Natalie, uh, take care."

She lifted her gaze from the table, and the elephant seemed to trip, fall and crash right on top of the table. Because shining in her gorgeous, sky-blue eyes was a world of misery and guilt and love and hopelessness, and I, who loved no one as much as I loved Natalie, felt it like a shovel to the head. "Take care, Andrew," she said briskly.

Both of us watched him walk away to rejoin his friends on the other side of the mercifully large restaurant.

"Want to go somewhere else?" Natalie suggested when Andrew was out of range.

"No, no, I'm fine. I like it here," I said heartily. "Besides, dinner should be out soon." We smiled at each other.

"Are you okay?" she asked softly.

"Oh, yeah," I lied. "Sure. I mean, I loved him and all, he really is a great guy, but…you know. He wasn't The One." I made quote marks out of my fingers.

"He wasn't?"

"Nope. I mean, he's a great guy and all, but…" I paused, pretended to think. "I don't know. There was something missing."

"Oh," she said, her eyes thoughtful.

Our dinners came. I'd ordered a steak; Nat had salmon. The potatoes were great. We ate and chatted about movies and our family, books and TV shows. When we got the check, Natalie paid and I let her. Then we stood up. My sister didn't look in Andrew's direction, just walked smoothly to the door in front of me.

But I glanced back. Saw Andrew staring at Natalie like a junkie needing a fix, raw and hurting and naked. He didn't see me looking—he only had eyes for Nat.

I caught up to my sister. "Thanks, Nattie," I said.

"Oh, Grace, it was nothing," she answered, perhaps a bit too emotionally for the circumstances.

My heart thudded in my chest on the elevator ride down. I remembered my fourth birthday. Remembered the barrettes. The Saturday-morning cuddling. Her face as I'd left for college. I remembered that hospital waiting room, the smell of old coffee, the glare of the lights as I'd promised God anything, *anything,* if He'd save my sister. I considered what was in Natalie's eyes when she looked up at Andrew.

I imagined what kind of character it took to walk away from what might be the love of your life for the sake of another. To feel the big kablammy and not be able to do a thing about it. I wondered if I had the selflessness for an act of that magnitude. I asked myself what kind of heart I really had. What kind of sister I really was.

"I had this very strange thought," I said as we walked back toward Natalie's apartment, arm in arm.

"So many of your thoughts are strange," she said, almost hitting our usual vibe.

"Well, this one is pretty out there, but it feels right," I said, stopping on the corner of the New Haven Green. "Natalie, I think you should…" I paused. "I think you should go out with Andrew. I think he might've met the wrong sister first."

Those amazing Natalie eyes flashed again—shock, guilt, sorrow, pain…and hope. Yup. Hope. "Grace, I would never…" she began.

"I know. I really do," I murmured. "But I think you and Andrew should talk."

I met Andrew for dinner a few days later. Told him the same thing I told Natalie. The same emotions flashed over his face as had flashed across hers, with one more. Gratitude. He put up a few gentlemanly objections, then caved, as I knew he would. I suggested they meet in person, rather than talk on the phone or email. They took my suggestion. Natalie called me the day after their first meeting, and in tones of gentle wonder, told me how they'd walked through New Haven, ending up shivering on a bench under the graceful trees in Wooster Square, just talking. She asked, repeatedly, if this was really okay, and I assured her it was.

And it was, except for just one problem, so far as I could see. I wasn't sure I was quite over Andrew myself.

CHAPTER NINE

ON SATURDAY MORNING, ANGUS shocked me into consciousness with his maniacal barking, clawing at the door as if a steak was being stuffed underneath it.

"What? Who?" I blurted, barely conscious. Glancing at the clock, I saw that it was only seven. "Angus! This house better be on fire, or you're in big trouble." Usually, my beloved pet was quite content to sleep squarely in the middle of my bed, somehow managing to take up two-thirds of it despite weighing a mere sixteen pounds.

An accidental look in the mirror showed me that my new hair tamer (which cost fifty bucks a bottle) clocked out after 1:00 a.m., which was when I went to bed the night before. So if in fact Angus *was* saving my life and our photo *did* appear on the front page of the paper, I'd better do something about that hair before rushing out into the flames. I grabbed an elastic, slapped my hair into a ponytail and felt the door. Cool. Opening it a crack, I smelled no smoke. Drat. There went my chance at meeting a hot fireman who would carry me out of the flames as if I were made of spun sugar. Still, I guessed it was a good thing that my house wasn't going up in flames.

Angus flew down the stairs like a bullet, doing his trademark Dance of the Visitor at the front door, leaping straight up so that all four paws came off the floor.

Oh, yes. Today was Bull Run, and Margaret was coming along. Apparently she felt the need to rise early, but I needed coffee before I could kill any Johnny Rebs. Or was I killing Bluebellies today?

Scooping up Angus, I opened the door. "Hi, Margaret," I mumbled, squinting at the light.

Callahan O'Shea stood on my porch. "Don't hurt me," he said.

The bruise around his eye had faded considerably, still there, but yellow and brown had replaced the livid purple. His eyes were blue, I noted, and the kind that turned down at the corners, making him look a little… sad. Soulful. Sexy. He wore a faded red T-shirt and jeans, and there it was again, that annoying twinge of attraction.

"So. Here to sue me?" I asked. Angus barked—*Yarp!*—from my arms.

He smiled, and the twinge became more of a wrench.

"No. I'm here to replace your windows. Nice pajamas, by the way."

I glanced down. Crap. SpongeBob SquarePants, a Christmas present from Julian. We had a tradition of giving horrible gifts…I'd given him a Chia Head. Then his words hit home. "Excuse me? Did you say you're replacing my windows?"

"Yup," he said, poking his head in the doorway and glancing around the living room. "Your father hired me the other day. Didn't he tell you?"

"No," I answered. "When?"

"Thursday," he said. "You were out. Nice place you've got here. Did Daddy buy it for you?"

My mouth opened. "Hey!"

"So. Are you going to move aside so I can come in?"

I clutched Angus a little tighter. "No. Listen, Mr. O'Shea, I don't really think—"

"What? You don't want an ex-con working for you?"

My mouth snapped shut. "Well, actually...I..." It seemed so rude to say it out loud. "No, thank you." I forced a smile, feeling about as sincere as a presidential candidate pledging finance reform. "I'd rather hire another guy...um, someone who worked for me in the past."

"I've been hired. Your father already paid me half." He narrowed his eyes at me, and my teeth gritted.

"Well, that's inconvenient, but you'll have to give it back." Angus barked from my arms, backing me up. Good dog.

"No."

My mouth dropped open. "Well, sorry, Mr. O'Shea, but I don't want you working here." *Seeing me in my pajamas. Stirring things up. Possibly stealing my stuff.*

He cocked his head and stared at me. "How cutting, Ms. Emerson, to think that you don't like me, and also how ironic, given that if anyone has reason not to like someone else, I'd say the votes go to me."

"You get no votes, pal! I didn't ask you to—"

"But since I have better manners than you, I'll reserve judgment and say only that I don't like your propensity for violence. However, I already took your father's money, and if you want these windows before hell freezes over, I have to put in an order from a specialty place in Kansas. And to be honest, I need the work. Okay? So let's drop the feminine outrage, ignore the fact that I've seen you in your unmentionables—" his eyes traveled up and down my frame "—and get to work. I have to measure the windows. Want me to start upstairs or down?"

At this moment, Natalie's BMW pulled into the driveway, causing Angus new seizures of outrage. I clutched him to me, his little form trembling, as he tried to heave himself out of my arms, his barks bouncing off the inside of my skull.

"Can't you control the wee beastie?" Callahan O'Shea asked.

"Quiet," I muttered. "Not you, Angus, honey. Hi, Natalie!"

"Hi," she said, gliding up the front steps. She paused, giving my neighbor a questioning look. "Hello. I'm Natalie Emerson, Grace's sister."

My neighbor took her hand, an appreciative grin tugging his mouth up on one side, making me dislike him all the more. "Callahan O'Shea," he murmured. "I'm Grace's carpenter."

"He's not," I insisted. "What brings you here, Nat?"

"I thought we could have a cup of coffee," she said, smiling brightly. "I've been dying to hear about this guy you're seeing. We haven't had a chance to talk since Mom's show."

"A boyfriend?" Callahan said. "I take it he likes things rough."

Natalie's silken eyebrows popped up an inch and she grinned, her eyes studying his shiner. "Come on, Grace, how about some coffee? Callahan, is it? Would you like a cup?"

"I'd love one," he answered, smiling at my beautiful and suddenly irritating sister.

Five minutes later, I was staring sullenly at the coffeepot as my sister and Callahan O'Shea became best friends forever.

"So Grace actually hit you? With a field hockey stick? Oh, Grace!" She burst into laughter, that husky, seductive laugh that men loved.

"It was self-defense," I said, grabbing a few cups from the cupboard.

"She was drunk," Cal explained. "Well, the first time, she was drunk. The second time, with the rake, she was just flighty."

"I was *not* flighty," I objected, setting the coffeepot on the table and yanking open the fridge for the cream, which I set on the table with considerable force. "I have never been described as flighty."

"I don't know, Natalie," Callahan said, tilting his head. "Don't those pajamas say flighty to you?" His eyes traveled up and down my SpongeBobs once more.

"That's it, Irish. You're fired. Again. Still. Whatever."

"Oh, come on, Grace," Natalie said, laughing melodically. "He's got a point. I hope Wyatt won't see you in those."

"Wyatt loves SpongeBob," I retorted.

Nat poured Callahan a cup of coffee, missing the daggers shooting from my eyes. "Cal, have you met Grace's new guy?" she asked.

"You know, I haven't," he answered, cocking his eyebrow at me. I tried to ignore him. Not easy. He looked so damn...wonderful...sitting there in my cheery kitchen, Angus chewing his bootlace, drinking coffee from my limited edition Fiestaware cornflower-blue mug. The sun shone on his tousled hair, revealing very appealing streaks of gold in that rich chestnut-brown. He just about glowed with masculinity, all broad shoulders and big muscles, about to fix stuff in my house...damn it. Who wouldn't be turned on?

"So what's he like?" Natalie asked. For a second I thought she was talking about Callahan O'Shea.

"Huh? Oh, Wyatt? Well, he's very...nice."

"Nice is good. And how was your date the other night?" she continued, stirring sugar into her coffee to make herself even sweeter. Dang it. Nat had called the other night, and I could hear Andrew in the background, so I'd cut the conversation short by saying I had to meet Wyatt in Hartford. Oh, the tangled web...Callahan's soulful blue eyes were looking at me. Mockingly.

"The date was good. Pleasant. Nice. We ate. Drank. Kissed. Stuff like that."

So eloquent, Grace! Again with Callahan's eyebrow.

"Grace, come on!" my once-beloved sister said. "What's he like? I mean, he's a pediatric surgeon, so obviously he's wonderful, but give me some specifics."

"Lovely! His personality is lovely," I said, my voice a little loud. "He's very—" another glance at Cal "—respectful. Friendly. He's incredibly kind. Gives money to the homeless...and um, rescues...cats." My inner voice, disgusted at my poor lying abilities, sighed loudly.

"Sounds perfect," Natalie said approvingly. "Good sense of humor?"

"Oh, yes," I answered. "Very funny. But in a nice, nonmocking way. Not snarky, sarcastic or rude. In a gentle, loving way."

"So this is a case of opposites attract?" Callahan asked.

"I thought I just fired you," I said.

His eyes crinkled in a grin, and my knees went traitorously soft.

"I think he sounds amazing," Natalie said with a beautiful smile.

"Thanks," I said, smiling back. For a second, I was tempted to ask her about Andrew, but with the burly ex-con in the room, I decided against it.

"Are you going to the battle today, Grace?" my sister asked, taking a sip of her coffee. Honestly, everything she did looked as if it was being filmed…graceful and balanced and lovely.

"Battle?" Callahan asked.

"Don't tell him," I commanded. "And, yes, I am."

"Well, sorry to say I have to head down to New Haven," Natalie said regretfully, putting her cup aside. "It was nice to meet you, Callahan."

"The pleasure was mine," he said, standing up. Well, well, well. The ex-con had nice manners…when Natalie was around, at any rate.

I walked her to the door, gave her a hug. "Everything good with Andrew?" I asked, careful to keep my tone light.

It was like watching a beautiful sunrise, the way her face lit up. "Oh, Grace…yes."

"Excellent," I said, pushing back a lock of her cool, silky hair. "I'm glad for you, honey."

"Thanks," she murmured. "And I'm so glad for you, Grace! Wyatt sounds perfect!" She hugged me tight. "See you soon?"

"You bet." I hugged her back, my heart squeezing with love, and watched her glide out to her sleek little car and back out of my driveway. She waved, then disappeared down the street. My smile faded. Margaret knew instantly that Wyatt Dunn was fictional, and Callahan O'Shea, a virtual stranger, seemed to guess it, too. But not Natalie. Of course, she had a lot riding on me being with a great guy, didn't she? Me being attached meant…well. I knew what it meant.

With a sigh, I returned to the kitchen.

"So." Cal tipped back in his chair, hands clasped behind his head. "Your boyfriend's a cat rescuer."

I smiled. "Yes, he is. There's a problem with feral cats in his area. Very sad. He wrangles them. Herds them up into crates, gets them to foster homes. Would you like one?"

"A feral cat?"

"Mmm-hmm. They say your pet should match your personality."

He laughed, a wicked, ashy sound, and suddenly, my knees were even weaker than the time I saw Bruce Springsteen in concert. "No, thank you, Grace."

"So tell me, Mr. O'Shea," I said briskly. "How much did you embezzle, and from whom?"

His mouth got a little tight at the question. "One-point-six million dollars. From my esteemed employer."

"One point… God's nightgown!"

My checkbook, I suddenly noticed, was lying right over there, on the counter near the fridge. I should probably put that away, shouldn't I? Not that I had a million dollars there or anything. Callahan followed my nervous gaze and raised his unbruised eyebrow once more.

"So tempting," he said. "But I've turned over a new leaf. Although those are gonna be hard to resist." He nodded at a shelf containing my collection of antique iron dogs. Then he stood up, filling my kitchen. "Can I go upstairs and measure the windows, Grace?"

I opened my mouth to protest, then shut it. It wasn't worth it. How long would windows take? A couple of days?

"Um, sure. Hang on one sec, let me make sure it… um…"

"Why don't you just come with me? That way, if I'm tempted to rifle through your jewelry box, you can stop me yourself."

"I wanted to make sure the bed was made, that's all," I lied. "Right this way."

For the next three minutes, I fought feelings of lust and irritation as Callahan O'Shea measured my bedroom windows. Then he went into the guest room and did the same thing, his movements neat and efficient, zipping the measuring tape along the frames, jotting things down in his notebook. I leaned in the doorway, watching his back (ass, let's be honest) as he opened a window and looked outside.

"I might need to replace some trim when I put these in," he said, "but I won't know till I take them out. These are pretty old."

I dragged my eyes to his face. "Right. Sure. Sounds good."

He came over to me, and my breath caught. God. Callahan O'Shea was standing within an inch of me. The heat shimmered off his body, and my own body seemed to soften and sway in response. I could feel my heart squeezing and opening, squeezing and opening. His hand, still holding the tape measure, brushed the back of mine, and suddenly I had to breathe through my mouth.

"Grace?"

"Yes?" I whispered back. I could see the pulse in

his neck. Wondered what it would be like to kiss that neck, to slide my fingers through his tousled hair, to—

"Can you move?" he asked.

My mouth closed with a snap. "Sure! Sure! Just... thinking."

His eyes crinkled in an all-too-knowing smile.

We went back downstairs, and a disappointingly short time later, Callahan O'Shea was done. "I'll put in the order and let you know when they come in," he said.

"Great," I said.

"Bye. Good luck at the battle."

"Thanks," I said, blushing for no apparent reason.

"Make sure you double lock the doors. I'll be home all day."

"Very funny. Now get out," I said. "I have Yankees to kill."

CHAPTER TEN

THE CANNON ROARED IN MY EARS, the smell of smoke sharp and invigorating. I watched as six Union soldiers fell. Behind the first line, the Bluebellies reloaded.

"This is so queer," Margaret muttered, handing me the powder so I could reload my cannon.

"Oh, shut up," I said fondly. "We're honoring history. And quit complaining. You'll be dead soon enough. A pox upon you, Mr. Lincoln!" I called, adding a silent apology to gentle Abe, the greatest president our nation ever saw. Surely he would forgive me, seeing as I had a miniature of the Lincoln Memorial in my bedroom and could (and often did) recite the Gettysburg Address by heart.

But Brother Against Brother took its battles very seriously. We had about two hundred volunteers, and each encounter was planned to be as historically accurate as possible. The Yankee soldiers fired, and Margaret dropped to the ground with a roll of her sea-green eyes. I took one in the shoulder, screamed and collapsed next to her. "It will take me hours to finally kick the bucket," I told my sister. "Blood poisoning from the lead. No treatment options, really. Even if I was taken to a field hospital, I'd probably die. So either way, long and painful."

"I repeat. This is so queer," Margaret said, flipping open her cell phone to check messages.

"No farbies!" I barked.

"What?"

"The phone! You can't have anything modern at a re-enactment. And if this is so queer, why did you come?" I asked.

"Dad kept harassing Junie—" Margaret's long-suffering legal secretary "—until she finally begged me to say yes just to get him to stop calling and dropping by. Besides, I wanted to get out of the house."

"Well, you're here, so quit whining." I reached for her hand, imagining a Rebel soldier seeking comfort from his fallen brother. "We're outside, it's a beautiful day, we're lying around in the sweet-smelling clover." Margaret didn't answer. I glanced over. She was studying her cell phone, scowling, which wasn't an unusual expression for her, but her lips trembled in a suspicious manner. Like she was about to cry. I sat up abruptly. "Margs? Is everything okay?"

"Oh, things are peachy," she answered.

"Aren't you supposed to be dead?" my father asked, striding toward us.

"Sorry, Dad. I mean, sorry, General Jackson," I said, flopping obediently back in the grass.

"Margaret, please. Put that away. A lot of people have worked very hard to make this authentic."

Margaret rolled her eyes. "Bull Run in Connecticut. So authentic."

Dad grunted in disgust. A fellow officer rushed to his side. "What shall we do, sir?" he asked.

"Sir, we will give them the bayonet!" Dad barked. A little thrill shuddered through me at the historic words.

What a war! The two officers conferred, then walked away to engage the gunmen on the hillside.

"I might need a break from Stuart," Margaret said.

I sat bolt upright once again, tripping a fellow Confederate who was relocating my cannon. "Sorry," I said to him. "Go get 'em." He and another guy hefted the cannon and wheeled it off amid sporadic gunfire and the cries of the commanding officers. "Margaret, are you serious?"

"I need some distance," she answered.

"What happened?"

She sighed. "Nothing. That's the problem. We've been married for seven years, right? And nothing's different. We do the same things day after day. Come home. Stare at each other over dinner. Lately, when he's talking about work or something on the news, I look at him and just think, 'Is this it?'"

An early butterfly landed on the brass button of my uniform, flexed its wings and fluttered off. A Confederate officer rushed by. "Are you girls dead?" he asked.

"Oh, yes, we are. Sorry." I lay back down, pulling Margaret's hand until she joined me. "Is there anything else, Margs?" I asked.

"No." Her eyes flickered away from me, belying her words. But Margaret was not one to offer something before she was ready. "It's just…I just wonder if he really loves me. If I really love him. If this is what marriage is or if we just picked the wrong person."

We lay in the grass, saying nothing more. My throat felt tight. I loved Stuart, a quiet, gentle man. I had to admit, I didn't know him terribly well. I saw him sporadically at work, usually from afar. The Manning students loved him, that was for sure. But family dinners tended to revolve around Mom and Dad bickering or Mémé's soliloquies on what was wrong with the world today, and usually Stuart didn't get a word in edgewise. But what I did know was that he was kind, smart and very considerate toward my sister. One might even say, if pressed, that he adored her a little too much, deferring to her on just about everything.

The sound of fleeing Union soldiers and the cries of triumphant Rebel soldiers filled the air.

"Can we go now?" Margaret asked.

"No. Dad's just now assembling the thirteen guns. Wait for it…wait for it…" I raised myself up on my elbows so I could see, grinning in anticipation.

"There stands Jackson, a veritable stone wall!" came the cry of Rick Jones, who was playing Colonel Bee.

"Huzzah! Huzzah!" Though supposedly dead, I couldn't help joining in the cry. Margaret shook her head, but she was grinning.

"Grace, you really need to get a life," she said, standing up.

"So what does Stuart think?" I asked, taking her proffered hand.

"He says to do whatever I need to sort things out in my head." Margaret shook her head, whether in admiration or disgust. Knowing Margaret, it was probably disgust. "So, Grace, listen. Do you think I could stay with you for a week or two? Maybe a little longer?"

"Sure," I said. "As long as you need."

"Oh, and hey, listen to this. I'm fixing you up with this guy. Lester. I met him at Mom's show last week. He's a metalsmith or some such shit."

"A metalsmith? Named Lester?" I asked. "Oh, Margaret, come on." Then I paused. Surely he couldn't be worse than my veteran friend. "Is he cute?"

"Well, I don't know. Not cute, exactly, but attractive in his own way."

"Lester the metalsmith, attractive in his own way. That does not sound promising."

"So? Beggars can't be choosy. And you said you wanted to meet someone, so you're meeting someone. Okay? Okay. I'll tell him to call."

"Fine," I muttered. "Hey, Margs, did you run down that name I gave you?"

"What name?"

"The ex-con? Callahan O'Shea, who lives next door to me? He embezzled over a million dollars."

"No, I didn't get around to it. Sorry. I'll try to this week. Embezzlement. That's not so bad, is it?"

"Well, it's not good, Margs. And it was over a million dollars."

"Still better than rape and murder," Margs said cheerfully. "Look, there's donuts. Thank God, I'm starving."

And with that, we tramped off the field where the rest of the troops already stood, drinking Starbucks and eating Krispy Kreme donuts. Granted, it wasn't historically accurate, but it sure beat mule meat and hoecake.

THAT NIGHT, I SPENT AN HOUR taming my thorny locks and donning a new outfit. I had two back-to-back dates via eCommitment…well, not dates exactly, but meetings to see if there was a reason to try a date. The first was with Jeff, who sounded very promising indeed. He owned his own business in the entertainment industry, and his picture was very pleasing. Like me, he enjoyed hiking, gardening and historical movies. Alas, his fa-

vorite was *300,* so what did that say? But I decided to
overlook it for the moment. Just what his business was,
I wasn't sure. Entertainment industry…hmm. Maybe he
was an agent or something. Or owned a record label or
a club. It sounded kind of glamorous, really.

Jeff and I were meeting for a drink in Farmington,
and then I was moving on to appetizers with Leon.
Leon was a science teacher, so I already knew we'd
have lots to talk about…in fact, our three emails thus
far had been about teaching, the joys and the potholes,
and I was looking forward to hearing more about his
personal life.

I drove to the appointed place, one of those chain
places near a mall that have a lot of faux Tiffany and
sports memorabilia. I recognized Jeff from his picture—he was short and kind of cute, brown hair, brown
eyes, an appealing dimple in his left cheek. We gave
each other that awkward lean-in hug where we weren't
sure how far to go and ended up touching cheeks like
society matrons. But Jeff acknowledged the awkward-
ness with a little smile, which made me like him. We
followed the maître d' to a little table, ordered a glass
of wine and started in on the small talk, and it was then
that things started to go south.

"So, Jeff, I've been wondering about your job. What
exactly do you do?" I asked, sipping my wine.

"I own my own business," he said.

"Right. What kind?" I asked.

"Entertainment." He smiled furtively and straightened the salt and pepper shakers.

I paused. "Ah. And how exactly do you entertain?"

He grinned. "Like *this!*" he said, leaning back. Then,

with a flourish and a sudden, sharp flick of his hands, he set the table on fire.

Later, after the firefighters had put out the flames and deemed it safe to return to the restaurant, a large portion of which was covered in the foamy fire retardant that had doused the "entertainment," Jeff turned beseechingly to me. "Doesn't anyone love magic anymore?" he asked, looking at me, as confused as a kicked puppy.

"You have the right to remain silent," a police officer duly recited.

"I didn't mean the fire to be so big," Jeff informed the cop, who didn't seem to care much.

"So you're a magician?" I asked, fiddling with the burnt end of a lock of my hair, which had been slightly singed.

"It's my dream," he said as the officer cuffed him. "Magic is my life."

"Ah," I said. "Best of luck with that."

Was it me, or did a lot of men leave in handcuffs when I was around? First Callahan O'Shea, now Jeff. I had to hand it to Callahan—he looked a lot better in restraints than poor Jeff, who resembled a crated ferret. Yes, when it came to handcuffs, Callahan O'Shea was— I stopped that train of thought. I had another date. Leon the teacher was next in line, so on I went, glad that the firefighters of Farmington were so efficient that I wasn't even late.

Leon was much more promising. Balding in that attractive Ed Harris way, wonderful sparkling blue eyes and a boyish laugh, he seemed delighted in me, which of course I found very appealing. We talked for a half hour or so, filling each other in on our teaching jobs, bemoaning helicopter parents and extolling the bright minds of children.

"So, Grace, let me ask you something," he said, pushing our potato skins aside to touch my hand, making me glad I'd splurged on a manicure/pedicure this week. His face grew serious. "What would you say is the most important thing in your life?"

"My family," I answered. "We're very close. I have two sisters, one older, one—"

"I see. What else, Grace? What would come next?"

"Um, well...my students, I guess. I really love them, and I want so much for them to be excited about history. They—"

"Uh-huh. Anything else, Grace?"

"Well," I said, a bit miffed at being cut off twice now, "sure. I mean, I volunteer with a senior citizen group, we do ballroom dancing with my friend Julian, who's a dance teacher. Sometimes I read to some of them, the ones who can't read for themselves."

"Are you religious?" Leon asked.

I paused. I was definitely one of those who'd classify herself as *spiritual* rather than *religious*. "Sort of. Yes, I mean. I go to church, oh, maybe once a month or so, and I—"

"I'm wondering what your feelings are on God."

I blinked. "God?" Leon nodded. "Um, well, God is... well, He's great." I imagined God rolling His eyes at me. *Come on, Grace. I said, "Let there be light," and bada-bing! There was light! Can't you do better than "He's great," for God's sake? Get it? For God's sake?* (I always imagined God had a great sense of humor. He'd have to, right?)

Leon's bright (fanatical?) blue eyes narrowed. "Yes,

He is great. Are you a Christian? Have you accepted Jesus Christ as your personal savior?"

"Well…sure." Granted, I couldn't ever remember anyone in my family (Mayflower descendants, remember?) ever using the term *personal savior…* We were Congregationalists, and things tended to stay a little more philosophical. "Jesus is also so…good." And now I had Jesus, raising His head as He hung on the Cross. *Wow. Thanks, Grace. This is what I get for dying up here?*

"Jesus is my wingman," Leon said proudly. "Grace, I'd like to take you to my church so you can experience the true meaning of holiness."

Check, please! "Actually, Leon, I have a church," I said. "It's very nice. I can't say I'm interested in going anywhere else."

The fanatical blue eyes narrowed. "I don't get the impression you've truly embraced God, Grace." He frowned.

Okay. Enough was enough. "Well, Leon, let's be honest. You've known me forty-two minutes. How the hell would you know?"

At the *H-E*-double hockey sticks word, Leon reared back. "Blasphemer!" he hissed. "I'm sorry, Grace! We do not have a future together! You're going straight to you-know-where." He stood up abruptly.

"Judge not," I reminded him. "Nice meeting you, and good luck with finding someone," I said. I was pretty sure God would be proud. Not just a quote from the Good Book, but turning the other cheek and everything.

Safely in my car, I saw with dismay that it was only eight o'clock. Only eight, and already I'd been in a fire and condemned to hell…and still no boyfriend. I sighed.

Well. I knew a good cure for loneliness, and its name was Golden Meadows. Twenty minutes later, I was sitting in Room 403.

"Her white satin chemise slid to the floor in a seductive whisper." I paused, glanced at my one-person audience, then continued. *"His eyes grew cobalt with desire, his loins burning at the sight of her creamy décolletage. 'I am yours, my lord,' she said, her lips ripe with sultry promise. Reaching for her breast, his mind raced...* Okay, that's a dangling participle if I ever heard one. His mind did not, I assure you, reach for her breast."

Another glance at Mr. Lawrence revealed the same level of attention as before—that is to say, none. Mr. Lawrence was nonverbal, a tiny, shrunken man with white hair and vacant eyes, hands that constantly plucked at his clothes and the arms of his easy chair. In all the months I'd been reading to him, I had never heard him speak. Hopefully, he was enjoying our sessions on some level and not mentally screaming for James Joyce. "Well. Back to our story. *His mind raced. Dare he take the promise of forbidden passion and sheathe his rock-hard desire in the heaven of her soft and hidden treasure?"*

"I think he should go for it."

I jumped, dropping my tawdry paperback. Callahan O'Shea stood in the doorway, shrinking the size of the room. "Irish! What are you doing here?" I asked.

"What are you doing here, is a better question."

"I'm reading to Mr. Lawrence. He likes it." Hopefully Mr. Lawrence wouldn't lurch out of his two-year silence and deny that fact. "He's part of my reading program."

"Is that right? He's also my grandfather," Callahan said, crossing his arms.

My head jerked back in surprise. "This is your grandfather?" I asked.

"Yes."

"Oh. Well, I read to…to patients sometimes."

"To everyone?"

"No," I answered. "Just the patients who don't get—" My voice broke off midsentence.

"Who don't get visitors," Callahan finished.

"Right," I acknowledged.

I had started my little reading program about four years ago when Mémé first moved here. Having visitors was a huge status symbol at Golden Meadows, and one day I'd wandered into this unit—the secure unit—and found that too many folks were alone, their families too far to visit often or just unable to stand the sadness of this wing. So I started reading. Granted, *My Lord's Wanton Desire* wasn't a classic—not in literary terms, anyway—but it did seem to keep the attention of my listeners. Mrs. Kim in Room 39 had actually wept when Lord Barton popped the question to Clarissia.

Callahan pushed off from the doorway and came into the room. "Hi, Pop," he said, kissing the old man's head. His grandfather didn't acknowledge him. My eyes stung a little as Cal looked at the frail old man, who, as always, was neatly dressed in trousers and a cardigan.

"Well, I'll leave you two alone," I said, getting up.

"Grace."

"Yes?"

"Thank you for visiting him." He hesitated, then looked up at me and smiled, and my heart swelled. "He liked biographies, back in the day."

"Okay," I said. "Personally, I think the duke and the prostitute are a little more invigorating, but if you say so." I paused. "Were you guys close?" I found myself asking.

"Yes," he answered. Callahan's expression was unreadable, his eyes on his grandfather's face as the old man plucked at his sweater. Callahan put his hand over the old man's, stilling the nervous, constant movement. "He raised us. My brother and me."

I hesitated, wanting to be polite, but curiosity got the better of me. "What happened to your parents?" I asked.

"My mother died when I was eight," he said. "I never met my father."

"I'm sorry." He nodded once in acknowledgment. "What about your brother? Does he live around here?"

Cal's face hardened. "I think he's out West. He's… estranged. There's just me." He paused, his face softening as he looked at his grandfather.

I swallowed. Suddenly, my family seemed pretty damn wonderful, despite Mom and Dad's constant bickering, Mémé's stream of criticism. The aunts and uncles, mean old Cousin Kitty…and my sisters, of course, that primal, ferocious love I felt for both my sisters. I couldn't imagine being estranged from either of them, ever.

"I'm sorry," I said again, almost in a whisper.

Cal looked up, then gave a rueful laugh. "Well. I had a normal enough childhood. Played baseball. Went camping. Fly-fishing. The usual boy stuff."

"That's good," I said. My cheeks burned. The sound of Callahan's laugh reverberated in my chest. No denying it. I found Mr. O'Shea way too attractive.

"So how often do you come here?" Callahan asked.

"Oh, usually once or twice a week. I teach Dancin' with the Oldies with my friend Julian. Every Monday, seven-thirty to nine." I smiled. Maybe he'd drop by. See how cute I looked in my swirly skirts, swishing away, delighting the residents. Maybe—

"Dance class, huh?" he said. "You don't look the type."

"And what does that mean?" I asked.

"You're not built like a dancer," he commented.

"You should probably stop talking now," I advised.

"Got a little more meat on your bones than those girls you see on TV."

"You should definitely stop talking now." I glared. He grinned.

"And aren't dancers graceful?" he continued. "Not prone to hitting people with rakes and the like?"

"Maybe there's just something about you that invites a hockey stick," I suggested tartly. "I've never hit Wyatt, after all."

"Yet," Callahan responded. "Where is the perfect man, anyway? Still haven't seen him around the neighborhood." His eyes were mocking, as if he knew damn well why. Because no cat-loving, good-looking pediatric surgeon would go for a wild-haired history teacher who enjoyed pretending to bleed to death on the weekends. My pride answered before my brain had a chance.

"Wyatt's in Boston this week, presenting a paper on a new recovery protocol in patients under ten," I said. Good Lord. Where had I pulled that from? All those Discovery Health shows were starting to pay off, apparently.

"Oh." He looked suitably impressed…or so it seemed to me. "Well. Any reason for you to hang around, then?"

I was dismissed. "No. None. So. Bye, Mr. Lawrence. I'll finish reading the book when your charming grandson isn't around."

"Good night, Grace," Callahan said, but I didn't answer, choosing instead to walk briskly (and gracefully, damn it) out of the room.

My mood was thorny as I drove home. While Callahan O'Shea was completely right to doubt the existence of Wyatt Dunn, it bugged me. Surely, were such a man to exist, he could like me. It shouldn't seem so impossible, right? Maybe, just maybe, somewhere out there was a real pediatric surgeon with dimples and a great smile. Not just magicians with tendencies toward arson and religious nut jobs and too-knowing ex-cons.

At least Angus worshipped me. God must've had single women in mind when he invented dogs. I accepted his gift of a ruined roll of paper towels and a chewed-up sneaker, praised him for not destroying anything else and got ready for bed.

I imagined telling Wyatt Dunn about my day. How he'd laugh at the bad dates—well, of course, there would be no bad dates if he were a real person—but still. He'd laugh and we'd talk and make plans for the weekend. We'd have a gentle, sweet, thoughtful relationship. We'd hardly ever fight. He'd think I was the loveliest creature to walk the earth. He'd even adore my hair. He'd send me flowers, just to let me know he was thinking of me.

And even though I knew quite well he wasn't real, I felt better. The old imaginary boyfriend was doing what he did best. I knew I was a good, smart, valuable person. If the dating pool of Connecticut failed to provide a worthy choice, well, what was the harm in a little visualization? Didn't Olympic athletes do that? Picture a perfect dive or dismount in order to achieve it? Wyatt Dunn was the same idea.

The fact that Callahan O'Shea's face kept coming to mind was purely coincidental, I was sure.

CHAPTER ELEVEN

"WHO IS JEB STUART?" Tommy Michener suggested.

"Correct!" I said, grinning. His teammates cheered, and Tommy, who was captain of his team, flushed with pride. "Pick again, Tom!"

"I'll stick with Civil War Leaders, Ms. Em," he said.

"Leaders for a thousand. This vice president of the Confederacy was sickly his whole life, never weighing more than one hundred pounds."

Hunter's team buzzed in. "Who is Jefferson Davis?" Mallory guessed.

"No, honey, sorry, he was the *president* of the Confederacy. Tommy, does your team have a guess?" The kids huddled together, conferring.

Emma Kirk, the day student with a crush on Tommy, whispered into his ear. I'd made sure they were on the same team. He asked her a question. She nodded. "Who is Little Aleck Stephens?" Emma said.

"Yes, Emma! Well done!"

Tommy high-fived Emma, who practically levitated in pleasure.

I beamed at my students. Civil War Jeopardy! was a hit. With a glance at the clock, I was shocked to see our time was almost over. "Okay, Final Jeopardy! everyone. Ready? This Pulitzer Prize–winning author, whose book details the rise and fall of the South as seen through one woman's eyes, never wrote another novel."

I hummed the theme from *Jeopardy!* with gusto, strolling back and forth between the two groups of kids. Tommy's team was kicking some serious butt; however my favorite student was showing off for Kerry, who was on the other team, and chances were he'd bet it all.

"Pens down. Okay, Hunter, your team had nine thousand points. Your wager? Oh, I see you've bet the farm. Very bold. Okay, Hunter. Your answer, please?"

He held up his team's wipe-away board. I winced. "No. Sorry, Hunter. Stephen Crane is not the answer. But he did write *The Red Badge of Courage,* which is about the Battle of Chancellorsville, so nice try. Tommy? What did you bet?"

"We bet it all, Ms. Em," he said proudly, glancing over at Kerry and winking. Emma's smile dropped a notch.

"And your answer, Tom?"

Tom turned to his team. "Who is Margaret Mitchell?" they chorused.

"Correct!" I shouted.

You'd think they'd won the World Series or something—screams of victory, lots of high fives and dancing around, a few hugs. Meanwhile, Hunter Graystone's team groaned.

"Tommy's team…no homework for you!" I announced. More cheering and high-fiving. "Hunter's team, sorry, kids. Three pages on Margaret Mitchell, and if you haven't read *Gone with the Wind,* shame on you! Okay, class dismissed."

Ten minutes later, I was seated in the conference room in Lehring Hall with my fellow history depart-

ment members—Dr. Eckhart, the chairman; Paul Boccanio, who was next in seniority; the unfortunately
named Wayne Diggler, our newest teacher, hired last
year right out of graduate school; and Ava Machiatelli,
sex kitten.

"Your class sounded quite out of control today," Ava
murmured in her trademark phone-sex whisper. "So
much chaos! My class could hardly think."

Not that they need to for you to give them an A, I
grumbled internally. "We were playing Jeopardy!" I
said with a smile. "Very invigorating."

"Very noisy, too." A reproachful blink…another…
and, yes, a third blink.

Dr. Eckhart shuffled to the head of the table and
sat down, an activity that took considerable time and
effort. Then he gave his trademark phlegmy, barking
cough that caused first-years to jump in their seats until
about November. A distinguished gentleman with an
unfortunate aversion to daily bathing, Dr. Eckhart was
from the olden days of prep schools where the kids wore
uniforms and could be locked in closets for misbehaving, if not beaten with rulers. He often mourned those
happy times. Aside from that, he was a brilliant man.

He now straightened and folded his arthritic hands in
front of him. "This year will be my last as chairman of
the history department at Manning, as you have doubt-
less all heard."

Tears pricked my eyes. I couldn't imagine Manning
without old Dr. E. Who would huddle in a corner with
me at trustee functions or the dreaded Headmaster's
Dinner? Who would defend me when angry parents
called about their kid's B+?

"Headmaster Stanton has invited me to advise the

search committee, and of course I encourage all of you to apply for the position, as Manning has always prided itself on promotion from within." He turned to the youngest member of our staff. "Mr. Diggler, you, of course, are far too inexperienced, so please save your energy for your classes."

Wayne, who felt that his degree from Georgetown trumped all the rest of ours put together, slumped in his seat and sulked. "Fine," he muttered. "Like I'm not headed for Exeter, anyway." Wayne often promised to leave when things didn't go his way, which was about twice a week.

"Complete your sentences, please, Mr. Diggler, until that happy day." Dr. Eckhart smiled at me, then gave another barking cough. It was no secret that I was a bit of a pet with our elderly chair, thanks to regular infusions of Disgustingly Rich Chocolate Brownies and my membership in Brother Against Brother.

"Actually, speaking of Phillips Exeter," began Paul, blushing slightly. He was a balding, brilliant man with glasses and a photographic memory for dates.

"Oh, dear," sighed Dr. Eckhart. "Are congratulations in order, Mr. Boccanio?"

Paul grinned. "I'm afraid so."

It wasn't that uncommon, prep schools poaching teachers, and Paul had a great background, especially given that he'd actually worked in the real world before becoming a teacher. Add to that his impressive education—Stanford/Yale, for heaven's sake—and it was no wonder that he'd been nabbed.

"Traitor," I murmured. I really liked Paul. He winked in response.

"That leaves my two esteemed female colleagues,"

Dr. Eckhart wheezed. "Very well, ladies, I'll expect you to submit your applications. Prepare your presentations in paper form, none of this computer nonsense, please, detailing your qualifications and ideas for improvements, such as they may be, to Manning's history department."

"Thank you for this opportunity, sir," Ava murmured, batting her eyelashes like Scarlett O'Hara.

"Very well," Dr. Eckhart said now, straightening his stained shirt. "The search begins next week, when we shall post the opening in the appropriate venues."

"You'll be terribly missed, Dr. Eckhart," I said huskily.

"Ah. Thank you, Grace."

"Oh, yes. It won't be the same without you," Ava hastily seconded.

"Indeed." He hauled himself out of the chair on his third attempt and shuffled out the door. I swallowed thickly.

"Good luck, girls," Paul said cheerfully. "If you'd like to have a Jell-O wrestling match, winner gets the job, I'd be happy to judge."

"We'll miss you so," I said, grinning.

"It's so unfair," whined Wayne. "When I was at Georgetown, I had dinner with C. Vann Woodward!"

"And I had sex with Ken Burns," I quipped, getting a snort from Paul. "Not to mention the fact that I was an extra in *Glory.*" That part was true. I'd been eleven years old, and Dad took me up to Sturbridge so we could be part of the crowd scene as the 54th Massachusetts Regiment left for the South. "It was the best moment of my childhood," I added. "Better even than when that guy from *MacGyver* opened the new mall."

"You're pathetic," Wayne mumbled.

"Grow up, little man," breathed Ava. "You don't have what it takes to run a department."

"And you do, Marilyn Monroe?" he snapped. "I'm too good for this place!"

"I'll be happy to accept your resignation when I'm chair," I said graciously. Wayne slammed his hands on the table, followed by some stomping, followed by his most welcomed departure.

"Well," Ava sighed. "Best of luck, Grace." She smiled insincerely.

"Right back at you," I said. I didn't really dislike Ava—prep schools were such tiny little worlds, so insulated from the rest of the world that coworkers became almost like family. But the idea of working under her, having her approve or disapprove my lesson plans, rankled. Watching her leave with Paul, her ass swinging vigorously under a too-tight skirt, I found that my teeth were firmly clenched.

For another minute or two, I sat alone in the conference room and allowed myself a tingling little daydream. That I got the chairmanship. Hired a fantastic new teacher to replace Paul. Revitalized the curriculum, raised the bar on grades so that an A in history from Manning meant something special. Increased the number of kids who took—and aced—the AP test. Got more money in the budget for field trips.

Well. I'd better get started on a presentation, just as Dr. Eckhart suggested. Tight sweaters and easy A's aside, Ava had a sharp mind and was much more of a political creature than I was, which would definitely help her. Now I wished I had chitchatted a bit more at last fall's faculty/trustee cocktail party, instead of hiding in the corner, sipping bad merlot and swapping obscure historical trivia with Dr. Eckhart and Paul.

I loved Manning. Loved the kids, adored working here on this beautiful campus, especially at this time of year, when the trees were coming into bloom and New England was at her finest. The leaves were just budding out, a haze of pale green, lush beds of daffodils edged the emerald lawns, the kids decorating the grass in their brightly colored clothing, laughing, flirting, napping.

I spied a lone figure walking across the quad. His head was down, and he seemed oblivious to the wonders of the day. Stuart. Margaret had emailed me to say that she'd be staying with me for a while, so I gathered things weren't better on that front.

Poor Stuart.

"WELCOME TO MEETING MR. *Right*," said our teacher.

"I can't believe we've been reduced to this," I whispered to Julian, who gave me a nervous glance.

"My name is *Lou*," our teacher continued plummily, "and I've been happily *married* for sixteen *wonderful* years!" I wondered if we were supposed to applaud. Lou beamed at us. "Every single *person* wants to find The *One*. The one who makes us feel *whole*. I know that my *Felicia*—" he paused again, then, when we failed to cheer, continued. "My Felicia does that for *me*."

Julian, Kiki and I sat in a classroom at the Blainesford Community Center. (Kiki's perfect man had dumped her on Wednesday after she'd called his cell fourteen times in one hour). There were two other women, as well as Lou, a good-looking man in his forties with a wedding ring about an inch wide, just so there'd be no misunderstandings. His rhythmic way of talking made him seem like a white suburban rapper. I shot Julian a condemning stare, which he pretended to ignore.

Lou smiled at us with all the sunny optimism of a Mormon preacher. "You're all *here* for a *reason,* and there's no *shame* in admitting it. You want a *man*…um, I am correct in assuming you also want a man, sir?" he asked, breaking off from his little song to look at Julian.

Julian, clad in a frilly pink shirt, shiny black pants and eyeliner, glanced at me. "Correct," he mumbled.

"That's *fine!* There's nothing *wrong* with that! These methods work for, er…anyway. So let's go *around* and just introduce *ourselves,* shall we? We're going to get pretty *intimate* here, so we might as well be *friends,*" Lou instructed merrily. "Who'd like to go first?"

"Hi, I'm Karen," said a woman. She was tall and attractive enough, dark hair, dressed in sweats, maybe around forty, forty-five. "I'm divorced, and you wouldn't believe the freaks I meet. The last guy I went out with asked if he could suck my toes. In the restaurant, okay? When I said no, he called me a frigid bitch and left. And I had to pay the bill."

"Wow," I murmured.

"And this was the best date I've had in a year, okay?"

"Not for *long,* Karen, not for *long,*" Lou announced with great confidence.

"I'm Michelle," said the next woman. "I'm forty-two and I've been on sixty-seven dates in the past four months. Sixty-seven first dates, that is. Want to know how many second dates I've been on? None. Because all those first dates were with idiots. My ex, now, he's already married again. To Bambi, a waitress from Hooters. She's twenty-three, okay? But I haven't met one decent guy, so I hear you, Karen."

Karen nodded in grim sympathy.

"Hi, I'm Kiki," said my friend. "And I'm a teacher in a local school, so is there a vow of confidentiality in this class? Like, no one's going to out me on the street, right?"

Lou laughed merrily. "There's no *shame* in taking this *class,* Kiki, but if you're more *comfortable,* I think we can all agree to keep our *enrollment* to *ourselves!* Please continue. What drove you to this *class?* Are you past *thirty?* Afraid you'll never meet Mr. *Right?*"

"No, I meet him all the time. It's just that I tend to… maybe…rush things a little?" She glanced at me, and I nodded in support. "I scare them away," she admitted.

Julian was next. "I'm Julian. Um…I'm…I've only had one boyfriend, about eight years ago. I'm just kind of…scared. It's not that I can't meet a man…I get asked out all the time." Of course he did, he looked like Johnny Depp, and already I could see the speculation in Karen's eyes… *Hmm, wonder if I could get this one to jump the fence…*

"So you're afraid to *commit,* afraid things won't work *out,* so you can't *fail* if you don't *try,* correct? All right!" Lou said, not waiting for an answer. "And you, miss? What's your name?"

I took a deep breath. "Hi. I'm Grace." I paused. "I'm currently pretending to have a boyfriend. My sister's dating my ex-fiancé, and to make everyone think I was fine with that, I told my family I've been seeing this fabulous guy. How's that for pathetic? And like you, Karen, I've been on some astonishingly bad dates, and I'm getting a little nervous, because my sister and Andrew are getting serious, and I'd really like to find someone. Soon. Very soon."

There was a moment's silence.

"I've made up boyfriends, too," Karen said, nodding her head slowly. "The best man I ever dated was all in my head."

"Thank you!" I exclaimed.

"I did it, too," Michelle said. "I even bought myself an engagement ring. It was beautiful. Exactly what I wanted. For three months, I wore that thing. Told everyone I knew I was getting married. It got so I was trying on dresses on the weekends. Sick, really. Looking back, though, it was one of my happier times."

"This brings up one of my *strategies*," Lou announced. "Men love women who are *taken*, so Grace, your little *ruse* isn't the worst idea in the *world*. It's a great way to get a man *intrigued*. A woman who is sought out by other *men* shows that she has a certain *appeal!*"

"Or a certain lack of *honesty*," I offered.

Lou guffawed heartily. Beside me, Julian winced. "I'm sorry," he whispered. "I thought this was worth a shot."

"It's only sixty bucks," I whispered back. "Plus we can get margaritas after."

"Let's get *going* with the class. Some of these *things* are going to sound a little *silly*, maybe, a little old-*fashioned*, but the name of the class is Meeting Mr. *Right*, and my methods *work*." He paused. "For you, Julian, I'm not so sure, but give it a try and let me know how it's going, okay?"

"Sure," Julian said glumly.

For the next hour, I bit my lip to keep from snorting and did not look at Julian, who was similarly struggling. Everything Lou said sounded silly, all right. Downright idiotic, sometimes. It was like we were stepping back in time to the 1950s or something. *Be feminine and proper.* An image of me clubbing Callahan O'Shea came to mind. So proper, so ladylike. *No swearing, smoking or drinking more than one small glass of wine, which should not be finished. Make the man feel strong. Make yourself as attractive as possible. Makeup at all times. Skirts. Be approachable. Smile. Laugh, but quietly. Flutter your eyelashes. Bake cookies often. Exude serenity and grace. Ask for a man's help and flatter his opinions.*

Gack.

"For example," Lou said, "you should go to the *hardware* store. There are lots of *men* at a *hardware* store. Pretend you don't *know* which *lightbulb* to choose. Ask for the man's *opinion*."

"Come on!" I blurted. "Lou, please! Who would want to date a woman who can't choose her own lightbulb?"

"I *know* what you're *thinking,* Grace," Lou sang out. "This is not *me.* But let's face it. *'You'* isn't working, or *'you'* wouldn't be in this *class.* Am I right?"

"He's got us there," Karen admitted with a sigh.

"THAT WAS FAIRLY *demeaning,*" I said, mimicking Lou's rolling speech pattern as we sat at Blackie's a half hour later, slurping down margaritas.

"At *least* it's *over,*" Julian said.

"Okay, stop, you two. He has a point. Listen to this," Kiki said, reading one of the handouts. "'When in a restaurant or bar, square your shoulders, look around carefully and say to yourself, *I am the most desirable woman here.* This will help you exude the confidence necessary to make men notice you.'" She frowned in concentration.

"I am the most desirable woman here," Julian said with mock earnestness.

"Problem is, you are," I answered, nudging him in the ribs.

"Too bad you aren't straight," Kiki said. "Then you and I could hook up."

"If I were straight, Grace and I would be married and have six kids by now," Julian said valiantly, putting his arm around me.

"Aw," I said, tilting my head against his shoulder. "Six, though? Seems like a lot."

"I'm gonna try it," Kiki said. "It's our homework, right? So here goes nothing. By the way, *I* am the most desirable woman here, and I'm exuding confidence." She smiled and stood up, then walked over to the bar, crossing her arms and leaning on the counter so her breasts swelled like ocean waves in a storm surge.

A man noticed immediately. He turned, smiled appreciatively and said something.

It was Callahan O'Shea.

My face flushed. "Crap," I hissed. God forbid that Kiki mention the class, for one, since Callahan would know I wasn't dating anyone, and for two...well...if Kiki was turning over a new leaf with men, shouldn't she know Callahan was recently released from prison? And should he know she tended to be a little wacko when it came to men?

"Maybe I should warn her," I murmured to Julian, not taking my eyes off the two of them. "That's my neighbor. The ex-con." I'd told Julian about Cal's past.

"Oh, I don't know. Embezzlement didn't sound so

bad," Julian said, sipping his piña colada. "And God, Grace. You didn't tell me he was so hot."

"Yeah, well…" My voice trailed off. Kiki said something, Callahan replied, and Kiki threw her head back, laughing. My eye twitched. "I…I'll be right back," I said.

Walking over to the bar, I touched Kiki's arm. "Kiki, can I talk to you a sec?" I said. I turned to my neighbor. "Hi, Callahan." I was already blushing. Wondered how my hair was. Dang it. I wanted to look pretty because Callahan O'Shea was looking at me.

"Hi, Grace," he said. He smiled…just a little, but enough. The man was just unfairly attractive.

"Oh, do you two know each other?" Kiki asked.

"Yes. We live next door to each other. He just moved in."

I hesitated, not sure I was doing the right thing. But Kiki had been my friend for years. Wouldn't I want to know if a guy I was interested in had just left prison? If she knew, she could make her own decision. Right?

Callahan was watching me. Dang it. I'd bet the farm that he knew what I was thinking.

"Kiki, Julian and I have a question," I finally said.

"Sure," she said uncertainly. I dragged her off a few paces, not looking at Cal. "Um, Kiki," I whispered, "that guy just got out of prison. For embezzling over a million dollars." I bit my lip.

She winced. "Oh, damn!" she said. "Isn't this typical? Leave it to me to pick the criminal. Crap. Of course he's gorgeous, too, right?"

"And he seems…well, he's…I just figured you should know."

"No, you're right, Grace. I have a hard enough time as it is, right? Don't need to date an ex-con."

With me trailing a step or two behind, Kiki went back to the bar and took her drink from the bartender. Callahan was watching us. His smile was gone. "Cal, nice meeting you," Kiki said politely.

His eyes flicked to me in a knowing glance, but he simply inclined his head in a courtly manner. "Have a good night," he said, turning back to the baseball game on the TV above the bar. Kiki and I hightailed it back to our table.

Our artichoke dip had arrived, and Julian was already eating, gazing across the restaurant with his soulful gypsy eyes at a good-looking blond guy who was returning his gaze with equal intensity.

"Go for it," I said, nodding toward the guy. "You're the most desirable woman here."

"He looks like that football player. Tom Brady," Julian murmured.

"How do you know who Tom Brady is?" I asked.

"Every gay man in America knows who Tom Brady is," he said.

"Maybe he *is* Tom Brady," Kiki said. "You never know. Go ahead, give it a shot. Make him feel manly and smart. Use those feminine wiles."

For a second, Julian seemed to consider it, then his shoulders dropped. "Nah," he said. "Why do I need a man when I have you two beautiful girls?"

For the rest of the night, I shot little glances at Callahan O'Shea's back as he ate a hamburger and watched the baseball game. He did not look back.

CHAPTER TWELVE

ON SATURDAY MORNING, I WAS once again wrenched out of bed by Angus's hysteria and staggered down the stairs to open the door. This time, it was Margaret, a suitcase in tow, a glower on her face.

"I'm here," she said. "Got any coffee?"

"Sure, sure, let me put it on," I answered, still squinting. I'd been up late last night watching all two hundred and twenty-nine smarmily glorious minutes of *Gods and Generals,* weeping copiously as General Jackson barked out his last delirious orders to First Virginia. I think it's fair to say I had a Confederate hangover, so Margaret in all her grouchy glory, first thing in the morning…ouch. I followed her as she stomped into the kitchen.

"So what happened?" I asked as I measured out coffee grounds.

"Here's the thing, Grace," Margaret said in her master and commander voice. "Don't marry a man you love like a brother, okay?"

"Brothers, bad. Got it."

"I'm serious, smart-ass." She bent over and scooped up Angus, who was chewing on her shoe. "I said to Stuart last night, 'How come we never have sex on the kitchen table?' And you know what he said?" Margaret glared at me accusingly.

"What?" I asked, sitting down at the table with her.

She lowered her voice to imitate her husband. "'I'm not sure that's sanitary.' Can you fucking believe that? How many men would turn down kitchen-table sex? You want to know when Stuart and I do it?"

"No, I absolutely do not," I answered.

"Monday, Wednesday, Friday and Saturday," she snapped.

"Wow," I said. "That sounds pretty good to—"

"It's in his daily planner. He puts a little star in the nine o'clock slot to remind him. Intercourse with Wife. Check."

"But still, it's nice that he—"

"And that's the whole problem, Grace. Not enough passion. So I'm here."

"At the home of passion," I murmured.

"Well, I can't just stay there! Maybe he'll notice me a little more now! Maybe not! I don't really care at this point. I'm thirty-four years old, Grace. I want to have sex on the kitchen table! Is that so wrong?"

"I know I wouldn't say so," came a voice. We both turned. Callahan O'Shea stood in the kitchen doorway. Angus exploded into his usual sound and fury, struggling to get out of Margaret's arms. "I knocked," Cal said, grinning. "Hi, I'm Callahan. The good-looking neighbor."

Margaret's expression morphed from furious to rapacious, a lion staring at a three-legged baby zebra. "Hi, Callahan the good-looking neighbor," she said in a sultry voice. "I'm Margaret the horny sister."

"The horny *married* sister," I inserted. "Margaret, meet Callahan O'Shea. Cal, my sister, pretty happily married for lo these many years, currently suffering from what I believe is called the seven-year itch."

"Hey, it has been seven years, hasn't it?" Margaret snapped out of her lustful daze. "So you're the embezzler, huh?"

"That's right." Cal inclined his head, then turned to me. "Not fit for decent company, right, Grace?"

My face went nuclear. Ah, yes. Kiki and the warning. Callahan's expression was decidedly cold.

"Grace, your windows came yesterday afternoon. If you want, I can get started today."

Closing my eyes, I tried to imagine this guy stealing my Victorian Santa collection. "Sure."

"How about if I only work when you're around?" he suggested. "That way you can keep an eye on your checkbook and family heirlooms, maybe pat me down before I go."

"Or I can do that," Margaret volunteered.

"Very funny," I said. "Install the windows. Will it take long?"

"Three days. Maybe five, depending on how the old ones come out. I might need a hand with that, if your boyfriend's around today."

Gosh. Almost forgot about that pesky boyfriend. Margaret looked at me sharply. "Mmm. He's working," I said, shooting her a silent warning.

"He doesn't seem to come around much, from what I've noticed." Cal folded his big arms and raised an eyebrow.

"Well, he's very busy," I said.

"What does he do again?" Callahan asked.

"He's a…" I really wished I'd picked something less sappy. "A pediatric surgeon," I said.

"So noble," Margaret murmured, smiling into her coffee cup.

Callahan's hair was sticking up on one side, and my fingers wondered what it would feel like to run through that silky, misbehaving, adorable mess. I told my fingers to stop daydreaming.

"So, sure, okay, you can start today, Cal," I said. "Would you like some coffee first?"

"No. Thank you," he said. So much for my peace offering. "Where do you want me to start? And do you want to make a sweep of the room first?"

"Okay, listen. I'm sorry I told my friend you just got out of the slammer. But you *are* an admitted criminal, so…"

"So?" he said.

I sighed. "So you can start in here, I guess."

"The kitchen it is." He turned and walked down the hall toward the front door.

When he was safely outside, presumably to get my first window, Margaret leaned forward. "Are you guys fighting? And why did you tell him you have a boyfriend?" she asked. "He's gorgeous. I'd do him in a New York minute."

"We're not fighting! We hardly know each other. And yes, he's gorgeous, but that's beside the point."

"Why? I thought you were looking to get laid."

"Shh! Lower your voice. I told him I was seeing someone."

"Why'd you tell him that?" Margaret took a sip of her coffee.

I sighed. "Natalie was over last weekend, asking all these questions about Wyatt…" Margaret, the least fanciful creature on earth, never did understand the comfort of my imaginary boyfriends. "Anyway. I don't think it's a bad thing for him to think there's a man who stops by occasionally. Just in case he's casing my joint."

"Wouldn't mind if he cased mine." I gave her a dirty look. "Right. Well. He's hot. Wonder if he's interested in an affair."

"Margaret!"

"Relax. Just kidding."

"Margs, speaking of dates, weren't you going to fix me up with the blacksmith? I'm getting a little desperate here."

"Right, right. Metalsmith. Lester. Weird. I'll call him."

"Great," I muttered. "I can't wait."

She took another sip of coffee. "Got anything to eat? I'm starving. Oh, and I brought some dirty laundry, hope that's all right. I just had to get out of the house. And if Stuart calls, I don't want to talk to him, okay?"

"Of course. Anything else, Majesty?"

"Can you pick up some skim milk? This half-and-half will kill me." Margaret was one of those people who ate nonfat cheese and didn't know she was missing anything.

Callahan came into the kitchen carrying a new window and leaned it against the wall.

"Are you married, good-looking neighbor?" Margs asked.

"Nope," came his answer. "Is that a proposal?"

Margaret grinned wickedly. "Maybe," she murmured.

"Margaret! Leave him alone."

"How much time did you actually serve, Al Capone?" Margs asked. "God, his ass in those jeans," she whispered to me, not taking her eyes off his backside.

"Stop it," I whispered back.

"Nineteen months," Cal answered. "And thanks." He winked at Margaret. My uterus twitched in response.

"Nineteen months on three-to-five?" Margs asked.

"Yup. You've done your homework," he said, smiling at my sister. My beautiful sister. Beautiful, red-haired, smart as a whip, razor-witted sister in a high-income bracket and a size four to boot.

"Well, Grace asked me to check you out, being that you're a threat to her security."

"Shut it, Margaret," I said, blushing.

"Any other questions?" Cal asked mildly.

"Have you had a woman since you got out?" Margaret asked, studying her fingernails.

"God's nightgown!" I yelped.

"You mean did I swing by the local whorehouse on my way into town?" Cal asked.

"Correct," Margaret affirmed, ignoring my offended squeaks.

"No. No women."

"Wow. How about in the big house? Any girl-friends?" she asked. I closed my eyes.

Callahan, however, laughed. "It wasn't that kind of prison."

"You must be so lonely," Margaret said, smiling wickedly at Cal's back.

"Are you done interrogating him?" I snapped. "He has work to do, Margaret."

"Party pooper," Margaret said. "But you're right. And I have to go into the office. I'm a lawyer, Callahan, did Grace tell you? Criminal defense. Would you like my card?"

"I'm completely reformed," he said with a grin that promised all sorts of illicit behavior.

"I know people in the parole office. Very well, in fact. I'll be watching."

"You do that," he answered.

"I'll help you get settled," I offered, hauling Margaret out of her chair and grabbing her suitcase. "You can't have an affair with him," I hissed once we were upstairs. "You will not cheat on Stuart. He's wonderful, Margaret. And he's heartbroken. I saw him at school the other day, and he looked like a kicked puppy."

"Good. At least he's noticing me now."

"Oh, for God's sake. You're so spoiled."

"I have to go to the office," she said, ignoring my last comment. "I'll see you for dinner, okay? Feel like cooking?"

"Oh." I took a deep breath. "I won't be here."

"Why? Date with Wyatt?" she asked, raising a silken eyebrow.

I reached up to smooth my difficult hair. "Um, no. Well, yes. We're going to Nat's for dinner. Double date."

"Holy Mary the Eternal Virgin, Grace," my sister muttered.

"I know, I know. Wyatt will end up in emergency surgery, bless his talented heart."

"You're an idiot. Hey, thanks for letting me crash here," Margs said at the door to the guest room, vaguely remembering that she should be grateful.

"You're welcome," I said. "Leave Callahan alone."

For the next few minutes, I found things to do upstairs, away from my neighbor. Took a shower. As the warm water streamed over me, I wondered what would happen if Callahan O'Shea walked in. Tugged his shirt over his head, unbuckled his belt, slid out of those faded jeans and stepped in here with me, enfolding me in his brawny arms, his mouth hot and demanding, his— I blinked hard, turned the water to cold and finished up.

Margaret headed into her office, calling out a cheerful goodbye to Callahan and me, seeming rather depressingly chipper about leaving her husband. I wrote up a quiz on the Reconstruction for my seniors, using my laptop and not the larger computer downstairs. Corrected essays from my sophomores on the FDR administration. Downstairs, the whine of the saw and thump of the hammer and the offhanded, tuneless whistle of Callahan O'Shea blended into a pleasant cacophony.

Angus, though he still growled occasionally, gave up trying to tunnel under my bedroom door and lay on his back in a puddle of sunlight, his crooked bottom teeth showing most adorably. I concentrated on my students' work, writing notes in the margins, comments at the end, praising them lavishly for moments of clarity, pointing out areas that could've used some work.

I went downstairs a while later. Four of the eight downstairs windows were already in. Cal glanced in my direction. "I don't think I'll have to replace those sills. If the windows upstairs are as easy as the ones downstairs, I'll be done Monday or Tuesday."

"Oh. Okay," I said. "They look great."

"Glad you like them."

He looked at me, unsmiling, unmoving. I looked back. And looked. And looked some more. His was a rugged face, and yes, handsome, but it was his eyes that got me. Callahan O'Shea had a story in those eyes.

The air seemed to thicken between us, and I could feel my face—and other parts—growing warm.

"I'd better get back to work," he said, and, turning his back on me, he did just that.

CHAPTER THIRTEEN

THE SECOND I OPENED THE DOOR, I knew that Natalie and Andrew were living together. Natalie's apartment had his smell, that baby shampoo sweetness, and it hit me in a slap of undeniable recognition. "Hello!" I said, hugging my sister, stroking her sleek hair.

"Hi! Oh, it's so good to see you!" Nat hugged me tight, then pulled back. "Where's Wyatt?"

"Hey, Grace!" Andrew called from the kitchen.

My stomach clenched. Andrew at Natalie's. So cozy.

"Hi, Andrew," I called back. "Wyatt got stuck at the hospital, so he'll be a little late." My voice was smooth and controlled. Bully for me.

"But he is coming?" Nat said, her brows puckering in concern.

"Oh, sure. He'll just be a while yet."

"I made this fabulous cream tart for dessert." Nat grinned. "Definitely wanted to make a good impression, you know?"

Natalie's apartment was in the Ninth Square section of New Haven, a rescued part of the city not far from the downtown firm where she worked. I'd been here, of course, helped her move in, gave her that iron horse statue for a housewarming gift. But things were different now. How long had Nat and Andrew been together? A month? Six weeks? Yet already his things were scattered here and there…a jacket on the coatrack, his running shoes by the door, the *New York Law Journal* by the fireplace. If he wasn't living here, he was staying over. A lot.

"Hey, there," Andrew said, coming out of the kitchen. He gave me a quick hug, and I could feel his familiar sharp angles. Angles that felt repugnant today.

"Hi," I said, stretching the old mouth in a grin. "How are you?"

"Great! How about a drink? A vodka gimlet? Appletini? White Russian?" Andrew's merry green eyes smiled behind his glasses. He'd always been proud of having bartended his way through law school.

"I'd love some wine," I said, just to deny him the exhibitionistic pleasure of making me a cocktail.

"White or red? We have a nice cabernet sauvignon open."

"White, please," I answered. My smile felt tight. "Wyatt likes cabernet, though."

At this moment, I was incredibly grateful to young Wyatt Dunn, M.D. This night would've been awful without him, even if he didn't exist in the corporeal world. I drifted over to the couch, Natalie chattering away about how she couldn't find tilapia anywhere today and had to go to Fair Haven to a little fish market down by the Quinnipiac River. I had to stifle a sigh at the picture of Natalie, a study of elegant beauty, riding her bike down to the Italian market, where, no doubt, the owner fussed over her and threw in a few biscotti, since she was so pretty. Natalie with the perfect hair and fabulous job. Natalie with the lovely apartment and Natalie with the beautiful furniture. Natalie with my ex-fiancé, telling me how she was dying to meet my imaginary beau.

I didn't relish the fact that I was lying to Natalie—and my parents, and grandmother and even Callahan O'Shea—but it was a far sight better than being Poor Grace, tossed over for her sister. Morally wrong to lie, but hey! If lying was ever justified, I'd have to say it was now.

For a brief second, another scenario flashed across the old brain cells. Callahan O'Shea sitting by my side, rolling his eyes at how Andrew was even now showing off in the kitchen, chopping parsley like a manic spider monkey. That Cal would sling his big, muscular arm around my shoulder and mutter, "I can't believe you were engaged to that scrawny jerk."

Right. That would happen, and then I'd win the Lotto and discover I was the love child of Margaret Mitchell and Clark Gable.

To distract myself, I looked around Nat's living room. My gaze stopped abruptly on the mantel. "I remember this," I said, my voice a tad tight. "Andrew, this is the clock I gave you, isn't it? Wow!"

And it was. A lovely, whiskey-colored mantel clock with a buttery face and elaborately detailed numbers, a brass key for winding it. I found it in an antiques shop in Litchfield and gave it to Andrew for his thirtieth birthday, two years ago. I planned the whole dang party, good little fiancée that I was. A picnic in the field along the Farmington. His work friends—*our* friends, back then—as well as Ava, Paul, Kiki and Dr. Eckhart, Margaret and Stuart, Julian, Mom and Dad, and Andrew's snooty parents, who looked vaguely startled at the idea of eating on a public picnic table. What a great day that had been. Of course, that was back when he still loved me. Before he met my sister.

"Oh. Yeah. I love that clock," he said awkwardly, handing me my wine.

"Good, since it cost the earth," I announced with a stab of crass pleasure. "One of a kind."

"And it's…it's gorgeous," Andrew mumbled.

I know it is, dopey. "So. You two are very cozy. Are you living here now, Andrew?" I asked, and my voice was just a trifle loud.

"Well, uh…not…I still have a few months on my lease. So, no, not really." He exchanged a quick, nervous glance with Natalie.

"Mmm-hmm. But obviously, since your things are migrating here…" I took a healthy sip of my chardonnay.

Neither of them said anything. I continued, making sure my tone was pleasant. "That's nice. Saves on rent, too. Very logical." And *fast.* But of course, they were in love. Who wouldn't be in love with Natalie, the fair flower of our family? Nat was younger. Blond, blue-eyed. Taller. Prettier. Smarter. Man, I wished Wyatt Dunn was real! Wished that Callahan O'Shea was here! Anything other than this echoing sense of rejection that just wouldn't fade away. I unclenched my jaw and took a seat next to my sister and studied her. "God, we just do not look alike, do we?" I said.

"Oh, I think we do!" she exclaimed earnestly. "Except for the hair color. Grace, do you remember when I was in high school and got that perm? And then colored my hair brown?" She laughed and reached out to touch my knee. "I was crushed when it didn't come out like yours."

And there it was. I couldn't be mad at Natalie. It was almost like I wasn't *allowed* to be mad at Natalie, ever. It wasn't fair, and it was completely true. I remembered the day she was referring to. She'd permed it, all right, permed that lovely, cool hair, then dyed it a flat, ugly brown. She was fourteen at the time, and had cried in her room as the chemical curls failed to produce the desired results. A week later, her hair was straight again, and she became the only brunette in high school with blond roots.

She'd wanted to be like me. She thought we looked alike—me, three inches shorter, fifteen pounds heavier, the accursed hair, the unremarkable gray eyes.

"There's definitely a resemblance," Andrew said. *Piss off, buddy,* I thought. *Here I am taking a class on how to meet a husband, dredging up men on the internet, lusting after a convict, and you have this* pearl, *you undeserving jerk.* Well. I guess the anger wasn't quite so gone after all. Not the anger caused by Andrew, that was.

He seemed to catch that thought. "I better check the risotto. I don't think it's going to thicken without some serious prayer." With that, he scurried off into the kitchen like a frightened crab.

"Grace, is everything okay?" Natalie asked softly.

I took a breath. "Oh, sure." I paused. "Well, Wyatt and I had a little fight."

"Oh, no!"

I closed my eyes. I really was becoming a masterful liar. "Yeah. Well, he's so devoted to the kids, you know?" *Yes, Grace, such a prick, your pediatric surgeon.* "I mean, he's wonderful. I'm crazy about him. But I hardly see him."

"I guess it's an occupational hazard," Natalie murmured, her eyes soft with sympathy.

"Yeah."

"But he makes up for it, I hope?" Nat asked, and I answered that yes, indeed he did. Breakfast in bed... strawberries, and the waffles were a little burnt, it was so cute, he was like a kid...the flowers he sent me (I had actually sent myself some flowers). The way he listened...loved learning about the classes I was teaching. The beautiful scarf he bought me last weekend (in fact, I did have a beautiful new scarf, except that I'd bought it for myself that day Julian and I went shopping).

"Oh, hey, did I tell you I'm up for chairmanship of the history department?" I said, seizing on a change of subject.

"Oh, Grace, that's wonderful!" my sister cried. "You would do so much for that place! It would totally come alive if you were in charge."

Then, on cue, my cell phone rang. I stood up, reached into my pocket, withdrew my phone and flipped it open. "It's Wyatt," I said, smiling at Nat.

"Okay! I'll give you a little privacy." She started to get up.

"No, stay!" I commanded, then turned to the phone. After all, she needed to hear this conversation...my end, anyway. "Hi, honey," I said.

"Hi, baby," said Julian. "I'm thinking of changing my name."

"Oh, no! Is he okay?" I asked, remembering to frown in concern, as I'd practiced in the rearview mirror on the way here.

"Something more manly, you know? Like Will or Jack. Spike. What do you think?"

"I think he's lucky you were his doctor," I answered firmly, smiling at my sister.

"Maybe that's too butch, though. Maybe Mike. Or Mack. Well, I probably won't. My mother would kill me."

"No, no, that's fine, honey! I understand. Of course she will! No, they both know what you do for a living! It's not like you're a…" I paused. "A carpenter or something. A mechanic. You're saving lives!"

"Down, girl," Julian coached.

"You're right," I said.

"What are you having for dinner?" my friend asked.

"Risotto, asparagus and tilapia. Some delicious tart my sister slaved over."

"I'll send some back with Grace!" Natalie called.

"Make sure I get that tart," Julian said. "I've earned it. Shall we chat some more? Want me to propose?"

"No, no, honey, that's fine. You have a great night," I said.

"Love you," Julian said. "Now say it back to me."

"Oh, um, same here." My face grew hot—I was not about to declare my love for an imaginary boyfriend. Even I wouldn't go that far. Then I flipped the phone closed and sighed. "Well, he can't make it. The surgery was more complicated than he thought, and he wants to stay close until the little guy's out of the woods."

"Ooh," Natalie sighed, her face morphing into something like adoration. "Oh, Grace, I'm so sorry he can't come, but God, he sounds so wonderful!"

"He is," I said. "He really is."

After dinner, Natalie walked me to my spot in the parking garage. "Well, I'm so sorry I couldn't meet

Wyatt," she said. "But it was great to have you here." Her voice echoed in the vast cement chamber.

"Thanks," I said, unlocking the car. I put the Tupperware containing Julian's generous slab of tart on the backseat and turned back to my sister. "So things are really serious with you and Andrew?"

She hesitated. "Yes. I hope that's okay with you."

"Well, I didn't want you to have a fling, Nat," I replied a bit sharply. "I mean, *that* would've hurt, you know? I just... I'm glad. This is good."

"Are you sure?"

"Yes. I am."

She smiled, that serene, blissful smile of hers. "Thanks. You know, I have to thank Wyatt when I do finally meet him. To tell you the truth, I think I would've broken up with Andrew if you hadn't been seeing someone. It just felt too wrong, you know?"

"Mmm," I said. "Well. I...I should go. Bye, Nattie. Thanks for a lovely dinner."

Rain came down in sheets as I drove home, my little car's wipers valiantly battling for visibility. It was a vicious night, colder than normal, windy and wild, much like the night my tire blew out. The night I first met Wyatt Dunn. I snorted at the thought.

I imagined, for one deeply satisfying second, that I'd kept my mouth shut in the bathroom at Kitty's wedding. That I'd let the guilt work its magic and admitted, yes, it *was* wrong, a woman shouldn't date a man who was once promised to her sister. Andrew would have been out of my life forever, and I wouldn't have to see his eyes light on Natalie's face with that expression of gratitude and wonder—an expression I can tell you quite honestly I never saw before. No, when Andrew had looked at me, there was affection, humor, respect and comfort. All good things, but no kablammy. I had loved him. He hadn't loved me back the same way.

Despite Margaret's sleeping presence in the guest room when I came home, and though Angus did his best to tell me that I was the most wonderful creature on God's green earth, the house felt empty. If only I did have that nice doctor boyfriend to call. If only he was on his way home to me now. I'd hand him a glass of wine and rub his shoulders, and he'd smile up gratefully. Maybe we'd cuddle on the couch there, then head up to bed. Angus wouldn't so much as nip Wyatt Dunn, because Angus, in this fantasy anyway, was an excellent judge of character and just adored Wyatt.

I brushed my teeth and washed my face and grimaced over my hair, then found myself wondering if the attic needed, well, a little visit. Yes. Sure it did. It was quite wet out, after all, though the hard rain had stopped around Hartford and it was just kind of foggy and damp now. Surely Callahan O'Shea wouldn't be out on his roof. This was simple homeownership...perhaps a window was open up there. It might rain again later. You never knew.

Callahan O'Shea *was* out there. *Good for you, Cal,* I thought. Not the type to let a little New England weather stop him from doing his thing.

He must've missed the outdoors in prison. Granted, he'd been in a Club Fed, apparently, but when I pictured him, he was in an orange jumpsuit or black-and-white stripes, in a cell with bars and a metal cot. (There just weren't enough movies featuring Club Feds, and so the one in my imagination was identical to the prison in *The Shawshank Redemption*.)

For one second, I imagined what it would be like to be down there with Callahan O'Shea, his arm around me, my head on his shoulder, and the image was so powerful that I could feel the thud of his heartbeat under my hand, his fingers playing in my hair. Occasionally, one of us would murmur something to the other, but mostly, we'd just be still.

"Don't waste your time," I whispered sagely to myself. "Even without the prison record, he's not your type." *Besides,* my irritating little voice told me, *he doesn't even like you.* Add to that the roiling discomfort I felt around the large, muscular man next door… no. I wanted comfort, security, stability. Not bristling tension and sex appeal. No matter how good it looked from here.

CHAPTER FOURTEEN

"Grace?"

Angus growled fiercely then bounded off to attack a moth. I looked up from the pansies I was potting on the back patio. It was Sunday morning, and Callahan O'Shea was back, standing in the kitchen at the sliding glass door. He'd gotten right to work this morning; Margaret was off for a run (she ran marathons, so there was no telling when she'd be back) so apparently Cal had no reason to hang around and flirt.

"I need to move the bookcase in front of the window. Do you want to move your little…things?"

"Sure," I said, getting up and brushing off my hands.

My "things" were mostly DVDs and collectibles. Wordlessly, I placed the items on the couch…a tobacco tin from the 1880s, a tiny cannon, a porcelain figure of Scarlett O'Hara in her green velvet curtain dress and a framed Confederate dollar.

"I guess you like the Civil War," he commented as he glanced at the movie cases. *Glory, Cold Mountain, The Red Badge of Courage, Shenandoah, North and South, The Outlaw Josey Wales, Gods and Generals, Gettysburg,* and the Ken Burns documentary, special edition DVD, a Christmas gift from Natalie.

"I'm a history teacher," I said.

"Right. That explains it," he said, looking more

closely at the movies. "*Gone with the Wind*'s never been opened. You have more than one copy?"

"Oh, that. My mom gave this to me, but I always thought I should see it on the big screen first, you know? Give the movie its due."

"So you've never seen it?"

"No. I've read the book fourteen times, though. Have you?"

"I've seen the movie." He smiled a little.

"On the big screen?"

"Nope. On TV."

"That doesn't count," I said.

"I see." He smiled a little, and my stomach tightened. We moved the bookcase. He picked up his saw and waited for me to move out of the way. I didn't.

"So, Cal...why did you embezzle a million dollars?" I asked.

"One-point-six million," he said, plugging the saw in. "Why does anyone steal anything?"

"I don't know," I answered. "Why did you?"

He looked at me with those dark blue eyes, weighing his answer. I waited, too. There was something in his face that told a story, and I wanted to hear it. He was sizing me up, wondering what to tell me, how to say it. I waited.

"Hi, honey, I'm home!" The front door banged open. Margaret stood there, sweaty and flushed and gorgeous. "Bad news, campers. Mom's on her way. I saw her car at Lala's Bakery. Hurry. I almost set a world record getting here before she did."

My sister and I bolted for the cellar. "Callahan, give us some help!" Margs ordered.

"What's wrong?" Cal asked, following us. At the

foot of the cellar stairs, he stumbled to a halt. "Oh, my God." He looked slowly around.

My cellar was the sculpture repository. Mom, alas, was generous with her art, and so my cellar was littered with glass girl-parts.

"I love it here," Callahan said distantly.

"Hush, you. Grab some sculptures and get upstairs. No time for chitchat," Margaret ordered. "Our mom will have a fit if she knows Grace hides her stuff. I speak from experience." Grabbing *The Home of Life* (a uterus) and *Nest #12* (ovary), my sister ran lightly back upstairs.

"Do you rent this place out?" Callahan asked.

"Stop," I said, unable to suppress a grin. "Just bring that upstairs and put it on a shelf or something. Make it look like it belongs." I shoved *Breast in Blue* into his hands. It was heavy—I should've warned him, and for a second, he bobbled the breast, and I grabbed for it, and so did he, and the end result was that we both were sort of holding it, our hands overlapping as we both supported the sculpture. I looked up into his eyes, and he smiled.

Kablammy.

My knees practically buckled. He smelled like wood and soap and coffee, and his hands were big and warm, and God, the way those blue eyes slanted down, the heat from his body beckoning me to lean in over *Breast in Blue* and just…you know…just… Really, who cared if he was an ex-con? Stealing, shmealing. Though I was distantly aware that I should probably change my expression from *unadulterated lust* to something more along the lines of *cheerful neighbor,* I was paralyzed.

A car horn sounded. Upstairs, Angus burst into a

tinny thunderstorm of barking, hurling his body against the front door, from the thumping sound of it.

"Hurry up down there!" Margaret barked. "You know what she's like!"

The spell was broken. Cal took the sculpture, grabbed another one and went upstairs. I did the same, still blushing.

I shoved *Hidden Treasure* onto the bookcase and lay *Portal in Green* on the coffee table, where it splayed most obscenely.

"Hello, there!" Mom called from the porch. "Angus, down. Down. Quiet, honey. No. Stop. Quiet, dear. No barking."

I picked up my dog and opened the door, my heart still thumping. "Hi, Mom! What brings you here?"

"I have pastries!" she chirped. "Hello, Angus! Who's a sweet baby? Hi, Margaret, honey. Stuart said we'd find you here. And oh, hello. Who are you?"

I glanced back. Cal stood in the kitchen doorway. "Mom, this is my neighbor, Callahan O'Shea. Callahan, my mother, the renowned sculptor, Nancy Emerson."

"A pleasure. I'm a big fan of your work." Cal shook my mother's hand, and Mom turned a questioning gaze on me.

"Dad hired him to put in some new windows," I explained.

"I see," said Mom suspiciously.

"I need to run next door and then head to the hardware store, Grace. Anything you need?" Cal said, turning to me.

I need to be kissed. "Um, nope. Not that I can think of," I said, blushing yet again.

"See you later, then. Nice meeting you, Mrs. Emerson." The three of us watched as he went out the front door.

Mom snapped out of it first. "Well. Margaret, we need to talk. Come on, girls. Let's sit in the kitchen. Oh, Grace, this shouldn't go here! It's not funny. This is serious artwork, honey."

Callahan O'Shea had placed *Breast in Blue* in my fruit bowl amid the oranges and pears. I grinned. Margaret snorted with laughter and opened the pastry bag. "Oh, goody. Poppy seed rolls. Want one, Grace?"

"Sit, girls. Margaret. What's this about you leaving Stuart, for heaven's sake?"

I sighed. Mom wasn't here to see me. I was her trouble-free daughter. Growing up, Margaret had been (and proudly still was) the drama queen, full of adolescent rebellion, collegiate certainty, academic excellence and a gift for confrontation. Natalie, of course, was the golden one from the moment of her birth and since her brush with death, her every feat had been viewed as miraculous.

So far, the only exceptional thing that had happened to me was my breakup with Andrew. Sure, my parents loved me, though they viewed becoming a teacher as a bit of an easy route. ("Those who can, do," Dad had said when I announced I'd forgo law school and get a master's in American History with the hope of becoming a teacher. "And those who can't, teach.") My summers off were treated as an affront to those who "really worked." The fact that I slaved endlessly during the school year—tutoring and correcting and designing lesson plans, staying well past school hours to meet with students in my office, coaching the debate team, going to school events, chaperoning dances and field trips, boning up on new developments in teaching and handling the sensitive parents, all of whom expected their children to excel in every way—was viewed as irrelevant when compared with all of my delicious vacation time.

Mom sat back in her chair and eyed her eldest child. "So? Spit it out, Margaret!"

"I haven't left him completely," Margaret said, taking a huge bite of pastry. "I'm just…lurking here."

"Well, it's ridiculous," Mom huffed. "Your father and I certainly have our problems. You don't see me running off to Aunt Mavis's house, do you?"

"That's because Aunt Mavis is such a pain in the ass," Margaret countered. "Grace is barely even half of the pain that Mavis is, right, Gracie?"

"Oh, thanks, Margs. And let me say what a privilege it was to see your dirty clothes scattered all over my guest room this morning. Shall I do your laundry for you, Majesty?"

"Well, since you don't have a real job, sure," she said.

"Real job? It's better than getting a bunch of drug dealers—"

"Girls, enough. Are you really leaving Stuart?" Mom asked.

Margaret closed her eyes. "I don't know," she said.

"Well, I think that's ridiculous. You married him, Margaret. You don't just leave. You stay and work things out till you're happy again."

"Like you and Dad?" Margaret suggested. "Kill me now, then. Grace, would you do the honors?"

"Your father and I are perfectly…" Her voice trailed off, and she studied her coffee cup as if a light was abruptly dawning.

"Maybe you should move in with Grace, too," Margaret suggested, raising an eyebrow.

"Okay, very funny. No. You can't, Mom." I shot Margs a threatening look. "Seriously, Mom," I said slowly. "You and Dad love each other, right? You just like to bicker."

"Oh, Grace," she sighed. "What's love got to do with it?"

"Thank you, Tina Turner," Margaret quipped.

"I'm hoping love has a lot to do with it," I protested.

Mom sighed. "Who knows what love is?" She waved her hand dismissively.

"Love is a battlefield," Margaret murmured.

"All you need is love," I countered.

"Love stinks," she returned.

"Shut up, Margs," I said. "Mom? You were saying?"

She sighed. "You get so used to someone…I don't know. Some days, I want to kill your father with a dull knife. He's a boring old tax attorney, for heaven's sake. His idea of fun is to lay down and play dead at one of those stupid Civil War battles."

"Hey. I love those stupid battles," I interjected, but she ignored me.

"But I don't just walk away, either, Margaret. We did, after all, vow to love and cherish each other, even if it kills us."

"Gosh. That's beautiful," Margaret said.

"But my word, he gets on my nerves, making fun of my art! What does *he* do? Runs around in dress-up clothes, firing guns. *I* create. *I* celebrate the female form. *I* am capable of expressing myself by more than grunts and sarcasm. *I*—"

"More coffee, Mom?" Margs asked.

"No. I have to go." Still, she remained in her chair.

"Mom," I asked cautiously, "why *do* you, uh, celebrate the female form, as you put it? How did that get started?" Margaret gave me a dark look, but I was a little curious. I was in graduate school when Mom discovered herself, as it were.

She smiled. "The truth is, it was an accident. I was trying to make one of those little glass balls that hang in the window or on a Christmas tree, you know? And I was having trouble tying off the end, and your father came in and said it looked like a nipple. So I told him it was, and he turned absolutely purple and I thought, why not? If your father had that kind of a reaction to it, what would someone else think? So I took it down to Chimera, and they loved it."

"Mmm," I murmured. "What's not to love?"

"I mean it, Grace. The *Hartford Courant* called me a postmodern feminist with the aesthetic appeal of Mapplethorpe and O'Keeffe on acid."

"All from a screwed up Christmas ornament," Margaret interjected.

"The first one was accidental, Margaret. The rest are a celebration of the physiological miracle that is Woman," Mom pronounced. "I love what I do, even if you girls are too Puritanical to properly appreciate my art. I have a new career and people admire me. And if it tortures your father, that's just gravy."

"Yes," Margs said. "Why not torture Dad? He's only given you everything."

"Well, Margaret, dear, I'd counter that by saying he's the one who got everything, and you of all people should appreciate my position. I became wallpaper, girls. He was more than happy to come home, be served a martini and a dinner I slaved over for hours in a house that was immaculate with children who were smart, well-behaved and gorgeous, then pop into bed for some rowdy sex."

Margaret and I recoiled in identical horror.

Mom turned a hard eye on Margaret. "He was completely spoiled, and I was invisible. So if I'm torturing him, Margaret, darling firstborn of my loins, you of all people might say, 'Well done, Mother.' Because at least he's noticing me now, and I didn't even have to go running to my sister's house."

"Youch," Margaret said. "I'm bleeding, Grace." Oddly, she was smiling.

"Please stop fighting, you two," I said. "Mom, we're very proud of you. You're, um, a visionary. Really."

"Thank you, dear," Mom said, standing up. "Well, I have to run now. I'm giving a talk at the library on my art and inspiration."

"Adults only, I'm guessing," Margaret murmured, taking Angus from my lap to make kissing faces at him.

Mom sighed and looked at the ceiling. "Grace, you have cobwebs up there. And don't shlunch, honey. Walk me to the car, all right?"

I obeyed, leaving Margaret, who was hand-feeding Angus bits of her roll.

"Grace," my mother said, "who was that man who was here?"

"Callahan?" I asked. She nodded. "My neighbor. Like I told you."

"Well. Don't go screwing up a good thing by falling for a manual laborer, dear."

"God, Mom!" I yelped. "You don't even know him! He's very nice."

"I'm just pointing out that you have a lovely thing going with that nice doctor, don't you?"

"I'm not going to date Callahan, Mother," I said tersely. "He's just some guy Dad hired."

Ah, shit. There he was, getting into his truck. He heard, of course. Judging from his expression, he heard the "just some guy Dad hired," not the "very nice" bit.

"Well, fine," Mom said in a quieter voice. "It's just that ever since Andrew and you broke up, you've been wandering around like a ghost, honey. And it's nice to see your young man has put some roses back in your cheeks."

"I thought you were a feminist," I said.

"I am," she said.

"Well, you could've fooled me! Maybe it's just that enough time passed and I actually got over him on my own. Maybe it's springtime. Maybe I'm just having a really good time at work these days. Did you hear that I'm up for the chairmanship of the department? Maybe I'm just doing fine on my own and it has nothing to do with Wyatt Dunn."

"Mmm. Well. Whatever," Mom said. "I have to go, dear. Bye! Don't shlunch."

"She'll be the death of me," I announced as I went back inside. "If I don't kill her first, that is."

Margaret burst into tears.

"God's nightgown!" I said. "I didn't mean it! Margs, what's wrong?"

"My idiot husband!" she sobbed, slashing her hand across her face to wipe away the tears.

"Okay, okay, honey. Settle down." I handed her a napkin to blow her nose and patted her shoulder as

Angus happily licked away her tears. "What's really going on, Margs?"

She took a shaky breath. "He wants us to have a baby."

My mouth dropped open. "Oh," I said.

Margaret never wanted kids. Actually, she said that the memory of Natalie hooked up to a respirator was enough to crush any maternal instincts she might've had. She always seemed to like kids well enough—gamely holding our cousins' babies at family gatherings, talking to older kids in a pleasingly adult way. But she also was the first to say she was too selfish to ever be a mother.

"So is this up for discussion?" I asked. "How do you feel?"

"Pretty fucking awful, Grace," she snapped. "I'm hiding at your house, flirting with your hunky neighbor, not speaking to my husband, and *Mom* is giving me lectures on marriage! Isn't it obvious how I feel?"

"No," I said firmly. "You're also bawling into my dog's fur. So spill, honey. I won't tell anyone."

She shot me a watery, grateful look. "I feel kind of...betrayed," she admitted. "Like he's saying I'm not enough. And you know, he's...he can be really irritating, you know?" Her breath started hitching out of her again. "He's not the most exciting person in the world, is he?"

I murmured that, no, of course he wasn't.

"And so I feel like he just hit me upside the head."

"So what do you think, Margs? Do you think you might want a baby?" I asked.

"No! I don't know! Maybe! Oh, shit. I'm gonna take

a shower." She stood up, handed me my doggy, who snagged the last bit of poppy seed roll from my plate and burped. And thus ended the sisterly heart-to-heart.

CHAPTER FIFTEEN

ON WEDNESDAY EVENING, I was getting ready for my date with Lester the metalsmith. He'd called at last, sounded normal enough, but let's be honest. With a name like Lester, being a member of an artisan's cooperative and having his looks summarized as *attractive in his own way*...well. My hopes were flying pretty low.

Nonetheless, I figured it wouldn't be the worst thing in the world for me to get out of the house. I could practice my feminine wiles on him, try a few of the techniques Lou had urged during our Meeting Mr. Right class. Yes, I was that desperate.

Margaret was working—since our chat over the weekend, she'd kept mum on the subject of her husband. Angus watched as I resignedly followed Lou's advice...a skirt short enough to show that, yes, I had fabulous legs. A little lipstick, a little holy water on the hair, and I was ready to go. I kissed Angus repeatedly, asked him not to feel jealous, lonely or depressed, told him he could watch HBO and order pizza, realized that I was far, far down the path to "Weird Dog Lady" and headed out.

Lester and I were meeting at Blackie's, and I figured I'd walk. It was a beautiful night, just a little cool, and in the west, there was the thinnest line of red as the sunset held on a little longer. I looked for a moment at my own house. I'd left the Tiffany lamp on for Angus, and my hanging porch light was on. The buds of the peonies were tight with promise...in another week or so, they'd burst into fragrant, lush blossoms that scented the whole house. The slate walk was edged with lavender, ferns and heather, and hostas huddled in a thick green mass at the base of my mailbox.

It was a perfect house, sweet enough to be featured on the cover of a magazine, cozy, welcoming, unique. Only one thing was missing—the husband. The kids. The whole adorable family I'd always envisioned...the one that was getting harder and harder to imagine.

You might wonder why I didn't sell the house after Andrew broke it off with me. It was, after all, supposed to be *our* house. But I loved it, and it had so much potential. The thought of not hearing the Farmington River shushing gently in the distance, of letting someone else plant bulbs and hang ferns on the front porch...I just couldn't do it. And yes, maybe I was holding on to the last piece I had of Andrew and me. We'd planned to be so happy here....

So rather than becoming our house, it became mine. That house was my grief therapy, and as I polished it and made it a sanctuary of comfort and beauty and surprising little delights, you can bet that I imagined my revenge on Andrew. That I'd meet someone else, someone better, smarter, taller, funnier, richer, nicer...someone who freakin' adored me, thank you so much. And Andrew would see. It was his stupid loss. And he could just be lonely and miserable for the rest of his stupid life.

Obviously, it didn't turn out that way, or I wouldn't be standing here on the sidewalk, a fake boyfriend on one hand, a metalsmith on the other, an ex-con who made my girl parts sit up and bark in the background.

"Get going," I told myself. Margaret might be a bit off love these days, but she wouldn't fix me up with a bad person. Lester the metalsmith. It was kind of hard to get excited about him. Lester. Les. Nope. Nothing.

Blackie's was packed, and immediately, I regretted arranging the date this way. What was I supposed to do, just start tapping men on the shoulder and asking if they were Lester the metalsmith? *Is there a metalsmith in the building? Please, if you're a metalsmith, report to the bar immediately.*

"What can I get you?" the bartender asked as I pushed my way forward.

"A gin and tonic, please?" I asked.

"Coming up," he said.

Well, here I was, once again trying to convey The Look, the confidence, the appeal, the *I'm just an amused observer of life* look that didn't say *Quite eager to find boyfriend so I won't have to be alone when sister marries ex-fiancé, which seems like it'll be happening soon, damn it. Good dancer a plus.*

"Excuse me, are you Grace?" came a voice at my shoulder. "I'm Lester."

I turned. My eyes widened. Heart rate stopped entirely, then kicked in at about one hundred and eighty beats per minute.

"You are Grace, right?" the man asked.

"Thank you," I murmured. As in "Thank you, *God!*" Then I closed my mouth and smiled. "Hi. I mean, yes. I'm Grace. Hello. I'm fine, thanks."

So I was a babbling idiot. So would you be, if you'd seen this guy. Dear God in heaven, oh, Margaret, thank you, because before me stood a man the likes that every woman on the face of the earth would want to devour with whipped cream and chocolate sauce. Black hair. Black gypsy eyes. Killer dimples. Shirt open to reveal swarthy skin and completely lickable neck. Like Julian, sort of, but more dangerous, less adorable. Swarthier. Taller. Heterosexual. Praise be.

The bartender handed me my drink, and I passed him a twenty in a daze. "Keep the change," I murmured.

"I got us a table," Lester said. "Over there, in the back. Shall we?"

He led the way, which meant I got to look at his ass as we twisted our way through the crowd. Vowing to send Margaret some flowers, do her laundry and bake her brownies, I mentally thanked her for fixing me up with Lester the metalsmith, who was so much more than "attractive in his own way."

"I was really psyched when Margaret called," Lester said, sitting down. He already had a beer, and he took a sip from it now. "She's so cool."

"Oh," I said, still in full idiot mode. "That's…yes. She is. I love my sister."

He grinned, and a little whimper came from the back of my throat.

"So you work at a school?" he said.

I gave myself a mental shake. "Yes, I do," I answered. "I'm a history teacher at Manning Academy."

I managed to complete several sentences on what I did and where, but I couldn't relax. This man was just unbelievably good-looking. His hair was thick and kind of long, waving gracefully around his face. He had incredible hands, strong and dark with long fingers and a healing cut I yearned to kiss better.

"So, Lester, what kind of metalsmithing do you do?" I asked, swallowing.

"Well, actually, I brought you one of my pieces. A little gift to say thanks for meeting me." He reached into a battered leather bag next to him and fumbled for something.

A gift. Oh! I melted like…well, like a hunk of molten metal, of course. He *made* me something.

Lester straightened up and put the object on the table.

It was beautiful. Made from iron, an abstract person rose up from the base, the metal twisting gracefully in a fluid arc, arms raised to heaven, iron hair flowing as if greeting a gust of wind on a summer day. "Oh, my gosh," I breathed. "It's beautiful."

"Thanks," he said. "That's one of a series I'm doing now, and they're selling really well. But yours is special, Grace." He paused, looked at me with those dark, dark eyes. "I think you're great, Grace. I'm hoping that we'll really connect. This is sort of a good faith gift."

"Wow," I said. "Yes." As in Yes, *I* will *marry you and bear us four healthy children.*

He grinned again, and I fumbled for my drink and drained it.

"Excuse me one second," Lester said. "I have to make one quick call, and I'll be right back. I'm so sorry."

"Oh, no, not at all," I managed. I could use the time to get myself under control, since I was practically teetering on the brink of orgasm. Who could blame me? Mr. Beautiful Gypsy Man *liked* me. Wanted a *relationship* with me. Could it really be this easy? Imagine bringing him home to meet the gang! Imagine having him as my date the next time Natalie and Andrew invited me over. Imagine Callahan O'Shea seeing me with Beautiful Gypsy Man! Wouldn't that be the coolest! Good God!

I snatched my cell phone from my bag and punched in my home number.

"Margaret," I muttered urgently when she picked up. "I love him! Thank you! He's amazing! He's not attractive in his own way! He's unbelievably gorgeous!"

"I just turned on *Gods and Generals*," Margaret said. "Do you really watch this crap?"

"He's amazing, Margs!"

"Okay. Glad to be of service. He seemed pretty hot to meet you. Actually, he asked me out first, but I flashed the wedding ring. I regret that now," she said, sounding mildly surprised.

"Oh, here he comes. Thanks again, Margs. Gotta go." I pushed End and smiled as Lester returned and sat down. My whole body pulsated with desire.

For the next half hour or so, we managed to talk. Actually, I was the one having a hard time of it and so tried instead to show that I was a good listener, despite the fact that I was barely paying attention, thanks to the lust that roiled inside me. Dimly, I heard Lester tell me about his family, how he became a metalsmith, where he showed in New York and San Francisco. He'd been in a long-term relationship (with a woman, which put any lingering fears to bed), but things hadn't worked out. Now he was looking to settle down. He loved to cook and couldn't wait to make me dinner. He wanted children. He was perfect.

Then his cell phone rang. "Oh, shoot, I'm sorry, Grace," he said with an apologetic smile, glancing at the screen of the phone. "I've been waiting for this call."

YOUR OPINION POLL
THANK-YOU FREE GIFTS INCLUDE:

▶ **2 ROMANCE BOOKS**
▶ **2 LOVELY SURPRISE GIFTS**

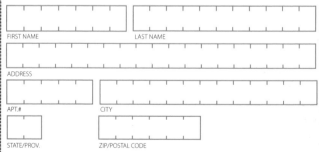

"No, no, go ahead," I said, sipping my G&T. *Do whatever you want, baby. I'm yours.*

Lester flipped open his phone. "What do you want, bitch?" he demanded, his face contorting with fury.

I choked and sputtered, lurching up straight in my seat. Around us, patrons grew still. Lester ignored us all.

"Well, guess where I am?" he barked, turning slightly away from me. "I'm at a *bar* with a *woman!* So there, you disgusting whore! And I'm going to take her back to our house and I'm going to have *sex* with her!" His voice grew louder and louder, cracking with intensity. "That's right! On the *couch,* in our *bed,* on the kitchen *floor,* on the goddamn *kitchen table!* How do you like that, you cheating, miserable skank?" Then he flipped his phone shut, looked at me and smiled. "So where were we?" he asked pleasantly.

"Uh…" I said, glancing around in frozen horror. "Was that your ex?" I asked.

"She means nothing to me anymore," Lester said. "Hey, feel like going back to my place? I can cook us some dinner."

All my internal organs seemed to retract in horror. Suddenly, I wanted no part of Lester's kitchen, thanks very much. "Gee…um, Lester. Do you think I'd be out of line if I suggested you, uh, weren't really over her yet?" I tried to smile.

Lester's face crumpled. "Oh, crap," he sobbed, "I still love her! I love her and it's killing me!" He lowered his head to the table and banged his forehead repeatedly, sobbing, snuffling, tears spurting out of his eyes.

I caught the eye of our waitress and pointed to my drink. "I'll have another," I called.

AN HOUR AND A HALF LATER, I finally walked Lester to his car, having heard all about Stefania, the coldhearted Russian woman who'd left him for another woman... how he'd gone to her house and bellowed her name over and over and over until the police were summoned and dragged him away...how he'd called her one hundred and seven times in a single night...how he'd defaced Russia from an antique map in the public library and had to serve a hundred hours of community service. I nodded and murmured, sipping my much-needed alcohol (I was walking home, what was the harm?). *Artists,* I thought as I listened to his tirade. I'd been dumped, too, yet you didn't see me crapping on anyone's lawn. Maybe Kiki would like him....

"So, hey. Good luck, Les," I said, rubbing my hands on my upper arms. The night had grown cooler, and mist hung around the streetlamps.

"I hate love," he declared to the heavens. "Just crush me now, why don't you? Kill me, universe!"

"Chin up," I said. "And...well. Thanks for the drinks."

I watched as he drove out of the parking lot—no way in hell I was getting in the car with him, no matter how benign his offer of a ride had been. Sighing, I looked at my watch. Ten o'clock on a Wednesday night. Another man down.

Drat. I'd forgotten my statue inside, and whether its maker was insane or not, I liked it. In fact, it might well have more value in the near future. *Metalsmith institutionalized. Prices soar.* I made a mental note to strangle Margaret as soon as I got home. She was a lawyer, after all. Maybe next time she fixed me up, she could run a quick background check.

I went back inside, retrieved my little statue, wove my way once again through the sea of bodies crammed into Blackie's and pushed the door to leave. It was stuck. I pushed harder and it opened abruptly, thudding against someone who was trying to come at the same moment.

"Ouch," he said.

I closed my eyes. "Watch where you're going," I muttered by way of greeting.

"I should've known it was you," Callahan O'Shea said. "Hitting the sauce, Grace?"

"I was on a date, thanks very much. And you're in no position to point fingers. An Irishman in a bar. How novel."

"I see we're drunk again. Hope you're not driving." His gaze wandered past me toward the bar. I turned to look. An attractive blonde woman gave him a little wiggle of her fingers and smiled.

"I'm not drunk! And I'm not driving, so don't worry. Enjoy your date. Tell her to order a double." With that, I walked past him into the chilly night.

Callahan O'Shea may have been an arrogant, irritating man, but I had to admit, he was right about my ability to hold my liquor. Granted, I had planned on having some food, but when the waitress did come by, Lester had been at the height of his tirade against love, and ordering buffalo wings seemed insensitive. Well, I wasn't exactly drunk, just a bit buzzed. Add to that the thick scent of lilacs, and it was actually a rather nice sensation.

The mist was heavier now, and I could only imagine what my hair was doing, but I could practically feel it spreading, growing, expanding like a feral creature. I sucked in more lilac-scented air and tripped—the price

of closing one's eyes on Peterston's erratic sidewalks—
but recovered nicely.

"I can't believe your boyfriend let you walk home
alone in this condition, Grace. Such a cad."

I scowled. "You again. What are you doing here?"

"Walking you home. I see we won an Emmy," Callahan said, tilting his head to get a better look at my
statue.

"This is a very lovely gift. From Wyatt. Who bought
it for me. And you don't have to walk me home."

"Someone should. Seriously, where's that boyfriend
of yours?"

"He has surgery in the morning and he had to go.
So he left."

"Mmm-hmm," Callahan said. "Why didn't he at least
drive you home? Did he have feral cats to round up?"

"I wanted to walk. I insisted. Besides, what about
your date? Did you just leave her all alone in the bar
like that? *Tsk, tsk.*"

"She's not my date."

"Yet I saw her wave to you in definite recognition
and anticipation."

"Yet she's not my date," he said.

"Yet I find that hard to believe," I said. "So who is
she, then?"

"My parole officer." Callahan grinned. "Now tell
Uncle Cal the truth, Grace. Did we have a little spat
with our boyfriend tonight?"

"No, we didn't spat. Spit—whatever. And that is
God's honest truth." Perhaps now was a good time to
change the subject. "Are you really Irish?"

"What do you think, genius?"

I think you're a jerk. Oops. May have said that aloud.

"Maybe you should stick with a nice Coke the next time you go out, hmm?" he suggested. "How many drinks did you have?"

"I had two gin and tonics—actually, one and a half—and I don't drink very often, so yes, maybe I'm feeling the effects. That's all." We came to a trestle bridge that crossed the railroad tracks.

"So you can't hold your liquor. How much do you weigh, anyhow?"

"Cal, it's a cardinal sin to ask a woman about her weight, so back off, bub."

He laughed, that ashy, deliciously naughty sound. "I love it when you call me 'bub.' And I'll call you 'lush,' how's that?"

I sighed loudly. "Listen, Callahan O'Shea of the lep-rechauns, thank you for escorting me this far. It's only a few blocks to home. Why don't you head back to your woman?"

"Because this isn't the greatest neighborhood and I don't want you walking home alone."

Aw. It *was* one of the scruffier parts of town…in fact, when a drug deal went down, it usually happened right here under the bridge. I sneaked a look at Cal's face. Aside from his being far too good-looking, I had to admit, he was being really…well, considerate.

"Thank you," I said. "You sure your date doesn't mind?"

"Why would she mind? I'm doing a public service."

Going down the metal steps of the little bridge, I slipped a little. Callahan reached out and grabbed me before any harm was done, and for a second, I just clung to his arms. Warm, solid, reassuring arms. Wouldn't mind staying here all night. He smelled good, too, dang it, like soap and wood.

He reached up and gently pulled something from my hair…a leaf. Looked at it for a second before dropping it. Resumed his hold on me, his hand warm on my upper arm.

"So. Your date," I blurted. "Um. She seems nice. Looks nice, I mean." My heart was flopping around like a dying fish in my chest.

Cal let go of my arms. "She's nice. Not my date, though. As I told you already."

"Oh." Relief flooded my knees, making them tingle painfully. No. I didn't want Callahan O'Shea to be dating anyone. And what did that say? We started walking once more, side by side, the mist cocooning us from the occasional headbeams that passed, muffling the sound of the cars. I swallowed. "So, Cal, are you…um…seeing anyone?"

He shot me a veiled glance. "No, Grace, I'm not."

"Not the marrying type, I guess? Don't want to settle down just yet?"

"I'd love to settle down," he said. "A wife, a couple of kids, a lawn to mow."

"Really?" I asked. Yelped, actually. Callahan struck me as the type who walked into the room while "Bad to the Bone" was playing. Mowing the lawn while the kiddies frolicked? Hmm. Hmm.

"Really." He shoved his hands in his pockets. "Isn't that what you and Dr. Wonderful want?"

"Oh. Uh, sure. I guess. I don't know." This was not a conversation I wanted to have while slightly inebriated. "It would be hard to be with a guy who's married to his work," I finished lamely.

"Right," Cal said.

"So you know, things aren't as wonderful as they seem," I added, surprising myself.

"I see." Cal turned to look at me. He smiled, just a little, and I looked down suddenly. I didn't know anything about this guy. Only that he was undeniably attractive. That he wanted to settle down. That he'd served time for criminal acts.

"Hey, Cal, are you sorry you embezzled that money?" I asked abruptly.

He tilted his head and considered me. "It's complicated."

"Why don't you just spit it out, Irish? What did you do?"

He laughed. "Maybe I'll tell you someday. We're almost home, anyway."

We're almost home. As if we had a place together. As if he might come in, and Angus wouldn't bite him. As if I might make us a snack—or he might—and we'd pop in a movie. Or not. Or we'd just go upstairs, heck. Take off a few articles of clothing. Get a little exercise.

"Here you go," Callahan said, walking up the path with me. The iron porch railing was slick and cold, and Callahan's hand on my back felt even warmer by comparison. Whoa. Wait a sec. His *hand* on my *back*. He was *touching* me, and man, it felt good, like a small sun was resting there, radiating heat into the far regions of my body.

I turned to him, about to say something—what, I had no idea. The sight of his smile, his downturning, lovely eyes, wiped all thought from my mind.

My knees went soft and tingly, and my heart swelled against my ribs in a warm surge. For a second, I could *feel* what it would be like to kiss Callahan O'Shea, and the strength of that image caused a buzz in the pit of my stomach. My lips opened slightly, my eyes fluttered closed. He was like a magnet, pulling me in.

"Good night, my little lush," he said.

My eyes snapped open. "Great! Good night, bub. Thanks for walking me home."

And with one more grin that I felt down to my bone marrow, he turned and left, back to the woman who was not his date, leaving me not at all sure if I was greatly relieved or hugely disappointed.

CHAPTER SIXTEEN

"Hey, Dad," I said one evening after school. Dropping by the family domicile was a habit of mine—sometimes you just can't learn from experience, right? The truth was, taken individually, my parents were great people. My father was methodical and reliable, as dads should be, I thought, and his love of the Civil War gave us a special bond. And my mother was a vibrant, intelligent woman. Growing up, she'd been a devoted mom, the kind who sewed our Halloween costumes and baked cookies from scratch. Granted, my parents had always seemed to do things separately; I had very few memories of them going out just the two of them. They had friends and socialized normally enough, but as far as a deep and abiding love or passion…let's just say that if it was there, they hid it well.

It worried me. What if that was the kind of marriage I ended up with, stifled and irritated with my spouse all day, wishing I'd chosen another life? Look at Margaret. Look at Mémé and her three husbands, none of whom she ever recalled fondly.

Dad was sitting at the kitchen table, his daily six ounces of red wine (for health reasons only) next to him. I let go of Angus's leash so my puppy could go see his second favorite person on earth.

"Hello, Pudding," he said, glancing up from the *Wall*

Street Journal. Then he caught sight of my dog. "Angus! How are you, buddy?" Angus leaped in the air, barking with love. "Who's a good boy, huh? Are you a good dog?"

"He's really not," I admitted. "He bit my neighbor. The carpenter."

"Oh, how are the windows coming along?" Dad asked, picking up Angus to better worship.

"They're done, actually." And I had to admit, I was disappointed. No more Callahan O'Shea in my house. "He did a great job. Thanks again, Daddy."

He smiled. "You're welcome. Hey, I heard you're Jackson at Chancellorsville."

"I get a horse and everything," I said, smiling modestly. Brother Against Brother's members included a stable-owner who would loan out horses here and there, so long as we passed a riding class. Alas, I was only allowed to ride Snowlight, a fat and elderly white pony with a fluffy mane and a narcoleptic tendency to lie down when hearing loud noises, which made my rallying the troops a bit less dramatic than planned. However, as Colonel Jackson, I was to be shot at this battle, so Snowlight's narcolepsy would come in handy.

"You were great at Bull Run, by the way," I said. He nodded in acknowledgment, turning the page of his paper. "Where's Mom?"

"She's in the garage," Dad answered.

"The studio!" Mom's voice could be heard clearly from the *studio*—she hated when we referred to it as garage, feeling that we were demeaning her self-expression.

"She's in the *studio!* Making her porno statues!" Dad bellowed back, slapping the paper down on the table.

"God help me, Grace, if I'd known your mother would have a meltdown when you kids left for college—"

"You know, Dad, you could try to be a little more supportive of Mom's—"

"It's not porn!" My mother stood in the doorway, her face flushed from the heat of her glassblowing fire. Angus raced into the garage to bark at her artwork.

"Hi, Mom," I said. "How are the, uh, sculptures coming along?"

"Hello, honey," Mom replied, kissing my cheek. "I'm trying to use a lighter glass. The last uterus I sold weighed nineteen pounds, but these light ones keep breaking. Angus, no! Stay away from that ovary, honey!"

"Angus! Cookie!" I said. My dog raced back into the kitchen, and Mom closed the door behind her, then went to the special doggy cookie jar they kept on hand for my dog (no grandchildren, you understand).

"Here you go, you sweet thing!" Mom cooed. Angus sat, then raised his front paws in the air, nearly causing Mom to faint with joy. "So sweet! Yes, you are! You're a sweet baby! You're my little Angus-Pooh!" Finally, she straightened up to look at her biological child. "So what brings you here, Grace?"

"Oh, I was just wondering if you guys had talked to Margaret lately," I said. Angus, miffed that the attention was no longer upon him, trotted off to destroy something. Since her little tear jag in my kitchen, I'd barely spoken to my sister, who'd been drowning herself even more than usual in work.

Mom gave Dad a sour look. "Jim, our daughter is visiting. Think you could drop your paper and pay attention to her?"

Dad just rolled his eyes and continued reading.

"Jim!"

"Mom, it's okay. Dad's just relaxing. He's listening, right, Dad?"

My father nodded, giving my mother a resigned stare.

"Well, about Margaret and Stuart, who knows?" Mom said. "They'll find their way. Marriage is complicated, honey. You'll find out someday." Mom flicked Dad's paper, earning a glare. "Right, Jim? Complicated."

"With you it is," my father grumbled.

"Speaking of marriage, honey, Natalie wanted to make sure everyone was free for brunch on Sunday, did she tell you?"

"Marriage? What?" My voice cracked.

"What?" Mom asked.

"You said, 'speaking of marriage.' Are they engaged?"

Dad lowered his paper and peered at me over his bifocals. "Would you be all right with that, Pudding?"

"Um, yeah! Of course! Sure! Did she say? She didn't tell me anything."

Mom patted my shoulder. "No, no, she didn't say anything. But, Grace, sweetie…" She paused. "It seems like it might be coming."

"Oh, I know! Sure! I hope it does come to marriage. They're great together."

"And now you have Wyatt, so it doesn't sting as much, right?" Mom said.

For a second, I almost blurted out the truth about Wyatt Dunn, saintly doctor. *I actually just made that guy up so Nat wouldn't feel so guilty, Mom, Dad. And oh, by the way, I may have a thing for the ex-con next door.* But what would they say to that? I could imagine their faces, the consternation, the worry, the fear that I'd chugged around the bend. The certainty that I wasn't over Andrew, that I'd been crushed beyond repair, that a crush on Cal indicated my wobbly emotional state. "Right," I said slowly. "I have Wyatt. And also papers that need grading."

"And I have to finish my *art*," Mom said, once again poking Dad's paper. "So make your own damn dinner."

"Fine! I'd love to! Your cooking has really gone down the drain, you know. Ever since you became an *artist*."

"Grow up, Jim." Mom turned to me. "Honey, wait. We want to meet Wyatt." She reached for the calendar that hung next to the fridge. "Let's make a date right now."

"Oh, Mom, you know how it is. He's so busy. And plus he's working in Boston a few days a week, um, consulting. Up at Children's. Oops, gotta go. See you soon. I'll get back to you on a date."

As I drove around town on my errands, Angus on my lap, helping me steer, it seemed like everyone's story— their how-they-met story—echoed in my head. My own parents had gotten together when Dad was a lifeguard and Mom had been swimming at Lake Waramaug, pretending to drown for her friends. She was sixteen at the time, just goofing around, and had Dad been a less literal person, he probably could've seen that. As it was, he hauled her out of the lake and, learning that her lungs were water-free, chastised her so fiercely that she burst into tears. And just like that, he fell in love.

Margaret and Stuart met during a fire drill at Harvard. It was a frigid January night, and Margs was clad only in her pajamas. Stuart wrapped her in his coat and let her sit on his lap so her feet wouldn't have to touch the snow. He carried her back into the dorm (and right into her bed, as the story went).

I wanted a story. I didn't want to say, "Oh, Daddy and I met on a website because we were both so damned desperate we couldn't think of anything else." Or, "I tricked Daddy into loving me by pretending I couldn't pick out my own lightbulb and wearing makeup at all times."

Andrew and I had had a story. A pretty great story. How many people could say they'd met their husbands while lying dead at Gettysburg, after all? It was damn cute. And of course, I reminded myself harshly, gently pushing Angus's head out of the way so I could see, Natalie and Andrew had a great story, too. *I was engaged to her sister, but one look at Natalie, and I knew I had the wrong Emerson girl! Hahaha!*

"Stop it," I told myself, my voice grating. "You'll find someone. You will. He doesn't have to be perfect. Just good enough. And, yes, Natalie and Andrew are probably going to get married. We know this. We are not surprised. We'll take the news very well."

But I couldn't shake the funk that lowered as I did my errands…grocery store, dry cleaner, wine shop for some good and cheap chardonnay. Everywhere I went, I imagined the story. At the package store: *He recommended some wine, we got to talking…I saved the bottle, see, it's over there, on the shelf.* Unfortunately, the man behind the counter at the package store was sixty years old, wedding ring in place, as well as a couple of hundred extra pounds. At the market: *We ran into each other at the Ben & Jerry's case, argued over which was better, Vanilla Heath Bar or Coffee Heath Bar, and we still can't agree.* But, no, the only person in front of Ben & Jerry's was a girl of about twelve, stocking up on Cinnamon Bun from the look of things. At the cleaners: *He was picking up a suit, I needed my Confederate officer's uniform...* Alas, the only one in the cleaner's was the sweet and tiny woman who owned the place. "Watch you don't get shot!" she said, handing me my dress grays.

"Getting shot is the whole point," I said. My smile felt forced.

When I got home, I stashed my groceries, took a box of tampons away from Angus and gave him a chew stick instead, poured a healthy glass of wine and went up to the attic with my uniform. Did I usually stow my uniform in the attic? Well, no, not until winter, usually, but it seemed like a good idea tonight. And I left the light off, because I knew the way by heart.

He was there. Callahan O'Shea was back on the roof, hands clasped behind his head, looking up at the sky.

We met when I clocked him with my field hockey stick. I thought he was robbing the house next door. Turned out he wasn't, simply a guy on his first night out of prison. What for, you ask? Oh, he stole over a million dollars.

Sighing, I tore myself away from the view and went back downstairs. Pictured Wyatt Dunn coming home, hugging me, resting his cheek against my hair. Angus wouldn't bite him or even bark. We'd sit down in my seldom-used dining room, and I'd pour him a glass of wine, and he'd ask to hear about my students, and I'd cheer him up by telling him about how I divided the class into Confederates and Union citizens and made them debate why their side was right, how the entire Southern side spoke in drawls and got the giggles when Emma Kirk said, "Fiddle-dee-dee."

So intense was my little daydream that when a knock came on the door, I almost expected it to be Wyatt, that I somehow conjured him. Angus went into his yapping frenzy, so I picked him up and peeked. It was Callahan O'Shea, down from the roof. My face went lava-hot.

"Hi," I said, clutching my dog, who growled fiercely.

"Hi," Callahan said, leaning in the doorway.

"Everything okay?" It was dark, after all.

"Yup." He just looked at me from those denim-blue eyes, and I noticed for the first time that his irises were flecked with gold. His shirt was a soft green, and the smell of freshly cut wood drifted toward me.

"What can I do for you?" I asked, my voice husky.

"Grace."

"Yes?" I breathed.

"I want you to stop spying on me," he said.

Dang it! I sucked in a guilty breath. "Spying? I'm not…I…I don't…"

"From the attic. Do you have a problem with me being up on my roof?"

"No! I just was…" *Hrrrr. Hrrrr. Yarp!* Angus was struggling to get out of my arms, giving me a great excuse to stall. "Hang on a second. Or just come in. I have to put Angus in the cellar."

I stashed Angus, took a few deep breaths, then turned to face my neighbor, who stood just inside the doorway, a sarcastic eyebrow raised. If eyebrows could be sarcastic, that is.

"Cal, I was just putting some things away up there. I

saw you and yes, I wondered what you were doing out there, okay? I'm sorry."

"Grace, we both know that you've been spying. Just knock it off."

"Well, someone has quite an ego, doesn't he?" I said. "I was putting away my general's uniform. Go upstairs and check if you want." Angus barked from the cellar, backing me up.

Callahan took a step closer and looked down at me—literally and figuratively, I imagined. His eyes wandered to my hair, then...oh, God...to my mouth. "Here's what I want to know," he said. "Why does that boyfriend of yours leave you alone so damn much?" His voice was soft.

My whole body responded with a giant, hot, pulsating throb. "Oh...well..." My voice was breathy. "I'm not sure that's gonna work out. We're, um...reevaluating."

Tell him you're free, Grace. Just say you and Wyatt broke up.

I didn't. Honestly, it was just too scary. My entire body was quivering with Callahan's nearness, and fear. Fear that he was playing me, all too aware that I was a heartbeat away from wrestling him to the floor and ripping off his clothes.

That stirring image was almost immediately replaced with another, much less desirable picture—Cal pushing me back and saying, quite firmly, *No, thanks,* that sardonic expression on his too-appealing face.

"So." My voice was brisk and teacherly. "Anything else, Mr. O'Shea?"

"No." But he looked at me, really looked, and it was awfully hard to maintain eye contact, let me tell you. Surely I was blushing, since my face was burning hot.

"No more spying," he finally said, his voice gentle. "Got it?"

"Yes," I whispered. "Sorry."

And then he turned and left, leaving me standing in the middle of my living room, shaky and feeling like my stays were a little too tight.

Okay, okay, I admitted that I was desperately attracted to Callahan O'Shea. And that was not a good thing. First of all, I wasn't sure he liked me very much. Secondly...well. It wasn't just the ex-con thing. Sure, if he'd beaten someone with a pipe or something, obviously he'd be out of the running. Embezzlement, yes, it was also a crime. But not that bad, right? If he was sorry...plus, he'd served his debt to society and all that crap....

No. It wasn't his past, though obviously I put a lot of weight on the past. It was the fact that my whole life, I knew what I wanted. Andrew had been The One, and look how that turned out. What I wanted now, God help me, was another Andrew, just without the whole sister-loving complication.

Callahan O'Shea was ridiculously appealing, but I'd never relax around him. He was not the type to look at me adoringly. He...he...ah, crap, he was just too *much*. Too big, too good-looking, too appealing, too *stirring*. I felt too many things around him. It was disturbing, really. He made me irritable and lustful and sharp when I wanted to be sweet and loving and soft. I wanted to be...well, like Natalie. And I wanted a man who looked at me the way Andrew looked at Natalie. Not like Callahan, who looked like he knew my every dirty little secret.

CHAPTER SEVENTEEN

I was working late at Manning one evening, putting together my presentation for the board of trustees, when Stuart paid me a visit.

"Hey, Stuart!" I exclaimed, getting up to kiss his cheek.

"How are you, Grace?" he asked politely.

"I'm okay," I said. "Have a seat. Want some coffee or anything?"

"No, thank you. Just a few minutes of your time."

Stuart looked awful. His eyes were shadowed and tired, and there seemed to be gray in his beard that wasn't there a few weeks ago. Although we worked at the same school, Stuart's office was in Caybridge Hall, a newer building on the southern side of the campus, far from Lehring, where the history department nestled appropriately in the oldest building at Manning. I rarely encountered Stuart at work.

I sat back behind my desk and took a deep breath. "You want to talk about Margaret?" I asked softly.

He looked down. "Grace..." He shook his head. "Has she told you why we're...apart?"

"Um..." I paused, not sure how much I should reveal. "She's said a few things."

"I brought up the idea of us having a baby," Stuart said quietly. "And she basically exploded. Suddenly, it seems, we're having all sorts of troubles that I was completely unaware of. I'm quite boring, apparently. I don't talk about work enough. She feels like she's living with a stranger. Or a brother. Or a ninety-year-old man. We don't have enough fun, we don't just grab a toothbrush and rush off to the Bahamas—and here she works seventy hours a week, Grace! If I suggested we fly off somewhere, she'd kill me!"

He certainly had a point. Margaret was mercurial, putting it kindly.

He sighed wearily. "All I wanted was to talk—just talk—about the idea of having a baby. We decided we wouldn't have kids when we were twenty-five, Grace. That was a long time ago. I figured we could revisit the idea. And now she said she's filing for divorce."

"A divorce?" I squeaked. "Oh, crap. I didn't know that, Stuart." I was quiet for a minute, then said, "But you know Margaret, buddy. She's all thunder and lightning. I doubt she really wants…" My voice trailed off. I had no idea what Margaret really wanted. On the one hand, I couldn't imagine her divorcing Stuart just like that. On the other, she'd always been impulsive. And completely unable to admit when she was wrong.

"What should I do?" he asked, and his voice broke just a little.

"Oh, Stuart." I got out of my seat and went to him, patted his shoulder awkwardly. "Listen," I murmured, "one thing she said to me was that…" *you only have sex on scheduled days…* I grimaced. "Um, maybe things were a little…routine? With you guys? So maybe a little surprise now and again—" *on the kitchen table* "—wouldn't be a bad thing. Just sort of to show that you really…noticed her."

"I do notice her," he protested, wiping his eyes with one hand the way men do. "I love her, Grace. I've always loved her. I don't understand why that's not enough."

Mercifully, my sister wasn't home when I got there. As Stuart pointed out, she worked a very long day. Bemused, I threw together some dinner, then went upstairs to change for Dancin' with the Oldies.

Callahan was busy these days at his own house, and I hadn't seen him since he busted me for spying. I looked out the window at the new shingles on the roof, the curving and lovely little deck in the back. For the past two days, he'd been doing something inside, so I hadn't been able to ogle him. Pity.

"Come on, Angus, buddy. Let's go," I said. I got my things and left the house, Angus trotting and leaping with delight at my side. He knew what Mommy's swirly-twirly skirt meant. I got in the car, put it in Reverse and backed out onto the street as I had done a thousand times before.

Unlike those thousand other times, however, I heard a horrifying metallic crunch.

Callahan's pickup truck was parked on the street, very close to my driveway. Well, okay, maybe not that close, but having gotten used to a clear runway ever since I'd lived here, I guess I took the turn kind of... yes. Okay. It was my fault.

I got out of the car to inspect the damage. Crap. I guessed that Callahan would be less than amused when I told him I'd just crushed his rear left taillight. Lucky for me, my own car was made of sturdy German stock, and there was only a little scrape where I'd hit the truck.

Glancing at my watch, I sighed, then dutifully trotted down the path to fess up.

I knocked briskly. No answer. "Callahan?" I called. "I just hit your truck!" Nothing. Fine, he was out. I didn't have a pen, either, dang it, and if I went inside, I'd be late for dancing. I was cutting it close as it was.

He'd have to wait. I ran back down the path, shooed Angus out of the driver's seat and headed off for Golden Meadows.

As I drove, Angus sitting on my lap, his adorable front paws resting on the steering wheel, I found myself wishing I was the single-mother type. I could just pop into a sperm bank and bingo. No man necessary. Life would be so much simpler.

I drove past the lake. The sun was setting, and a pair of Canada geese cruised in for a landing, their graceful black necks outstretched. The minute they touched water, each swam to the other, checking that the other was safe. Beautiful. That was the kind of tenderness I wanted. Super. I was now envying geese.

Pulling into the visitors' lot at Golden Meadows, I bucked up a bit. This place was good for the spirit. "Hi, Shirley," I said to the receptionist as I went in.

"Hello, Grace." She smiled. "And who have we here? Why, it's Angus! Hello, honey! Hello! Do you want a cookie?" I watched in amusement as Shirley convulsed in delight at the sight of my dog, who was extremely popular here. Angus, knowing he had a captive audience, raised his right paw and tilted his little head as Shirley swooned with joy.

"You sure you don't mind watching him?" I asked as Angus delicately (we were in public, after all) ate the proffered cookie.

"Mind? Of course not! I love him! Yes, I do! I love you, Angus!"

Smiling, I walked down the hall. "Hey, everyone!" I called as I went into the activity room where we held Dancin' with the Oldies each week.

"Hello, Grace!" they chorused. I hugged and kissed and patted, and my heart was eased a good bit.

Julian was there, too, and the sight of my old buddy made me just about burst into tears. "I miss you, ugly," I said to him. Dancin' with the Oldies hadn't met last week, due to a conflict with a free blood pressure screening.

"I miss you, too," he said, pulling a face. "This dating thing isn't working for me, Grace. I say forget it."

"What happened?" I asked.

"A whole lot of nothing," he answered. "It's just... I'm not meant to be with anyone, I think. Romantically, anyway. It's not the worst thing to be alone, is it?"

"No," I lied. "Not at all! Come over for *Project Runway* tomorrow, okay?"

"Thank you. I've been so lonely." He gave me a sad smile.

"Me, too, buddy." I squeezed his hand in relief.

"Okay, good people!" Julian called, patting my head and pushing Play. "Tony Bennett wants you to 'Sing, You Sinners'! Gracie, let's jitterbug!"

Three dances later, flushed and panting, I took a seat next to my grandmother. "Hello, Mémé," I said, giving her withered cheek a kiss.

"You look like a tramp," she hissed.

"Thank you, Mémé! You also look so pretty today!" I said loudly.

My grandmother was odd...her utmost pleasure in life was to put other people down, but I knew she was also proud of the fact that I came here, that everyone loved me. She might not have a kind word to say, but she liked having me around nonetheless. Somewhere in her sour old soul, I believed, was Nice Mémé, a woman who just had to have a little affection for her three grand-daughters. So far, though, Mean Mémé had gagged and bound Nice Mémé, but you never knew.

"So what's new, Mémé?" I asked, sitting next to her.

"What do you care?" she answered.

"I care. A little. I'd care more if you were nice to me once in a while."

"What's the point? You're just after my money," she said, waving her liver-spotted hand dismissively.

"I thought two hundred years of hard living would've used up your money by now," I answered.

"Well, I have plenty. I buried three husbands, missy, and what's the point of marriage if you're not making money?"

"That's so romantic, Mémé. Really. I have tears in my eyes."

"Oh, grow up, Grace. A woman your age doesn't have time to waste. And you should show me more re-spect. I might cut you out of my will."

"Tell you what, Mémé," I said, patting her bony little shoulder, "you take my portion and you spend it. Go on a cruise. Buy yourself some diamonds. Hire a gigolo."

She harrumphed, but didn't look my way. Instead, she was watching the dancers. I might've been wrong, but it seemed that her pinkie was keeping time to "Papa Loves Mambo." My heart swelled with unwilling sym-pathy. "Want to dance, Mémé?" I asked softly. She could, after all, walk pretty well. The wheelchair was more for effect—she was better able to ram people if her center of gravity was lower.

"Dance?" she snorted. "With whom, dimwit?"

"Well, I'd—"

"Where's that man you're always talking about? Scared him off, did you? I'm not surprised. Or did he fall in love with your sister?"

I flinched. "Jesus, Mémé," I said, my throat thickening with tears.

"Oh, get over it. It was a joke." She glanced at me with disdain.

Still stunned, I moved away, accepting a rather stiff waltz from Mr. Demming. Mémé was my only living grandparent. I never met my biological grandfather— he was the first of the husbands that Mémé buried, but I loved him in theory, since my father had an arsenal of wonderful stories about him. Mémé's other two husbands had been lovely men; Grandpa Jake, who died when I was twelve, and Poppa Frank, who died when I was in graduate school. My mom's parents had died within months of each other when I was in high school. They, too, were quintessentially wonderful people. But because the fates were cruel, the only surviving grandparent I had was as mean as camel spit.

When Dancin' with the Oldies was done, Julian kissed my cheek and said farewell. Mémé watched and waited, vulturelike, so I could follow her, slavelike, to her apartment. I knew from experience that if I told her she'd hurt my feelings, she'd just make it worse, tell me I had no sense of humor and then call my dad to complain about me. Resigned, I took the handles of her wheelchair and pushed her gently down the hall.

"Edith," Mémé said loudly, stopping a fearful looking woman in her tracks. "This is my granddaughter, Grace. She's visiting me. Grace, Edith is new here." A

Grinchy smile spread over her face. "Did *you* get any visitors this week, Edith?"

"Well, actually, my son and his—"

"Grace comes every week, don't you, Grace?"

"I do. I help with the ballroom dancing class," I said. "You'd be more than welcome to come."

"Oh, I love dancing!" Edith cried. "Really? I can just stop in?"

"Seven-thirty to nine," I answered with a smile. "I'll look for you next week."

Mémé, irritated that she wasn't having better luck making Edith feel inferior, began her hacking cough-on-demand to get the attention back to herself.

"So nice to meet you," I said to Edith, taking my cue to continue pushing the wheelchair. We continued through the foyer.

"Stop," Mémé commanded. I obeyed. "You there! What do you want?"

A man was coming down one of the hallways that led off the main foyer. It was Callahan O'Shea.

"If you're thinking this would be a good place to rob, let me set you straight, young man. We have security cameras, you know! Alarms! The police will be here in seconds."

"You two must be related," Callahan said drily.

I smiled. "My grandmother. Eleanor Winfield, meet my neighbor Callahan O'Shea."

"Oh, the Irish." She sneered. "Don't loan him any money, Grace. He'll drink it away. And for God's sake, don't let him in your house. They steal."

"I've heard that," I answered, grinning. Cal smiled back and there it was, that soft, hot feeling in my stomach.

"We had an Irish maid when I was a child," Mémé continued, looking sourly at Callahan. "Eileen, her name was. Or Irene. Possibly Colleen. Do you know her?"

"My mother," he said instantly. I choked on a laugh.

"She stole seven spoons from us before my father caught on. Seven."

"We loved those spoons," he said. "God, the fun we had with your spoons. Eating, hitting each other on the head, throwing them at the pigs in the kitchen. Happy times."

"It's not funny, young man," Mémé sniffed.

I thought it was funny. In fact, I was wiping my eyes, I was laughing so hard. "Visiting your grandfather, Callahan?" I managed to ask.

"That's right," he answered.

"How's he doing? Think he wants me to come back and finish with the duke and Clarissia?"

Cal grinned. "I'm sure he does."

I smiled back. "For a second, I thought you were here about your truck."

His smile dropped. "What about my truck?"

I felt my face warming. "It's hardly noticeable."

"What, Grace?" His voice was hard.

"Just a little dent," I answered, cringing a little. "Maybe a broken taillight." He scowled. "Actually, it's definitely…hey. I have insurance."

"You need insurance," he muttered.

"Grace! Take me back to my apartment," Mémé ordered.

"Easy, Pharaoh," I said. "I'm talking to my neighbor."

"So talk to him in the morning." She glared up at

Callahan. He glared back, and I found myself grinning again. I liked a man who wasn't scared of Mémé, and there weren't many around.

"How'd you get here, Cal? I'm assuming you didn't drive."

"I rode my bike," he answered.

"Would you like a ride? It's dark out," I said.

He looked at me for a second. Then the corner of his mouth pulled up in a smile, and my lady-parts buzzed once more. "Sure. Thank you, Grace."

"You shouldn't give him a ride, Grace!" Mémé snapped. "He's likely to strangle you and dump your body in the lake."

"Is this true?" I asked Callahan.

"I was thinking about it," he admitted.

"Well. Your guilty secret is out."

He smiled. "Allow me." He took the handles of Mémé's chair and started off. "Which way, ladies?"

"Is that Irishman pushing me?" Mémé demanded, craning her neck around to see.

"Oh, come on now, Mémé," I said, patting her shoulder. "He's a big, brawny, good-looking guy. You just sit back and enjoy the ride."

"You sound like a tramp," she muttered. But she did, bidding us a sharp good-night at her apartment door. She stared pointedly at Callahan until he took the hint and walked a few paces down the hall so as not to see the heaps of gold lying about in her dragon lair and thus be tempted to rob her blind.

"Good night, Mémé," I said dutifully.

"Don't trust that man," she whispered. "I don't like the way he looks at you."

I glanced down the hall, tempted to ask just how he looked at me. "Okay, Mémé."

"What a sweet old lady," Callahan said as I rejoined him.

"She's pretty horrible," I admitted.

"Do you visit her a lot?" he asked.

"Oh, yes, I'm afraid."

"Why?"

"Duty," I answered.

"You do a lot for your family, don't you?" he asked. "Do they do anything for you?"

My head jerked back. "Yes. They're great. We're all really close." For some reason, his comment stung. "You don't know my family. You shouldn't have said that."

"Mmm," he said, cocking his eyebrow. "Saint Grace the Martyr."

"I'm not a martyr!" I exclaimed.

"Your sister moved in with you and bosses you around, your grandmother treats you like dirt, but you don't stick up for yourself, you lie to your mother about liking her sculptures…yes, that sounds pretty martyrish to me."

"You have no idea what you're talking about," I snapped. "To the best of my knowledge, you have two relatives, one of whom isn't speaking to you and one who can't. So what do you know about family?"

"Well, looky here. She has teeth after all." He sounded perversely pleased.

"You know, you are certainly not obliged to take me up on my offer of a ride, Callahan O'Shea. Feel free to ride your bike and get hit by a car for all I care."

"And with you on the road, there's a good chance of that happening, isn't there?"

"I repeat. Shut up or go home alone."

"All right, all right. Settle down," he said. I walked faster, irritated, my dancing shoes tapping loudly on the tile floor.

We walked back to the front desk to fetch my wee beastie from Shirley. "Was he a good boy?" I asked her.

"Oh, he was an angel!" she cooed. "Weren't you?"

"What sedative did you use?" Callahan asked.

"You're the only one he doesn't like," I lied as Angus bared his crooked little teeth at Callahan O'Shea and growled his kitten-purr growl. "He's an excellent judge of character."

It was raining outside, a sweet-smelling rain that would have my peonies (and hair) three inches taller by morning. I waited, still miffed, as Cal unchained his bike from a lamppost and wheeled it to my car. I popped open the trunk and waited, but Cal just stood there, getting rained on, looking at me.

"Well?" I asked. "Put it in."

"You don't have to give me a ride if you don't want to, Grace. I made you mad. I can ride my bike home."

"I'm not mad. Don't be dumb. Put your bike in the car. Angus and I are getting wet."

"Yes, ma'am."

I watched as he picked it up and maneuvered it in. It wouldn't fit all the way, so I made a mental note to drive slowly so as not to damage two forms of Callahan's transportation in one night, then got in the car with my dog. A quick look in the rearview mirror assured me that, yes, my hair was in fact possessed by evil spirits. I sighed.

"You're cute when you're mad," Callahan said as he got in.

"I'm not mad," I answered.

"It's all right with me if you are," he answered, buckling his seat belt.

"I'm not!" I practically shouted.

"Have it your way," he said. His arm brushed mine, and a hot jolt of electricity shot through my entire body. I stared straight ahead, waiting for it to fade.

Cal glanced at me. "Does that dog always sit on your lap when you're driving?"

"How's he going to learn if he doesn't practice?" Callahan smiled, and I felt my anger (yes, yes, so I was still a little bit mad) fade away. The lust remained. I backed (carefully) out of my parking space. Callahan O'Shea smelled good. Warm, somehow. Warm and rainy, the ever-present smell of wood mingling in an incredible combination. I wondered if he'd mind if I buried my face in his neck for a while. Probably shouldn't do that while I was driving.

"So how's your grandfather doing these days?" I asked.

"He's the same," Cal answered, looking out his window.

"Does he recognize you, do you think?" I asked, belatedly realizing that that was none of my business.

Callahan didn't answer for a second. "I don't think so."

A hundred questions burned to be asked. *Does he know you were in prison? What did you do before prison? Why doesn't your brother speak to you? Why'd you do it, Cal?*

"So, Cal," I began, taking a left on Elm Street, Angus helping me steer, "how's your house coming along?"

"It's pretty nice," he said. "You should come over and take a look."

I glanced at him. "Sure." I hesitated, then decided to go for it. "Callahan, I was wondering. What did you do in your pre-prison life?"

He looked at me. "I was an accountant," he said.

"Really?" I'd have guessed something outdoor-related—cowboy, for example. Not a desk job. "Don't want to do that again, then? Kind of boring, is it?"

"I lost my license when I broke the law, Grace."

Oh, crap, right. "So why *did* you break the law?" I asked.

Cal merely looked at me. "Why do you want to know so badly?"

"Because!" I answered. "It's not every day you live next door to a convicted felon."

"Maybe I don't want to be thought of as a convicted felon, Grace. Maybe I want to be thought of as the person I am now. Make up for lost time and leave the past behind and all that crap."

"Ah, how sweet. Well, I am a history teacher, Mr. O'Shea. The past matters very much to me."

"I'm sure it does." His voice was cool.

"The best indicator of the future is past behavior," I intoned.

"Who said that? Abe Lincoln?"

"Dr. Phil, actually." I smiled. He didn't smile back.

"So what are you saying, Grace? You expect me to embezzle from you?"

"No! Just…well, you obviously felt the need to break the law, so what does that say? It says something, but since you won't open your mouth and speak, I don't know what it is."

"What does your past say about you?" he asked.

My past was Andrew. What did it say? That I wasn't a good judge of character? That when compared with Natalie, I didn't measure up? That I wasn't quite good enough? That Andrew was a jerk?

"There's the lake," I commented. "If you're planning on dumping my body there, you'd better get to it."

His mouth pulled up in one corner, but he didn't answer.

We pulled onto our street. "About your truck," I said. "I'm really sorry. I'll call my insurance agent tomorrow."

"I take it you have him on speed dial," Callahan said.

"Very funny."

He laughed, an ashy, low laugh that hit me right in the pit of my stomach. "Thanks for the ride, Grace," he said.

"If you ever want to confess your sins, I'm available."

"Now you've gone from a martyr to a priest. Good night, Grace."

CHAPTER EIGHTEEN

"IT'S...UH, BEAUTIFUL," I said, blinking down at the ring. Oh, heck, it was. The diamond was about a carat, maybe a little more, a nice chunky thing, pear-shaped, pretty setting. I loved it. I *owned* it, in fact. Well, no, that's not quite true. I *owned* its twin, which sat in my jewelry box at home, waiting for me to pawn it. For heaven's sake. Couldn't Andrew be a little more original? I mean, come on! He'd picked sisters to become his fiancées...at least he could've picked out different rings, for crying out loud.

"Thanks," Nat said, blissfully unaware that we now had matching engagement rings from the same man. We were sitting in the backyard of our parents' house, just Nat and me. The rest of the gang was inside—Andrew, Mémé, Margaret, Mom and Dad.

"You're sure this is okay with you?" Natalie asked, slipping her hand into mine.

"The only thing that's not okay is you constantly asking if I'm okay," I said a bit sharply. "Really, Natalie. Please stop." Then, guilty at my irritation, I squeezed her hand. "I'm glad you're happy."

"You've been just amazing, Grace. Getting Andrew and me together...that was above and beyond the call."

You're telling me. I gave a snort, then glanced at my little sister. The sun was shining on her hair, her

dark gold eyelashes brushing her cheeks as she gazed
at her ring.

"So have you set a date?" I asked.

"Well, I wanted to ask your opinion on that," she
said, looking at me. "Andrew and I kind of felt it should
be soon. Get it out of the way, you know? Then we
could just be married. Nothing huge. Just the family
and a few friends and some dinner afterward. What
do you think?"

"Sounds pretty," I said.

"Grace," she began hesitantly, "I was wondering if
you'd be my maid of honor. I know the circumstances
are pretty weird, but I had to ask you. And if you don't
want to, of course I understand. But ever since I was
little, I always imagined it would be you. Margaret as
a bridesmaid, of course, but you as my number one,
you know?"

It was impossible to say no. "Sure," I murmured.
"I'd be honored." My heart was beating in slow, rolling thumps, making me feel a little ill.

"Thank you," Nat whispered, hugging me. For a minute, it was like we were little again, her face warm and
smooth against my neck, me petting her silky blond
hair, breathing in the sweet smell of her shampoo.

"I can't believe you're getting married," I whispered,
a couple tears slipping out of my eyes. "I still want to
give you piggyback rides and braid your hair."

"I love you, Grace," she murmured.

"I love you, too, Nattie Bumppo," I said around the
rock in my throat. My little sister, whom I had helped
bathe and diaper, whom I'd read to and cuddled, was
leaving me in one of the most profound ways a sister
could. For twenty-five years, I had been Natalie's fa-

vorite person, and she'd been mine, and now that was changing. When I was with Andrew, let's face it, he hadn't deposed Natalie from the throne in my heart. Sure, I loved him…but Natalie was *part* of me. Part of my soul and heart, the way only sisters could be.

Dozens of memories flashed through my head. Me at age ten, when I'd had my tonsillectomy, waking up from a restless, narcotic-induced sleep to find that Natalie had drawn eighteen pictures of horses for me, laying them on my bedroom floor, propping them on my chair and desk so everywhere I looked, I'd see horses. The time I beat up Kevin Nichols when he put gum in her hair. Me leaving for William & Mary, and Natalie's face contorting with the effort of smiling so I wouldn't see that she was, in fact, sobbing.

I loved her, and had always loved her, so much that it hurt. I could not—would not—let Andrew come between us.

She squeezed me hard, then sat up. "I can't believe I still haven't met Wyatt," she said.

"I know," I seconded. "He's dying to meet you, too." Wyatt was, alas, at a medical convention in San Francisco. I'd briefly flirted with the idea of telling my family Wyatt and I had broken up, then I decided I needed him a little longer. This morning, I'd searched *medical conventions* and *surgeons* on the internet and found one in the City by the Bay. Extremely convenient.

"Things are good with you two?" Nat asked.

"Oh, I guess. He works too much. If there's one fly in the ointment, it's that." My evil plan was to plant these seeds so I could ease everyone into the idea of a breakup. "He's always at the hospital, and now he's up in Boston... He's so devoted to his work. I guess it's the classic complaint of the doctor's wife."

Oops. Hadn't actually meant to say that last sentence. Natalie's face glowed even more beautifully, if possible.

"Do you think you guys might get married?"

Oh, crap. "Um, well...I don't know. The work thing is something we have to figure out. And of course, I've been burned before."

And again. Didn't mean to say that last bit. Natalie flinched.

"I mean, I've picked the wrong guy before, so I want to be careful and all. Make sure he's the right one."

"But you think he is?"

I tipped my head, pretending to consider the question. After all, Wyatt and I were going to have to break up. Rather soon, in fact, since obviously I couldn't keep this up forever. "He's..." I smiled at Natalie in what I imagined was modest adoration. "He's pretty wonderful, Nat. I just wish we had more time together."

The back door banged open, and Margaret appeared before us. "Grace, your dog just broke a vulva. And Mom wants you to come in and eat, anyway." She fisted her hands on her hips. "And did it ever occur to you two that I might be jealous of your little club? Christ Almighty and His five sacred wounds, girls! Can't I be included once in a while?"

"She swears like some ex-nun turned sailor," Natalie murmured.

"Yeah. You have to wonder how she spends her free time," I seconded.

"Quit your whining," Nat called to our big sis. "You two are living together, so don't talk to me about clubs, okay?"

Margaret tromped over to us. "Move over, favorite," she grumbled, shoving my shoulder so she could sit down. "Is everything okay out here? I've been spying through the windows."

"Everything's great. I'm Nattie's maid of honor," I said. It felt okay. Yes. It would be fine.

"God's sandals, Natalie! You want Andrew's former fiancée to be your fucking maid of honor?"

"Yes," Nat answered calmly. "But only if she wants to be."

"And I do," I said, sticking my tongue out at Margaret.

"So? What am I, Nat? Can I maybe sweep up for you? Maybe I could do dishes at the reception and peek out at you once in a while, if you don't think I'll be blinded with your golden beauty, your majesty."

"God, listen to her," Nat giggled. "Would you be my bridesmaid, Margaret dear?"

"Oh, gosh, thanks, yes. I can't wait." Margaret shot me a look. "Maid of honor, huh? Freaky."

"Margs, you've met Wyatt, right?" Natalie asked.

Margaret stuck her tongue in her cheek. "Sure," she answered. I closed my eyes.

"What do you think?" Nat sat up straighter, grinning. She always did love girl talk.

"Well, aside from that sixth toe on his left foot, he's pretty cute," Margs said.

"Very funny," I answered. "It's barely a nub, Natalie."

Natalie was laughing. "What else, Margs?"

"Well, the way he sucks on Grace's ear is pretty disgusting. Especially in church. Yick."

"Come on, I'm serious," Natalie wheezed, wiping her eyes.

"That wandering eye freaks me out."

When our mother came out to find what was keeping her girls, she found us helpless with laughter on the bench under the maple tree.

My good humor remained as Angus and I walked home along the Farmington. A path meandered through the state forest that bordered the river, and though the gnats were out, they were harmless enough if I ignored them. Angus trotted ahead on his long leash, stopping frequently to pee, sniff and pee some more, making sure that all the other dogs who came down this path would know that Angus McFangus had been there before them.

Natalie and Andrew had set a date after poring over Mom's calendar. June fourth, the day after Manning's graduation. Four weeks from now. Four weeks to break up with my imaginary boyfriend, four weeks to possibly find a date for yet another wedding. I imagined being stag at this one. Bleecch. Yet the thought of turning myself inside out to find someone was equally distasteful.

Angus barked and trembled. Up ahead, someone was fly-fishing in the river, hip boots on, the long line of his pole arcing out in a golden, serpentine flash. The sun shone on his messy hair, and I smiled, somehow not surprised to see my neighbor.

"Catching anything, or are you just trying to look pretty?" I called.

"Howdy, neighbor," he called back. "Haven't caught a thing."

"You poor slob." I picked my way over the rocks to get closer. "Don't blind me with your hook, okay?"

"Why? Seems like I owe you a few cuts and bruises," he said, sloshing over toward me. Angus began yarping. "Quiet, you," Cal said sternly, which set Angus off into hysterics. *Yarpyarpyarpyarp! Yarpyarpyarpyarpyarp!*

"You have such a way with animals," I said. "Do small children burst into tears at the sight of you?"

He laughed. "What are you doing out here, Grace?"

"Oh, just headed for home," I answered.

"Want to sit for a while? I have cookies," he said temptingly.

"Are they homemade?" I asked.

"If by *homemade,* you mean *bought at the bakery,* then yes," he answered. "They're good. Not compared to your brownies, though. Those things were out of this world. Worth all the pain I had to go through to get them."

"Aw. Well, that was such a nice compliment, maybe I'll bake you some more." I sat on a rock that jutted over the river, holding Angus on my lap, where he growled at the man in front of us.

"Why don't you let Angus off the leash?" Cal suggested.

"Oh, no," I said. "He'd go right for the water and get swept away." I hugged my little pal a little closer. "We don't want you to drown, do we, sweet coconut baby? Hmm? No. We don't."

"Some of us do," Callahan said. The cookies were from Lala's—sad, really, that I could recognize baked goods from twenty yards—crumbly and delicious peanut butter cookies with crystals of sugar sparkling in the crisscross marks.

Cal offered a cookie to Angus, who snapped it up, catching part of Cal's finger. Cal jerked his hand back, sighed, looked at the wounded extremity and held out his finger for my inspection. Two tiny drops of blood showed.

"You poor thing," I said. "Shall I call 911?"

"Why don't you call a lawyer?" he said, raising an eyebrow. "Possibly Margaret. Your dog is becoming a menace. Between the two of you, I can't believe I'm still alive."

"Tragic, really. Well, you'll be moving soon, right?"

"Yup. I'm sure you'll miss me."

Dang it. I would miss him. The sun shone on his hair, illuminating all the shades of brown and caramel and gold. It wasn't fair that this guy could look like an ad for *Outdoor Living,* oozing sex appeal in wader boots and a flannel shirt. The sleeves were rolled up to reveal his tanned forearms. His lashes were golden and straight and really just pointlessly attractive, and my girl-parts were begging me to do something.

I cleared my throat. "So, Cal, how's your love life? I happened to see you again with that blonde from the bar."

"Spying again, Grace? I thought we had an understanding."

I sighed in exasperation. "She was right on the front porch. I was weeding." I paused. "You kissed her."

"On the cheek," he said.

"Mmm-hmm. Which some women find very romantic." He said nothing. "So? What about the lawn you want to mow?"

"That's kind of a crude way to refer to sex, isn't it, Grace?"

I blinked, then laughed. "I meant what you said that time. You wanted a wife, some kids, a lawn to mow."

"And I do." He cast the line out again, not looking at me.

"So how's the search going?" I asked.

"Not bad," he answered after a beat or two. Angus growled.

Not bad. What did that mean? "Well." I stood up and brushed off my jeans. "Thanks for the cookie, mister. Good luck with your fishing. For the wife *and* the trout."

"Have a nice day, Grace."

"You, too."

As I walked the rest of the way home, I tried to talk myself out of lusting after Callahan O'Shea. Reminded myself that he wasn't husband material, not for me. We weren't compatible. Because…um…well, because…

Let's face it. Callahan O'Shea was very fun to look at, that was true. Maybe he liked me. He *flirted* with me…a little. Sometimes. He flirted more with Margaret, to be honest. I'd seen them talking the other day, laughing like old friends over the back fence. Regrettably, I'd been on the phone at the time, so I hadn't been able to eavesdrop.

One thing was certain, however. I did not feel safe around him. Not that he would rob me, no, of course not. But if Andrew had broken my heart, imagine what Callahan O'Shea could do to it. Crush it until there was nothing left but rubble. Let's be honest. For someone like me—the little schoolteacher who danced with old people, loved Civil War movies and playing pretend—to be with someone like him, this vital, vaguely dangerous man who radiated and bristled with sex appeal… it had to be a bad idea. A disaster waiting to happen.

I just wished I could stop thinking about it.

CHAPTER NINETEEN

IT WAS QUITE A RELIEF to have Julian back as a regular feature in my life. And not only did I have him, but also the handsome and debonair Tim Gunn, since *Project Runway* was on. Margaret had deigned to come downstairs, I'd made popcorn and brownies, and it was the happiest I'd felt in a good while.

This week had been tough at school. The kids were dying to do anything but learn, and the seniors' year had basically ended once they'd heard from the colleges. I understood, had shown *Glory* instead of making them work, but still. I couldn't do nothing, either, which was what Ava was doing...letting the seniors text their friends and gossip, despite the fact that classes wouldn't end for weeks.

Speaking of Ava, her presentation to the board had been (from her own account, anyway) dazzling. The fact that she was sleeping with the chairman (according to Kiki, seconded by Paul and hinted at by Ava herself) certainly wasn't hurting her cause. My presentation was soon, and I'd been going over it feverishly, wondering if I should pull back on the changes I wanted to make, stick with the status quo a bit more.

On the dating front, eCommitment had offered up a mortician whose passion was taxidermy (understandable, I guess, but that didn't mean I had to date him) and an unemployed man who lived in his parents' basement and collected Pokémon cards. Come on! I was tired of looking. Granted, I hadn't been at it very long, but I wanted a break. I'd break up with Wyatt and just tell my family he was a workaholic, the end. Then I could relax and just enjoy life. I thought it was a great plan.

"Which one is that again?" Margaret asked, stuffing more popcorn into her mouth. She was supposedly working on a brief and did indeed have a yellow legal pad next to her, but it was forgotten as she succumbed to the siren call of my favorite show.

"That's the one who made his mother a gown when he was six," Julian answered, stroking Angus's back. "The prodigy. He's cute, too. I think he might be gay."

"Really," Margaret said. "Hmm. A guy who designs women's clothing. Gay. Who knew?"

"Now, now. No need for stereotypes," Julian chided.

"Said the gay male dance instructor," Margaret added, grinning.

"Replied the angry, driven, heterosexual female defense attorney," Julian countered.

"Retorted the man who spends thirty minutes on his hair each day, owns three cats and knits them sweaters," Margaret said.

"Sniped the beautiful, bitter workaholic who walked out on her mild-mannered husband, essentially castrating him," returned Julian. They grinned fondly at each other.

"You win," Margaret said. "The angry hetero concedes to the dancing fairy." Julian batted his impressive eyelashes at her.

"Children. Stop your bickering or there's no ice cream for you," I said, spreading my middle-child peacekeeping karma among them. "Oh, look, Tim's giving them the challenge." We fell silent, hanging on Tim Gunn's every word. Of course, that was when the phone rang.

"Don't get it," hissed Julian, turning up the TV from the remote.

I disobeyed after glancing at the caller ID. "Hey, Nat."

"Hi, Gissy! How's it going?"

"I'm great," I said, trying to listen to the show. Ooh. Dresses out of materials found at the dump. This would be a good one.

"What are you doing?" Natalie asked.

"Oh, um, we're just watching *Project Runway*," I answered.

"He's there? Wyatt's there?" Natalie squealed.

"No, Julian's here. Wyatt's in, um, Boston."

Julian's head snapped around, and he scootched closer to me so he could listen. *Project Runway* went into commercial.

"Well, listen, I wanted to ask you a favor. Andrew and I are going to come up on Friday for a family dinner. You know, the Carsons and you guys, and I wanted to make sure you could make it. With Wyatt."

I winced.

"I think he can finally get away, don't you, Grace? I mean, there are other doctors in Boston, right?" She chuckled.

"Uh, dinner? With the Carsons?" Margaret recoiled at the name, Julian looked stricken. They remembered the Carsons. I simulated shooting myself in the temple.

"Um…Friday?" I gestured to Margaret and Julian for help. "Gee, we, um…we sort of have plans."

"Grace, come on!" Natalie said. "This is getting ridiculous."

You have no idea, I thought.

Margaret jumped up and pried the phone out of my hand. "Nat, it's Margs." Margaret listened for a second. "Well, shit, Nat, did you ever think that maybe Grace is afraid Wyatt will fall for you, too?"

"Stop! That's not nice. Give me the phone, Margaret." I wrestled the receiver out of my older sister's hand and spoke soothingly to my younger sister. "I'm back, Nattie."

"Grace, that's not true, is it?" she whispered.

"Of course not! No!" I glared at Margaret, then lowered my voice. "I can tell you this, because I know you'll understand." Margaret sighed loudly. "Nat," I continued, "you know how Wyatt and I don't get to spend too much time together. And I told him I was losing patience. So he made these special plans..."

Nat was quiet for a minute. "Well, I guess you need a little time alone together."

"Exactly. You understand. But tell the Carsons I said hello, and of course I'll be seeing them soon at the wedding and all that."

"Okay. Love you, Grace."

"Love you, too, honey." I clicked End and turned to my other sister and friend. "Wyatt and I are going to have a big fight," I announced.

"Poor bastard. If only he wasn't so committed to healing children," Margaret said.

"I'm sure he'll be heartbroken," Julian said kindly.

I went into the kitchen for a drink of ice water, Angus pattering after me, hoping for a cookie. I obliged, knelt

down and made my little dog sit up for his treat, then
gave it to him and patted his head.

I was tired of Wyatt, tired of Margaret, too, tired of
my parents' bickering, tired of mean old Mémé, tired of
Natalie and Andrew. For a second, I remembered Callahan O'Shea asking me if my family did anything for
me. Well. I was tired of thinking about him, too, because that just got me all hot and bothered and tingly
in places long neglected, and then I didn't sleep well,
which made me feel more tired than ever.

When Natalie's wedding was over, I was going to
take a nice long vacation. Maybe go to Tennessee, see
some of the battle sites down there. Maybe go to England. Or Paris, where I could possibly meet a real-life
Jean-Philippe.

Angus rested his sweet head on my foot. "I love you,
McFangus," I said. "You're Mommy's best boy."

Straightening up, I couldn't help but check out Callahan O'Shea's house for signs of life. A soft light
glowed in an upstairs window. Maybe a bedroom window. Maybe he was having sex with a potential wife.
If I went upstairs, to the attic, for example, I might
be able to see…or if I just bought some really good
binoculars…or if I climbed up the lilac tree and went
hand-over-hand along the drainpipe, then, yes, I'd have
a perfect view of what was in that room. God's nightgown, I was pathetic.

"Grace." Margaret stood in the kitchen doorway.
"Hey, you okay?"

"Oh, sure," I said.

"Listen, I'm sending you and Julian out for dinner,
okay? As a thank-you for letting me be such a pain in

the ass and stay here." Her voice was uncharacteristically kind.

"That's nice of you."

"I'll have Junie make reservations, okay? Somewhere really swanky. Order lots to drink, get two desserts, the works." She came over to me and put her arm around my shoulder, and from the porcupine sister, it was a horribly tender gesture. "And you can have all the more fun thinking of how you're missing the Carsons."

ON FRIDAY NIGHT, JULIAN and I were shown to a lovely table at Soleil, a beautiful restaurant overlooking the Connecticut River in Glastonbury. It was the kind of place I'd never eat in—very modern and expensive. We passed not only a glassed-in wine storage room on our way to our table, but a special, clear glass freezer full of designer vodka. On one end, the kitchen was exposed so we could see the chefs working madly away, sliding plates under the lights, chattering away in French. Our waiter, whose name was Cambry, handed us menu after menu—wine list, today's specials, martini list, regular menu, staff picks, each bound in leather and printed in an elegant font. "Enjoy your meal," he said, gazing at Julian. My friend ignored him, as was his custom.

"Look at this place, Grace," Julian said as we pored over the martini list. "Just the sort of place Wyatt would take you."

"You think? It's a little too high pressure for me."

"But he wants to impress you. He adores you."

"That's not enough, Wyatt," I said with mock seriousness. "I understand how devoted you are to your work, but I want more. You're a lovely man. Good luck. I'll always care for you, but goodbye."

Julian placed both of his hands over his heart. "Oh, Grace, I'm so sorry. I'll always love you and regret that my work came between us, but I cannot abandon those poor children to some ham-handed caveman when I alone possess the necessary..." Julian's head whipped around as a waiter passed. "Oh, that looks good. What is that, salmon? I think I might order that." Julian looked back at me. "Where was I?"

"It doesn't matter. It's over. My family will be crushed." My buddy laughed. "Julian," I said more quietly, "you know how you said we weren't going to keep looking for a man?"

"Yeah?" he said, frowning.

"Well, I still want a man."

He sat back in his seat and sighed. "I know. Me, too. It's just so hard."

I sat back. "I have a crush on my neighbor. The ex-con."

"Who wouldn't?" Julian muttered.

"He's just a little..."

"Much?" my friend suggested.

"Exactly," I agreed. "I think he might like me, but as for doing anything about it, I'm just too..."

"Chickenshit?"

"Yes," I admitted. Julian nodded in sympathy. "But what about you, Julian? You must have to fight men off with a stick. The waiter keeps looking at you. He's cute. You could talk to him, at least."

"Well, maybe I will."

I gazed out the window at the river. The sun was sinking into a spectacular pile of buttery clouds, and the sky was pale peach and rose. It was lovely, and I felt myself relaxing.

"Okay, give it a try, Grace," Julian said, once we'd ordered dinner (he'd ignored the cute waiter) and were sipping our cool and unusual martinis. "Remember Lou from Meeting Mr. Right? We already know rule number one."

"I'm the most beautiful woman here," I said obediently.

"Yes, Grace, but you have to feel it. Sit up straight. Stop shlunching."

"Yes, Mother," I said, taking another sip.

"Rule number two. Look around the room and smile, because you know that every man here would be lucky to have you, and you can have any man you want."

I did as told. My eyes stopped on an elderly man, well into his eighties. Sure, *he'd* be lucky to have me. As proven with Dave of the Leg Bag, I had a certain *je ne sais quoi* when it came to older men. But would the bartender, who looked hauntingly like a young Clark Gable *sans* moustache, feel that way?

"'Believe in yourself,'" Julian intoned. "No, Grace, you're doing it wrong. Look. What's the problem?"

I rolled my eyes. "The problem is that it's stupid, Julian. Put me next to, I don't know, Natalie, for example, or Margaret, for another, and I'm *not* the most beautiful woman in the room. Ask Andrew if he was lucky to have me, and he'd probably say hell yes! Because if it weren't for me, he'd never have met his darling bride-to-be."

"Ooh! Are we having our period? Sit and watch, darling," Julian said, ignoring my diatribe. I watched sulkily as my buddy sat back in his seat and gazed around the room. Bing, bang, boom. Three women at three different tables stopped midsentence and blushed.

"Sure, you're great with *women*," I said. "But you don't want to date *women*. Think I didn't see you just about crawl under the table when our waiter was fawning all over you? Try it on the guys, Julian."

He narrowed his lovely eyes at me. "Fine." His own face grew a little pink, but I had to give him credit for trying.

And sure enough, his eyes met our waiter's, who snatched a plate from the kitchen counter and practically vaulted over a table to get to us. "Here you are," he breathed. "Oysters Rockefeller. Enjoy."

"Thank you," Julian said, looking up at him. The waiter's lips parted. Julian didn't look away.

Well, well. Would my friend actually break his self-imposed chastity and find Mr. Right after all? Smiling, I took a bite of the oysters—yummy—and decided to check my messages while the two good-looking men gazed soulfully at each other. Gracious! Julian was actually initiating conversation! Would wonders never cease.

I'd turned off my phone in last period today when giving my freshmen a test and hadn't turned it back on. I wasn't a cell phone lover, to be honest. Many was the day that I forgot to turn it on at all. But wait. This was odd. I had six messages.

I'd never had six messages before. Was something wrong? Had Mémé died? An unexpected wave of sadness hit me at the idea. Hitting the code for my voice mail, I glanced out the window and waited as Julian and Cambry the waiter flirted.

"You have six new messages. Message one." My older sister's voice came on. "Grace, it's Margaret. Listen, kid, don't go to Soleil tonight, okay? I'm really

sorry, but I think Junie told Mom where you were going
when Mom called my office this afternoon. I guess
Mom's all hell-bent for leather to meet Wyatt, and she
made a reservation for tonight. With the Carsons. So
don't go there. I'll pick up the tab somewhere else, just
charge it. Call me when you get this."

The message was left at 3:45.

Oh…my…God.

Message two. "Grace, Margs again. Mom just called
me. The dinner is definitely at Soleil, so head somewhere else, okay? Call me." That one was at 4:15.

Messages three through five were the same, I dimly
noted, though Margaret's language deteriorated as they
went on. Horror rose like an icy tide. Message six was
as follows. "Grace, where the hell are you? We're leaving for the stupid restaurant right now. The Carsons,
Andrew, Nat, Mom and Dad and Mémé. Call me! Our
reservation is at seven."

I looked at my watch. It was six-fifty-three.

Julian and Cambry were laughing now as Cambry
wrote his phone number on a piece of paper. "Julian?"
I said, my voice barely a whisper.

"One sec, Grace," said Julian. "Cambry and I—"
Then he saw my expression. "What is it?"

"My family is on their way. Here," I said.

His eyes popped. "Oh, shit."

Cambry looked at us, confused. "Is there a problem?" he asked.

"We need to leave right away," I said. "Immediately.
Family emergency. Here." I fumbled in my pocketbook for the gift certificate Margaret's secretary had
printed off the internet. Dread raced through my veins.

I couldn't be found here. I couldn't! I'd just tell the family we'd gone somewhere else. That was it. No problem.

Just as we stood up to go, I heard the horrible sound of my mother's nervous society laugh. *Ahahaha! Ahahaha! Oooh...ahahaha.* I looked at Julian. "Run," I whispered.

"We need another exit," Julian said to Cambry.

"Through the kitchen," he answered instantly. The two of them were off, me right on their heels, when the strap of my pocketbook snagged on the chair of a nearby diner. He looked up.

"Oopsy," he said. "You're caught, honey." *In more ways than one, mister.* I flashed him a panicked smile and tugged. The strap didn't come free.

Years of dance training made Julian lithe and fast as a snake. He zigged and zagged through the tables toward the busy, open kitchen, failing to notice I wasn't with him.

"Here you go," said the diner, sliding the strap off the back of his chair. And just as I turned to gallop after my friend, I heard my mother's voice.

"Grace! There you are!"

My entire family walked in. Margaret, wide-eyed. Andrew and Nat, holding hands. Dad pushing Mémé's wheelchair, followed by Mom. And the Carsons, Letitia and Ted.

My mind was perfectly blank. "Hi, guys!" I heard myself saying in that out-of-body way. "What are you doing here!"

Nat gave me a hug. "Mom insisted that we crash. Just to say hello, not to spoil your special night." She pulled back to look at me. "I'm really sorry. I told her no a million times, but you know how she is."

Margaret caught my eye and shrugged. Well, hell, she tried. I could feel my heart thumping in sick, rolling beats, and hysterical laughter wriggled like a trout in my stomach.

"Grace, darling! You've been so secretive!" Mom burbled, her eyes darting to my table, where two martinis and an order of oysters Rockefeller sat abandoned. "I told Letitia here about your wonderful doctor boyfriend, and she said she couldn't wait to meet him, and then I had to tell her that *we* haven't met him, and then I thought, well, I'll just kill two birds with one stone. You remember the Carsons, don't you, dear?"

Of course I remembered them. I got to within three weeks of being their daughter-in-law, for heaven's sake. Someday, a long, long time from now, I might forgive my mother. On second thought, no. In my experience, Mr. and Mrs. Carson were aloof, undemonstrative people, completely devoid of humor. They never expressed anything but the coolest politeness toward me.

"Hi, Mrs. Carson, Mr. Carson. Good to see you again." The Carsons smiled insincerely at me. I returned their smile with equal affection.

"What are you eating? Are those oysters? I don't eat shellfish," Mémé boomed. "Disgusting, slimy, riddled with bacteria. I have irritable bowel syndrome as it is."

"Grace, honey, I'm sorry if we're horning in," Dad murmured, giving me a kiss on the cheek. "Your mother went a little berserk when she heard you weren't coming. Don't you look pretty! So where is he? As long as we're here."

Andrew caught my eye. He knew me pretty well, after all. He tilted his head to one side and smiled curiously.

"He's…uh…he's in the bathroom," I said.

Margaret closed her eyes.

"Right. Um, not feeling that well, actually. I'd better go check on him. Tell him you're here."

My face burned as I walked (and walked, and walked, God, it seemed to be taking forever) through the restaurant. In the foyer, Cambry gestured down the hall toward the restrooms. Sure enough, there was Julian, lurking just inside the men's room, peering out through the cracked door. "What should we do?" he whispered. "I told Cambry what was going on. He can help us."

"I just told them Wyatt's not feeling well. And you're playing the part of Wyatt." I glanced back toward the dining room. "Jesus, Mary and Joseph on rye bread, here comes my dad! Get in a stall. Hurry up!"

The door closed, and I heard the sound of a stall door slamming as Dad lumbered down the hall. "Honey? How's he doing?"

"Oh, well, not so good, Dad. Um, he must've eaten something that didn't agree with him."

"Poor guy. Helluva way to meet your sweetheart's family." Dad leaned amiably against the wall. "Want me to check on him?"

"No! No, no." I pushed the men's room door open a crack. "Hon? You doing okay?"

"Uhhnnhuh," Julian said weakly.

"I'm here if you need me," I said, letting the door close again. "Dad, I really wish you guys hadn't come. This is—" *a ridiculous farce* "—our special night."

He had the decency to look ashamed. "Well, your mother…you know how she is. She felt the whole family should be there to show the Carsons…well, that you're okay with everything."

"Right. And I am," I said, cursing myself. I should've just gone to the stupid dinner, said that Wyatt had plans or emergency surgery or something. Instead, here I was, lying to my father. My dear old dad who loved me and played Civil War with me and paid for my new windows.

"Dad?" I said hesitantly. "About Wyatt…"

Dad patted my shoulder. "Don't worry, Pudding. It's embarrassing, sure, but no one will hold a little diarrhea against him."

"Well, the thing is, Dad—"

"We're just glad you're seeing someone, honey. I don't mind admitting that I was worried about you. Breaking up with Andrew, well, that was one thing. Everyone's heart gets broken once or twice. And I knew it wasn't your idea, honey."

My mouth dropped open. "You did?" I'd taken such pains to tell everyone that it was mutual, that we just weren't sure we were right for each other…

"Sure, Pudding. You loved him, clear as day. Letting your sister date him…" Dad sighed. "Well, at least you found someone else. The whole way here, Natalie was chattering on and on about how wonderful your young man was. I think she still feels pretty guilty."

Well. There went my feeble desire to confess. A man came down the hall and paused, looking at us.

"My daughter's boyfriend is sick," Dad explained. "The runs." I closed my eyes.

"Oh," the man said. "Um…thanks. I guess I can wait." He turned and headed back to the dining room.

Dad pushed the door open a little. "Wyatt, son? This is Grace's dad, Jim Emerson."

"Hello, sir," Julian mumbled in a lower than normal voice.

"Anything I can get for you?"

"No, thanks." Julian threw in a groan for authenticity. Dad winced and let the door close.

"Why don't we go back, too, Dad?" I suggested. I cracked the door again. "Honey? I'll be back in a sec."

"Okay," Julian said hoarsely, then coughed. Frankly, I thought he was overdoing it a bit, but hey. I owed the guy my firstborn. Dad took my hand as we went back to the dining room, and I gave him a grateful squeeze as we approached my family, who was now seated around a large table. The Carsons frowned at the menu, Mémé inspected the silverware, Mom looked like she could levitate with the amount of nervous energy buzzing through her. Andrew, Nat and Margaret all looked up at me.

"How's he doing?" Natalie asked.

"Not that great," I said. "A bad oyster or something."

"I told you. Oysters are filthy bits of rubbery phlegm," Mémé announced, causing a nearby diner to gag noticeably.

"You're looking well, Grace," Mrs. Carson said, tearing her eyes from the menu. She tilted her head as if impressed that I hadn't slashed my throat when her son dumped me.

"Thanks, Mrs. Carson," I said. For about a month, I'd called her Letty. We had lunch together once to talk about the wedding.

"I have some Imodium in here somewhere," Mom said, fumbling through her purse.

"No, no, that's okay. It's more of…well. We're going to head home. I'm so sorry. Wyatt would just love to meet everyone, but you understand." I stifled a sigh. Not only was I dating an imaginary man, he had diarrhea, as well. So classy. Definitely the kind to make Andrew jealous.

Wait a second. To the best of my knowledge, Wyatt Dunn was not invented to make anyone jealous. I glanced at Andrew. He was looking at me, still holding Natalie's hand, and in his eyes was a hint of something. Affection? His mouth tugged up on one side, and I looked away.

"I'll walk you to the car," Natalie said.

"Stay here," Margs all but barked. "He doesn't want to meet you under these circumstances, dummy." Natalie sank back down, looking wounded.

I kissed my mother's cheek, waved to Mémé and finally left the dining room. Cambry the waiter was waiting outside the bathroom door. "You can leave the back way," he murmured, pushing open the bathroom door. "Julian? Coast is clear."

"I'm so sorry," I said to my friend. "And thank you," I added, pressing a twenty on Cambry. "You were really nice."

"You're welcome. It was kind of fun," Cambry said. He led us to another exit, farther away from the main dining room, shook hands with Julian, holding on a little too long.

"Well, I know I had a good time," Julian announced as we pulled out of the parking lot. "And, Grace, guess what? I have a date! So every cloud has a silver lining."

I glanced at my buddy. "You were great in there," I said.

"Faking diarrhea is a specialty of mine," he said, and with that, we laughed so hard I had to pull over.

CHAPTER TWENTY

"WHY WOULD YOU TEACH the American Revolution at the same time as the Vietnam War?" asked Headmaster Stanton, frowning.

Ten of us—the headmaster, Dr. Eckhart, seven trustees and me—sat around the vast walnut conference table in Bigby Hall, the main administrative building of Manning, the one that was featured on the cover of all our promotional brochures. I was making my presentation to the board of trustees, and I felt ill. I'd been up till 2:00 a.m. perfecting my talk, practicing over and over till I thought I had it right. This morning, I'd gotten up at six, dressed in one of my Wyatt outfits, taking care to combine conservatism with creativity, tamed my hair, ate a good breakfast despite the churning stomach and now was wondering if I should've bothered.

It wasn't going well. I'd finished my talk, and the seven members of the board, including Theo Eisenbraun, Ava's reputed lover, stared at me with varying degrees of confusion. Dr. Eckhart appeared to be dozing, I noted with rising panic.

"That's an excellent question," I said in my best teacher voice. "The American Revolution and the Vietnam War have a lot in common. Most history departments teach chronologically, which, to be honest, I think can get a little stale. But in the Revolution, we have a situation of an invading foreign army up against a small band of poorly armed citizens who won the war through cunning use of the terrain and just a simple refusal to give up. The same can be said for Vietnam."

"But they happened in different centuries," said Adelaide Compton.

"I'm aware of that," I said, a bit too sharply. "I feel that teaching by theme and not simply by timeline is the way to go. In some cases, anyway."

"You want to teach a class called 'The Abuse of Power'?" asked Randall Withington, who'd been a U.S. senator for our fair state some time ago. His already-florid face seemed a bit more mottled than usual.

"I think it's a very important aspect of history, yes," I said, cringing internally. Senator Withington had been ousted on charges of corruption and, er, abuse of power.

"Well, this is all very interesting," said Hunter Graystone III, who was Hunter IV's father and a Manning alumnus. He indicated my fifty-four-page document—curriculum for all four years, required courses, electives, credits, budget, field trips, staffing suggestions, teaching strategies, the role of parents, meshing the history curriculum with other subjects. I'd color-coded it, included pictures, graphs, charts, had it printed up and bound at Kinko's. Mr. Graystone had yet to open it. Damn it. I'd given Hunter a B on his midterm (quite fair, let me tell you), and Mr. Graystone had reminded me of this very fact when I introduced myself a half hour ago. "Why don't you just sum things up for us, Ms. Emerson?"

Dr. Eckhart looked up—not asleep, thank goodness—and gave me a little nod of encouragement.

"Sure," I said, trying to smile. "Well, here it is in a

nutshell." Taking a deep breath, I decided to give it all I had, my blank-faced audience aside. "I want Manning students to understand the impact of history on where we are today. I want the past to come alive for them, so they can appreciate the sacrifices that have gotten us to this point." I looked around at each board member in turn, willing them to *feel* my love for the subject. "I want our students to learn from the past in a way much more profound than memorizing dates. I want them to feel how the whole world shifted because of the act of a single person, whether it was Henry VIII creating a new religion or Dr. King calling for equality on the steps of the Lincoln Memorial."

"And who is Dr. King?" Adelaide asked, frowning.

My mouth dropped open. "Martin Luther King, Jr.? The civil rights activist?"

"Of course. Right. Go on."

Taking a steadying breath, I continued. "So many kids today see themselves as isolated from even the recent past, disconnected from their country's policies, living in a world where there are too many distractions from true knowledge. Text messaging, video games, online chatting…they all detract from living in this world and understanding it. These kids have to see where we've been and how we got here. They have to! Because it's our past that determines our future—as individuals, as a nation, as a *world*. They have to understand the past, because these kids *are* the future."

My heart pounded, my face was hot, my hands shook. I took a shaking breath and folded my sweaty hands together. I was finished.

No one said anything. Not a word. Nothing, and not

in a good way. Nope, it was fair to say there was the proverbial sound of crickets.

"So...you believe the children are our future," Theo said, suppressing a grin.

I closed my eyes briefly. "Yes," I said. "They are. Hopefully, they'll have the ability to think when the fates call on them to act. So." I stood up and gathered my papers. "Thank you all so much for your time."

"That was...very interesting," Adelaide said. "Er... good luck."

I was assured that I'd be notified if I got through the next round. They were, of course, looking outside Manning, yadda yadda ding dong, blah blah blah. As for making it to the next round, my chances were dubious. Dubious at best.

Apparently, word of my impassioned speech got out, because when I ran into Ava later that day in the Lehring staff room, she smiled coyly. "Hello, Grace," she said. Blink...blink...here it comes...and, yes, blink. "How was your presentation to the board?"

"It was great," I lied. "Very positive."

"Good for you," she murmured, washing out her coffee cup, singing as she did. "'I believe the children are our future...teach them well and let them lead the way—'"

I gritted my teeth. "How did yours go, Ava? Did the push-up bra sway the board in your favor, do you think?"

"Oh, Grace, I feel sorry for you," she said, pouring herself some more coffee. "It's not my cleavage they loved, hon. It's my way with people. Anyway. Best of luck."

At that moment, Kiki stuck her head in the door. "Grace, got a minute? Oh, hi, Ava, how are you?"

"I'm fantastic, thanks," Ava half whispered. Blink. Blink. And blink again.

"You okay?" Kiki asked when I came into the hall and closed the door behind me.

"I'm crappy, actually," I said.

"What happened?"

"My presentation didn't go very well," I admitted. All that work reduced to a Whitney Houston song. To my irritable disgust, my throat tightened with tears.

"I'm sorry, kid." She patted my arm. "Listen, do you want to go to Julian's Singles' Dance Night this Friday? Take your mind off your troubles? I still haven't met someone. God knows why. I've been trying those methods from Lou like they were sent from Mount Sinai, you know?"

"Kiki, that class was dumb, don't you think? Do you really want to trick a guy into dating you by pretending you're someone you're not?"

"Is there another way?" she asked. I sighed. "Okay, okay, I know. But come to the dance with me. Please? Just to distract yourself?"

"Yick," I answered. "I don't think so."

She lowered her voice. "Maybe you'll find someone to take to your sister's wedding," she suggested, evil, black-hearted woman that she was.

I grimaced.

"It's worth a shot," she cajoled.

"Satan, get thee behind me," I muttered. "Maybe. I'm not promising, but maybe."

"Okay, great!" She glanced at her watch. "Dang it, I have to run. Mr. Lucky needs his insulin, and if I'm late, he craps all over the place and then has seizures. Talk to you later!" And she was off, running down the hall to the medical disaster that was her cat.

"Hello, Grace."

I turned around. "Hi, Stuart! How are you? How's everything?"

He sighed. "I was hoping you'd tell me."

I bit down on a wave of impatience. "Stuart, um... listen. You need to do something. I'm not your intermediary, okay? I want very much for you guys to work this out, but you need to take action. Don't you think so?"

"I just don't know what action to take," he protested, taking off his glasses to rub his eyes.

"Well, you've been married to her for seven years, Stuart! Come on! Think of something!"

The door to the teacher's lounge opened. "Is there a problem here?" Ava's chest said. Well, her mouth said it, but with the amount of boob she was showing today, who could pay attention?

"No, no problem, Ava," I said shortly. "Private conversation."

"How are you, Stu?" she purred. "I heard your wife left you. I'm so sorry. Some women just don't appreciate a truly decent man." She shook her head sadly, blinked, blinked, blinked, then sashayed down the hall, her ass swaying.

Stuart stared after her.

"Stuart!" I barked. "Go see your wife. Please."

"Right," he muttered, tearing his eyes off Ava's butt. "Will do, Grace."

LATE THAT EVENING, I SIGHED, triple circling *would of* in red pen and writing *would HAVE* in the margin of

Kerry Blake's paper. I was correcting papers on my bed, as Margaret was using the computer to play Scrabble downstairs in my tiny office. Would of. Come on!

Kerry was a smart enough girl, but even at the age of seventeen, she knew she'd never have to really work for a living. Her mother was a Harvard grad and managing partner at a Boston consulting firm. Her father owned a software company with divisions in four countries, which he often visited in his private jet. Kerry would get into an Ivy League school, regardless of her grades and test scores. And, barring some miracle, if she did decide to work instead of take the Paris Hilton route, she'd probably get some high-paying job with a great office, take three-hour lunches and jet around to meetings, where she'd do a negligible amount of work, taking credit for the grunts who worked under her. If Kerry didn't know a past participle from a preposition, no one would care.

Except me. I wanted her to use her brain instead of coast on her situation, but Kerry didn't really care what I thought. That was clear. The board of trustees might well share her ennui.

"Grace!" Margaret's voice boomed through the house, making Angus jump. I swear, my older sister was becoming more and more like Mémé every day. "I'm making whole grain pasta with broccoli for dinner. Want some?"

I grimaced. "No, thanks. I'll throw something together later on." Something with cheese. Or chocolate. Possibly both.

"Roger that. Oh, shit. Stuart's here."

Thank *God*. I leaped to the window, Angus bouncing merrily behind me. Sure enough, my brother-in-law was coming up the path. It was almost dark, but his standard white oxford glowed in the dimming light. I moved out into the hallway to eavesdrop better, shutting the door behind me so Angus wouldn't blow my cover. Margaret stomped to answer the soft knock. I could see the back of her head, but no more.

"What do you want?" she asked ruthlessly. I detected a note of pleasure under her tone…Stuart was finally *doing* something, and Margaret appreciated that kind of thing.

"Margaret, I think you should come home." Stuart's voice was quiet, and I had to strain to hear. He didn't say anything else.

"That's it?" Margaret barked, echoing my own thought. "That's all you've got?"

"What more would you like me to say, Margaret?" he asked wearily. "I miss you. I love you. Come home."

My eyes were suddenly wet.

"Why? So we can stare at each other every night, bored out of our minds?"

"I never felt that way, Margaret. I was very happy," Stuart said. "If you don't want to have a baby, that's fine, but all these other complaints…I don't know what you want me to do. I'm no different from how I've always been."

"Which may be the problem," Margaret said sharply.

Stuart sighed. "If there's something specific you want me to do, I'll do it, but you have to tell me. This isn't fair."

"If I tell you, then it doesn't count," Margaret retorted. "It's like planned spontaneity, Stuart. An oxymoron."

"You want me to be unexpected and surprising," Stuart said, his voice suddenly hard. "Would you like it if I ran naked down Main Street? How about if I started shooting heroin? Shall I have an affair with the cleaning woman? Would that be surprising enough?"

"You're being deliberately obtuse, Stuart. Until you figure it out, I have nothing to say. Goodbye." Margaret closed the door and leaned against it, then, a second later, peeked out the transom window. "Goddamn it," she muttered. I heard the sound of a car motor starting. Apparently, Stuart was gone.

Margaret caught sight of me, crouched at the top of the stairs. "So?" she asked.

"Margaret," I began cautiously, "he loves you and he wants to make you happy. Doesn't that count, honey?"

"Grace, it's not that simple!" she said. "He'd love it if every night of our life was the same as the night before. Dinner. Polite conversation about literature and current events. Sex on the prescribed days. The occasional dinner out, where he takes half an hour to order a bottle of wine. I'm so bored I could scream!"

"Well, here's what I think, roomie," I said, my own voice growing hard. "He's a decent, hardworking, intelligent man and he adores you. I think you're acting like a spoiled brat."

"Grace," she said tightly, "since you've never been married, your opinion really doesn't count a whole heck of a lot right now. So mind your own business, okay?"

"Oh, absolutely, Margs. Hey, by the way, how much longer do you think you'll be staying?" Sure, it was bitchy, but it felt good.

"Why?" Margaret said. "Am I cutting in on your time with Wyatt?" With that, she stomped back into the kitchen.

Ten minutes later, feeling that I really should have control of my own house and shouldn't have to hide in my bedroom, I went downstairs. Margaret was standing at the stove, stirring her pasta, tears dripping off her chin. "I'm sorry," she said in a small voice.

"Sure," I sighed, my anger evaporating. Margaret never cried. Never.

"I do love him, Grace. I think I do, anyway, but sometimes I just felt like I was suffocating, Grace. Like if I started screaming, he wouldn't even notice. I don't want a divorce, but I can't be married to a piece of cardboard, either. It's like we work in theory, but when we're actually together, I'm dying. I don't know what to do. If just once he could move outside the stupid box, you know? And the idea of a baby..." She started to sob. "It feels like Stuart wanting a baby means I'm not enough anymore. And he was the one who was supposed to adore me."

"Which he does, Margs!"

She didn't listen. "Besides, I'm such a bitch, Grace, who would want me for a mother?"

"You're not a bitch. Not all the time," I assured her. "Angus loves you. That's a good sign, isn't it?"

"Do you want me to move out? Stay at a hotel or something?"

"No, of course not. You know damn well you can stay with me as long as you want," I said. "Come on. Give us a hug."

She wrapped her arms around me and squeezed fiercely. "Sorry about the Wyatt crack," she muttered.

"Yeah, yeah," I said, squeezing her back. Angus, jealous that there was love and it wasn't directed at him, began leaping and whining.

Margaret stepped back, breaking our hug, grabbed a tissue and wiped her eyes. "Want some dinner?" she offered. "I made enough for us both."

I looked at what she called dinner. "I try to avoid eating rope," I said, getting a little grin in response. "I'm actually not hungry. Think I'll just sit outside for a bit." I poured myself a glass of wine, patted her shoulder to assure her I wasn't mad and went out with my dog into the sweet-scented night.

Sitting in an Adirondack chair, I looked around my yard. Angus was sniffing the back fence, patrolling the perimeter like the good guard dog he was. All the flowers I planted last year were coming up beautifully. The peonies along the back fence were heavy with blooms, the sugary smell of their blossoms heady in the night. Bee balm waved over near pine trees that shielded me from 32 Maple, and on Callahan's side, the irises rose in graceful lines, white and indigo, vanilla and grape scented. The lilacs along the eastern side of the house had faded, but their scent was indescribably lovely, calming and invigorating at the same time. The only sound was of the Farmington River, full and fast at this time of year, gushing over the rocks. A train whistle sounded somewhere, its melancholy note underscoring the loneliness that shrouded my heart.

Why couldn't people be happy alone? Love took your heart hostage. I'd sell my soul for Margaret and Natalie, my parents, Julian, even sweet little Angus, my faithful friend. As proven by my recent actions, I'd do anything to find someone who'd love me with the same wholeheartedness I wanted to love him. Those distant days with Andrew seemed like they'd happened to someone else. And even if I did find someone, what guarantee was there that it would last? Look at my parents, so pissed off with each other all the time. Margaret and Stuart…seven years crumbling away. Kiki, Julian and me, all floundering.

I seemed to be crying a little bit. I wiped my eyes on my sleeve and took a healthy slug of wine. Stupid love. Margaret was right. Love sucked.

"Grace?"

My head jerked up. Callahan O'Shea was out on his roof, looking down at me like a blue-collar *deus ex machina*.

"Hi," I said.

"Everything okay?" he asked.

"Oh…sure," I said. Feeble, even for me.

"Want to come up?"

My answer surprised me. "Okay."

I left Angus examining a clump of ferns, went through the little gate that separated my backyard from the front and headed for Callahan's back deck. The fresh boards, sharp and clean-smelling, glowed dimly in the night, and the metal rungs of the ladder were cool under my hand. Up I went, peeking over the roof to where my neighbor stood.

"Hi," he said, taking my hand to help me.

"Hi," I said back. His hand was warm and sure, and I was glad, never being a huge fan of ladders. That hand made me feel safe. Just one hand, that was all it took. It was with great reluctance that I let it go.

A dark-colored blanket was spread on the rough shingles. "Welcome to the roof," Callahan said. "Have a seat."

"Thanks." Self-consciously, I sat down. Cal sat next

to me. "So what do you do out here?" I asked, my voice sounding a bit loud in the quiet, cool air.

"I just like to look at the sky," he answered. But he wasn't looking at the sky. He was looking at me. "I didn't get to do that a lot in prison."

"The sky's pretty," I said. *Clever, Grace. Very witty.* I could feel the warmth of his shoulder next to mine. "So."

"So." He was smiling a little, and my stomach did a slow, giddy roll. Then he stretched out so that he was lying on the blanket, clasping his hands behind his head. After a second's hesitation, I did the same thing.

It *was* pretty. The stars were winking, the sky velvety and rich. The river's lush song was pierced by a night bird of some kind, trilling softly every few minutes. And there was Callahan O'Shea, the solid warmth of him just inches from me.

"Were you crying before?" His voice was gentle.

"A little," I admitted.

"Everything all right?"

I paused. "Well, Margaret and Stuart are having a tough time of it these days. And my other sister, Nat— remember her?" He nodded. "She's getting married in a few weeks. I guess I was just feeling sentimental."

"You and that family of yours," he commented mildly. "They sure have a choke hold on you."

"They sure do," I agreed glumly.

The far-off bird trilled again. Angus barked once in reply. "Were you ever married?" Callahan asked.

"Nope," I said, staring at the hypnotic stars. "I was engaged a couple of years ago, though." God. A couple of years ago. It sounded like such a long time.

"Why'd you call it off?"

I shifted to look at him. Nice, that he assumed it had been my decision. Nice, but untrue. "I didn't, actually. He did. He fell for someone else." Funny...saying it like that didn't sound all that bad. *He fell for someone else.* It happened.

Callahan O'Shea turned his head. "Sounds like he was an idiot," he said softly.

Oh. *Oh.* There it was again, that warm, rolling squeeze of my insides. I swallowed. "He wasn't that bad," I said, looking back at the sky. "What about you, Callahan? Ever get close to the altar?"

"I was seeing someone before prison. I guess it was serious." His voice was level, unperturbed.

"Why'd you guys break up?" I asked.

"Well, we were struggling a bit as it was," he answered. "But me being arrested was the final nail in my coffin."

"Do you miss her?" I couldn't help asking.

"A little," he said. "Sometimes. It's like our happy times were in another life, though. I can barely remember them."

His statement so echoed my own earlier thoughts about Andrew that my mouth opened in amazement. He must've noticed my shocked expression, because he smiled. "What?" he asked.

"Nothing. I just...I know how that feels." We were quiet for another minute, then I asked him another question, one I'd wondered about more than once. "Hey, Cal, I read that you pled guilty. Didn't you want to go to trial?"

He kept his eyes on the sky and didn't answer for a second. "There was a lot of evidence against me," he finally said.

As I had once before, I got the impression that Callahan wasn't telling me all there was to tell. But it was *his* crime, *his* past, and the night and being here were just too comfortable to press on. I was out on the roof with Callahan O'Shea, and it was enough. It was, in fact, lovely.

"Grace?" God, I loved the way he said my name, his voice deep and soft and with just a hint of roughness in it, like distant thunder on a hot summer night.

I turned my head to look at him, but he was just staring at the stars. "Yes?"

He still didn't turn my way. "Are you finished with the cat wrangler?"

My heart jolted, my breath froze. For a flash of a second, I imagined telling Callahan the truth about Wyatt Dunn. Imagined him turning to look at me, his expression incredulous, then disgusted, rolling his eyes and muttering something less than flattering about my emotional state. I sure as hell didn't want that. Callahan O'Shea was asking if I was done with Wyatt because he...yes, there was no denying it...he was interested. In me.

I bit my lip. "Um...Wyatt's...he was better on paper than in real life," I said, swallowing hard. Not exactly a lie. "So yeah. So we called it quits."

"Good." Then he did turn to look at me. His face was serious, his eyes unreadable in the dim light from the stars. My heart slowed, and suddenly the smell of lilacs was dizzying. Cal's lashes were so long, his eyes so lovely. And it was scary, too, looking at him like that, so close and available, so warm and solid.

Very slowly, he reached out to touch my cheek with the backs of his fingers. Just a little caress, but I sucked in a sharp breath at the contact. He was going to kiss me. Oh, God. My heart clattered so hard it practically bruised my ribs. Cal smiled.

Then Margaret's voice split the quiet air. "Grace? Grace, where are you? Nat's on the phone!"

"Coming!" I called, abruptly lurching to my feet. At the realization that his mistress was on the roof, Angus exploded into yarps, breaking the quiet into shards of noise. "Sorry, Cal. I—I have to go."

"Coward," he said, but he was smiling.

I took another step closer to the ladder, then stopped. "Maybe I could come back up here again sometime," I said.

"Maybe you could," he agreed, sitting up in one quick, graceful move. "I hope you do."

"Gotta run," I breathed, then scuttled down the ladder as fast as I could. Cal's low, ashy laugh followed me as I trotted into my own yard where Angus finally quieted. My heart thundered as if I'd run a mile.

"What were you doing out there?" Margaret hissed as I burst onto the patio. "Were you up there with Callahan?"

"Hi, Margaret," Cal called from his roof.

"What were you guys doing up there?" she called back.

"Monkey sex," he answered. "Wanna give it a try?"

"Don't tempt me, Bird Man of Alcatraz," she said, shoving the phone into my hand.

"Hello?" I panted.

"Hi, Grace. I'm sorry. Was I interrupting?" Nat's voice was small.

"Oh, no. I was just…" I cleared my throat. "Just talking to Callahan next door. What's up?"

"Well, I was wondering if you were free this Saturday," she said. "Do you have anything at school? Or any battles?"

I went through the slider into the kitchen and glanced at my calendar. "Nope. All clear."

"Think you'd like to go dress shopping with me?"

My head jerked back slightly. "Sure!" I said heartily. "What time?"

"Um, maybe around three?" Nat sounded so hesitant that I could tell something was wrong.

"Three would be great," I answered.

"You sure?"

"Yes! Of course, Bumppo. Why do you sound so weird?"

"Margaret said maybe I should cut you a break and go without you."

Good old Margs. My older sister was right—it would be awfully nice to skip out on this particular wedding event, but I had to go. "I want to come, Nat," I said. Part of me did, at any rate. "I'll see you at three."

"Why do you baby her so much?" Margaret demanded the minute I hung up. Angus raced in, almost tripping her, but she ignored him. "Tell her to open her eyes and think of someone else for a change. She's not lying in a hospital bed anymore, Grace."

"I know that, Margaret dear. But for crying out loud, it's her wedding dress. And I'm over Andrew. I don't care if she's marrying him, she's our little sister and we should both be there."

Margaret dropped into a kitchen chair and picked up Angus, who licked her chin with great affection. "Princess Natalie. God forbid she think of someone else for a change."

"She's not like that! God, Margs, why do you give her such a hard time?"

Margaret shrugged. "Maybe I think she needs a little hard time once in a while. She's lived a charmed life, Grace. Adored, beautiful, smart. She gets everything."

"Unlike your poor, orphaned, troll-like self?" I asked.

"Yes, I'm all soft edges and peachy glow." She sighed. "You know what I'm talking about, Grace. Admit it. Nat has glided through life on a fluffy white cloud with a fucking rainbow over her head while blue-birds sang all around her. Me, I've stomped through life, and you…you've…" Her voice broke off.

"I've what?" I asked, bristling.

She didn't answer for a second. "You've hit a few walls."

"Andrew, you mean?"

"Well, sure. But remember when we first moved to Connecticut, and you were kind of lost?" Sure I remembered. Back when I was dating Jack of Le Cirque. Margaret continued. "And that year you lived with Mom and Dad after college, when you waitressed for a year?"

"I was taking time off to figure out what I wanted to do," I bit out. "Plus, waitressing is a life skill I'll always have."

"Sure. Nothing wrong with that. It's just that Nat's never had to wonder, never been lost, never doubted herself, never imagined that life would be anything less than perfect for her. Until she met Andrew and finally found something she couldn't have, which you ended up giving her. So if I think she's a little self-centered, that's why."

"I think you're jealous of her," I said, smarting.

"Of course I'm jealous of her, dummy," Margaret said fondly. Honestly, I would never figure Margaret out. "Hey," she added, "what were you doing up on that roof with Hottie the Hunk Next Door?"

I took a deep breath. "We were just looking at the sky. Talking."

Margaret squinted at me. "Are you interested in him, Grace?"

I could feel myself blushing. "Sort of. Yes. Definitely. I am."

"Mmm-hmm." Margs gave me her pirate smile. "So?"

"So nothing. He's a huge improvement on Andrew the Pale. God, imagine screwing Callahan O'Shea. Just his name practically gives me an orgasm." She laughed, and I smiled reluctantly. Margaret stood up and patted my shoulder. "Just make sure you're not doing it to show Andrew that there's a man who wants what's in your pants, okay?"

"Wow. That's so romantic, I think I might cry."

She grinned again like the pirate she should've been. "Well, I'm beat. I have to write a brief and then I'm hitting the hay. 'Night, Gracie." She handed me my wee doggie, who rested his head on my shoulder and sighed with devotion. "And, Grace, one more thing as long as I'm doing the big sister shtick." She sighed. "Look. I know you're trying to move on and all that crap, and I don't blame you. But no matter how great Cal looks without a shirt, he's always going to have a prison record, and these things have a habit of following a person around."

"I know," I admitted. Ava and I had both made it to the second round of interviews for the chairmanship, much to my surprise. I still wasn't entirely hopeful, but Margs was right. Callahan O'Shea's past would matter at Manning. Maybe it shouldn't, but it would.

"Just be sure you know what you want, kiddo," Margs said. "That's all I'm saying. I think Cal's pretty damn fun, and you could probably use some fun. But keep in mind that you're a teacher at a prep school, and this just might matter to the good people at Manning. Not to mention Mom and Dad."

I didn't answer. As usual, Margaret was right.

CHAPTER TWENTY-ONE

"I've been commissioned to do a sculpture of a baby in utero for Yale New Haven's Children's Hospital," Mom announced the next night at dinner. We were at the family domicile—me, Margaret, Mémé, Mom and Dad—eating dinner.

"That sounds nice, Mom," I said, taking a bite of her excellent pot roast.

"It's coming along beautifully, if I do say so myself," she agreed.

"Which you do say, every half hour," Dad muttered.

"I almost died in childbirth," Mémé announced. "They had to put me under. When I came to three days later, they told me I had a beautiful son."

"My kind of labor and delivery," Margaret murmured, knocking back her wine.

"The problem with the sculpture is that the baby's head keeps breaking off—"

"Less than reassuring for the expectant mothers, I'm guessing," Margaret interjected.

"—and I can't find a way to keep it on," Mom finished, glaring at Margs.

"How about duct tape?" Dad suggested. I bit down a laugh.

"Jim, must you constantly belittle my work? Hmm?

Grace, stop shlunching, honey. You're so pretty, why do you shlunch?"

"You can always tell breeding by good posture," Mémé said, fishing the onion out of her martini and popping it into her mouth. "A lady never hunches. Grace, what is wrong with your hair today? You look like you just stepped out of the electric chair."

"Oh, do you like it, Mémé? It cost a fortune, but, yes, electrocution was just the look I was going for. Thanks!"

"Mother," Dad said, "what would you like to do for your birthday this year?"

Mémé raised a sparse eyebrow. "Oh, you remembered, did you? I thought you forgot. No one has said a word about it."

"Of course I remembered," Dad said wearily.

"Has he ever forgotten, Eleanor?" Mom asked sharply in a rare show of solidarity with Dad.

"Oh, he forgot once," Mémé said sourly.

"When I was six," Dad sighed.

"When he was six. I thought he'd at least make me a card, but, no. Nothing."

"Well, I thought we'd take you out to dinner on Friday," Dad said. "You, Nancy and me, the girls and their boys. What do you think? Does that sound nice?"

"Where would we go?"

"Somewhere fabulously expensive where you could complain all night long," Margaret said. "Your idea of heaven, right, Mémé?"

"Actually," I said on impulse, "I can't come. Wyatt's presenting a paper in New York, and I said I'd go down to the city with him. So sorry, Mémé. I hope you have a lovely night."

Granted, yes, I'd been planning to tell the family that

Wyatt and I had parted ways—Natalie's wedding would demand attendance, and obviously Wyatt couldn't show, being imaginary and all. But the idea of spending a Friday night listening to Mémé detail her nasal polyps and having Mom and Dad indulge in their endless bickering, sitting in the glow of Andrew and Natalie while Margaret sniped at everyone...nope. Callahan O'Shea was right. I did a lot for my family. More than enough. Wyatt Dunn could give me one last excuse before, alas, we were forced to break up for good.

"But it's my birthday." Mémé frowned. "Cancel your plans."

"No," I said with a smile.

"In my day, people showed respect to their elders," she began.

"See, I was thinking the Inuit have it right," Margaret said. "The ice floe? What do you say, Mémé?"

I laughed, receiving a glare from my grandmother. "Hey, listen, I have to go. Papers to grade and all that. Love you guys. See you at home, Margs."

"Cheers, Grace," she said, toasting me with a knowing grin. "Hey, does Wyatt have a brother?"

I smiled, patted her shoulder and left.

When I pulled into my driveway ten minutes later, I looked over at Callahan's house. Maybe he was home. Maybe he'd want company. Maybe he'd almost kiss me again. Maybe there'd be no "almost" about it.

"Here goes nothing," I said, getting out of the car. Angus's sweet little head popped up in the window, and he began his yarping song of welcome. "One second, sweetie boy!" I called, then walked over to 36 Maple. Right up the path. Knocked on the door. Firmly. Waited.

There was no answer. I knocked again, my spirits

slipping a notch. Glancing down the street, I noticed belatedly that Cal's truck wasn't there. With a sigh, I turned around and went home.

The truck wasn't there the next day, or the next. Not that I was spying, of course…just glancing out my window every ten minutes or so in great irritation, acknowledging the fact that…yikes…I missed him. Missed the joking, the knowing looks, the brawny arms. The tingling wave of desire that one look from Callahan O'Shea could incite. And God, when he touched my face that night on the roof, I'd felt like the most beautiful creature on earth.

So where was he, dang it? Why did it bug me so much that he'd gone off for a few days? Maybe he was back in an orange jumpsuit, stabbing trash on the side of the freeway, having broken parole somehow. Maybe he was a CIA mole and had been called up to serve, like Clive Owen's assassin character in *The Bourne Identity.* "Must go kill someone, dear…I'll be late for dinner!" Seemed to fit Callahan more than being an accountant, that's for sure.

Maybe—maybe he had a girlfriend. I didn't think so, but I just didn't know, did I?

On Friday night, tired of torturing myself about Callahan, I decided that going to Julian's singles' night with Kiki was a better way to spend my time than wondering where the hell Callahan O'Shea had gone. I was supposed to be in New York with Wyatt, and Margaret was growling in the kitchen, surrounded by piles of paper and an open bottle of wine, complaining about having to go to dinner with our family.

And so it was that at nine o'clock, instead of watching Mémé wrestle food past her hiatal hernia and listening to my parents snipe, I was instead dancing to Gloria Estefan at Jitterbug's singles' night. Dancing with Julian, dancing with Kiki, dancing with Cambry the waiter and having a blast.

There were no men here for me...Kiki had claimed the only reasonably attractive straight guy, and they seemed to be hitting it off. Apparently, Cambry had brought a lot of his friends, so aside from a scattering of middle-aged women (Julian's usual crowd for this event), the night had taken on a decidedly gay-man feel.

I didn't mind a bit. This only meant that the men danced well, dressed beautifully and flirted outrageously in one of the unfairnesses of life—gay men were generally better boyfriends than straight guys, except on the sex front, where things tended to fall apart. Still, I'd bet a gay boyfriend would at least tell me if he was going out of town for a few days. Not that Callahan was my boyfriend, of course.

I let the music push those thoughts away and found that after a while, I was twirling, laughing, showing off my dancing skills, being told I was *fabulous* again and again by Cambry's pals.

As the music pulsed in my ears and I salsa-stepped with one good-looking guy after another, I felt a warm wave of happiness. It was nice to be away from my family, nice not to be looking for love, nice to be just out having fun. Good old Wyatt Dunn. This last date was definitely our best.

When Julian went to the back to change the music, I followed him. "This is great!" I exclaimed. "Look at all the people here! You should make this a regular thing. Gay Singles' Night."

"I know," he said, grinning as he shuffled through

his song list. "What should we do next? It's ten o'clock already. Man! The night has flown by. Maybe some slower stuff, what do you think?"

"Sounds good to me. I'm beat. This is quite a bit livelier than Dancin' with the Oldies. My feet are killing me." Julian grinned. He looked as ridiculously handsome as ever, but happier, too. The shadow that made him so tragically appealing seemed to have lifted. "How are things with Cambry?" I asked.

Julian blushed. "Fairly wonderful," he admitted shyly. "We've had two dates. I think we might kiss soon."

I patted my friend's arm. "I'm glad, honey," I told him.

"You're not feeling…neglected?"

"No! I'm happy for you. It's been a long time coming."

"I know. And, Grace, you'll—" He looked up suddenly, his expression changed to one of horror. "Oh, no, Grace. Your mother's here."

"What?" I said, instantly imagining the worst. Mémé had died. Dad had a heart attack. Mom was tracking me down to break the news. *Please, not Nat or Margs,* I prayed.

"She's dancing," Julian said, craning his neck. "With one of Cambry's friends. Tom, I think."

"Dancing? Is my father here?" I stood behind Julian, peeping over his shoulder.

"I don't see him. Maybe she just…felt like dancing," he said. "Oh, she's coming our way. Hide, Grace! You're supposed to be in New York!"

I slipped into Julian's office before my mother could see me. Mature? No. But why ruin a happy night when good old hiding would do the trick? I pressed my ear against the door so I could hear.

"Hello, Nancy!" Julian's voice, purposefully loud, came to me easily. "How nice to see you!"

"Hello, Julian dear," Mom said. "Oh, isn't this fun! Now, I know I'm not single, but I just felt like dancing! Is that all right?"

"Of course!" Julian said heartily. "You'll leave a few broken hearts behind, but of course! Stay a while! Have fun! Shall we dance?"

"Actually, sweetheart, could I use your phone for one second?"

"My phone? In my office?" Julian practically yelled.

"Yes, dear. Is that all right?"

"Um, well, sure! Of course you can use the phone in my office!"

With that, I leaped away from the door, jerked open the closet door and popped in, closing the door behind me. Just in the nick of time.

"Thanks, Julian dear. Now you go! Shoo! Don't let me keep you from your guests."

"Sure, Nancy. Um, take your time." I heard the door close, smelled the leather from Julian's jacket. Heard the beeping of the phone as my mother called someone. Waited with thudding heart.

"The coast is clear," she murmured, then replaced the receiver.

The coast is clear? Clear for what? For whom? I was tempted to crack the closet door, but didn't want to give myself away. After all, not only was I *not* in New York City with my doctor boyfriend, but I was hiding in a closet, spying on my mother. The coast was clear. That did not sound good.

Crap. I knew things weren't great with my parents, but then again, that was the norm. Did Mom have someone on the side? Was she cheating on Dad? My poor father! Did he know?

Indecision kept me standing where I was, my throat tight, heart galloping. I realized I was gripping the sleeve of Julian's coat. *Calm down, Grace,* I urged myself. Maybe *the coast is clear* didn't sound quite as clandestine as I thought. Maybe Mom was talking about something else...

But, no. The office door opened again, then closed.

"I saw you dancing out there," came a man's gruff voice. "You're that sculptor, aren't you? Every man was watching you. Wanting you."

Okay, well, *that* statement wasn't true. I frowned. Every man out there, save about two, was gay. If they were watching my mother, it was for fashion tips.

"Lock the door." Mom's voice was low.

My eyes widened in the dark closet. God's nightgown! I clenched the sleeve more tightly, my fingernails digging into the soft leather.

"You're so beautiful." The voice was hoarse...but familiar.

"Shut up and kiss me, big boy," Mom ordered. There was silence.

Cold with dread, I cracked the door the smallest fraction and took a peek. And just about peed my pants.

My parents were making out in Julian's office.

"What's your name?" my father asked, breaking off from the kiss and looking at Mom with smoky eyes.

"Does it matter?" Mom said. "Kiss me again. Make me feel like a woman should."

My astonishment turned to horror as dear old Dad

grabbed my mother and kissed her sloppily…oh, God, there was tongue. I jerked back, shuddering, and closed the door as quietly as I could…not that it mattered, they were moaning rather loudly…and stuffed the jacket sleeve into my mouth to keep from screaming, a massive case of the heebie-jeebies rolling through me from head to toe. My parents. My parents were *role-playing*. And I was stuck in a closet.

"Oh, yes. More. Yes," my mother groaned.

"I want you. Since the moment I walked into this seedy little joint, I wanted you."

I jammed my fingers in my ears hard. *Dear God,* I prayed. *Please strike me deaf right now. Please? Pretty please?* I could, of course, just open the closet door and bust them. But then I'd have to explain what I was doing in there in the first place. Why I was hiding. Why I hadn't revealed myself sooner. And then I'd have to hear my parents explain what they were up to.

"Oh, yes, right there!" my mother crooned. My fingers weren't working, so I tried the heels of my hands. Alas, I could still hear a few words. "Lower…higher…"

"Ouch! My sciatica! Not so fast, Nancy!"

"Just stop talking and do it, handsome."

Oh, please, God. I'll become a nun. Really. Don't you need nuns? Make them stop. At the sound of another groan, I tried to go to my happy place…a meadow full of wildflowers, guns firing, cannons booming, Confederate and Yankee soldiers dropping like flies…but no.

"Oh, baby," my mother crooned.

I could not stay in here and listen to my parents doing the wild thing, but just as I was about to burst forth and stop them in the name of decency, my mother (or God) intervened.

"Not here, big boy. Let's get a room."

Thank you, Lord! Oh, and about that nun thing... how about a nice fat donation to Heifer International instead?

I waited a few more minutes, taking cleansing breaths, then risked another look. They were gone.

The door burst open and I flinched, but it was just Julian.

"Everything okay?" Julian exclaimed. "Did she find you? She didn't say a word, just scooted out the door." Julian took a better look at me. "Grace, you're white as a ghost! What happened?"

I made a strangled noise. "Um...you might want to burn that desk."

Then, eager to leave this office and never return, I sidled past him, waved to Kiki, who was still dancing with the straight guy, and headed for home. As I drove, shuddering, feeling that Satan had cigarette-burned a hole into my soul, there was part of me that was...*shudder*...quite happy that my parents...*gack*...could still get it on. That there was more than irritation and obligation driving their marriage, no matter how yucky it was for their child. I rolled down the window and took a few gulps of the clean spring air. Perhaps a strong dose of hypnotherapy could erase this night from my mind forever.

But yes. It was good to know that my parents still, er, loved each other.

Shudder. I pulled into my driveway.

Callahan's house was still dark.

CHAPTER TWENTY-TWO

THE NEXT DAY, I FOUND MYSELF once again sitting in the bosom of my family—Margs, Natalie and the sexpot formerly known as my mother were dress shopping at Birdie's Bridal.

Well, Mom and Natalie were dress shopping. Margaret and I were drinking strawberry margaritas from a thermos Margs had thoughtfully brought along as we sat in the dressing room, waiting for Natalie to emerge in another dress. Actually, dressing room was a misnomer. Dressing hall, really, because Birdie's had couches, an easy chair, coffee table and a huge, curtained area for the bride to try on dresses before coming out to dazzle her entourage.

"You've earned this," Margaret muttered, taking a slug herself straight from the thermos.

"I really have," I agreed. Mom and Nat were behind the curtain, Mom fussing away. "A little tuck in here, move your arm, honey, there…"

Mom seemed so normal today. I wondered if she was thinking about almost *shtupping* Dad at Jitterbug's last night. Blecch. Or perhaps she was remembering the day she and I went wedding dress shopping. Margaret had had a deposition, Nat was still at Stanford, so it was just Mom and me, and we'd had a lovely time. Granted, I bought the first dress I tried on…not really the princess bride–type, to be honest, and one white dress looked about as good as another. (I'd kind of been hoping for a hoop skirt, sort of like the one Ms. Mitchell described Scarlett wearing in Chapter Two of *Gone with the Wind,* but Mom's look of incredulity had squashed that one.) I barely remembered what my actual wedding dress really looked like, aside from being white and simple. I'd have to sell it on eBay. Wedding dress: Never been worn.

"Ooh, that one's pretty, too!" I chirruped as Nat emerged from behind the curtain. She looked like a bride should…flushed, beaming, eyes sparkling, sweetly modest.

"The first one was better," Margaret said. "I don't like those froufrou things along the neckline."

"Froufrou's out," I seconded, taking another slug of my drink.

"I don't know," Natalie murmured, staring at herself. "I kind of like froufrou."

"It's nice froufrou," I amended hastily.

"You look beautiful," Mom announced staunchly. "You could wear a garbage bag and you'd look beautiful."

"Yes, Princess Natalie," Margaret said, rolling her eyes. "You could wear toad skins and you'd be beautiful."

"Sack cloth and ashes, I was thinking," I added, earning a gratifying snort from my older sister.

Nat grinned, but her eyes were distant. "I don't care what I wear. I just want to be married," she murmured.

"Blecch," said Margaret. I grinned.

"Of course you do," Mom said, patting her shoulder. "I felt the same way. So did Margaret."

"Did I?" Margaret mused.

Mom, belatedly aware that perhaps there were other feelings to be considered, glanced at me with a nervous smile. I smiled back. Once, yes, I'd felt that way about marriage. Once, being married to Andrew was all that I'd wanted, too. Nights of movies and Scrabble games, weekends spent antiquing or on the battlefield, leisurely sex on a bed strewn with sections of the *New York Times*. A couple of kids down the road. Long summers spent vacationing on Cape Cod or driving across country. Yadda yadda ding dong, blah blah blah.

And sitting here, admiring my sister, I could finally see that, even back then before Andrew's revelation, all those imaginings had felt a little…thin. I'd pictured that future with a determination that should've clued me in. It was all too good to be true.

"How was your overnight in the city, Grace?" Natalie asked, snapping out of her daze.

I glanced at Margaret, who'd been clued in before. "Well, I'm sorry to say that Wyatt and I are—" I paused for regretful effect "—taking a break."

"What?" Natalie and Mom chorused.

I sighed. "You know, he's such a great guy, but really, his work is just too demanding. I mean, you guys never even got to meet him, right? What does that say about the kind of husband he'd be?"

"Crappy," Margaret announced. "Plus, I never thought he was all that."

"Quiet, Margaret," Mom said, coming to sit at my side to administer a few maternal pats.

"Oh, Grace," Natalie said, biting her lip. "He sounded so wonderful. I—I thought you were madly in love. You were talking about getting married a little while ago!"

Margaret choked on her drink. "Well," I said, "I just don't want a husband who can't really, um, be devoted to the kids and me. You know. Running off all the time to the hospital was getting a little old."

"But he was saving children's lives, Grace!" Natalie protested.

"Mmm," I said, taking a sip of margarita. "True. Which makes him a great doctor, but not necessarily a great husband."

"Maybe you're right, honey. Marriage is hard enough," Mom said. I forced myself not to picture last night, but of course, it was seared onto my eyelids, Mom and Dad…bleccch!

"How are you taking it, Grace?" Margaret asked, as she'd been instructed in the car ride here.

"You know, I'm actually fine with it," I answered blithely.

"You're not heartbroken?" Natalie asked, kneeling in front of me, a vision in her white dress.

"No. Not even a little. It's for the best. And I think we'll stay friends," I said, getting an elbow in the ribs from Margaret. "Or not. He might be transferring to Chicago. So we'll see. Mom, how's your art coming along?" A subject guaranteed to take the focus off my love life.

"It's getting a little dull," Mom said. "I'm thinking of going male. I'm tired of all those labias and ovaries. Maybe it's time for a good old-fashioned penis."

"Why not flowers, Mom? Or bunnies or butterflies? Does it have to be genitalia?" Margs asked.

"How are we doing in here?" Birdie of Birdie's Bridal bustled in holding another dress. "Oh, Natalie, honey, you look dazzling! Like an ad in a magazine! Like a movie star! A princess!"

"Don't forget Greek goddess," Margaret added.

"Aphrodite, rising from the waves," Birdie agreed.

"That would be Venus," I said.

"Oh, Faith, here's your dress," Birdie said, handing me a rose-colored, floor length dress.

"It's Grace. My name is Grace."

"Try it on, try it on!" Nat said, clapping her hands. "That color will be gorgeous on you, Grace!"

"Yes, maid of honor. Your turn to be super special," Margaret growled.

"Oh, get over it," I said, rising from the couch. "Try on your dress, Margaret, and behave."

"Yours is right here," Natalie said, swatting Margaret on the head. Birdie handed Margs a dress a few shades paler than mine, and Margaret and I went into separate dressing rooms to try our garments on.

Behind the curtain I went. I hung the dress on a hook, slid out of my jeans and T-shirt, glad for the new bra and panties set that kept me from feeling like a total slob. I slipped the dress over my head, freed my hair from the zipper and managed to rescue my left breast from where it got stuck in the bodice. There. A tug here, a push there, and I was zipped.

"Come on, let's see!" Natalie called impatiently.

"Ta-da!" I said gamely, coming out to join my sisters.

"Oh! Gorgeous! That is really your color!" Nat cried, clapping her hands. She'd put on another wedding dress, a shimmering white silk creation with a demure neckline, a snug bodice that glistened with beads and a huge, puffy skirt. Margaret, fast and efficient at everything she did, was already waiting, looking sulky and gorgeous in her pale pink.

"Come on, Grace," Mom said. "Stand with your sisters and let's see how you look."

I obeyed. Stood on the little dais next to cool, blonde, elegant Natalie Rose. On Nat's other side was Margaret, her reddish gold hair sleekly cut into a stylish bob, sharply attractive, thin as a greyhound, cheekbones to die for. My sisters were, simply put, beautiful. Stunning, even.

And then there was me. I noticed that my dark hair hadn't taken kindly to the weather today and was doing its wild-animal thing again. A few dark circles lurked under my eyes. (Who could sleep after Mom and Dad's foreplay?) In the past few months, I'd managed to gain weight in my upper arms, courtesy of all that quality time with Ben & Jerry's. Based on the one picture we had of her, I looked like my great-grandmother on my mother's side, who'd immigrated from Kiev.

"I look like Great-Grandma Zladova," I commented.

Mom's head jerked back. "I always wondered where you got that hair," she murmured in wonder.

"You do not," Natalie said staunchly.

"Wasn't she a washerwoman?" Margaret asked.

I rolled my eyes. "Great. Nat is Cinderella, Margaret is Nicole Kidman and I'm Grandma Zladova, laundress to the czars."

Ten minutes later, Birdie was completing the sale, Mom was fussing over headpieces, Margaret was checking her BlackBerry and I needed a little air. "I'll meet you outside, Nat," I said.

"Grace?" Natalie put her hand on my arm. "I'm sorry about Wyatt."

"Oh," I said. "Well, thanks."

"You'll find someone," she murmured. "The right one will come along. It'll be your turn soon."

The words felt like a slap. No, more than the words was…damn it, my eyes were stinging…the pity. In all the time since Andrew and I broke up, Natalie had felt sympathy, and guilt, and a whole lot of other feelings, no doubt, but she'd never *pitied* me. No. My younger sister had always, *always* looked up to me, even when my chips were down. Never before had she given me the kind of look I was getting now. I was Poor Grace once more.

"Maybe I'll never meet someone," I said tartly. "But hey. You and Andrew could use me as a nanny, right?"

She blanched. "Grace…I didn't mean it like that."

"Sure," I said quickly. "I know. But you know, Nat, me being single isn't the worst thing in the world. It's not like I lost a limb."

"Oh, no! Of course not. I know." She smiled uncertainly.

I took a deep breath. "I…I'll be outside," I said.

"Okay," she chirped. "Meet you at the car," she said, then went back to our mother and her wedding dress.

WHEN I GOT HOME FROM DRESS shopping, I was limp from the effort of all that damn fun. Dinner and drinks had followed the dress shopping, full of good cheer and talk of the wedding. We were joined by a few other female relatives—Mom's sisters and, alas, Cousin Kitty, Queen of the Newlyweds, who gushed and beamed about how wonderful it was to be married. For the third time, that was…numbers one and two hadn't been so great, but that was in the past, of course, and now Kitty was an expert on Happily Ever After.

In just a few weeks, Andrew and Natalie would be husband and wife. I couldn't wait. Seriously, I just wanted to be done with it. Then, finally, it'd seem like a new chapter of my life could start.

Angus clawed at the kitchen door to be let out. It was raining now, thunder rumbling distantly in the east. Angus wasn't one of those dogs who feared storms—he had the heart of a lion, my little guy—but he didn't like being rained on. "Come back soon," I said.

The minute I opened the door, I saw the dark shape against the fence at the end of my property. Lightning flashed. A skunk…damn it! I lunged after my dog. "No, Angus! Come here, boy!"

But it was too late. My dog, a blur of white ferocity, streaked across the backyard. Another flash of lightning showed me that the animal was a raccoon. It looked up in alarm, then was gone, under the fence in a hole that Angus had probably dug. A raccoon could do serious damage to my little dog, who wasn't smart enough to know better. "Angus! Come! Come, boy!" It was no use. Angus rarely obeyed when in pursuit of another animal, and just like that, he, too, was gone, under the fence, after the raccoon.

"Damn it!" I cursed. Turning around, I ran back into the house, grabbed a flashlight then ran back outside, into Callahan's yard to avoid having to climb over the back fence in my own yard.

"Grace? Everything okay?" The back porch light came on. He was back.

"Angus is chasing a raccoon," I blurted, running past the deck without stopping, tearing down Cal's yard to the woods, my breath coming in gasps already. Visions of my adorable little dog with his eye torn out, with slash marks down his back, blood staining his white fur... Raccoons were fierce, and this one could very well tear up my little dog. It had looked much bigger than Angus.

"Angus!" I called, my voice high with fear. "Cookie, Angus! Cookie!"

My flashlight illuminated the raindrops and dripping branches of the state forest. As I crashed forward, twigs snapping in my face, a new fear lanced my stomach. The river. The Farmington River was a hundred yards away, full and dark from the spring rains and snowmelt. It was more than strong enough to sweep away a small and not-very-bright dog.

Another light flashed next to mine. Callahan, wearing a slicker and Yankees cap, had caught up.

"Which way did he go?" he asked.

"Oh, Callahan, thank you," I panted. "I don't know. He went under the fence. He tunnels. I usually fill them in, but this time...I...I..." Sobs ratcheted out of me.

"Hey, come on. We'll find him. Don't worry, Grace." Callahan slipped his arm around my shoulder, gave me a quick squeeze, then aimed his light overhead into the canopy branches.

"I don't think he can climb, Cal," I said wetly, rain and tears mixing on my face as I looked up.

Cal smiled. "The raccoon can, though. Maybe Angus treed him. If we find the raccoon, maybe we'll find your little dog."

Smart idea, but after five minutes of shining our flashlights into the branches, we had found neither the raccoon nor my dog. There was no sign of him, not that

I was a tracker or anything. We were closer to the river now. That which had once sounded sweet and comforting now sounded menacing and cruel...the uncaring river rushing past, carrying anything along with it.

"So where have you been the past few days?" I asked Callahan, shining my light under a fallen branch. No Angus.

"Becky needed me to do a quick job down in Stamford," he answered.

"Who's Becky?"

"The blonde from the bar. She's an old friend from high school. Works in real estate. That's how I found this house."

"You could've let me know you were going out of town," I said, glancing at him. "I was worried."

He smiled. "Next time I will."

I called Angus again, whistled, clapped my hands. Nothing.

Then I heard a distant, sharp bark, followed by a yelp, that sickening surprised cry of pain. "Angus! Angus, buddy, where are you?" I called, tripping forward toward the direction of the cry. It came from upriver. In the river? I couldn't tell.

It was hard to hear over the noise of the rain and flowing water. Images of Angus when I first bought him, a tiny ball of shivering, coconutty fluff...his bright eyes staring at me each morning, willing me to wake up...his funny little Super Dog pose...the way he slept on his back with his paws in the air, his crooked little bottom teeth showing. I was crying harder now. "Angus!" I kept calling, my voice harsh and scared.

We came to the edge of the river. Usually I thought it so beautiful, the rushing, silken water, the stones beneath, the flashes of white where the current collided with a rock or branch. Tonight, it was sinister and dark as a black snake. I guided my beam over the water, dreading the sight of a little white body being swept along.

"Oh, shit," I sobbed.

"He probably wouldn't go in," Cal said soothingly, taking my hand. "He's dumb, but he's got some instincts, right? He wouldn't drown himself."

"You don't know Angus," I wept. "He's stubborn. When he wants something he just doesn't stop."

"Well, if he's chasing the raccoon, the raccoon would have enough sense, then," Cal said. "Come on. Let's keep looking."

We walked along the river, through the woods, farther and farther away from home, calling my dog's name, promising treats. There were no more yelps, just the sound of the rain hissing through the leaves. I didn't have socks on, and my feet were freezing inside my plastic gardening clogs, which were covered in mud. This was all my fault. He dug all the time. I knew this. Usually, I checked the fence line on weekends for just this reason. Today, I hadn't. Today, I'd been dress shopping with stupid Natalie.

I didn't want to picture life without my dog. Angus who slept on my bed after Andrew left me. Angus who needed me, waited for me, whose little head popped up in the living-room window each and every time I came home, overjoyed at the miracle of my very being. I'd lost him. I should've filled in that stupid hole, and I didn't, and now he was gone.

I sucked in a ragged breath, tears, hot and endless, cutting down my rain-soaked face.

"There he is," Cal said, shining his light.

He was right. About thirty yards west of the river, Angus stood next to a small house that, like mine, backed up to the state forest. He was sniffing a tipped over garbage can and looked up at the sound of my voice. His tail wagged, he barked once, then went back to investigating the trash.

"Angus!" I cried, lurching up the slight hill that separated me from my dog. "Good puppy! Good boy! You worried Mommy! Yes, you did!" He wagged his tail in agreement, barked again, and then I had him. Gathering my dog in my arms, I kissed his soggy little head over and over, tears dropping into his fur as he wriggled and nipped me in delight.

"There you go, then," Cal said, coming up behind me. He was smiling. I tried to smile back, but my mouth was doing that wobbling contortion thing, so I didn't quite pull it off.

"Thank you," I managed. Callahan reached out to pet Angus, who suddenly realized that his nemesis was there, turned his little head and snapped.

"Ingrate," Cal said, giving my dog a mock scowl. He bent down and scooped the trash back into the garbage can, then set it aright.

"You've been really great," I said shakily, clutching my dog against my chest.

"Don't sound so surprised," Cal returned.

We walked down the driveway of the house to the street. I recognized the neighborhood—it was about half a mile from Maple Street, a bit posher than where Cal and I lived. The rain gentled, and Angus snuggled up on my shoulder, doing his baby impression, cheek against my neck, front paws on my shoulder. I stretched

my jacket around his little body and thanked the powers that be for the safety of my dopey little dog, whom
I loved more than was probably advisable.

The powers that be, and Callahan O'Shea. He came
with me on this cool, rainy night and didn't leave till
we found my dog. Said nothing irritating like, "Oh,
he'll come back." Nope. Callahan had stuck with me,
reassured me, comforted me. Picked up trash for me. I
wanted to say something, though I wasn't sure what, but
when I glanced at my strong, solid neighbor, my face
burned hot enough to power a small city.

We turned onto Maple Street, and the lights of my
house glowed. I glanced down. Cal and I were covered
in mud from our feet to our knees, and soaked to the
skin. Angus resembled a mop more than a dog, his fur
soaked and matted.

Cal noticed my glance. "Why don't you come over
to my house?" he suggested. "We can get washed up
there. Your house is kind of a museum, isn't it?"

"Well, not really a museum," I said. "It's just tidy."

"Tidy. Sure. Well, want to come over? It won't matter if we get my kitchen dirty. I'm still working on it."

"Sure. Thanks," I said. I had been wondering about
the house, what it was like inside, what Callahan had
been doing. "How's that been going, anyway? You flipping the house and all?"

"It's going fine. Come in. I'll give you a tour," he offered, reading my mind.

CAL LET ME IN THE BACK DOOR.

"I'll get a couple towels," he said, taking off his work
boots and disappearing into another room. Angus, still
on my shoulder, gave a little snore, making me smile. I

slipped off my filthy gardening clogs, pushed my hair out of my face with one hand and took a look around.

Cal's kitchen was nearly done. A trestle table with three mismatched chairs overlooked a new bay window. The kitchen cabinets were maple with glass panes, and the counters were made from gray soapstone. Spaces gapped where the appliances would go, though there was a two-burner stove and a dorm-size fridge. I should definitely invite him over for dinner, I thought. Seeing as he was so nice to me. Seeing as he'd held my hand. Seeing as I had the hots for him and couldn't seem to remember the reasons that I'd once thought Callahan O'Shea made a bad choice.

Cal came back into the room. "Here," he said, taking my sleeping pooch from me and wrapping him in a big towel. He rubbed the dog's fur, causing Angus to blink sleepily at the strange man holding him. "No biting," Cal warned. Angus wagged his tail. Cal smiled.

Then he kissed my dog on the head.

That was it. Without even quite realizing that I'd moved, I found that my arms were somehow around Callahan's neck, that I'd knocked off his Yankees cap, that my fingers were in his wet hair, that I was squishing Angus and that I was kissing Callahan O'Shea. Finally.

"It's about time," he muttered against my mouth. Then he was kissing me back.

CHAPTER TWENTY-THREE

His mouth was hot and soft and hard at the same time, and he was so solid and warm, and he was licking my chin while he kissed me…or no, wait. That was Angus, and Callahan laughed, a low, scraping laugh. "Okay, okay, hang on," Cal murmured, pulling back. One of his hands held Angus, the other cupped the back of my head. Oh, crap, my hair. The man could lose a finger in there. But he gently disentangled himself, then set my damp little dog on the floor and straightened up, looking at me in the eyes. Angus yarped once, and then he must've run off somewhere, because I heard his toenails clicking away. But I wasn't looking at anything except the man in front of me. His lovely, utterly kissable mouth, the slight scrape of razor stubble, those downward slanting, dark blue eyes.

Now those were eyes I could look into for a long, long time, I thought. The heat of him shimmered out to me, beckoning, and my lips parted.

"Want to stay over?" he asked, breathing hard.

"Sure!" I squeaked.

And then we were kissing again. His mouth was hot and fierce on mine, my hands clenched his hair. His arms went around me, crushing me against him, and God, he felt good, so big and safe and a little scary at the same time, so masculine and hard. And his mouth, oh, Lord, the man knew how to kiss, he kissed me like I was the water at the end of a long stretch of burning sand. I felt the wall against my back, felt his weight pressing against me, and then his hands were under my wet shirt, burning the damp skin of my waist, my ribs. I tugged his shirt out of his jeans and slid my hands across the hot skin of his back, my knees practically buckling as his mouth moved to my neck. Then his hand moved a little higher and my knees did buckle, but he held me against the wall and kept kissing me, my neck, my mouth. All that time in prison must have made Callahan O'Shea a little desperate, and the fact that he was with *me*, kissing *me*...it was overwhelming. A man like this. With me.

"You sure about this?" he asked, pulling back, his eyes dark and his cheeks flushed. I nodded, and just like that, he kissed me again and lifted me, his hands cupping my ass, and carried me into another room. One with a bed, thank God. Then Angus yarped and jumped against us, and Callahan laughed. Without putting me down, he gently shoved my dog out with his foot and closed the door with his shoulder.

So it was just the two of us. Outside the room, Angus whined and scratched wildly. Cal didn't seem to notice, just set me down, slid his hands up my face and stepped closer, erasing the space between us.

"He's going to ruin that door," I whispered as Cal nuzzled my neck.

"I don't care," he muttered. Then Callahan O'Shea pulled my shirt over my head and I stopped worrying about my dog.

Whatever urgency he'd felt before seemed to melt, and suddenly things moved in slow motion. His hands were so hot on my skin, and he bent to kiss my shoulder, sliding the strap of my camisole down, his five-o'clock shadow scraping the tender skin there, his mouth hot and silky smooth. His own skin was like velvet, his hard muscles sliding underneath with hypnotic power.

Without me quite realizing that we'd moved, I found that we'd made it to the bed, because he was pulling me down with him, smiling that wicked, slow smile that caught me in the stomach. Then his hand moved to the waistband of my jeans, playing there before cleverly undoing the button. He kissed me again, hot and slow and lazy, and then he rolled over so I was on top of him, his big muscular arms around me, and I kissed that smiling mouth, slid my tongue against his. God, he tasted so good, I just couldn't believe he'd been living next door to me for all these long, lonely weeks when there was this kind of kissing waiting for me. I heard him groan deep in his throat as he wove his fingers into my wet hair, and I pulled back to see his face.

"About time," he whispered again, and after that, there was no more talking.

An hour later, my limbs were filled with that almost-forgotten, heavy sweetness. I lay on my side, my head on Callahan's shoulder, his arm around me. I sneaked a peek at his face. His eyes were closed, those long, straight lashes brushing the tops of his cheeks. He was smiling. Possibly asleep, but smiling.

"What are you looking at?" he murmured, not opening his eyes. Not sleeping, but apparently omniscient.

"You're pretty gorgeous, Irish," I said.

"Would it break your heart to hear that I'm actually Scottish?"

"Not if it means I can see you in a kilt." I grinned. "Plus, then you're related to Angus."

"Great," he said, still smiling. My heart expanded almost painfully. Callahan O'Shea. I was in bed, naked, with Callahan O'Shea. Pretty damn nice.

"Scottish, hmm?" I asked, tracing a line on his shoulder.

"Mmm-hmm. Well, Pop's Scottish. My father was Irish, I guess. Hence the mick name." He opened his eyes like a lazy dragon and grinned. "Any other questions at the moment?"

"Um, well…where's the bathroom, Cal?" I asked. Not exactly the most romantic thing, but nature was calling.

"Second door on the left," he said. "Don't be long."

I grabbed the afghan that had been neatly folded at the bottom of the bed and ventured into the hall, wrapping myself in the blanket as I went. There was Angus, asleep on his back in front of the fireplace in the living room, which was illuminated only by the kitchen lights spilling in. My dog was snoring. Good boy.

In the bathroom, I flicked on the light and blinked, then winced as I saw my reflection. Jeez Louise! A streak of mud lined my jaw, my forehead bore a red stripe from the twig that had caught me in the face, and my hair…my hair…it looked more like wool than hair. Rolling my eyes, I finger-combed it a bit, wet it down on the left side, took care of business and washed my hands. Noticed that my feet were rather dirty. Washed those, one at a time, in the sink.

"What are you doing in there?" Cal called. "Stop rifling through my medicine cabinet and get back to bed, woman!"

The mirror showed my grin. My cheeks glowed. I rewrapped the afghan around my shoulders—modesty, you know?—and walked back down the hall to Callahan's room. At the sight of me, he lurched abruptly into a sitting position.

"It's the rain," I said, running a hand over my hair. "It goes a little crazy in the rain."

But he simply looked at me. "You're so beautiful, Grace," he said, and that pretty much sealed the deal.

I was rather crazy about Callahan O'Shea.

THE NEXT MORNING, I OPENED one eye. The clock on the night table read 6:37 a.m. Callahan was asleep next to me.

It took a minute for that to sink in, and as it did, I felt a glow in my chest. Callahan O'Shea was sleeping next to me. After shagging me. Three times. Ahem! And quite fabulously, I might add. So much so that the second time, I'd awakened Angus, who then tried to tunnel under the bedroom door to ascertain why his mistress was making all that noise.

Not only that, it was…fun. Hot and steamy, yes, that I'd expected from a guy like Callahan O'Shea. But maybe I hadn't expected that he'd make me laugh. Or to tell me how soft my skin was, his voice in a tone of near wonder. When I woke up somewhere around 3:00 a.m., he'd been looking at me, smiling like I was Christmas morning.

"Hey, Cal?" I whispered. He didn't move. "Callahan?" I kissed his shoulder. He smelled *so* good. God, three times last night, you'd think I'd have had enough. "Hey, gorgeous. I have to go." I thought about adding *honey,* but that felt a little…sweet. Bub, maybe. Not honey. Not yet. "Wake up, bub."

Nope. Nothing. I'd worn him out, poor lad.

I realized I was grinning. Ear to ear. Maybe humming a bit. Felt a little Cole Porter coming on. With one more kiss and one more look at the beautiful Callahan O'Shea, I slipped out of the warm bed and tiptoed out of the room, gathering my mud-stained clothes as I went. Angus bounced up in the living room the minute he saw me. "Shh," I whispered. "Uncle Cal's still sleeping."

Taking a quick look around the living room, I could see that Callahan had been hard at work. The floors still held the faint bite of polyurethane, and the walls were painted a pale gray. Planks of some sort were piled in the corner, and beveled wooden trim framed two of the four living-room windows.

It was a lovely home, or it would be when he was finished. The fireplace tiles were painted blue, and though the stairs leading to the second floor had no railing, they were wide and welcoming. It was the kind of home that had been carefully built, with surprising little windows with deep sills, crown molding and a pattern inset in the oak floors. The kind of house that just wasn't made anymore.

Angus whined. "Okay, boy," I whispered. In the kitchen, I found a pen and piece of paper by the phone. "Dear Mr. O'Shea," I wrote.

Thank you ever so much for your kind assistance in helping me find my beloved Angus last night. I trust you slept well. I have the unfortunate duty of fighting off the Yankee hordes this morning at Chancellorsville (also known as Haddam Meadows on Route 154 just off of Route 9, should you be interested in watching us drive back the Northern aggressors). Should I survive unscathed, I very much hope that our paths will cross again in the near future. Very best wishes, Grace Emerson (Miss).

Dumb or cute? I decided it was cute and tucked it by the phone. Then I took one more peek at the gorgeous sleeping man, picked up Angus and let myself out. My dog needed a bath, and so did I.

CHAPTER TWENTY-FOUR

"THIS WAY, FIRST VIRGINIA!" I called, safely aboard Snowlight. Granted, the fat little white pony was not exactly a warrior steed, but he was better than nothing.

Margaret trotted up to my side. "I really need to stop doing this," she said, pulling at the corner of her wool uniform. "I'm dying here."

"Actually, you're supposed to die over there, by the river," I corrected.

"I can't believe this is your social life," she said.

"Yet here you are, tagging along." I turned toward my troops. "'Who could not conquer, with troops such as these?'" I quoted loudly. My soldiers cheered.

"So you went to bed early last night," Margs commented. "Lights out, Angus quiet, and it was only 9:30 p.m. when Mom dropped me off."

"Yup. Early to bed, early to rise," I said, my face prickling with telltale heat. Margs had found me this morning in the kitchen, hair wrapped in a towel, red bathrobe firmly cinched, very proper. She'd driven down to the battlefield herself, since she had a deposition in Middletown at two, so I hadn't had the chance to tell her of recent developments with Hottie the Hunk Next Door.

"Hey, I met a guy in court and thought you might

want his number," Margaret said, aiming her rifle at a Union soldier.

"Oh, wait, don't fire," I said. "Snowlight will fall asleep if you do. He has narcolepsy." I patted the pony's neck fondly.

"Gentle Jesus of the three iron nails, Grace," Margs muttered. She pointed her gun at the soldier and said, without much conviction, "Bang." The soldier, well aware of my steed's shortcomings, fell with obliging dramatics, clawed the ground for a few seconds, then lay tragically still. "So, should I have him call you?"

"Well, actually, I don't think I'll be needing anyone's number," I said.

"Why?" Margs asked. "Did you find someone?"

I looked at her and smiled. "Callahan O'Shea."

"Holy shit," she yelped, her face incredulous. At that moment, Grady Jones, a pharmacist by day, fired a cannon from fifty yards away, and Margaret dropped dutifully to the ground. "You slept with him!" she exclaimed. "With Callahan, didn't you?"

"A little quieter, please, Margaret, you're supposed to be dead, okay?" I dismounted from Snowlight and gave him a carrot from my pocket, stalling so I could talk to my sister. "And, yes, I did. Last night."

"Oh, shit."

"What?" I asked. "What about 'Grace, you deserve some fun'?"

Margaret adjusted her rifle so she wasn't lying on it. "Grace, here's the thing. You do deserve fun. You definitely do. And Callahan is probably a tremendous amount of fun."

"He is. So what's the problem?"

"Well, fun's not really what you're looking for, is it?"

"Yes! It...well, what do you mean?"

"You. You're looking for happily ever after. Not a fling."

"Quiet down! You're supposed to be dead!" snapped a passing Union soldier.

"This is a private conversation," Margaret snapped back.

"This is a battle," he hissed.

"No, honey, this is called *pretending*. I hate to break it to you, but we're not really in the Civil War. If you'd like to feel a bit more authentic, I'd be happy to stick this bayonet up your ass."

"Margaret! Stop. He's right. Sorry," I said to the Union soldier. Luckily, I didn't know him. He shook his head and continued, only to be shot a few yards later.

I looked back down at my sister, who had draped her arm across her face to shield her eyes from the sun. "About Callahan, Margs. He happens to be looking for the whole shmear, too. Marriage, a couple of kids, a lawn to mow. He said so."

Margaret nodded. "Well. Good for him." She was quiet for a minute. Shots rang in the distance, a few cries. In another minute, I'd have to remount Snowlight, join a reconnaissance party and catch a little friendly fire in the arm, resulting in a gruesome amputation and my eventual death, but I lingered a little longer, the sun beating on my head, the sharp, sweet scent of grass rising all around us.

"One more thing, Gracie." Margaret paused. "Did Callahan ever tell you exactly what happened with his embezzlement?"

"No," I admitted. "I've asked once or twice, but he hasn't told me."

"Ask again," she advised.

"Do you know?" I asked.

"I know a little. I did some digging."

"And?" I demanded.

"He ever mention a brother to you?" Margaret asked, sitting up and squinting at me.

"Yes. They're estranged."

Margaret nodded. "I bet they are. It seems the brother was the president of the company Cal embezzled from."

God's nightgown! I guess my stupefaction showed, because Margaret reached out to pat my shin. "Ask, Grace. I bet he'll come clean now, since you're bumping uglies and all."

"Such a way with words. No wonder juries love you," I murmured automatically.

"General Jackson! Your opinion is required over here!" called my father, and so I remounted and left my sister to nap in the grass.

For the rest of the battle, my mind fretted over Margaret's little bombshell, and though I went through the motions, being Stonewall Jackson was a bit wasted on me this day. When I finally took the bullet, taking care to slide off Snowlight as he fainted from fear at the barrage of blanks, I was relieved. I uttered the General's poetic last words… "'Let us cross over the river and rest in the shade of the trees,'" and our battle was over. Granted, it actually took Stonewall Jackson eight days to die, but even Brother Against Brother wasn't willing to spend a week reliving the deathwatch.

BY THE TIME I CAME HOME, it was almost five o'clock. It felt like I'd been away from home for days, not hours. Of course, last night, I'd been at Callahan's. The very thought weakened the old knees, and a pleasant tightness squeezed my chest. But now, mingling with that was knowledge that it was time for Cal to tell me about his past.

First, though, I had a dog to worship, a dog who was leaping repeatedly at my side, barking to remind me just who my true love was supposed to be. I apologized profusely to Angus for my absence (despite the fact that my mother had come by and fed him hamburger meat, taken him for a walk, brushed him and given him a new and very jaunty red bandanna). Grand-maternal devotion apparently not enough, Angus had chewed up a slipper to punish me for my absence. He was a bad doggy, but I didn't have the heart to say so, him being so dang adorable and all.

A hard knock came at the front door. "Coming!" I said.

Callahan O'Shea stood on my front porch, hands on his hips, looking mad as hell.

"Hi," I said, blushing in spite of his expression. His neck was beautiful, tanned to the color of caramel, just waiting to be tasted.

"Where the hell have you been?" he barked.

"I—I was at a battle," I said. "I left you a note."

"I didn't get a note," he said.

"I left it by the phone," I replied, raising my eyebrows. He scowled, quite steamed, apparently. It was rather adorable.

"Well, what did it say?" he demanded.

"It said…well, you'll read it when you get home," I said.

"Was this a one-night stand, Grace?" His voice was irritable and hard.

I rolled my eyes. "Come in, Cal," I said, tugging his hand. "I wanted to talk to you anyway, but, no, this wasn't a one-night stand. God's nightgown! What kind of girl do you think I am, huh? First things first, though. I'm starving. You want to order a pizza?"

"No. I want to know why I woke up alone."

He sounded so mad and sullen and adorable that I couldn't suppress a smile. "I tried to wake you, bub. You were out cold." He narrowed his eyes. "Look, if you want me to go over and show you the note, I'll be happy to."

"No. It's fine." He didn't smile.

"Fine, huh?"

"Well, no, Grace, it's not fine. I stomped around all day, not knowing where you were. I practically scared your mother to death when I came over, and she wouldn't unlock the door to talk to me, and, yes, I'm in a pretty crappy mood."

"Because you didn't find the note, Grumpy. Which was very cute, if I do say so, and gave no indication of a one-night stand. Now how about that pizza, or should I chew off my own arm? I'm starving."

"I'll cook," he grunted, still glaring.

"I thought you were mad at me," I reminded him.

"I didn't say it would be good." Then he wrapped his arms around me, lifting me so my toes were off the ground, and kissed the stuffing out of me.

"Dinner can wait," I breathed.

Oh, it wasn't the smartest thing to do, given that we had Things To Discuss, but come on! Those soft blue eyes, that tousled hair… Did I mention he carried me? All the way up the stairs, over his shoulder, caveman style? And he wasn't even out of breath at the top? Come on! And God, the way he kissed me, urgent, hungry kisses that melted my bones and heated my core to the point that I didn't even notice Angus chewing on Cal's leg until he started laughing against my mouth, then grabbed Angus and put him out in the hall, where my little dog barked twice before trotting off to destroy something else.

Looking at Callahan there, leaning against my bedroom door, his shirt unbuttoned, his eyes heavy-lidded and hot...well, I almost didn't need the sex, if I could just stare at him, that little smile finally playing at the corner of his mouth... Actually, what was I saying? I *did* need the sex. No point in wasting a man who looked at me like that.

Margaret was sitting on the chaise lounge on the patio when we came downstairs a good while later. Angus lay sprawled on her lap, groaning occasionally as she stroked his fur.

"I heard zoo noises," Margs called, turning her head as we entered the kitchen. "Figured it was safer to stay outside."

"Want a glass of wine, Margaret?" I asked.

"Sure," she said listlessly.

Callahan did the honors, opening the fridge as if he lived there and getting out a bottle of chardonnay. "This okay?" he asked.

"That's great," I said, handing him the corkscrew. "Thanks, bub. And not just for uncorking the wine."

He grinned. "You're very welcome. To all my skills. Want me to cook something?"

"Yes, I do," I said. "Margs, you want to eat with us?"

"No, thanks. The pheromones alone in there would choke me."

I opened the screen door and sat next to my sister, sliding my bare feet against the brick of the patio. "Everything all right, Margaret?" I asked.

"Stuart's on a date," she announced. "With your co-worker, Eva or Ava or some other sex-kitten, porn-star name."

My mouth dropped open. "Oh, Margs. Are you sure it's a date?"

"Well, he's having dinner with her, and he took great pains to remind me who she was." Her voice deepened to impersonate Stuart's formal voice. "'You remember, Margaret. Rather attractive, teaches history with Grace...' Asshole." Margaret's mouth gave a telltale wobble.

"You know, she might just be trying to butter him up for his support on her being chairman of our department," I suggested. "She must know he's friends with the headmaster."

"He wouldn't go against you, Grace," she replied.

"I'm harboring his wife. He might," I said. She didn't say anything else. I glanced at Callahan through the screen door. He was chopping something at the counter, and he looked so *right* there that it made me a little dizzy. Then I immediately felt a pang of guilt for feeling so happy when Margaret was suffering.

"Margaret," I said slowly, turning back to my sister, who was staring at her knees, "maybe it's time for you to go back to Stuart. Get some counseling and all that. Things aren't getting any better with you staying here."

"Right," she said. "Except it would look like I'm crawling back because I'm jealous, which is true, now that I think of it, and I don't want to give him the satisfaction of thinking that if he's going to cheat on me,

I'll come to heel like some trick dog." Angus barked in solidarity. "If he wants me back, he should bloody well do something!" She paused. "Other than screwing another woman," she added.

"What can I do?" I asked.

"Nothing. Listen, I'm going down cellar, okay? To watch one of your geeky movies or something, is that all right?"

"Sure," I said. "Um, I might stay over at Cal's tonight."

"Okay. See you later." She got up, gave my shoulder a squeeze and went into the kitchen. "Listen, Shawshank, you need to talk to my sister about your sordid past. Okay? Have fun." She took her glass of wine and disappeared down cellar.

I sat alone on the patio, listening to the birds begin their evening chorus. The peace of the season, the smell of freshly cut grass, the gentling sky made me so happy. From the kitchen came the sounds of Callahan cooking, the hiss of something in the frying pan, the cheerful clatter of plates. I felt such a surge of…well, it was too early to say *love,* but you know. Contentment. Pure, underrated contentment. Angus licked my ankle as if he understood.

Cal opened the door and brought out our plates, setting one in my lap. An omelet and whole wheat toast. Perfect. He sat down in the chair vacated by Margaret and took a bite of toast. "So. My sordid past," he said.

"Maybe I should know what you did that landed you in prison."

"Right," he answered tightly. "You should know. You eat, I'll talk."

"I just think I should hear it from you, Cal. Margaret knows—"

"Grace, I was planning to tell you today, okay? That's why I was ticked when you weren't around. So eat."

Obediently, I took a bite of the omelet, which was hot and fluffy and utterly delicious. Giving him what I hoped was an encouraging smile, I waited.

Cal put his plate down and turned his chair so it faced me better. He sat leaning slightly forward, his big hands clasped loosely in front of him, and stared at me for a minute, which made chewing a bit awkward. Then he sighed and looked down.

"I didn't exactly embezzle the money. But I knew about it, I didn't report the person who did embezzle it, and I helped it stay hidden."

"Well, then, who took it?" I asked.

"My brother."

I nearly choked. "Oh," I whispered.

For the next half hour, Callahan told me a pretty fascinating story. How he and his brother, Pete, owned a large construction company. About Hurricane Katrina and an endless supply of reconstruction the government was paying for. About the frenetic nature of the business, the orders that went missing, the insurance claims, the criminal underbelly of New Orleans. And then, one night, how he found a Cayman Islands account under his own name with $1.6 million in it.

"Holy crap, Cal," I breathed.

He didn't answer, just nodded.

"What did you do?"

"Well, it was four in the morning, and I was fairly stunned, seeing my own name there on the computer screen. I was afraid to look away, too, thinking my brother—because it couldn't have been anyone but him—that he might move the money. Or spend it. God, I don't know. So I opened another account and transferred the whole amount."

"Aren't those accounts password protected and all that?" I asked. (I did read John Grisham, after all.)

"Yeah. He used our mother's name. He never was really smart when it came to PIN numbers and that kind of thing. Always used his birthday or our mom's name. Anyway, I figured I'd confront him, and we'd find a way to get the money back to where it belonged. We were working in the Ninth Ward, rebuilding neighborhoods, and I figured we'd just slip the money back in."

"Why didn't you call the Feds or the police?" I asked.

"Because it was my brother."

"But he was cheating all those people! And he was using you to do it! God, the Ninth Ward was hardest hit of anyone—"

"I know." Cal sighed and scrubbed his hand through his hair. "I know, Grace. But…" His voice trailed off. "But he was also the brother who let me sleep in his room for a year after our mom died. The one who showed me how to hit a baseball and taught me to drive. He always said we'd go into business together. I wanted to give him a chance to make things right." Cal looked at me, his face looking older, and sad. "He was my big brother. I didn't want him to go to jail."

Yes. I also knew about putting family before common sense, didn't I? "So what happened?" I asked more quietly. "What did he say?" I set my empty plate aside.

"Well, what could he say? He was sorry, he got caught up in it all, everyone else was doing it… But he agreed that we'd just funnel the money back into the projects and make things right." He paused, remembering. "Unfortunately for us, the Feds had been watching the company. When I moved the money, I gave them a trail, and they pounced." He looked down and shook his head.

"Did your brother go to jail, too?" I asked softly.

Cal didn't look up. "No, Grace. He testified against me."

I closed my eyes. "Oh, Cal."

"Yeah."

"Did you…what did you do?"

Another weary sigh. "My brother had taken steps, you know? My name was all over this, and it was his word against mine. And I was the accountant. Pete said even if he'd wanted to, he wouldn't have known how to do it, I was the college boy and all that. The prosecutors found him a lot more convincing, I guess. My lawyer said the world wasn't going to go easy on someone who stole from Katrina victims, so when they offered a plea, I took it."

Angus jumped onto my lap, and I petted him, thinking. "Why didn't you ever tell me this before, Cal? I would've believed you."

"Would you?" he asked. "Doesn't every convict say he's innocent? That he was set up?"

He had a point. I didn't answer. "I have no way of proving that I didn't do exactly what my brother said I did," he added quietly.

My heart ached in a sudden, sharp tug as I tried to imagine what it would feel like to be turned in by Margaret or Natalie. To be betrayed by one of them. I couldn't. Yes, of course Nat had fallen for Andrew, but that wasn't her fault. I never thought so, anyway, and I knew my sister. But to have your own brother send you to jail for his crime...man. No wonder Cal had an edge when it came to discussing his past.

"So you were going to tell me all this? Even without Margs digging around in your records?"

"Yes."

"Why now? Why not all the other times I asked?"

"Because we started something last night. I thought we did, anyway." His voice was hard. "So that's the story. Now you know."

We sat in silence for a few more minutes. Angus, weary of being ignored, yarped once and wagged his tail, inviting me to adore him. I petted his fur idly and adjusted his bandanna, idly noting that he'd eaten Cal's omelet while we were talking.

"Cal?" I finally said.

"Yeah." His voice was flat, his shoulders tight.

"Would you like to have dinner with my family sometime?"

He didn't move for a second, then practically sprang across the distance between us. His smile lit up the gloom. "Yes."

He wrapped his big arms around me and kissed me hard, and Angus nipped him. Then we cleared the dishes and went to his place.

CHAPTER TWENTY-FIVE

THE NEXT DAY WAS MEMORIAL DAY, so I didn't have to crawl out of Cal's bed at the crack of dawn. Instead, we walked down to Lala's for pastries and meandered back along the Farmington.

"Do you have plans this afternoon?" Callahan asked, taking a long pull from his coffee.

"What if I did?" I asked, tugging Angus's leash so he wouldn't eat or roll on the poor dead mouse at the edge of the path.

"You'd have to cancel them." He grinned, slipping his arm around my waist.

"Oh, really?"

"Mmm-hmm." He wiped a little frosting off my chin, then kissed me.

"Okay, then. I'm yours," I murmured.

"I like the sound of that," he said, kissing me again, long and slow and sweet, so that my knees wobbled when he let me go. "I'll pick you up around two, but I have to run now. The appliances are being installed today."

"You're almost done with the house, aren't you?" I asked, a sudden pang hitting my heart.

"Yup," he answered.

"What happens after that?"

"I have another house to work on, couple towns

north. But if you want, I can come back and lie on the roof of this house so you can spy on me. If the new owners don't mind."

"I never spied. It was more of a gazing thing."

He grinned, then glanced at his watch. "Okay, Grace. Gotta run." He kissed me once more, then went up the path to his house. "Two o'clock, don't forget."

I let out some line on Angus's retractable leash so my puppy could sniff a fern and took a pull of my own coffee. Then I headed back home to correct papers.

As I sifted through my kids' essays, I had an uneasy thought. I needed to tell the Manning search committee about Callahan. He was, after all, in my life now, and I should be upfront about that. However it happened, Cal had served time in a federal prison, had covered up a crime, even though his intentions had been honorable. That wasn't something I should try to hide. That was also something that would probably tank whatever chance I had at becoming chairman of the history department. Nonprofit institutions tended to frown on embezzling and felons and prison records, especially where impressionable children were concerned.

MY SHOULDERS DROOPED at the thought. Well. I had to do it just the same.

At two o'clock sharp, Cal came up the walk. "You ready, woman?" he called through the screen door as Angus leaped and snarled from the other side.

"I have four papers left to grade. Can you wait half an hour?"

"No. Do it in the car, okay?"

I blinked. "Yes, Master." He grinned. "Where are we going?"

"You'll find out when we get there. When do you think this dog will like me?"

"Possibly never," I said, picking up my dog and kissing his head. "Goodbye, Angus, my darling boy. Be good. Mommy loves you."

"Ouch. That's really...wow. Sad," Cal said. I punched him in the shoulder. "No hitting, Grace!" he laughed. "You need to get those violent urges looked at. God. I never got beat up in prison, but I move in next to you, and look at me. Hit by sticks, bitten by your dog, my poor truck dented..."

"Such a baby. I'd think prison would've toughened you up a bit. Made you a man and all that."

"It wasn't that kind of prison." He smiled and opened his truck door for me. "We did have tennis lessons. No shivving, though. Sorry to disappoint you, honey."

Honey. I sort of flowed into the truck. Honey. Callahan O'Shea called me honey.

Ten minutes later, we were on the interstate, heading west. I took out a paper and started to read.

"Do you like being a teacher?" Callahan asked.

"I do," I answered immediately. "The kids are fantastic at this age. Of course, I want to kill them half the time, but the other half, I just love them. And they are sort of the point of teaching."

"Most people don't love teenagers, do they?" He smiled, then checked the rearview mirror as we merged.

"Well, it's not the easiest age, no. Little kids, who doesn't love them, right? But teenagers—they're just starting to show signs of who they could be. That's really great to watch. And of course, I love what I teach."

"The Civil War, right?" Callahan asked.

"I teach all areas of American history, actually, but yes, the Civil War is my specialty."

"Why do you love it? Kind of a horrible war, wasn't it?"

"Absolutely," I answered. "But there was never a war where people cared more about their cause. It's one thing to fight a foreign country, a culture that you don't know, cities that you've never visited, maybe. But the Civil War...imagine what would drive you to raise troops against your own country, the way Lincoln did. The South was fighting for rights as individual states, but the North was fighting for the future of the nation. It was heartbreaking because it was so personal. It was *us*. I mean, when you compare Lincoln with someone like—"

I heard my voice rising, becoming that of a television preacher on Sunday morning. "Sorry," I said, blushing.

Callahan reached over and squeezed my hand, grinning. "I like hearing about it," he said. "And I like you, Grace."

"So it's more than the fact that I was the first woman you saw out of prison," I said.

"Well, we can't discount that," he said somberly. "Imprinting, they call it, right, Teacher?"

I swatted his arm. "Very funny. Now leave me alone. I have papers to grade."

"Yes, ma'am," he said.

And grade them I did. Cal drove smoothly, not interrupting, commenting only when I read a snippet out loud. He asked me to check his MapQuest directions once or twice, which I did, quite amiably. It was surprisingly comfortable.

About an hour later, Callahan pulled off the highway. A sign announced that we'd arrived in Easting, New York, population 7512. We drove down a street lined with a pizzeria, hair salon, package store and a restaurant called Vito's. "So, Mr. O'Shea, why have you brought me to Easting, New York?" I asked.

"You'll see it in about a block if these directions are right," he said, pulling into a parking space on the street. Then he hopped out and opened my door. I made a mental note to thank Mr. Lawrence the next time I read to him. Callahan O'Shea had beautiful manners. He took my hand and grinned.

"You look very confident," I said.

"I am," he answered, kissing my hand. All the qualms I'd felt about his past and my chances at the chairman job vanished, replaced with a tight band of happiness squeezing my chest. I couldn't remember the last time I'd felt so light. Maybe, in fact, I'd never felt this good.

Then I saw where Cal was taking me, lurched to a halt and burst into tears.

"Surprise," he said, sliding his arms around me in a hug.

"Oh, Cal," I snuffled into his shoulder.

A small movie theater stood just down the block, brick entrance, wide windows, the smell of popcorn already seducing the senses. But it was the marquee that got me. Framed in lightbulbs, black letters against a white background were the following words: *Special Anniversary Showing! See It As It Was Meant To Be Seen!* And below that, in huge letters...*Gone with the Wind*.

"Oh, Cal," I said again, my throat so tight I squeaked. The teenager behind the counter stared wonderingly at me as I wept, while Cal bought us tickets, popcorn and root beer. The place was mobbed—I wasn't the only one, apparently, who yearned to see the greatest love story of all time on the big screen.

"How did you find this?" I asked, wiping my eyes once we were seated.

"I searched it on the internet a few weeks ago," he answered. "You said you'd never seen it before, and it made me wonder if it ever got shown anymore. I was just going to tell you, but then you finally jumped me, so I figured I'd make it a date."

A few weeks ago. He'd been thinking about me weeks ago. Wow.

"Thank you, Callahan O'Shea," I said, leaning in to kiss him. His mouth was soft and hot, and his hand slid behind my neck, and he tasted like popcorn and butter. Warm ripples danced through my stomach until the white-haired lady sitting behind us accidentally (or purposefully) kicked our seats. Then the lights dimmed, and I found that my heart was racing. Cal grinned, gave my hand a squeeze.

For the next few hours, I fell in love with Scarlett and Rhett all over again, my emotions as tender and raw as when I was fourteen and first read the book. I winced when Scarlett declared her love to Ashley, beamed when Rhett bid for her at the dance, cringed when Melly had her baby, bit a nail as Atlanta burned. By the last line, when Katie Scarlett O'Hara Hamilton Kennedy Butler raised her head, once again determined to get what she wanted, unbowed, unbroken, I was out and out sobbing.

"I guess I should've brought some Valium," Callahan murmured as the credits rolled, handing me a napkin, since I'd run out of tissues when Rhett joined the Confederate troops outside of Atlanta.

"Thank you," I squeaked. The white-haired lady behind us patted my shoulder as she left.

"You're welcome," Cal said with that grin that I was coming to love.

"Did you like it?" I managed to ask.

He turned to me, his face gentle. "I loved it, Grace," he said.

IT WAS ALMOST NINE WHEN WE got back to Peterston. "You hungry?" Callahan asked as we passed Blackie's.

"I'm starving," I said.

"Great." He pulled into the parking lot, got out and took my hand. Holding hands had to be one of the most wonderful things God ever invented, I thought as we went into the restaurant. A small but undeniable claim on someone, holding hands. And holding hands with Callahan O'Shea was thrilling and comforting at the same time, his big hand smooth and callused and warm.

We found a booth, and Cal sat next to me, rather than across. He slid his arm around my shoulder and pulled me close, and I breathed in the clean, soapy smell of him. Damn. I was in deep.

"Want some wings?" he asked, scanning the menu.

"You are definitely getting shagged tonight," I said. "First *Gone with the Wind,* now buffalo wings. I can't resist you."

"Then my dastardly plan is working." He turned and kissed me, that hungry, hot, soft kiss that was like caramel sauce, and I thought to myself that for the rest of my life, I would remember this as the most perfect, most romantic date I or any other woman had ever had. When

I opened my eyes, Callahan O'Shea was grinning. He pinched my chin and turned back to the menu.

I looked around the restaurant, smiling, feeling that the world was a beautiful place. A good-looking guy caught my eye and raised his beer glass. He looked familiar. Oh, yes. Eric, the window washer from Manning who loved his wife. And wasn't she cute. They were holding hands. Another happy couple. Aw! I waved back.

"Hello there, Grace," came a soft voice. I looked up and tried to suppress a grimace.

"Hi, Ava," I said. "How are you?" My voice was chilly. She had, after all, gone on a date with Stuart.

"Very well, thank you," she purred, looking at Callahan. Blink...blink...and blink again. "I'm Ava Machiatelli."

"Callahan O'Shea," my boyfriend said, shaking her hand.

"I heard you had dinner with Stuart the other night," I said.

"Mmm." She smiled. "Poor lad. He needed a little... company." My teeth clenched. Damn Stuart for being just another typical man, and damn Ava for being the kind of woman who had no morals when it came to sex.

Ava turned and waved toward the bar. "Kiki! Over here!" She turned back to Cal and me. "Apparently, Kiki broke up with someone over the weekend and is feeling rather devastated," she said. "I'm administering margaritas."

Kiki joined us, looking indeed quite tragic (and a little tipsy). "Hey, Grace. I called you about ten times today. Remember that guy from Jitterbug's? Well, he dumped me!" Her voice broke. She turned her gaze to

Callahan. "Hi—" Her voice broke off abruptly. "My God, it's the ex-con!" she exclaimed, heartbreak forgotten.

"Nice to see you again," Cal said, raising an eyebrow at her.

"Ex-con?" Ava said.

There was an uncomfortable pause. I didn't say anything...visions of trustees danced in my head. Shit.

"Embezzling, right?" Kiki said, shooting me a decidedly cool look. Ah, yes. I'd warned her off Callahan for just that reason. Damn it.

"That's right," Cal said.

Ava's eyes lit up. "Embezzling. Fascinating."

"Well," I said. "Nice seeing you guys. Have fun."

"Oh, we will," Ava said with a huge smile. "So nice to meet you, Callahan." And with that, they returned to their table.

"Everything okay?" Cal asked.

"They work at Manning," I said, watching as Ava and Kiki sat at a table not too far away.

"Right."

"So now everyone will know I'm dating an ex-con," I said.

"I guess so." His eyes were expectant.

"Well," I said briskly, squeezing his hand. "I guess I *am* dating an ex-con. So there you go." Ava's and Kiki's heads were together. My stomach hurt. "So. Buffalo wings it is."

Unfortunately, I wasn't hungry anymore.

CHAPTER TWENTY-SIX

I WENT TO SCHOOL EARLY the next morning, straight to the headmaster's office.

I wasn't fast enough.

"Grace. I was expecting you," Dr. Stanton said as I sat in front of his desk like a repentant student. "I had a rather disturbing phone call from Theo Eisenbraun this morning."

"Right," I said, sweat breaking out on my forehead. "Um…well, I wanted to tell you myself, but I guess the news is out. But yes, I just started dating someone, and he, uh, served time for embezzlement."

Dr. Stanton sighed. "Oh, Grace."

"Dr. Stanton, I'd hope that my credentials stand on their own," I said. "I love Manning, I love the kids, and I really don't think my personal life should have anything to do with how I'm viewed as a teacher. Or, um, as a potential department chairman."

"Of course," he murmured. "And you're quite right. We value you tremendously, Grace."

Right. We both knew I was screwed. If I'd had any chance of getting the chairmanship, it was gone now. "The search committee is meeting this week, Grace. We'll let you know."

"Thanks," I said, then went on to Lehring Hall, to my casket-size office, and sat in the old leather chair

Julian and I had found at a yard sale. Damn it. Glum, I gnawed on a fingernail, staring out the window at the beautiful campus. The cherry blossoms waved thick and foamy, as if the tree branches had been sprayed with pink whipped cream. Graceful dogwood blossoms seemed to float on the air, and the grass glowed emerald. It was Manning's most beautiful time. Classes ended next Wednesday, with graduation two days after that. The day before Natalie and Andrew's wedding, actually.

Being chairman might've been a stretch for me—I was only thirty-one, after all, and I didn't have a doctorate in history. Add to that the fact that I just wasn't a political creature with minimal administrative experience, aside from heading up the curriculum committee. Maybe I'd never had a chance at all.

Still, I had made it to the final round. It might've just been a courtesy to a Manning faculty member. But if being with Callahan O'Shea had tanked my chances... well. He was worth it. I hoped. No. I knew. If being passed over for chairman was the price I had to pay, so be it. Thus resolved, I left my poor fingernail alone, sat up straight and booted up my computer.

"Hello, Grace." Ava blinked sleepily from the doorway, a knowing smile on her glossy lips. "How are you this morning?"

"I'm perfect in every way, Ava, and you?" I slapped a chipper smile on my face and waited.

"I heard you met with Dr. Stanton this morning." She grinned. Nothing was secret at a prep school. "Dating an ex-con, Grace? Not much of a role model for the young minds of Manning, is it?"

"Well, if we're examining morals, I'd say it beats dating a married coworker, Ava. One wonders."

"One does," she murmured. "The search committee meets Thursday, you know."

"I heard they already made their decision," came a rusty voice. "Good morning, ladies."

"Good morning, Dr. Eckhart," I said.

"Hello, there," whispered Ava.

"A word, please, Ms. Emerson?" he croaked.

"Ta-ta," Ava said, then swung off down the hall, her lush bottom straining the seams of her skirt.

"Have you heard?" I asked as Dr. Eckhart came into my office.

"Yes, I've heard, Grace. I'm here to reassure you." He broke off into a coughing fit, sounding, as he usually did, as if he were trying to expel a small child from his lungs. When he caught his breath, he smiled with watery eyes. "Grace, many of our own board members have had a brush with the law, especially concerning matters of creative financing. Try not to worry."

I gave the old man a halfhearted smile. "Thanks. Have they really reached a decision?"

"From what I've heard, they're finalizing the package this afternoon, but yes, I was told they agreed on someone last week. I recommended you, my dear."

My throat tightened. "Thank you, sir. That means more to me than I can say."

The chimes rang for first period. Dr. E. shuffled off to Medieval History with his sophomores, and I went down the hall to my seniors. Two more Civil War classes with them, then they'd be out in the world. Many of them, I'd never see again.

I pushed open the door and went in, my arrival unnoticed by my students. Hunter IV lounged in front of Kerry Blake, who was wearing a cropped, low-cut shirt that wouldn't have looked out of place on a prostitute, but which probably cost a week of my salary. Four students were checking their BlackBerry, despite the rules against having them in class. Molly, Mallory, Madison and Meggie were trying to out-impress each other with their summer plans—one was going to Paris to intern at Chanel, another would be mountain climbing in Nepal, one had plans to white-water raft on the Colorado, and one would be, in her words, committing slow suicide by spending the summer with her family. Emma sat staring at Tommy Michener, who was dozing with his head on the desk.

Maybe I wasn't as good a teacher as I thought. For all my best intentions, had I really taught these kids what I wanted them to learn? Would they ever understand how important it was to know our past? And add to that the fact that I'd just killed my chances of becoming chairman, and I felt something inside me snap.

"Good morning, princes and princesses!" I barked, earning a gratifying jump from many of them. "This weekend, my lovely children, is the reenactment of the Battle of Gettysburg." Groans. Eye rolling. "You are required to attend. Failure to do so will result in an F in class participation, which, as I'm sure you remember, is worth one third of your grade, and even though you've all gotten into college, I do believe you're supposed to maintain a healthy grade point average. Am I right? I am. Meet me in front of the building Saturday morning, 9:00 a.m."

Their mouths hung open with horror, and for a second, they were unable to find their voices. And then came the chorus. "It's not fair! I have lacrosse/soccer/ tickets! My parents will—"

I let them protest for a minute, then smiled and said simply, "Nonnegotiable."

WHEN I GOT HOME THAT afternoon, Angus was looking cuter than ever, so I figured a waltz was in order. Scooping my little dog up into my arms, I swooped around the living room, one-two-three, one-two-three, humming "Take It to the Limit" by the Eagles, one of Angus's favorites. "'So put me on a highway, and show me a sign,'" I sang. Angus began to croon along. As I said, it was one of his favorites.

I wasn't sure why I felt so happy, given that my chances of being history chair were smaller than ever. "I guess there's more to life than work, right, McFangus?" I asked the Wonder Pup. He wriggled in delight.

It was true. In just a little while, Natalie and Andrew would be married, putting the final nail in the coffin of Andrew and me. Summer was fast approaching, the time of reading and relaxing and battling down South.

And Callahan O'Shea was my boyfriend. A warm tide of happiness rose from my ankles on up. Callahan O'Shea was looking for a wife, kids and a lawn to mow. I figured I might just be able to help him out on that quest.

"Can I cut in?"

Speak of the devil, there he was on my porch, sinful grin in place. Angus stiffened and yarped in my arms.

"Come on in," I said, setting down my faithful beastie, who leaped onto Cal's ankle with great enthusiasm. *Hrrr. Hrrr.* Cal ignored him, took my hand and put his hand on my waist.

"I don't really know what I'm doing," he admitted, his eyes crinkling most appealingly as he tried to execute a box step, stepping on my foot.

"I'll teach you," I said. The back of his neck was warm under my hand, and the lovely smell of wood and man and sweat made my heart beat a little faster. The tide of happiness became a flood.

"I always kind of liked the eighth-grade shuffle myself," he said, pulling me into a hug. Our feet barely moved…well, except when Cal tried to shake Angus off. My hands drifted down Cal's back…I figured I'd cop a feel, why not…when I touched paper.

"Oh, right," Callahan said, stepping back. "This is yours. The mailman put it in my box by mistake." He pulled an envelope from the back pocket of his jeans and handed it to me.

The envelope was thick and creamy, my name done in stylish calligraphy, the ink a dark green. "This must be my sister's wedding invitation," I said, opening it. Sure enough, it was. Stylish and classic, just like Natalie. I smiled a little at the pretty design, the traditional words. *Together with their parents, Natalie Rose Emerson and Andrew Chase Carson warmly request the honor of your attendance*… I looked up at Callahan. "Want to be my wedding date?" I asked.

He smiled. "Sure," he said.

Sure. Just like that. Such a contrast from the superhuman effort I'd put into finding a date for Kitty's wedding. I paused. "Um, I don't think I told you this, Cal, but remember I said I'd been engaged once?" Cal nodded. "Well, it was to Andrew. The guy who's marrying my sister."

Cal's eyebrows bounced up in surprise. "Really?"

"Yup," I said. "But once he and Natalie met, it seemed pretty clear that she was the one for him. Not me."

He didn't say anything for a minute, just looked at me, frowning slightly. "Are you okay with them being together?" he asked finally. Angus shook the cuff of his jeans.

"Oh, sure," I answered. I paused. "It was really tough at first, but I'm fine now."

Cal studied me for another minute. Then he bent, picked up Angus, who replied with a growl before gnawing on Cal's thumb. "I'd say she's more than fine, wouldn't you, Angus?" he asked. Then he leaned in and kissed my neck, and it dawned on me in a sweetly painful rush that I was crazy in love with Callahan O'Shea.

CHAPTER TWENTY-SEVEN

BUT BEING CRAZY ABOUT HIM didn't mean things were perfect.

"I think we should just wait a little bit," I said to Cal a few days later as we drove to West Hartford.

"I think it's a bad idea," he said, not looking at me. We were on our way to that most distressing of family gatherings—Mom's art show. Well, actually, most of my family gatherings were distressing, but Mom's shows were special. However, it was the only night before Nat's wedding that my family could get together. The official Meet the Family horror show.

"Callahan, trust me. It's my family. They're going to…well, you know. Flip a little. No one wants to hear that their baby girl is dating a guy with a record."

"Well, I do have a record, and I think we should just get it out in the open."

"Okay, listen. First of all, you've never been to one of my mother's shows. They're weird. My dad will be tense as it is, Mom will be fluttering all over the place… Secondly, my grandmother is deaf as a stone, so I'd have to yell, and it's a public place and all that. It's just not the time, Cal."

I'd told my parents and Natalie that I was dating the boy next door. I hadn't told them anything else.

My parents were concerned, thinking I had dumped

a perfectly good workaholic doctor for a carpenter. That was bad enough...wait till they found out about his nineteen months behind bars. Not that there were bars at his prison, but such a distinction was going to be lost on the Emerson family, whose line could be traced back to the *Mayflower*.

"I'm actually surprised you haven't told them yet," Cal said.

I glanced over at him. His jaw was tight. "Listen, bub. Don't worry. I'm not trying to hide anything. I just want them to know you and like you a little bit first. If I walk in and say, 'Hi, this is my boyfriend who was recently released from prison,' they'll have kittens. If they see what a great guy you are first, it won't be so bad."

"When will you tell them?"

"Soon," I bit out. "Cal. Please. I have a lot on my mind. School's ending, I still haven't heard about the chairmanship, one sister's getting married, the other's ready to jump out of her skin... Can we just let my folks meet you without dumping your prison record on them? Please? Let me have one major crisis at a time? I promise I'll tell them soon. Just not tonight."

"It feels dishonest," he said.

"It's not! It's just...parceling out information, okay? We don't have to go around introducing you as Callahan O'Shea, ex-con. Do we?"

He didn't answer for a minute. "Fine, Grace. Have it your way. But it doesn't feel right."

I took his hand. "Thanks." After a minute, he squeezed back.

"YOU'RE DATING THE HELP? You threw over that nice doctor for the help?" Mémé's expression was that of a woman who'd just bitten into a lizard. Actually, of a lizard biting into a lizard. She wheeled a little closer, hitting a pedestal and causing *Into the Light* (supposedly a birth canal, but actually more resembling the Holland Tunnel) to wobble precariously. I steadied it, then looked down at my disapproving grandmother.

"Mémé, please stop calling Callahan the help, okay? You're not in Victorian England anymore," I started. "And as I said—" here I took a breath, weary with the lie "—Wyatt, though a very nice man, just wasn't a good fit. Okay? Okay. Let's move on."

Margaret, lurking nearby, raised an eyebrow. I yearned for more wine and ignored her *and* Mémé, who was once again labeling the Irish as beggars and thieves.

Chimera Art Gallery was littered with body parts. Apparently, Mom wasn't the only one who was doing anatomy these days, and she was quite irritable that another artist was also featured (joints…ball-and-socket, gliding and cartilaginous, not nearly as popular as Mom's more, ah, intimate items, most of which looked like they belonged in a sex shop). I dragged my eyes off *Yearning in Green* (use your imagination) and sidled over to Callahan, who was talking to my father.

"So! You're a carpenter!" Dad boomed in the hearty voice he used on blue-collar workers, a little loud and with an occasional grammatical lapse to show that he, too, was just an average joe.

"Dad, you hired Cal to replace my windows, remember? So you already know he's a carpenter."

"Restoration specialist?" Dad suggested hopefully.

"Not really, no," Callahan answered evenly, resisting Dad's efforts to glam him up. "I wouldn't say a specialist in anything, though. Just basic carpentry."

"He does beautiful work," I added. Cal gave me a veiled look.

"What I wouldn't give to trade in my law books for a hammer!" Dad trumpeted. I snorted—in my memory, at least, it had always been Mom who did the needed household repairs; Dad couldn't even hang a picture. "You always a carpenter?" my father continued, dropping a verb to demonstrate his camaraderie with the working man.

"No, sir. I used to be an accountant." Cal looked at me again. I gave him a little smile and slipped my hand in his.

My mom, apparently having overheard, pounced on us. "So you had a *revelation, Callahan?*" she asked, caressing a nearby sculpture in a most pornographic way. "The same happened with me. There I was, a mother, a housewife, but inside, an artist was struggling for recognition. In the end, I just had to embrace my new identity."

"Dance hall hussy?" I muttered to Margaret. I'd told Margs about our parents' attempted tryst—why should I suffer alone?—and she snorted. Mom shot me a questioning look but dragged Cal over to *Want,* describing the wonders of self-expression. Callahan tossed me a wink. Good. He was relaxing.

"Hey, guys! We made it!" My younger sister's mellifluous voice floated over the hum of the crowd.

Natalie and Andrew were holding hands. "Hi, Grace!" my younger sister said, leaping over to hug me.

"What about me?" Margaret growled.

"I was getting there!" Nat said, grinning. "Hello, Margaret, I love you just as much as I love Grace, okay?"

"As you should," Margs grumbled. "Hi, Andrew."

"Hi, ladies. How's everyone?"

"Everyone's suffering, Andrew, so join the crowd," I said with a smile. "Nice of you guys to come."

"We wanted to meet Callahan officially," Natalie said. "You and Wyatt were together for what, two months? And I never got to even shake his hand." Nat looked over at Cal. "God, Grace, he is really gorgeous. Look at those *arms*. He could pick up a horse."

"Hello, I'm standing right here," Andrew said to my sister. I smiled at my wineglass, a warm glow in the pit of my stomach. *That's right, Andrew,* I thought. *That big, strong, gorgeous man is your replacement.* I wondered what Cal would think of my ex. Cal glanced over at me, smiled, and the glow became a lovely ache. I smiled back, and Cal returned his attention to my mom.

"Crikey, look at her," Nat said to Margaret. "She's in love."

I blushed. Andrew caught my eye, a questioning eyebrow raised.

"I'm afraid you're right, Nat," Margs replied. "Grace, you're in deep, poor slob. And hey, speaking of poor slobs, Andrew, make yourself useful and get us more wine."

"Yes, sir," Andrew answered obediently.

"By the way," I said, "Mom wants you to pick out a wedding present. A sculpture." I lifted an eyebrow.

"Oh, sweetie, let's pick fast," Natalie said. "The smallest one, whatever it is. My God, look at that. *Portals of Heaven.* Wow. That is large." They meandered off.

Dad approached Margs and me. "Gracie-Pudding," he said, "can I have a word?"

Margaret heaved a sigh. "Rejected again. People wonder why I'm so mean. Fine. I'll just go browse the labias." Dad flinched at the word and waited till she was out of hearing range.

"Yes, Dad?" I said, picking up a shoulder joint to admire. Oops. It came apart in my hands.

"Well, Pudding, I just have to ask myself if maybe you broke things off prematurely with the doctor," Dad said, watching me fumble the joint parts. "Sure, he has to work a lot, but think of what he's working on! Saving children's lives! Isn't that the kind of man you want? A carpenter...he...well, not to be snobby or anything, honey..."

"You're sounding pretty snobby, Dad," I said, trying to fit the humerus (or was it the ulna? I got a B- in biology) back into the socket. "Of course, you think being a teacher is akin to being a field hand, so..."

"I think nothing of the sort," Dad said. "But still. You'd probably make more picking cotton."

Callahan, having been released from my mother's death grip, came over to me.

"Here y'are!" Dad barked heartily, slapping Callahan on the back hard enough to make his wine slosh. "So, big guy, tell me about yourself!"

"What would you like to know, sir?" Cal asked, taking my hand.

"Grace says you used to be an accountant," Dad said with an approving smile.

"Yes," Cal answered.

"And I take it you went to college for this?"

"Yes, sir. I went to Tulane."

I gave Dad a look that was meant to convey *See? He's*

really nice and also *Lay off the questions, Dad.* He ignored it. "So, Callahan, why'd you leave—"

Mom interrupted. "Do you have family in the area, Callahan?" she asked, smiling brightly.

"My grandfather lives at Golden Meadows," Cal answered, turning to her.

"Who is he? Do I know him?" Mémé barked, wheeling closer and almost toppling a breast from a nearby pedestal.

"His name is Malcolm Lawrence," Cal answered. "Hello, Mrs. Winfield. Nice to see you again."

"Never heard of him," Mémé snapped.

"He's in the dementia unit," Callahan said. I squeezed his hand. "My mother died when I was little, and my grandfather raised my brother and me."

Mom's eyebrows raised. "A brother? And where does he live?"

Cal hesitated. "He…he lives in Arizona. Married, no kids. So not much family to speak of."

"You poor thing!" Mom said. "Family is such a blessing."

"Is it?" I asked. She clucked at me fondly.

"You. Irishman." Mémé poked Cal's leg with a bony finger. "Are you after my granddaughter's money?"

I sighed. Loudly. "You're thinking of Margaret, Mémé. I don't really have a lot, Cal."

"Ah, well. I guess I'll have to date Margs, then," he said. "And speaking of sister swapping," he added, lowering his voice so only I could hear.

"Hi, I'm Andrew Carson." The Pale One approached, my glowing, beautiful sister in tow. Andrew pushed up his glasses and stuck out a hand. "Nice to meet you."

"Callahan O'Shea," Cal returned, shaking Andrew's

hand firmly. Andrew winced, and I bit down on a smile. *That's right, Andrew! He could beat you to a pulp.* Not that I was a proponent of violence, of course. It was just true.

"It's great to see you again, Callahan," Natalie said.

"Hello, Nat," Cal returned with a smile, the one that could charm the paint off walls. Natalie blushed, then mouthed *Gorgeous!* I grinned back in complete agreement.

"So you're a...plumber, is it?" Andrew said, his eyes flicking up and down Cal's solid frame, a silly little grin on his face, as if he were thinking, *Oh, yes, I've heard of blue-collar workers! So you're one of those!*

"He's a carpenter," Natalie and I said at the same time.

"It's so great to work with your hands," Dad boomed. "I'll probably do more of that once I retire. Make my own furniture. Maybe build a smokehouse."

"A smokehouse?" I asked. Cal smothered a smile.

"Please, Dad. Don't you remember the radial saw?" Natalie said, grinning at Callahan. "My father almost amputated his thumb the one time he tried to make anything. Andrew's the same way."

"That was a rogue blade," Dad muttered.

"It's true," Andrew said amenably, slipping an arm around Natalie. "Grace, remember when I tried to fix that cabinet when we first moved in together? Practically killed myself. Never tried that again. Luckily, I can afford to pay someone to do it for me."

Natalie shot him a surprised glance, but he ignored it, smiling insincerely at Cal. Who didn't smile back. Well, well. Andrew was jealous. How pleasing. And how classy of Cal, not to rise to his bait. Still, I could feel him tensing next to me.

"Such a shame to waste your education, though, son," Dad continued. Oh, God. He was doing his "Earn a Decent Wage" speech, one that I'd heard many times. And by decent wage, Dad didn't mean the simple ability to pay your own bills and maybe sock a little away. He meant six figures. He was a Republican, after all.

"Education is never wasted, Dad," I said hastily before Cal could answer.

"Are you from around here, Calvin?" Andrew asked, tilting his head in owlish fashion.

"It's Callahan," my guy corrected. "I'm originally from Connecticut, yes. I grew up in Windsor."

"Where'd you live before you moved back?" Andrew asked.

Callahan glanced at me. "The South," he said, his voice a little tight. I tried to convey my gratitude by squeezing his hand. He didn't squeeze back.

"I love the South!" my mother exclaimed. "So sultry, so passionate, so *Cat on a Hot Tin Roof!*"

"Control yourself, Nancy," Mémé announced, rattling her ice cubes.

"Don't tell me what to do, old woman," Mom muttered back, knowing full well that Mémé was too deaf to hear.

"So why'd ya leave accounting?" Dad asked. Cripes, he was like a dog with a bone.

"Maybe we can stop interrogating Cal for now, hmm?" I suggested sharply. Cal had grown very still next to me.

Dad shot me a wounded look. "Pudding, I'm just trying to figure out why someone would trade in a nice secure job so he could do manual labor all day."

"It's an honest question," Andrew seconded.

Ah. Honest. The key word. I closed my eyes. *Here it comes,* I thought. I was right.

Callahan let go of my hand. "I was convicted for embezzling over a million dollars," he stated evenly. "I lost my accounting license and served nineteen months at a federal prison in Virginia. I got out two months ago." He looked at my father, then my mother, then Andrew. "Any other questions?"

"You're a convict?" Mémé said, craning her bony neck to look at Cal. "I knew it."

BY THE TIME THE GALLERY SHOW was over, I had managed to tell my family about Cal's situation. Granted, I did a piss-poor job, given that I was completely unprepared. I'd been planning to figure out something a bit more convincing than *It's not as bad as it sounds…* Plus, Margs had abandoned me, saying there was an emergency at work and she wouldn't be home till midnight at the earliest.

"Happy?" I asked Callahan, getting into the car and buckling myself in with considerable vigor.

"Grace, it's best to be honest right up front," he said, his face a bit stony.

"Well, you got your way."

"Listen," he said, not starting the car. "I'm sorry if it was uncomfortable for you. But your family should know."

"And I *was* going to tell them! Just not tonight."

He looked at me for a long minute. "It felt like lying."

"It wasn't lying! It was introducing the idea bit by bit.

Going slow. Considering the feelings of others, that's all."

We sat in the idle car, staring ahead. My throat was tight, my hands felt hot. One thing was clear. I was going to be spending a lot of time on the phone for the next day or so.

"Grace," Callahan said quietly, "are you sure you want to be with me?"

I sputtered. "Cal, I shot myself in the foot for you this week. I told the headmaster of my school that I was dating you! I'm taking you to my sister's wedding! I just don't think you need to walk around with a scarlet letter tattooed on your forehead, that's all!"

"Did you want me to lie to your dad?" he asked.

"No! I just…I wanted to finesse this, that's all. I know my family, Cal. I just wanted to ease them into the idea of your past. Instead, you went in with guns blazing."

"Well, I don't have a lot of time to waste."

"Why? Do you have a brain tumor? Are there blood-hounds tracking you at this very moment? Is an alien spaceship coming to abduct you?"

"Not that I'm aware of, no," he answered drily.

"So. I'm a little…mad. That's all. I just… Listen, let's go home. I have to make some calls. And I should stay at my place tonight," I said.

"Grace," he began.

"Cal, I probably have twenty messages on my machine already. I have to correct the final essays for my sophomores and post all my classes' grades by next Friday. I still haven't heard about the chairmanship thing. I'm stressing. I just need a little alone time. Okay?"

"Okay." He started the car, and we drove home in

silence. When we pulled in my driveway, I jumped out of the car.

"Good night," he said, getting out.

"Good night," I answered, starting up the walk. Then I turned around, went back and kissed him. Once. Another time. A third. "I'm just a little tense," I reminded him in a gentler voice, finally pulling back.

"Okay. Very cute, too," he said.

"Save it, bub," I answered, squeezing his hand.

"I just couldn't out-and-out lie, honey," he added, looking at the ground.

Hard to be mad at a guy for that. "I understand," I said. Angus yarped from inside. "But I really do have to work now."

"Right." He kissed my cheek and walked over to his place. With a sigh, I went inside.

CHAPTER TWENTY-EIGHT

A FEW HOURS LATER WHEN my parents had been called (if not soothed) and my schoolwork was done, I found myself once again staring over at Cal's house from my darkened living room.

When I told Dr. Stanton about Callahan this week, I'd done it with the idea that Callahan would be part of my future. It was funny. A couple of months ago, when I pictured the man I'd end up with, I was still picturing Andrew. Oh, not his face…it wasn't that obvious. But so many of his qualities. His soft voice, gentle sense of humor, his intelligence, even his flaws, like how inept he was at changing tires or unclogging a sink. Now, though…I smiled. Callahan O'Shea could change a tire. He could probably hot-wire an entire car.

I stroked Angus's head, earning a little doggy moan in response and a love bite to my thumb. When I was alone with Callahan, I was crazy about him. When his past came into my narrow little world of teaching and family…things were a little harder. But as Cal had pointed out, at least it was done now. Everyone knew. No more parceling out of information. There was something to be said for that.

A soft knock came on my front door, and I glanced at the clock. Eight minutes past nine. Angus had fallen too deeply asleep to go into his usual rage, luckily, so I tiptoed to the door, turning on a light as I went, figuring it was Callahan.

It wasn't.

Andrew stood on my porch. "Hey, Grace," he said in his quiet voice. "Do you have a minute?"

"Sure," I answered slowly. "Come on in."

The last time Andrew had seen the home we were going to live in together, it had been only half-Sheetrocked, wires and insulation exposed, the kitchen just a gaping hole. The floors had been rough and broken in places, the stairs stained and dark with age.

"Wow," he said, turning in a slow circle. Angus popped up from the couch. Before he could maul Andrew, however, I picked him up.

"Want a tour?" I asked, clearing my throat.

"Sure," he answered, ignoring Angus's purring snarls. "Grace, it's beautiful."

"Thanks," I said, bemused. "Well, here's the dining room, obviously, and the kitchen. That's my office, remember, it was a closet before?"

"Oh, my God, that's right," he said. "And wow, you knocked down the bedroom wall, didn't you?"

"Mmm-hmm," I murmured. "Yup. I figured...well, I just wanted a bigger kitchen."

The original plan was that there'd be a downstairs bedroom, you see. We were planning to have at least two kids, possibly three, so we planned on both upstairs bedrooms being theirs. Then, later, when our clever children went off to college and Andrew and I got older, we wouldn't have to worry about schlepping up and down the stairs. Now what was once going to be a bedroom—our bedroom—was my office.

My Fritz the Cat clock ticked loudly on the wall, tail swishing in brittle motion. *Tick...tick...tick...*

"Can I see upstairs, too?" Andrew asked.

"Of course," I said, holding Angus a little tighter. I followed Andrew up the narrow stairs, noticing how he was still so scrawny and slight. Had I once found that endearing? "So this is my bedroom," I said tersely, pointing, "and there's the guest room, where Margaret's staying, that's the door to the attic—I haven't done anything up there yet. And at the end of the hall is the bathroom."

Andrew walked down the hall, peeking in the various doorways, then stuck his head in the loo. "Our tub," he said fondly.

"My tub," I corrected instantly. My voice was hard.

He gave a mock grimace. "Oops. Sorry. You're right. Well, it looks beautiful."

We'd found the old porcelain claw-foot tub in Vermont one weekend when we'd gone antiquing and bed-and-breakfasting and lovemaking. It had been in someone's yard, an old Yankee farmer who once had his pigs use it as a water trough. He sold it to us for fifty bucks, and the three of us had practically killed ourselves getting it into the back of Andrew's Subaru. I found a place that reglazed tubs, and when it came back to us, it was shiny and white and pure. Andrew had suggested that, while it wasn't yet hooked up to the plumbing, maybe we could get naked and climb in just the same. Which we had done. A week later, he dumped me. I couldn't believe I'd kept the thing.

"It's amazing. What a great job you've done," he said, smiling proudly at me.

"Thanks," I said, heading downstairs. Andrew followed. "Would you like a glass of water? Coffee? Wine? Beer?" I rolled my eyes at myself. *Why not just bake the man a cake, Grace? Maybe grill up a few shrimp and a filet mignon?*

"I'll take a glass of wine," he said. "Thanks, Grace."

He followed me into the kitchen, murmuring appreciatively as he noticed little details—the crown molding, the cuckoo clock in the hall, the cluster of heavy architectural stars I'd bolted to the wall behind the kitchen table.

"So why the visit, Andrew?" I asked, carrying two glasses of wine into the living room. He sat on the Victorian sofa that had cost so much to reupholster. I took the wing chair, handed Angus a misshapen hunk of rawhide to discourage him from eating Andrew's shoes and looked at my sister's fiancé.

He took a deep breath and smiled. "Well, this is a little awkward, Grace, but I felt I should…well, ask you something."

My heart dropped into my stomach, sitting there like a peach pit. "Okay."

He looked at the floor. "Well, I…this is uncomfortable for me." He broke off, looked up and made one of his goofy faces.

I smiled uncertainly.

"I guess I'll just blurt this out," he said. "Gracie, what are you doing with that guy?"

The peach pit seemed to turn, scraping my insides unpleasantly, and my smile dropped from my face as if it was made from granite. Andrew waited, a kindly, concerned expression on his face. "What do you mean?" I asked, my voice quiet and shaky.

Andrew scratched his cheek. "Grace," he said very

softly, leaning forward, "forgive me for asking this, but does this have something to do with Natalie and me?"

"Excuse me?" I asked, my voice squeaking. I reached for my dog and lifted him to sit protectively on my lap. Angus dropped the rawhide and growled obediently at Andrew. Good dog.

Andrew took a quick breath. "Look, I'll just come right out with this, Grace. That guy doesn't seem, well, right for you. An ex-con, Gracie? Is that really what you want? I…well, I never met the other guy, Wyatt, was it? The doctor? But from what Natalie said, he sounded great."

I closed my eyes. *Natalie never met him, you dope. I never met him.* But God knew Natalie had a lot dependent on me dating Wyatt Dunn, so perhaps her imagination had gotten the better of her. As mine had with me.

"Grace," Andrew continued, "this guy… I have to ask myself if you're doing this out of…well…"

"Desperation?" I suggested with a bite.

He winced slightly but didn't correct me. "You've been…well, generous, Grace," he said. "I'm sure the whole situation with Natalie and me has been…uncomfortable. It has been for me, anyway, so I can only imagine how it's been for you."

"How kind of you to consider my feelings," I murmured. The peach pit scraped deeper.

"But—what's his name again? The embezzler?"

"Callahan O'Shea."

"Well, Grace, to me it just seems like he's not for you."

I smiled tightly. "Well, you know, Andrew, he does have this one really wonderful quality. He's not in love with my sister. Which, you know, I find quite refreshing."

Andrew flushed, acknowledging that with a half nod. "Point taken, Gracie. But even with—"

"And I feel compelled to mention," I said, my voice taking on my *silence in the classroom* tone, causing Angus to whine sympathetically, "that my love life is no longer any of your business."

"I still care about you, that's all," he protested softly, and in that moment, I wanted to kick him in the nuts.

"Don't trouble yourself, Andrew," I said, trying to keep my voice from breaking with rage. "I'm fine. Callahan is a good man."

"Are you sure, Grace? Because there's something I don't trust about him."

I set Angus down and looked steadily at Andrew. "How interesting that you should say that, Andrew. After all, look what happened with you and me. I thought you loved me. I thought we were pretty damn perfect together. And I was wrong. So it's funny. You don't trust Callahan, and I don't quite trust you, Andrew, and I have no idea what you're doing here right now, questioning my taste in men."

He started to say something, but I cut him off. "Here's what I know about Callahan. He uncovered a crime and he tried to make it right. At the same time, he was trying to protect his brother. He risked everything for the person he loved best, and he got screwed in the process."

"Well, that's a nice spin, Grace, but—"

"It's not spin, Andrew. Have *you* ever risked anything? You…" My voice grew choked with anger, my heart thudding, face burning. "You asked me to marry you, knowing I was head over heels for you and knowing damn well you didn't feel the same way. But you figured it was time to settle down, and there I was, ready, willing and able. Then you met my sister, fell in love, never said boo about it. Instead you waited until three weeks before our wedding to call things off. Three weeks! Jesus, Andrew! Think you might have spoken up a little sooner?"

"I never—"

"I'm not finished." My voice was hard enough to cause his mouth to snap shut. "Even with Natalie, you just sat back and did nothing. Yet she's the love of your life, isn't she? But if it weren't for me, you would never have even spoken to her again."

His face reddened even more. "I said I'm grateful for how you got Nat and me together."

"I didn't do it for you, Andrew. I did it for her. You, though…you didn't fight for her, you didn't try to talk to her…you just sat there like a fern or something, doing nothing."

His shoulders slumped. "What was I supposed to do?" he said, his voice small. "I wasn't about to date my ex-fiancée's sister. I didn't want to put you in a bad spot."

"And yet here you are, a week away from marrying her."

He sighed, slumping back against the sofa, and ran a hand through his pale blond hair. "Grace, you're right. I never would've even spoken to Natalie without your blessing. The last thing I wanted to do was hurt you more. I thought it was the right thing to do. Wasn't it?" He looked so genuinely confused that I wanted to shake him.

Then I saw the tears in his eyes. The sight took the fight out of me, and I drooped back against my chair. "I don't know, Andrew. It was a complicated situation."

"Ex*act*ly," he said, and *God,* I was sick of him! For the past three years, I'd been obsessed with Andrew, happily and miserably, and enough was enough.

"Listen," I said wearily. "I guess I appreciate your concern over Cal, but…well, you just don't get a say, Andrew. I'm none of your business anymore."

He smiled, a little sadly. "Well, you'll be my sister-in-law soon. You are my business, a little."

"Save it, pal." But I said the words with a smile. For Nat's sake.

He set his wineglass on the coffee table and stood. "I should go," he said, looking around again. "The house is beautiful, Grace. You did a wonderful job."

"I know," I said, opening the door.

He went out on the porch, and I followed, closing the screen door so Angus wouldn't get out. Andrew turned back to face me. "You'll always be special to me, you know," he said, not looking in my eyes.

I paused. "Well. Thank you."

He put his skinny arms around me and gave me a stiff hug. After a second, I patted his shoulder. Then, quite out of the blue, Andrew turned his head and kissed me.

It wasn't a romantic kiss…not quite. Too puckery. But neither was it a brother-in-law peck on the cheek. In typical Andrew fashion, he hadn't been able to decide. Idiot.

I jerked back. "Andrew, are you out of your mind?"

"What?" he said, his quirky eyebrows raised.

"Well, call me crazy, but I don't think you should ever do that again, okay? Ever."

"Shit. Sorry," he said, grimacing. "I just—I'm sorry. Force of habit. I don't know. I just...forget it. I'm really sorry."

I just wanted him gone. "Bye, Andrew."

"Good night, Grace." Then he turned and walked down the steps to his car. He opened the door, got in, started the car and waved, then backed down the driveway.

"Good riddance," I muttered. I turned to go into the house, then started in fright.

Callahan O'Shea was standing at the border of our yards, looking at me with an expression that made me surprised I hadn't burst into flames.

CHAPTER TWENTY-NINE

"CALLAHAN!" I STAMMERED. "Hey! You surprised me."

"What the hell was that?" he growled.

I waved my hand dismissively. "That was nothing." *He just doesn't think you're good enough for me, that's all.* "Want to come in?"

"Grace," he bit out. "It didn't look like *nothing*. It looked like your sister's fiancé just kissed you. The guy you were going to *marry!*"

"So I've got a lot of 'splainin' to do?" I said. He narrowed his eyes. Aw! He was jealous! Funny how pleasing that can be, isn't it? Unfortunately, Callahan didn't seem to share my amusement. "Well, don't just stand there brooding, Mr. O'Shea. Come in. You can grill me all you want."

With a muttered curse, he came up the steps and into the house, not even glancing down as Angus launched himself through the air to attack. Instead, he took in the wineglasses on the coffee table. The scowl deepened.

"It's not what you think," I said.

"And what do I think?" Callahan asked tightly.

"You think…" I squashed a smile. "You think Andrew's hitting on me."

"That seemed obvious."

"Wrong. Sit down, Cal. Want some wine?"

"No. Thank you." He sat in the spot recently vacated

by Andrew. "So? Why was he here? And does he always kiss you on the mouth?"

I nestled into my chair and took a sip of my wine, considering my honey. Yep. Definitely jealous. Perhaps now wasn't the time to say I found it incredibly sexy. "Andrew hasn't kissed me for a long, long time. Why he did tonight, who knows? He said it was force of habit."

"That's the stupidest thing I ever heard."

Angus growled, his teeth firmly sunk into Cal's work boot.

"You're jealous, aren't you?" I couldn't help asking.

"Yes! I am, actually! You loved that scrawny little idiot, and he came over tonight and kissed you. How am I supposed to feel?"

"Well, for one, you should feel happy, because as you said, Andrew's a scrawny little idiot. And you're the opposite."

Callahan started to say something, then stopped. "Thanks." The corner of his mouth pulled up.

"You're welcome." I smiled.

"Do you still have feelings for him, Grace?" he asked carefully. "Tell me right now if you do."

"I don't. As you said, scrawny little idiot."

Callahan considered me for a moment, then reached down to dislodge Angus's teeth from his shoes. "Go see your mommy," he said. Angus obeyed, leaping onto my lap and curling in a tight circle. Callahan sat back and looked at me, his face considerably more at ease than when he first came in. "Does it worry you? Andrew kissing someone who's not Natalie?"

I thought on that. "No. The first time those two saw each other, they fell in love, just like that. Kablammy, like they were hit by lightning."

"Or a field hockey stick," Cal added.

Oh. *Oh*. My heart swelled. "Anyway," I said, blushing. "Andrew came over because he was…" I paused. "Concerned."

"Because you're dating someone with a record?"

"Correct." I stroked Angus's sweet, bony head, earning a little groan in response.

"So the man who left you for your sister has a problem with my morals."

"Bingo." I smiled across at my sweetie. "And I told him I thought you were pretty wonderful and quite honorable, and I may have mentioned how great you look without your clothes on." Callahan smiled. "Plus, I told him one of the things I liked best was the fact that you hadn't fallen for Natalie *or* Margaret, so I thought you might be a keeper."

"Grace," Cal said seriously, leaning forward, "I can't imagine falling for Natalie or Margaret. Not after meeting you."

My throat tightened abruptly. No one…*no one*…had ever compared me with my sisters and found me superior. "Thanks," I whispered.

"You're welcome," he murmured, gazing into my eyes. "You want me to find Andrew and beat him up?"

"Nah," I said. "It'd be like shooting fish in a barrel."

He laughed, then reached down to retie the work boot Angus had mauled. "You planning to tell Natalie that her fiancé's going around kissing people?"

I thought about that for a second, playing with my puppy's fur. "No. I honestly don't think it meant anything. I mean, really, Angus has given me a more passionate kiss than that one." *Not to mention you, bub,* I added silently. "I think it was just a reflex."

"What if it wasn't?" Cal asked.

My head jerked back. "It was. I'm sure. He loves Natalie! They're crazy about each other. You saw that."

Cal hesitated, then gave a nod. "I guess."

He guessed? Everyone could see that Natalie and Andrew were meant to be. It was obvious. Wasn't it?

Angus snapped awake from his brief nap and leaped off my lap, trotting into the kitchen to see if God had miraculously refilled his bowl.

Callahan leaned back against the couch, looking like a contender for Sexiest Man Alive. In all the time I'd spent with Andrew, I could honestly say I'd never felt like this...the thrilling rush of Cal's presence mingling with the comfort that came from the certainty that he... well...he liked me. He chose me. He *wanted* me. He even put up with Angus.

"So how's your family taking the news that Princess Grace is dating an ex-con?" he asked, grinning a little.

I decided not to tell him about Dad's eleven-point argument on why Cal was a bad idea or the fact that Mom had already talked to a private investigator. "They'll get used to it."

"I guess they thought your cat-wrangling pediatrician was a better choice, huh?"

Those words were Arctic water on my heart. Oh, yeah. Wyatt Dunn, M.D. "Um...well." I nibbled on a thumbnail. "Callahan. About that."

"What?" Cal said, grinning. "Don't tell me he dropped by for some kissing, too."

My stomach twisted. "No, no. Um, Cal. As long as we're talking. I need to tell you something. Something you might not like." I realized I was chewing my thumb again and put my hands in my lap. Taking a deep breath, I looked into Callahan's eyes.

The smile slipped off his face, leaving it blank and inscrutable. "Go ahead," he said silkily.

"Well...this is actually kind of funny," I said, attempting a chuckle. My heart raced in a manic patter. "Here's the thing. I...I never actually dated Wyatt Dunn. The doctor. The pediatric surgeon."

Cal didn't move. Didn't even blink.

"Yeah," I continued, swallowing twice, my mouth dry as Arizona in July. "Um...I...I made him up."

The only sound was Fritz the Cat, ticking away, and the jingle of Angus's tags as he snuffled around the kitchen. *Tick...tick...tick.*

"You made him up."

"Well, yeah!" A panicky laugh burst out of my tight throat. "Of course! I mean, come on! You suspected, right? A good-looking, single, straight pediatric surgeon? I could never get a guy like that!"

Oh, boy, did that ever come out wrong.

"But you could get a guy like me." Callahan's voice was dangerously calm.

Shit. "I...well, I didn't mean it that way. I meant that there's no such animal. He's...you know. Too good to be true."

"You made him up," Cal repeated.

"Mmm-hmm," I squeaked, clenching my toes in discomfort.

"Tell me, Grace, why would you do something like that?" The calm in his voice was downright ominous.

I didn't answer for a minute. The day I made up Wyatt Dunn seemed a long, long time ago. "Well, see, we were at a wedding." As quickly as I could, I told him about the comments, the bouquet toss, Nat in the bathroom. The words fell out of my mouth like hailstones. "I guess I didn't want Natalie thinking I wasn't over Andrew," I said. "And to be honest—" Cal lifted a sardonic eyebrow but remained silent "—I was tired of everyone looking at me like I was…well, the dog no one wants at the pound."

"So you lied." His voice was very quiet. He sat still as a bronze statue, and my heart raced a little faster, making me feel ill. "To your entire family."

"Well, you know, it made everyone feel better. And Margaret knew," I mumbled, looking to the floor. "And my friend Julian. And Kiki, actually."

"I seem to remember you on at least one date with this man," Cal said. "And flowers…didn't he send you flowers?"

My face was so hot it hurt. I glanced at Callahan's face. "I, um, sent them to myself. And…I pretended to be on a date or two." I winced, then cleared my throat. "Cal, look. It was dumb, I know that. I just wanted everyone to think I was okay."

"You lied, Grace," he said, his voice no longer so quiet. Getting a bit loud, in fact, and one could even say rather angry. "I can't believe this! You lied to me! You've been lying for months! I asked you if you were done with that guy, and you said you weren't seeing him anymore!"

"And I wasn't, right?" My nervous laugh came out like a dry heave. "Yes, right. I lied. I did. It was a mistake, probably."

"Probably?" he barked.

"Okay, it was definitely a mistake! I admit it, it was

stupid and immature and I shouldn't have done it, but my back was against the wall, Cal!"

"I've got to hand it to you, Grace." His voice was flat and calm. "You're a great liar. I did suspect, you're right. But you convinced me. Well done."

Youch. I took a quick breath. "Cal, listen. It was juvenile. I know that. But cut me some slack here."

"You lied to me, Grace. You lied to just about everyone you know!" He jammed a hand through his hair and turned away from me. My temper started to bubble. It wasn't *that* bad. No one was hurt. In fact, it's fair to say that my lie spared people from worrying over poor tragic Grace who was dumped. I know it had made *me* feel better.

"Callahan, look," I said more calmly. "I did a stupid thing, I admit it. And I hate to be the one to tell you this, Callahan, but people are flawed. Sometimes they do dopey things, especially around people they love. Surely you've heard of such occasions."

This earned me another glare, but he remained silent. No slack, no understanding, no sympathy. And so, alas, I continued talking, my voice rising.

"I mean, come on, Cal. You're not perfect, either. Remember? You yourself did a stupid thing to protect someone you loved. I have to say, it's a little ironic, getting a morality lecture from you, of all people!"

"And just what does that mean?" he asked, his mouth tight.

"It means you're the ex-con who covered up a crime for his brother and just got out of clink two months ago!"

Oops. Probably shouldn't have said that. His face

went from tight to completely furious. And calm. It was a horrible combination.

"Grace," he said quietly, standing up. "I can't believe I was so wrong about you."

It was like a punch in the heart. I jolted out of my chair, standing in front of him, my eyes flooding with tears. "Wait a second, Callahan. Please." I took a deep breath. "I'd think that you of all people would understand. We were both doing the wrong thing for the right reason."

"You're not over Andrew," he stated.

"I most certainly *am* over Andrew," I said, my voice shaking. I *was*. And it killed me that he didn't believe that.

"You lied so people would think you were, and you kept lying, and you're still lying, and you don't even see that there's something wrong with this picture, do you?" Cal stared at the floor like he couldn't bear to look at me. When he spoke next, his voice was quieter. "You're lying to your family, Grace, and you lied to me." He dragged his eyes up to mine. "I'm leaving now. And just in case it's not clear, we're done."

He didn't slam the door. Worse, he closed it quietly behind him.

CHAPTER THIRTY

"THIS IS, LIKE, SO LAME." Kerry's expression combined disgust, incredulity and martyrdom the way only a teenager's could.

"I thought we got to ride horses," Mallory whined. "You said we were in the cavalry. That guy has a horse. Why can't I have a horse?"

"Picture us dismounted," I said tightly. Suffice it to say, my mood over the past forty-eight hours had been poor at best.

My righteous indignation had faded about ten minutes after Callahan had closed the door with such finality, leaving hot shards of shock flashing across an echoing emptiness. Callahan O'Shea, who thought I was beautiful and funny, who smelled of wood and sun, didn't want anything more to do with me.

Last night, despite Julian and Margaret's best efforts to distract me with a *Project Runway Season 1* DVD marathon and mango martinis, I'd sat in a daze of self-disgust, not eating, not drinking, tears leaking out of my eyes as Tim Gunn urged on the troops in the background. Well into the wee hours of this very morning, hard little sobs hiccuped out of me like pebbles until I finally fell asleep around 6:00 a.m. Then, realizing I'd ordered my Civil War class to attend the Gettysburg reenactment, I jolted out of bed, drank three cups of cof-

fee and now stood before them, a sickly caffeine buzz
in my head, an ache in my chest.

"Children, the Battle of Gettysburg lasted for three
days," I said, dressed in my Yankee blues. "When it was
over, fifty-one *thousand* men would be dead. The Confederates' line of wounded stretched fourteen miles. Ten
thousand injured. One in three men killed. The bloodiest battle in American history. The beginning of the
end for the South."

I looked into the eleven dubious faces before me.
"Look, kids," I said wearily. "I know you think this is
lame. I know we're in Connecticut, not Pennsylvania.
I know that having a couple hundred oddball history
geeks like me running around, firing blanks, isn't the
real thing."

"So why'd you make us come?" Hunter asked, earning an admiring "Like, exactly!" from Kerry.

I paused. "I want you to try…just try, just for the next
couple hours, to put yourselves as best you can in the
minds of those soldiers. Imagine believing in something
so passionately that you'd risk your life for it. For an
idea. For a way of life. For the future of your country,
a future you knew you might never see. You're here,
you lucky, nice, well-fed rich kids, because you stand
on the shoulders of this country's history. I just want
you to feel that, just a little bit."

Kaelen and Peyton rolled their eyes in unison. Hunter
discreetly checked his cell phone. Kerry Blake examined her manicure.

But Tommy Michener stared at me, his mouth
slightly open, and Emma Kirk's eyes were solemn and
wide.

"Let's go, kids," I said. "Remember, you're part of

First Cavalry now. General Buford is over there. Do what he says, and just…well. Whatever."

With a few groans and giggles, the kids straggled after me. I got them in line with the other Brother Against Brother members. General Buford (better known as Glen Farkas, an accountant from Litchfield), rode his horse up and down the line. The kids sobered at the sight of the snorting bay mare, the sword flapping at the general's side. Glen was really good at this.

"When does it start?" Tommy whispered.

"As soon as General Heth attacks," I whispered back.

"My heart's kind of pounding," Tommy said, grinning at me. I patted his arm, smiling back.

And here they came. The Rebel yells pierced the air, and over the hill streamed dozens of Confederates.

"Onward, men!" called General Buford, wheeling his horse. And with a mighty yell, First Cavalry followed, Tommy Michener at the front of the pack, his empty musket held high, yelling at the top of his lungs.

Five hours later, I was driving the Manning minibus back to school, grinning like an idiot.

"That was so cool, Ms. Em!"

"Did you see me nail that guy with my bayonet?"

"I was actually, like, scared!"

"I thought that horse was gonna trample me!"

"Tommy and I took over that cannon! Did you see that?"

"And when those other dudes came up behind us, when we were, like, losing it?"

Kerry Blake kept up her ennui, but the rest of them were chattering like wild monkeys. And I was soaring. Finally. Finally, the subject we'd been studying all semester had had a tiny impact on their polished, protected worlds.

Once at Manning, they piled out of the car. "I'll email you a copy of that picture, Ms. Em," called Mallory. Even though modern inventions were frowned upon at reenactments, we'd bent the rules and taken a picture in front of a cannon. My kids and me. I'd have it blown up, frame it and put it in my office, and if I was head of the department, I'd…

Well. Chances were, I wasn't going to be head of the department. The announcement still hadn't been made, but telling Dr. Stanton about Callahan O'Shea had pretty much killed my chances. I wondered if I should tell him I wasn't seeing my ex-con anymore. But no. If I wasn't going to get the promotion because of some guy I was or wasn't seeing, I guess I didn't really want it.

Maybe Callahan had cooled off, I thought as I drove home. Maybe he'd see my point. Maybe he'd been missing me, too. Maybe my lie didn't seem so bad, now that some time had passed. Maybe—

As I turned onto my street, I saw a real estate sign up in front of Cal's house. My heart stuttered. Yes, I'd known Cal was planning to sell the house. I just hadn't thought it would be so soon.

The front door opened, and a woman emerged…the blonde from the bar. His real estate friend. Callahan followed right behind.

Margaret's car was not in the driveway, which meant no backup for me. She had a big case pending, so chances were she was at her office. I was on my own. I opened the car door and got out.

"Hey, Cal," I called. My voice was fairly steady.

He looked up. "Hi," he said, closing his front door behind him. He and the woman came down the walk where I'd once smacked Callahan O'Shea with a rake.

"Hi, I'm Becky Mango, as in the fruit," she chirped, sticking out her hand.

"Hi," I said. "Grace Emerson, as in Ralph Waldo." Well, didn't I sound nice and snooty. "I live next door," I added, glancing at Callahan. He was looking at the new landscaping, which had gone in this past week. Not at me.

"Beautiful house!" Becky exclaimed, gazing at my place. "If you ever want to sell it, give me a call!" She stuck her hand in her bag and pulled out a card. *Becky Mango, Mango Properties Ltd. Licensed Realtor.* The logo matched the one on the For Sale sign.

"Thanks. I will," I said, then turned to the brooding male next to her. "Cal, do you have a minute?"

He looked at me, those blue eyes that had once smiled so wickedly now so guarded. "Sure," he said.

"Callahan, I'll see you next week?" Becky asked. "I think I might have a property you'd be interested in down in Glastonbury. Real fixer-upper, going on the market next month."

"Okay. I'll call you." We both watched as she got in her car and drove off.

"So you're...you're done here?" I asked, though the answer was rather obvious.

"Yup." He slung his bag into the bed of his pickup truck.

"Where to now?" My eyes stung, and I blinked hard.

"I'm working on a place up in Granby," he said. "I'll be in the area until my grandfather...as long as he's

around." He took his keys out of his pocket, not looking at me. "But I don't think he's long for the world."

My throat tightened. Cal's last relative, except for
the estranged brother. "I'm sorry, Cal," I whispered.

"Thank you. Thank you for visiting him, too." His
dark blue eyes flickered to mine, then dropped to the
driveway once more.

"Callahan," I said, putting my hand on his warm,
solid arm. "Can we just...can we talk?"

"What about, Grace?"

I swallowed. "About our fight. About...you know.
You and me."

He leaned against the truck and folded his arms.
Body language not promising, folks. "Grace, I think
you're...I think you have things you need to work out."
He started to say something else, then stopped, shaking
his head. "Look," he continued. "You've been lying to
me since the day we met. I have a problem with that. I
don't know if you're over Andrew, frankly, and I don't
want to be your rebound fling. I was looking for...well,
you know what I was looking for." He looked at me
steadily, his expression was neutral.

A wife, a couple of kids, a lawn to mow on weekends.
"Cal, I..." I stopped and bit my thumbnail. "Okay. You
have a thing about honesty, so I'll be honest now. You're
partly right. I made up the boyfriend because I wasn't
completely over Andrew. And I didn't want anyone to
know because it made me feel so...small. So stupid,
carrying a torch for the guy who dumped me for my
sister. Even pretending that I had a great boyfriend was
better than people knowing that. Having people think
some wonderful guy out there adored me...it was a
nice change."

He gave a half nod, but didn't say anything.

"When Andrew fell for Natalie…" I paused, then went on. "I loved him, he didn't love me quite so much, then he took one look at Nat, who's basically perfect in every way and my baby sister, too, and he fell in love with her. That's hard to get over."

"I'm sure it is," he said, not unkindly.

"But what I'm trying to say is that I *am* over Andrew, Callahan. I know I should've told you the truth about Wyatt, but—" My voice cracked. I cleared my throat and forced myself to continue. "I didn't want you to see me as someone who got traded in."

He sighed. Looked at the ground and shook his head a little. "I was thinking about that time I walked you home from Blackie's," he said. "You were on a date, weren't you?" I nodded. "I bet you were pretty…desperate."

"Yup," I admitted in a whisper.

"So I was just about your last shot, wasn't I, Grace? Your sister's wedding was coming fast, and you hadn't found anyone. The ex-con next door was the best you could do."

I flinched. "No, Cal. That's not how it was."

"Maybe," he said. He didn't say anything more for a minute, and when he did, his voice was gentle. "Look, if you are over Andrew, I'm glad for you, Grace. But I'm sorry."

Well, dang it. I was going to cry. Tears burned my eyes, and my throat hurt like I was being strangled. He noticed. "To be really blunt here," he said very quietly, "I don't want to be with someone who lies to make herself look better. Someone who can't tell the truth."

"I did tell the truth! I told you everything," I squeaked.

"What about your family, Grace? You planning on coming clean with your folks? With Andrew and your sister?"

I cringed at the thought. Like Scarlett O'Hara, I'd been planning on thinking about that tomorrow. Or the next day. Possibly never. It's fair to say that I was hoping the Wyatt Dunn fantasy would just fade into the past.

Callahan glanced at his watch. "I have to go."

"Cal," I said, my voice breaking, "I really would like you to forgive me and give me another chance."

He looked at me a long moment. "Take care of yourself, Grace. I hope you work things out."

"Okay," I whispered, looking down so he wouldn't see my face crumple. "You take care, too."

Then he got in his truck and drove away.

BACK IN THE HOUSE, I SAT at my kitchen table, tears dripping off my chin, where Angus cheerfully licked them off. Great. Just great. I blew it. How I ever thought my Wyatt-Dunn idea was a good one was completely beyond me. I should never have… If only I'd… Next time I'd just…

Next time. Right. It occurred to me in a dizzyingly painful flash that guys like Callahan O'Shea didn't grow on trees. That God had thrown a man down right next door, and I'd spent weeks in judgment. That just like my best friend Scarlett O'Hara, I hadn't seen what was right in front of my face. That any guy who'd drive an hour and a half so I could see *Gone with the Wind* was worth ten—a hundred—of the type of guy who'd string me along until twenty days before our wedding.

It's about time, Callahan had said the first time I'd kissed him. He'd been waiting for me.

The thought caused a hard sob to ratchet out of me. Angus whined, nuzzling his little face against my neck. "I'm okay," I told him unconvincingly. "I'll be fine."

I blew my nose, wiped my eyes and stared at my kitchen. It was so pretty here. Actually, now that I looked at it, it was rather...well, perfect. Everything had been chosen with an eye toward getting over Andrew—colors that would soothe my heartache, furniture that Andrew would never like. The whole house was a shrine to Getting Over Andrew.

And yet it wasn't Andrew I kept seeing here. Nope. I saw Callahan sitting in my kitchen, teasing me about my pajamas...Callahan holding my mother's sculptures in his big hands...Cal shaking Angus off his foot, or sinking onto his knees because I hit him with the field hockey stick or cooking me an omelet and telling me everything about his past.

Before long, someone was going to buy the house next door. A family, maybe, or an older couple, or a single woman. Or even a single man.

I knew one thing. I didn't want to see it. Almost without realizing it, I fished out the business card in my pocket and grabbed the phone. When Becky Mango answered, I simply said, "Hi, this is Grace Emerson and we just met. I'd like to sell my house."

CHAPTER THIRTY-ONE

MANNING'S GRADUATION WAS the same day as Natalie's rehearsal dinner. Classes had ended a week after Gettysburg, and I gave everyone except Kerry Blake an A+ for their participation. Kerry got a C, bringing her final mark to a dreaded B- and resulting in seven phone calls to the school from her enraged parents. As his final act as chairman of the history department, Dr. Eckhart upheld my grade. I would really miss that man.

The hall echoed as I made my way down to my classroom, which I'd spent yesterday cleaning. For the summer program in August, I'd be teaching a class on the American Revolution, but for the next two months, I wouldn't be here. The familiar end-of-term lump came to my throat

Looking around the room, I smiled at the sight of the picture, which Mallory had not only given me, but matted and framed, bless her heart. My seniors, my First Cavalry. I would never see most of those kids again. Maybe a few emails from some of my favorites for the next six months or so, but most of them would leave Manning and not return for years, if ever. But I planned on making a battle reenactment a permanent requirement for my class.

My gaze wandered to the huge copy of the Gettysburg Address, another of the Declaration of Independence, which I read aloud on the first day of school, in every class, every year. And in my continual effort to get the kids to feel a connection to our country's history, I'd shamelessly covered the walls with movie posters. *Glory. Saving Private Ryan. Mississippi Burning. The Patriot, Full Metal Jacket, Flags of Our Fathers.* And on the back of the door, *Gone with the Wind,* tawdry enough that I felt it should be hidden from direct view. Scarlett's bosom was scandalously exposed, and Rhett's eyes bored into hers. Now that I'd seen the movie, I loved that poster more than ever.

The lump in my throat grew. Luckily, I was interrupted by a gentle knock on the door. "Come in," I called. It was Dr. Eckhart.

"Good morning, Grace," he said, leaning on his cane.

"Hello, Dr. Eckhart." I smiled. "How are you?"

"A bit sentimental today, Grace, a bit sentimental. My last Manning graduation."

"It won't be the same without you, sir," I said.

"No," he agreed.

"I hope we can still meet for dinner," I said sincerely.

"Of course, my dear," he said. "And I'm sorry you didn't make chairman."

"Well. Sounds like they picked a winner."

The new department chair was someone named Louise Steiner. She came to Manning from a prep school in Los Angeles, had significantly more administrative experience under her belt than either Ava or I and held a doctorate in European history and a master's in American. In short, she'd kicked our butts.

Ava had been furious enough to break up with Theo Eisenbraun, Kiki told me. Ava was actively interviewing at other prep schools, but I didn't really think she'd leave. Too much work, and Ava never was much of a worker.

"Will you be going to Pennsylvania this year?" Dr. Eckhart asked. "Or any other battle sites?"

"No," I answered. "I'm moving this summer, so no travel for me." I hugged the old man gently. "Thank you for everything, Dr. Eckhart. I'll really miss you."

"Well," he harrumphed, patting my shoulder. "No need to get emotional."

"Hello? Oh, damn, I'm sorry. I didn't mean to interrupt." Both Dr. Eckhart and I looked up. An attractive woman in her fifties with short gray hair and a classy linen suit stood in my doorway. "Hi, I'm Louise. Hello, Dr. Eckhart, nice to see you again. Grace, isn't it?"

"Hi," I said, going over to shake the hand of my new boss. "Welcome to Manning. We were just talking about you."

"I wanted to meet you, Grace, and talk about a few things. Dr. Eckhart showed me a copy of your presentation, and I loved the curriculum changes you came up with."

"Thank you," I said, shooting a look at Dr. E., who was examining his yellowed fingernails.

"Maybe we can have lunch next week, talk about things," Louise suggested.

I smiled at Dr. Eckhart, then looked back at Louise. "I'd love to," I said sincerely.

WHEN THE CAPS HAD BEEN THROWN and the children celebrated the accomplishment of not having flunked out, when the graduation brunch was over, I made my way back to the parking lot. I had about two hours to shower, change and head on over to Soleil, the site of my faked date with Wyatt Dunn and where Natalie's rehearsal dinner would take place.

"Another school year gone," said a familiar voice.

I turned. "Hi, Stuart." He looked…older. Grayer. Sadder.

"I hope you have a nice summer," he said politely, looking at a particularly beautiful pink dogwood.

"Thanks," I murmured.

"How's…how's Margaret?" His gaze flickered to mine.

I sighed. "She's tense, jealous and difficult. Miss her?"

"Yes."

I looked at his sorrowful face for a beat or two. "Stuart," I asked quietly, "did you have an affair with Ava?"

"With that piranha?" he asked, looking shocked. "Goodness, no. We had dinner. Once. All I talked about was Margaret."

What the heck. I decided to throw him a bone. "We'll be at Soleil in Glastonbury, Stu. Tonight. Reservations are for seven-thirty. Be spontaneous."

"Soleil."

"Yup." I looked at him steadily.

He inclined his head in a courtly nod. "Have a lovely day, Grace." With that, Stuart walked away, the sun shining on his graying hair. *Good luck, pal,* I thought.

"Ms. Em! Wait up!" I turned to see Tommy Michener and a man, presumably his father, judging by the resemblance between them, coming toward me. "Ms. Emerson, this is my dad. Dad, this is Ms. Em, the one who took us to that battle!"

The father smiled. "Hello. Jack Michener. Tom here

talks about you all the time. Says your class was his favorite."

Tommy's dad was tall and thin, with glasses and salt-and-pepper black hair. Like his son, he had a nice face, cheerful and expressive, sort of an Irish setter enthusiasm about the both of them. His grip was warm and dry when he shook my hand.

"Grace Emerson. Nice to meet you, too. You have a great kid here," I said. "And I don't say that just because he adores history, either."

"He's the best," Mr. Michener said, slinging his arm around Tommy's shoulders. "Your mom would be so proud," he added to his son, a little spasm of pain crossing his face. Ah, yes. Tommy's mom had died the year before he came to Manning.

"Thanks, Dad. Oh, hey, there's Emma. I'll be right back," Tommy said, then bolted off.

"Emma, huh?" Mr. Michener said, smiling.

"She's a great girl," I informed him. "Been nursing a crush on your son all year."

"Young love," Jack Michener said, grinning. "Thank God I'm not a teenager anymore." I smiled. "Did Tom tell you he's majoring in history at NYU?"

"Yes, he did. I was so pleased," I answered. "As I said, he's a fantastic kid. Really bright and interested. I wish I had more students like him."

Tommy's dad nodded in enthusiastic agreement. I glanced at my car. Jack Michener made no move to leave, and being that he was the father of my favorite senior, I decided I could chat a little longer. "So what do you do for a living, Mr. Michener?"

"Oh, hey, call me Jack." He smiled again, Tommy's open, wide grin. "I'm a doctor."

"Really?" I said politely. "What kind?"

"I work in pediatrics," he said.

I paused. "Pediatrics. Let me guess. Surgery?"

"That's right. Did Tom tell you that?"

"You're a pediatric surgeon?" I asked.

"Yes. Why? Did you think it was something else?"

I snorted. "No, well...no. I'm sorry. Just thinking of something else." I took a deep breath. "Um...so. How rewarding your work must be." The irony sloshed around my ankles in thick waves.

"Oh, it's great." He grinned again. "I tend to log in too many hours at the hospital—hard to leave sometimes—but I love it."

I bit down on a giggle. "That's wonderful."

He stuffed his hands in his pockets and tipped his head. "Grace, would you like to join Tom and me for dinner? It's just the two of us here today..."

"Um, thanks," I said, "but I can't. My sister's getting married tomorrow, and tonight's the rehearsal."

His smile dropped a few notches. "Oh. Well, maybe some other time?" He paused, blushing. "Maybe even without Tommy? We live in New York. It's not that far."

A date. The pediatric surgeon was asking me out on a date. A burst of hysterical laughter surged up my throat, but I clamped down on it just in time. "Um... wow, that's really nice of you." I took a quick breath. "The truth is, I'm..."

"Married?" he said with a no-hard-feelings shrug.

"No, no. I just broke up with someone, and I'm not over him yet."

"Well. I understand."

We were quiet for a second, both of us mildly embarrassed. "Oh, here comes Tommy," I said, relieved.

"Excellent. It was great meeting you, Grace. Thanks again for all you did for my son."

Tommy enveloped me in a hug. "Bye, Ms. Em," he said. "You're the best teacher here. I've had a crush on you since my first day of class."

I hugged him back chastely, my eyes wet. "I'll really miss you, buddy," I said honestly. "Write to me, okay?"

"You bet! Have a great summer!"

And with that, my favorite student and his pediatric surgeon dad left, leaving me more bemused than ever.

CHAPTER THIRTY-TWO

"Ahahaha. Ahahaha. Oooh. Ahahaha." Mom's society laugh rang out loud and false over the table.

"Hoohoohoohoo!" Andrew's mother, not to be out-faked, chortled right back. From the other side of the table, Margaret kicked me meaningfully, making me wince in pain.

"Aren't you glad you're not marrying into that family?" she hissed.

"So glad," I whispered back.

"Margaret, are you drunk?" Mémé asked her loudly. "I had a cousin who couldn't hold her liquor, either. Disgraceful. In my day, a lady never overindulged."

"Aren't you glad those days are gone now, Mémé?" Margaret quipped. "Would you like another Rusty Nail, by the way?"

"Thank you, dear," Mémé said, mollified. Margaret signaled the waiter, then made a mocking toast to me.

"Oh, yes, a toast!" Natalie cried. "Honey, make a toast!"

Andrew stood up, his parents gazing at him with servantile adoration. "This is such a happy day for us," he said. Awkwardly. His eyes paused on me, then moved on. "Nattie and I are so happy. And we're so happy that you're all here to share our happiness."

"I know I'm happy," I muttered to Margs, rolling my eyes.

"Hardly a great orator, is he?" she said, loud enough for our mother to hear. Mom covered with another round of "Ahahaha. Ahahaha. Oooh. Ahahaha."

The waiter appeared with our appetizers. Looking up, I saw it was Cambry. "Hey!" I exclaimed. "How are you?"

"I'm fine," he said, grinning.

"I hear we're all having dinner next week chez Julian."

"If he doesn't bolt," Cambry answered, setting down the oysters Rockefeller in front of me.

Julian was in a relationship. Granted, the mere word caused him stomach cramps and a cold sweat, but he was dating, and even he couldn't find much fault with Cambry, who was waiting tables while he finished law school.

"You hang in there," I said. "You're good for him. He hardly ever wants to come over and watch *Dancing with the Stars* these days. I should probably hate you."

"Do you?" he asked, raising a concerned eyebrow.

"No, of course not. But you have to share. He's been my best friend since high school."

"Duly noted," he said.

"Grace, I thought the oysters here caused food poisoning," Mémé bellowed, causing a nearby diner to spit abruptly into his napkin.

"No, no!" I said loudly. "No. They're great. So fresh!" I smiled encouragingly to the napkin spitter and took a bite as he watched nervously.

"Well, didn't they just about kill your doctor?" Mémé asked, turning to the Carsons, who were smiling politely. "He was in the toilet for twenty minutes," she informed them, as if they hadn't been there. "The trots, you know. My second husband had stomach problems. We couldn't leave the house some days! And the smell!"

"It was so bad, the cat fainted," Margaret intoned.

"It was so bad, the cat fainted!" Mémé announced.

"Okay, Mother," Dad said, his face burning. "Perhaps that's enough."

"Ahahaha. Ahahaha. Oooh. Ahahaha," laughed Mom, her eyes murderous upon her mother-in-law, who was knocking back another cocktail. Personally, I'd never been fonder of Mémé, for some reason. Cambry was struggling unsuccessfully to hide his laughter, and in a rush of warm sincerity, I said a quick little prayer that he and Julian would make it. Even if it meant I had no one to cushion my loneliness, poor lonely spinster that I was. Perhaps Angus needed a wife. Maybe I could have his little snipping reversed and I could become a dog breeder for people who loved to have things destroyed by adorable barking balls of fur. Or not.

I looked down the table at Natalie. She wore a pale blue dress, and her smooth, honey-colored hair was swept up and held with the kind of clip my own hair ate like a Venus flytrap. She looked so happy. Her hand brushed Andrew's over a roll, and she blushed at the contact. Aw. Then she caught my eye, and I smiled at her, my beautiful sister. She smiled back.

"Grace, where's Callahan?" she asked abruptly, her head snapping around to look for him. "Is he coming separately?"

Drat. The truth was, I'd been kind of hoping not to have to discuss it. I hadn't mentioned my breakup to anyone but Margaret. For two reasons. One, I'd been holding on to the hope that Cal might, well, forgive me, realizing that I was the one for him and he couldn't live without me. And two, I didn't want to rain on Nattie's parade. She'd be worried about me, cluck and pat my back and puzzle over how someone could not want to date her big sister. Someone other than Andrew, that was.

Lucky for me, I'd just taken a bite of my oysters, so I grinned and pointed and chewed. And chewed. Chewed a bit more, stalling as the oyster was ground into flavored saliva.

"Who's Callahan?" asked Mrs. Carson, turning her beady eyes on me.

"Grace is dating someone wonderful," Mom announced loudly.

"A convict," Mémé said, then belched. "An Irish convict with big hands. Right, Grace?"

Mr. Carson choked, Mrs. Carson's slitty eyes grew wider with malicious glee. "Well," I began.

"He used to be an accountant," my father said heartily. "Went to Tulane."

Margaret sighed.

"He's a handyman, right, Grace?" Mémé bellowed. "Or a gardener. Or a lumberjack. I can't remember."

"Or a coal miner. Or a shepherd," Margaret added, making me snort.

"He's wonderful," Mom said firmly, ignoring both her eldest child and Callahan's criminal past. "So, er, handsome."

"Oh, he is!" Natalie said, turning her shining eyes to the Carsons. "He and Grace are so good together. You can tell they're just crazy about each other."

"He dumped me," I announced calmly, wiping my

mouth. Across the table, Margaret choked on some wine. As she sputtered into her napkin, she gave me a thumbs-up.

"The gardener dumped you? What? What did she say?" Mémé asked. "Why are you mumbling, Grace?"

"Callahan dumped me, Mémé," I said loudly. "My ethics aren't up to snuff."

"The prisoner said that?" Mémé barked.

"Pish!" my mother said. No one else said a word. Natalie looked like I'd clubbed her over the head.

"Thanks, Mom," I said. "Sorry to say, I think he's right."

"Oh, Pudding, no. You're wonderful," Dad said. "What does he know, after all? He's an idiot. An ex-con and an idiot."

"An ex-con?" Mr. Carson wheezed.

"No, he's not, Dad. He's not an idiot, that is. He *is* an ex-con, Mr. Carson," I clarified.

"Well," Mom said, her eyes darting between the Carsons and me, "do you think you might get back with your pediatric surgeon? He was such a nice young man."

Wow. Amazing how a lie could be so powerful. I looked at Margaret. She looked back, lifted an eyebrow. I turned back to my mother.

"There was no pediatric surgeon, Mom," I said, enunciating so Mémé could hear. "I made him up."

You know, it was almost fun, dropping a bomb like that. Almost. Margaret sat back and smiled broadly. "You go, Grace," she said, and for the first time in a long time, she looked genuinely happy.

I sat up a little straighter, though my heart was thudding so hard I thought I might throw up. My voice shook...but it carried, too. "I pretended to date someone so Natalie and Andrew wouldn't feel so guilty. And so everyone would stop treating me like I was some sort of abandoned dog covered in sores."

"Oh, Grace," Nat whispered.

"What? Grace, you can't be serious!" Dad exclaimed.

"I am, Dad. I'm sorry," I said, swallowing hard. Here it was at last…my confession. I started talking again, and my voice grew faster and faster. "Andrew broke up with me because he fell in love with Natalie, and it hurt. A lot. But I was getting over it. I was, and if they wanted to be together, I didn't want to be the reason they stayed apart. So I made up Wyatt Dunn, this impossibly perfect guy, and everyone felt much better, and I just ran with it because to tell you the truth, it felt great, even just pretending I had a boyfriend who was so wonderful. But then I fell for Callahan, and obviously I had to break up with Wyatt, and then, that night that Andrew came over and kissed me on the porch, Cal was really unhappy about that, and we talked and then I ended up telling him about Wyatt Dunn. And he dumped me. Because I lied."

My breath came in shaky little gasps, and my back was damp with sweat. Margaret reached across the table and put her hand over mind. "Good girl," she murmured.

Natalie didn't move. The Carsons' heads swiveled to gape at their son, who looked like he'd just been shot in the stomach, eyes wide with horror, face white. The rest of the restaurant was so quiet, you could almost hear the crickets cheeping.

"Wait a minute, wait a sec," my father said, his face slack with confusion. "Then who was I talking to in the bathroom that night?"

"Shut it, Jim," my mother hissed.

"That was Julian, pretending to be Wyatt," I said. "Any other questions? Comments? No? Okay, then, I'm going out for some air."

On shaking legs, I walked across the restaurant, past the now-silent diners, my face on fire. As I entered the foyer, Cambry leaped over to open the front door. "You are one magnificent creature," he said in an admiring voice as I walked out.

"Thanks," I whispered.

He had the grace to leave me alone. I was shaking like a leaf, my heart thudding. Who said that confession was good for the soul? I wanted to throw up. Going over to a small bench that sat in the restaurant's front garden, I sat down heavily. Pressed my cold fingers against my burning cheeks and closed my eyes, just trying to breathe normally. In and out. In and out. Not hyperventilating or passing out would be enough for now.

"Grace?" Natalie's voice was timid. I hadn't heard her footsteps.

"Hey, Nattie," I said wearily without looking up.

"Can I sit with you?" she asked.

"Sure. Of course." Natalie sat next to me. When she slipped her hand into mine, I looked down at our entwined hands. Her engagement ring caught the light. "My ring looked just like this," I murmured.

"I know. Who buys the same ring for sisters?"

"He probably didn't remember the one he gave to me. He can't even pick out matching socks."

"Pathetic," she murmured.

"Men," I muttered.

"So dumb."

I agreed…in Andrew's case, anyway. "Did he tell you about that kiss?" I whispered.

I hadn't meant to ruin anything for Natalie. Should've thought about that before I opened my mouth.

She was quiet for a moment. "Yes, he told me." A mockingbird twittered above us, a long stream of notes.

"What did he say?" I asked, more out of curiosity than anything.

"He said it was a lapse in judgment. That being in the house with you, having seen you with another guy…it made him feel a little jealous."

I sneaked a glance at my sister. "What did you think about that?"

"Well, I thought he was an asshole, Grace," she said, making my mouth drop open in shock. "It was our first fight. I told him he'd screwed up our lives enough already, and kissing you was unacceptable. Then I slammed a few doors and stomped around for a while."

Natalie's face was red. "How refreshing," I murmured.

She snorted. "And I was…jealous. Not that I had a right to be, given what I did to you."

I squeezed her hand. "You can't help the big kablammy," I said.

Natalie shot me a questioning glance.

"You know," I said. "The thunderbolt. Just one look, that's all it took, all that garbage." I paused. "But you made up, obviously. You guys are okay, right?"

She gave a little nod. "I think so," she whispered, looking straight ahead and squeezing my hand a little tighter. Her eyes were full of tears. "Grace, I'm so sorry that of all the people in the world, I had to fall for him.

That I hurt you." She drew a shaking breath. "I never said it, but I'll say it now. I'm so, so sorry."

"Well, you know, it really sucked," I admitted. It was a relief to say the words.

"Are you mad at me?" Two tears slipped down her cheeks.

"No," I assured her. Then I reconsidered. "Well…not anymore. I tried not to be. I was more mad at Andrew, to be honest, but yeah, part of me was just screaming. It wasn't fair."

"Grace, you know you're my favorite person in the world. The last person I'd ever willingly hurt. I never meant to. I never wanted to. I hated that I fell for Andrew. I hated it." She was crying harder now.

I slipped my arm around her, pulling her so that our heads touched as we sat, side by side, not looking at each other. I didn't like to have my sister crying, but maybe she just needed to. And maybe I needed to see it. "Well," I admitted softly, "it hurt. Quite a bit. I didn't want you to know it. But I'm over that now. I really am."

"Making up Wyatt…" Her voice trailed off. "I think that might be the nicest thing anyone's ever done for me. And man, I jumped all over that." She gave a grim laugh. "I kind of suspected he wasn't real, you know. You had me up until the bit about the feral cats." She grinned.

I rolled my eyes. "I know."

Nat sighed. "I guess I didn't want to know the truth." We were quiet for a moment. "You know, Grace," she said softly, "you don't have to watch out for me anymore. You don't have to protect me from every sad emotion."

"Well," I said, my own eyes filling. "I kind of do. That's my job. I'm your big sister."

"Forget the job," she suggested, reaching out to tuck a wayward strand of frizz behind my ear. "Forget that you're the big sister. Let's just be plain old sisters. Equals, okay?"

I looked into the blue, clear sky. Ever since I was four, I'd been watching out for Natalie, admiring her, protecting her. It might be nice, just…just liking her. Instead of adoration, friendship. Equals, like she said.

"Like Margaret," I mused.

"Oh, God, don't be like Margaret!" she blurted with mock earnestness, and we both burst into laughter. Then Nat opened her purse and handed me a tissue— of course, she was armed with a cunning little tissue pack with roses on the cover—and we sat for another minute, listening to the mockingbird, holding hands.

"Grace?" she said eventually.

"Yeah?"

"I really liked Callahan."

Hearing that was like pressing on a bruise to see if it still hurt. It did. "Me, too," I whispered. She squeezed my hand and had the sense not to say anything else. After a moment, I cleared my throat and glanced around at the restaurant. "Want to get back?"

"Nah," she said. "Let everyone wonder. Maybe we could fake a cat fight, just for fun."

I laughed. My Nattie of old. "I missed you," I admitted.

"I missed you, too. It's been so hard, wondering if you're really as okay as you seemed, but afraid to ask. And I've been jealous, you know. You and Margs, living together."

"Oh, well, then, you can take her. You and Andrew," I said. "For as long as you want."

"He wouldn't survive the week." She grinned.

"Nattie," I said slowly, "about us being equals…" She nodded encouragingly. "I want you to do me a favor, Nat."

"Anything," she said.

I turned a little to better face her. "Nat, I don't want to be maid of honor tomorrow. Let it be Margaret. I'll be your bridesmaid, go down the aisle and all that, but not maid of honor. It's too weird, okay? A little pimpish, you know?"

"Okay," she said instantly. "But make sure Margaret doesn't roll her eyes and make faces."

"I'm sorry, I can't guarantee anything," I said with a laugh. "But I'll try."

Then I stood up and pulled my little sister to her feet. "Let's go back, okay? I'm starving."

We held hands all the way back to our table. Mom hopped up like an anxious sparrow when she saw us. "Girls! Is everything all right?"

"Yes, Mom. We're fine."

Mrs. Carson rolled her eyes and gave a ladylike snort, and suddenly, our mother wheeled on her. "I'll thank you to wipe that look off your face, Letitia!" she said, her voice carrying easily through the restaurant. "If you have something to say, speak up!"

"I'm…I don't…"

"Then stop treating my girls like they're not good enough for your precious son. And Andrew, let me say this. We only tolerate you because Natalie asked us to. If you screw up any of my girls' lives again, I will rip out your liver and eat it. Understand me?"

"I...I definitely do understand, Mrs. Emerson," Andrew said meekly, forgetting that he was supposed to call Mom by her first name.

Mom sat back down, and Dad turned to her. "I love you," he said, his voice awed.

"Of course you do," she said briskly. "Is everyone ready to order?"

"I can't eat beets," Mémé announced. "They repeat on me."

WE ALMOST GOT THROUGH the dinner without further incident. In fact, I was trying to resist the urge to lick my bowl clean of crème brûlée when there was a commotion at the front of the restaurant.

"I'm here to see my wife," came a raised voice. "Now."

Stuart.

He came into the dining room, dressed in his usual oxford and argyle sweater vest, tan trousers and tasseled loafers, looking like the gentle, sweet man he was. But his face was set, and his eyes, God bless him, were stormy.

"Margaret, this has gone on long enough," he announced, ignoring the rest of us.

"Hmm," Margaret said, narrowing her eyes.

"If you don't want to have a baby, that's fine. And if you want sex on the kitchen table, you'll get it." He glared down at his wife. "But you're coming home, and you're coming home now, and I will be happy to discuss this further once you're naked and in my bed." He paused. "Or on the table." His face flushed. "And the next time you leave me, you'd better mean it, woman, because I'm not going to be treated like a doormat. Understand?"

Margaret rose, put her napkin by her plate and turned to me. "Don't wait up," she said. Then she took Stuart's hand and let him lead her through the restaurant, grinning from ear to ear.

CHAPTER THIRTY-THREE

THE MINUTE I CAUGHT SIGHT of Andrew, I saw it.

Trouble.

The organ played Mendelssohn's "Wedding March," the fifty or so guests, most related to either the bride or groom, stood and turned to look at us, the freaky Emerson sisters. There was Stuart, looking smugly blissful, the expression of a man who saw a lot of action last night. I grinned at him. He nodded and touched his forehead with two fingers in a little salute. There were Cousin Kitty and Aunt Mavis, who both smiled with great false sympathy as I passed. Resisting the urge to give them the finger (we were in church, after all, and *Mayflower* descendants and all that crap), I looked ahead and, for the first time that day, saw the groom.

He ran a hand through his hair. Pushed up his glasses. Coughed into his fist. Didn't look at me. Bit his lip.

Uh-oh. This did not look like a man whose dreams were all about to come true. This was more than the discomfort of standing in front of dozens of people. This was bad.

I gave Andrew a questioning look, but he wouldn't meet my eyes. His gaze bounced around the church, flitting from guest to guest like a housefly bouncing against a window, relentlessly seeking escape.

I hiked my skirt up a bit and stepped onto the altar,

then made room for Margs. "We have a problem," I whispered.

"What are you talking about? Look at her face," she whispered back.

I looked at Natalie, beautiful, glowing, her sky-blue eyes shining. Dad looked tall and proud and dignified, nodding here and there as he walked his baby girl down the aisle to the grand music. "Take a look at Andrew," I whispered.

Margaret obeyed. "Nerves," she muttered.

But I knew Andrew better than that.

Nattie got to the altar. Dad kissed her cheek, shook Andrew's hand, and then sat down with Mom, who patted his arm fondly. Andrew and Natalie turned to the minister. Nat was beaming. Andrew...not so much.

"Dearly beloved," Reverend Miggs began.

"Wait. I'm sorry," Andrew interrupted, his voice weak and shaking.

"Holy Mary, Queen of Heaven," Margaret breathed. "Don't you dare, Andrew."

"Honey?" Nat's voice was soft with concern. "You okay?" My stomach clenched, my breath stopped. Oh, God...

Andrew wiped his forehead with his hand. "Nattie...I'm sorry."

There was a stirring in the congregation. Reverend Miggs put a hand on Andrew's arm. "Now, son," he began.

"What's wrong?" Natalie whispered. Margaret and I moved as one to flank her, instinctively wanting to protect her from what was about to come.

"It's Grace," he whispered. "I'm sorry, but I still have feelings for Grace. I can't marry you, Nat."

A collective gasp came from the assembled guests.

"Are you fucking kidding me?" Margaret barked, but I barely heard her. A white roaring noise was in my ears. I watched as the blood drained from Natalie's face. Her knees buckled. Margaret and the minister grabbed her.

Then I dropped my bouquet, shoved past Margaret, and punched Andrew as hard as I could. Right in the face.

The next few minutes were somewhat unclear. I know that Andrew's best man tried to pull him to safety (my punch had knocked him down) as I repeatedly kicked my once-fiancé and very nearly brother-in-law in the shins with my pointy little shoes. His nose was bleeding, and I thought it was a great look for him. I remember my mother joining me to beat him about the head with her purse. She may have tried to rip out his liver and eat it, but I didn't remember the details. Vaguely, I heard Mrs. Carson screaming. Felt Dad wrap his arms around my waist as he bodily dragged me off Andrew, who was half lying on the altar steps, trying to crawl away from my kicks and Mom's ineffective but highly satisfying blows.

In the end, the groom's guests scuttled out the back, leaving the Carsons, the best man and Andrew, a handkerchief pressed to his face, huddled on one side. Natalie sat stunned in the first pew on the bride's side, surrounded by Margaret, me, Mom and Dad as Mémé herded people out of the church like some geriatric border collie in a wheelchair.

"Left at the altar," Natalie murmured blankly.

I knelt in front of her. "Honey, what can we do?"

Her gaze found mine, and for a minute, we just

looked at each other. I reached out and took her hand. "I'll be okay," she whispered. "It's okay."

"He's not worth your spit, Nattie," Margaret said, stroking Natalie's silky hair.

"Not worth the tissue you used to blow your nose," Mom seconded. "Bastard. Idiot. Penis-head."

Nat looked up at Mom, then burst out laughing, a hysterical edge to her voice. "Penis-head. That's a good one, Mom."

Mr. Carson came over warily. "Um, very sorry about all this," he said. "Change of heart, obviously."

"We got that," Margaret snapped.

"We're sorry," he repeated, looking at Natalie, then at me. "Very sorry, girls."

"Thanks, Mr. Carson," I said. He nodded once, then went back to his wife and son. A moment later, the Carsons were gone, out the side door. I hoped vigorously that we'd never see them again.

"What do you want to do right now, honey?" Dad asked.

Nat blinked. "Well," she said after a minute, "I think we should go to the club and eat all that good food." Her eyes filled once more. "Yes. Let's all do that, okay?"

"You sure?" I asked. "You don't have to be brave, Bumppo."

She squeezed my hand. "I learned from the best."

AND SO IT WAS THAT THE EMERSON side of the guest list went to the country club, ate shrimp and filet mignon and drank champagne.

"I'm better off without him," Nat murmured as she drank what had to be her fifth glass of champers.

"I know that. It's just gonna take a while for that to sink in."

"Personally, I hated him from the day Grace brought him home," Margs said. "Smug little weenie. Estate law, please. Such a sissy."

"How many men are stupid enough to dump two Emerson girls?" Dad asked. "Too bad we're not mobbed up. We could have his body dumped in the Farmington River."

"I don't think the Mafia accepts white Anglo-Saxon Protestants, Dad," Margaret said, patting Nat's shoulder and pouring her more champagne. "But it's a sweet thought."

Nattie would be okay, I could tell. She was right. Andrew didn't deserve her, and he never had. Her heart would heal. Mine did, after all.

I wandered over to sit with Mémé for a bit. She was watching Cousin Kitty, who was as sensitive as a rhino, dancing with her new husband to "Endless Love." "So what do you think of all this, Mémé?" I asked.

"Bound to happen. People should be more like me. Marriage is a business arrangement. Marry for money, Grace. You won't be sorry."

"Thanks for the advice," I said, patting her bony shoulder. "But really, Mémé, were you ever in love?"

Her rheumy eyes were faraway. "Not especially," she said. "There was a boy, once...well. He wasn't an appropriate match for me. Not from the same class, you see."

"Who was he?" I asked.

She gave me a sharp look. "Aren't we nosy today? Have you gained weight, Grace? You look a little hefty in the hips. In my day, a woman wore a girdle."

So much for our heart-to-heart. I sighed, asked

Mémé if she wanted another drink and wandered off to the bar. Margaret was already there.

"So?" I asked. "How was the kitchen table?"

"It actually wasn't that comfortable," she said, grinning. "You know, it was muggy last night, the humidity made me stick like Velcro, so when he actually—"

"Okay, that's enough," I broke in. She laughed and ordered a glass of seltzer water.

"Seltzer, hmm?" I asked.

She rolled her eyes. "Well, when I was living at your house, I kind of decided that maybe a baby...well, maybe it wouldn't be awful. Someday. Maybe. We'll see. Last night he said he wanted a little girl just like me—"

"Is he insane?" I asked.

She turned to look at me, and I saw her eyes were wet. "I just thought that was the sweetest thing, Grace. It really got to me."

"Yes, but then you'd have to raise it. The Mini-Margs," I said. "That man must really love you."

"Oh, shut up, you," she said, laughing in spite of herself. "The baby idea seems kind of...well. Kind of okay."

"Oh, Margs." I smiled. "I think you'd be a great mom. On many levels, anyway."

"So you'll babysit, right? Whenever I have spit-up in my hair and a screaming baby in my arms and I'm ready to stick my head in the oven?"

"Absolutely." I gave her a quick hug, which she tolerated, even returned.

"You doing okay, Grace?" she asked. "This whole Andrew thing has come full circle, hasn't it?"

"You know, if I never hear that name again, I'll be glad," I said. "I'm fine. I just feel so bad for Nat."

But she'd be okay. Even now, she was laughing at something my father said. Both my parents were glued to her side, Mom practically force-feeding her hors d'oeuvres. Andrew wasn't worthy of her.

Or of me, for that matter. Andrew never deserved me. I could see that now. A man who accepts love as if it's his due is, in a word, a jerk.

Callahan O'Shea...he was another matter altogether.

"So what are your plans for the summer?" Margs asked. "Any offers on the house yet?"

"Two, actually," I answered, taking a sip of my gin and tonic.

"I have to say, I'm surprised," Margs commented. "I thought you loved that house."

"I do. I did. I just... It's time for a fresh start. Change isn't the worst thing in the world, is it?"

"I guess not," she said. "Come on, let's go sit with Nattie."

"Here they are!" Dad boomed as we approached. "Now the three prettiest girls in the world are all together. Make that four," he quickly amended, putting his arm around Mom, who rolled her eyes.

"Dad, did Grace tell you she's selling her house?" Margaret asked.

"What? No! Honey! Why didn't you tell me?"

"Because it's not a group decision, Dad."

"But we just put new windows in there!"

"Which the Realtor said would help it sell," I said calmly.

"Where are you going, then?" Mom asked. "You wouldn't go far, would you, honey?"

"Nope. Not far." I sat next to Nat, who was doing that mile-long stare I had mastered myself a year and a half ago. "You okay, kiddo?" I asked.

"Yeah. I'm fine. Well, not fine. But you know." I nodded.

"Hey, did you ever hear about the history department job?" Margs asked.

"Oh, yes," I answered. "They hired someone from outside. But she seems great."

"Maybe she'll give you a raise," Dad speculated. "It'd be nice if you earned more than a Siberian farmer."

"I was thinking of picking up work as a high-class hooker," I said. "Do you know any politicians who are looking?"

Natalie laughed, and the sound made us all smile.

A while later, after dinner had been served, I headed into the ladies' room. From the stalls came the voice of my smug cousin Kitty.

"…so apparently, she just was pretending to date someone so we wouldn't feel sorry for her," Kitty was saying. "The doctor was completely made up! And then there was something about a convict she'd been writing to in prison…" The toilet flushed, and Kitty emerged. From the next stall came Aunt Mavis. Upon sighting me, they both froze.

"Hello, ladies," I said graciously, smoothing my hair in the mirror. "Are you enjoying yourselves? So much to gossip about, so little time!"

Kitty's face turned as red as a baboon's butt. Aunt Mavis, made of stronger stuff, simply rolled her eyes.

"Do you have any questions about my love life? Any gaps in your information? Anything you need from me?" I smiled, folded my arms across my chest and stared them down.

Kitty and Mavis exchanged a look. "No, Grace," they said in unison.

"Okay," I answered. "And just for the record, he was on death row. Sorry to say, the governor turned down his stay of execution, so I'm on the prowl again." I winked, smiled at their identical looks of horror, and pushed my way into a stall.

When I rejoined my family, Nat was getting ready to go. "You can stay with me, Bumppo," I said.

"No, thanks, Grace. I'll stay with Mom and Dad for a few days. But you're sweet to offer."

"Want me to drive you?" I asked.

"No, Margs is taking me. We have to make a stop first. Besides, you've done enough today. Beating up Andrew...thanks for that."

"My pleasure," I said with complete sincerity. I kissed my sister, then hugged her a long, long time. "Call me in the morning."

"I will. Thanks," she whispered.

Walking to my car, I fished the car keys out of my bag. What seemed like aeons ago, I had promised my little old lady friends at Golden Meadows that I'd stop by tonight. They wanted to see my fancy dress and hear how the wedding went. Well, Dad had taken Mémé home before dinner. Chances were, the residents of Golden Meadows knew quite well how the wedding went.

But I figured I'd go just the same. Tonight was the Saturday Night Social. I could probably scare up someone to dance with, and though he wouldn't be under eighty years old, I felt like dancing, oddly enough.

I drove across town and pulled into Golden Meadows's parking lot. There was no sign of Callahan's battered pickup truck. I hadn't seen him since the day he left Maple Street, though I had stopped in to see his grandfather. As Cal had mentioned, the old man wasn't doing well. We'd never even finished the book.

On impulse, I decided to stop in and see Mr. Lawrence. Who knew? Maybe Callahan would be there. Betsy, the nurse on duty, buzzed me in with a wave. "You just missed the grandson," she said, cupping her hand over the receiver.

Drat. Well, Callahan wasn't my reason for coming, not really. I walked down the hall amid the familiar, sad sounds of this particular ward—faint moans, querulous voices and too much quiet.

Mr. Lawrence's door was open. He was asleep in his hospital bed, small and shrunken against the pale blue sheets. An IV, new from the last time I'd come by, snaked from a clear plastic tube into his arm, and tears pricked my eyes. I'd been coming to Golden Meadows long enough to know that in cases like this, an IV usually meant the patient had stopped eating and drinking.

"Hi, Mr. Lawrence, it's Grace," I whispered, sitting down next to him. "The one who reads to you, remember? *My Lord's Wanton Desire?* The duke and the prostitute?"

Of course, he didn't answer. To the best of my recollection, I'd never heard the voice of Cal's grandfather. I wondered what he'd sounded like when he was a younger man, teaching Cal and his brother to fly-fish, helping them with their homework, telling them to finish their vegetables and drink their milk.

"Listen, Mr. Lawrence," I said, putting my hand on

his thin and vulnerable arm. "I just wanted to tell you something. I was dating your grandson for a little while. Callahan. And basically, I screwed things up and he broke up with me." I rolled my eyes at myself, not having planned on a deathbed confession. "Anyway, I just wanted to tell you what a good man he is."

A lump came to my throat, and my voice dropped back to a whisper. "He's smart and funny and thoughtful, and he's always working, you know? You should see the house he just fixed up. He did such a beautiful job." I paused. "And he loves you so much. He comes here all the time. And he's...well, he's a good-looking guy, right? Chip off the old block, I'm guessing."

The sound of Mr. Lawrence's breathing was barely audible. I picked up his gnarled, cool hand and held it for a second. "I just wanted to say that you did a great job raising him. I think you'd be really proud. That's all."

Then I leaned over and kissed Mr. Lawrence's forehead. "Oh, one more thing. The duke marries Clarissia. He finds her in the tower and rescues her, and they live...you know. Happily ever after."

"What are you doing, Grace?"

I jumped like someone had just pressed a brand against my flesh. "Mémé! God, you scared me!" I whispered.

"I've been looking for you. Dolores Barinski said you were supposed to come to the social, and it started an hour ago."

"Right," I said with a last glance back at Mr. Lawrence. "Well, let's go, then."

So I wheeled my grandmother down the hall, away from the last link I had to Callahan O'Shea, knowing that I would probably not see Mr. Lawrence again. A few tears slipped down my cheeks. I sniffed.

"Oh, cheer up," Mémé snapped omnisciently from her throne. "At least you have me. That man isn't even related to you. I don't know why you even care."

I stopped the wheelchair and went around to face my grandmother, ready to tell her what a sour old pain in the butt she was, how vain and rude, how selfish and insensitive. But looking down on her thinning hair and wrinkled face, her spotted hands adorned with too-big rings, I said something else.

"I love you, Mémé."

She looked up, startled. "What's wrong with you today?"

"Nothing. I just wanted to tell you."

She took a breath, frowning, her face creasing into folds. "Well. Are we going or not?"

I smiled, resumed pushing and headed to the social. It was in full swing, and I danced with all my regulars and a few people I didn't recognize. I even took Mémé out for a spin in the wheelchair, but she hissed at me that I was making a fool of myself and wondered loudly if I'd had too much to drink at the club, so I took her back. Eventually. After two songs, that is.

My dress was admired, my hands were patted and held, even my hair was deemed pretty. I was, in other words, happy. Nat was heartbroken, and my own heart wasn't doing too well, either. I'd ruined something lovely and rare with Callahan O'Shea and made an idiot of myself in front of my family by faking a boyfriend. But that was okay. Well, the idiot part was okay. Callahan, though…I'd miss him for a long time.

CHAPTER THIRTY-FOUR

WHEN I GOT HOME FROM Golden Meadows, it was nearly ten. Angus presented me with two rolls of shredded toilet paper, then trotted into the kitchen to show me where he'd vomited up a few wads. "At least you did it on the tile," I said, bending down to pet his sweet head. "Thank you for barfing in the kitchen." He barked once, then stretched out in Super Dog pose to watch me clean.

"I hope you'll like our new place," I said, donning the all-too-familiar rubber gloves I used when cleaning Angus's, er, accidents. "I'll pick us out a winner, don't you worry." Angus wagged his tail.

Becky Mango had called yesterday. "I know this might be weird," she said, "but I was wondering if you might be interested in the house next door to you. The one Callahan fixed up? It's just charming."

I'd hesitated. I loved that house, heaven knew. But I'd already lived in a house that was all about one failed relationship. Buying Cal's, though it cost roughly the same as mine, would've been too Miss Havisham for me. No. My next house would be about my future, not about my past. "Right, Angus?" I said now. He barked helpfully, then burped and flipped onto his back, craftily suggesting that I take a break from cleaning up his vomit to scratch his tummy. "Later, McFangus," I murmured.

I blotted up his little mess, taking care not to let my hem get soiled. It was a pretty dress, but I was planning on taking it to the Salvation Army. I never wanted to see it again. That, and my wedding dress. Maybe Nat would want me to bring hers, too.

Tomorrow, I'd start packing. Even though I hadn't found a house yet, I'd be moving soon. I could go through all my old tag sale finds, maybe have a sale of my own. Fresh start and all that.

As I cleaned with Windex the last traces of barf off of the floor and stuffed the paper towels into the trash, Angus leaped to his feet and flew out of the room in an explosion of barking. *Yarp! Yarpyarpyarp!*

"What's wrong, honey?" I asked, coming into the living room

Yarpyarpyarp!

I peeked around the curtains through the window and my heart surged into my throat so hard I nearly choked.

Callahan O'Shea was standing on the front porch.

He looked at me, raised an eyebrow and waited.

My legs barely held me as I opened the front door. With a snarl, Angus launched himself on Cal's work boot. Cal ignored him.

"Hi," he said.

"Hi," I whispered.

His gaze went to my hands, which were still protected by the rubber gloves. "What are you doing?"

"Um…cleaning up dog puke."

"Pretty."

I just stood there. Callahan O'Shea. Here. On my porch, where we'd first met.

"Mind calling off your dog?" he asked as Angus, his mouth clamped onto a good part of Cal's pant leg, swung his little head back and forth, growling his kittenish growl.

"Um...sure. Of course," I said. "Angus! Down cellar, boy! Come on!" My knees were shaking, but I managed to pick up Angus and shove him through the cellar door, down with the girl-part sculptures. He whined, then accepted his fate and grew quiet.

I turned back to Callahan. "So. What brings you to the neighborhood?" My throat was so tight my voice squeaked.

"Your sisters paid me a visit," he said quietly.

"They did?" I asked, my mouth dropping open.

"Mmm-hmm."

"Today?"

"About an hour ago. They told me about Andrew."

"Right." I closed my mouth. "Big mess."

"You beat him up, I hear."

"Yes, I did," I murmured. "One of my finer moments." A thought occurred to me. "How did they know where to find you?" Callahan had certainly not left a forwarding address with me.

"Margaret called her pals at the parole office."

I bit down on a smile. Good old Margs.

"Natalie told me I was an idiot," Callahan murmured, his voice low enough to cause a vibration in my stomach.

"Oh," I squeaked, leaning back against the wall for support. "Sorry. You're not an idiot."

"She told me how you came clean with everyone." Cal took a step closer to me, and my heart thudded so hard I felt like I might imitate Angus and throw up myself. "Said I was an idiot if I was going to just walk away from a woman like you."

Callahan took my limp hand and removed the rubber glove, smiling a little as he did. He repeated the action on the other hand, I found myself staring at our hands, because it was hard to look in Cal's eyes.

"The thing is, Grace," he said gently, holding my sweaty hands in his own much more appealingly dry ones, "I didn't really need to hear it. I'd already figured that out."

"Oh," I breathed.

"But I have to admit, I thought it was nice that your sisters were finally doing something for you, instead of the other way around." He tipped up my chin, forcing me to look into his pretty eyes. "Grace," he whispered, "I *was* an idiot. I should know better than anyone that people get stupid around the folks they love. And that everyone deserves a second chance."

I sucked in a shaky breath, my eyes filling with tears.

"Here's the thing, Grace," Cal said, a smile playing at the corner of his mouth. "Ever since that first day when you smacked me in the head with your field hockey stick—"

"You just can't let that go, can you?" I muttered.

He grinned fully now. "—and even when you hit me with the rake and dented my truck, and when you were spying on me from your attic and your dog was mauling me, Grace, I always knew you were the one for me."

"Oh," I whispered, my mouth wobbling like crazy. Not my best look, to be sure, but I couldn't help it.

"Give us another chance, Grace. What do you say?" His smile told me he was fairly sure of the answer.

Instead of answering, I just wrapped my arms around him and kissed him for all I was worth. Because when you meet The One, you just know.

EPILOGUE

Two years later

"WE ARE NOT NAMING OUR SON Abraham Lincoln O'Shea.
Think of something else." My husband pretended to
scowl at me, but his look was somewhat marred by
Angus licking his chin. We were lying in bed on a Sunday morning, the sun streaming in through the windows, the smell of coffee mingling with the sweet scent
drifting from the small vase of roses on the night table.

"You already rejected Stonewall," I reminded him,
rubbing my enormous stomach. "Stonewall O'Shea.
There certainly wouldn't be any other little boys in kindergarten with that name."

"Grace. Your due date was four days ago. Come on.
Be serious. This is our child. And if he has to have a
Civil War name, it's got to be Yankee. Okay? We're both
from New England, after all. Angus, get your tongue
out of my ear. Yuck."

I giggled. When we first moved in together, Callahan took Angus to an eight-week-long obedience
course. Children need structure, Cal had told me, and
ever since, the dog had been insanely devoted to him.

I tried again. "How about Ulysses S. O'Shea?"

"I'd settle for Grant. Grant O'Shea. That's a compromise, Grace."

"Grant O'Shea. Nope. Sorry. How about Jeb?"

"That's it, missy." He pounced, tickled, and a second later we were making out like a couple of teenagers.

"I love you," he whispered, his hand on my tummy.

"I love you, too," I whispered back.

Yep, we got married. I got the boy next door. And for that matter, the house next door, as well. Cal said it didn't seem right that it belong to anyone but us, and we bought it together, two weeks after Natalie's non-wedding.

Living next door to my old place didn't bother me a bit. I was grateful to that house, where my sore and sad heart had slowly mended. It was where I first met my husband, after all.

Speaking of Natalie, she was doing fine. She was single still, working a lot, and seemed happy. She dated a little here and there, but nothing serious yet. Stuart and Margaret had become parents about a year ago—James, a colicky baby who cried the first four months of his life before transforming into a dimpled, chubby little Buddha of smiles and drool, and Margaret loved him beyond reason.

"God, you smell good," Cal muttered from the region of my neck, which he was nuzzling most pleasantly. "Want to fool around?"

I looked at him, his long, straight lashes and perpetually tousled hair, those soft, dark blue eyes...*I hope our son looks just like him,* I thought, and my heart ached with such love that I couldn't answer. Then there was a different ache, and soggy feeling to go with it.

"Honey?" Callahan asked. "You okay?"

"You know what? I think my water just broke."

Thirty minutes later, Cal was trying to get me out

the front door as Angus barked maniacally in the cellar, enraged at the unceremonious way Callahan had dumped him there, but Cal was in no mood for niceties, racing around like the house was on fire. I knew from Margaret's long and gruesome labor, which she enjoyed discussing in great detail, that the baby would probably take the better part of a day to come. The obstetrician had said the same thing, but Cal was convinced that I was about to squat and push his child out right here and now...or worse, on the side of the road between here and the hospital.

"Do you have my lollipops?" I asked calmly, consulting my list from birthing class.

"Yup. I sure do." He looked nervous—*terrified* might have been a better word—and I found it quite adorable. "Come on, honey, let's go. Baby's coming, don't forget."

I gave him a pointed look. "I'll try to remember, Callahan. What about my pretty bathrobe? My hair's going to be bad enough. At least I can look nice from the neck down." I looked back at the list. "Don't forget the camera, of course."

"Got it, Grace. Come on, sweetheart. Let's not have the baby in the hall here."

"Cal, I've had two contractions. Relax." He made a noise in the back of his throat, which I kindly ignored. "Did you remember the baby clothes? That little blue sleeper with the dog on it?"

"Yes, honey, please, I checked the list already. Think we can leave for the hospital before the kid turns three?"

"Oh, my focal point! Don't forget that." The birthing instructor had said to bring an object to concentrate on during the contractions, something I liked looking at.

"Got it." He reached up over the front door and took

down the focal point—my field hockey stick, which Cal had hung up the day we moved in. "Okay, sweetheart. Let's go meet our boy. Want me to carry you? It's faster. I'll do that. Just put your arm around my neck, honey. Come on. Let's go."

Nineteen and a half very impressive and memorable hours later, we learned several things. One, I could be very, very loud when the situation demanded it. Two, while Cal was pretty amazing during labor and delivery, he also tended to cry when his wife was in pain. (Just when you think you can't love a guy any more…) And three, ultrasounds are still wrong once in a while.

Our boy was a girl.

We named her Scarlett.

Scarlett O'Hara O'Shea.

* * * * *

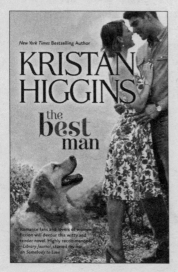

New York Times **bestselling author**

shannon stacey

is back with a tantalizing new trilogy!

**He won't stay put for a woman,
and she won't chase after any man....**

"This is the perfect
contemporary romance."
—*RT Book Reviews* on
Undeniably Yours

New York Times Bestselling Author

shannon
stacey

all he ever
needed

"Books like this are why I read romance."
—*Smart Bitches, Trashy Books* on *Exclusively Yours*

Available wherever books are sold!

HARLEQUIN®HQN™
™ www.Harlequin.com

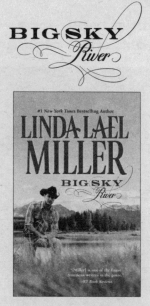

A remarkable true story about an unlikely hero

One of *Publishers Weekly*'s Top 10 Memoirs of 2012!

—

"A DOG NAMED BOO…touched my heart."
—Brett Witter, *New York Times* bestselling coauthor of *Dewey* and *Until Tuesday*

How One Dog and One Woman Rescued Each Other—and the Lives They Transformed Along the Way

REQUEST YOUR FREE BOOKS!

2 FREE NOVELS
FROM THE ROMANCE COLLECTION
PLUS 2 FREE GIFTS!

YES! Please send me 2 FREE novels from the Romance Collection and my 2 FREE gifts (gifts are worth about $10). After receiving them, if I don't wish to receive any more books, I can return the shipping statement marked "cancel." If I don't cancel, I will receive 4 brand-new novels every month and be billed just $5.99 per book in the U.S. or $6.49 per book in Canada. That's a savings of at least 25% off the cover price. It's quite a bargain! Shipping and handling is just 50¢ per book in the U.S. and 75¢ per book in Canada.* I understand that accepting the 2 free books and gifts places me under no obligation to buy anything. I can always return a shipment and cancel at any time. Even if I never buy another book, the two free books and gifts are mine to keep forever.

194/394 MDN FVU7

Name _____ (PLEASE PRINT)

Address _____ Apt. #

City _____ State/Prov. _____ Zip/Postal Code

Signature (if under 18, a parent or guardian must sign)

Mail to the **Harlequin®** Reader Service:
IN U.S.A.: P.O. Box 1867, Buffalo, NY 14240-1867
IN CANADA: P.O. Box 609, Fort Erie, Ontario L2A 5X3

Want to try two free books from another line?
Call 1-800-873-8635 or visit www.ReaderService.com.

* Terms and prices subject to change without notice. Prices do not include applicable taxes. Sales tax applicable in N.Y. Canadian residents will be charged applicable taxes. Offer not valid in Quebec. This offer is limited to one order per household. Not valid for current subscribers to the Romance Collection or the Romance/Suspense Collection. All orders subject to credit approval. Credit or debit balances in a customer's account(s) may be offset by any other outstanding balance owed by or to the customer. Please allow 4 to 6 weeks for delivery. Offer available while quantities last.

Your Privacy—The Harlequin® Reader Service is committed to protecting your privacy. Our Privacy Policy is available online at www.ReaderService.com or upon request from the Harlequin Reader Service.

We make a portion of our mailing list available to reputable third parties that offer products we believe may interest you. If you prefer that we not exchange your name with third parties, or if you wish to clarify or modify your communication preferences, please visit us at www.ReaderService.com/consumerschoice or write to us at Harlequin Reader Service Preference Service, P.O. Box 9062, Buffalo, NY 14269. Include your complete name and address.

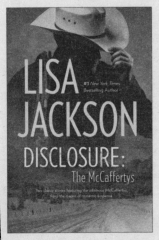

LINDA HOWARD

77569 TROUBLE	___$7.99 U.S.	___$9.99 CAN.
77430 MACKENZIE'S HEROES	___$7.99 U.S.	___$9.99 CAN.
77429 MACKENZIE'S LEGACY	___$7.99 U.S.	___$8.99 CAN.

(limited quantities available)

TOTAL AMOUNT	$ _____
POSTAGE & HANDLING	$ _____
($1.00 FOR 1 BOOK, 50¢ for each additional)	
APPLICABLE TAXES*	$ _____
TOTAL PAYABLE	$ _____

(check or money order—please do not send cash)

To order, complete this form and send it, along with a check or money order for the total above, payable to Harlequin HQN, to: **In the U.S.:** 3010 Walden Avenue, P.O. Box 9077, Buffalo, NY 14269-9077; **In Canada:** P.O. Box 636, Fort Erie, Ontario, L2A 5X3.

Name: _____

Address: _____ City: _____

State/Prov.: _____ Zip/Postal Code: _____

Account Number (if applicable): _____

075 CSAS

*New York residents remit applicable sales taxes.
*Canadian residents remit applicable GST and provincial taxes.

HARLEQUIN® HQN™
™ www.Harlequin.com

PHLH0113BL